MORE BEAST THAN
PRINCE CHARMING...

BEAUTIFUL SINNER

VOL.2

ELENA M. REYES

SUMMARY

These Men Are More Beasts Than Prince Charming...

Beautiful Sinner Volume 2 features three full-length novels packed with blood-pounding mafia romances where love is obsession and loyalty is laced with violence.

These men don't beg. They take.

And when their women are threatened...

They'll burn the world to the ground until they're back where they belong —pinned beneath them.

P.S. Read this if you love morally gray, unapologetic antiheroes who love hard and f*ck dirty.

Includes: YOURS, RISQUE, & OWN

DEDICATION

For the girlies who crave danger in a tailored suit and wicked lips that whisper... **"Mine."**

You know who you are. This one's for you.

CONTENTS

RISQUE

OWN

TRIGGER WARNINGS

This book contains dark elements that some readers may find triggering. These men are brutal and unapologetic; please read at your own discretion.

THIS IS A MAFIA ROMANCE SERIES AND YOU WILL FIND THE FOLLOWING:

EXPLICIT VIOLENCE
ON PAGE DEATH
EXPLICIT SEX (SPICY) SCENES
SEXUAL SPANKING
TORTURE/GORE
OBSESSED MEN
AGE GAP
FORCED PROXIMITY
SOME KIDNAPPING
MILD STALKING
VERBAL ABUSE BY ENEMY
MISOGYNY (NOT BY MMC)
TOXIC FAMILY

CRIMINAL ACTIVITY
VULGAR LANGUAGE

JAVIER LUCAS

I'm a man with an immoral compass. A convicted killer in one country and the right-hand to the devil in another.

Javier Lucas offers death without mercy—something my enemies don't live long enough to tell, but the carnage left behind paints a brutal story. He has no soul. No regrets. This is who I am, and I embrace the darkness that flows through my veins while blood stains my skin.

And I've never wanted more until...

Our eyes met and my world took a pause. One flirty exchange and I vowed to tame her wildness.

Fate is a word I now believed in.

Because it led me to her. To my beautiful little criminal.

GLOSSARY OF SPANISH/COLOMBIAN SLANG:

Muñeca = Doll

Linda = Beautiful or Pretty

Hijueputa = Son of a bitch

Parce = Friend

Güevon = Lazy person

Brujeria = Voodoo/Witchcraft

Mamita = Term of endearment for a mother or used as a cat-call for hot girl. The same word could be used either way and has different meanings depending on how it's used.

Listo = Done

We're a brutal explosion of lust and hunger,
this raw uncontrollable yearning that I call home.

~Javier Lucas

JAVIER

COLOMBIA THREE YEARS AGO...

THE STALE STENCH of old wounds greets my senses the moment I step inside the semi-darkened room. It's overpowering and undeniably human. That beginning stage of decomposition where lesions fail to heal and infection sets in, rotting a person from the inside out.

It's a scent I know. One I understand.

Because for every action, there is an often more damning consequence that even the most corrupt fear. All men have a weakness. One soft spot which renders them useless, and no one is immune to the karma of divine justice.

I'm here today as an example of that.

You pay in life for your wrongdoings.

My eyes sweep the room, and I nod at the man responsible for my role in today's proceedings. Alejandro, my cousin, sits just a few feet from the center in an opulent golden chair that doesn't fit within these walls while villagers gather around. Men and women line the back wall of an old abandoned building on the outskirts of Bogota while waiting on justice to be served.

Two men are on trial for their misdeeds and are tied together by greed. Stupidity.

For stealing from those who trusted—put faith in the empty words of a low-life opportunist.

Because you don't bite the hand that feeds. You don't take away the only source of sustenance these families have by emptying the poppy fields while using their labor under false direction—telling them it was a direct order—and attempting to sell the flowers to a European company whose loyalty lies with our family.

A novice mistake, and they'll pay with their lives for two reasons. One, for being scum. And the other, for trying to go behind his boss's back and making that idiotic purchase.

Everyone's watching the two men bound and gagged—bruised and bloodied—with horror-stricken expressions on their faces as the men take me in. The assholes wait, they beg with their eyes for a mercy they'll never receive.

Instead, the closer I get, the more they tremble. The smile on my face eviscerates whatever shred of hope they held on to.

I don't feel bad for them. Not at all.

I wouldn't be here if they were honorable men.

Hushed whispers meet my ears then, the murmurs of witnesses filling the space as I stop beside a small rolling cart. There's a tray atop it with two bullets, a .45 caliber Glock, and a machete.

It's all I'll need.

"That family is nothing but an infestation of roaches in need of extermination."

I catch that, and my attention snaps in the direction of the idiot who spoke. It's not hard to pick him out amongst the group. Not when the two women beside him take steps to the side with wide eyes. They're watching him, and then flick their eyes to me and then back again. Back and forth three times, and then they all but run toward the opposite side when I move in his direction.

There's a gulp, and two palms go up in supplication.

"Say it again, Güevon," I hiss out, my hand wrapped around his neck before his next inhale. My fingers tighten and his breathing becomes choppy, chest rising and falling fast—fighting to regain the missing oxygen he needs to live. There's a choking sound that slips from his parted lips while his body fights to break my hold, and still, I won't budge. I don't lose my stance even when his legs go weak. If anything, I take joy in the feel of his life slipping away beneath my fingertips.

I revel in the moment rationality sets in, and how easy it is to lose one's mortality becomes a haunting truth; he has no choice but to confront.

"Por favor, I didn't—" His fingernails try to break the skin at my wrist but fail. No strength whatsoever.

"I won't ask you again." Bringing my face closer to his, I arch a brow. "Repeat."

"Can't breathe," he chokes out, voice low while the color of his face reminds me of a fallen tomato out on the fields: dirty and ripped open under a heavy boot. It's a pathetic response that further fuels my dislike of him. Of his type.

A man without a backbone. Without conviction.

The kind that runs at the first sight of a fight but will feed the fire until someone snaps.

"If you can talk, you can breathe." Multiple guns click and many avert their eyes as I tilt my head to the side, catching sight of Alejandro walking over from the corner of my eye. "What did you say?"

"Q'hubo, Andresito?" My cousin stops beside us and I look over, catching the smirk on his face. He's calm and collected, methodically dissecting the idiot in my hold. "You have something to say?"

"No."

"Louder." Alejandro nods and I release the man, letting him fall to his knees. At once, his hand comes up and he rubs his neck, glaring at us from his position. "Didn't your father ever teach you manners? How to respect those above you?"

"You'll never be him." The hand on the ground bracing his weight tightens into a fist, his teeth grinding as he spits out words through them. He's amusing to watch, at least.

"An abusive adulterer? Is that who I should admire?"

"Fuck you," Andresito hisses out a second before the bottom of my foot meets his face. A swift kick and he's thrown back, landing on his back with an arm at an awkward angle. "Hijueputa!"

"Watch. Your. Mouth." My fingers twitch, and I hold myself back from putting a bullet between his eyes. We're not innocent—there's enough blood on my family's hands to cover a stadium, but his crimes are worse. Behind the disguise of a poppy farmer, Don Andres also dabbled in human trafficking and kept a horde of prostitutes at his disposal by forced addiction. Andresito knows this. His wife knew this. "I won't repeat myself."

"He ruined us!" The kid tries to wipe his face, but only succeeds in spreading the blood flowing from his nose across his lips and cheek. "My family is—"

"You're a bunch of sick fucks."

At my words, his eyes narrow and he tries to stand. "Maybe I'll return the favor?" He's unsteadied, almost drunk-like, and can barely manage to kneel with his face screwed up in anger. "He killed mine and I'll kill—"

"You." I finish for him, pulling my Ruger from the holster around my chest. His father died at Alejandro's hands, and he'll meet his end at mine as a second later I pull the trigger, killing the sole male heir to Don Andres's small estate. A few garbled breaths, and those scared eyes are on mine as his body stills and his life's essence seeps from the wounds. One to his neck and the other his chest; two bullets exit his body and ricochet off the concrete ground, his blood marking those closest to his corpse. "Anyone else have something to say?"

Not a word. Not so much as a sound.

"We apologize for this small inconvenience." Alejandro's voice reverberates throughout the space as he clasps my shoulder, giving it a small squeeze before releasing. His men lower their drawn weapons, and mine returns to its place. "Let's proceed."

"Agreed." Nothing else is said while he retakes his seat, and my attention turns to the men on the floor, a puddle of urine now surrounding their scared forms. That, and the rivulets of blood winding down to the divot at the center that leads to drainage in the cement floor. "How are you two holding up? Need anything?" Their response is a muffled sound and I look over at the man closest to their forms. "Remove the gag."

"Of course, sir." Alejandro's guard tears the covering, then moves back into formation, gun in hand and finger on the trigger.

"Gracias." He nods, and I tilt my head in Francis's direction. "I'm not going to repeat myself."

"I can explain, Javier. Just hear me out."

My eyes narrow and I pick up the machete, admiring the smooth wooden handle and slick blade. Not too heavy. Unbreakable if used with force. "That's not what I asked, Francis."

"Please."

"How have you been?"

"C-could be better."

"And whose fault is that?" Placing the machete back upon the tray, I prepare my single-use gun by loading the two bullets and cocking it with the barrel pointing at Francis.

I've known him for years.

I've welcomed him to share a meal or two with my family.

I offered him a job when his father fell ill, and later when he passed, my family took care of the bill. *Ungrateful son of a bitch.*

"I'm sorry." It's a whisper; two pathetic words that earn him a bullet to his right shoulder. His cry of pain reverberates throughout every inch of this room as his life's essence begins to flow.

At first, the .45 bullet's entry and exit create a small splash, but soon it begins to flow downward, staining his exposed skin.

He's a human map of bruises and cuts, of swollen flesh and pain. From where I stand, it's easy to make out the broken ribs and the fragment poking through the skin.

My cousin doesn't take kindly to thieves.

And while it's his product the men stole, these two are mine. I'm not the head of this operation, never want to be, but I do command respect.

Taking lives is my profession. My passion as a private Sicario.

But more than that, I am a Lucas first, and it was my mother they ran over with a pickup while rushing out of the field.

They left her for dead.

They left a woman whose life revolved around taking care of loved ones broken and now bound to a wheelchair.

"Fuck your apology." *One bullet down.* "Now, let's play a round of truth or death."

"We can find a solution, Javier. She didn't die—"

"You'd already be dead otherwise." The man beside him weeps, and I look over. "Something you want to say, Mr. Gil?" His head shakes back and forth fast, a bit of bloody spittle flying out with the frantic move. "Then be a good boy until I address you. Understood?"

"Yes." Low and meek.

"Speak up. You still have your tongue."

"Yes, sir."

At my nod, he lowers his head and sits stone still. "Tell me, Francis. Tell me why you did it?"

"He offered me money and a lot of American pussy."

"The world is full of opportunities, culicagado. Some good. Some bad." I take the remaining steps between us and poke the still-hot barrel of the Glock into his wound. He squirms, trying to move away while I dig deeper, forcing the tip inside the hole by force. Tears run down his grimy face, his nose running as the skin stretches and eventually gives way. One hard push, and the muscles there buckle. The barrel is deep enough to stay upright without my hand and I let go, crouching down to his level. Eye to eye. "The outcomes vary by scenarios. Investing in real estate is profitable, but stealing from those you owe your life to becomes a death sentence."

"Please don't kill me. I-I'll work off the debt."

"Open that mouth again out of turn, Gil, and I'll slit your throat," I say without looking over, and when he doesn't utter another sound, I smile at Francis and tap the handle. "Get up."

"I'm bound, Javi—" He doesn't finish as the back of my hand connects with his face, forcing his head to the side.

"There's enough slack for you to stand." Gil looks up at me and begins to rise before Francis, but I shake my head. One kneels while the other struggles to find footing, taking longer than my patience has time for, and I pull the gun out and hold it to his temple as positive reinforcement.

Once again, his scream rends the air and his body recoils, but Francis is smart enough to rise to his feet. "That's better."

"What can I do to make this right?" His low words meet my ears and I smile, rubbing the stained red barrel down his cheek and then tapping the skin there. "I don't want to die, Javier. Please."

"So, you want to make a deal? Is that right?" At my words, he nods. "Okay."

"Okay?" There's a hint of relief mixed with trepidation in his tone, and there should be. Nothing is ever as simple. Not in our life. "I'll do whatever it is you ask."

"You sure about that?"

"Yes." No hesitation, and I catch the nervous flinch from Gil. The way he folds into himself.

That man isn't a complete idiot; he just made the mistake that so many do. Greed isn't an awful trait; the problem lies in taking from the wrong hands because those at the top have been where you are.

The most notorious criminals start somewhere. An attack on our business isn't a foreign occurrence—it's something our family has prepared for —but not choosing their victim wisely will be a costly error.

"There's a bullet in the magazine, Francis. Just one." He nods and I hand the Glock over, taking a step back. "Kill him."

There's an important choice to be made here:

Be brave or fight.

Shoot him or me.

Not that he would ever set a single foot outside this warehouse, but when the will to survive is strong, you'll try anything. A few beats of silence follow, the sole cause of noise coming from the man still kneeling on the cold and dirty floor.

Gil begins to recite words that are familiar to me. A prayer from the Catholic church while Francis raises a shaking hand. There's a line on forgiveness for one's sins—on repenting for harmful thoughts—and throughout both, the man remains breathing.

Sweat beads on both sets of brows, and those in the room to witness don't dare speak.

"Shoot him."

"Javier, I'm—"

"Unable to follow simple instructions?" Because playing the role of a monster and being one are two vastly different things. "Is that what you're telling me?"

"I can do it." His shaking limbs say otherwise. His expression is one of utter fear.

"Then get closer and use both hands to steady the shot." Not that his injured shoulder helps, but it amuses me to see him grit his teeth while doing as I say. "You have five seconds to shoot."

Francis closes his eyes, and I move closer. He exhales roughly, and I smirk. "That's five." Before he can react, I have the Glock back in my hand and Gil lies dead with a bullet hole to the side of the head. Fragments scatter with the force of the blast. A lifeless body. Cold, vacant eyes.

I drop the gun between his bare feet and wait.

No reaction. Not so much as a twitch of a muscle.

My eyes flick to Alejandro, and he presses a button on his phone. At once, the buzz of speakers fills the space and Francis's voice filters through the room.

"I told you this would be easy, parce. These people are mindless slaves. If the Lucas family says jump, they fall into line and ask how high." The sound of an engine turning can be heard, and then the seat belt alarm follows shortly after. His companion doesn't give more than a grunt in answer, giving Francis the opening to run his mouth. I've listened to this recording. *"Cocky assholes sit comfortably atop while we do all the work."*

"But isn't your dream to be them?" Gil asks. A lighter sparks and you can hear his deep inhale from a cigarette. *"That's why you're doing this, no? The money, power, and easy pussy attached."*

"Always for a willing whore!" Both men laugh, but then Francis sobers. *"But apart from that, I said yes because both Alejandro and Javier denied me the money I needed. They cost me my wife, and I'm returning the favor by taking a client and making them lose a lot more than the fifty thousand dollars I asked for."*

"They couldn't spare fifty?" Gil's tone is incredulous with a hint of amusement. *"That's nothing to them. Not even a blip on their accounts."*

"It isn't."

"Then why say no?"

"Javier—"

"Turn it off." Alejandro does and then tosses the device to land beside the gun. Francis looks down at both, face pallid. "Say it again."

"Say what?" He doesn't look up at me.

"Finish what you said on the recording."

"You know?"

"We do." Every single member of my family does.

"How?" Now his eyes meet mine, and in them I find defeat. "I didn't talk around—"

"The pickup Gil offered was one of ours, you dumb motherfucker. It was a loaner he got from Emiliano a day before under the guise of being here on vacation. An idiot move, for a man who didn't hide his tracks well."

"Why?"

"We let you empty the fields. We let you make the transaction with him."

"I'm sorry."

"You will be." I take the few steps toward the tray with the machete and pick it up, slapping the metal against my palm before turning back to him. He's a mess: bloody and weak. "But this was the risk you were willing to take when you decided to rise against us, and all because we wouldn't give you the money needed to silence your mistress."

"It wasn't supposed to end like this." Francis hangs his head, shoulders slumped. "In and out is what he promised me and with the move, Ana would forgive me. She'd come back."

"Why put yourself in this position?" I ask, but the answer is of no true importance.

"Because I'm an idiot."

"Very true."

Francis takes in a deep breath and lets it out slowly. "For what it's worth, Javier, I'm so sorry about what happened to your Mrs. Ida…how we left her there. I regret that more than you'll ever know."

"And I'll see you in hell one day, parce." With that, I swing the machete clear across his chest, tearing open his flesh from shoulder to rib.

Blood spills and his scream of pain overtakes every inch of the room while those inside begin a slow clap. One by one, the witnesses make their approval heard as the noise level drowns out Francis's pain. "Mercy or pain?"

"Pain."

"Pain."

"Pain."

It's a chant that grows louder, the small windows rattling, and I nod, lifting the machete high again. The next strike is down his injured shoulder, embedding deep before I leave a matching slice across the opposite arm.

The puddle beneath him grows. The strength in his body is depleted and he slumps forward on all fours. "Please end me, Javier."

"It'll come sooner than you think." One by one, I leave cuts across his body from the neck down. His face is left alone and only so his family can bury him without further trauma.

"Thank you." Those are his final words as the last blow is delivered to the back of his neck. My blade stays lodged as he falls, the final breath escaping while his mouth is now stained by the blood trickling from the corner.

"Let this be a lesson to those who ever try to rise against the Lucas family. Next time, I won't be as forgiving." Faces nod and people turn toward the door as the seconds begin to pass. They go back home to their families while Alejandro's men begin to remove the bodies, and it's when Gil is placed inside a bag and wheeled out that my cousin approaches once more, a damp towel in his hand. "Thanks, primo."

"Our get-togethers have always been entertaining."

"Would you have it any other way?"

"No." Alejandro claps me on the shoulder then, a laugh booming out of him. "You remember our last trip to Mexico?"

"How can I forget." There's a smirk across my face as I remember what led to the showdown with a local cartel boss. "Who knew turning down a gold-digger would cause such a mess. I lost my favorite gun in that exchange."

"There's a replica in the car for you."

"It's the least you can do." We both let out a chuckle, making our way outside and toward my SUV where I pause to admire the gaudily wrapped box atop the hood. "The paper is hideous."

"Shut it and smile."

"I'm going to miss you, asshole."

"And it won't be the same without you here." He turns and leans against the front grill. "Are you sure about Chicago?"

"I'm a wanted man."

"Aren't we all in this family?"

"True." I mimic his stance, and we both watch the sun begin to set across the skyline. "But something is pulling me in that direction, and I'm following my instincts. Besides, I've been made a very lucrative offer."

"How good?"

"Enough to keep me occupied for a year."

"And you trust this person?"

"He comes highly recommended." It's the best I can give him, and he nods. In this business, no one has morals and everyone has ulterior motives —myself included.

"Just remember that this will always be home, Javier."

"And blood is always thicker than water."

JAVIER

TWO MONTHS LATER…

THE ASHER BUILDING is synonymous with wealth and opulence, and yet, I know the truth behind these walls. Things hidden in plain sight that those walking past would never imagine the man behind a CEO's desk is capable of.

But then again, I'm not most people, and word travels fast within certain circles.

All it takes is the right connection—the right person pulling the strings—and doors open with endless possibilities for the right price. A price Mr. Asher is all too willing to pay for a man with my particular set of skills.

A young woman sitting at the receptionist's desk looks my way as I walk through the main entrance and head straight for the elevator. She's smart enough to not draw attention my way just as the guards ignore my existence. Instead, she quickly looks away and helps an elderly woman asking to speak with the investment specialist inside the branch.

No one speaks to me, and I don't wait long as the door opens a few seconds after I press the button, letting me inside a wide and empty car. The walls are glass and as I ascend, I take notice of multiple cameras on each floor and the heavy security watching all who enter.

To someone who doesn't know any better, it's a simple system—common—while I know the quality of the equipment will rival that of the White House. The sensors are there to read more than activity. More than account for who comes and goes.

At this point, someone inside the security room knows the size of my cock and to what side it hangs.

There is no privacy within these walls, and I respect that. Respect the man who's taken his family's bank and turned it into a profitable money laundering empire for corrupt and unapologetic businessmen around the world. Men like my cousins who could profit from the services offered.

He's dangerous, but I have no soul. He's wealthy, and I have no fear.

I pass floor after floor until reaching the last, and the door opens. Two letters stand out across from me; a large golden M and A that lead to a small hallway where a desk awaits. There's no one sitting there—no one to let their boss know I'm here, and just when I take a step past the table, my world stops.

Literally. Unequivocally.

"Take another step and I'll shoot you." There's a hint of amusement in her tone, and the decadent sound sends a rush of excitement down my spine. Every nerve ending vibrates as her scent, a sweet and floral tone, infiltrates my senses. The owner of the voice is close, invading my personal space, and my nostrils flare—my cock giving a harsh jerk behind the confines of my zipper. *What the fuck?* "Now, the question here is…are you feeling frisky?"

"Those are dangerous words for a…" I begin but trail off when she steps into my line of sight, hand on her hip and eyes, challenging. *Fuck.* This woman is beautiful: a tiny doll with a hint of wickedness behind those seafoam eyes and a taste of depravity in every sinful curve.

Because I take her in.

All of her.

From her dark auburn hair to the dangerous heels on her tiny feet; this woman is perfection. At no more than five feet and three inches, she draws something from deep within that makes me throb where I stand, but it's the cockiness—that tiny curl of her upper lip that brings forth the asshole in me.

I take a step forward, loving the way her chest expands.

I lick my bottom lip, savoring the way she follows the movement with unveiled interest.

Who is she?

"Who are you?" she asks without pause. No shame in the way she watches me.

"I'll tell you after I meet with your boss, Muñeca." There's a slight narrowing of her eyes and purse to her top lip at my words, and they make me want to bite her. To keep pushing her buttons to see if she snaps—if she scratches. "So be a good girl for me and let him know Javier Lucas is here."

"What did you just say? What did you call me?" My eyes skim down her front and pause on a small name tag attached to her white silk top. "I think I heard wrong."

"Mariah," I croon low, savoring her name on my tongue and the small hitch in her breath. There's a slight tremble that she quickly hides behind a rigid back when I close the space between us. "Muñeca…my little doll, I asked that you do your job and announce me. I promise to reward you after."

"Step back," she hisses through gritted teeth, her expression angry, but I catch the straining of two little nipples against her top. The goose bumps on her arms. "I'll give you to the count of—"

"Mariah, let me know when Mr. Lucas arrives," a male voice says from the doorway at the far back of the room. It startles her, and she jumps back as if burned while I hold my ground, never taking my eyes off of her. Never addressing the man I came here to see.

"He's here, Malcolm." I don't like the way she says his name. The familiarity and ease when she should address him as her superior and nothing else.

"You mean Mr. Asher?" The bite in my tone isn't missed by either, and I feel the man's eyes on me. Sense when he comes closer, and if I were a lesser man, I'd cower back.

But I'm not. Never will be.

"Is there a problem here between you and my cousin, Mr. Lucas?"

Cousin? She's his cousin? I'm better than to miss an important fact like this.

For the first time in my life, I'm speechless—a bit embarrassed—and all I can manage is a shake of my head, and yet, pulling my attention away from her is impossible. The jealousy that burns through me like molten acid unnerves me, but at the same time, excites me. It's shaken me, and by the coquettish look in those beautiful orbs, Mariah knows this.

Finds my reaction amusing. *Motherfucking dangerous.*

"Mr. Lucas seems to take his formalities extremely serious, Malcolm. Cut him some slack. It might be a cultural thing." My eyes narrow at her words, but her cousin merely chuckles to my right where he seems to be taking in my fumble.

"Is that so, Javier?"

"Not at all." I flick my attention in his direction for ten seconds— moments where I take in the familial resemblance and smirk—before meeting Mariah's challenge head-on. "I've just been caught off guard by your cousin's beauty. That's all."

"I am spectacular, *cousin*," she says, and then fucks me in a way that tests my control. I'm left hanging by a very thin thread and every muscle in my body tenses, coils when her delicate fingers land on my chest while closing the distance between us. There's playfulness in her words while her body language teases. "Can't fault the man for having impeccable taste."

"You are trouble."

"And I think you like challenges." With that she walks past me, leaving me in the open room with the man I came to work for and a hard cock.

"*Christ.*"

"Is not affiliated with my family." Malcolm gives my shoulder a quick squeeze before turning toward his office, and I follow, walking through and taking a seat on the other side of his desk. And while I try to gather my thoughts and explain my behavior, Asher walks over to a small bar on the back wall and pours a few fingers' worth of clear liquid into two glasses.

He hands one to me and I immediately bring it to my lips, taking in the floral with a hint of citrus notes in the gin. "Thank you."

"You're welcome." His first sip is slow, and I expect the narrowing of his eyes when he swallows. Once, twice...on the third, Malcolm tosses back the spirit and walks around to his chair, taking a seat with the Chicago skyline as his backdrop. "Now, tell me why I shouldn't shoot you."

"That's the second time within thirty minutes someone in your family has threatened to do so."

"And we won't hesitate, either."

"Neither will I."

Malcolm doesn't react as one would expect with my threat. No. Not at all.

Instead, his smile widens and his narrowed eyes crinkle at the corner from amusement. "You've got balls, Javier. More than you should for a man outside of his country."

"What's that supposed to mean? Outside of my country?"

"Simply put?"

"Speak your mind, but I will do the same."

He's smirking, not a single thread of fear. "This isn't territory the Lucas family controls, nor is this a diplomacy. I hired you because I know you're the best and will be an asset to me."

"An asset?" Because my understanding is that I'd be in charge of his security for the next twelve months with a payout well over three million American dollars. I'm here to shape his guards and implement what I've done back home. "Explain yourself, Asher."

"I've done my homework."

"That makes two of us."

"Then you know I put out the call after the job you did for a client. News travels fast, and I'm not an easy man to impress." Placing the glass down, he rubs his chin. Dissecting me. Waiting for me to ask a question that will never leave my lips. I'm not a man who worries about the whys or maybes. Instead, I match his composure and wait.

And wait.

His patience matches mine and, in this game, neither is willing to bend. I know why he wanted me and why the call came, but the change in negotiation came much sooner than I expected.

"Ask me."

"How long?" There's no need for me to elaborate and he sits forward, opening the drawer to his right and pulling out two items: a file and a knife. Both are pushed my way and I open the folder, reading the contents inside. He's been busy. Most of the offenses here are well accounted for and I've never denied or hidden them, but it's the last page that makes me pause. "Who gave this to you?"

There's no mistaking the venom in my tone nor the tensing of my muscles for what it is…

A threat. A warning.

"I paid that contract out, Javier. No harm will come to them."

"Who did this, Malcolm?" I grit out through clenched teeth, crushing the paper in my hand. "Who the fuck was stupid enough to put a hit on the women in my family?"

"It's taken care of—"

"No. It isn't." With that, I stand, roughly pushing the chair back, and turn to leave, but before I reach the door, the knife once atop his desk embeds itself in the wall closest to me. My reaction is just as volatile, full of ire, and I grip the handle in my hand and pull it out. It's a beautiful piece, and by the weight, I can attest that it's solid gold. The blade is sleek, sharp, and I return the favor with a quick flick of the wrist.

"You haven't been dismissed, Javier. Sit down."

"Next time, I won't miss."

"Then you aren't interested in taking a walk with me and meeting the name on the sheet you've crumbled in your rage?" That stops me in my tracks. No rebuttal. Not a single word as I retake my seat, eyes on him with a neutral expression.

Malcolm Asher played his cards well, and I'm not stubborn enough to walk out with the silent offers he's made.

"I'm listening."

"Look at the last line and read it aloud."

"Castro Acevedo."

"Do you know him?" A nod is my response, seething at the nerve of this son of a bitch. Castro Acevedo works with the presidential family in Colombia, an enemy to mine. They all are. "This came as a direct order the moment you left the country. They want you to come back."

"I know they do."

"So much so, that they sent Acevedo here."

"Here?"

"Here."

"Where is he?"

"I'll give him to you on two conditions." And there it is. His upper hand. Malcolm stands then and takes his jacket off, placing it carefully over his chair. Then the cufflinks come off and the sleeves are rolled up. He doesn't answer me while he does this but does push across another piece of paper.

A smaller one with a single line written in neat penmanship.

THREE YEARS AND TEN BODIES. DO YOU ACCEPT?

"I can, but I have a stipulation of my own." Grabbing a pen from beside his stapler, I scribble my condition and slide it across.

I'LL CONCEDE TO AN OPEN CONTRACT WITH NO END DATE UNDER MY DISCRETION AFTER THE THREE YOU REQUEST, BUT IN RETURN, YOU DON'T INTERFERE.

"You're walking a very thin line, Lucas. My cousin isn't—"

"I want the chance to get to know her, Malcolm," I interject before he says something that will destroy any agreement we could arrive at. The click of his gun is quickly followed by mine as two hands raise, and we hold our ground. "I'd never disrespect her like that."

"Give me one good reason why I should allow this?"

Because while I don't believe in love at first sight, I won't deny she's caught my attention. That her sass has lit something within, and I want to see how dangerous her touch will be to:

My body. My mind.

I want her to burn me alive.

Keeping those thoughts to myself, I hold his stare. He might be the boss in Chicago, dominate the global market of finances, but I'm not some peon or low-level thug who came begging for a job off the streets. I'll give respect but demand it just the same.

It's the only way this agreement will work. I'd hate to hurt him or anyone in Mariah's family.

"First, she's a grown woman and makes up her own mind. Head of your family or not, I won't allow you to take choices away from her."

"And second?" There's less hostility in his tone, and my stance relaxes a bit.

"She undid me." I'm not going to beat around the bush or deny it. "Simple as that."

For a few beats of the clock, we remain quiet. Each holding the other's gaze. Our weapons are drawn.

"That honesty could get you in trouble."

"I'm not afraid."

"And it's the only reason I'll concede to your request." Malcolm places his gun atop the desk, and I do the same. "Welcome to the Asher family, Javier."

"Gracias." I extend a hand and he takes it, giving it a hard squeeze.

"You hurt her, and I'll kill you."

"I hurt her, and I can guarantee she'll pull the trigger herself." At my words he throws his head back and laughs, shaking his head while picking up his gun and mine, handing over the latter. "Smart man."

"Now, where do I sign?"

"Your word suffices, but I do believe you're owed a signing bonus."

Mariah

I'M IN TROUBLE.

So much trouble since the moment he walked onto my floor and knocked the very breath from my lungs. My palms are sweaty, and my chest feels tight. My knees feel weak, and the delicate slip of lace covering my mound has been rendered useless.

And all because of one man. A very self-assured and dangerous man.

"*Christ*, Mariah. Get ahold of yourself," I mumble under my breath, hand on the wall beside the elevator shaft after pressing the down button. For the next two hours, this floor will be closed to all foot traffic while they talk, and we await orders inside of a hidden room beneath the building where a selected few meet their fate.

The good.

The bad.

Their end.

The sound of his voice caresses my skin while the sound of footfalls over the marble floor follows. It's faint—melodic—and I shiver. Goose bumps break out across my skin while I lean my head on the wall and close my eyes.

Breathe in. Breathe out. *Never show weakness.*

It's the mantra I've been reciting since the day I learned who my family is. What they are—what I'm capable of without remorse.

However, thinking and doing it are two very different things because I've never been affected by a man like this. *Not even by him.*

I've never felt the rush of excitement or the lick of heat settle low in my abdomen with such ferocity from his mere presence.

At the moment, I feel like the virgin I'm not and haven't been in years. And while I've only slept with one man, a worthless jerk no longer walking this earth, I feel unsure of myself.

Nervous. Jittery. Unable to comprehend how one devilish smirk could get under my skin with such ease. How with one look from a pair of soulful brown eyes I lost more than my composure.

His height made me feel dainty.

His muscles made me breathless.

But what's more dangerous than his looks is the slickness of his mouth and the challenge he presents. Because this man with his white, open-at-the-collar dress shirt and black slacks wasn't intimidated by me or who my family is. His cockiness was playful while his stare was a silent promise to devour his prey…

Me. I'm his prey.

The private elevator that leads to the lowest level of the Asher building opens then, and I let out a breath I didn't know I'd been holding. Each step inside is a bit shaky, and more so when the lingering scent of his cologne infiltrates my senses.

Fuck. It's earth and rain mixed with a hint of spice that causes my thighs to clench and another stuttered breath to escape. "He can't work here." *Malcolm will have to find someone else.* But as those words run through my mind, a pang of remorse follows. I can't help my attraction to him, even if he equally pisses me off.

If anything, it's the danger—the demand in his tone that excites me.

He's not going to *yes, ma'am* me because of my last name.

He isn't what I expected to arrive today, and I feel off my game.

The large metal door opens, and the men within greet me with a nod of their head. They're standing against the back wall, watching a man tied to a chair in a three-piece suit whose facial expression gives way to his fear and a bloody encounter with his captors.

We know why he's here, but he doesn't. We've given him the accommodation he deserves while he's returned our kindness with whining and unnecessary tears.

"Has he been given anything to eat or drink since last night?" I ask Carmelo, a trusted guard. He's standing closest to Acevedo and without the customary all-white coveralls that Malcolm demands his cleanup crew wear.

"Not—"

"Please, Miss," he interrupts Carmelo, looking at me from the one eye that isn't swollen shut. "This is a mistake. Help me out of here, and you'll be rewarded by the Colombian president."

Carmelo raises his hand to strike the idiot, but I give him a minute shake of the head and he stands down. Instead, he retakes his position of silence while biting back a chuckle.

"Will he, now?"

"Yes." Relief colors his features as he thinks I'm intrigued by the offer. He has no idea who I am. "You'll never work another day in your life."

"Never?" I keep my voice low, almost sweet and innocent. He's buying it too. "I'd be rich?"

"Beyond your comprehension, *linda*." Because calling me beautiful is supposed to win me over. *Idiot.*

"But what if my taste runs a little more—"

"Whatever you want."

"Morbid," I finish off with a glare, and his lips snap shut. His shoulders slump and eyes close, a few stray tears falling down his bruised cheek. "Why the tears, Acevedo? Why the sudden plea for mercy when you were willing to murder women and children to hurt the Lucas men?"

"What is he to you?"

"You've always been a curious one, Castro," Javier answers for me, his voice reverberating throughout every square inch of the room as he steps through the threshold, and the horror-filled expression on our guest is comical. His body shakes and a pitiful cry escapes a set of chapped lips while a breath gets caught in my throat.

My pulse races. My nipples tighten. My core clenches.

Lord help me.

"How? Why?" Acevedo looks to me for answers, but I merely shrug and take my place beside a silent Malcolm. My cousin's standing a bit to the left, leaving Javier to run this show, but remains within everyone's line of sight.

"Because you sold your soul to the devil and he delivered you to me." Javier steps forward while slowly undoing the buttons of his shirt and slips the garment off his shoulders. He's precise in his movements, adorable while placing the neatly folded dress shirt atop a small table close to Acevedo.

There are no weapons in sight. No way for him to exact revenge, but the prospect of what those muscles—the bulging cords of tattooed flesh— can do leave me breathless.

"Javier, I was just following commands." It leaves Acevedo in a low whisper, but the silence of the room makes it so we all hear clearly. "Quintero—"

"Fucked you without lubrication," he spits out, face contorted in rage before softening when he looks in my direction. The action is fast, and the softness that flickers in those warm orbs pulls a smile from my lips. It's brief, this moment we share, before he looks away and the killer I've heard so much about makes an entrance.

He's magnificent. Overwhelming.

Perfect.

"Please." Tears and snot and the faint scent of urine are unmistakable in the room. "Please don't kill me."

"You accepted the offer Quintero made."

"But I never carried it out!" Javier just smiles, walking around his form once before stopping at his right wrist. Without pause, he undoes the rope keeping Acevedo in place and then the other. Both feet are next. "Please, Javier. I didn't touch anyone; that has to mean something!"

"Stand up."

"Just listen...*fuck!*" The first strike is straight to his mouth and two teeth fly out, landing near Malcolm's feet. The next is to his neck and he chokes out a cry, bending at the waist with both hands up in an attempt to defend himself while his legs give out.

Javier doesn't let up, though. Blow after vicious blow is landed on Acevedo's upper body and the back of his head. Javier's knuckles are white and bruised. His chest is heaving, his mouth curled into a sinister grin.

He's brutally beautiful and my walls clench when he drives a knee in to the bent man's face.

"You knew exactly what you were accepting, Castro." Fisting Acevedo's hair, Javier forces the bleeding man to meet his stare from his position on his knees. There's a gash across the bridge of his nose and the swelling has already begun, but it's not enough for the assassin now working for the head of the Asher family. Bloodthirst is real, and he's given in to the need for vengeance. "I warned you once in the past, and there won't be a second chance."

With that, he lifts a leg and brings Acevedo's face down to his knee repeatedly. Over and over without pause, he breaks the man's face down to the point it's nothing but a bloody mass of cuts and broken bones.

And even then, he continues until our guest's nose caves in and all his front teeth fall out. Both men are a mess, but it's the beast standing that holds me captive—spellbound—and unable to look away as he smiles and then lands another direct strike to Acevedo's jaw.

There's a sickening crunch, a splash of red that decorates the floor, and then a body falls limply, making the most disturbing gurgling sound. Each breath becomes more shallow than the last. Each second his body struggles, you see the life drain from his eyes until there's nothing left but a broken man and the victor standing over his frame with his eyes set on me.

Around us, Malcolm's men quickly move as they begin the process of decontamination...

Water is turned on, and the floor near Javier is flushed out.

The body is removed in a large black bag.

My cousin leaves without a word.

And while the world carries on, we watch each other. Take in the rise and fall of our chests and the mirroring want that's left me breathless, a bit nervous and unsure.

"We need to talk, Muñeca." *Why do I like it so much when he calls me that?* I'm already shaking my head before he finishes, ignoring the clench in my core, and take a few steps back. There's mirth in his eyes, but he doesn't follow, choosing instead to tilt his head while licking his lips. I'm inspected from head to toe. His stare feels like a soft caress. "But not today."

That catches me off guard and I pause mid-step, my face scrunching up in confusion. "What?"

My sputter amuses him, and the jerk lets out a low, throaty chuckle. "I said, not today."

"Then why are you wasting my time," I grit out through clenched teeth, hands balled at my sides while fighting to ignore the pictures adorning his upper body, more so the black and white angel of death design that looks like the counterpart to my fallen angel. They're both Gothically haunting yet beautiful. A mated pair. *This is ridiculous, chica. Snap out of it.* "Better yet, I'll see you around. I have better things to do than—"

"I'll be picking you up tomorrow night for dinner, Mariah."

"I'm not going out with you." What kind of game is he playing?

Javier rubs a hand across his chest, spreading the fresh blood across the dark angel. "You will."

"What makes you so sure? I'm not a woman who lowers her standards."

At my words, he takes the steps between us and grips my chin. His hold isn't hard or meant to hurt, but to prove how much he affects me, and he does. I'm jittery and sensitive between my thighs, and goose bumps rise across my flesh. But more damaging to my psyche is the hungry way he watches me. Memorizes my face while cataloging each reaction with that devilish smirk across his lips.

I'm screwed. More than.

"Be a good girl, Muñeca. Don't fight me."

"You haven't earned the right to make demands on my time."

"I own your time, Mariah. Learn to accept that." Then the bastard lowers his head and kisses my reddening cheek, rendering me speechless. Unsettled. Angry at his cockiness.

Then on the next breath, I'm turned on by the heat in his eyes and command in his tone.

This sudden urge to test his patience and conviction is a dangerous game, and I find myself meeting his stare without an ounce of fear. Without a care for the consequences.

Because I'm not a wilting flower, and I'm ready to play if he is.

"To own me, you have to catch me first, Mr. Lucas. Are you worthy?"

"I'd kill every man in this city if you so much as asked."

Christ, those words stir something deep within me, but I walk away before impulses become problems down the road. Each step away from him is harder than the last, but I make my way back to my floor without looking back.

He doesn't follow me inside the elevator. He doesn't demand I respond, but I am aware of his heated stare and then the near suffocating presence he exudes the moment he steps onto the CEO's floor an hour later. Javier doesn't talk to me as he strides past my desk fully clothed and without a single hair out of place.

No blood. No slick remarks. Not so much as a look in my direction before slipping inside of Malcolm's office. It bothers me, this ignoring my narrowing eyes and the small huff that escapes, but more so when a few minutes later my phone rings with my cousin's extension blinking.

"Yes, boss?"

"Two coffees, please, and bring in the Bernard file."

"Right away." I'm already grabbing the folder he needs, anticipating it earlier in the day, and closing the bottom drawer before locking it. There's certain client information that can't be lost or tampered with—stolen—and I only keep on hand the bare necessities at all times.

No one knows where we store physical documents except Malcolm and me. They have no access to the hidden room with restricted access a floor below. Most never realize that this building has an entire floor blocked off and that the elevator shaft skips it.

It was designed that way. Made to appear as though the vault room downstairs was its separate floor when in fact, it connects with one small step changing the elevations.

With the file in my hand of a notorious French art smuggler worth a billion from trading in the black market, I head to the small kitchen on the other side of the wall behind me. It's not large, but it gets the job done for what we need; coffee being the main focus.

That, and pastries from a small Hungarian bakery my family loves to visit. There isn't a single house that bears the last name Asher who doesn't have a never-ending stock, and I plate a few while pressing the start button on the Keurig.

While it percolates, I make a conscious decision to let Javier use my mug. A shiny and pink and full of glitter unicorn cup that my aunt gave me after our Black Friday hunt last year.

"Good-looking jerk," I mutter under my breath, filling both cups before adding creamer, sugar, and the pastries to the tray. "Should've just…*Jesus*!" I scream, almost dropping their refreshments. "How long have you been standing there?"

My tone is accusatory, my posture defensive, but Javier only grins at me while pulling the tray from my hands and placing it on a small dinette table to his left. "Long enough."

"For what?" I'm shaking, but not from fear. His scent envelops me in a web of want.

"To hear the need in your voice."

"You mean repulsion?"

"You and I both know that's a lie." Closer, he takes the three steps separating us and grips my hips with both hands. "And the feeling is very mutual, sweetheart."

"Let go," I hiss out and then bite back my disappointment when he does. His warmth is gone. He's now by the door, holding it open with the back of his foot with the full tray in his hands. "What game are you playing at?"

"Hurry up with that file, Muñeca. Asher wants to go over it with me and I don't have all day to wait."

"You motherfu—"

"Watch the words that leave that pretty little mouth."

"Or what?"

"Or you'll find yourself praying to a different God." Then he winks before walking away, leaving me an angry, frustrated, and intrigued ball of nerves that follows a few minutes later while plotting his demise.

I'm not going to let him get one over on me.

He should be afraid. Very afraid.

JAVIER

S HE'S GLORIOUS IN her indignation.

Beautiful and majestic while placing the file down atop Malcolm's desk with more force than necessary while glaring at me. *So sexy in her anger.* There's something about her that's gotten under my skin, and the more I see of her sweet lips and dangerous eyes, the more I want.

To taste. To bite. To bend her over and show her how good it could be.

Every instinct within me fights to bring her closer, to not question the why, but I hold my stance with a stoic expression on my face. Her every action draws me in, and the dare in her eyes fuels a fire I've never experienced before.

I'm not one to date and have never given a single fuck about settling down.

Not in this life. Not when your next day is never guaranteed and leaving a family behind is irresponsible. So I've kept to myself and when the need arose, I found a willing woman who understood the no-questions-asked and no-repeats rule.

Moreover, I've seen it before in my family when Alejandro's father was incarcerated for being an honest man. Women and kids suffer. Most end up repeating the cycle because that's all they'll ever know. Because they'll always be the product of what society deems to be scum.

I'll make an exception for her, though. That thought has been running through my mind since our little exchange earlier in the day.

"Will that be all, boss?" It leaves her on a sneer directed at me, and I bite back a smirk.

"Yes." Asher's eyes are on me, watching my reactions, while I continue to ignore anything but her. "Just make sure we're not disturbed. You can head out whenever you want."

"Wish I could, but I'm meeting someone for dinner nearby. It would be a waste of time to drive—"

"Who?"

"None of your concern, Mr. Lucas. Remember that." The glare is gone, and the sass is back. It's there in the swing of her hips as she passes by my chair on her way out and then the quick look of triumph when I reach out and stop her, my grip of her wrist firm. "Is there something you need?"

"There is." I rub my thumb along the veins of her wrist, enjoying the tiny little flutters at the pulse point. The softness that overtakes her features and an almost inaudible sigh that makes me swallow back the demand to submit and clear her calendar. *Not yet. Not here.* "Do you have regular milk for the coffee? Could you get some for me?"

"I'm not your—"

"Play nice, Mariah." It's on the tip of my tongue to tell our boss to fuck off, but I take in a deep breath and let it out slowly. "He's new and valuable."

"My pleasantries will cost extra."

"I'll remember that." She doesn't pull her hand away from me during their exchange. Instead, I notice the small step in my direction. The leaning of her hip. "We do have milk, Javier. Is two percent okay?"

"That would be fine."

"Then I'll be right back."

Neither of us moves until a throat clears and our heads turn toward an amused CEO. "Was that for today's coffee or tomorrow's?"

"My apologies." Reluctantly, I release my hold and she nods, giving me a quick smile before exiting. There was no mention of the milk I requested or if she'd be back, but I watch that door, hoping to catch another glimpse of the little demon.

"You know…" Malcolm begins, and I tilt my head so he knows I'm listening "…I thought this would be a mistake and I'd kill you before the week was over."

"That's a funny assumption."

"The dead part?"

"The part where you think I'd go down easily."

"I don't underestimate you, Javier. That's where it becomes dangerous for you." At those words, I shift my attention to him and arch a brow. "Your heart is black, and I hired you for that quality, but watching my cousin run you around will be the highlight of my days. Just don't let it interfere with work. You do, and the consequences won't be agreeable."

"Understood."

"Good." He waves a hand in the air. "Now, go get your milk because she's not coming back."

"Not necessary." Picking up my lukewarm cup of coffee, I bring it to my lips and take a large sip. "I take it black and without sugar. That was just to annoy her."

"She's not a wilting flower. Her bark is darker than her bite."

"I'm counting on that."

THE FIRST THING I notice as I exit Malcolm's office a few hours later is the lack of movement. No one's here. No noise. Nothing but the sweet lingering scent of her perfume and the temptation it causes.

It pulls me in the direction of her desk where it's stronger, where I can almost feel Mariah's fire surround me, and I sit in her chair.

A little creepy? Maybe.

Do I care? Not one bit.

The first thing I take notice of is how organized—uncluttered—her items are. Not so much as a pen is out of place and I remedy that by repaying the little beauty for making me hard all afternoon.

For each time she walked into his office with a file.

For each time she brushed past my arm, extending herself while placing an item down in front of him.

My muñeca could've walked around but chose not to. So I'm choosing to do this.

I pull out a pen with my name monogrammed and leave it in her holder. Then, I take hers. All ten of them. A simple switch that will annoy her, and so will the flipping of file placements.

What's on the left will move to the right and vice versa.

"She's going to kill you."

"More than likely." I'm scribbling a note for her to find before standing from her seat and facing an amused Malcolm. "I'm not afraid."

"Don't say I never gave you fair warning. I think I've more than done that today."

"Understood." Patting my pocket with her pens, I smirk. "Now, have a good evening."

The elevator's already waiting when I press the arrow down, and as I step through, my phone rings. It stops at the third ping and then starts again once I press the button for the lobby.

Not many people have this number, so I pull it out and answer without looking at the caller ID. "Hello?"

"Mijo!" Mom's excited voice comes through the line, wind rustling on her side. "How are you? Are you eating okay?"

"I'm good. Can't complain too much." The large metal doors close and the metal box begins to descend as I lean back. "I'm pretty settled in now and I've made the necessary moves. Have you thought about my proposal?"

"Not interested."

"Think of it as a mini-vacation." I want her out of the country for a few months. "Just enough time for you to relax, maybe cook me a meal or two—"

"I know what you're doing, and it's unnecessary." There's a hint of annoyance in her tone, that motherly don't-argue-with-me-on-this that almost makes me laugh, but I rein it in. If I go that route, I'll lose. Ida Lucas is the most stubborn woman I know. "Besides, I'm staying with your aunt Sara for now. Alejandro picked me up yesterday against my will."

"Did he, now?" The doors open and I step out, nodding at the guard beside the entrance. He has an envelope in his hand and casually slips it into mine before I cross the exit. I know what's inside: my ID for clearance, a key to a company SUV, and a monetary donation for agreeing to his terms. "When was this?"

"Did you give the order?" she counters, and I can imagine her arched brow and the drumming of nails atop the wheelchair's arm. "Am I being shipped off next, too?"

"Mamita, I had nothing to do with that. I swear." Lies. All lies, and she knows this. Her huff over the line tells me as much, but at the moment I'm left with few options. With Quintero Jr. coming into power as the next Colombian president, we're on the defensive. Their family hates ours, and the feeling is mutual. "Listen, come and visit me here and see for yourself how well I'm living. Even cook me a meal or two?"

"That's the second time you mention food."

"Just miss yours."

"No." There's a pause between us, the silence heavy right before she sighs. "I love you, Javiercito. Love you more than my own life, but I need you to accept something. I was born in Colombia and I'll die here...that family nor their hijueputa obsession with mine will send me running."

"One week?" It's a compromise. The parking garage is up ahead and I walk toward it, ignoring the passersby and the one lady in her fifties that sends me a wink.

"Three days."

Pausing at the Asher garage entrance, I look up toward the sky. "Five, and—" I'm cut off by the sudden bump to my side and the sharp pain at my hip. The hit isn't hard, but I do lose my balance and end up staring at the car's owner with my front bent over and hands splayed over the hood, phone still caught between car and shoulder.

Her eyes dance with mirth.

Her lips quirk up into a devilish grin.

Mariah's the epitome of trouble and simply asks me to move out of her way with the flick of her wrist. The action is meant to be condescending, but I catch the sly lick of her lips when I bite my own.

I'm not mad. Not at all.

She hit me with her car, and I'm hard. Throbbing.

Get out of my way, she mouths, and I shake my head. She's revving the engine, and I grin.

"Javier! Mijo!" Mom's voice gets louder with each unanswered call of my name, and it's the worry in her tone that pulls me back from lustful thoughts. It's enough to make me stand and move to the side—to give the beautiful little criminal a bow as she stops and lowers her window beside me.

"You might want to take care of that. It looks painful?" She's not the least bit worried about her actions or the fact I'm going to be bruised where her sports car met my flesh. No, her eyes devour me where I stand and the heat behind her hooded stare is thrilling. More satisfying than every throat I've slit.

"I will." My voice is rough and my cock flexes behind my zipper. "You have a good night."

"You, too." Her brows furrow and lips pout at my dismissal, driving past me when I don't say anything else.

But now isn't the time. Not yet.

I'm going to confuse and overwhelm and then conquer Mariah. I'm going to own and enjoy her.

"Que fue eso?" Mom asks in my ear, and I laugh at the simple yet arduous question: *what was that?*

"That was your future daughter-in-law hitting me with her car."

She gasps, the sound a mixture of excitement and awe. "What did you say?"

"I met someone crazier than me." *And I'm infatuated after one encounter.* Crazy but true, and yet, I'm following my gut on this one. Something is driving me toward her, and I'll let it.

"Give me a month or two and I'll come."

"Now you want to come. Wait…why so long?"

"One, yes. And two, none of your business."

"What are you up to, woman? Do I need to call Alejandro?"

A loud giggle comes through her end of the line and I smile. "Quit it and send me a picture of this beautiful, crazy girl."

"I'm still calling."

"Don't ruin my small getaway with your aunt, kid. I need some relaxation near the coast."

"Two months."

"Deal, Javi. Now be the gentleman your father never was."

My face scrunches up in disgust at her insinuation. "I'm going to ignore that last statement."

"Put a ring on it first, Javier. Mother knows best."

Mariah

"**Y**OU'RE KIDDING ME?" My friend Allison asks between fits of giggles later that night, her margarita sloshing—spilling over the rim and dirtying her white silk blouse. She's more than amused by my encounter with Javier; the certifiable she-hoe is jealous and excited. "He sounds delicious."

"He is." No point in denying it. I'm sure it's written across my face and highlighted by the lights above our table inside of our favorite taco bar. There aren't many people here tonight and I'm glad. The decibel of her gossiping battle-cry is embarrassing.

Especially since my shame surrounds me like a halo, and now that the lust-induced fog he created has receded, I'm left exposed. Open to judgment by one of the few people that know my past and the promise I made that night.

Someone who's been trying to get me to agree to a blind date for a month now. *I'll never hear the end of this.*

"Height, eye color, and to the right or left?"

The mere question makes my body flash hot from jealousy—an aggravating feeling that I fight to push back. It takes me a minute, breathing in and out slowly while forcing my expression to remain friendly. She's not buying it; her smirk only intensifies my annoyance.

"At least six foot three, warm brown, and don't ever ask me that again."

"Possessive much?" The gleam in her eyes makes me want to hit her, but I settle instead for a subtle middle finger and shrug. "Girl, I'm liking him more and more. This level of feisty looks good on you." Bringing the glass to her mouth, she takes a large sip, smiling before it turns into a petulant pout. "Now, if only Malcolm would marry me, we could double date."

"Not happening." Two voices answer, and she goes from red to white to near blue as my cousin slips into a seat beside mine, shocking her.

"You suck!"

Malcolm rolls his eyes, not sparing her outburst much thought. They've always been that way, though. Allison says something, he blows her off, and then she whines.

One day she'll get it. He's just not into her, and the man isn't subtle about it. Malcolm isn't cruel, but his disinterest shows clear as day.

He doesn't trust women after Karina.

The woman who catches his eye has to be near sainthood to put up with his grouchiness.

"You're crashing our dinner and you're going to ignore me?"

"Option one or two," he says, impassive eyes on mine. I know what he's asking. Life or death.

He can't— "Don't touch him." It leaves me through gritted teeth and clenching hands, the stem of my glass breaking. It pierces my hand, the sting surprising me while he just nods, stands, and leans down to kiss my forehead.

"Take the day off and sleep in."

"That's it?" Not telling me it's a bad idea. Not warning me about fraternizing.

"It's all I needed." For a brief second his eyes soften before he exits, Carmelo walking out behind him.

In the background, I hear Allison chirping about Malcolm and his suit and something about handsome cocky men, but I can't focus past the emotion of something happening to Javier. It's left this raw mark on me. Hurt me, and I hate it.

I feel vulnerable, something I vowed to myself to never feel for a man again.

Walk away, Mariah. Men like him are all the same.

"Are you even listening to me?" Alli's staring at me with a raised brow, and all I can do is down what's left of my margarita in one go, clean my hand with the nearest napkin, and ask a passing waiter for the check.

"Let's go."

"Go? Go where?" Any other time I'd find her expression comical—as if I've grown a second head and she isn't sure whether to call for help or display me like a circus attraction. "Mari, we need to—"

"Figure out my next move and take me to get stitches."

"Oh shit!"

"Indeed."

A SUDDEN KNOCK on my door wakes me from a nap. I've been crashed out on my large sofa with a soft afghan, ignoring the world and all my duties while trying to push the memories of the last twenty-four hours out of my mind.

His presence.

His effect on me.

The person on the other side of the door pounds louder, the rhythmic *tap tap tap* grinding my gears and I throw the blanket off, stretching my arms high and causing my back to arch and release a soothing pop. I'm a bit stiff, but it feels good to do so, and I move my neck from side to side to do the same.

A few quick cracks and I throw my legs over the edge, stumbling a bit to the door. "I'm coming!"

All noises cease and I quickly grab my Glock, the one I keep by the entrance table, and stand on the tips of my toes to look through the peep-hole. It's a young man with an old trucker hat and a shirt that matches the company logo. He's holding a delivery bag and I stand back, tucking the gun in the waistband of my spandex shorts.

Maybe Malcolm sent this?

With that thought, I open the door partway and look at the kid with a raised brow. "Can I help you?"

"Delivery for a Mariah Asher," he squeaks out, and I fight back a smile. All men are the same, and with how little I answered the door in, I'm surprised the looks-to-be high schooler hasn't drooled a bit. Because I know I'm a beautiful woman, that I turn heads, but I don't live in a land of delusion where appearances make you untouchable. I can hold my own, and I'm just as deadly as Malcolm when pushed.

"That's me. Who sent you?"

His eyes sweep down quickly over my crop top, and he swallows hard. "No name, ma'am. I was just told to deliver and—"

Whatever explanation he has dies the moment a dominating presence makes itself known. He's here, standing but a few feet from me with a handsome smile on his face, taking me in as I do him, though, when he reaches the expanse of bare skin—between my crop top and the waistband of my shorts—his expression turns predatory.

Javier's eyes narrow and he takes a step closer. Just one, and I feel him as though he'd pressed every square inch of his muscular frame against mine.

"Hello, Muñeca."

"How?" is all I manage to get past the sudden dryness of my mouth and the shaking of my limbs. He's standing there looking devilish in a pair of grey sweats and a University of Chicago hoodie with a smirk across his tempting lips.

He's wearing my alma mater. He's becoming a weakness.

There's just something about a man dressed down, comfortable, and unable to hide the muscles beneath. To hide the hardness between his legs.

It's the highlight of the cold months for women all across the world. A special treat we enjoy without being obvious, though, he seems to know where my mind is as a touch of pink grazes my cheek.

"I'm here for our date." Javier bites his bottom lip, eyes softening while perusing my figure. He pauses at my chest, then hips, before spending a little extra time on my thighs and the nonexistent gap there.

I'm curvaceous, and he likes it. More than, and his heavy-lidded eyes are a tell.

"How do you know where I live?" I ask instead, fighting my smile back at his audacity. At the hint of possessiveness in his stance. Because I can't deny to myself that his unexpected visit is a bit sexy. Pushy, yet cute. "How sure are you that I won't shoot you?"

Javier shrugs, placing a hand on the delivery boy standing a few inches from him. He doesn't look at him when turning him away. Not so much as a word when pointing toward the elevator bank down the hall, where the kid scurries off to. "I'm sure you can, but a little wound doesn't scare me."

"Wanna bet?"

"Let me in, beautiful." He takes a step forward but I hold my stance, hand on the doorknob. "Are you going to deny me this meal?"

"I'm tempted to." But I don't want to deny him. A large part of me wants to drag him inside and do something that I shouldn't. *Why?*

Why is he getting under my skin?

Why am I curious?

Why is the thought of turning him away unattractive?

"You will." Then he wrecks me. Utterly destroys my resolve by jutting his bottom lip out in a pout.

"Get in here," I hiss out, pulling the door open and stepping back. "Hurry up before I regret it."

"Gracias, Muñeca." The moment he crosses my threshold, I shiver. But more so when he stops an inch from me and lays a kiss on my forehead. "Point me in the direction of the kitchen."

"Right through there." I'm pointing behind me where an archway opens into my kitchen, but my eyes are on him. On the way he bends and picks up the bags with our food. On the way he passes by me and his scent surrounds me—hugs me while I lean over just a bit.

I slightly stumble. His chuckle pulls me from almost tripping and I close my eyes, gritting my teeth and clenching my uninjured hand. A mistake, since it causes a whimper to slip and for the man in question to rush back to my side.

It's then he notices my injured hand, the bandage a little red from the few beads of blood that seeped through the six stitches over my palm. His touch is soothing, a gentle sweep of fingers over my wound that calms and excites. Sends my nerves into overdrive.

Javier doesn't say anything, but those warm brown eyes stare into mine, gauging my reaction, and when he's happy with what he sees, I'm swept up and into strong arms. I'm cradled against his hard, warm chest. He's kissing my temple while striding back to my kitchen.

"I'm okay," I say, voice low, feeling almost shy for a second as he deposits me atop a counter stool and disarms me on my next breath. Javier takes my gun and places it beside me; I can feel his gaze as if it were a caress. "It's just a small cut."

Two fingers tip my face up, and my breath catches in my throat at the look of lust mixed with pride. His face is close to mine. His exhale is my inhale. "Still unacceptable."

"Javier, I—"

"Let me feed you, Mariah."

"Okay."

JAVIER

"*O*KAY."

The word sounds like heaven coming from her plump lips. She was granting me entrance into her life with it, a soft agreement that I'd be around from now on getting to know her. And if tomorrow her attitude returns and her eyes challenge me, I'm not backing down.

Not after holding her close and receiving the small smile she's giving me.

Because there's something about this fiery beauty that calls to me—that pulls me in closer with each interaction. I know it's fast and dangerous for me as I now work for her cousin, but I like tempting death and I'm unafraid of the possible repercussions.

"So what did you bring me?" Mariah's peeking at me from beneath long lashes and my cock jerks, the movement caught by her. The sweatpants do little to hide my length and girth and the little demon licks her lips, unaware of her reaction. There are goose bumps across her flesh and hard nipples pressing against the thin strap of fabric she calls a shirt, high-lighting the piercings there.

My mouth waters and I swallow hard, fighting back the desire to nip each nipple. "Do you like your food spicy or mild?" There's no mistaking the hunger in my tone, nor the way I admire her body. "Anything in partic-ular you don't like?"

"Hot." It's breathy. "Very hot."

"Good girl."

"And no onions if possible. Just not the biggest fan."

"As you wish." We're more alike than I thought, and I hide my smile because I hate the vegetable and order everything without it. It's another coincidence that I plan to take full advantage of without her knowing, like the fact we live in the same building, my unit being two floors below hers. "Is tea okay, or do you want a Coke?"

"Tea, please." So complacent. So sweet. Such a little liar.

Pulling out the first container from the Thai place I found a few days after moving here, I begin to lay them out on her counter. Because nothing in life is simple, and she'll put up a fight. It's in her nature to do so, just like it is for me. This life hardens you—family ties will hold you down—and Mariah will give me as good as I gift tenfold while smirking and taunting me with what she believes I'll never own.

It's a dare I'll accept. Be there every fucking step of the way, and when reality smacks and she's left choking for air, I'll pat her back with a grin.

There's a reason we are both here, and I won't let her stand in my way of putting together this enigma and the feelings she evokes.

"Do you like green papaya—"

"I love it! I've been known to eat an entire container all by myself." Her little squeal is so far removed from the woman I met earlier yesterday, but I like it. More than I probably should, but this is another side to her, and uncovering each is fast becoming an obsession. "This place has the best, too. Did you get any drunken noodles? And chopsticks? Can't eat this without chopsticks."

"You're beautiful when you smile." The smile drops and she eyes the gun and then me, trying to figure out who's faster if push came to shove. *Dangerous little criminal.* "I'm not taking your piece, calmate."

"What does that mean?" she asks after a minute of silence, watching me dish her meal onto paper plates I brought with me. Noodles, salad, and my newest addiction: chicken basil fried rice.

Setting her food down, I reach back into the bag and produce a few sauces and the chopsticks she needs. "It means to calm down. Now eat."

"I'm not that—" A loud growl comes from her stomach, and I raise a brow. "Fine. I'm starving...are you happy?"

"Very." Plastic fork in my hand, I grab the container of rice and dig in. No talking. No glares. We eat in silence while watching the other. I'm leaning against the counter behind me and she's perched like the queen she is in her seat, eyes happy while enjoying a little takeout with me.

This feels right.

"Can't use chopsticks?" Mariah asks, bringing me away from that thought. *I'm so at ease with her.* She's patting her stomach after finishing two-thirds of her plate and eyes the rest of the salad. "Are you clumsy..." Mariah picks up her iced tea and brings it to her lips, sipping while assessing me "...or a messy eater?"

Wiping my mouth with a napkin, I mock glare. "No. Just never used them."

"So, the big bad man isn't good at something."

"I'm good at plenty."

"Tell me one?"

"Ruffling your feathers." At my words, her eyes narrow. "And you? What are you good at, Ms. Asher?"

"Shooting. I have a very precise shot."

"Always with the threats." I tsk, shaking my head. "After all I've done for you."

"Done for me?" There's a curse that slips through thin lips and a twitch in her hand, but I don't back down. I'm getting to know her through each interaction. With the gestures that come naturally and not the composed heat at work. "Please enlighten me here. What exactly have you done again?"

"Saved you from a boring existence." A flush of red sweeps across her cheeks and her breathing accelerates, chest rising rapidly. It's a beautiful sight.

This woman in a simple pair of shorts and top, with her nipples hard and the barbells through them rubbing against the cotton, fuming at me while trying to dispel her truth. "Now, it's my turn to ask the second question."

"Hit me." Yeah, I'm under her skin, and she hates to crave it.

"What's your guilty pleasure?"

"Life hack videos that make no sense." Mariah takes another bite from her salad and then tilts her head to the side. "Weirdest food you've eaten?"

"I'd say fugu on a trip to Japan."

"You ate a poisonous fish?"

"Yes." At my blasé response, her eyebrows shoot up to her hairline. *Cute.* "It was quite the experience."

"How so?"

"My cousin, Emiliano, ate too much and couldn't feel his tongue and lips all night. Let's just say he drooled on himself more than once."

"Oh my God!" Snickers erupt from her, shoulders shaking while a small palm meets the countertop. "That's priceless."

"His wife didn't think so." I snort, and that only causes her to laugh harder. Full-on belly laugh. "She ran him down the street with a flip-flop after he left a trail of spit down her cheek. He went in for a quick kiss and left a nasty mess."

"That's mean," she tries to say with a straight face but fails and falls into another fit of giggles. "Why did you let him eat so much? Shouldn't you have—"

"We warned him. The chef warned him." Bringing the can of soda to my lips, I take a quick drink. "But Emiliano, being the stubborn mule he is, decided that a little venom couldn't hurt and that the tingling feeling on his lips was fun. That was all on him."

"Still messed up."

"My turn."

Her amusement dies and she juts out her jaw. "Hit me."

"Favorite animal?"

"I'm a dog lover and miss owning one." Sadness flashes in her eyes, but she looks away and finds whatever is above my head fascinating. "My Frenchie passed away six months ago."

"I'm sorry to hear that, doll. My condolences—"

"And you? Favorite animal?"

"Wild? Jaguar. Domestic? Dog." Seeing we're no longer eating, I pick up our trash and clean up, storing the leftovers in her fridge. I'm thankful now to have bought two containers of the green papaya salad, not knowing it was her favorite. "I have a Doberman back home."

"Are you bringing him to the States?" Once again, those seafoam eyes meet mine and my skin prickles with electricity—this almost dominating force that makes me take a step closer. And closer. I don't stop until I'm around the counter and sitting beside her curvaceous form.

Knees touching. Arms brushing.

Why am I so intrigued by you?

"No. Chulo is staying with my mother in Colombia." Her expression is soft and inviting, and all I want to do is kiss her. Taste her. "I'll miss my little Parcerito, but she needs him more. He's a great dog and very protective of her."

"Chulo? That's a weird name." That teasing tone does nothing but excite me, but I don't fall into her trap, choosing instead to just roll my eyes. Something out of character for me, but that's what she's doing— breaking my normal behaviors and replacing them with childishness. *She's trouble.* "What does it mean?"

"That he's the most handsome good boy out there."

"Doesn't sound very threatening or protective."

"It's meant to be that way. Always confuse your opponent. What they see is never what you are."

"Hmmm," is her response before jumping down from her perch, the stool a little high for her, and I find the action cute. Adorable even. Walking around to her Keurig, she opens the pod holder beside it and peruses the contents. Seconds turn to minutes. Our breathing and the sound of plastic pods jiggling against each other fills the space before she huffs and turns. Green eyes on mine, she purses her lips. "Would you like some coffee?"

"No, thank you." This is my cue to leave. Mariah is a difficult woman, the few interactions we've had prove as much, but I know when to back off. When to strike. There's something hidden behind those eyes—a little wariness she fights to conceal—but I see her. All of her, and plan to erase every doubt with my actions. "I'll be heading out."

If she's surprised by my words, her expression doesn't show it, but body language never lies. Tense muscles, hands clenching, and the tapping of her right foot. I wouldn't be surprised if she's unaware of these actions, but I'm loving every single one.

Fight all she wants; I've gotten to her.

"Let me walk you out."

"No need. I know the—"

"That wasn't a request," she grits out, chin jutted out. Gorgeously defiant.

"Of course." Without waiting for her, I turn and head in the direction of the front door. And I'm almost there when she sighs, causing me to smile.

I stay silent, though. Waiting to see what she does or says.

"By the way…why a jaguar?" Mariah asks suddenly a few seconds later. Her curiosity makes me pause and look back, causing the little beauty to bump into my back. "I never asked you to stop walking."

"You asked me a question." Before she can step back, I turn and hold her close. Breathe her in. "I'm being thoughtful."

"How so?" A small shiver runs through her as my fingers grip her hips and run soothing circles over the flesh there.

"By giving you my undivided attention." Dipping my face down to hers, I lay a kiss on her cheek and then the other, loving the sudden rush of goose bumps and her stuttered breath. "And to answer your question, I love jaguars because they're deadly yet regal. Dominant over their habitat while bowing to no other predator." Another tiny peck, this time right on the tip of her nose and I turn, leaving her apartment before I bend her over the entry table and bury myself to the hilt.

This was a win.

The beginning of something that holds a wicked promise.

I'm going to wear you down, Muñeca.

JAVIER

"RIGHT THIS WAY, Mr. Bennett." I step aside, and the three people I picked up this morning at the airport walk into the conference room on the executive floor. They're an affluential family from California, a Silicon Valley genius with a penchant for walking a fine line between the ethical and immoral while spoiling Mrs. Bennett. He's here with his wife and one guard, a man I've been watching from the moment they put a single foot inside the all-black SUV I drive.

His attention isn't on security or asking me what has been done to assure his boss's safety, but instead, on her. The wife. She's unaware—face pinched tight in anger while holding her husband's hand—but I saw, and by the clenching of her husband's jaw, so did he.

What are they playing at?

"Thank you, Javier," the wife answers, and the other two enter with nothing more than a nod in my direction. Not that I give a single fuck as the object of my frustration walks toward me with a stoic expression on her stunning face. The same expression was saved solely for me since our mini date in her apartment.

All five feet and three inches of perfection in her high-waisted black skirt, white cap-sleeved top, and red stilettos saunter in my direction with her hair down and the ends curled. With ruby lips and the sweet scent of flowers surrounding her—infiltrating my senses. Embedding itself into my DNA.

Mariah is teasing me. Avoiding me; a week of silence unless work-related and even then, the responses are minimal and to the point.

Her stubbornness doesn't deter me, though. Not one bit.

I find her adorable.

"Morning."

"Morning," she says, looking past me and toward the table where our guests will sit. "Excuse me." Before she can sweep by me, I grab her wrist and pull us back just outside the door and to the left where we are out of sight.

Mariah's back meets the wall in a soft thud, and I stand a mere inch or two from her, soaking up her decadent scent and the heat radiating from her body. Our eyes lock and breaths mingle.

A shiver rushes through her and flows through me as I lean in, lips hovering, but before they touch, I lift my face and kiss her forehead. At the contact, a stuttered breath escapes and I smile against her soft skin.

"Ignore me all you want, Muñeca. It won't change a thing."

Ignore the pet name, Mariah. "Move."

"One day you'll beg me to stay." With that, I push back and walk into the room. I take a seat beside Malcolm while she walks in a few seconds later, face flushed, and sits across from me with narrowed eyes.

Malcolm gives me a quick look, questioning if everything is okay, and I nod. He's not asking about his cousin, but the other people in the room.

I've already sent him my observation in a text and have the clearance to proceed as I see fit, should something occur during their stay in Chicago.

It's a trust he's given me. I might be his right hand here, something I never saw myself doing—not even for my own family—but the woman beside him has left me no choice.

I'll play my role while making sense of my sudden need for her presence in my life.

Because it's true what they say; there's more value in a single drop of your woman's come than a million pounds of gold. I want her taste in my mouth. I want to own her pleasure.

It's a compulsion I can't control and don't want to.

This game—ignoring me for seven fucking days—has done nothing to deter me.

If anything, she's poured gasoline onto this fire.

Malcolm stands, fixing his cufflink before extending a hand. "Good to see you, Kyle..." his attention then turns to the wife "...Clarissa."

"Likewise, my friend."

"It's been a long time," they answer in unison and then smile, the first one I've seen since picking the couple up, but that drops again when the manila folder in front of Asher is opened. That's when Clarissa's expression darkens and she turns her head toward her spouse, openly glaring. "This isn't necessary, Kyle. Please stop this nonsense."

"No." The response is cold. His body is tense and he's breathing harshly. "We need to make sure you're protected at all costs. Everything of mine is yours, but this makes it lawfully binding."

"Please." There's a broken plea, the tone of a woman who's hurting, and I flip my eyes to the security guard standing just behind her chair. They sit two chairs from mine with hers being the closest, and the way he hovers seems possessive, almost challenging.

Fingernails drumming on the table pull my attention, back toward the owner and Malcolm nods, the action barely perceptible, but acknowledging what I see.

"Any questions before we begin?"

"No."

"Yes."

"Go on, Clarissa," Asher says, giving her his undivided attention and I notice the guard's hands clench from the corner of my eye as I turn to look at Mrs. Bennett. "What concerns you?"

"I just see no need for this. Nothing will happen to my husband."

There's a tinge of anxiety in her tone and her husband reaches out, intertwining their fingers and placing their united hands atop the table. "It's just a precaution. Nothing else."

"Your money means nothing to me." Her face turns toward his. "I need you safe and with me."

For some reason, I look at Mariah at that moment and take in the almost wistful expression on her face. The smile curling at the corner of plump lips and the quiet sigh that escapes. As if feeling my eyes on hers, she looks over and at once, a flush of pink dances across her soft skin—from her cheeks to the very top of her chest where the silk of her top begins.

You okay, I mouth, and she nods quickly before turning her attention back to Malcolm's clients.

"...do this for me." I catch the end of Kyle's sentence and then watch as the woman beside him nods, but her eyes become glassy.

"Fine."

"Thank you."

"Clarissa, I understand your concerns, but let me assure you that this is a necessary step for any man in your husband's shoes. This isn't to lead him toward an impending ending, but to give him the peace of mind that you'll be taken care of no matter what." Malcolm pushes the envelope in her direction, and I move it the rest of the way, grabbing a pen from the pile at the center of the table between us.

She looks my way with a forced smile in thanks before picking up the pen. "I'm doing this for you, not because I want to."

"I know, love."

Mrs. Bennett signs her name and then closes her eyes. She takes in a deep breath and lets it out slowly before staring into his eyes. "I did that for you, but if you ever—"

She's cut off by a sudden curse from behind her and a bullet that lodges itself high on the wall across from where they sit. Her screams rend the air and so does the sound of multiple guns being cocked, but it's a missed shot, and I have her guard on the floor with my weapon drawn to his temple before anyone has time to dislodge.

My foot is on his hand with the weapon; I aim for his shoulder and then a knee. The first makes him writhe, while the second splatters the back of my leg and hip.

No one moves, but I see Clarissa's going into shock and then the appreciation on Kyle's face when I bend and knock the man unconscious with the butt of my Glock. I also notice the sudden paleness in my muñeca's face, but I can't acknowledge it right now.

I'll deal with her after the room is cleared. That flash of worry doesn't sit right with me.

"How? What the?" Bennett lifts his crying wife from her chair and walks Clarissa to the other side of the room, an arm possessively around her midsection. He's shielding her from the scene, her face buried in his chest and body shaking.

"Kyle, get her out of here. I'll meet you later."

"Yeah, we'll head back to the hotel. I'll—"

"No." Malcolm holds up two fingers. Plan B is in effect, which is the use of a backup escape for clients of this nature. "Use my penthouse. I'll have someone drive you."

"Are you sure?"

"Yes."

"Thank you, Malcolm." Asher nods at this and I send Carmelo a text, telling him to drive the Bennett's to the private condo Malcolm keeps near the office. They both begin to step out of the room, but Kyle pauses just within the threshold to look back at me. "I owe you my life, Javier. You noticed he was off right away and protected us both. Thank you."

I nod at him and they walk out, leaving the three of us standing on different sides of the table. My side has a man who's grumbling beneath my foot and bleeding.

"Tell me," Malcolm asks.

"The idiot is obsessed with Mrs. Bennett and doesn't hide his reactions well. I noticed his body language when they got in the car; hard breathing, glaring, and when Kyle kissed her cheek, his hand flexed over the gun at his waist."

"How can he keep him on his payroll? Why didn't he see this?" Mariah's talking, but her hand with the gun shakes, and without a second thought, I leave the idiot on the ground and make my way to her. I take the Glock and lay it on the table, squeezing her fingers with mine.

Her reaction isn't what I expect from her. Not from someone accustomed to our way of life.

Shit happens, but you never waver or lose composure. *What's wrong, Muñeca?*

"You okay there, cousin?"

"I am." Voice a little stronger—steadier, she pulls her hand from mine, eyes avoiding. "This just makes no sense."

"Kyle will get his chance to explain tonight. Have this idiot taken downstairs and keep two guards in the room at all times."

"Done." With a final glance in her direction, I walk out and call the team working in the cells below the bank. The phone rings twice before someone picks up and silently waits. "You have a pick-up and delivery."

"Yes, sir," the guard answers, and the dial tone follows. It takes them four minutes to reach this floor and another three to remove the semi-conscious man, now with a bag covering his head. They take a private elevator, the one used only by those who work security or the Ashers themselves, and disappear as if they've never been here.

Behind me, in the room, I can hear mutterings and a few hissed whispers, but I pay the two cousins no mind and move toward my own office beside Malcolm's. It's a decent-sized room, the view behind my chair fantastic, but it feels complete a few minutes later when an angry Mariah storms into the room.

Her chest rises and falls fast. Her lips are thinned and the looks she's giving me are cold.

"How can I help you, Ms. Asher? Is there something you need?"

"You could've been shot," she spits out, hands clenching at her sides.

"Why do you care?" I challenge, standing to match her heated stare and lean over with two hands atop my desk. Not one to back down, Mariah does the same and puts her face a few inches from mine, nostrils flaring and always challenging.

"It was reckless of you to knock him down like that, forcing his arm toward your body, while the gun was in his hand." Each word is coated with venom and is gritted out through clenched teeth. Her anger is palpable, but clearer to see is that she cares about my safety. "We don't need that kind of shitstorm. If word gets out about what happened here…"

"I know how to do my job."

"You're an egotistical idiot."

"Why do you care if I get shot?"

"I-I don't."

"Liar."

"Fuck—" she doesn't get to finish her insult as I grab the back of her neck and quickly press my lips to hers. *She's poison and fire, and I want nothing more than to be consumed by her.* The kiss is fast and heated—decadent in a sweetness uniquely hers, but I don't let her melt into me after a moan slips from her mouth to mine.

Instead, I pull back and watch her even though every cell of my DNA demands I retake those swollen lips and devour. Instead, I breathe in her intoxicating scent and lick my lips, savoring the last hint of her taste while Mariah flushes and her red lips part.

There's shock in her eyes. There's a hunger that matches mine, too.

Mariah knows I want her. Just like I know she wants me.

But more than that, there has to be a level of respect—trust—for this to work. I'm not a punching bag, and she isn't a toy. In our world, stupid reactions can be costly.

So I stand upright and level her with a blank expression. "Next time, please knock."

"Are you kidding me?"

"No. I'm not." Walking around my desk, I stride to the door and pause just within the threshold. "I don't take kindly to being questioned on both my common sense and professionalism. Don't make that mistake again."

Mariah saunters over, hand on her hip and face close to mine. Her heels giving her the height needed to reach my chin. "Or what?"

Always challenging. Always pushing.

Leaning down enough that my lips graze her ear, I exhale roughly. She shivers, and I bite back a smile. "Or I'll put you over my knee and give you the spanking you need. I'm going to enjoy reddening those sweet cheeks, Muñeca."

Mariah

I WANT TO kill him.

I want another kiss and the feelings his lips on mine evoke.

I want what I shouldn't—the path I refuse to travel—and walk out without another word. Without another glance in his direction, no matter how much my body craves it. Craves him.

It's late enough in the morning that I stride to my desk and grab my purse, heading for the elevator without letting Malcolm know that I'm stepping out. *Screw it.* I'll deal with every missed call later, and push the down button, opening the doors. I'm thankful no one is inside and without being stopped, I make it out of the building within minutes, walking down the sidewalk and merging with the passing crowd.

I have no destination in mind, but the further I walk from the Asher building, the more my mind wanders down dangerous roads brought to the forefront by Javier's actions.

What if he got shot? What if I lost him?

Those thoughts have been plaguing me since the scuffle and for some reason, it throws me head first into my past. Down a rabbit hole that leads to a memory I've fought hard to bury even though the two men couldn't be further apart.

One is successful, determined, and proud.

The other was spoiled, unworthy, and unfit to run the family business.

It's late when I make it home, much later than I expected I'd be when I left this morning. With Thiago Rivera arrested and the scandal over confirmed family ties to both the mob and cocaine traffickers, we've been moving information and money all day.

Moving to offshore accounts. Clearing all bank records. Wiping every server with information that can be traced back to them and Asher Holdings.

We made sure that anything unclean is no longer accessible, and not even the best hacker in the FBI can find a speck of dirt on our client.

And while I'm tired and hungry, I gladly do my part as a shareholder and family member.

Slipping my heels off, I relish the feel of the cool hardwood flooring beneath my feet before tossing my keys in a bowl atop an entry table. My purse sits beside it.

"Guess he went out," I mutter under my breath, undoing the top few buttons of my blouse while making my way to the kitchen. Food would be amazing, but a glass of wine will hit the spot, along with a bath.

However, the second I grab a glass and a bottle of Malbec from the wine cooler, the lights flicker on. "What the hell!" I scream, whirling around with a hand on my chest. I'm gasping, narrowing my eyes at Lane. "You scared the bejesus out of me."

"Where were you?" His tone is eerily calm, his body language tense.

Nothing new in that department as of late. He's changed in the last few months—demanding and possessive, but not in a way most women find sexy. This isn't an I love you and want to keep you by my side while cherishing you *sort of way.*

No. Not one bit.

After giving him my virginity, it's been a never-ending battle of wills, and I'm growing tired.

Fighting isn't a turn-on. Explaining my every move isn't foreplay.

"Hey, babe." I leave the unopened bottle and walk to him, winding my

arms around his neck to placate him. It fails. My touch doesn't calm him and the feel of him gives me no comfort in return. Maybe I should break it off already. Why am I even trying? *"You didn't need to wait up for me. Did you get my text earlier?"*

His hands snake around me, one hand on my hip while the other grips my hair. He's smiling, eyes soft, and I think for a flash that he'll make this bad feeling go away when a sharp hiss escapes me. With my hair wound tight around his fist, he yanks my head back so hard that tears gather, and fear settles over my limbs.

Lane has never hurt me, but I'm not feeling safe anymore. I don't trust him, and that dangerous edge he's been teetering on between obsession and unhealthy sends chills down my spine.

One day he's sweet. The next, he treats me as though I'm an enemy.

He's nothing like the man I began seeing two years ago.

"Where the fuck were you?"

"You're hurting me." My voice is steady, eyes on his, unwavering. Because you don't back down from an aggressor. You don't show fear or weakness. "Let go, and get out."

A dark chuckle leaves him, his fingers tightening, and I feel as strands of hair are pulled from their follicles. His other hand leaves my hip and sweeps across my cheek in a caress. "You don't know what pain is, princess."

That's when the scent of alcohol greets me—when I notice the blood-shot eyes and rumpled clothing.

"Get out and leave. Don't force my hand," I hiss out, heart beating fast while I walk us backward three steps. There's an empty wine glass on the counter and a gun that I keep inside the entry table; if I could just get to—

Blinding pain sears my right cheek and eye, the impact forcing my head to the side, but his hold only forces me back. His eyes are angry, not even a hint of the man I thought I knew and cared for.

Another point of contention between us:

He loves me, but I don't reciprocate. Those words have never passed through my lips, and it angers him. More reason to call it quits. I should have never waited so long.

"If I ask you again, you won't like the outcome."

"At work."

"Do you think I'm stupid?"

"It's the truth." I'm calm—almost chilling—as Lane lowers his face to mine, lips hovering. The stench of liquor is near nauseating, and his touch makes my skin crawl. *"Ask Malcolm if you don't believe me."*

"Malcolm," he spits out with so much venom, spittle flying over my lips and chin. *"That son of a bitch would lie for his slutty little cousin. He's as much of a bitch as you are."*

Ignore the insult. *I repeat this in my head a few times, remembering all the lessons drilled into my head since the age of ten by my uncle, even though my father, his brother, didn't think it was necessary:*

Breathe.

Don't underestimate your aggressor.

Kill without mercy.

Taking in a steadying breath, I let it out slowly while keeping my eyes locked on his. "You knew we had to finalize everything for the Rivera De Leon family. Why are you being like this?"

"Who is Ivan? Why is he sending you a gift basket?" Lane releases my hair, and I relax a bit—then choke. His fingers tighten around my throat, cutting off the air while my fingernails dig into his skin.

He hisses but doesn't let go. My vision gets a bit hazy behind my tears, but I don't cave. I've been groomed all my life to defend myself when the time came, and it always would.

You don't escape our world unscathed.

I take another step back and he follows, unwilling to release his hold. Another, and he brings his hand down across my other cheek, catching the corner of my mouth and breaking the skin. The metallic taste fills my mouth. The flash of pain almost makes me stumble, but I regain myself and take two more steps back.

And on that final move back, Lane slams me into the counter, the force knocking over the bottle and emptying its contents all around us. It breaks in half, the top slicing my arm and I grit my teeth, holding back the pain.

I grab the sharp glass and wrap my fingers around the unbroken opening.

He doesn't see it. Lane's too busy breathing hard against my neck, right below my chin where he's pressing his lips, a complete contrast to his other actions.

His lips part and the kiss is tender. Almost worshipping.

I hate his touch. I don't want this.

"Who is he, Mariah?" Teeth scrape against my skin and I shudder; I feel disgusted, and sadness fills my chest. Lane isn't giving me another out, and I close my eyes. "How long have you been fucking him behind my back?"

"Don't force my hand, Lane. Please leave."

"How fucking long!" he screams and snaps his teeth over my neck. His bite hurts. It burns as the stupid man breaks the skin.

"Forgive me." And on my next breath, I shove the broken, jagged glass into his neck. Push it in a little deeper before he can step back and scream out from the shock and pain.

Lane stumbles, his hand coming up to his chest, not paying attention to me. I kick him. With all the strength I have, I land my foot on his chest and run to the front door.

He's grunting; I hear him stumble and the crash of something glass. Then his footsteps come near, and it's as I make it to the entryway table and grab my Glock that he appears in my line of sight.

He takes a step my way and I remove the safety, pointing the barrel at his chest. "Stop." My voice is shaky, my emotions threatening to overtake me as I let the first few tears fall. "Last chance."

Lane laughs, the action causing blood to spurt and stain my floor. "You wouldn't."

"Leave."

"Not before I kill you." And he means it. The hate in his eyes sears me. The threat isn't without intent; his position as next in line for the Molly empire his father built makes him a dangerous man with the means to do just that.

It's why our union interested both his family and mine. My father to be precise.

The Asher's don't need them, but I won't deny that they're useful at times.

Then, everything happens fast. One second, I'm swallowing back a sob, and the next, I'm pulling the trigger four times. Two to the chest. Two to the stomach.

Lane falls back on impact, his head banging against the archway behind him and groans. Blood quickly pools, and his shirt is proof of how little time he has left.

The gun slips from my hand and I walk over, kneeling beside his head, and push the hair back. His eyes are still aware—wide and scared.

"Ivan is De Leon's youngest son, Lane. He sent a basket to everyone who worked on clearing their money and file, not just me." My tears fall on his cheek, and his expression fills with remorse. "I never cheated."

"I'm sorry." It's low and hoarse. Our eyes stay locked for a few minutes, but then his close and don't reopen. His chest no longer rises and falls. He's gone.

"I am too."

"Are you okay?" someone says, and I snap back to the present, pushing back the thoughts I've fought to bury. Lane was my first and only boyfriend. My first kill.

Did I love him? No. Not a single part of me belonged to him—not like a woman loves her man—but regret still lingers over my actions and stupidity to stay and please others. To make him happy while I became wary and miserable.

I should've broken it off before then.

I should've seen that Lane needed help.

I should've, but didn't.

His demons had nothing to do with me, and yet, I became his focus and allowed it to go that far.

My eyes focus on the person in front of me, and I'm shocked it's Javier. "How did you find me? Are you stalking me?" The latter leaves me in an accusatory tone, which causes his brow to raise.

"No. I'm not."

"Then how..." my words trail off as I look behind him and realize where I am. I'm back outside of the Asher building, a few steps from the door, and have no recollection of how I arrived. Squinting a bit, I make out the receptionist and she's looking at me from her desk with concern stretched across her face. *"Christ,* I'm a mess today."

"Just today?" Javier jokes, his hand on my shoulder, squeezing it. I didn't realize it was there, nor do I know where I went or how long I've been standing here. "Hey, look at me."

"I'm heading back inside." I rebuff him, shrugging his hand off. His touch, no matter how small, feels good, and it's for the best I keep him at bay.

Men like him are dominant and distrustful. They come and go as they please, while the women stay behind to clean and cook—to give the world around them the illusion of perfection.

Perfect wife.

Perfect kids.

Perfect house with a large yard and a beautiful dog running around.

I've seen it from my father. And while my mother has always remained quiet, I refuse to let anyone else hold that power over me. It's why I admire Malcolm's mom. My aunt doesn't play by those rules and refuses to let her husband or son become that sick.

Because this misogynistic idea, the illusion of a killer being a family man, gives him a reputable status. It makes him dependable and trustworthy, something that no criminal is.

I will kill anyone who crosses those I love without remorse.

And the sole reason I regret killing Lane? His mother.

The pure look of horror and devastation in that woman's eyes when Malcolm turned the body over and gave them three days to leave the country still haunts me. Gail was devastated to lose her only child, and the raw pain of her wails made me realize that I never want to be in her shoes.

To be that vulnerable.

"No!" Gail stands, eyes blazing in anger and despair. "This isn't true. Tell me it's not true, Mariah!"

"I'm sorry," I answer, my voice low. A little unsteady; her pain makes my chest clench. I feel bad for her. His mother, even though she was overindulgent and turned a blind eye to Lane's bad behavior—her son's many addictions—genuinely loved him. That was her baby, her only child, that I killed. "He's gone."

"You fucking—"

"Tom, I'd be very careful about how you finish that sentence."

Malcolm sits forward in his chair, hands flat atop his desk. "Disrespect her, and your wife will be burying two bodies, not one."

"Nephew," my father says suddenly, hands up as if to pacify the situation. "Leave this to me. It's my daughter at fault here and who needs to make amends to the Dermots." That stung, a sob catching in my throat at the look of disgust he sent my way. In his eyes, I messed up. He's afraid of the Dermots for some reason. "Mariah needs to pay for her crime. I'll make sure they're not to—"

"Not another word before I lose my last shred of patience with you. I'm not your brother, nor do I hold qualms over hurting one of my own." At Malcolm's words, Dad steps back and sends me a murderous glare. Something my cousin catches. "Stay in your lane, and keep those eyes on the ground. She's above you and always will be."

"Do you not have a heart?" Lane's mother steps in front of her fuming husband, her fingernails digging into his arm, a silent plea to keep composure. There's more he wants to say, insult me, but can't. Not with Malcolm here, and more so with the six fully armed guards standing post. Their Molly operation, while quite large, only holds that power because my family has allowed them to flourish with the agreement that they know their place and pay a due, giving them rights to a certain area. I was just a bonus. "She killed our son and you—"

"You should thank her for being merciful."

Both Lane's parents and mine gasp, but it's Tom's face I focus on. He's turning red in anger. Hate. "You seem to forget that we hold power in this city, too, Asher. Chicago is—"

"Mine." Malcolm interrupts, standing from behind his desk, and walks toward a small storage cabinet in the room. Inside there are a few guns, a knife, a ring, and a glass used when certain business agreements are made.

It's an old-school tradition. You sign with blood, not ink.

A collective intake of breath and the glass shatters upon impact, creating a small hole where it met the wall. It's a symbolic gesture. Their accord is over.

"You've fooled yourself into believing you are more than what you are. All of you. It's the same mistake Lane made the night he attacked my family, in her home, intending to end her life." His back is to the room,

voice controlled, and yet you feel his ire. The evil that lurks beneath the surface and his enemies cower from. "You are nothing but what I allow. One word from me, and your entire life can be burned to the ground with you inside the building. Or in your case, Uncle, the home I've allowed you to keep. I'm being more than courteous here, at Mariah's request, by letting you all live. Because had he succeeded or ran, I would've made you watch me dismember him limb by limb while alive."

Neither set opens their mouths, but their eyes speak volumes. Fear. Almost choking panic at his words.

If they stay here another minute, he'd order their execution on the blatant disrespect alone.

"Leave." At that, all four parents snap their eyes my way. I don't give them a chance to refute my demand or negotiate. I'm saving their lives, even if they don't see it. "Take your son's body, sell what you can, and get out of the country within the next forty-eight hours. Do not look back. Do not come back."

"Mariah, sweetheart," Mom says, voice low and contrite. And I believe it, too. Problem is that she's a product of a male-dominated home where his word is the law and his demands reign king. She has no real backbone. "Baby, please stop this nonsense. This isn't how I brought you up."

"I think it's better for all involved if you two leave as well." Tears gather in her eyes, hurt, and disappointment flowing down each cheek, but I'm not moved. Not this time.

Lane's dad opens his mouth, the retort on his tongue sure to be coated in venom, but he's interrupted by a guard stepping inside. There's a body over this employee's shoulder, the body-bag hiding their identity, but everyone knows.

"Heed her warning. My cousin's more generous than I am." Malcolm snaps a finger, and the body is placed at the Dermots feet. His mother's eyes fill with tears that fall as a hurt-filled wail escapes her chest. Her husband, though, shows a little more composure. There's sadness, but overpowering the pain is hate. He's scared, but the disdain is just as powerful. "She asked me to return him to you, and now I have. So do as she bravely suggests. Leave. Don't further tempt me to break my promise."

"You have our word," Mr. Dermot says, and her cries grow louder. He

understands that this means their entire operation must leave—every member of the family—or face the repercussions. With his arms around her midsection, he turns, and they make it to the door where one of their men, a distant cousin, awaits to take Lane.

And when they step across the threshold, Malcolm claps once. "The clock is ticking. For you as well, uncle."

Two steps are all he lets me take before snatching my wrist and pulling me against his strong chest. "What's wrong?"

"Let go."

"Talk to me."

"Respect my boundaries, Mr. Lucas."

"Understood." And all of a sudden, I hate that word. Despise how easily he gives in to my request. *This yo-yo'ing is going to drive me crazy.* Javier makes me want to run to him and then away, far away, because I'm not ready to let the walls down I've built around myself.

This is for the best. Has to be.

"Good." Snatching my arm from his hold, I continue toward the door. He doesn't say anything, just lets me walk away, and it confuses the hell out of me, but then a hiss meets my ears and I shiver.

"For now."

JAVIER

MALCOLM GIVES ME a nod before entering the opulent establishment near the Asher building the next morning at ten. The Bennett meeting had to be pushed back due to medical reasons, and while I still don't believe his wife is okay after what occurred, extending this another day isn't feasible.

Not when dealing with the sentencing and execution of a man.

Mistakes can be costly. Destructive.

Walking through the lobby, I make eye contact with each man standing beside the three exits and nod. We're in the heart of the Loop, a few minutes from Malcolm's financial building, and I'm impressed with the surveillance I've seen thus far. Not that it can't be improved, but he has a solid foundation I can work with.

He owns it, provides all security for it, and only those trusted business associates that pass through frequently—are allowed to reside within.

I had the choice of an apartment here but chose wisely without knowing.

Mariah can run but can't get far. She has no idea how close we are.

How easily this predator can reach his prey.

Because that's what this dance feels like; a game of cat and mouse I don't plan to lose.

"They're waiting and the room is ready," Mariah says from beside him, looking straight ahead while matching his steps. I'm two behind them and watching their dynamic, taking in their reactions from the moment they entered my SUV. They speak through looks and short answers, but behind the professional demeanor is respect and familial love.

"Thank you. Make sure Mr. Bennett is down in five."

"Already sent him a text, and he's downstairs." She's checking her phone, but I catch the tilt of her head and the slight look back from the corner of her eye. "The guard is also in attendance and awake."

"Perfect. That'll be all." Malcolm stops at the elevator and puts a key to the panel. "Take Javier's car and head back. I need you to work on the Frederick contract."

"Are you sure?" Now she does look back and meets my stare. I'm not hiding or avoiding. "I'm more than happy to—"

"Positive." He kisses her cheek, pulling her attention away from me, and I hate it. Loathe her looking at anyone that isn't me, but I keep my reactions at bay. This feeling—this rage-fueled jealousy—isn't something I've faced before. It makes me see red. Yearn to feel the life essence of whoever holds her gaze on my fingertips. "I want the twins in and out of my office before they start trying to sell me bullshit I neither care nor have time for."

"I know." Mariah laughs and its warmth settles around me, calms the devil within, while my expression remains blank. She sneaks another look after a minute, almost like she can't help herself, and narrows her eyes at my demeanor. *What kind of reaction are you looking for, Muñeca? Are you thinking about our kiss?* However, the longer we stare, the more I see what lurks behind those pretty orbs. Something is bothering her. Maybe a hint of annoyance for being asked to leave. "The food has been ordered and the files are ready. We'll be using conference room two for this one."

"Will they need an escort to the office?" She doesn't respond to him, too busy trying to read me. The only things she gets from me, though, are a raised brow and a nod in her cousin's direction. "Mariah," he says, and still nada. Not even an acknowledgment of her name.

"Pay attention, Muñeca." That snaps her out of it and with a quick wave to Malcolm, she rushes out without answering. My eyes follow her the entire way. "I'll be picking them up."

"You two are becoming quite entertaining to watch." He enters the elevator and Carmelo and I follow, not another word spoken on the matter. We ascend to the sixty-eighth floor, and the doors open into a spacious living space with nothing but a large conference table at the center. The room has floor-to-ceiling windows that line the outer walls from one side to the other, the view showing us a slightly overcast day with an uninterrupted view of city landmarks and skyline.

Mr. Bennett sits at one end of the table while the guard is placed at the center, tied to a chair and gagged. His face is swollen and a tooth is missing, and while both men hold enraged expressions, one person is missing.

The wife. The victim.

"How is she?" Malcolm asks, sitting down at the other end while I take my place right across from the aggressor. "Will she be joining us?"

"No." Kyle doesn't explain further, and no one probes. Instead, we turn to look at the one person who does owe an explanation. "Speak," Bennett hisses through clenched teeth a minute later, and the man flinches a bit before composing himself. "Tell me why you earned the bullet in my gun."

Nothing. No answer.

And all it does is piss me off. More so because no matter what country you're in, it seems that disrespect is a common trait that all assholes share.

There's a paperweight at the center of the table and before anyone asks him again, I pick it up and throw it. It lands near the bridge of his nose and a gash appears, the blood rushing to the surface before falling to his lip and filling his mouth.

"The next blow, I'll aim for your eye with my knife. Answer him," I say, tone even and low.

He trembles, his fear palpable. "I love her."

"What did you just say?" Kyle stands, the chair scraping harshly against the floor. His hands come down atop the glass table, the force making it shake while his lip curls up into a snarl. "Repeat that, Douglass."

Douglass swallows hard, coughing a bit. "I fell in love with Mrs. Bennett."

"Did she reciprocate?" Malcolm asks, holding a hand up to Kyle who moves in Douglass's direction. He pauses with a minute nod and waits. We've already discussed how to handle him. Get what we want. "Or is this a gut feeling?"

"I knew the day she hired me." Douglass smiles. It's wistful, yet there's ire lingering beneath the surface. His disdain for Mr. Bennett is clear. "She's sweet and kind. Nothing like this asshole who spends more time making enemies than paying attention to his wife. I was there when he wasn't. I saw the smile slip from her face each time he canceled a dinner date or weekend away." No one misses the way Kyle flinches slightly back at that, and it further fuels Douglass. "It was me," he sneers, and I find his backbone almost comical. Any other man would've pissed his pants by now. "Always me."

"So, she led you on?" At my question, all three look at me, but my focus is on the guard. "Are you saying she's a—"

"Don't you fucking dare!" He's struggling against his bindings, the rope cutting into his skin. "Clarissa is an angel."

"How so if she's toying with your emotions?"

"She's too innocent and pure to realize I've been—"

"Planning to kill her husband, kidnap her, and then force her into a relationship while you gain access to their millions?" Silence. Utter silence. Malcolm asked me to dig and I did, finding out more than they expected. This runs deeper than a simple infatuation. "Or does the name Jorge Wendell ring a bell?"

Kyle's head snaps in my direction. "What does my business partner have to do with this, Javier?"

"Why don't you explain, Douglass? Tell him what Wendell's secretary told me for a few thousand dollars."

"She wouldn't." His voice wavers.

"She did." Carmelo steps forward then. He hands Malcolm the two files I gathered in the two hours before arriving here. "Cindy was more than willing to fax me what I needed, too."

"No!"

"What the fuck is going on?" Kyle growls out, storming toward Douglass and fisting his hair. He pulls the dark blond strands hard, forcing the guard's head back while staring at me. "Tell me."

Malcolm slides the folder over; it's open and the top page shows the forged signatures on paperwork, making it seem Mrs. Bennett is unstable and needs a guardian. That Kyle was putting Wendell in charge of everything if anything happened to him.

"The plan was to kill you via robbery gone wrong." The disdain in my voice is noticeable. I take offense to shitty criminals playing the bullshit badass role. "With you out of the picture and then the filing of this paperwork, Clarissa would've been under their thumb. Wendell gets the company and other business ventures/assets, while Douglass gets your wife and a 50/50 split of the money. The sick fuck is obsessed with her, and more so, after being ignored. Isn't that right?"

"Fuck you!"

Kyle turns his head up to the ceiling and takes in a deep breath. He holds it for ten seconds, his hands clenching twice before his right hand pulls a gun from the back of his pants.

We don't stop him. We don't even draw our weapons.

Instead, we watch silently as he bends and puts his mouth near Douglass's ear. Kyle whispers something to him; it's too low for anyone to hear, but the guard becomes enraged just long enough for Bennett to pull the trigger and his body to go limp.

A bullet in each eye and brain matter scatters behind the body on the pristine floor.

"We'll be leaving tonight on an extended holiday," Kyle says, not looking at us but watching every drop of blood seep from the bullet wounds, a small smile on his face. "Do you need anything from us?"

"No. You're set." Malcolm gives me a nod, and I text the cleanup crew to come and eradicate all traces of this meeting. "Have a good vacation, and please send my regards to Clarissa."

"Thank you both." With that, he walks out and we stand, heading back downstairs toward Carmelo's car while the Bennett's prepare for their departure.

IT'S near nine at night by the time I make it home, and the front door hasn't fully closed before my jacket is tossed aside and my tie pulled off. I'm shrugging everything off, leaving the piles for tomorrow, while heading toward my bathroom.

I'm in need of a quick shower. A release before ending my night with a little taste and tease.

The lights flick on as I enter the large, all-white bathroom with an over-sized shower that extends from one wall to the opposite. Its large subway tiles in marble cover almost every inch, from wet areas to the dry with hardware in gold to compliment the stone.

Turning the handle toward the hot water, I step back and remove my boxer briefs before stepping inside. It's been a long day; from meetings and training for Malcolm's guards to Mariah's haughty, cold shoulder.

One I returned. Then, I sat back and watched the fight to ignore me become the search for any reason to get closer. No matter where I turned, she was in my line of sight or near enough to touch.

Hair up in a messy bun.

Glasses perched on the end of her nose while biting a pen.

Giggling at something.

The coquettish minx made sure to punish me, but I held back. My not giving in caused her frustration and a few muttered curses thrown my way, but it'll be worth it soon enough.

Heat fills the room, and I step beneath the waterfall showerhead. The hot water slides down my limbs and hard cock, caressing my skin and causing a shiver to rush down my spine.

I grab my bodywash and loofah on the small alcove to my right, pouring a large drop in to the sponge before rubbing it across my chest. The suds glide lower and over my pelvis before they kiss my balls.

I'm throbbing. In pain. My hand fisting over the tight skin, knuckles strained white, before pumping once. Then again. Just knowing that she's a few floors from me...

"Fuck," I hiss out, my strokes becoming rougher with each twist down and then up. My eyes close and I throw my head back, picturing her sultry eyes and sinful smirk before leaving for the day. Mariah was bent over her desk while looking for something, giving me the perfect view of her ass and hips while talking on the phone, ignoring my presence. "Delicious little beauty."

Her skirt was mid-thigh and tight with no visible panty line, and instead, I got a peek of the soft skin between her thighs through the small slit with a pleat at the back. Perfect and round, and my mouth waters as I remember how the fabric moved with her, rising a little higher on her thighs until I groaned.

A little more, and I'd see the round cheeks I want to bite. Smack. Smear my come across.

Heat licks at my balls and with each pump of my hips, the pleasure increases, and more so when Mariah's evil grin flashes behind closed lids. She'd turned around to face me then, back slightly arched and with a hand on her hip.

"Need something, Mr. Lucas?" Tone breathy, she looks at me from head to toe, pausing a bit at the thick bulge in my pants. My suit jacket's over the back of my office chair and I'm not hiding her effect on me. Fuck that—she caused it and I want her to see.

To hunger for it.

For her plump little mouth to water.

"Do you?" I counter, my voice husky. Deeper. "Need help?"

"I have fingers for that. No help needed."

"But sometimes a little assistance makes the task sweeter. Dirtier."

"Are you speaking from experience?" She licks her lips and my cock jerks, a bead or two of liquid rolling down the tip. "Is using your hands something you do a lot?"

"I'm going to make you pay for that," I grunt low, tightening my grip before swiping my thumb across the sensitive head. *Christ,* that feels good and I pinch the tip, the sudden jolt of pain giving me another minute or two. My hips don't stop pumping, fucking my fist while imagining it's her tight cunt and the slap of skin is my hips slamming into parted thighs. "Slowly break you down until my cock is all you know."

"Do you think of me when you do?"

"Son of a bitch." That memory of her words—the look in her eye when whispering—brings me over the edge. My palm slams against the wall, holding myself up while come shoots from the tip, dribbling down the wall and to the drain below.

It takes me a minute or two to calm my breathing and for my cock to stop twitching, and I step out, wrapping a towel around myself. My bedroom's past this door and the bed is my destination, where I was smart enough to toss my phone before giving in to the need for pleasure.

"Now, I want the tease." Towel thrown aside, I get comfortable with a pillow behind my head and send the first message.

What are you wearing? ~

Mariah

I'm lying in bed, staring at my ceiling and thinking about the text that came in a few seconds ago. I won't deny the sender has piqued my curiosity, that gene all women have when it comes to deciphering the unknown, and my finger hovers over the screen without looking. *Do I ignore or answer?*

Because this can go one of two ways: the person is a creep, or someone is sending a little naughtiness to their other half. Moreover, I'm nosy, and trying hard to ignore the little voice inside my head that wishes this was Javier messaging me and not a random stranger.

His kiss, that quick and will-crumbling touch of his soft lips on mine, has messed with my head. With my goal and wants and the desire to stay single—unattached to any man, because I am. Javier seems to be near whenever my defenses are low and always on my mind when out working and protecting our family's interest.

He's loyal when he doesn't need to be. He isn't some nobody looking to come up.

I've read his file front to back, looked up the Lucas organization in Colombia, and I can't come up with a single plausible reason for his determination to be here. To work for the Asher's when his name is respected, feared, and admired.

He's here because of me. A thought I'm fighting to ignore. It's not plausible. *But what if?*

Because there's no denying our attraction, this pulsing energy that fills me when we touch. Moreover, his kiss stole every reason why this can't work and turned it into doubts on why it shouldn't. *Jesus, help a girl out here. Amen.*

Indecisiveness lasts but so long, and I'm further tempted/thankful when another ping draws my attention to the screen.

> Are you waiting for me? ~Unknown

Definitely someone trying to reach their lover. Something I'll never have, and it makes me jealous—hate how untrusting I've become. Giving two years of my life to a man that treated me like an enemy, a cheating whore, broke something within me that turns away from any possibility for more. *Then why flirt with Javier? Why is he different?*

An answer I don't possess, or maybe I don't want to acknowledge how much the man affects me. How his indifference, the way he doesn't take my abuse, both excites and scares me.

I'm never going to be dependent on a man, but I won't deny that having someone be my equal is a yearning that Lane tampered with. The last thing I want is a controlling asshole or to be forced into a mold I neither find attractive nor need.

I'll never be arm candy. I'll never want to be the perfect little housewife.

"Even dead, the jerk ruins my fun," I grumble, typing out a quick response to the sender before tossing the device beside me.

> You have the wrong number. ~Mariah

Their response is immediate and I furrow my brows, reaching blindly and bringing the lit-up screen to my face. I read the message once, twice—three times, and a little smile curls on my lips. Because there are only two people in my life that keep their responses short and to the point, and my cousin wouldn't send something like this.

Malcolm's messages are solely concerning work.

And if it's family-related, I get a call, and even that only lasts long enough to be told what to expect or where to show up in as much of a loving way as the ever-present grouch can express.

> No. I don't. ~Unknown

> Then who wants to know what I'm wearing?
> ~Mariah

Stretching a bit, I let myself sink into the bed and wait. I don't know how he got this number, but a part of me is happy he did. This way I can flirt, play, and maybe get to come without everything that comes attached to the title of being his.

Because the last thing I want is another possessive man laying claims.

Liar.

Another ping reverberates throughout the room, and I'm beyond grateful to ignore that little voice inside my head.

> A wolf who isn't hiding his hunger. ~Unknown

My stomach clenches and toes curl with that simple response. I also find myself typing back without hesitation, a smirk on my lips.

> Should I be afraid of the big bad wolf? ~Mariah

A minute passes and nothing. Then another. And just when I'm ready to toss the phone aside, annoyed that he didn't respond to my taunt, a message comes in.

I'm going to eat, bite, and make you scream my
name. ~Unknown

Christ, I shiver. The undisguised hunger—the unadulterated want gives me a high I've never encountered before. Not at this level. This feeling of euphoria mixed with danger that I need to chase and conquer. Push a little further no matter how wrong this could end.

His fire might destroy me.

Is that a threat~ Mariah

It's a promise, Muñeca. ~Javier

And then an attachment pings on my device, and I click the link like an idiot. Like the in-lust little girl I am.

The picture's a close-up of his mouth and chin with day-old stubble across a lickable, defined jaw. Then there's the way he bites his bottom lip, teeth embedded into the corner, making him smirk in a way that causes goose bumps to rise across my skin.

I feel feverish. Excited.

I'm in trouble.

Can you catch me? ~Mariah

You'll always be within my reach. ~Javier

THIS MAN IS GOING to drive me to the point of instability where people snap, and reactions have costly consequences.

Like now; this is stupid. A bad choice on my part.

The beginning of what can only be described as my fallout.

And why? Because I'm sitting on the grass against a building my cousin owns with a vast field in my direct line of sight. I'm here to watch him exactly five days from my demand to be left alone. For him to respect *my* boundaries when I didn't follow the same protocol.

I can't seem to stay away. I keep trying to find ways to get close.

During meetings. During his two p.m. coffee break.

"He's going to think I'm certifiable." *He's no saint, either.* Which is true, and his smirk while dropping a handful of Hershey's kisses atop my desk on his way to his office, Cafe Con Leche in hand, tells me as much. Javi is enjoying my indecisiveness, which aggravates me.

It's a vicious cycle of hot and cold, and I'm screwed.

He also knows I'm here; knew the very moment I sat down and my eyes wandered down his tattooed upper body. I saw the small shiver rush through him. I saw the way he tilted his head in my direction, the flex of his pecs while he addressed those here today for training.

This group is new. All men that have come with some level of vouching by associates to Malcolm.

Moreover, he's aware of my small and newly discovered fetish. Watching him put men on their knees, crying out in pain while tapping out, is something I find sexy. Extremely. Almost obsessively.

The way he stands in front of the guards, no shirt on, and demanding they follow through with the new moves he's shown them; a mixture of boxing meets mixed-martial arts, and each segment follows a new technique.

It's a little chaotic. The moves are meant to cause harm, and yet, I'm salivating as he takes the youngest in this bunch to the center where they've put a large mat over the grass and squares off.

Sweat glistens across his chest.

His muscles ripple while he waits for the other to charge forward like the idiot he is. Because fighting isn't about brawn or weight.

Anyone can be brought to their knees no matter the size. Which is what happens next.

One second, he's charging like a raging bull, and the next, the young guard is flat on the ground, facing down, while Javier locks his arm in a hold. He pulls back and the man groans, gritting his teeth while Javi continues to teach. The group surrounding them comes closer—they're hanging on his every word while Javi points out pressure points with his free hand.

I can't make out his voice from here, but I follow the movement of his lips. The way he signals the lines and position of his body and arm, the way it's tucked and crossed over his opponent in a way that's near impossible to escape.

I could escape.

And God, I'm tempted to challenge him. Show him just how equal we are.

"Pair off," I hear him call out and I lift my eyes to his, fighting back the urge to admire every solid inch of his physique. His brown eyes are narrowed, lips curling up into a small snarl while listening to something one of the new men to his right says.

Whatever it is, he doesn't like it.

His face contorts, and the demon behind the facade of perfect makes an appearance. Javier is glorious in his anger. His movements are precise and meant to cause more than harm.

With a quickness no one predicts, the guard flies over his back and lands harshly on the ground, away from the mat. Head bouncing, he's disoriented while Javi mounts and pins his arm with one hand and his knees in a kimura, ignoring the cry to stop and doesn't let go until breaking the forearm in two.

And as the man cries, Javi proceeds to break the other.

No one stops him. No one dares to protest.

Instead, they watch him land punch after punch on a defenseless man until he's unconscious and bloody, face swollen and rapidly bruising.

My feet carry me closer on their own accord, pausing only when his angry eyes meet mine. "Any one of you disrespect Miss Asher, and Malcolm will be the last person you should fear. I'll personally empty a clip into your skull."

Jesus. I shiver. My thighs clench.

White-hot desire pulses through my womb, and I step back and then again, all the way to my belongings on the grass with my eyes on him the entire time.

This, my reaction to his protectiveness and possessiveness, proves I'm weak when it comes to him. I'm a ticking time bomb.

Want. Need. Hunger.

Those three words describe me to a 'T' and he knows. Mirrors those feelings.

How can I win a losing battle?

***

COME MONDAY MORNING, there's a cup of coffee from my favorite little shop near the office; a quaint location owned by a lady older than dirt and run by her granddaughter. It's hipster meets old European vibes, and I can't get enough of their eclairs.

I've been known to buy half a dozen per visit, and the box in front of me holds seven with a note above in neat penmanship.

ONE IS FOR ME.
I'LL BE BY ON MY COFFEE BREAK TO PICK IT UP.
~ JAVI ~

"Stupid attractive man." I'm smiling as I bring the cup to my lips, almost moaning as the rich cappuccino greets my caffeine-deprived body. There's a hint of almond to this one, just the right amount without over-powering, and reminds me of my mom's favorite biscotti.

The one thing we have in common is our sweet tooth.

"Do you and your coffee need a moment?" Malcolm says from beside me all of a sudden and I yell, almost dropping my coffee. There's a hint of amusement in his eyes, and I'm tempted to kick his shin or stomp his foot with my heels.

"Shut it."

"Did you bring me anything?"

"Nyet." He's eyeing the box of pastries, a frown on his face. "These are a gift, and since you were a jerk, the answer is no."

"That's not very nice."

"And neither are you," I counter, bringing the cup to my lips and taking a hearty sip of the perfect temp brew. "Not sharing."

"I can always make you go get some." He's sipping from his favorite traveling mug. It's expensive, ridiculous for what it is, but the damn thing keeps his Jamaican special blend the perfect temp for a few hours.

He does not start his day without it.

Coffee is a religion in our family.

"You're going to be that petty?" Malcolm merely raises a brow, and I huff. "Fine. Grab one and go."

"Two, and I pay for the lunch you'll be ordering for Javi."

"I'm not—"

"Liars never make it into heaven, little cousin."

"Neither do murderers and pitiful eclair extortionists."

He shrugs. Not one care is given. "I know what would make his day."

"What's that?" It slips before I can stop myself, and his grin widens. I'm starting to get annoyed with him. "Just for your amusement's sake."

"Lying is a nasty habit, Mariah." For a second, he turns serious, watching me through narrowed eyes. "You need to stop living in the past and comparing every man to Lane and his dipshit failures. He wasn't a real man, just another child hiding behind his mother's skirt while breaking every plate on the table."

"It's not that—"

"I know you. Remember that."

Nodding, I sigh, because he's right. I'd already thought to do something nice for Javi. Not today, but maybe Friday before they head out to Nevada. "Where?"

"Paisa on the green."

"I'm not even sure what that is."

"For him, a taste of home."

<hr>

MY PLAN TO set up a lunch delivery for this week became an impossibility as a soft alert came from our FBI informant, causing protocol *blink* to go into effect. The IT department came onto the executive floor, wiping down every trace of the Frederick file.

The twins lied when Malcolm asked about possible investigations into their business.

"Antonio, I couldn't care less about the possibilities you're claiming when nothing you've presented says the FDA backs your findings. Are you under watch? Is there any possibility of a probe at your lab?"

The man sweats, a few beads trickle down the side of his head. "N-no."

"Lying will cost you in the end. I can't move the amount you want if it's seized." From the corner of my eye, I watch Javi stand and walk out. He comes back a minute or two later with two files that Malcolm takes from his hand. I don't know what's in those folders, and my brows furrow. "Final chance."

"Malcolm," Mildred, the other twin, calls softly. She's sitting forward, another button on her shirt undone while her finger traces her collarbone. Pathetic and useless. "Why the distrust? We've been friends for a year and—"

"Answer the question or leave."

"No. No investigations." Though she doesn't meet his stare now, instead, Mildred looks at her brother through hardened eyes. "Everything is clean and ready to be moved. We have a private account offshore in the Bahamas."

"And that means nothing to me." Malcolm pushes the folders toward them, sitting back in his seat while they read through the contents. "I chose the where, how, and when. Not you." Mildred tries to protest, her brother shaking his head, but my cousin carries on. "If you lie, at any point, I'll take ownership until my fee is paid. Ten million per infraction. Understood?"

"That's outrageous!" she yells, standing from her seat. The rough movement causes her chair to tip back and for her brother's face to become pale. "I'm not giving you—"

"We'll sign."

"Are you kidding me?" Mildred glares at her brother not a full second after he agrees, face red with anger. "We can't just give him—"

"Shut it and sit down, Mildred!" Antonio's voice thunders: it's the

angriest I've never seen him. "We need him, and I won't get fucked in the ass because you think the world should bend at your feet. I'm the president, not you."

"If this goes south, I'll spit on your grave," she hisses, her face turned and I hear a low sniffle that's out of character, but I don't question it. Mildred has always been off to me. Instead, I focus on the apologetic expression her brother gives Malcolm.

"I don't want your apologies." My cousin nods at the group of pens atop the table. "Sign before I change my mind. Those are my stipulations. Take them or leave them."

They took, and now we overthrow after removing all traces of the contract in this country. I've sent the files out this morning via private courier to the office in Costa Rica.

"Ready to head out, Muñeca?" Javi asks from the edge of my desk, pulling my attention from the scheduling I had to adjust due to today's bull. My neck cracks as I look at him, my head throbbing a bit from hours upon hours of tracing every last chunk of info with the IT department. "You look exhausted."

"I will be in a minute. Why?"

"I'm waiting to walk you out before heading out to pick up the twins."

"They're not hiding under a rock in Utah?"

"Hiding in plain sight approximately twenty minutes from here."

Nodding, I ignore the sudden bout of butterflies at his smile. At the softness in his eyes. "Who's going? Should I prepare a statement or—"

"Not necessary, beautiful. I already put something together for you in case we're intercepted by anyone watching the place." Javi places a USB flash drive beside my pen holder that l left right where he left it and he smirks every day it stays that way. Sure, it pissed me off, but at the same time, I find his knack for finding ways to get under my skin annoyingly endearing. "They shouldn't, but it's just a precaution."

"Okay." I grab the small device, shut my computer down, and open my purse, leaving the USB inside a small pocket. "My car's in the—"

"I've moved mine beside yours. It's not an issue."

"Thank you." *Christ,* I find him sexy when thoughtful.

"Muñeca, never thank me for taking care of you. It's my pleasure."

And damn me if I didn't blush right then. I like the sound of being his more than I should. Love the thought of him being there for me.

Not because I'm weak, but because it makes *him* happy to be near me. Because I'm his focus.

He's going to break my walls down, and I'm starting to question if I need them.

JAVIER

I ARRIVE AT the private penthouse the Frederick twins keep in Chicago. It's in a nice area, less than half an hour from the Asher building, where they hide in plain sight. Not in Utah like they hope we'd think, burning daylight hours that could lead to their escape.

Because it's hard to find an ant in a pile where possibly millions surround the guilty one, but I have a skill many don't.

Patience.

In Colombia, I took personal care of my family's enemies. Politicians and cartel members, it made no difference and there are plenty of places to hide but give a rat confidence, and it shows its face. Security gives comfort and the feeling of untouchability; that's when I strike.

The lobby is busy when I step inside. Multiple heads turn to look—the group of women checking in begins to whisper and giggle, but I don't pause or encourage.

I'm here for the twins, with Carmelo as added encouragement if need be.

And while I'll never hit a woman, if I have to make her brother suffer so she complies, so be it. They brought this upon themselves.

"What floor?" Carmelo asks, stepping into the empty elevator cart.

"Penthouse." At my response, he presses the needed button using a pen and leans back, adjusting the two boxes in his left hand. And so do I, pulling my phone out and bringing up Mariah's number.

There's been a subtle change in her over the last few days. She's been a tiny bit softer toward me, and I love it—revel in the rosy tint that sweeps across her cheeks when I bring my daily offering of chocolate or coffee.

A bribe? Maybe.

But there's something so delicious about those innocent reactions.

So unlike her normal demeanor, and yet, Mariah is letting me in. Little by little. One interaction at a time.

> Whatcha doing, Muñeca? ~Javier

Immediately three dots appear.

> Thinking. My mind keeps going around in a
> circle. ~Muñeca

> About? ~Javier

For a second or two no sign of her typing, but then her next words fuck with my head. My dick.

> Here I am, all alone inside of this large bath with
> bubbles and a glass of wine thinking about you.
> About the one kiss you stole and how much I
> liked the way you taste. ~Mariah

Fucking tease. Motherfucking destroyer of my will.

A low hiss escapes, my cock swelling at the mere thought. She's going to pay for this.

That little demon knows what she's doing. This game of hot and cold—taunt and chase that she both loathes and yearns for.

With one hand she pushes me away, and on her next breath, pulls me closer.

Close enough to touch but not bend over.

I could be back home in thirty and at her door in five more.

A throat clears, and I look over at Carmelo. "I'm a little hungry."

"We can stop after." My response is a little strained, my thoughts jumping between my needs and responsibility. "Anything in mind?"

This mindless conversation is needed, and I focus on him and not the throbbing of my length, the pulse in my veins that's thankfully hidden behind my suit jacket.

"Dominican if you're down?" My response is a nod, and he smiles. The guy's young and ambitious, but smart and hard-working—reminds me a little of the men in my family. It's also why I've taken him under my wing; he could go places in a business like this if he remains loyal. "I hope the crying doesn't last long. This woman is too extra for me."

"Agreed," I say, nodding absentmindedly while staring at my phone's screen. Mariah sent me a picture while he interrupted me, and I wish I hadn't clicked on it. Not now, when I can't rush back and punish my Muñeca for this infraction.

The pic is of her in a large free standing tub with bubbles covering her body and just enough of her breasts, that the two tips aren't visible. *How did she manage to get such a perfect shot?* I see them, though. Can make out their dusty rose color and their slight pebbling. The way her skin has broken out in goose bumps and the smirk on her lips just below the edge of the picture where she cut the image off.

Tonight she's going to see what I'm like when pushed too far.

> I'll be picturing you just like this tonight when I come with your name on my lips. ~Javier

Pocketing my phone, I close my eyes for a second. Breathe in and out through my nose—focus on why I'm here and not where I want to be.

With her.

Between her thighs.

Tasting her every moan.

My phone pings twice, but I don't look. Instead, I wait for the door to open and exit with Carmelo two steps behind while thinking of everything I find unattractive.

And my mom's seventy-year-old neighbor in a swimsuit at her birthday cookout does it. I'm soft before I'm three steps onto their floor.

There are two doors here: A and B, with the latter being our first stop. The twins each own a unit, but scum always sticks together.

Antonio will try to protect her, while Mildred will shove him in the way to save her hide. Their dynamic is a bit sick and predictable, something I'll use to my advantage.

It's why I put on a pair of gloves and press the doorbell. No fingerprints. No cameras are on; they scrambled the moment we walked in via the company's hacker.

"Hey, Ant? Can you get the door?"

"I'm on the phone!" Antonio calls back, and a shrill scream follows. Then there's the stomping of feet and a high-pitched *asshole* before the door is swung open.

She didn't look. Didn't see the added work Carmelo put in by stopping a random delivery guy and taking the two boxes of pizza, tipping the pimple-faced kid two hundred bucks to walk away.

"Oh shit." Mildred gasps, backing up with her hands shaking a second before trying to slam it closed.

The hardwood hits my shoe as I kick it back, causing it to smash against the wall, and a scream rends the air. It's full of fear. Of a pathetic attempt to get sympathy. "Please."

Mildred falls to her knees, shaking. The tears pooling in her eyes are real, but that doesn't stop her from arching her back, showing us that her fake tits are free to ogle. Tries and fails to distract me.

Disgusting.

"Get up," I hiss, walking in and closing the door after Carmelo enters. He drops the pizza boxes beside her legs, the sound loud but her whimper is louder. "I won't ask you again, Mildred. On your feet."

"Okay." Meek. Submissive. Bullshit.

"I'll go escort Mr. Frederick to the living room," Carmelo says, Glock in hand and safety off. He cocks it in her direction, and she jumps to her feet, rushing beside me. "You got that?"

"I do." Removing her hand from my arm, I push it off none too gently and point down the hall. "Don't touch, and walk."

"Let us explain. We can come to an—"

"Get him. I'll be there." Once he's out of sight, Mildred fingers the bottom of her top, trying to play the card of a willing tease, but stops all movements when I pull out my gun and wave it in the direction of Antonio's voice. "Walk."

The corridor isn't long, opening into a spacious, unused kitchen with access to the main living space.

"This is all a misunderstanding." *Those* words annoy me. Famous last words said by every lying asshole I've dealt with.

"Don't speak unless I ask you a question. Understood?"

"Millie!" Antonio rushes to her side, cradling her face and checking her for injuries. His concern is almost touching, a little too personal and not brotherly.

But then again...

"Your wife is fine, Mr. Frederick. Please have a seat."

He tenses while she lets out a panicked whimper, his eyes on her wide ones. "What did you say?"

"What part didn't you understand?" I take a seat on an oversized chair across from them and Carmelo does the same on another beside me. We're the picture of relaxation while understanding sets in for them. "She is your wife, no?"

"Mildred is my sister," he thunders, snapping around to face me with a false bravado that brings a smile to my face. "Who the fuck do you think...*fuck!*" His knee buckles and Antonio drops, biting his lip to the point of breaking skin from the pain.

I settle the Glock back down on my thigh. "I'll aim higher next time. Watch your tone, Mr. Frederick."

"Please don't!" Not-Mildred falls beside him, cradling his head. "We'll give you whatever you want, no questions asked. We'll leave the country and disappear, too."

"You two have a lot of explaining to do to Mr. Asher and have an appointment within the hour. Clean up, get your emotions under control, and don't even think of drawing attention to yourselves when we exit through the garage." Hope fades from his face. I know that this penthouse goes from top to underground parking without needing to bypass the lobby or gym floors. "And if I were you, I'd pray. Beg your God to have mercy because lying is the ultimate sin."

FIVE PEOPLE SIT inside Malcolm's office an hour later.

Malcolm and me.

Antonio and his wife, not-Mildred.

And finally, the real Mildred herself.

No one's talking. No one has explained as of yet, but the way Mr. Frederick looks at his sister, you'd think he'd seen a ghost. That, or a mistake.

"You three have ten minutes to make me understand this mess," Malcolm says calmly, sitting back in his seat, a Desert Eagle and knife within reach atop the table while his eyes remain on the real Mildred. It's a little unnerving how much the two women look alike, from the bleach-blonde hair to their grating, high-pitched voices. Their clothing is similar, and the way they sit with one leg crossed at the knee and hands in their lap is not a coincidence.

"Antonio hired someone to kill me a little over a year ago, but the marksman failed." At the sister's words, there is no outrage or explosive defense from her sibling. His wife, though, is staring daggers at her and biting back whatever retort is on the tip of her tongue.

His fingers are gripping his wife's, and the strength used to keep them in his grasp makes them turn a purplish red from the pressure.

"Is that true?"

"Yes, Malcolm. I did." And while I give him credit for not denying, there's no remorse either. "Mildred knows the reason, too."

"I see." There are three files in front of him and he begins to read the one furthest to the left, nodding his head before flipping to the next page. This goes on for a few minutes. He's reading and the ones across from us wait, two with fear and the third a little smug.

There's something about the real Mildred Frederick that doesn't sit right with me, though.

For someone betrayed by her brother and usurped by his wife, she's cocky, not hurt.

Unafraid. A little taunting. *What are you really after here?*

"So you see, Malcolm, it's—"

"Not another word unless spoken to, Ms. Frederick," I interrupt, letting Asher finish his reading. Her eyes narrow and lips thin; I raise a brow and almost smile at the way she backs down.

He puts the first file down and then picks up the middle, ignoring the group. Malcolm doesn't see the way Antonio sweats or the way his wife's lips move in silent prayer.

Instead, he takes his time, reading the paperwork his team gathered after I found a discrepancy in Ms. Frederick's signature. I'll give them that it was a good match, but all it takes is one wrong loop to catch someone's eye. My eye.

Before taking on jobs as a hitman in Colombia, I oversaw the contracts that Alejandro signed with a fine-toothed comb.

It's a necessity when millions are on the line.

This time, though, when putting down the next folder, he doesn't pick up the third. Instead, his gaze meets Antonio a second before a shot is fired from his gun. It's a clean entry and exit with his shirt staining red at the shoulder this time.

"Explain yourself."

"He thought that—"

"I wasn't talking to you, Mildred." Malcolm flicks his eyes toward her for a second, stare hard and challenging. "Understood?" She nods, and he goes back to Antonio. "Well, Mr. Frederick? I'm waiting."

"What she said is true. I did try to kill her for the company, and because of an issue she created two years ago."

"What issue?" Something in the way he says the words pulls my attention from the idiots across from us. There's a hint of undisguised irritation mixed with ire I didn't expect from someone who shows little to no emotion.

"My sister slept with an almost married man and the family was not happy."

"Hmmm." That's all he says before turning to the wife. "What's your gain in this?"

"He's my husband and needed help."

"Nothing else, Delia?"

"No." She looks at her husband and a tear falls. Not fake or to gain sympathy like before. This time, Delia is showing her emotions without any bullshit attached. "I simply love him and did what I had to."

"I need more than that, Mrs. Frederick. Tell me why you'd go along with such a stupid plan and try to deceive me?"

"Because when you love someone, you help them no matter the cost."

"Even if that's your life?"

"Yes." Delia's eyes close, and more tears fall while her husband watches. His expression is one of repentance. Of utter sadness, which has caught Asher's notice as well. There's more to this story than greed.

"Okay." That's all before lifting his gun a second time and firing again, this time hitting Antonio's ear and blowing the body part clean off. Blood spurts out, staining his wife's clothes and skin. "You forfeited your life the moment you signed those papers inside my office, and I plan to collect my pound of flesh. Mildred," he calls the woman without taking his eyes off a frantic Delia putting her hands on the head wound, trying to slow the bleeding, "choose her punishment, and I'll carry out the sentence. You have three minutes to decide."

The couple is horror-stricken by this, a whimper escaping the wife while Mildred tries to hide her glee. But I saw the look that flashed in her eyes before she took on a more stoic expression. She's enjoying this.

Most in her position would show hurt and betrayal. Would demand a better explanation, instead of glaring when Delia began to talk—the contempt and threat behind the heated look made the other woman a bit nervous.

After a minute, Mildred gives Asher a pleading look from beneath her over-mascaraed eyes. "They're my family, and I should be the one to—"

"Don't test my patience, Ms. Frederick. I've been compliant enough."

"Maybe we can come to a better agreement? I'll watch?"

"No."

"Malcolm, you're being difficult for no reason."

"Time's up. Javi, have them removed and transferred to a holding cell until I decide."

"Done." I stand from my seat and step out the door where Carmelo is waiting, talking with another two guards working at the bank this evening. "Take Antonio and his wife downstairs. We'll be down in a minute."

"Together or separate?"

"Keep them together for now, and no further injuries during transport. Understood?" All three men nod and walk inside, helping Antonio—nearly carrying him—while Delia follows amid sobs, body-shaking cries for leniency that no one reacts to.

Once they exit, I retake my seat and then take the last file, which Malcolm holds out for me.

"Please be reasonable," Mildred tries again, a whine in her tone. "What they did to me deserves retribution. Taking my life—my company—to make his wife happy deserves death. I'm only alive to tell my tale because of incompetence on their part."

"How did you survive a so-called hitman?" I ask, keeping my voice neutral when I'm anything but. Her audacity knows no bounds after sleeping with an almost married man, Mariah's ex to be exact.

Inside, I'm fuming as I meet her cold stare. Beyond irate.

My beautiful little criminal almost married this asshole, Lane Dermot, while he cheated. Lied. Put my girl at risk.

There isn't much of an explanation in this file. The one sheet only holds a few words, but they're enough to make my finger twitch.

I could kill her so easily.

But I don't. That pleasure will only be Mariah's. My beauty deserves the right to tell me her story—for me to earn her trust—and I'll wait because there's no doubt in my mind she's worth it.

"Since when does the help intervene in your business dealings, Mr. Asher?"

"Since he's family, Ms. Frederick."

Her plastic nose wrinkles at that while appraising me. "How are you related again?"

"One, you never asked, and I never explained. Two, he's Mariah's other half."

I'm not surprised by his words. His mind is working out logistics like mine.

Connecting dots she'd rather stay hidden.

"She's married?" Voice low and bitter, Mildred looks away, but I see her hands clench into tight fists.

"Answer my earlier question, Mildred." After putting the file face down atop the table, I rub two fingers across my bottom lip. "How did you survive?"

"I caught him cutting the brake lines of my car and staged an accident with the help of friends." Monotone. A rehearsed line and a lie. Most hitman will go for a personal approach and cutting lines is too far removed, a cop-out. "It was best to lay low after that and not tempt fate twice."

"Makes sense." Malcolm taps his fingers on the glass top, nodding to himself. "Smart move on our behalf."

"Now, about my company and my brother's betrayal..."

"What about it?" he asks with an amused chuckle at the end.

"How much will it cost to have the rights returned and—"

"Not a dime."

"Really?" Mildred smiles. Too cheery. Too easy to pick apart. "That's great, even though I am more than willing to pay with my flesh if you so inquire."

"Not interested in either your money or flesh. The company stays in my possession and so does your family. I'll execute and return the cadavers once I'm ready. You may see yourself out now."

"You're an ''

"Out." Her eyes narrow at my command, but the cocked gun makes her storm out a second later. She's muttering curses through gritting teeth. Demanding that whoever is still outside gets out of her way while the clacking of heels disappears down the hall.

"You saw what I saw, Lucas?"

"I did." My eyes narrow at the folder he gave me. "She's dirty and has help."

"So, the next question is: kill her now or let her hang herself?' At this, I meet his eyes. Malcolm doesn't realize that while I've never hurt a woman physically, if it relates to Mariah and her safety, I'd strangle one without a single ounce of remorse.

"Let her hang herself." There's an understanding between us. "The entire situation is fucked up—full of holes, and I'd rather know all the players involved than shoot blindly."

"Agreed."

"There's also the matter of Mariah's connection. She needs to know." This is something I won't back down from. I give exactly two fucks about his position in this family. When it comes to her, all bets are off. I'm protective of the woman to the point of blind madness if it ever came to that.

"Tell her." Asher stands and removes his suit jacket, then takes off his tie. "I'll handle the two downstairs in the meantime."

I follow his lead and type a message to Carmelo to bring the car around. Owing him dinner gives me the perfect excuse to pick up some dessert and personally deliver it to my muñeca later tonight. She has a sweet tooth I'll exploit if it gives me more time with her.

That, and I can explain today's event.

"They know something we don't."

"Not for long."

Mariah

I'VE BEEN HOME for less than three hours and the place is clean, the laundry that's been inside of the dryer for two days is now folded, and I have a pan of chicken enchiladas in salsa verde bubbling in the oven.

I've also taken a bath and played a game of *teasing the killer* that brought me more pleasure than the orgasm that followed. Not because it wasn't good, but because I wanted *his* hands on me. *His* fingers pumping in and out slowly, edging me, until I fell apart in his arms.

It's getting harder and harder to deny this uncontrollable attraction. To pretend my body doesn't call out for his.

Because there's something about this man—Javier's mere presence—that undoes me and leaves behind a mass of need willing to forget promises made to herself. To forget her past and want *more*.

Of him. Of us. Of a future together.

"I'm on a roll tonight," I mutter low, the hint of sarcasm heavy, and it's because I'm still restless for some reason. Two orgasms didn't quell the inkling churning that something is wrong.

My mind won't stop. Keeps dissecting Antonio and Mildred's behavior and then bounces to Javier and his last message.

> I'll be picturing you just like that tonight when I come with your name on my lips. ~Javier

A shiver rushes through me and I shake my head, trying to rid myself of the images I used to come.

Javier on a bed. Cock in a tight first. His head thrown back while groaning my name.

"Oh God," I whimper low, thighs clenching—the pulse between my legs racing. *Christ, Mariah! Focus. We need to focus.*

Right. I need to think. Clear my mind.

It takes a few deep breaths for my body to relax, and I recall the twins' visit. Their mannerisms were the same: over-the-top rich and expectant. Nothing stood out. Nothing that could raise a red flag.

Those two aren't the best actors and it makes no sense. None.

Because even at their most narcissistic, faking documents and getting into unapproved—illegal human testing—isn't their deal. They've never shown this level of criminality, their specialty being seizing federal grants for what they claim will be breakthrough testing that funds their expensive taste while doing minimal effort and research.

Are they overindulgent assholes? Yes.

Are they obnoxious? No doubt.

Feeling unaccomplished and more than a little stuck, I refill my glass of wine and walk to the living room, taking a seat facing my floor-to-ceiling windows. The buildings surrounding mine are lit up, and the evening sky has begun to turn dark.

It's beautiful. Peaceful.

I take a sip and then another. My knees are bouncing and fingertips drumming against the glass in my hold.

Why can't I control this restlessness brewing inside of me?

Like I know something is wrong.

Or maybe it's the confusion Javi creates. Maybe it's the electricity that shocks my senses and warms my bones when we touch. Maybe it's his persistence, that longing that matches my own.

But however I look at it, it all starts and ends with him.

I worry about him when he's out with Malcolm.

I look forward to the daily coffees and the flirty looks.

How do I fight something that I feel is inevitable? *You don't.*

I've been tempting him—pushing him to take and break the last of my walls down. A truth that is both hard to swallow and freeing. With his possessiveness and slick grin, Javier has infiltrated every corner of my mind and heart until the two became needy for his presence.

"Girl, you need to stuff your face and finish that bottle before you do something stupid. Calling him is no bueno in this state." I'm even nodding to myself, which further cements how crazy Javier Lucas makes me. "Especially since you're looking for issues with the Fredericks past the federal investigation. Remember that clear heads don't make mistakes."

I can deal with Javi and my feelings after. Much later.

A knock at my door pulls my attention and I stand, appreciative of the distraction even though I'm not expecting anyone. But what's worse is the sudden giddiness that hits my chest at the thought that maybe it's Javi. *So much for wanting to delay?*

Ignoring my subconscious, I look down at my body and I'm glad I chose the small sleep shorts and ribbed tank in a mint color. It's soft and looks sweet, but the lace edging and thin material give the like-second-skin fabric a sheer quality.

Another knock, and I fluff my hair. "Coming!" I yell out, and no other taps on my door are heard. Moreover, I don't look through the peephole or check the security camera, pulling the doorknob and opening it fully. "What the?"

No one is here. No sign of life down the corridor either.

However, what I do find is a bouquet of all-black roses in a large glass vase with no note. Picking up the large arrangement, I bring it inside and place it atop my entry table, digging through the stems for anything that tells me where it came from.

Yet there isn't anything.

"Must be a mistake." It's the only plausible explanation because no one is stupid enough to send me flowers that symbolize death or new beginnings. Because the two are tied together.

For every death, there is a birth.

For every ending, there's a start awaiting the chance to commence.

I close the door and take the flowers with me to the kitchen where I turn the oven off, pour another glass of wine, and sit while my food cools off a bit. And while I wait, I watch the flowers.

They're not helping my earlier thoughts. It's the opposite. They further unsettle me.

Who left them outside my door? Why?

Maybe a neighbor lost a family member? I know the lady three doors down has an elderly mother, but still, while the flowers themselves are beautiful, the meaning isn't loving or comforting.

So while I eat, I stare at them. While I wash my dishes and set them on the mat to dry, I stare at them. They don't leave my line of sight through my fourth glass of wine, and I'm so lost in my thoughts that when the ringer chimes, I jump in my seat.

At once I jump down from my barstool and rush to the door, not caring about my lack of clothing or the untamed mass of curls—the two long spirals that continually fall over my right eye now that it's dry.

It's one of the reasons I never leave my hair in its natural state. Too untamed. Wild.

"Should've straightened—" My whining is interrupted by three quick raps against my door, and I flick my eyes to the clock on the wall. *Jesus,* how did I lose two hours? It's late. A little past nine-thirty, and I pull the door open in hopes of catching...

"Fuck, Muñeca."

SHE'S TRYING TO kill me.

Destroy what little patience I have left, and before the threadbare cord snaps, I'm on her, pushing her back and slamming the door closed with my foot. The loud sound makes her jump, but my lips swallow the delicious gasp.

"Motherfuck, baby. You drive me insane." The bag with dessert is somewhere on the floor, the thud barely registering as my arms bring her closer. "Need to feel you. Taste you."

She's nodding against my mouth while her chest rubs against mine, the two stiff peaks and their piercings making me shiver. The feel of her makes me forget what I came to talk to her about. It makes me forget the little punishment I'd planned for her teasing earlier.

"Javi, please," leaves her on the sweetest little whimper, a needy sound that settles on the tip of my cock. I'm pulsing. Throbbing behind the zipper of my slacks. "Just please!"

"Tell me what you need and it's yours," I say into the kiss, twining my tongue with hers again and flip us around. Mariah's back meets the door while my right hand wanders, caressing the soft skin where her thin tank has risen, and I pull back just long enough to catch the sight of her like this.

Swollen lips and hooded eyes.

Chest heaving.

Hair natural and wild, a perfect mass of curls to wrap around my fist.

The bare skin just above her indecent sleep shorts exposes the start of a tattoo I didn't know was there.

Fuck. What she does to me.

The hand not exploring her hip and skimming lower tangles in her hair and I angle her head back, tilting it to my liking. I savor the challenge still present in her eyes and the parting of those bee-stung lips, but more than that, is that she's letting me take control.

Mariah doesn't fight my possessive hold or dominating touch. If anything, my muñeca melts into me as I slant my lips over hers, growling in satisfaction.

The sound is animalistic. Hungry. Thankful for her trust.

Lips hovering, sweeping softly, I stare into those gorgeous sea-foam eyes. "Tell me, Mariah. Just ask and it's yours."

"Touch me." Two simple words, and they wreck any semblance of rationality I have left. She's all I see, smell, and feel, and on her next exhale, I grip her hips a little tighter.

My nails dig in right before I lift that tight body, bringing her warmth to just above my cock and her legs around my waist. I flex and she shivers, her small fingers embedding themselves into the hair at my nape while her perfectly white teeth bite down on my lip.

The action is one of aggression, a fight against my domination that I counter with a thrust of my hips, pinning her and enjoying the sweet heat seeping through those almost nonexistent shorts. Her nails scratch my neck, and I can feel the skin break as pleasure rips through me.

"Make me bleed, Muñeca. I'll just make you pay for it with tears later on." Another flex and she shivers; tightening those thighs, I drop my hand to the right leg, squeezing the skin there.

Mariah is perfect in my eyes.

Supple yet lithe, toned yet curvaceous, and I follow the curve of flesh until her bare cheek meets my fingertips. I caress her, palming it roughly before delivering the first of many smacks.

"Oh, *Christ*."

"Javier, Muñeca." Another spank, this time a little harder. And fuck me if she doesn't moan. Arching her body in a way that presses her cheek deeper into my palm. "My needy girl only moans for me. My name."

"I—"

"Say it. Cry out for me."

She doesn't comply. Instead, she throws her head back with her eyes closed. Denying me what's rightfully mine.

Her. All of her.

Punishment it is, then.

Before she can protest, I have her legs on the ground and her body facing the door. She shakes, goose bumps rising across her skin, and I use my nose to push aside a few curls and expose her neck.

Her scent is sweet against the sweep of my lips, and her hips roll as my teeth sink in, leaving behind the perfect indentation of my mouth.

"What're you...*fuck*," Mariah cries out when I dig a little deeper and my hands traverse her front from her flat stomach to her breasts, cupping one in each hand.

I squeeze them. Feel their weight.

And when she whines at my slowness, I slap each tip with a bit of force. The metal of her piercings beneath the thin shirt makes my mouth water and I swallow hard, forcing myself to stay on course and not play a little longer.

I'll beg her to feed me each little tip later.

Much later.

Instead, I rake my teeth down to the center of her back between her shoulder blades and pause, ripping the offending top down the middle. And as the tattered pieces fall to the ground, so do my knees.

Immediately I take in the two dimples right above her ass and I kiss each, licking a path from right to left, and then I drag my tongue lower, right beneath the shorts that are both a blessing and a curse.

"Javi." It leaves her on a sacred whisper. The perfect combination of fear and desire. Of giving in to your wants and needs while handing over the control.

"You're always safe with me." It's a vow. The truth.

"I know."

"Good girl." One hard tug, and the tiny shorts covering her pool at her feet. Then it's my turn to groan when I take in the lack of underwear, just a thin little string between her cheeks, and the scent of her arousal. "*Motherfuck.*"

Sliding my hands up her calves, I follow the path my fingertips take and memorize every inch of bare skin I touch. I revel in the sigh of my name and the gyration of her hips when she presses her thighs together, looking for a small reprieve from the throbbing between them.

She's wet for me. Swollen, and I confirm this a second later when one hand doesn't pause at her inner thighs and cups her pussy through the lace of her G-string.

The soft material is soaked, clinging to her mound.

Slick heat. So soft.

"We should...I need..." with the tips of my fingers I rub tight little circles over her clit and stop "...more. Just more."

"As you wish." Sitting back on my haunches, I remove my hands from her body and admire her just like this. At my mercy. So beautiful and mine.

"What? No," she whines, a petulant sound that makes me smile. "Why are you stopping?"

"Spread your legs and bend over. Hands on the wall." One of her hands slips down and between her thighs, the tips of her fingers barely visible from where I sit. *Bad girl.* I don't say anything, but quickly land a harsh smack to the top of her right asscheek. Blood rushes to the surface as the sound of flesh meeting flesh reverberates throughout the room. "Don't make me repeat myself, Muñeca. Spread them." Mariah bends and spreads, but I want more. I want her asshole and pussy on display and legs shaking from anticipation. "Wider."

Perfection. She's an absolute wet dream become reality, and I lean forward when the two holes I plan to worship meet my line of sight. I trace a finger over the heated flesh where my palm print adorns her skin and travel down, slowly, learning her every moan and sigh as I meet the area where ass meets thigh and then walk my fingertips to the dip at the center.

Heat sears my skin and her wetness coats me as I caress each inner thigh and then pause at the entrance to my heaven. She's clenching, body shaking, and I've barely touched her.

"This changes everything," I say, tone harsher than I intend, but having her like this—at my mercy—is more than a heady feeling. I'm entranced. Owned just as much as I own her. "Tell me you understand this."

"Javier, we should talk—"

"Tell me you understand, Mariah. No more running or avoiding." I kiss each cheek and then lay one right over her puckered hole, flicking my tongue across the sensitive skin twice before waiting for a response. A hard shiver runs through her, her body swaying above me, and I grip her waist with one hand to steady her. She's aroused and needy and ready for more, but my words take away her docility— she wants to fight me or anything that demands her trust. Stubbornness is something we share, and I'll fight just as hard and dirty to possess her. "Say it, or I walk."

"Then I'll take care of myself," she grits out, trying weakly to push back against my hold. "You can leave...*Javi*!"

"Louder." The pathetic string she calls underwear is in my fist, the front digging into the sopping, swollen flesh of her cunt. One rough tug, and it snaps. "Let everyone in this building know I'm the one making you scream."

"No."

"Don't deny me, beautiful."

"Make me." Two words. They tell her truth, expose the push she needs from me, and yet they're the wrong words to tell a man barely hanging on to sanity and I land another smack to the round globes mere inches from my face. Then another, I leave her skin hot and body undulating, seeking the release only I'll give her.

Mariah tries to close her thighs, but before they touch, I palm and push them apart. The sight before me is almost obscene. Depravedly exquisite.

"You wanted this. Just remember that."

I don't give her a chance to answer, to further ignite me with her sharp tongue, and I bury my face between the two rosy cheeks. My tongue tastes her, flicking against the soft rosebud in a silent promise to be back before descending lower.

She's sweet and slick, soaking my lips and chin.

I lick her from back to front, pausing briefly at her pussy's entrance—dipping my tongue inside—before sliding down to her clit. The tiny bundle of nerves throbs against my tongue, coming out of its hood to greet my growls against the swollen flesh.

I become a savage for her. Take without care because she's woven her brujeria and I'm a proud slave for her.

With her clit between my lips, I bring a finger to her flexing hole and dip it inside to the first knuckle. Her walls pulse, hole fluttering around my finger to pull me in deeper, and I give my girl just that.

Son of a bitch she's tight. So soft.

I pull the digit out coated in her sweetness and slam it back in, pumping it a few times before adding a second.

The slam of her hand on the wall is loud, and the way she rises onto the tips of her toes, both wanting to escape my touch while grinding against my face is a privilege to experience.

"Oh my God!" she cries out suddenly, and I chuckle against her clit before raking my teeth once again down the hood, adding a little more pressure before pulling back and admiring the view of her slick thighs, flexing rosebud, and the vice-like grip on my fingers.

"You always call out to me." It's a hiss, my fingers slipping out long enough to slap the length of her pussy, fingertips landing over the throbbing bundle. The barely contained snarl, the undisguised hunger in my tone causes a rush of wetness to spill into my palm and down my wrist, a few drops marking the floor. *The little demon.* "Do you like it rough? Do you like to beg?"

Before she can open her mouth in protest, I'm gripping her hips and flipping her around to face me. Our eyes meet, my hungry ones on her heavy-lidded ones, and I slowly make my way back to her pussy, spreading her labia with my tongue as her lips part. She's panting, chest rising rapidly while I suck the first then second lip into my mouth, starving for more of the wetness coating her bare skin.

So pretty and pink. So mine.

"Motherfucking answer me, Muñeca. Are you testing my patience?"

"Please, Javi." *Christ*, her voice is all soft with a hint of desperation that pierces my gut and further stiffens my cock. I'm so fucking hard. Throbbing, I raise her right thigh over my shoulder with one hand while releasing myself with the other.

The cold air meets the swollen, angry head and I hiss, bringing two fingers to her opening and push them inside—pumping them in and out rapidly and I'm rewarded with a rush of wetness that I use to lube my cock.

With my fingers soaked in her, I bring my face once again against her core and breathe her in, rubbing my nose over her clit.

Above me she's whining, arching her back and pulling on her nipples while my tongue follows the same path, using the flat of my tongue to catch every drop and bring her closer to the edge.

"I'm so close."

"Give me what's mine." My voice doesn't drown out the sound of my hips meeting my hand, cock piercing through the tight fist as I forget about anything but her. Her taste. Her scent. Her scream as I bite down on her clit hard enough to make her come. "Good girl."

There's nothing I find sexier than your trust.

"..." Her lips part but no words escape. She's lost to her pleasure, riding my tongue while I continue to fuck my fist.

I'm so close. Just need...

Mariah grips my hair hard, a few strands breaking as she pulls me closer—holds me to her while a second orgasm rips through her lithe frame.

"Fucking hell, Muñeca," I growl, tightening my hold to almost the point of pain, and come overflows my palm and lands on the floor below.

At the same time, her legs give out and she slides down into my lap, letting me wrap her in my arms.

We sit there for a while. Just breathing. Calming racing hearts when the bag with dessert catches my attention and hers.

It doesn't look ruined, the container and bag not broken, and I clear my throat. "We need to talk."

Mariah

"WHAT ARE YOU thinking about, beautiful?" Javier asks, and I'm pulled back from my thoughts. Everything he's said, the giant mess created by the twins, spins in my mind. Sadly, this makes more sense than the behavior displayed by who I now know isn't Mildred.

Because while she remained aloof this time, there wasn't the usual glare or underhanded comment she passed as a compliment in the hallway after I showed them out. A behavior that I'd roll my eyes at in the past, I found the lack of strange.

Mildred and I never spent time together outside of the necessary business meetings, but the woman has always been unpleasant. Always miserable in my presence.

However, I get it now. Mildred was nothing but the bitter other woman.

Lane couldn't leave me, not without dealing with consequences his parents couldn't spare him from. Christ, he made me the fool of the story, and even with that, this delusional bitch had the gall to be angry with me as if I'd taken something from her.

You killed him. I did. And would again to protect myself.

"Just thinking," I answer truthfully, giving him a small shrug before taking a sip from my lukewarm coffee. We're in my living room and dressed somewhat; I'm wearing his shirt while Javi remains bare-chested and tempting.

There's no awkwardness. No regret. No self-reproach when I've fought so hard to keep him at bay.

Instead, I feel at peace even though the situation with the Fredericks leaves a sour taste in my mouth—ire in my veins—but it's contained with him by my side. Not even the memory of my parents betrayal and the disdain on the Dermots face make my heart clench like before. Instead, I find myself thinking rationally, not acting on impulse while enjoying the view in the seat across from mine.

Javier's tan muscles and the small amount of chest hair across his pecs are on display, and I'm memorizing each. My gaze travels lower and across beautiful tattoos, unashamed, and I count each indentation that leads to a delicious 'V' I want to run my tongue across.

He's a bit of a distraction, but I like it. Secretly love the fact he refuses to let me be.

A throat clears and once again I meet his eyes, feeling the slight heat sweep across my face. I've never been a person who blushes, but this man has that effect on me. He makes me lose my train of thought and the ability to send him to hell.

He has no idea he's already won.

"Be specific, Mariah. You've been silent for twenty minutes, and your facial expressions range from lust to anger. And before you answer, that lust better be for me."

"And if it isn't?" I challenge back, loving the way his nostrils flare and jaw clenches. Testing his patience is a turn-on, and the earlier result was worth every minute we've fought so far. Subtly, I rub my thighs together, but he catches the act and raises a brow, smirk in place. "Answer me, Muñeca," he croons, and goose bumps rise, a stuttered breath caught in my throat as I choke back a groan. He has me with that nickname. The effect is always the same as liquid heat rushes through my veins and settles in my core. *The day he realizes this, I am screwed.* "If I parted those thick little thighs and ran a finger down your folds, I'd find you wet. More than eager." *Abort. Abort before you climb into his lap and ride that beautiful thickness you watched him abuse.* "And while God knows how badly I want you on my tongue again, I'm concerned with your reaction to the Mildred situation. You're being too passive for the fiery woman I know."

His expression is one of sincere concern and I offer a small smile back, a different feeling taking over me. It flutters, feels like a thousand and one butterflies dancing within, and I melt back into my seat. Not just because of the magnificent orgasm he gave me, but because he came here with the intent to talk—keep total honesty between us—and that's something I appreciate.

He's proving day by day to be everything his reputation preceeds and so much more. Javier Lucas is everything I find attractive, and my walls crumble with each look, that gentle way his eyes sweep over me with affection so sweet I can't fight against it.

After a few beats of silence, I give him the same honesty back. "It's a lot to take in, Javi."

"Are you upset about the nature of their relationship?" There's a hint of jealousy there, some tensing of his muscles, but I won't call him out on it.

"Not in the least." There's no hesitation from me and he nods, relaxing back a bit. "But I am curious here…"

"That's all I know, Mariah. Do I have the file? Yes." Figured as much. Getting information on anyone is just a matter of time and connections. "However, I haven't read it. I'm waiting for you to fill in the blanks."

"Thank you."

"You deserve my respect."

Again, my heart thumps harshly at his words. My smile widens. "Then my next question is how much time do you have to give?"

His scent surrounds me, his shirt keeping me warm and I inhale deeply, taking him into my lungs and holding it there. There's a yearning within me that I can't control. He makes me forget the past and live for the present.

Really live. Want the *more* I've been running from.

"My entire life."

My eyes close at those three simple words and the heavy implication behind them. "That's a long time, Javi. Are you sure?"

"I am." Now he is the one without hesitation. His conviction makes me happy until I remember the topic of conversation and the earlier surprise left outside my door. My brows furrow as my mind runs and coincidences don't seem so innocent. *Mildred.* "What is it?"

Something tells me what I'm about to say will piss him off, but if he's honest with me, then I'll always return the favor.

"Earlier tonight, I received a bouquet of roses." Javier's hands clench at my words, but he nods for me to carry on. I meet his stare and keep it there. "They were left outside the door, black from the flowers to the vase, and without a note."

"Hijueputa," he grits out, and I won't deny that hearing him swear in Spanish is a turn-on. Javier doesn't do it often, speak in his native tongue, but I wish he would. It also makes me want to find ways to provoke it.

Bend me over and call me your little doll.

And had someone else spoken to me the way he does, I'd have knocked out a tooth or ten by now, but with him, it's not demeaning. It feels warm. Full of this sweetness that makes my core clench whenever he calls me his *Muñeca.*

"Are you paying attention, Muñeca?"

The always-present tingles spread, and I fight the need to whimper. I'm still sensitive. Feel the slight burn from his five o'clock shadow on my inner thighs.

Dear God, please help me get it together. This isn't the time to give in to temptation. Amen.

"What was the question?"

He tsks, but there's no real annoyance in his features. Instead, there's a hint of a smirk. As if he knows where my mind has been. "When did the flowers appear, Mariah?"

With a sheepish grin, I shrug. No denying it. "A little before I pulled my dinner from the oven. I was sitting right where you are now, looking at the early evening sky when a knock came. They didn't ring the doorbell but knocked hard instead."

"So it should be on the doorbell recorder?"

"It should." Why didn't I think of that? *Hard to think with his mouth between your thighs.* "Let me grab my phone. Be right back." I'm rushing to the kitchen before the words finish leaving my lips. I need a moment to collect myself. To gain a bit of decorum.

This isn't the time to be anything but what I am: an Asher.

Opening the faucet, I grab a paper towel and dip it under the water before squeezing off the excess and running the dampness over my heated neck, my cheeks, and lower across the top of my breasts. The coolness feels good, but his shirt on me smells of him and it isn't helping me control my libido.

He's woodsy scents mixed with a hint of cigar and heavy liquor. He's sex and danger, and I'm sniffing the collar and abandoning the paper towel, closing my eyes to enjoy the moment. The thoughts and images running through my mind are of him on his knees—worshipping me—but the reel quickly morphs to another fantasy.

I'm praying at *his* temple. Tasting what is mine.

"I need to change."

"You okay in there?" Javi calls out from the other room and I squeak, the embarrassing sound bringing me back to the situation at hand. Wearing this shirt isn't a smart choice. It's disastrous for my common sense, and I walk out sans phone.

"Be right back." My answer comes out high-pitched while walking toward my room. The plan is to lose the shirt and get myself together before further embarrassing myself.

And I make it inside without issue. I begin undoing the buttons and notice his lack of response, but it's as I get to the last button that two hands come up from behind and stop me, a deep rumble leaving his chest in displeasure.

"No." His face appears next to mine a second later, his cheek rubbing against mine. "Don't take it off."

"But I can't think straight." It leaves me before I can stop it, and I'm embarrassed. This isn't who I am, but with him, my defenses are nonexistent—an afterthought.

"I don't want you to think straight." Javi's hands leave mine and he begins to put each button back through a hole, lingering a little longer when he reaches the one between my exposed breasts. "Lord knows I'm unstable in your presence. Completely fucked by a slip of a girl that threatens daily to shoot me while the mere image makes me hard as fuck."

A harsh shiver rocks me, his nose skimming the length of my neck, causing goose bumps to rise across my flesh. I know I'm supposed to be looking at the video, talking about the discrepancies found in the twins' file and the possibility of who their donor could be, but when his lips follow the path back up to my jaw and he nips the skin, I lose composure.

That tiny spark of pleasurable pain makes me the aggressor. I'm the one who's salivating for a taste.

With his shirt on and a bold little grin, I turn around and drop to my knees. His eyes turn nearly black—dilated and hungry—as he watches me undo two of the buttons he closed.

My mouth waters as the bulge in his pants expands, twitches beneath my gaze. That's the only part of him that moves; he's stone still as I open his pants and lower the zipper, the angry, purple head greeting me while a drop of pre-come slips down the thick shaft.

"Hands behind your back and don't move," I breathe out, voice just above a whisper as I sweep a finger across the deep V, following the sharp indent from right to left and then back again.

"Muñeca," he groans, the pain in his voice causing my eyes to snap up to his. *Christ*, he's beautiful and masculine and complying with my wishes without a single complaint. Instead, his eyes are reverent. Hold so much affection. "Baby, I can't promise to give you full control, but I'll try. For as long as I can, I'll do what you ask."

Mariah

MY RESPONSE IS a small kiss on his right hip and then left, traversing the skin with the tip of my tongue before going lower. There, I leave an open-mouthed kiss at the base of his cock and another up the length, laving the tight skin until my parted lips caress the engorged head.

The bead at the slit glides across my lips and I can't stop myself from licking his essence, getting my first taste, and I hum. He's salty-sweet with a hint of earth, igniting my hunger in a way I've never experienced before.

"Don't. Move." The unrestrained yearning in my voice makes him shiver, but he doesn't move. Doesn't grab me when I take the first two inches into my mouth and let his weight settle on my tongue.

He's silky smooth, angry veins desperate for my touch. He's tense muscles and gritted teeth, watching me behind dilated eyes as a rumble builds in his chest.

I feel vibrations straight down to my core.

I'm wet and throbbing and my lack of underwear—the cool air in the room over my slick thighs gives away my desire to do this.

I need to taste him.

To have him lose control and take. To let him fuck my mouth.

Another inch and his thighs tense, the pants sitting just below his ass stretching, and I rake the blunt of my nails down his skin, pulling them down to his feet as my mouth takes him in deeper. I don't pull off to catch a breath or to tease her with a little teeth; instead, I slowly take him down to the back of my throat and swallow, not pausing until my nose touches the base.

"Fuck." Javi hisses, eyes on mine as I touch the edge of his balls with the tip of my tongue. Spit rolls down his shaft and sack. It pools on the floor right in front of his shoes and I hollow my cheeks, pulling back slowly until the only thing that connects us is a string of spit. "God, you're perfect. Made for me."

Large hands twitch and I raise a brow, blowing a little on the bulbous tip. "I said don't move."

"You have five minutes, sweet girl." The deep vibration of his voice carries throughout the room, and I feel a rush of wetness coat my lips at the threat in his words. He excites me. "Four and a half."

Swiping a finger across the slit at the tip, I bring it to my mouth and hum. "Can you make it that long, Javi?"

"Do your worst."

"I plan to." *I'm going to use every single trick I've watched porn actresses do.* Gripping the bottom of his shirt, I rip the buttons off and leave the two sides open, exposing my perky breasts to his eyes. The piercings glint in the room's low lighting, my chest heaving as I put half his length back into my mouth and hollow my cheeks. I bob my head while my hands wander my body, from my collarbone to the edge of my mound and back again, pausing to cup a tit in each hand.

I squeeze them, and he grunts.

I pull the piercings, tugging hard enough to make me groan around his length, and a curse bellows from him.

"Son of a bitch, Muñeca. God, baby…just a little deeper." He's shaking, body fighting to grab me and take, but he needs that extra push. "Open that sweet little throat for me."

A large part of me wants to do just that, but I don't. Instead, I slow down and pull off, keeping just the head between my lips while I pinch a nipple and bring the other hand between my thighs. I also slide closer and lean back, the tip of his shoe sitting just below my pussy.

I'm hot and swollen. Soaked, and as I slip a finger through my soft lips, his hand fists my hair and tips my head back. Angry eyes meet my excited ones, and his lip curls up into a sneer. "That wasn't nice, linda."

"Are you going to punish me?"

"No."

"Then what?"

"I'm going to watch you come as I use your pretty little mouth." Pulling away, he bends at the waist and gives me a kiss that curls my toes and sets my blood on fire. It's fast and perfectly messy, but it's over too soon and then I find myself choking on his cock on my next breath.

Javi's stroke is near punishing, and with my hair wrapped around his fingers, I'm held still while he strokes in deep. He holds still when his balls meet my chin, tapping two fingers against the bulge in my throat and I swallow hard, breathing through my nose and ignoring the urge to gag.

I'm at his mercy. Being used by him.

I love it more than I should, but I can't help and rub my clit a little harder while he stares down my body and begins to thrust in time with my fingers. "Faster, Mariah. Get yourself off while sucking my cock." The two fingers on my throat become his hand and he wraps it tight, moaning each time he strokes in and feels himself expand my throat.

"I'm close," I whimper around his shaft, spit dribbling down the side of my mouth and he wipes up the mess, pushing his thumb inside my mouth, further stretching me. I'm full. His taste dances on my tongue, but it's when he pumps his thumb twice and then drags the glistening digit to my left nipple and pulls the piercing that I come.

I scream around him, eyes closed, and rubbing my clit faster as my orgasm takes me over. Pleasure grips me out of nowhere, the hold nearly painful as the pulsing wave consumes me until becoming a throb, and my body feels as if I've been electrocuted by a thousand pinpricks. But that's when I start coming back to my senses and the guttural groans above me become clear.

Javi's fucking my mouth with wild abandon. No stopping. No concern, he strokes in and out at a rapid pace while bottoming out each time, using my hair to guide my mouth.

He feels larger, his growls harsher, and when our eyes connect again, he stills. "Motherfuck."

Spurt after spurt glides down my throat and I swallow fast, making sure to not spill a single drop.

WE'RE SITTING in my bed an hour later, naked and with our legs crossed at the ankles. He's to my left and quiet, humming now and then some tune I don't recognize, and eating his slice of tiramisu while my phone lies between us. No shame. Not a care as his dick twitches each time my eyes wander lower.

And they do. A lot.

He's muscles and control and danger.

He's tattoos and a few scars that only serve the purpose of raping my psyche.

And while I've fought this thing between us, I know that here, like this, was inevitable. Javier Lucas didn't take my no at face value and pushed and pushed until my will gave in. He's been persistent enough for the both of us and while I still have a few reservations, I'm at peace with what's happened.

Happy. Excited.

Is this fast? Yes.

Does my attraction to a man like him make sense after what happened before? No.

Moreover, he's never given me a reason to doubt his word. He's a man of integrity.

"I'm not a piece of meat, you know." Javi's rough voice breaks my appraisal, and I blush when the words hit me. I look away and toward my turned-off TV hoping for a miracle to break the now heated flush that covers down to the tops of my breast. "Not that I usually mind when it comes to you, but you promised an explanation and a search through your front door security feed."

"You suck," is my mature reply and he snorts, hand on my knee while his body shakes beside mine. "I do." His hand sweeps higher, pausing just at the edge of my core and squeezes, grip firm. "And I'll be more than happy to remind you after."

A hard shiver rushes through me at the same time I slap his arm. "Maybe I don't want you to show me."

"You do."

"So cocky."

"I see no point in denying that." Placing his now empty plate on the nightstand with his unoccupied hand, he shifts to face me a little, a subtle turn of hips that pushes those long, calloused fingers against my still-sensitive clit. "We both know who we are and where we stand; the only thing I need clarification on is the murder of Lane Dermot."

"You swing without lubing me up first."

His chuckle warms me even when I should be annoyed. "Always aim to please."

"All right, dork. How much do you know?"

All traces of amusement die and he's back to being the stone-faced killer I met weeks ago. "Nothing but what I told you. Please fill in the blanks."

"Okay. But first…" I put my plate down and reach for the large afghan I keep on my bed at all times, pulling it over my naked body "…for distractions' sake."

"I'd rather you don't."

"I'd rather a few things as well, but they're not conducive to this conversation." Javi grunts but doesn't pull my blanket away. Instead, he gives me his attention and waits with patience for me to begin. "Lane and I met years ago when I was still in high school, and we became friends. You know, the kids of affluent families that didn't fully abide by the law and run in the same social circles, we bumped into each other a lot. He was older than me, a jerk to most and spoiled, but never disrespectful toward me."

"How long did you date?"

"Two years, and no, I didn't love him then or now." For some reason, I'm ashamed to admit my faults to this man. To let him see me as anything but a smart, fierce, and independent woman. "My reality now isn't what it was back then, Javi. I made bad choices. Let others dictate my life."

"Malcolm?" There's venom in his tone, and while I still don't meet his eyes, I grab his hand and intertwine our fingers. Squeeze them. "Did he force you?"

"No. He hated Lane."

"Then who?"

"My parents."

"I haven't met them." Not a question, although his raised brow and pursed lips show displeasure. He's demanding an explanation without uttering the words, but I read those warm brown eyes, and the anger in them isn't directed at me.

"And you more than likely won't for a long time." Sighing, I reach over to the bedside table and pick up my bottle of water, twisting the cap off and taking a long pull. It gives me a small reprieve, the moment needed to explain the dynamic he isn't aware of. "They've been exiled to Europe for the foreseeable future by Malcolm for their role and the audacity to try and pin the incident on me."

"Incident?"

"I killed Lane the night he attacked me in this apartment two years ago. A few days before our anniversary/engagement dinner was to be held."

JAVIER

PRIDE SURGES THROUGH my chest at her words.

She put the dog down with mercy because had he still been alive today—breathing and walking this earth—I'd have hunted him down and left his entrails for Mildred to find.

"Do you threaten all the men you meet?" I say, and she giggles a bit, the tension in her shoulders dropping. *Is she worried I'd think differently of her?* Because if anything, I'm in awe of her and fuming at her parents.

How could they sell their child out this way?

"Are your parents active members on the Asher board?" Because if they are, I'll talk to Malcolm and make the bounty on their heads worthy of his acquiesce. Not that it will stop me, but I don't want Mariah to lose anyone she cares about.

"No." A wayward curl glides across her shoulder and I bring my hand up to her face, turning to fully face her and push it back, tucking the loose strand behind her ear. She shivers, and I see the two hard little tips beneath the blanket. "After going behind Malcolm's back and making a deal to expand territories—overthrow two other families that deal in the city in exchange for helping my father claim my cousin's rightful place, everything was taken. Money, properties, and access to all Asher dealings and buildings around the globe. They've been left with a small monthly allowance to live off and that's it."

"Do you talk to them?" Sadness flashes in those seafoam eyes briefly, but just as fast it's gone. "Miss them?"

"Not since my last birthday seven months ago." Mariah pulls her hand from mine and stands, the blanket tightly wrapped around her lithe frame, and walks toward the bathroom. Her foot is over the threshold when she pauses and turns her head slightly, just enough for me to see the pain that lingers from their actions, and I vow at that moment to take it all away. To give her the life she deserves with a faithful man at her side. "That's the day I buried them after being blamed for destroying their lives. They rather I'd died instead of the asshole who nearly choked me to death."

My muñeca slips inside the bathroom with the door closed, and I give her the time she needs. No matter how much my body wants to follow her inside the running shower or pull her close, I pick up our plates instead and run them to the kitchen.

While she's soaping up and touching what is mine, I bring us a bottle of water each, find her bottle of ibuprofen, and fix the sheets and covers. She's upset. I know there's more that needs to be discussed—the flowers and Mildred—but for tonight, I'll hold her and make sure she understands that no matter what…

I'm here.

And twenty minutes later when she comes back into the now pitch-black room and slips under the covers, I mold my body around hers. Keep her warm and kiss the crown of her head, humming a song that reminds me of her. Her beauty.

Moreover, when her breathing evens out and body melts into mine, I follow. Allowing my eyes to close and sleep to claim me.

"Why are you staring at me, Muñeca?" My eyes are closed, but I feel hers on me. Like a heated caress, they've been traveling from my face to chest and lower, while tiny fingers walk up each indentation of my abdomen.

She's been counting the six over and over. Skipping, sliding—tapping my skin softly with the pad of her fingertips. She moves away, and immediately I miss her warmth and the horny little hums of approval that follow.

I've been awake for a while, since before dawn, enjoying the bit of quiet that surrounds us. Reveling in her touch.

It's my favorite time of day. The few hours between sunrise and my alarm blaring when the world stills and I can think—dissect and plan—and today is no different.

Our conversation still weighs heavily on my mind. Her taste and touch still linger on my flesh.

"Christ, Javier! You scared me."

"You're the one being sneaky, not me. Very inappropriate, linda." Turning my head in her direction, I pucker my lips but still don't open my eyes. "Morning."

It takes her a few minutes, but she pecks my lips, grazing her teeth down my bottom lip. "Buenos dias."

I can't stop the smile that spreads across my lips as my eyes greet her bashful ones. Mariah's without makeup, her hair a mess of curls, and she's wearing nothing but a thin silk slip. She's fresh-faced and sleep-rumpled, but God, she's beautiful.

My other half. Mine.

"*Fuck*, you're perfect," I groan, gripping the back of her neck and pulling her down to my lips. The kiss is softer than the others we've shared, yet deeper, and I find myself turning until I'm fully lying on top of her, my hips cradled by her thighs.

There's no rush. No desperate touches as if the other person would vanish. Instead, we savor and explore. Caress and moan as I press the blunt head of my cock against her clit. The tip glides smoothly across, her wetness mixing with my pre-come, and if I shift a little lower, there's no stopping me from snapping my hips and claiming what's mine.

And I want to. Fuck, I do.

But not yet. Not until we put everything on the table because this beautiful criminal beneath me isn't a one night stand. She's not a quick fuck.

Mariah has quickly become my everything, and I'm not fighting the craziness that consumes—obliterates rationality.

Fuck it being too fast.

Fuck the way she fights me.

Fuck everything, because, in the end, it'll be worth it. She is worth it.

I care about her. *More than.*

"We need to stop," I grit out, flexing against her one last time, and sit back when her tiny hands move to grab me. "There's somewhere we need to be within the next hour."

There's a pout on her lips, and those seafoam orbs narrow. "Where? Nothing's going on until after two, and Malcolm gave us the morning off."

It's my turn to narrow my eyes. "I was never told this."

Not that I'm giving her much of a notice on my plans, but there's something I need to see just as bad. For my peace of mind. For her safety.

"That's because I told him we'd be late last night before my shower." Rising from the bed, a strap of her gown slipping down her shoulder, Mariah grips my jaw. "And I'm not done kissing you, Javi. Not yet."

Christ, this beautifully dangerous woman tempts every single cell in my body. Knows what to say. Knows how to light me on fire with the faintest of touches.

We have plans for her. She's more than a fuck.

"I'll give you all the kisses you want after my surprise."

"What's it going to cost me?"

"Two hours in a ring with me."

I thought she'd protest, but I'm dead wrong. Her eyes light up and her body vibrates with excitement as she scrambles off the bed, pushing me over in her haste. And all I can do is laugh. She's certifiably adorable, and when she comes back thirty minutes later showered and dressed in a pair of lavender-colored yoga pants and a sports bra, I rethink these plans.

How the fuck am I supposed to test her fighting skills when all I can picture is bending her over and plowing deep?

"Again. Harder this time." I'm moving around her, ducking my arms, holding the focus mitts just out of her reach. She's breathing hard and sweaty, the few tendrils that slipped from her bun plastered to the side of her face and neck. An elegant neck where a few drops of perspiration glide down to the edge of her...

Her fist connects with my chin, and it stings. She's caught me off guard and looks smug. Her grin is cocky. "I think you need to focus, Javi. Or do I need to find another trainer?"

Thank God the gym used by Malcolm's employees is empty and no one is allowed inside until I give the okay. All cameras are off and the lights are dimmed, leaving just enough brightness where we can see the other move. *No one sees her like this but me.*

"I'm going to make you pay for that," I hiss, ducking her next punch and tapping her right thigh when she stumbles a bit, losing her footing while chasing me. "Think you can handle me?"

"Bring it, pretty boy."

"Noted." Holding a hand up, I take the mitts off and toss them aside along with my shirt a few seconds after. She wants to play, then so be it. "You can throw a decent punch, princess, but can you dodge them?"

Something about what I said doesn't sit right with her. Darkness overtakes her features, hate and ire her stance.

She's stiff, chest heaving in a way that worries me. "Never call me that again, Lucas."

"What that, *princess*?" Her reaction is the same: anger. A sudden blinding rage that makes me pause. I'm not going to call her out, not now, but I'll push because whatever just overcame her mind is dangerous.

Mistakes cost lives. And it's unacceptable that anything should happen to this woman.

"Don't." It's a hiss. A warning. Nodding, I slip off my sneakers and tuck the strings of my joggers inside the waistband, taking away anything that could get caught in the fight she's bringing my way. Her chest heaves, eyes bore into mine, but Mariah isn't seeing me.

I still don't have the full story of her history with Lane, but something tells me this has to do with him or her parents—their role and involvement with him is what's setting her off. I'm also wondering if she's ever truly dealt with her anger toward the assholes.

"Or what?" At my response, her nostrils flare and eyes narrow. "Something you want to say?"

"Quit it, Javi. This isn't a box you want to open."

"I'm not afraid, Muñeca." I circle her, knocking her left hand from her hip on purpose. "You want to vent, do it. You want to strike, do it."

"Back off." Two words spit out through clenched teeth.

"Get it off your chest." Rather now than during a dangerous situation. Mildred, in my eyes, is a threat, a weak one, but stupid people cannot be discounted. They're careless. Ballsy. "Why do you hate the word—"

"Fuck you." And she reacts without thinking, charging me with all her strength and I let her, taking the brunt of our fall and cradling her close. Mariah's angry, eyes a bit red-rimmed while landing an elbow across my chin, knocking my face to the side. "Never call me what those pieces of shit did. Not you. Never you."

"Why?" Before she can land another blow, I have her hand in mine and roll her off me. She's on her back when I stand, eyes following me, and I wave her up. "Again. Don't let your emotions rule you."

"Maybe we should stop for today."

"Get up. Don't make me be an asshole this early."

"Why do you care?" The ire from a few minutes ago has cleared a bit but still lingers.

"Because I'd rather you get pissed at me than make a costly mistake out there." Her features soften at that, and I nudge her shin with the tip of my sock-covered foot. "Now, get up or I'll mount you." Cheeks flushing a bit, she does as I ask and gets into a fighter's stance, leaning most of her weight on the right leg. Another mistake. You don't favor one side more than the other, and I sweep Mariah's feet out from under her.

"What the hell?" She lands with a thud, but there's a hint of a smile on those sweet lips.

"No one outside these walls will grant you mercy, baby." I take two steps back and crook a finger. "Up."

"You're going to pay for that, Javi." And there's my girl. Focusing on me. On what's important. Grinning like the Cheshire Cat, Mariah brings her two hands up to block my attack while balancing her core, feet planted firmly on the ground. *Much better.*

But there's still an opening on her left and I strike toward her thigh, not giving her the full force of my blow but enough to cause her to stumble back. She catches herself, arms never lowering and when I go for the right rib area, she counters and lands her punch.

My stomach contracts, but I keep a proud smile on my lips. "Think you can knock me down?"

"Bet you two hundred bucks I can."

"I won't go easy on you."

"I'd be pissed if you did." This time when she charges, Mariah changes position at the last second and kicks the back of my knee. My weight drops, but before she can get me down I return the favor, chuckling as her leg buckles.

"That was good, but not enough."

"You're a jerk."

Before she can continue to berate me, I tackle the brat and cover her body with mine. "Never claimed to be anything but an asshole, sweetness."

"That's what you want others to think, Javi, but I see you." Those words pause me, and she takes the distraction as her opening, flipping our position with a hard buck of her hips, turning us so I'm on my back and looking up. I'm left marveling at the cheeky grin and the bright eyes of this incredible woman. "No one else has bothered to make me talk about shit I hate. No one else pushes me to deal with what I feel when ignorance is an easier solution."

"Muñeca, I—"

"I know you pay attention. I know you care." Mariah lowers her face to mine and kisses the tip of my nose, then each cheek before pecking my lips. "You're so much more than what I thought, Javier. Thank you."

Bringing a hand up, I cup the back of her neck, keeping her lips hovering over mine. "For what?"

"For doing more for me than those who were supposed to love me. Those who called me *princess*," she spits the word out with so much venom and tears in her eyes. This is her letting me fully in. A beautiful olive branch. "That was Dad's nickname for me growing up, and Lane adopted it. It wasn't meant to be loving, more demeaning as he thinks all women are beneath the men in their lives."

"I'm not them."

"I know." Another soft smile. A sweet sigh. "You have the possibility to be my everything, and that scares me."

"I'd never hurt you."

"And I don't think I'd recover if you ever did."

Mariah

"WHAT TIME ARE you getting off?" Javi asks, pulling into the Asher building parking structure a few minutes before two in the afternoon. I'm in the passenger seat and fighting back a giggle, keeping my face neutral after the semi-argument we had outside of the women's shower where he all but demanded to drive us in today. An exchange I lost after the jerk jutted his bottom lip out while sweaty, chest glistening and those damn joggers hanging low.

I could make out the outline of his thick cock, and it made getting my point across a near impossibility. Couldn't think straight when he twitched and grew, and I had to yell out a *yes* before disappearing inside to take a cold shower.

Turning the ignition off, he sits quietly and I follow suit. His spot is next to my empty one and two down from the ones Malcolm keeps for certain clientele. We never host more than one family at a time, and no more than four members of their organization are allowed upstairs together.

A precaution for them. For us.

"Should be out by five. I left everything he'd need today on his desk before logging off last night."

"Any plans?"

"No."

"You do now," he says simply. Just like peppering the weather into any conversation.

But more comical is that I nod and inspect my nail polish. The one nail that I chipped a corner of. "What are you in the mood for? I can stop on my way home and—"

"I'm asking you out on a date, Muñeca."

My heart flutters inside my chest and I smile, turning my face toward him. "A date?"

"Si." His grin matches mine and he holds his palm up to me. I place mine atop his, and it's only when our fingers intertwine that he fully relaxes. "How does a nice dinner with you and me and alcohol mixed in sound? And to sweeten the pot, there will also be some witty banter and a lot of sexual innuendos."

"You piqued my interest. Booze is muy important."

"You're adorable when sprinkling Spanish into our conversations." Before I can respond, Javi lets my hand go and exits the SUV, coming around to my door. He opens it and leans in, lips a hair's breadth from mine. "It's one of the reasons I adore you. Everything you do to me is precious."

He's killing me here. "Thank you."

"That blush is also delicious." His voice is deeper Husky.

"And about that dinner?" Because the sweet nothings are making it difficult to breathe and the urge to pull him into the back seat is becoming maddening. "Seven okay, or—"

Javier places his keys into my hand and brings the closed fist to his lips, nipping each knuckle. "Take the car and be ready at seven."

"Okay." My expensive schooling has flown out the window.

"Good girl." Another bite before kissing the slight mark. "I'll see you in a few hours."

It's then I notice another black car parked just behind us with dark tints.

It's my cousin's car, and before slipping inside the passenger side, Javier looks back at me and winks.

They drive off, and I'm still sitting here contemplating life.

The taillights are out of sight, and I shake my head.

That man was made to disrupt my life.

"AFTERNOON," I say, stepping off the elevator and onto a floor below Malcolm's office. There are three people here today, which surprises me, and a network of computers as they run scans for anything we might've missed. *But why three of them?* "Everything okay?"

"Morning, Ms. Asher," the youngest of the trio answers. He's a recent college grad with hacking skills coveted by the government, but he's protected under Malcolm's employ as a security expert. It's keeping them back for the time being in hopes he comes willingly, but there are other plans already in the works for an unfortunate disappearance. Erik takes a sip from his Starbucks cup before turning back to the largest of the eight monitors and hits three keys, the keyboard on his lap almost slipping off but he catches it and then turns to fully face me. He's a punk, a bit of a smartass at times, but dependable and has earned our trust. "Just going over video footage I swiped from the Fredericks laboratory in Utah dating two years back. Mr. Asher approved this."

He seems a bit nervous, and I arch a brow. "You found something?"

"You can say that." Without looking at the screen, he presses a combination of keys and the video changes to a cropped one. The length of time reads just over five minutes with a date stamp of two years ago, and when he hits play, I understand why he's a bit tense.

Lane is walking into the building with his arm around Mildred and my father to his left. They walk past the security guard all smiles, as if this is a normal occurrence, and my blood boils within my veins.

Not for Lane, but because of my father.

Another betrayal. Another example of how little I mean to him.

"Did Malcolm see this?" My voice is hollow. Monotone.

"Getting the disc ready now." Again he presses a few keys, and another short clip begins. The date is after Lane's death and my father is there with Mildred, and it's his arm around her waist, her lips he kisses. *Sick bastard.* At once my stomach churns, bile rising to my throat, but I swallow it back and pretend as if I'm not affected. *Can't show weakness.*

"Burn two copies. I want one."

"Of course, Ms. Asher." The other two don't say a word and shrink back a bit when I turn to walk over to the elevator. It's best I exit now and not after I discover someone else from my side of the family is in on this clusterfuck. "Do I take it upstairs?"

With my hand on the up button, I look back at Erik from over my shoulder. "Please."

"You got it, boss."

"Thank you." The doors close behind me as I slip inside, and I allow a single tear to fall. My father being involved is not a coincidence, and the Fredericks have been doing more than testing at that lab. I bet money on it.

But the question now remains on each key player's purpose?

How many more people are involved?

Why use me?

MY REFLECTION in the mirror later that evening doesn't represent what's going on inside of me. The things that make the most sense hurt after I watched the burned copy Erik made me.

My father's involvement. Mildred's hate toward me.

I'm angry. I feel betrayed. There are more questions than answers now.

And yet, as I watch the girl in the mirror pass the straightener through another stray auburn curl, I don't recognize her. She's here, but not. She's aware, yet a part of her hungers for the one thing that will sever all ties to those who brought her into this world.

Revenge. Blood. Peace.

All these years, I believed my father to be harsh and at times a sexist jerk, but this goes beyond that. He made me a pawn—a movable piece in a game I wasn't aware of playing.

Another pass, and I twist my wrist when reaching the end, giving the bottom of the strand a bit of wave. It swishes into place when I release it, joining the others as the wild girl from this morning that Javier admired is put away and Mariah Asher takes center stage.

This woman looking back at me is everything she's been taught to be, but behind the ire is a shine in her eyes that hasn't been there before. For the first time in a long time, she doesn't feel alone and the small curl to her lips and hint of a blush destroys all notion of the persona she's let herself hide behind for fear of:

Love.

A four-letter word that can destroy even the strongest. That if she embraces, will end *her*.

"It's just dinner with him. Doesn't need to be anything more." A lie. Even to myself I lie, and it's pathetic because a second later when the doorbell rings and I look through the phone app to see who's at my door, my heart races and that tiny smile grows at the sight of him.

I know this is fast.

I know things won't be perfect.

It's a somersault of emotions running rampant through me—a battle between my heart and mind where both agree that no matter the leap, things could end badly and leave me with a broken heart.

However, I trust the man on the other side of the door wearing a bowtie and a smirk more than those of my flesh and blood. Deep down I know— feel it in my bones—that he wouldn't deceive nor put me in danger and right now, that's good enough for me.

With him, it's the opposite. Javier would avenge me even against Malcolm if it ever came to that.

Give him an honest chance. Taking in a deep, cleansing breath, I press the green button on the screen and wait for the crackle to talk. "Be right out. Give me five."

"You get three and a half, Muñeca. Not a second more."

JAVIER

S HE LOOKS STUNNING and nothing like the happy girl I left a few hours ago. Something is off. The softness I've come to crave as much as I love the snark that rolls off her tongue with venomous ease—gone.

Mariah's sitting across from me inside of a riverfront restaurant enjoying a glass of Malbec while we wait for our starters to arrive: a crab and corn chowder for her, and bacon-wrapped scallops for me. We've made conversation, admired the interior of the steakhouse, but still, I sense that she's holding back, and I don't like it.

I don't like the lack of eye contact and how the Chicago river outside these windows holds her attention. How she looks at me for a second or two and then turns to find something random to comment on.

"Those lamps are from…what?" my girl asks with her face scrunched up in false confusion while pretending I'm the one with the issue.

"I'm waiting for you to tell me." At my words, she looks away briefly and those rosy pink lips purse. "Talk to me."

"Nothing is—"

"Don't." The low hiss makes her look back, and the expression on her face is contrite. Guilty. "There's nothing I hate more than a liar, Muñeca. Please, just don't."

"Can we talk about it later?"

"No." Reaching across the table, I take her hand and entwine our fingers. "Talk to me. What's eating you up?"

Emotions fly across her face: contentment, anger, hurt, and the last… confusion. "To be honest, I don't know where to start, and I also don't want to ruin our date."

"The only thing that could ruin my night is you walking away, Mariah." And there's the sweetness I've been missing. The way her eyes become soft and her cheeks pull up slightly while those eyes, those beautiful seafoam orbs look at me as if I'm her salvation.

It's humbling. Makes me feel like a king.

"Thank you," she says lowly, the delicate fingers between mine giving a small squeeze. She's looking at them, her smile a bit wistful. "Can we talk after dinner, though? All I need right now is to pretend that everything is okay and that decisions with no turning back don't need to be made."

"Mariah."

Her head pops up, eyes meeting mine. "Yeah?"

"You're not alone, beautiful. Whatever it is, we'll face it together." Suddenly, Mariah stands from her seat and before I can ask what's wrong, she's in my arms sitting astride my lap. We're in a private corner with the perfect outside view, and I feel complete when her arms squeeze me to her. The reaction is the complete opposite of what I know of her thus far, but I welcome it and hold her tighter. Give her the comfort she needs without question. "I got you, sweetheart. Whatever it is."

"Then I say start sharpening your knives because it seems I have enemies."

"Say the word and I'll kill them all. Lay their corpses at your feet."

"I know," she whispers and lays a tiny kiss just below my Adam's apple. "You're so different than what I thought you'd be, and I've never been happier to be wrong." Another kiss and then nip to my chin. "Please don't ever prove me right."

"You have my word." That pleases her, and she hums a cute little sound at the back of her throat before laying the next kiss on my lips. It's small. Nothing inappropriate, although I want nothing more than to devour her. To take until there's nothing left but my imprint on her soul.

"Thank you."

"Never thank me for taking care of what I consider mine." A throat clears and we look up, finding the waiter holding a large tray with our starters and salad. He smiles at us and I pat her thigh to stand, but before she moves to the opposite side, I pull her chair beside mine with my shoe. "That's better."

Mariah sits, but her amusement is clear and I'm thankful the darkness clouding her has receded. It's not gone, but she's getting a reprieve from whatever put her there. "You, Mr. Lucas, are a cheeseball."

I wink, and she giggles a bit. "Take that back, Muñeca."

"Can't, Javi."

"Why not?"

"You asked me to never lie."

And what's worse, my glare doesn't affect her at all. Instead, I'm gifted a cheeky grin full of defiance. "You're a brat."

"Are you complaining?" No. Never. I prefer her happy and at ease; unafraid to call me out and give back just as hard as she receives. My silence is her answer, and she blows me a kiss before grabbing the spoon beside the small bowl now in front of her, dipping it into the creamy soup and bringing some of it to her mouth. The second she closes her lips around the spoon and moans, my pants tighten—cock painfully pressing against the zipper of my slacks. "This is amazing."

I'm thankful for the long linens covering me, and I reach below to adjust myself. "Enjoy, beautiful."

"Want to try?"

"No," I say, and my voice comes out husky, hunger palpable in the one-word response.

"Behave, Javier. We're in public."

"My lack of decorum is your fault. Not mine."

A small snort escapes her then, and I can't hold in my laughter either. "We have issues."

"Normal is boring." Cutting a piece of my scallop, I bring it to my lips and pause. "Now eat, Muñeca."

Her brows furrow then, and I raise a brow in question. "Umm, have you noticed we haven't put our dinner orders in?"

"That's because I called ahead and ordered for the two of us."

"You don't know—"

"Mariah, I am nothing if not prepared." I cut another piece of the scallop and offer it to her which she takes, a low moan escaping at the taste. "I've planned this for a few days, and a little birdy informed me of your likes and dislikes. I also got her blessing."

"Who?" The perplexed expression is adorable.

"Someone with baby pictures of you and a love for gossip."

"You met my aunt?" A delicious blush spreads across her cheeks and lower, causing me to bite back a groan.

"Maybe."

"Whatever she said is a lie."

"Eat, baby girl. You have all the time in the world to prove that you're not a closeted romantic."

***

It's ten p.m. by the time we make it back to our building, and she looks exhausted. More than, and I know things are weighing heavy on her mind —the truths being uncovered are cutting deep, but she's not alone and I'll gladly bear the brunt of her pain. Of her madness.

Moreover, when I told her tonight she wasn't alone, I meant it.

The good. The bad. The insanity.

I want it all.

To help her welcome the rage I see simmering beneath the surface and embrace every emotion tearing her apart. Because if she doesn't, it will consume her. Eat her from the inside out, and I'll be fucked before I let that happen.

Moving to this country, I never expected to meet a woman like her. To care as deeply as I do.

But I do. This heartbroken woman I'll put back together owns me.

Our eyes meet once I'm parked. Her gaze is questioning while mine is expectant, needing her to ask. "It's late, Javi."

"It is."

"Then why don't you use one of my parking spaces? The owner could come back and—"

"Hush." Getting out, I come around to her side and pull her out the second the door is open. Then, we're chest to chest and lips hovering; her scent embeds itself into my DNA while those sinful lips match my grin, a tiny coquettish smirk that says everything we don't.

We are crazy.

She's my person.

Insanity feels right.

Mariah leans in closer and pecks my lips once. "Are you going to walk me up or stay?"

Goose bumps arise where my fingers touch her warm skin, rubbing soothing circles on her hip where the dress she wore has a small cutout. "It's getting harder and harder to leave each night."

"Then don't."

"That's a very tempting offer." My fingers tighten on her hip, and she giggles. "A dangerous one."

"I'm not afraid."

"That word shouldn't exist in your vocabulary."

Mariah shrugs, her smile fading a bit. "The world is an ugly place."

"And yet, you're the beauty in mine." At my words, heat rises to her cheeks, and her eyelids flutter closed. "You're making letting you walk a near impossibility."

"Then let me take you home tonight. Let me wake up with you in my arms tomorrow."

"Yes." With the tip of two fingers, she pushes me back and makes the move to slip back into my car, but I press the key fob, locking the door. Her gaze is questioning, but instead of voicing them, she simply places her hand in mine and waits. "Ready when you are."

"Thank you." No further words are exchanged as I pull us inside and head straight toward the elevator. I can feel her stare, wondering why I'm pressing the number two floors down from hers as we ascend, and then more so when it dings a minute later when reaching our destination.

She's compliant, though. Putting things together without any signs of outward rage.

And when I stop at the number that reads 1522 down the hall and to the left of the elevator, the hand not holding mine smacks my arm. "Why doesn't this surprise me."

Not a question, and I don't treat it as such either. Instead, I smile down at her. "Because you believe in fate as much as I do."

Cheeky little criminal arches a brow, lip twitching. "Do I? Or are you just my stalker?"

"Yes, you—" I'm cut off by a phone ringing inside my pocket, and I freeze. No one in this country knows this number, and those who do in Colombia would only use it if something went wrong.

"Javi, are you okay?"

"Take my keys and make yourself comfortable. I need to take this." Whatever she sees in my face has Mariah nodding and letting us in, not mentioning or questioning my sudden change in demeanor. "I'll be right back."

There's a balcony across the living room, and I don't pause my steps until the door is wide open and I'm leaning against the veranda, hitting the redial button. It rings twice and I hear the commotion, the yells in the background of anger and pain.

"Hola? Javier?" I've never heard my cousin sound anything but in control, but right now, he's angry—hurting—and dread fills my bones.

"Alejandro, what's going—"

"Primo, I need you back on a plane tonight. Your mom—"

"What happened?" I hiss through clenched teeth, my grip so tight on the plastic in my hand it groans. "Just spit it out."

"I'm sorry." I can just make out the words my aunt screams, and my world crumbles. Blinding pain overtakes my chest and the phone slips, landing on the floor a second before I feel Mariah wrap her warm arms around me. Holding me as the words I heard set in.

"Talk to me. What's wrong, baby?" Any other day the term of endearment would've made me smile—call out the beauty beside me—but I don't. Can't.

Instead, I repeat the four words that help her understand.

"My mother's been shot."

Mariah

HE'S BEEN GONE seventy-two hours, and I miss him. It's a foreign feeling, this urgency that pushes me out of bed at eight a.m. on a Sunday and toward my closet with only one goal in mind...

Go to him.

Javier needs me. I know he does.

I can feel it. This oppressive force sitting atop my chest that demands I comply and follow my heart.

It's been there since yesterday's phone call. His news broke my heart. His sadness nearly bowled me over as the longing to hold him grew with each hurt-filled word out of his mouth.

"Javi, baby? How are you? How's your—"

"She passed early this morning of complications from a blood clot in her lungs." His words are monotone, lifeless, and tears prick at my eyes. I can feel his pain as if it were my own. *"She's resting now, Muñeca, and that's all that matters. I'm just sad she never got to meet you and love..."* Javier pauses, and I can hear the shuddering breath escape him, the near

desperate sigh he allows to slip through. "I'll call you later. We're heading to the funeral home now and then meeting with—"

"Don't worry about me. I'll be here when you're ready."

"I miss you, beautiful."

The second the line disconnected, I was hit with every emotion in the span of seconds. From anger to sadness to despair to giddiness at him missing me, and then loss. Javier's mother is dead, and it tore me in two for different reasons: selfishness and understanding.

Selfishness because I'll never meet the woman that made him who he is today.

Understanding because I've been where he is now with someone I loved deeply.

My grandmother was taken from us out of pure selfishness, a hit gone wrong against Malcolm's dad not knowing that the passenger in the car was old and here for a simple visit.

One bullet and my Mimi was gone, leaving us here to grieve and later demand the blood of every person involved. From the financial institution's owner—a competitor trying to force us to sell—to the hired shooter: they paid with their lives and that piece-of-shit company.

"Alexa, call Malcolm!" I yell out, grabbing items in a rush before stuffing them in my bag. I'm not even sure what's making the cut, but my goal isn't organization here; it's speed.

The first ring barely finishes when an audible click follows. "What time is your flight?" he says in greeting, not sounding surprised in the least. Not upset either.

"Haven't booked It yet." I grab my passport from a small safe I keep in my closet along with two guns and other important papers. "I'm packing now and just heading—"

"The jet will be ready when you are. Do you need a ride?"

My eyes narrow at the speaker. "Why are you being so easy about this?"

"Because he needs you more than I do at the moment, little cousin." My eyes tear up, but I blink back those tears. Very few people ever see the softer side to this man, but those closest to him have the privilege.

Malcolm shows he cares with actions, and this right here is his way of accepting Javier as family.

Not just as an employee. Not just as someone I'm casually dating.

Are we dating? Is he my boyfriend? The title doesn't sit right with me. Doesn't describe his place in my life adequately.

"I'll still be available for scheduling and meetings through Skype. Refreshments can be catered and—"

"No."

"What do you mean, *no*?" I pause mid-zip of the carryon luggage, my eyebrows scrunching up in confusion. "You know we can't have a temp in there. People are nosy, and I'd hate to go to jail this close to my birthday for killing a snitch."

"Mom's covering." *Thank you, Jesus!* She held the position before me, helping her husband run Asher Holdings until the day he stepped down. "We've already discussed the upcoming week and moved a few things around." The sound of papers being shuffled comes through the line, followed by the creak of a chair. "So don't worry about anything."

"But when—"

"Not another word about work."

"Thank you," I breathe out, letting the worry about work melt away. If anyone can run that office better than me, it's his mother.

"Just make sure he's okay and knows we're here if needed." With that, he hangs up and I smile. His acceptance of Javier makes me feel at ease—comforted by the knowledge that someone I admire finds him worthy.

"Welcome to Colombia," a man greets me with an outstretched hand the second I exit the airport. He's smiling, dressed all in black while a younger, female version of him stands against a black F350, studying me closely. No smile. No frown. "How was the flight?"

"Emiliano or Alejandro?" I ask, remembering a photo Javier showed me of his cousins one day while scrolling through his phone. They'd sent it to him and after I accused him of being stuck-up, I was shut down with the snapshot in question. All three were standing side by side with goofy drunk grins, but I was too busy staring at Javi to understand who was whom. He'd been younger in the photograph, but still just as handsome while wearing that grin I hate to love.

"Emiliano, Miss—"

"Mariah. Just Mariah." His grip is firm before dropping my hand and grabbing my bag, motioning with his free hand to get inside. "You want the front or back?" I ask the girl, but she doesn't answer, choosing instead to climb into the second row and buckling up.

I know who she is and why she's upset.

It's hard to lose someone you love—watch them take their final breath —while another close relative moves away without plans for a return. So many changes for a girl still in her teens surrounded by blood and carnage —her life path paved by the choices of others.

She's a victim in this. A survivor of a night that killed one and left the young woman with a scar she'll forever carry.

I see so much of myself in her.

And while my father didn't directly pull triggers or slice throats, he did lead many toward their demise.

Our last name is a blessing and a curse. A weight we carry and a stigma we can never escape.

"The drive is about two hours." Emiliano slips into the driver's seat and presses the keyless start beside the steering wheel. He's not looking at me. Instead, he's frowning at Lourdes through the rearview mirror. "Do you need to stop for anything?"

"No." At my curt response, he looks over with a questioning look, but I shake my head at him. "Does he know I'm here?"

"Are you okay?" *Christ*, men can be dense at times. It's obvious his sister is uncomfortable and doesn't trust me—she doesn't know me—and shouldn't be expected to open her arms easily. Not in our world. "You seem upset, Mariah."

"Please answer the question, Emiliano."

"Can you answer mine?" His expression is one of a lost puppy, but before I can respond, Lourdes takes her seatbelt off and leans forward.

"Oh, dear God!" she grits out, her head is closer to mine than his, and I see the moment her glare turns to tears. "She's just saying lay off with the reprimanding looks my way. I'm not talking because I dislike her, but because I don't have the energy. It's all too much…" Her hiccuping pause is filled with pain and before the first tear falls, I'm jumping from the front to the back and hugging her tight. *Thank God I'm small and flexible.* A shuddering breath escapes her, and the small hands clenched at my sides open and grip; she's holding on to me while letting go of what's eating her inside.

"Lourdes, please. Not now, sis." Emiliano pulls out from the curb, his voice tense as are his shoulders. "Just keep it together until—"

"Just drive. I'll handle her." If he's inclined to argue, I don't know. He simply zips his lips and nods. However, a few minutes later I catch the thankful expression at a red light when he turns to look at us.

His eyes soften when he sees his little sister's tears and the way my arms embrace her. *Thank you,* he mouths, and I know at that moment I've made a friend in him.

After a while, when the sobs turn into sniffles, Lourdes tries to move back. Her face is blotchy, expression embarrassed. "My apologies. I don't know what—"

"Stop." Gently, I wipe my fingers under her eyes. "You have every right to be upset. Javi told me what happened, and I'm so sorry for what you've gone through." At the mention of his name, another round of tears fall. Her chest heaves and her tiny frame trembles, and it breaks my heart. "Breathe, Lourdes. No one is upset with you."

"I should've done more to save Mama Ida." It's low, a whisper full of recrimination and pain that leaves her exposed. Lourdes blames herself because she's here and my Javi's mother isn't.

"How?" Tipping her face up to meet my eyes, I raise a brow. "Sweetie, they sent men there with high-round capacity weapons and one goal. There was nothing you could've done, and it's a blessing you weren't harmed."

"But Javi won't even look at me!"

"Because he feels guilty for not being here." That makes her pause. Her watery eyes are stunned and mouth open, as if to speak. She doesn't, though. For the next few minutes, nothing comes out except the occasional sniffle and I leave her alone to dissect my words.

In all her guilt, Lourdes never paused to analyze what others might think, and she just accepted the worst. Especially about her cousin. A cousin, who in my understanding, is sometimes closer to her than her brothers.

"Does he really?" she asks after a while, leaning into me, and I wrap my arm around her shoulders, hugging her tight. My response is a sad smile, and her brows scrunch up. "But that makes no sense. How can he protect us when we were ambushed and—"

"Apply that same explanation to your situation, kiddo. You did nothing wrong." Lourdes gives me a minute nod. "Good. Now rest up until we get there. Javi needs us to be strong and give him space when needed."

"You're good for him."

"I hope I'll be."

"You will." Her conviction warms my heart, and the sucker gives a harsh thump in agreement. This—us—is crazy and unpredictable and dangerous, but I wouldn't change a single thing about it. In not making sense, we fit. In not being afraid to be who we are, we become stronger.

That man has become my person.

Mine.

"Thank you," I say, and we both close our eyes after. She's lost within her thoughts, and I vow to let him know how I feel soon.

Because I love him. Completely and unequivocally, I'm head over heels for that murderous sweetheart.

I'M shaken awake by a hand on my arm. The movement jostles me, pulling me from the nap the car's movements lulled me into and my eyes snap open.

"Morning, sleepyhead," Lourdes smiles, and it's genuine and she looks sweet. Nothing like the hurt girl from a little while ago. "Are you ready to see him, or want to freshen up first?"

"What has you in a sudden good mood?" I ask, stretching a bit before stepping out in front of a beautiful two-story home where armed guards stand at every corner with rifles strapped across their chests. "It's a good look on you."

"He's going to flip when he sees you."

"And that makes you happy?"

"I know he misses you." She flicks her eyes behind us before leaning over conspiratorially. "Javier's mentioned you at least fifty times a day since arriving and looks at his phone twice as much. You're the half of his soul keeping him together."

JAVIER

MY MIND IS a dangerous place to be, and losing myself within is taking its toll. I'm angry and hurting and still not able to fully process that the woman who brought me into this world is now gone.

That I wasn't here to protect her as a good son should.

That Ida Lucas was taken from us by a selfish son of a bitch wanting revenge over the death of a thieving asshole I killed a few months back. The same thieving asshole that left her in a wheelchair.

Two brothers. Each stole from her things that could never be replaced:

Her ability to walk. Her life.

"We'll find him, Javi," Alejandro vows, the hand on my shoulder squeezing tight. "I swear on my life that we'll find him."

"Rats never stay hidden for long." He nods and I pick up my glass, throwing back the last of the Aguardiente before standing. "Call Tito and up the reward through the surrounding barrios. I want his head on a spike within twenty-four hours."

"Listo."

"I'll be in my room. Let me know if..." *Fuck*, my heart thumps and palms sweat at the sight of her. My beautiful little criminal with a coquettish smile and warm eyes is standing just inside the doorway to the study watching me. *How did she get here? How did she know I needed her?*

Mariah's looking a bit nervous, a little rumpled from what I guess is traveling, but here. She's here, and it hits me then just how much I've been yearning for.

Her. Just her.

"Hi." Mariah's voice is soft, and I let it surround me. Soothe me. "Miss me?"

"Come here." My voice is rough with the sudden emotions rushing through me. I'm holding a hand out for her and every finger shakes, arm muscles twitching until her dainty hand wraps around my rough one.

Then it's calm, and I breathe.

No words are exchanged as I lose myself in her seafoam eyes, letting her presence give me the one thing I've been missing since Alejandro's call: peace. A small semblance of what I've had with her these last few weeks, and right now, I feel blessed to have her standing in front of me.

"You never answered my question, Javi." There's a playful tsk that comes from the back of her throat, a mock glare, but it's the twitch of her glossy lips that pulls a chuckle from me. "Making me wait is unacceptable."

"It is." I lift her hand and kiss each knuckle. "I've more than missed you, sweetheart. I've been a little lost without you."

It's the truth, and I'm not ashamed to admit it.

There are times in our lives where showing weakness is a strength, and being honest with the woman that's come to own my soul is one of them. So I let her see me. See the pain that's settled into my heart and I can't deal with alone.

"That's because we don't work well without the other." Rising to the tips of her toes, Mariah kisses my chin and then pulls back, releasing my hand. "It's why I'm here, Javi. I'm here for you...whatever you need."

Without waiting for my reply, she looks over at a silent Alejandro and walks over, giving the usually serious man a quick hug. She says something to him—it's too low for me to hear, but he smiles and walks toward the room's entrance with a knowing expression on his face.

And when he's right beside me, my cousin pauses his steps. "She's one of the good ones, Javier. Treat her right."

"I know."

"Good."

Then it's just the two of us, and the tension rises for a completely different reason. My missing her goes deeper than just the physical. It goes past carnal hunger or the way we challenge each other.

"Show me your room." Hips sway toward me and I follow the movement, admiring how beautiful she is in a simple pair of jeans and an old Spice Girl's shirt. "You look like you need some rest."

"Let me show you around first. You have to be starving—" Her finger over my lips shuts me up, and I raise a brow.

"Room. Now." Then the naughty little thing mimics my stance, brow, and all. This makes me want to bite her. "Comprende?"

"You're lucky I like you."

"And you're just lucky I'm a saint."

"Saint, my ass." With that, I toss her over my shoulder and walk out of the room with her whisper-cursing me all the way to the master bedroom at the top of the stairs with the large double doors. No one stops me or asks who she is, but I catch the smile on Lourdes's face and Emiliano smirking. Even their mother looks amused during a time when sadness is all we've felt.

"I'm going to whoop you, Javi. Put me down."

"No." I kick the door closed with my foot and march over to the bed.

"Javier Lucas, I swear to all that…shit!"

I'm looking down on her breathless form now atop my bed, her eyes bright. "You were saying, Muñeca?"

Tiny fingers wave. "Hi."

"Hi." Lowering my body to hers, I nuzzle my nose to hers and peck those sweet lips. "I'm happy you're here."

"There's nowhere else I'd rather be." Voice low and breathy, Mariah slips her arms around my neck and tugs on the hair at my nape. "I've missed you."

"Missed you too." I skim my lips across hers, slowly, softly, while taking her upper lip between my own. A soft bite. A little lick. Mariah releases a tiny whimper then, exhaling against my mouth, and deepens the kiss.

She's hungry. As desperate as I am, she pulls back a few seconds later and rests her forehead against mine. The soft look on her face makes my chest feel tight, and my heart beats wildly for her.

"I'm so sorry I didn't come sooner, Javi." Seafoam eyes turn watery, and I shake my head. Her tears are something I can't handle at the moment and she sees that, fighting back her own emotions for me. I know how she feels without her uttering a single word. Can read her even when she hides behind a persona that's cold and distant when Mariah is anything but.

"You're here now, and that's all that matters to me. To my family."

A different kind of need settles in the room then and I let her wrap those small, yet strong arms around me and pull me close. There are no more words. No need to express.

For the first time since coming back to my country, I let myself sink into the bed and gratefully take comfort in my Muñeca. And as her fingers run through my hair, tugging a bit near the ends, I rest.

Fall asleep in her arms with her heart beating beneath my ear. *I love you.*

THE NEXT TIME my eyes open, the room is dark and yet, I know it's early. There's a rooster somewhere on the property greeting the sun while annoying everyone here. There's a heaviness that settles in my chest knowing what the following hours will bring, but a soft sigh to my left calms me.

Soothes and comforts my soul.

Motherfuck, she's beautiful. Mariah's asleep while wearing an old soccer shirt from my teenage days she pilfered from one of my drawers with a bedsheet carelessly strewn across the back of her thighs. *It seems I hogged the comforter.* There's also the matter of a leg bent at the knee and an arm wrestling the pillow beneath her head in a serious choke-hold from my viewpoint, and I've never been more jealous of a sack of cotton in my life.

I want my chest to be where she rests her head. I want to be who she seeks for comfort.

I love you. Three little words that slam back to the forefront of my mind as her arrival replays in my mind:

Seeing her standing at the entrance to my study here.

The feel of her lithe body against my harsher planes.

Hearing those words just before falling asleep, the way she lulled me with gentle touches and the soft scent of her favorite lotion.

My beautiful little Muñeca. "I love you, too."

A soft knock on the door pulls my attention toward the bedroom door. "Javi?" Lourdes calls, her voice low. "You up?"

Mariah stirs on the bed, her eyebrows scrunching up, but they relax when I lean over and kiss her forehead. "Go back to sleep, sweetheart. There are still a few hours before we leave." She doesn't answer; instead, she snuggles deeper into the covers I place over her.

"If you're sleeping, cough, primo." Lourdes taps her fingernails on the door. "One cough and I'll—" The door opens before she finishes, and I chuckle at the small squeak she emits. "That's rude!"

"Hush, kid. Let's not wake her up yet." Closing the door softly, I walk past her and down the stairs, heading straight for the kitchen. My little cousin follows silently, heading straight for the fridge to pull out the creamer and milk before turning to grab our mugs. We've done this a time or a hundred, and I'm surprised she didn't seek me out before today. Her feelings of guilt are written all over her face and actions—she's haunted by memories that break my heart. "Now or after?"

"After. I'm still trying to gather my thoughts."

"Okay." Alejandro is a true coffee snob, and every family member has a setup that rivals the most expensive coffee houses around the world. The blends are rich while mine is a darker roast than what the others prefer, but I'll need the caffeine today more than other days. "Are you drinking from mine?"

"Not if I want to live." Lourdes snorts, reaching inside a small drawer next to the Keurig my mother wanted and that I bought last Christmas. She pulls out a pod of the mild stuff and preps her cup while I make mine, meeting at the coffee island a few minutes later where she pours the cream into mine and I cut us a slice of pound cake to dip.

Taking a sip from my coffee, I wait for her to start, but she doesn't. Instead, she fidgets and looks past me to the clock on the microwave. "Talk to me, Lourdes."

A heavy sigh escapes her, but her sad eyes meet mine. Tears gathered at the corners. "I'm so sorry, Javi. So sorry for not protecting, Mamita Ida." My mouth opens to refute her, to explain it's not her fault, but Lourdes shakes her head while holding a hand up. This is what she needs. To get this off her chest. "Rationally, I know I'm not at fault, but the fact I'm here and she's not isn't easy to swallow. She saved me that night. She pushed me down and fought with me to stay hidden at all costs and I…I should've done more. Dragged her out of the house if it came to that." Tears fall freely from her face and her lips tremble, but I let her get it all out. Lourdes needs this. "I failed you, Javi. Please don't hate me."

"No, you didn't."

"Yes, I—" Before the stubborn girl can finish her idiotic thought, I pull her into a hug and let her sob it out. Her body shakes and cries fill the room, and when Alejandro walks in to see what's going on, I shake my head and he leaves. This has been bottling up inside her, and I feel like utter shit because thoughts like these should never have crossed her mind.

A teenager doesn't stand a chance against high-caliber weapons and a group of men sent to kill. If anything, the men working security that night —two out of the three—who decided to head out for food instead of standing watch, are responsible. As accountable as the man who gave the order to kill an innocent woman.

Once her bawling turns to low sniffles, I pull back and take a seat. Lourdes does the same after I move her stool with my foot, and then she looks at me. "I could never hate you, bug. Never."

"I'm so sorry."

"Stop apologizing for something you had no control over. You didn't pull the trigger."

"I should have—"

"You did what my mother told you to do, and I'm thankful you listened." Picking up my mug, I take a sip of coffee and grimace. She put way too much sugar in this, but I swallow with a small smile. The last thing I want is to hurt her feelings. "What happened is horrible and God knows I'd give my life to have been able to save hers, but I was elsewhere and that's my burden to carry. I should've been here for you both and—"

"Don't you dare apologize!" Lourdes hisses, face hard, and I'm surprised by this sudden flip in her mood. "Mariah told me you'd feel guilty, that you were probably holding stuff in for my benefit, but dammit, this isn't on you. My brothers didn't know. Our security messed up. It's just one giant mess, and that woman upstairs is amazing."

Teenage girls are hard to follow. We went from crying to angry to now a small giggle.

Lord, please don't repay my sins with daughters.

"What did my Muñeca say?" This for some reason fills me with guilt. This beautiful, selfless, and utterly perfect-for-me-woman flew here to be my support, and I fell asleep on her. *When did they talk? What happened while I was knocked out?*

"The same thing you just did, but in a more eloquent way." Lourdes takes a sip from her mug and immediately adds more sugar. A lot more sugar. "She's smart and so sweet, Javi. Don't mess it up."

"I won't."

"He won't," we answer in unison, and my body turns in her direction. Mariah's sleep-rumpled and still wearing my shirt, just with a pair of tights beneath. "Got any more coffee? I woke up with a minor headache."

"Let me find you something for that. Be right back," Lourdes gets up and turns to rush out but stops and hugs me instead. It's a quick one, but I feel her relief and I kiss her forehead before nudging her toward the door.

"Mom's bathroom should have something for that."

"Okay." She brushes by Mariah and surprises us both by giving her a quick kiss on the cheek. "Thank you, new cousin."

My girl's shocked, but I'm not. She's too lovable for her own good.

I've been powerless against her after her threat to shoot me the day we met.

"Hi."

"Morning, linda." A hint of a blush crosses her cheeks, and she shuffles closer when I crook a finger, pulling her between my parted legs at the counter. Her warmth seeps into my skin. Her touch sets my heart ablaze. "How bad is it?"

"Mild. Don't worry." Her hands cup my face, thumbs sweeping beneath my eyes. "You sleep okay?"

"Like the dead."

"You snored like it, too." A sweet little snort escapes her, and I grip her hips, digging my fingers in when it turns into giggles. "Stop it."

"Take that back."

"Never."

"Then I'll never stop."

"Is this your way of saying you want to keep me?"

Letting go of her side, I bring my right hand to the back of her neck and hold her to me. Lips against lips. Breathing each other in. "I plan to do more than keep you, Mariah. I'm going to love you until the day I die, and even death won't stop or diminish what I feel for you."

"Good." She nibbles my bottom lip and then pulls back. "Because we will be revisiting these words in a few days."

"They won't change."

"And I won't leave your side."

Mariah

HE'S BEEN HOLED up in his study for the last twenty-four hours.

Alone and hurting. Needing space after lowering his mother to the ground, while the rest of the house—his family—entertains me. They don't need to, but they do, and I stifle a laugh when his aunt Sara brings out another photo album dedicated to the Lucas men in their baby years.

"And here's Javier running from Ida after he decided to redecorate their living room at the time with finger paints." The little boy in the picture couldn't be older than six and had a shitty grin on his face as his mother ran behind him with a flip-flop in her hand. "Can you believe he paused for ten seconds, hand on his hip, while I took the picture and his mom closed in? Ida wanted to kill him, while I laughed my butt off." She pauses for a moment, an innocent expression on her face when Alejandro sits across from us on the lanai. "Everything all right, mijo?"

"How many has she subjected you to, Mariah?" I hold up three fingers in response and she smacks my shoulder, a mock-outraged gasp coming from her place beside me. Chulo's on the floor beside my feet and looks up then, his eyes connecting with mine as if to say *they are all crazy*, then plops down. He's been by my side since we met the night I arrived.

Sweetest good boy you'll ever meet.

"And he's the rascal of the family, Chulo." Lourdes stops in front of a large dog bed that looks like a sofa and is fit for royalty. It's huge and looks soft, and I'm almost jealous of how comfortable the large Doberman seems to be. After Javi went to sleep and my confession, the small slip of the tongue right after his eyes closed, I became restless. Hungry. And the knock at the door from Lourdes saved me from waking the lightly snoring man. "He's a sweetheart, but be careful until he gets to know you. He's protective of the family and was hurt trying to protect Mamita Ida."

Not listening to her, I kneel in front of the sweet boy and hold my hand out. Chulo looks at it, his teeth showing for a few seconds before there's a soft lick, and then another. His tail wags the more he's allowed to greet me —make a new friend—before nudging my hand to give him a good old-fashioned head scratch.

"Aren't you the cutest thing, Chulo? Such a good boy." The dog gives me the sweetest look and I melt, as completely owned by the dog as I am the owner. And because I can't help myself, I bend over and kiss the top of his head. "I'm so going to want to take you home with me."

"You truly are one of us."

At this I look up, head tilted to the side. "What do you mean?"

"We aren't the easiest bunch."

"My family will give yours a run for its money." Chulo crawls closer, setting his head atop my lap for more scratches. "But then again, crazy embraces lunacy without question."

"Don't I know it." Leaning down, she runs her fingers through Chulo's back. "It's why I think you two were meant to be. You understand him, and he gets you."

"Shame on you, Madre. Just, shame." Alejandro's voice pulls me away from the memory, and I look between the mother and son duo. He's serious, while she's outspoken and sweet.

"Zip it, Alejandro." Sara nudges my shoulder after turning the page, a younger version of the man across from us in black and white. He's dressed like a cowboy, boots and all while cheesing it at the camera beside Emiliano. The older brother's wearing a horse costume, the head in his hand, and it's large and goofy. "How cute were they? My boys—"

"Are going to dig up the old family albums my mother kept hidden in her closet." Everyone turns to look at Javier at the entrance to the back terrace. He's smiling a bit but looks exhausted and as if he's had more than a drink or two, and yet, his eyes are sharp when they settle on me and his dog's proximity. "You ready for that kind of smoke, Aunt Sara?"

"You wouldn't dare!"

"Try me." I'm amused by their banter, and my shoulders shake when she slams the book shut and hides it behind her. "That's better. Don't embarrass me in front of my Muñeca."

"I thought it was adorable," I say, and all eyes turn my way. The men have their eyes narrowed while Sara's glisten with tears. "The Lucas men as kids were total badasses."

"Is she mocking us, primo?" Alejandro asks, sitting forward with an evil smirk on his face.

"I think she is." Javi walks closer, stopping a few feet from me and his dog quickly takes a stance in front of me. "And look at this; she's stolen my best friend too."

"Total disrespect." Alejandro tsks while his mom shakes her head, a few tears falling, and my heart clenches because I know this is hard. It was her sister we put to rest yesterday and her daughter that could've been killed, and yet, she's here and entertaining me as if I'm the most important person here. *She's doing what Ida would've done had I been blessed with meeting her.*

"We should teach her a lesson." Javi comes a little closer and my eyes narrow, lip curls into a mock-sneer. "Lucas men are to be respected at all times."

"Really?" Taking her hand in mine, I squeeze it while Sara rolls her eyes. She wipes away the fallen tears discreetly while Javi focuses on his pet, silently commanding Chulo to pick his side. *God bless the women of this family with endless patience.* "My threat from the first day still stands, Javier, and I'll extend it if I must."

"What threat?" Lourdes walks out holding a tray with coffee and my newest addiction: pan de Bono. It's always to be eaten a few minutes out of the oven and is soft, the bread and cheese combination melting in your mouth, and I can't get enough of these. Placing the tray on the coffee table between the seats, she hands me my cup first and then Javier's, her mother and brother grabbing their own. "I feel like this is a story that needs to be told."

"Quit being nosy, kid."

"Don't ruin our fun, nephew," Sara says, but her attention is on me. "What threat are you talking about, Mariah?"

"You want to do the honors?" I ask and he shakes his head, smiling at me in that boyish way that makes my heart flutter. However, it's his eyes that captivate me. There's sadness in them, a pain he can't escape, but a sliver of love remains and it's directed at me. As if I'm what's holding him together and it's a heady feeling, to know that my being here gives him a semblance of peace—comfort. "Are you sure? I'm giving you a chance to look good here."

"Go on." He waves a hand around us. "Tell them how horrible you've been to me."

My glare makes his family grin. "Threatening to shoot you isn't the worst thing I could've done."

"You did what?" Lourdes screams, laughing at the annoyed look on her cousin's face. "That's priceless."

"I need all the details." That came from Sara.

"You've gone soft, primo." Alejandro had to add his two cents in.

I shrug, taking a sip from my cup. "Not the first or last time, either. It's almost a daily occurrence and a bit of foreplay for him," I mumble the last part under my breath, but they heard and coupled with my slight embarrassment at the slip, they all crack up. And it's worth it because for that brief moment they're not thinking of death and violence or retribution.

Moreover, I'd gladly become a comedian to watch him let go even if it's just for a moment.

"Good morning, Muñeca," he whispers from behind me, his arm and leg thrown over my body. I'm almost pinned in place by Javier—the little spoon to his giant one—and the vibrations from his chest when he speaks cause goose bumps to rise across my flesh. "You ready to start the day?"

"No." I'm being honest. Being here has been amazing the last week, but I am exhausted and in need of more than the seven hours of sleep I got last night. Javier's home where we are all staying is grand and beautiful, sitting on almost thirty acres of farmland that needs tending to.

He has horses and pigs and chickens—crops of marijuana that he and Alejandro cultivate and then test the strains before any sales occur.

Then, there is his mother's house near the large stream that runs along the back end of the property. Where she was killed, and Lourdes terrorized. He's had it demolished in the last few days after a day spent taking out what he wanted to keep, and what his aunt wanted as mementos.

It was a grueling day. The women cried and the men comforted, but it was in my arms that night that Javier truly let go.

He allowed himself the few tears that fell before rage took root instead. And I embraced it; his anger and need for revenge.

"What are you thinking, Javi?" I cup his face, needing to keep his troubled eyes on mine. "Quit worrying about anything but what you need. Tell me, and we'll find a way."

"Let it go. I'm fine."

"Bullshit." I'm pushing him. Have been doing it since he came out of isolation, and after the emotional days he's had, Javier will snap if he doesn't accept—confront his emotions. "And we're not leaving this room until you're honest with me. Nothing you say will make me see you differently or leave; I'm here for the long haul."

"I'm hanging by a thread, sweet girl, and don't want you to—"

"I accept all of you."

"Thank you." His eyes soften, the slightly, red-rimmed edges crinkling when he smiles. A genuine one, and not the fake/forced one he puts on for the women of this family. Not because they need to be coddled, but because he cares and wants to shoulder their pain.

"Let me help and then thank me."

"Help with what?"

"I want the bloodied bodies of those responsible at your feet."

His laughter shakes us both while fingers explore across my chest and down, not stopping until removing his leg and slipping a finger beneath the edge of my panties. "You can always sleep for a bit in the car. We have about a three-hour car ride from here to my surprise."

"A surprise?" I whimper out when he slides down to just above my clit, tapping the sensitive area to the beat of a song only he knows the notes to. "Where are we—"

"No questions." This time he slaps my flesh with three fingers, his hand stretching the delicate lace. "I want you to nod and give me a kiss before getting ready with the clothes I left out for you yesterday." Lips just below my ear, he nips the skin there and then soothes the sting with a flick of his tongue. "Can you do that for me, Ms. Asher?"

"Yes." I'm rewarded with tight circles on my clit. They range from soft to rough—a vicious cycle that brings me to the edge sooner than I thought possible. Just the tip of two fingers are touching me, circling the throbbing bundle of nerves while his mouth attacks my neck with bites and licks.

I'm moaning for him. Fighting to turn around and kiss him—touch him —but his hold on me doesn't allow anything but *his* control. One of his hands is on my hip while the other strums my clit, I'm powerless, unable to do more than cry out in pleasure each time he brings me to the edge.

"You're perfect for me, Mariah," he groans against my neck, his breathing harsh and cock hard against my backside. "Mine."

"Javi," I mewl on a breathless whisper, clinging to his forearm as the first wave of bliss knocks into me. For a second or two, I can't breathe and cling to him, undulating as he wrings every last drop of pleasure and then when there's nothing left, Javi dips below and pumps his fingers inside me twice.

They're glistening when he brings them to his lips, inhaling deep before sucking each until no trace of my wetness is left. "Fuck, baby girl. So sweet." My core clenches and he grips my chin with the same fingers, turning my face toward his. I smell myself on his lips and fingers. I can feel a small trail of wetness on my ass just above where the head of his cock flexes. "I'm going to enjoy you today, Mariah. All of you, before you leave tomorrow."

"Please." It's all I can manage past the sudden dryness of my mouth, the heat of my skin.

"Good girl." Another clench and he smiles as if he knows my body is crying out for him. To feel him buried deep. "Now, go get dressed for me, and no panties. I want access to your body all day."

JAVIER

"WE'RE HERE, MARIAH," I say, softly stroking her cheek while the beautiful girl beside me stirs, arching her back while beginning to stretch. My eyes roam down her body, admiring her every curve and dip displayed in the simple cotton dress I've put her in.

It's soft against her skin; a light pink number with small pearl buttons down the middle of her chest flares a bit at her hips and ends just above her mid-thighs. And she wears the simplicity so well.

The two stiff points adorned by the nipple shield—I can make out the jeweled circular ring around each tip and my mouth waters. I also can't stop myself and lower my hand from her face, brushing my knuckles down the right and then left breast, smiling when she sighs and those seafoam eyes open.

She's looking at me with hunger. Mirroring my need.

"Where are we?" Her voice is husky, tinged with the last dregs of sleep. Warm eyes look around and her head tilts, wondering why we're out in the middle of nowhere with a large waterfall behind us that crests over a large lake. There's also a modest home, not lacking in luxury but the size is meant for intimacy and not hosting people.

It's a place I come when needing to regroup. To calm the raging ire that at times consumes me, but today, I'm here to share it with her. To show her more of who I am.

"This place belongs to me."

"Really?" Her question isn't because she doubts the money I have, but more of why the seclusion. "Are you here to kill me and dump the body?" Mariah lets out a cute giggle, the movement causing her breasts to jiggle and my knuckles to press a little harder over each tip.

Her laugh turns into a moan; the sound sends a shiver down my spine. Makes my cock throb.

"I'm here to eat you, Muñeca."

"Should I be afraid?"

"For my sanity? Absolutely." With a single sharp slap over her right tit, I cup her face and bring her closer, almost touching my lips before I stand, and just like I knew she would, Mariah follows. I'm barely touching her, but she's following my body further away from the car, walking closer and closer to the water's edge.

A mist greets our legs and I pause, groaning when her body doesn't stop. Instead, my beauty presses the length of her short frame against my harsher planes and then rises onto the tips of her toes, lips right where they belong.

On mine. Touching. Licking the seam when I don't part them for her.

"Kiss me."

"No." Fire flashes in her orbs, the challenge I've needed making itself present. And I push. Yank the proverbial chain of her pleasure with my denial. "We're here to have lunch and nothing more."

Frustrations sparks. Confusion.

But today is about her. What I know she needs.

Mariah is so used to having control that losing the tight leash around her neck—stepping out of the mold she's been forced into by other's careless mistakes—scares her. But she craves it. Silently, she wants to let go and not worry about the consequences, nor the opinion of others about who she should be.

I'm going to gift her what she's freely given me by just being here when I needed her the most. My Muñeca isn't meant to be controlled but cherished. She's meant to fly.

And I'm going to unleash and welcome the craziness with open arms because I am her home. Her peace. Her love.

"You're serious?" Confusion mars her features for a second—she doesn't understand my putting on the brakes, but I'm doing it for her. Apart from enjoying the day just the two of us, I want her to relax and enjoy herself. To yearn for and enjoy my touch as the hours pass. "But aren't you the one that asked for easy access?"

"I did."

"Then why—"

"Because I enjoy having free access to that lightly tanned flesh and the wetness that coats your inner thighs." Mariah inhales sharply, chest heaving. "Because when I touch you, I'm not going to ask for permission or deal with obstacles delaying the inevitable."

"And what's that?"

Lowering my face down to Mariah, I bypass her pouting lips and kiss the shell of her ear. "My cock buried deep inside that tight little cunt while your screams of pleasure disturb the peace of every beast that roams this jungle. I'm going to take you, baby. Fuck you. But first, I'll prove that you're my queen first and whore after."

Then, I walk away. Give her a moment to collect her thoughts and calm the shivers.

MARIAH ENTERS the house an hour later, and she's calm. A little too calm.

I smile when her small body sits beside me on the couch, relaxing into my side while slipping beneath my arm. Hugging herself to my bare chest. She's collected, and her body isn't showing outward signs of arousal, but fuck, I can smell it. This sweet little whisper of *her* that infiltrates my senses as if she's touched what's mine—

Bringing her delicate hand to my lips, I leave open-mouthed kisses over each tip and catch the hint of her taste. *Bad girl.* "Are you hungry, Mariah?"

"A little." Voice low and a bit meek, she looks up at me from beneath long lashes with a wisp of contriteness in her expression. *You know I know.* "Is there anything you'd like me to make?"

"No need." And because I can, I wrap my lips around her middle and pointer fingers, sucking once and pull back. Mariah's orbs become heavy-lidded and body rigid, and then her nipples poke through again. *Christ, they're perfect.* "I'm here to cater to you, sweetheart."

"I don't mind, though. We can cook together and—"

"You've done enough." My girl's smart enough to not argue—deny—her theft and then nods. "Why don't you rest for a bit."

"Can I take a shower or a bath?"

"No."

"Why?"

"Are you uncomfortable?" At my question, she squirms a bit and I smirk. "You touched yourself and will now sit there in your wetness and wait. No complaining. No begging."

"I can always take a dip in the lake." Not a threat, but a statement. Pushing to see if I snap and give her the one thing she needs. Craves.

Me. My touch. My cock.

"Go ahead. See what happens if you do."

No response. No pushing me away.

Instead, Mariah purses her lips and tries to relax back into my arms. She can't, though.

My denial makes her wet. More than the pathetic orgasm she might've had a few minutes prior.

"I didn't come," she says this low, so low I almost missed it, but I can't deny the fire that rushes through my veins at her confession. "Just couldn't finish."

"Why?"

"Because I need you." On her next intake of breath, Mariah finds herself on her back, looking up at me with wide excited eyes. "Hi," she says and it's breathless, her chest expanding, and every inhale rubs the two pointy tips on her chest against mine. For me to feel the metal surrounding each nipple.

"You love to tease and push, baby girl." I'm throbbing, my cock pressed tightly against her mound. "I hope you're prepared to deal with the consequences of this disrespect."

"Please." One word, and the last thread of patience left in me snaps. "Take what is yours."

Closing my eyes, I nod and breathe in deep.

I had plans for us. I wanted to cook and spoil and make love to her slowly.

"I'm going to ask for your forgiveness now." My voice is rough and my body shakes, but I keep my eyes soft when I look down at her. She's every-thing to me, and I need her to understand this—know that no one comes before her. "Because once I'm inside of you, there will be nothing in this world that can pull me away."

"Javi, I trust you. I—"

"I love you more than my own life, Mariah."

A warm hand cups my jaw, and she pulls me down to her, my lips just touching hers. "I love you, too. In an almost obsessive crazy way and without control. All I want is you. All I think about is you."

"Motherfuck." It's a rough exhale. A harsh shiver that runs from the top of my head and settles on my swelling cock. I'm throbbing—pulsing within the warmth of my girl's parted thighs.

She makes me lose touch with reality.

With the regime I've followed since the day I made my first kill.

I'm hers to do with as she pleases, and when she kisses me again, I give in. Lose myself in her touch and scent, in the way her plump lips feel against my own. *Jesus*, she's sweet and soft and explores my mouth with a keening mewl—almost begging for more of me. My touch. My cock.

"I'm going to spend the rest of my life spoiling you, beautiful. I'll live for you." Her hips undulate at that, and the thin fabric of her dress slips over her hips, exposing her cunt to the cool air. She hisses and I pull my lips from hers, looking down to the soft pink flesh. "So fucking pretty."

"Please."

"What do you need?" I'm rewarded with another horny little sound, but right now I need more. "Use your words."

"Kiss me. Touch me."

"Like this." With the tip of two fingers, I part her labia at the same time I retake her lips. I swallow her moans. Taste her need. She's wet and pliant, her noises filling the room with a symphony that I wish to spend the rest of my life listening to. "Or like this?"

"All of it as long as it's with you."

"Til death do us part." I slip a finger inside and pump it a few times. Then add another. Mariah's tight, walls clenching, and I smile against her mouth, deepening the kiss—her tongue battles mine for dominance, but gives in when I bite her lips.

We're a brutal explosion of lust and hunger, this raw, uncontrollable yearning that I call home. She's my reason and purpose.

"Javi," she moans, a reverent sound when I nip her chin and down the path to her neck. Her skin flushes under my ministration, her nipples hard, and I bite one while slipping from her small hole. Wetness coats my fingers and I rub her clit with the pad of my middle finger. "More."

Tight circles. Pressing down hard.

"Take your tits out," I hiss out, giving each tip a lick over the cotton and pull back. Shaky hands do as I say and undo the top three buttons slowly, teasing me, but I'm past the point of patience.

I smack her clit, and she opens the next two a little faster. *This won't do.*

Grabbing the bit of undone fabric in my hands, I rip it down the middle.

Buttons scatter. A gasp escapes her.

The look in her eyes is intoxicating, and I take a moment to look at her just like this:

She's on her back and looking up at me with hooded eyes, tits on display and her pussy lips wet with desire. This woman is my heaven. My weakness. Mine.

"You're so fucking beautiful, Muñeca."

"And you're perfect for me," she whimpers, spreading her thighs wider on my couch. "I love you."

"I love you, too." Kneeling between her parted thighs, I place a finger at her mouth and dip it between wet lips. Her breath is warm and her tongue soft. Her throat bobs and I trace a path down to the center of her chest before cupping a tit, my fingernail flicking the metal adorning the pebbled tip, and then the other before taking it between my lips, my tongue lapping at the sensitive flesh.

"More." One of her hands embeds itself into my hair and tugs me closer, holding me against her breast. And I suck harder, flipping between the two tips until her free hand slips between us and pulls at the drawstring of my shorts, pushing the waistband low enough that the engorged head slips out. "No foreplay. I want you just like this."

I can feel her heat. If I snap my hips, I'd be buried deep.

Mariah traces the head while her thighs try to push the basketball shorts lower. They don't move much, but just enough to rub the first few inches over her clit before I bite down on the flesh between her breasts.

She screams and I pull back, admiring the perfect indentation of my teeth.

I want her body littered with these. With my mark.

My cock throbs, and I look down in time to catch the sight of a little pre-come falling onto her skin. *So fucking beautiful.*

"I'll love you slowly later." I take my hands from her body long enough to remove my shorts and then toss them aside somewhere, could care less where they land. Her dress is torn. It hangs on either side of her body and I plan to frame the fabric after. I'll carry a piece of it in my wallet wherever I go.

That's how obsessed with her I am. No shame, either.

"And I'll let you baby me all you want."

"Good girl." Rubbing the head of my cock from clit to slit twice, I pause at her entrance. A whimper escapes her, thighs spreading wider—she's gorgeously indecent. "Now, hold on."

I'm inside her in one fluid motion, buried to the hilt as her fingernails dig into my arm. She's arching and bucking against the intrusion while I pull out and slam back in.

No pause. No waiting for her to adjust.

My baby takes my cock so prettily with a cry on her lips and her wetness dripping down to my balls. Her eyes roll back, neck pushing against the cushions. She's shaking. Breaths labored.

"Baby," Mariah moans, pulling me down until our chests are flushed and I anchor her to the couch with my hips. Fucking her with hard strokes, and when she clenches, I slip a hand beneath and grip an asscheek.

"You feel so good, Muñeca. So tight." I flex my hips and then pull out slowly, dragging my cock against her walls before slamming back in. A delicious clench comes from her core, nearly choking my girth. "Again. Do that again."

My pace is near punishing and every thrust pulls from her a cry of pleasurable pain that hits me in the chest like a sledgehammer. I'll live the rest of my life worshipping her just to hear those sounds again and again.

She's my reward. My fucking life.

"Kiss me, Javi. I'm so close." The nails on my arm move down to my back and the blunt tips rake down to my ass. She grips me, forcing my hips to pound deeper—harder—until those perfect thighs shake. They tremble and squeeze my sides. "Need them."

And I comply because this woman owns me.

I kiss her with every bit of the passion and love and hunger I hold for her. Mariah's tongue is soft and she makes a whiny noise at the back of her throat when our tongues twine. She tries to fight for dominance, to control the kiss, but one sharp bite to her bottom lip and two things happen:

She clenches around me and screams into my mouth; I swallow each cry as the sound of her pleasure grows and juices soak my cock. My balls are heavy and the slap of skin on skin is loud, but it's the way she closes her eyes and smiles that breaks me.

Every muscle in my body coils tight, but I never stop pounding into her, pulling out every last drop of come. Her pleasure comes before mine, and I revel in each spasm. Own her with each snap of my hip.

But when those seafoam-sated eyes focus on me again, a groan escapes and I lose control.

"Motherfuck, Mariah. So tight. So wet." I slam in a final time and hold myself deep inside, filling her with ropes of come. The euphoric peak knocks the breath from my chest, and I bury my face in her neck, kissing every bit of skin I can reach.

We stay that way for a while. My body on hers and her arms holding me tight.

There's no rush. No thoughts of her impending flight tomorrow morning where I'm not joining her.

She'll be in Chicago, and I'll be here hunting.

Painting the streets with blood.

I'm going to miss you, Muñeca.

I NEVER THOUGHT leaving him would be this hard, but it is, and I can't fight back the tears that spring to my eyes. I can't help but hold him a little tighter while around us the world carries on without pause; the people walking through this large terminal are either looking for food and drink, or a wall plug to charge their electronics. Because no matter what airport or country you're in, it's always the same, except this one time when it feels as though my chest is caving in

I'm going to miss him. I'm going to need him to come back.

This stubborn, beautiful man that's swept me off my feet and I've been unwilling to fight off as he took possession of my being. I love him. Completely and without pause, my heart belongs to Javier Lucas.

"I'll be back before you know it, Muñeca." His arms tighten around me and his lips press to the crown of my head. "Trust me, you'll be back to kicking me out—begging me to leave Chicago again within a week."

"Or I kick your ass." It's mumbled against his shirt, but the deep rumble of his laugh lets me know he heard. "Promise."

Javi pulls back just enough to tip my chin up with two fingers, his soft eyes staring deep into mine. "I love you, Mariah Asher. I love and need you and can't breathe right when you're not near. Nothing can stop me… not even God himself, from coming back to you. Trust me."

"I do." My reply is without hesitation, and it earns me one of those cocky smirks that I adore. "Find them, Javier."

"We already—"

He stops talking when I shake my head and pull him down low enough that I can reach the shell of his ear. "You're not understanding me." I take a moment then to just breathe him in, soothe my soul with his touch, before exhaling against his skin. "Baby…" Javi's fingers tighten their hold; they dig into the bruises from last night and I whimper, the sound just as needy as I am, but now is not the time. When I leave, go back to Chicago, I need him to focus on my request. To carry it out before coming back to me. "Baby, I need you to find them and kill each slowly. I need you to make them suffer, dismember them limb by limb until there's nothing left but the horror-filled expression on their faces before taking their last breath. And when it's done, and the country knows to never cross a Lucas again…come *home*."

He releases a shuddering breath, but I don't stay to hear his confirmation. Instead, I extricate myself from his hold and walk toward the boarding area and wait to be called. It doesn't take long, and just when I cross the entrance to the tunnel, I look back and immediately find his eyes.

Javier's been watching. He's giving me a look full of promise.

But more than that is the subtle nod. It's his agreement to my terms.

A WEEK HAS COME and gone without news from Colombia.

No local coverage of violence abroad. No Spanish-speaking networks discussing political unrest of affluent families with ties to criminal activities.

Not a damn thing, and I was losing my mind with worry.

This is also why I didn't notice the large bouquet of black roses sitting just outside my door after work. Again, there wasn't a note or a card from the shop making the delivery, but it's now clear to see this isn't a mistake.

Someone wants my attention, and the first person that crosses my mind is Mildred.

She slept with Lane and possibly my father. She's still roaming around according to Malcolm, and while I'm sure in part it has to do with her twin still being alive, my gut tells me there's more.

That *I'm* that more.

Pulling out my phone, I dial Malcolm, but it goes straight to voicemail. *Crap, he's still probably in the meeting with the Jameson family.* The customary bland and impersonal message comes through the line followed by a beep to respond.

"Call me when you get this. I just got another delivery." He'll know what I'm talking about and I hang up, looking down at the screen again with this uncontrollable urge to call Javier. My finger swipes down the contact list, hovering just above the call button beside his name. "Screw it."

It rings after a few seconds. And rings three more times.

No answer. Nothing.

All I receive is a generic instruction to call back because his inbox is full.

"Guess not, then." With the bottom of my foot, I nudge the arrangement inside and leave it on the floor beside the entrance. I'm sure Malcolm will send someone later to pick it up, and I'd rather not get my fingerprints on it. "Hopefully he'll call later."

Without pause, I toe off my slingbacks and leave them there as well, walking barefoot toward my room. My phone is still in my hand and my attention is garbage, which explains why after changing and heating some leftover spaghetti, I pick up the video call without checking the caller ID first.

Dad's face is the last one I want to see, but there he is, smiling. "Why were you out of the country, Mariah? Where have you been?"

"That's none of your concern."

He bristles at my detached tone. "You will always be my concern, daughter of mine."

"You forfeited that right two years ago. I have nothing else to say on the matter."

"Watch your tone," he hisses through clenched teeth, glaring at me with so much hatred and disappointment. "You seem to have forgotten your place, Mariah. You are my daughter, and you will respect me."

"Respect is earned." A text from Malcolm blinks on the screen and I hit ignore. "Now, what do you want? Calling isn't something you do and when it occurs, it's because you need something from me."

"Why were you in Colombia with Javier Lucas?"

My blood runs cold at that. *How the hell...*

"Are you having me watched?" His lack of a response gives me the answer I need, and while inside I'm fuming—wanting to strangle the man—my expression remains unemotional. Cold. "I guess this is a trait passed down from generation to generation."

"Are you fucking that—"

"Where is my mother?" Dad doesn't like that I interrupted nor my line of questioning, but I couldn't care less and match his icy glare. "What did you do to her?"

"She isn't of your concern."

"And my life isn't of yours."

"Mariah," he spits out, but his attention isn't on me but someone on the other side of the phone. It's a woman's voice, speaking low, but I catch part of their reflection in the windowpane behind my father. She's familiar. Someone I'll be paying a visit to soon.

"Get to the point." Walking to the fridge, I pull it open and take out a can of pop. "Some of us would like to eat dinner in peace."

His eyes snap back to mine and the woman turns her face, but I do catch a better look. *Mildred, you stupid bitch.* "I'm not above hurting my daughter and you're pushing me, sweetheart. Back down and do as you're told if you want to see your mother again."

Popping the top, I take a large sip. Noisily, which I know annoys him. "What is this going to cost me?"

"Malcolm is currently holding control of the Frederick's laboratory in Utah. Get me the—"

"No."

"The fuck did you just say?"

"I said no." Then I take another sip and smile. "Mom isn't dead, and I will find her."

"The hospital will never release her without my signature."

"Maybe, but you just signed your death warrant." Disconnecting the call, I quickly press the number for Malcolm and wait. It rings twice before there's an audible click.

"Did he call you?"

"He did. Much sooner than I expected."

"Was anyone with him?" His ire matches my own. A familial betrayal cuts deep and the punishment is served without mercy, something I am okay with.

"Mildred."

"Okay. See you tomorrow." We hang up and I go on with my evening. Within the last week, we've watched videos, gone through endless files, and started the search for my mother. Mildred Frederick and my father have been corroborating for the last few years on unapproved medical testing for a few viral strands that have been slowly growing overseas but haven't hit the States, and yet, their end goal is a worldwide bidding war.

That's their goal, but I have mine.

I want their blood on my hands.

<hr>

"THANK YOU FOR YOUR TIME." For the sixth time today, I hang up the phone and close my eyes. It's taken me a few days to narrow down my mother's location after Dad's video call, and she isn't in a mental institution. She isn't in Europe either.

Looking down my list, I cross off another women's shelter in Indiana and sigh.

For some reason, she's back in her home state and hiding. Using cash and prepaid cards, but facial recognition has come a long way and Erik found a video clip of her at the aquarium with a group of kids no older than eight.

My mother wasn't dressed as the society queen she once was. In a pair of dark-wash jeans and cream-colored blouse, she walked with the group from exhibit to exhibit while answering what she could—helping this one little girl in particular that seemed too small to play with the others.

"Why hasn't he called me?" I ask aloud, rubbing my temples when footsteps approach. They're heels, the clacking loud within the open space, and I look up in time to watch Mildred try and sneak past my desk. "Take another step and adhere to the consequences."

Mildred's head snaps in my direction, face pinched tight in anger. "What did you say?"

"Are you deaf?" Shuffling the list of numbers in Indiana under a financial report, I raise a brow. "Well?"

Crossing her arms over her chest, she turns to fully face me. "No. I'm not."

"Then you know I both find both irritating and disgusting," I sneer, catching Malcolm's imposing figure standing just within the entrance to his office. "Leave."

"You have balls for a secretary."

"And we both know you spread those legs for anyone, my father being one of them." Standing from my seat, I open the drawer to my right and pull out a gun with two bullets. "Married men. Engaged men. Do you sleep with family members too?"

Her face goes from furious to near ghostly white. Fake tears gather at the corner of her eyes. "How could you say something like that to me? I'm a respected member of—"

"Please cut the bull, Mildred. We both know what cloth you are cut from." Picking up my Glock, I pull the clip out and insert the two bullets before resetting with the safety off. "Why are you here? And don't give me some line about an appointment because you don't have one. You have two minutes to explain."

She fidgets, eyeing the weapon in my hand. "Malcolm called me to go over our merger. We've come to an understanding."

"Lie. Try again."

"It's the truth, Mariah. Call him and ask."

"Again, that's a lie. One more chance." I raise my hand and point toward her chest.

Mildred shakes, but her eyes are full of hate. Her animosity is palpable and so is her greed. "I came to talk to Malcolm about *my* brother and company. We need to come to an amicable agreement."

"Is that so?" My cousin steps forward now, a smile on his face and Mildred calms immediately.

"Yes." Her response is low and meek, and he's the epitome of gracious when holding a hand out. "I'm very sorry for showing up without a prior appointment, but please, I need—"

"No worries, Ms. Frederick." His eyes snap to mine and harden a bit for her benefit. "Put the gun away and show some respect, Mariah. She is a customer and must be treated as such. Understood?"

"Of course, Mr. Asher."

She's smiling at his reprimand. She enjoys me being put in my place.

Stupid fucking woman.

Mildred is pushing her luck with me, and if she catches me on the wrong day, I'll be the one putting a bullet between her eyes.

JAVIER

"**H**AVE YOU HAD any news on his whereabouts?" I ask Malcolm, holding the phone between my ear and shoulder while Alejandro and Emiliano hold a meeting inside the family compound. We've been here for the past two weeks, smoking out those responsible for my mother's death, while they try and hide.

I know where the three men are:

The shooter. The enabler. The general of Colombia's army.

They've been lying low and I haven't. The country—the president—wants me for my crimes but don't have a shred of possibility without cause and evidence. You can't be proven guilty of words alone, and the citizens demand proof of the murders committed.

"Her father is in Athens, Georgia."

"And the whore?" Because I'm well aware of the second set of roses Mariah received, even though the stubborn woman hasn't spoken of the incident. Nor did she tell me of her encounter with Mildred a few days ago. I might not be there, but I have ways of keeping tabs. "Has she left the state?"

"According to Mildred, she was heading home last night to Utah. She's put her home on the market and there's been an offer." He chuckles, the sound of papers shifting coming through the line. "Her plane landed two hours ago in Atlanta where she rented a sports car, and she is on her way to see my uncle."

"How many are tailing her?"

"Three, and two on him." At his response, I hum, scratching the five-day-old stubble on my chin. "They're too cocky and reckless. Antonio was honest in what he's shared so far."

"He's been useful," I admit. "Has his sister asked for the body again?"

"No. My word that he's dead sufficed."

"And the Dermots?" Both Lane's mother and father were killed last week—an unfortunate incident at their vacation home in Italy. House fires are a dangerous thing, and unfortunately for them, I traveled to the Italian countryside to play with matches. "Does Mariah know? Are the other two making any moves?"

"Negative, but her brother did warn us before you left. They're staying quiet as all avenues begin to close."

"Evening, gentleman." Malcolm steps into the room, nodding at the guards standing watch. "Antonio. Delia."

"Boss," his men answer in unison while I grab a chair and take a seat, keeping my eyes on the bloody man in front of me. He fidgets. She whimpers.

"The food has been ordered as Mr. Lucas requested." Carmelo hands over the credit card I'd given him and I pocket the plastic square, not taking my eyes off Antonio and Delia. These two know more than they let on, and I'm not taking any chances with Mariah's safety.

"Thank you, kid."

Malcolm drags a chair beside mine and we wait. And wait. No one in the room says a word until Mrs. Frederick breaks the silence. "Is there any scenario in this where we don't lose our lives?"

An honest question, and Malcolm nods. "There's always an open option, but the outcome lies solely at your feet."

"What do you need?" she asks, gripping her husband's hand tightly in hers. "Name the price and it's done."

"The truth," I answer for him after having discussed this development. "We want the full story, Antonio. Why did you try to kill Mildred and then turn your wife into her replica?"

The male twin sighs, rubbing a hand down his face, wincing from the pain of Malcolm's bullet. "My sister was sleeping with Lane Dermot and working with his family on a shady contract with an overseas investor. The laboratory was being used as their personal tester, playing with viral agents that we've yet to encounter as a society—creating and testing—for a profit. This wasn't about the betterment of the world, but a fat profit. One she was going to use to order Mariah's death."

Every muscle in my body locks down and beside me, Malcolm is just as angry. Fire burns through my veins while the need for vengeance—her blood—grows. "What else? Who else is involved?"

"Her father."

"That son of a bitch," Malcolm hisses, fingers twitching on the gun sitting atop his thigh. "Why did you do it? Jealousy or anger?"

"Fear." Antonio looks over at his wife and his expression softens. It's full of so much remorse. "I was afraid that if the Ashers caught wind, we'd go down with her sinking boat. It was only a matter of time before the shit hit the fan, but I never thought I'd be the catalyst."

"Which brings me to my next question…" Asher sits forward, eyes hard on the couple "…why try to move money through me if you're being investigated? What kind of game are you playing?"

"I'm not." Antonio shakes his head rapidly, sweat dotting his upper lip. His wife isn't any better; her body's shaking and leg bouncing. "I came to you because we had to keep up the appearances of nothing being wrong. Had we gone with a different financial institution; more flags would've been raised. You would have asked around or demanded to know the why."

"And the federal investigations?"

"Mildred." Delia spits out the name with so much venom. "She sent them to the lab, even though we stopped all experiments the day I switched into this role. He screwed us on the records we kept in boxes down in the basement, but no active work was being done at the time."

"But trust me, my sister is cunning. And when push comes to shove, she'll hide to save herself.

Alejandro snaps his fingers and I look up, pulled from the memory of a few weeks back. My hunch about Mildred Frederick was on point, and the woman didn't disappoint. Rats never stay hidden for long, and I know she's digging around. Looking for payback.

"Parce, look at the screen." Emiliano points, and I pay attention to the footage playing on the giant TV screen. It's of a small, worn-down home a half an hour from the Presidential palace, inside of a community owned by the central bank of Colombia's owner. He hasn't remodeled it since the purchase, nor do people reside within the subdivision's gates. The home on the screen is large, and in its prime, I'm sure cost a pretty penny, but that's not my focus.

There are four cars parked outside, but not all seem occupied as the drivers begin to step out.

"What the hell is going on?" I ask, and on his end of the line, Malcolm's gone silent so I can understand my cousins.

"Three bodies inside." Alejandro takes a sip from his water, eyeing the screen.

"What's the fastest ETA?" I ask them while the man behind the wheel of a black Hummer gets down, his eyes darting around. Moreover, it's when he knocks on the door that the camera angle changes. This is a live feed from a front-door transmission, and I smile.

We have the shooter on the screen.

Then the enabler opens the door.

And I hear the clear voice of the General coming up from behind my mother's killer.

Alejandro hums, fingers typing on his phone. "Taking back roads and avoiding the expressway, I say twenty minutes at the most."

"Suit up." They nod at my command and empty the room, going in search of what we'll need for this. We won't take security or have these three picked up; I'll take my pound of flesh without pause the second I enter that home.

"My guess is you're heading out to play a game of catch?" Malcolm chuckles, and the clink of a glass follows the question. "Alone or with a team?"

"Absolutely, Asher. It's my favorite pastime. My cousins enjoy it as well."

He chuckles and then sighs. "Be careful and keep a cool head."

"Always." I know he's not being intrusive or trying to tell me how to handle myself. I've gotten to know him on a personal level while here; our phone calls and worry over Mariah has created a bond that we both appreciate. He's family to me. He cares about everyone who bears my last name since I signed the contract, but more so since my mother's passing. "Besides, I can't give your cousin a reason to shoot me. I'm planning to grow old and grey with her."

"Good."

"What? No warnings to slow down and—"

"Come home and marry the woman, Javi. She's not letting you go."

"And I was never leaving. I'll text you later." With that, I hang up and pull up her contact.

> I love you with all my heart, Muñeca. I'll be home soon. ~Javi

THE GATE to the community has two armed guards standing out front and they're busy talking when we pull up. They're laughing, the one to the left throwing a punch to the arm of his friend after a joke, and completely oblivious of the three men stepping out of their cars until Alejandro slams the door.

Then two sets of eyes are on us, weapons pointing our way. "Who are you? This is private property and—" Two bullets and they hit the ground, a hole in each forehead. The silencer from my gun doesn't make much noise, and the hard cement cradles the impact of their corpses.

"Right or left?" Emiliano asks, and I tilt my head toward the right, following the sound of Vallenato playing loudly. The beat pulses as the male singer declares his love for a woman who he's never so much as kissed, while the off-key voice of a heavy smoker follows.

The sound of splashing water comes from a home three down from where we stand, and it's quickly followed by laughter. Female giggles and male chuckles as someone shrieks. And begs.

"Please stop this! I don't want to get in!"

"Don't be such a spoilsport, Luisa." It's one of the men, his speech a bit slurred. "It's just water. Nothing will happen to your hair."

"Take me home."

"No."

We share a look before taking account of the car with two guards sitting inside. This old, black beater wasn't in the video earlier, but I recognize the uniform and its military. They're young, more than likely just following orders, but it doesn't stop Alejandro from killing the two with a single shot that travels from one head to the other, a straight shot through the ear.

Their heads slump forward, and I nod, impressed. "Nice one."

"I'm an environmentalist." He shrugs, and I chuckle. Asshole.

"Front door or back?" Emiliano asks, and I point toward the main entrance. And we find it unlocked when entering the home a few minutes later. The music is louder from here and the place is trashed, dirty, but the men seem to be enjoying themselves.

It's a straight shot from the front door to the sliding glass that leads out back, and I step out first amidst empty liquor bottles. It's disgusting, the stale stench a little nauseating, but I'm smiling as I shoot the enabler from my place just over the threshold. He falls forward and into the pool, his blood spreading out.

The women scream. The two still alive scramble for a weapon.

"You four need to get the fuck out of here." Alejandro points the end of his Colt at the group of college-age women panicking on the pool's steps. "You have two minutes to gather your shit and run." They don't move and he sends out another shot. This time it hits the cheap speakers beside the drink table. "Hagale."

They try to rush past us, not taking a single item with them, and Emiliano takes their phones. "The keys to the Hummer are on the kitchen counter. Grab them and go. Understood?"

"Si, and we won't say anything," a small brunette answers and the girls leave without further prompting, leaving the two assholes in nothing but their boxers outside. They have guns, but their hands shake. They're scared, but don't have enough common sense to try and escape through the back door a few feet from them.

It makes sense when I look around and find a table with cocaine and a few cut lines on a mirror. *Fucking idiots.* "Please have a seat."

"What's the meaning of this?" General Gustavo Mijares asks, his hand flailing. "Do you know who I am? What I can do to you without repercussion?"

Emiliano pulls a knife from his back pocket and grabs it from the tip; a flick of the wrist and it embeds itself into the military man's arm. His scream rends the air while the man beside him seems to have gone mute. "Watch the tone."

"Gentlemen, can't we talk this out?" Gino asks, his hands up. "Let's all relax and have a drink. No need for violence."

"I'll accept your drink, but it comes with a condition." I walk over and pull up a chair right across from him. "Everything in life comes with a price."

"Of course, but first we drink."

"Do we drink to Francis or my mother?" Both men pale, but Gino's hand on the bottle tightens, knuckles turning white. "A loving woman or a piece-of-shit thief?"

"Javier, we've both lost." A shot is poured, and he pushes it in my direction. "It's time to let go and move on. We're even."

"Did you hear, primos? We're even."

"We heard." They each follow my lead and take a seat, weapons now atop the table. "Seems worthy of a celebration...don't you think, Gustavo?"

"Yes." His tone is nervous. He doesn't trust us.

"Great!" Gino picks up a small mirror beside him and without pause does another line, wiping his hand across his nose to dust off the excess. "Do you two want a shot?"

"We do." Then they empty every single bullet inside of Gustavo. Two guns. One clip each. And as the general begins to fall face forward, I lean across the table and fist his hair in my hands.

He's breathing is near nonexistent. Gustavo's body is heavy as his last seconds draw close, and I take the blade on the table, holding the sharp end to his neck, and slice it across. One quick pull from right to left and his neck is open, nearly chopped-off, as the blood rushes out from the large wound.

"Say hello to the devil for me." His eyes are wide with horror. His lips are bloody, a trickle of red sliding down the corner of his mouth before there's an infinite nothing.

The general is dead, and his accomplice pisses his pants. "Please don't." *Pathetic.*

"I think it's time I collect my favor."

"W-what can I do for you?" he stutters, body shaking so hard his teeth rattle as the reality sets in. As his fear begins to dominate.

"We're going for a ride."

THE ROAD we're driving down an hour later is deserted. Barren. And I spend my time just watching Gino; the way tears roll down his cheeks and his chin quivers. The low prayer that slips past his lips and burns my skin.

A man who killed an innocent woman will never receive the pardon he begs for.

He's unworthy of forgiveness.

We're in his car, an older model full-sized van with two captain's chairs and a large sliding door beside my seat. The vehicle is spacious. Somewhat clean.

"Javier, please. Let's be reasonable." His hands are clenching, body racking with sobs. "We both made mistakes here. Let's forgive and forget."

"Silence."

"Come on, parce—"

"Fucking idiot." I kick him in the mouth, my combat boot knocking out a few front teeth and I rub the sole against his mouth, making him swallow back the red substance. "Die with dignity."

"I don't want to die!" He wails, now fighting me. His weak attempts only make this sweeter.

"Did you know my mother was supposed to fly out in two weeks to Chicago? We'd planned it, but it'd become difficult when she caught a small cold and we decided to push it back." This time my foot kicks his chest and he falls over, trying to breathe through the burn. "She was supposed to meet my girl and love her as much as I do."

"I'm sorry."

"Your apologies mean shit," I snarl, lip curling up in disgust. In pure hatred for this piece of shit not worthy of breath. Gino coughs when I remove my foot, but his reprieve is short lived when I lean forward and land the first punch to his face. I don't stop after one and rain down blow after blow to his mouth, nose, and the corner of his left eye.

The skin becomes red, his flesh breaking just above his orb and still, it's not enough.

My fist doesn't pause. My anger won't simmer.

"Por favor. No more."

"I'll only stop when you're dead." The car picks up speed then and I look up, catching Alejandro's eyes in the rear view mirror. He nods and Emiliano turns in his seat, reaching back to open the van's door. "Thank you."

"Enjoy yourself."

"Oh, I will." Then I'm leaning the bitch over and smirk as his screams rend the open road. He's cursing, crying, but nothing fills my heart with peace like the sound of flesh rubbing off on asphalt. His face leaves behind a bloody streak from one end to the other, and back again when we make a circle back. Gino's body convulses in pain, fighting and squirming, and the scent of his piss infiltrates my senses when he soils himself again.

I pull him up, and half his face and scalp is gone. His eyeball is missing.

"..." he slurs, but it's unintelligible and I scrunch up my face in mock concern.

"What was that?" His head lulls back, and spit mixed with blood dribbles down his chin. *So nasty.* "You want more?"

Head shaking, a few tears roll down his good eye. "No."

"Si."

"Please...compassion."

For a second, I nod. Give him false hope before elbowing him in the one eye he has left and lowering him a final time out of the van's door. I'm holding him a little above the moving asphalt. His squinting eye is trying to focus on me, his body no longer fighting.

"Javi, I—"

"Thank me."

It takes him a moment, but he does. It's low and weak and I shoot him twice in the head before dumping his body over.

It bounces off the paved road, lying still and waiting for the birds to arrive. They don't take long; the scavengers wait nearby on trees and watch —wait for opportunities to present themselves.

"Are you heading straight to the airport from here?" Emiliano says as the sight of Gino's corpse becomes distant, and I turn my face to meet his eyes. "Or are you picking anything up? We can handle the cleanup alone."

"I'm taking Chulo. She loves him."

"Then I'll text Lourdes to have him and your bags ready. Let's get you back to Mariah."

Closing my eyes, I nod and sit back. Relax a bit knowing I'm going home.

I miss you, Muñeca.

Mariah

IT'S ALMOST TWO in the afternoon and I'm restless. Unable to sit still while this invisible pressure weighs on my chest. *What is wrong with me?*

Something inside me is unable to rest, and for a Friday afternoon that makes no sense. Not when I have the weekend off and Malcolm demands I disconnect from work.

No phone calls. No helping with last-minute demands from clients.

My eyes flick to my cell phone, and I glare at the screen. Javier hasn't called in days, and I'm fearing the worst while hoping for the best. This uncertainty is gnawing at my gut, and I'm going to punch him in the mouth before kissing him stupid the next time I see him.

No contact in days is unacceptable. *You go silent when hunting.* One of the few lessons my father imparted that I understand. Distractions can get you killed, and while I hate it—loathe the silence—I understand the why.

Touching someone's mother is forbidden, and when that line is crossed you act swiftly and without humanity. No conscious thought.

I'm still going to give him hell for making me—

"You look like you need a coffee break," my cousin asks, standing in front of my desk with a cup of coffee from my favorite shop, but all it does is make me miss Javier more. Wish that he were here bugging me instead; pushing me and taking my body as he did the night before I flew back.

I'll never forget that cabin deep in the jungle. The way he fucked me, then loved me and fed me a delicious dinner in bed afterward.

I want that man again. The side of him that only I'll see when the day is over and we no longer have to respond to titles and expectations.

I miss him. I love him.

"Thanks." Grabbing the cup, I bring it to my lips and take a sip. My brows furrow and head tilts to the side; the brew is too perfect. Just the right temp and sugar versus caffeine ratio. It also reminds me of every cup Javier has brought me thus far.

Of his smiles when I'd grumble.

Of his knowing eyes when I'd bite back a caffeinated moan.

"Nice to see you smile."

"Unless you have some kind of cake behind your back, shut it." And the gloating jerk only nods toward my desk and the open light pink box that sits there. They're from the same bakery as my drink, and containing the baked goods I've been craving for the past seven days of this week. "How?"

"Just thought you'd need a pick-me-up. You've been off for days." He's staring at me pointedly, and I feel a twinge of shame. This isn't a life I don't understand, I know to expect the unpredictability, but it doesn't negate that when someone you love is involved, things change.

"That bad?" I ask sheepishly, giving him innocent eyes that he sees through.

"Do you want the truth or a bullshit-praising deviation of reality?"

"Touché." Taking another sip, I breathe in deep and let it out slowly. "Has he contacted you?"

"Not in days, but we both know he's fine." The concern in his tone catches me off guard, and I raise a brow. "Just because I don't cry into my cereal doesn't mean I don't like the guy, Mariah. He's good to and for you. That's enough for me."

"So, you approve?"

"Do you need my approval?"

"No." He laughs at my response while bringing his wrist up, checking the time on his watch. "Shut everything off; we have somewhere to be."

On instinct, I check the notepad to my right and don't see anything scheduled for this afternoon. "We don't have—"

"Shut it down and gather your things. We're cutting out early."

"Sure thing, boss. Let me jump into action," I say with false elation laced with sarcasm.

"Good. And hurry." And to be a jerk, he takes my box of goodies because he knows I'll follow.

I'm half tempted to flip him off but choose instead to roll my eyes and do as he says. There's not much to do and I log off, tear the page off my notepad, and store the items no longer needed. *Clear space, clear head.*

"Where are we going?" I ask a few minutes later as we head down to the main floor and then exit through the back. The employees we pass smile at us—some have a knowing look, but no one stops or asks questions. "Did something happen? Is everyone okay?"

"Keep walking, Mariah. No more questions."

"Malcolm—"

"Trust me." And he hits right where I'll never argue. He's like my brother and has never lied to or hurt me.

"Okay." We walk down a private stretch of sidewalk that leads to the company garage in silence. It's quiet out, the sole noise coming from the distant horn or a street vendor calling out to sell his hot food items.

He doesn't pause at the door on this side of the building, just turns the handle without inputting the code. I'm surprised but don't voice it, choosing instead to bide my time.

"Keys?"

"Sure." Digging them out from my purse, I hand them over and hear the click of my alarm a few seconds later. I don't park far from the entrance and we make it to the vehicle within a minute or two. "Can I have them back now or are you driving?"

He doesn't answer and once again checks his watch. "Give me a sec."

"Malcolm, this is getting weird. Even for you."

"Hush, nerd."

"Suck it, donkey face." I'm smiling at the end of our exchange, more so because we haven't used these nicknames since high school. He was as much a jerk then as he is now. "But seriously, cousin. What's going on?"

"Always so many questions, Muñeca." My entire being freezes, eyes closing as his voice wraps around me and the drink in my hand crashes to the ground. I don't turn to look around for him, I don't so much as breathe, but then he's there. Right behind me. His warmth seeping into my pores. "Aren't you going to welcome me home?"

"You've rendered her speechless, Lucas."

"I should do it more often. Look at that—no arguing."

"I'm going to kick both your...oh shit!" I'm whirled around before I can finish my threat and his lips meet mine, breathing life back into my body. At once I'm hot and needy and I whimper into his mouth, gripping his dress shirt to keep him where he is.

Where he should always be. With me. Touching me.

A sense of relief so profound fills my lungs, and I breathe right for the first time since leaving Colombia. Javier is home and I'm drawing in his taste, clinging to him like the needy woman he's made me.

Our tongues twine, a loving caress and I moan. "When."

"A few hours ago," he growls into my mouth, his kisses desperate. Hungry. "Had to pick up Chulo first, but I'm here. I came back for you."

"I love you."

"I love you too, beautiful."

"And I'm taking the dog home. I don't want to see either of you until next Tuesday." Turning my head, I meet my cousin's stare and there's a warmth there that surprises me. "Go be happy."

Stepping out of Javier's arms, ignoring his protest, I walk over to Malcolm and hug him tight. He wraps his arms around me and squeezes just as hard, and then steps back, grabbing the leash my man's holding.

Oh shit! Chulo is here!

"He's already in Malcolm's car with Carmelo. We'll see him in a few days."

"Really?" I'm smiling so big and I know we have so much to discuss, but just having him here, makes my life brighter. Everything can wait.

Right now, I just need him. To be us for a few hours, and then I'll talk him into picking up my dog.

Because I'm claiming him. Chulo is mine.

"Yes, linda. He's comfy and warm and getting ready to be spoiled by you."

"That dog is brilliant." Turning my head back in the direction of Malcolm, I find the area empty. "Where did he—"

"He's gone, babe. Now kiss me." Javier doesn't wait for me. His mouth slants over mine and I give in to his taste. The softness of his lips is a contrast to his aggressiveness—as if he can't help himself—and Javier devours me. And I lose myself to him, to the feel of his cock hard and thick against my abdomen. Of the coolness of my car as the metal meets my back, his body covering my front while hands wander.

He's gripping my right thigh with one hand and palming the back of my neck with the other. Dominating my senses. Controlling and pulling moans from deep within my chest.

I don't know how long we stand there kissing and don't care. Either way, this is what I've been missing. That is until we hear the click of a gun and freeze.

"Isn't this sweet," a voice says from behind him, and a quick flash of fear runs through me. Mildred tsks when we don't disengage and turn to face her, but I feel the gun in Javi's jacket and finger the cold metal, gripping it tight right before he turns.

His back is against my front, his muscles coiled tight. "Leave, Ms. Frederick. Killing so soon after being gone so long isn't on my agenda for the day."

"Step aside."

"Last warning."

"Why do you defend the whore?" she spits out, and I take in her appearance. *The hell happened to her?* Mildred is dressed all in black and her lip is busted, a large bruise forming at her jaw. "It's because of her that I've lost it all."

"I thought you were pulling my strings. That I'd be the one to lose it all?"

"You took him from me." Tears fall and leave mascaraed tracks down her cheeks while her hand shakes. She looks unstable. "Had you kept out of my business—had you left Lane alone—I'd be a happy bride right now with a kid on the way. Instead, I'm alone on our anniversary and you'll end up dead by my hands."

"You mean, with you going to jail?"

"With your father burying his child." Something about the way she says *father* catches my attention. It's full of hurt and bitterness.

"Did he leave you? Is that why you're pulling the dramatic act?" Antagonizing her isn't ideal, but right now I'm seeing red. Seething at this bitch for interrupting our sweet reunion and I step from behind my love, standing shoulder to shoulder while keeping his Glock out of sight. "Or is he sleeping with someone else?"

Fury flashes in her eyes, but she tamps it down with a fake smile. "I'm going to enjoy killing you, and then I'll end your mother."

"Mildred, this is your final chance. Walk." Javi reaches for my hand, trying to grip the gun. She's too busy glaring to see the exchange, but he doesn't miss the way I hold on tighter. This kill is mine; I'm not backing down.

"I want her dead," Mildred sneers and lifts her shaking hand with the barrel pointing at my head.

"The feeling is mutual." Still, I hold my ground without showing my weapon. Showing your hand before it's time can be a costly mistake. "But I'm going to give you the opportunity I never offered Lane. Walk, run...leave Chicago and never come back."

The mention of his name cuts her deep; I've come to understand within the last few weeks that she did love him, just had a shitty way of showing it.

"Fuck you," she screeches and the gun in her hand goes off, the bullet aimed at me while I return fire with a quick flick of my wrist. It all happens so fast. One second she's standing, while the next, her vacant eyes watch us with three bullet holes decorating her head.

"I keep warning people that my shot is better than most." Her discharge never touched me and I smile, until I look over and catch the sight of red on Javier's shirt and the sudden buckling of his knees. "Baby?"

"I love you," he whispers, and my world stops. This can't be fucking happening.

"Look at me," I yell out as footsteps approach and then surround us. They're barking out orders and closing the garage down, and while I'm somewhat aware of Malcolm's voice through a phone's speaker, I don't react. My sole focus is on the man gritting his teeth as the stain grows. "Javier, baby...focus on me."

"I love you." He slumps back and I help him against my car, cradling his head as paramedics arrive with the police close behind. They load him on a stretcher and I try to follow, but with me being the shooter, one of the officers arrested me without questioning or watching the video recording.

Javier is taken to the closest hospital.

I'm being taken to the nearest precinct.

God, please let him be okay. Please don't take him from me.

I HAVEN'T FULLY stepped inside the precinct when I catch sight of a man I know and well. His eyes meet mine and they widen, then narrow on the man beside me walking as if he's made the bust of the century.

"What's the meaning of this!" Captain Hall bellows and all movement inside ceases; the man he's talking to also turns to look and grimaces at the image of my tears and the handcuffs on my wrists. "What the hell are you doing?"

"Captain, we answered a call for help at the garage for Asher Holdings," Officer Millstone answers, his chest puffing out with pride. He's young. Too eager. *Moron*. I'm seething in these cuffs, but I keep my composure. The faster we get things cleared up, the faster I can get to Javi. "Shots were fired as reported, and we discovered a deceased female upon arrival. There was also a wounded man nearby who's been taken to Northwestern Medical. She—"

"Is the fucking victim."

"What?" The hand on the small of my back shakes. "She's our suspect."

"No, she isn't." Hall flicks his eyes to me, and the look in them is apologetic. Embarrassed. Scared. "Had you done your job properly, you would've asked for video footage and known that the deceased shot first and accosted the couple. Ms. Asher acted in self-defense and if you don't get those handcuffs off within the next fifteen seconds, the only job you'll have in my department is in clerical."

Millstone jumps into action and the restraints come off; his face is ashen when I turn to raise a brow. "Ms. Asher, I apologize. This was a huge mistake and I—"

"Drive me to the hospital and we'll be even. No stopping for shit."

"Captain, can I—"

"Go." Hall is exasperated, embarrassed, and I'll talk Malcolm into not retaliating. But later. Much later. "Get her there and back quickly. Head straight to my office. I'll be waiting."

"Yes, sir."

"You'll be arresting me again if we don't get to that damn hospital, Officer. And that is not an empty threat." He gulps, then nods. Hall turns, and I catch a hint of a blush on his cheeks and it takes everything in me not to snap.

Lord, now is not the time to test my patience. Please get me to Javi.

I breathe a little calmer once we are on our way.

"WHAT THE HELL HAPPENED?" Malcolm hisses beside me the second I walk through the emergency rooms doors. He's been waiting outside, knowing I was close after Officer Millstone was kind enough to return my belongings that he confiscated from the ground near my car. "Who the fuck arrested you?"

"Not now."

"Mariah, I need—"

"To give me a moment to see if the man I love is okay." The tears come then, and I'm pulled into his chest, his lips at the crown of my head, but I don't understand what he's mumbling. "What?"

"I said, he's—"

"Malcolm, I swear to God if you tell me he's anything but fine, I'll shoot *you.*"

The man chuckles and gives me another quick squeeze before stepping back. He looks amused, mostly angry, but there's a hint of mirth there too. "So this is why he finds your threats so amusing. I get it."

"You are skating on very thin ice."

"*You* have anger issues, dear cousin."

"It's hereditary." I close my eyes and breathe in and out. And in and out. *Until you know everything is okay, you keep your composure. Rip him a new one later.* "Now… Where. Is. He?"

"Getting the wound cleaned and stitched up."

"So, he's okay?"

"Yes." Malcolm entwines our fingers and pulls me along behind him. I'm not paying attention to the where or if we turn right or left and how many doorways we cross; I feel lost until his eyes meet mine and his lips stretch into a soft grin. "Go on. I'll be in the waiting room while you two talk. And don't worry, Carmelo has Chulo."

My feet are rooted to the ground, though, and Javi gives me a concerned look. "Come here, Muñeca. I'm okay." A sob catches in my throat, and the nurse tending to what I now see is a large shoulder wound gives me a sympathetic look. It's just all too much. So much could've gone wrong. "Stop for a second."

"Sir, I just need to close the last two stitches. It'll be…never mind."

With his warm brown eyes on my seafoam ones, Javier rips off the medical tape and the dirty gauze used to clean up the wound. There's a green nylon string with a small pair of scissors clamped in place for her to administer the next suture, but he lets it dangle while walking closer.

Another step, and tears drip down my eyes in relief.

His scent infiltrates my senses, and I shake with this profound need to grab him and never let go.

And then he's the one touching me.

Javi's hands cup my face while ignoring what I'm sure is searing pain. He doesn't care. He only rubs his thumbs across my cheeks and collects my tears with soft brushes before his lips meet mine and soothe the ache that's making it hard to breathe.

"I can't live without you, Javier. I'm sorry I didn't see—"

"Shut up and kiss me." And just like a few hours ago, I give in to my need and kiss him with everything I am and what I'll be by his side. Each swipe of my tongue is an apology for not being careful. Each nip of his bottom lip is a promise to never leave his side. "Fuck, I love you."

Pulling back, I rest my forehead against his chin. "More than my own life."

We stay that way for a few minutes, his presence helping me calm down, and then I take his hand and walk him back toward the bed. I peck his lips and instruct him to lie down. I lay my head beside his ear while the woman works, and it's while his hand plays with my fingers that I get the courage to ask the one question that's been plaguing me since coming back from Colombia.

It's what I need. How I want to spend the rest of my life.

"Javier Lucas," I breathe out slowly against his cheek, and his head tilts in my direction. "Will you marry me?"

"Yes." No hesitation. No doubts.

"Today?"

"This very minute if we can find someone to officiate."

"Thank you."

Plump lips curl up into the happiest little grin. "Shouldn't it be me who thanks you?"

"No." The shake of my head is minute, and I use the movement to nip his jaw. "Because I feel like the luckiest woman in the world right now. You've given me you, and that's all I'll ever need to be happy. To feel complete."

"I'll never stop loving you, Muñeca."

"And I'll be more than thankful to have a good shot." His boisterous laughter fills the room and I smirk. No more of the heavy for today. Not when I'll move heaven and earth to marry him today. "Scare me like this again, and I'll shoot you. That's a promise."

"Wouldn't dream of it, dear." Javier rolls his eyes but in them, I see nothing but love and devotion. The same emotions I'm drowning in. "I'll just have to find other ways to annoy you."

"Good boy."

205

EPILOGUE 1
JAVIER

"WHERE DID YOU go?" Mariah asks, her voice thick with sleep as I kick off my boxer briefs. She's naked and warm, much like I'll be in a minute, and cuddled up on my side of the bed. I find the action amusing—sexy. "What could he have possibly needed at this time of night?"

"I visited the Foster residence to extend a formal invitation to his house tomorrow."

Mariah lifts her head and arches a brow. "At this time of night?" Why would he—"

"Because he's interested in one London Foster."

"Say what, now? He's interested in the sister?" My wife turns in my arms, her lips spread into this megawatt smile that means nothing but trouble. "When did they meet? Is she as pretty as the picture in her file?"

"What file?"

Her grin is sheepish and her eyes wide with mock innocence. "I might've made one after they moved to town cataloging the terms of their agreement. The men in that family are shady, low-end criminals, but the girl is not involved. If anything, she's too sweet and afraid of them."

"Does Malcolm know this?"

She scoffs, squirming a little closer, and my dick perks up at her nearness. At the way her ass jiggles while she plays the *I'm only trying to get comfortable* card. Brat. "Of course not. That man is too stubborn for his own good."

"What's that supposed to mean?" My hand falls to her hip and then lower to her thigh; I lift it, and she moans when my cock slips between her bare lips. When the head kisses the wetness that is only for me and settles at her entrance. The tiny hole clenches in anticipation, but I don't enter. Just touch it. Savor the feel of her sweet juices coating my tip. "What are you planning, Muñeca?"

"Nothing."

Lying is a mortal sin for me, and yet she pushes. *So bad. So mine.* "Liar."

"It was just in case they meet, or something goes wrong."

"Like what?" I slam in to the hilt and she clenches, her breath caught in her throat from the force of the punishing stroke. "Tell me." No response. Not so much as a breath escapes her, and I take that as a challenge. "This one is on you."

Pulling out, I push Mariah's hip forward and pin her there. Her back arches while she tries to fight my hold, wanting to be fucked for being bad, but unwilling to give in.

Good thing for her she has a husband who doesn't mind dominating, bringing her to tears with his cock.

"Javi, I—"

"*I* what?" Short little jabs slip the engorged head just past her opening a few times, but I don't penetrate. I want to hear this explanation. *Why is she keeping tabs on that family when I'm doing the same for our family's sake?* "Tell me."

"Please fuck me."

"Answer the question, Mariah." Fuck, she looks so good like this.

Needy and hungry and her entrance clenching in search of me. "Tell me why you've been—"

"Because Earl asked me to make sure she doesn't get mixed up in their drama. He's a family friend on her mother's side and is worried. *Christ...*" She's struggling against me. Her eyes over her shoulder meet mine and they're angry and desperate "...keep denying me, and I'll take care of this myself."

"Is that a threat?"

"Yes." My smirk is dark and my intentions dirty; she knows this. Lives for it. "You can't stop...oh *fuck*!"

"Louder, baby. Scream for me." My thrusts don't allow her time to adjust or take a breath; I'm fucking her fast and hard and holding her down with my weight after spreading that thigh higher. I hold it to the bed, fingers digging in, and yet, my precious doll only whimpers out a *"More."*

Always more.

"Javi, I'm..." she trails off, lips going slack when I slip a hand between us and touch her throbbing clit in time with my thrust. No lead in or gentle circles. I press two fingers down and use every punch of my hips to massage—bring her closer to the orgasm I denied her earlier in the night.

She's hiding something from me, and I don't like it.

"You close, Mamita?" Her response is a whiny, keening sound. She loves it when I speak Spanish and I'm not above using it when necessary. "Tan bonita mi muneca. Tan rica."

"Oh God..." another delicious clench and I feel her clit swell the second goose bumps erupt all over her heated flesh "...just need—"

"What?"

"Tell me."

I smile against her sweaty neck, closing my eyes as the power I hold over her slams into me and rocks me to the core. I'll never deny how heady it is to own her love. To experience her greed for me every single moment of the day.

"I love you more than my own life." No sooner has the last word slipped past my lips than Mariah comes and hard—her pussy tightens around my cock like a vice and I find myself holding still—letting her fuck herself back on me with short strokes.

She's massaging me. Her heat enveloping me.

And when her small hand slips beneath her hips and holds me to her, I come.

Spurt after spurt rushes out and deep into her core. I fill her and still, it's not enough.

I want her round with my child. I want to have everything she's not ready for…*yet.*

"Javi, I'm dead," my girl whimpers a while later and I laugh, pulling out and falling beside her on the bed. She's insane and a little mental at times, but I wouldn't change a single hair on her head. "I needed that."

"You ready to tell me what you're hiding now?" Secrets and lies are the one thing I'll never allow between us. Not with how far we've come. "Are you still—"

"I found my mom."

That's the last thing I expected and I sit up, pulling her into my lap in the middle of the bed with the sheets strewn around us. Her mother's disappearance has been bugging her since the last time she spoke with her father.

A man whose body, sans head, was found in a lake by the police a week after we said *I do*. No motive or suspects have been found, but that's because Malcolm is nothing but an irate perfectionist. Especially, after finding out the black roses were coming from him and his whore as a scare tactic.

The flower shop owner was a friend of her father.

Moreover, I took pleasure in hanging the widowed-shop owner and watering the sunflowers with his blood.

"Where is she?"

"In Indiana." She buries her face in my neck; I feel the few tears fall and begin to think the worst. "She's living under an alias and working as a caretaker in a women's shelter. The kids love her, and she seems happy. Happier than I've ever seen her."

"I can have the car ready in ten minutes, linda."

"That won't be necessary, Papi. I'm not going to see her."

"Why?" I'm surprised by this. I'd give anything to see my mother again.

"Because she's at peace, and I never want to take that away from her. I'm okay as long as she's safe."

We've had people look into her whereabouts over the last few years. We've dug and dug and searched high and low, but the truth is she's hiding and doesn't want to be found after Mariah's father forced her into a mental institution in London. For seven months under the guise of her being schizophrenic, her Mom was forced medications and endured treatments not meant for someone with a clean bill of health.

A lie he told after slipping those in charge a few bills, and it wasn't until the owner went to trial for a wrongful death case that my mother-in-law escaped. Vanished without much of a trace.

Tipping her face up to mine, I kiss her nose and then peck her lips. "Are you sure?"

"I am."

"You're amazing, sweetheart. She's lucky to have you as a daughter."

"And I am blessed to have you as my husband. So lucky that I want to start trying for that baby?"

"Yeah?" My grin matches her. It's dopey and happy and I'm fucking hard again. "Right now?"

"Why not?" Mariah laughs, turning her in my lap to straddle my legs. "I want a little mini Javi throwing tantrums and harassing kids on the playground."

"What about a mini Mariah threatening to shoot everyone she meets?"

"The possibilities are endless." It leaves her on a moan, her hips gyrating against the bulbous, angry tip. "But as long as I have you—"

"I want them all," I finish for her and then take those soft lips with my own, sending a silent vow to God above to never let me lose her. Our connection. She's my life, and I plan to spend my life showing her each day that I live and breathe for her love.

EPILOGUE 2
Mariah

"READY TO COME CLEAN, little cousin?"

My head whirls back, a gasp slipping from my lips at the sight of Malcolm. He's the one I've been worried about the most, disappointing him by not confiding a secret we've kept long enough.

That I've made Javi keep.

You hurt him, too.

Christ, my eyes well with tears and my lips open to speak, but no words come out. How do I explain my selfishness? How do I explain that I kept them away from the happiest day in my life?

"Malcolm."

"Stop," we say in unison, but the annoying jerk just wipes off my eyes with a soft expression. "I'm not mad."

"You're not? And what exactly are you *not* mad about?"

"I was there the night you said your *I do's* in the hospital room."

What the? "But we never saw you." It's the only thing my brain can muster. That, and a contrite expression.

He's always been there for me.

More like a brother than a cousin.

"It's a lucky coincidence that I was." He's smiling and relaxed. No anger or reproach in his tone. "After dealing with a phone call from the DA's office over the incident with Mildred, I stopped to check in on Javier. To thank him for saving someone I love."

"London's made you a softie with emotions," I tease, not used to seeing this side of him often. Malcolm shows his affection with actions and not words, unless you're his wife. The way he fawns over her is quite adorable to watch.

"I'd shoot you, but your husband might quit."

"That's my line, jerk!" I yell in mock-indignation. "Besides, Javi always double-crosses me."

"Do I?" The man in question wraps an arm around my waist then, pulling me against a hard chest. One I love. One I can't sleep without cuddling on. When I don't answer, he chuckles against the crown of my head. "What's freaking her out? Coming out, or the pregnancy?"

I've never turned around so fast in my life. My eyes meet his: my wide ones on his soft, molten chocolate ones. "You know?"

"I do." Javi brings both hands up to my face, cupping my cheeks. His lips are spread into a wide smile, the softest expression over his chiseled features. "At first, it was just a suspicion, but after the week of nothing but Buffalo wings for dinner with a coconut cake for dessert, I knew. You love coconut, but not in a cake."

"I'm sorry. I—"

He shuts me up with a kiss. It's soft and sweet and warm; our lips connect, and all my worries disappear. I'm tethered to him. My world begins and ends with him.

Softly, Javier nibbles on my bottom lip before pulling back when a throat clears, a sheepish grin on his face. "My apologies for forgetting you exist."

"I'll remember that the next time London comes to have lunch at the office." He's trying to sound annoyed, but I hear the happiness in his tone.

Real happiness, and after nipping Javi's jaw and removing his hands from my face, I turn to face him. "Take a moment and come inside when you're ready. We'll keep them inside."

"We?" I squeak, worried someone else knows.

"London knows, Mari. And don't worry, no one is upset, nor will we let them give you shit."

"I'm sorry I hid this from you."

"Shut up." Pulling me in for a quick hug, he kisses my forehead before gently pushing me back. Right back where I belong. With Javier. Always my Javier. "Congratulations, Lucas family. I'm looking forward to meeting my godchild."

"I didn't ask you?" I laugh, feeling so happy to finally share this.

"Not asking. I'm claiming my rightful spot." With that, Malcolm turns and heads back inside, slipping into the kitchen through our sliding glass doors.

"How far along are you?" Javi asks. His hands grip my hips, fingers expanding to caress my small bump.

"A little over a month."

He hums in the back of his throat. "And everything is okay? You've seen the OBGYN?"

No anger. Never reproach.

"We're healthy and right where we should be." Closing my eyes, I inhale deeply and let it out slowly, savoring his manly scent. Javi is my home, and being close to him gives me the peace and stability I need at the moment. He centers me. Assuages and fortifies my soul. "I'm sorry for not telling you sooner, but so much—"

"I'm not upset, Muñeca. You've been nervous and taking on so much." His words soothe me. Calm me of the fear I've been trying to fight against. "But I need you to understand that no matter what, you're not alone. We handle this together. Everything together."

"In sickness and health, we are one."

"We are one."

We've been here before, eight months ago when we lost our first little one. It was an accident. One of those things you can never prepare for— it's out of your hands—and no matter how much you think *what if the drunk asshole who slammed into my car didn't drink that night,* it's useless.

Nothing changes the outcome after the fact.

He decided to drive drunk after a coke bender.

He decided to hit his wife and then leave her locked in their basement.

He made a decision that changed our lives.

But more than that, we faced the heartache on our own, while Javier made an example of the unscathed driver. He made sure the man never made it to court, killing him outside his home with an old rusty ax his wife provided.

"I love you, Javier. So much." My voice breaks a bit, and he turns me, wrapping me in an embrace. His forehead on mine. "Please know that I never meant to hide you or our babies. Both of them," I whisper, tasting his every exhale. Letting the tears fall, because I know no matter what, he's my rock. My haven. "All I ever wanted was a bit of normalcy. To keep this perfect little bubble we've created where I'm me and you take me with every quirk."

"I do that with pride, Mariah. You're mine."

"Always yours."

Warm fingers sweep across my cheeks, clearing the traces of my emotions and then healing every fear with a kiss on my lips. Just one pec settles me. Just a simple touch to let me know he's here.

I'm not alone. I'm loved. I'm protected.

"Are you ready to let them know?

"I'm ready to marry you again." He tilts his head, brows furrowed, but before he can ask, I'm slipping to one knee. Our new rings are in my pocket; a special set I had made with our wedding date inscribed along with our babies' due dates. "So will you make an honest woman of me again and renew our vows?"

"You had this planned." Not a question. I see the small shiver that rushes through him.

"Yes."

"Yes."

"Yes, you will, or yes, I'm crazy."

Javi doesn't respond. Instead, I'm lifted off the ground and swept off my feet. He's a determined man with a smile on his face that sends my heart into a frenzy as he rushes inside and comes to a stop in front of our family.

Everyone watches us with a smile, not understanding his erratic breathing and my goofy grin.

"We've been married for over three years now and I'm sorry we've kept it hidden. I don't apologize for loving her, for living for her, and anyone who gives her shit will deal with me." My face heats up while silence surrounds us. I peek up and catch a few people with surprised expressions and others that look smug. My aunt and uncle look smug. *Do they know?* "Now, I'm going to take my *wife* upstairs, thank her for giving me this beautiful life—the baby growing within—and then renew our vows. Do not interrupt, or I will shoot you."

"Oh my God!"

"My baby!"

"Jesus, Javi," I giggle, smacking his shoulders while those in the room begin to protest. However, one look from the man I love, and they file out and into the backyard with London leading the pack. She's smiling, winking at me, and gives us a thumbs up before closing the door.

The music begins a second later.

Laughter seeps through the glass.

And it's exactly how our first wedding should've been, surrounded by those we love. Full of happiness and... *oh fuck!*

"But first, you'll choke on my cock..." Javi's lips are at my ear, nipping and teasing with the tip of his tongue "...while I eat your pretty little pink pussy. I want your juices on my face, your release on my tongue before I impale you and watch you shatter all over again. I want your sobs of pleasure and sweaty skin. I want to worship, then fuck you until you break, and then, *I do* is the only thing that will slip past those lips."

"Yes, please." It leaves me on a moan. A breathless plea, and Javier nods against my neck.

"Your wish will always be my command, Muñeca."

OUTTAKE 1
MALCOLM

I'M STANDING JUST outside of Javier's hospital room with a man I'm all too familiar with.

I caught him here, wandering down the halls and stopping just outside this room where I have just enough space between the door's opening to witness what's happening inside.

My little cousin is incredible, and I smile.

"She's always done things her way," I say, and the man tries to answer but I push the barrel of the gun deeper against his neck. "You should be proud of the woman she is, Uncle."

"Let me go."

"To your death, sure." The wedding officiant begins to speak, and I listen, taking in the goofy smiles on their faces and the way her eyes light up with laughter when he pokes her side. And while I'll never admit this to her, hiring—arranging that first meeting with Javier has been my wisest decision to date.

He's good to her. Has taken away the sadness that lingered in her eyes for so long after Lane and her parents betrayal.

"You need to stop this. That man—"

"Is your future son-in-law, although you'll never meet him."

The man dressed as a priest begins to read from his bible about love. He explains that the emotion is given freely and is honest—it's not jealous and does not boast nor does it strike down or hurt the other person. He talks about kindness and hope. Of unity and family.

A tear falls from Mariah's eye and she catches it before Javier notices. His eyes are on the officiant while my cousin shows a moment of weakness, of missing her family, but when he looks over and sees her frown, his concern erases all traces of hurt.

He mouths, *are you okay?*

And she replies, *always with you.*

"The rings?" the man asks, and both have sheepish grins. "You don't have any?"

"This was a last-minute thing, and she proposed." Javi shrugs, his grin cocky. "Ms. Mariah here stole my thunder, once again."

"I did not. You're just slow."

"You two will be just fine." He produces something from his pocket that looks like small rubber bands and places one in each hand. "Now, repeat after me and use these as place-holders. I'm sure you'll have your real sets before the week is over."

"Guilty." Javier looks at Mariah with a soft expression. One you don't see in men who hold no qualms in ending a life. Who's itching for revenge. "I brought my parents set home with me. I'd like to use those for now."

"I'd be honored, babe."

"You see that, asshole?" I hiss into my uncle's ear, my finger pulling the trigger but no bullet dislodges. The clip inside has three at the most, and he got lucky this time. "That's love. That's the look she'll wear on her face for the rest of her life."

"He's not worthy."

"And these are your last few minutes on this earth," I remind him. "I'm considering this a wedding gift to the happy couple after all the trouble you've caused with your deceased whore."

"What?" The gun is pressed so tight to his jugular that it comes out a low garble. "What did you do to Mildred? Where is she?"

"Dead." Javi looks over and I catch his minute nod of approval. The evil in his eyes, a quick flash that's gone before Mariah notices the exchange. "The same your friend—the supplier of the black roses—will encounter. Mariah killed Mildred. Javier will end Grant."

"No. No, she can't be—"

"By the power vested in me by the state of Illinois, I now pronounce you husband and wife. You may kiss the bride." Their lips meet, and I hit my uncle across the forehead with the butt of my Desert Eagle, creating a nasty gash right across the bridge of his nose. And as they kiss, I drag him back toward the stairwell where Carmelo stands guard. He sees the unconscious man and jumps into action, carrying his weight like a sack of potatoes over his shoulder.

"Where to?"

"My home. I'm in the mood to play."

OUTTAKE 1
JAVIER

"THIS IS UNNECESSARY, Javier." It's the eighth time she's said this since I placed her inside my SUV, adding kidnapping charges to my already long rap sheet. *Fuck it.* I don't care and my cock enjoyed the way she pouted at the end of her ridiculous statement.

Now, what's unnecessary is her notion to fight my every gesture. She's stubborn. Always on the defense.

You like it, though. And fuck me, I do.

Besides, this complaint falls on the nicer side of her conversational skills at the moment; a monologue I hum to here and there, so she knows I'm listening. And I am...

Each objection.

Each annoyed sigh.

Each curse.

Each motherfucking time she bites her bottom lip in exasperation, I'm left fighting the demonic urge to pull over and take her over the center console. Or part those glossed lips and let her feel the weight of my cock on her tongue.

She has no idea how each provocation heightens my need for her.

How hard I am behind my zipper.

"Time to get this over with," she whispers under her breath, but I hear it loud and clear and there's a lilt of anxiety that doesn't sit right with me. Mariah fidgets a bit in her seat, the just above-the-knee skirt she's wearing in a soft pink shimmying up her thighs, exposing more flesh. I swallow hard and she sighs. "No time like the present since I wasn't given a choice."

Pulling into the parking space closest to the E.R. entrance, I shut off the ignition and turn to look at her. Fully appreciate the vibrancy of her eyes, the high rosy cheeks, and then the curve of her pouty, sensuous lips. "I am your choice."

"Says who?"

"Me." I'm attuned to her moods, react to her emotions and right now, the little coquette is fighting back a smile. And yet, there's a hint of unease there I don't like. "Are you—"

"Have I ever told you that I despise hospitals and needles?"

"No." That's not something I'd forget about. Ever.

"Well, it's true." My eyes narrow and hers widen, giving me that phony innocent look all women use to their advantage at some point in their life. "Can I come back another time? I'm not ready."

Oh, she's good.

"Whatever you want," I croon, reaching over to tuck a stray piece of hair that's fallen from her high ponytail. Then, I begin to play. Tit for tat. Tilting my head to the side, I furrow my brows and frown. "You do look pale. Are you okay, Muñeca?"

I don't miss the small shiver at the nickname or the way she bites the inside of her cheek. "If I am, it's because needles squig me out. Just not a fan of being poked and prodded."

Her lips turn into a small frown and it hits me: she's serious. Mariah's uncomfortable and that creates a pang—tightness in my chest—and I rub the spot. "Why didn't you tell me, sweetheart? I'll never make you do something you don't want to do."

Her shrug is sheepish. "Couldn't give you more ammo to use against me."

No sooner has the last word passed through her lips that Mariah jumps down from the SUV, and rushes inside. For a second, I'm lost to her words and the way her answer makes me feel, but I'm hot on her heels the moment that car door slams closed.

A nurse inside the lobby looks up the second we almost run into her desk. I'm breathing hard and Mariah is slightly glaring—we don't look like the most trustworthy individuals—and the woman merely raises a brow in question.

"I'm here to get my stitches removed."

"They can wait a day or two," we speak in unison and the lady continues to just watch us. The expression on the poor nurse's face would be comical any other day, but the tremble of my muñeca's hand evaporates any amusement.

She really does hate this. Moreover, I'm the asshole forcing her.

"Babe, we really don't—"

"Is Samuel available?"

"Who the fuck is—"

"He's on shift tonight. Let me page him." The nurse is quick to press a few buttons on her phone, cradling the receiver when the link clicks. "Dr. Pains, are you available for a suture removal? Umm, I don't…let me ask her." She makes eye contact with my girl. "Name, ma'am?"

"Mariah Asher."

"He'll be right up." The young woman looks like she ate a lemon, her lips pursing a bit. "Must've heard you because he didn't give me the chance to finish."

"Thank you, I'll wait over—"

"What in God's name are you doing in my E.R., squeaks?" *Who the fuck is he calling squeaks and why is Mariah smiling at this clown?*

"Need these out." My muneca holds her palm out, showing the small line of stitches from her accident at the restaurant. The day I came into her life like a frustrating hurricane and she broke a glass, according to Malcolm. He snitched the next day with another threat to treat her right. "Can you help?"

She bats her lashes and my eyes narrow. She leans over a bit and I nearly pick her up, throw her over my shoulder, and march the fuck out.

"Mariah, I think it's best if we leave," I grit out and all three heads turn my way. Two wary, while she's all innocence. *And wasn't she afraid a minute ago?* "Trust me on this."

"No."

"Yes."

"Mariah…"

"Javier…"

"Do you two need a minute?" Dr. Pains asks, his lip twitching. "Or can I take care of *my* patient?"

The way he says *my* almost costs him his life, and were it not for Mariah, I would've shot the prick. Her hand grabs mine, entwining our fingers, and the harsh squeeze she gives them settles me—calms me down enough to not open fire inside the public building.

"Come on," she sighs, rolling her eyes and I'm tempted to bite the brat. "Let's get this over with."

"Fine."

"Good." Pains walks toward the two doors with the keycard access needed and waves the plastic square in front of the reader. They open and we walk through, following the prick to an empty room near the back of a long hall where he points to the bed. "Sit and breathe. You know the drill."

I cut my eyes to him; eyes narrowed. "Say it politely or I'll—"

"Ms. Asher, can you please sit down and extend your palm facing up over the tabletop?"

"Thank you, Sam." *Now she calls him Sam, too.* This woman is pushing my buttons. All of them. "Anything else you need me to do?"

"Muñeca," I warn, this is past the realm of what I can take. "Quit it."

"Quit what?" She bats her lashes and looks at me with that wide and innocent look that stirs something within. The kind that makes me want to drop to my knees and worship at her altar. "You brought me here. Isn't this what you wanted?"

"I'm—"

"Close your eyes and breathe," the doctor interrupts and Mariah's bottom lip trembles. She does as he asks, but the sudden jitters make me feel like shit all over again.

I'm going from jealousy to anger to guilt all within the span of a few minutes; she's going to drive me insane. Certifiable.

A lone tear falls and that's it. That's my limit.

"Touch her and I shoot." Fuck it, I use her line. "We're out, babe. Grab your things."

"But, Javi—"

"No but, Mariah. I will not sit here and let you be miserable." Cupping her face with one hand, I wipe her tear with my thumb. "This is unacceptable."

"It is." Another tear falls from her eye and my chest constricts. *God, what is she doing to me?* "But you know what's even more messed up?"

"No," I whisper, afraid to further upset her.

"It's messing with my desk, you jerk. Don't. Touch. My. Stuff."

"What did you just say?" The doctor is laughing beside us while her eyes are alight with mischievous amusement. "Muñeca, I'm—"

"What my cousin is trying to say," Samuel interrupts me once again and I'm close to snapping his neck. I'm trying to compute, but coming up short past the tears and threat over her desk and—"

"Your desk."

"Si."

"This is over your desk?"

"Once again…*si.*"

"And he's your cousin?"

Mariah tries to smirk, but it comes out as a squishy grin when I squeeze her jaw. Not hard, but enough to create a kind-of-cute ducky face. "He is."

"Are you fucking kidding me?"

"No." Turning her face with my hand still holding her jaw, she waves at Samuel. "Meet Dr. Samuel Pains. He's my mother's late sister's son."

"I'm going to kill you."

"Not really."

I turn her attention back to me and laugh. The chuckle is a bit dark. A little sinister, and when she raises a brow in challenge, I let go and step back. "Run."

"What?" A shiver rushes through her. My threat excites her.

"Run, Muñeca. Because I plan to do more than bite."

CALLUM JAMESON

I'm the new KING of London, but it's her body I crave to CONQUER. Her enemies have become my own. Her body is my favorite toy.

We were never supposed to meet, but then there she was across the bar sitting beside my cousin's newest obsession. A small little beauty with a grin on her sweet lips and a low-cut top meant to tease—to destroy a man's self-control. She didn't see me, but I took in every sensual inch while placing a target on her head.

Our paths will cross, and she'll fight, but I'm a man of my convictions. My vow is unbreakable.

I'll be back for you, my Venus.

CALLUM

"DISPOSE OF THE two separately."

"The two?" the man on his knees asks. These whimpered words slip through busted lips, the sound is amusing—a little whimsical—and I smile down at him. This is someone I've known my entire life, I grew up with the bloke, but greed is a dangerous disease and he let it consume him.

You don't steal from a Jameson.

You don't run from one either.

My family has a certain code we live by, and Jonathan Bryce broke every commandment.

Outside of his connection to me, he's no one of real importance, a normal man working a boring desk job with a wife who's pregnant and a dog who bares his teeth at him each time he walks through the door. The animal is a good judge of character. Can smell the bollocks that reek from this man's pores while he lies to his wife about where he's been and with whom.

He's useless, yet many overlook the shortcoming; the flat he lives in belongs to her, while the car he drives was a gift from me on his last birthday. His employment is another gift he didn't deserve then, and much less now as the family business isn't worth shit under his care.

Three simple responsibilities he couldn't provide for himself, and it stems from a gambling problem he refuses to accept.

Bryce loves football yet chooses the wrong team each bloody time, and as a mate, I've bailed him out more than a handful of times. Killed so he would be spared. I gave my protection because I felt bad for those he'd leave behind if a bookmaker took back a failed payment in blood.

He shared meals with the Jamesons.

He was allowed perks that weren't his to imbibe in.

And yet, he bit the hand that feeds.

Jonathan Bryce stole from me, and all for a night of basic sex with a whore's used pussy.

At the sight of my smirk, John pisses himself once again. *Disgusting.* "Please, Callum. It doesn't have to end like this, brother. Let me work this off. Or better yet, let me just call Mum. My family's good for it, and she'll wire you—"

His mouth snaps shut after kissing the two large rings on my fingers, the skin further tearing from the blow. "This is your mess, mate. Not theirs."

"Please." It's low. A cry. "It's not that big of a deal. Ezra was in on it. He—"

"No." Another plea sits heavily on his bloodied tongue, but I shake my head. He's afraid and has every reason to be. My friendship was an honest one, no strings attached on my end, but he abused the power it came with. I let him live in my shadow, and now I'll take away his right to breathe just the same. "You knew the consequences and took the risk anyway. Did you think someone loyal to the family, a hacker of all fucking things, wouldn't protect himself? I've seen the video. I heard every word that came out of your mouth."

His eyes drop to the ground, expression contrite. *Too late.* "I'm sorry."

"Lying to me will only make this worse."

"I don't want to die."

"And yet you've failed to give me a single reason why I should take pity, Jonathan."

"My unborn daughter." Bloody spittle lands on my trousers while I finger the edge of the blade in my hand. It slices the pad of my thumb, a few drops dripping down the metal and onto the handle while he watches, unmoving. Paralyzed. "She will need me."

"How sure are you about this?" I scratch my jaw. "What are you willing to bet?"

From the corner of my eye, I see one of the cleaners with me stop a few steps to my right with a familiar briefcase in hand. I'm not the only one who notices his presence, and I chuckle at the sight of Jonathan moving closer to me. An idiot move. *I'm the reaper. His executioner.* Jonathan's bloodied face tips up, his hands gripping my pant leg while tears roll down each cheek.

A true disappointment.

"She will need me."

"You can do better than that, arsehole."

For every action, there is an equal consequence you must accept and confront with pride. In my world, to hide, beg, or cry is a disrespect. More so than the offense that led you to your sentencing.

"I'm their sole provider. Neither would survive—"

Pursing my lips, I tilt my head to the side and give him a small sense of hope. As if I'm considering his idiocy—pretending for those few seconds that I don't know the kind of pathetic wanker he grew up to be. He's mistaken my friendship for something it's not, and even if he were family, I'd slit his throat just the same after a betrayal of any kind.

There's nothing above loyalty. Not even familial ties.

"Liar," I spit out through clenched teeth, and he stumbles back on his haunches, trying to crawl away but the stomp of my boot on his left knee stops him. Four times, and a scream rends the air; he's quick to grab the injured leg but stops when the tip of the knife in my right hand presses against his forehead, digging in just enough to bring blood to the surface of the small incision. "You're not worthy of the family you had, Jonathan.

Melissa deserves better than you, and I'll make sure they're both taken care of. She'll never work two jobs again, nor will she continue to pay for your mistakes."

"If I don't return home, she'll call the cops. There's a file—" He trails off when the briefcase is opened and a second later a manila folder is tossed at his feet. He makes no move to grab it, but tears do fall when a few seconds later a dial tone fills the warm building I own a few hours outside of London. The area is all private farmland, almost two hundred acres of untouched property with a few buildings at the center that I use for personal storage. There's one road in and one out with security around the clock to take care of my cars, a few small planes, and my private collection of war memorabilia—weapons used throughout history to be exact, including a tank used during the Gulf War.

"That file?" The knife's tip digs in a little deeper.

His expression is one of disbelief—betrayal—but that soon turns to abject horror when his pregnant wife's voice comes through the line. "Is it done, Callum?"

"Not yet," I say before slicing down from forehead to cheek while puncturing his eyeball.

"Fuck!" His scream, full of anguish, makes pleasurable goose bumps rise across my flesh. The darkness within my soul is feeding off the echoes that surround us in the large, open space. The cut isn't deep enough to cause blindness, not that he'll be alive to enjoy the sights and sounds of life outside these walls, but enough to make him hiss in pain and tear up—each track down his cheek turns a reddish-brown as the dirt on his face mixes with his blood. "No more. I've learned my lesson."

"We have a request I must oblige." Maybe it's because of the cut or the realization that he's truly dispensable, but Jonathan's face drops and his shoulders slump. He's the poster child for someone who's disingenuously ashamed, yet either way, I pat his head like one would a dog and wag the knife in his face as one would a finger. "Someone needs to hear the verbal confirmation of your blessing."

"Are you taking the piss?" Her laugh is sardonic, completely ignoring his pain-filled yell, but I can still make out *her* tears. The anguish Jonathan has caused. "Do my words really matter?"

"Yes." Yet I'm not the one she's asking. Her question is directed to the piece of shit on his knees crying like a git. "Give me your vote."

She takes a deep breath, and I plunge the blade of my knife from one cheek to the other and leave it there while her husband whimpers. Paints the ground red with his blood one drop at a time, the sprinkling reminding me of one of those designs made by a macabre artist I admire from Seattle. "I've been a widow since the day after we said *I do*. It's time to recoup my full freedom."

"No!" Jonathan yells out without thinking, ripping the flesh on each cheek apart. His mouth fills with blood, it rolls down his neck and onto the dirty collar of the light pink polo he's wearing. "Love, please. Please don't abandon me. You're my—"

"I'm tired of bailing you out," she says lowly, the words full of so much hurt, and for the first time, I see true repentance on his face. *Too late.* "Your family's legacy is gone because of your selfishness, you bloody bastard. The dealerships are under insolvency proceedings, the houses are being sold to pay back the money you stole, and all while your mum had a heart attack at the care home after finding out what you did. While you were busy shagging..." She chokes on a sob, the pain raw, and if I had a better conscience, I'd forgive him for her. But I don't. I won't. "She's been in a coma while you were busy bending over a woman that isn't the one you promised to love and cherish."

"I'm sorry." His split lip wobbles, his entire frame shaking. "I'm so fucking sorry."

"No. You're not."

"Melissa, I know I've hurt you. That I've—"

"Wasted enough years of my life." The woman on the other end takes in a deep breath, the silence looming from the line before a painful sigh escapes her. "I can't do this anymore, and neither can your mum. You can go in peace knowing we'll be better off."

"I'll make this right. Just please—"

"You're only sorry you were caught, Jonathan. Goodbye." The dial tone follows, and the sorrowful scream that leaves him shakes his entire frame. And I'm humanitarian enough to give him a second to come to terms with his reality. His death sentence was handed out by the same person to whom he tied his life to, and then proceeded to hurt by breaking each of those sacred vows.

And while I'm not a man who believes in love or spending my life with one woman, I respect those who do. I respect those vows. I've seen in my life what a good woman can do for a man in my aunt and uncle's relationship, my own parents not being the best example, but *those* two made it work. She was his true right hand before he stepped down and Casper took over as the head of our family.

Classy and poised—nothing like the women that cross my path.

They want an easy fuck with the hopes of taming my cock and bank account. To become a Jameson.

I fuck and leave. No strings attached. No commitment.

Pussy doesn't rule my life. I scratch the itch when the need arises and that's as far as it goes.

"Call her back." It's no more than a whisper, but I hear, and I also don't respond. "Call her!"

My hand extends out, palm side up while my eyes hold his. His anger is rising, and I find the false bravado amusing to an extent. It also doesn't last long as a second later my favorite toy is placed in my hand by the cleaner just slightly behind me.

The heavy leather feels good in my palm, centers me, and I breathe in deeply while letting its coiled length fall to the ground. The slapping sound isn't muted, and the subtle hint of a *clink* makes Jonathan's ire lose all strength, going from hot to a shivering form sitting atop his own mess.

He knows what this is. He was with me when I acquired the specially made whip.

"Vest off."

"I'll leave the country. I'll disappear."

"Shirt. Off," I spit out from between clenched teeth, and the guard who's been standing at the ready to help dispose of Jonathan comes forward. Within seconds, he rips the bloody garment from Jonathan's body, the fabric digging into his skin and my old friend hisses, feebly attempting to push my employee's hands away. But then again, he's always been a weak man. Once done, the guard looks at me, and I nod in appreciation. "Stand back."

"Yes, sir."

My thumb rubs against the handle, feeling the small button there, but I refrain from pressing it.

Instead, I take two steps back while dragging the thick leather against the harsh concrete, my eyes on the man I once called family. There are cuts and bruises, the holes on his cheek are a nasty color already, and his chest bears the brunt of an earlier kick to his sternum.

"Don't. Come on, mate...not—" He doesn't get to finish as my wrist flicks forward and the first lash lands across his upper torso, the skin there welting and in some spots ripping. *And this was a soft strike.* No real force was applied. The second and third are much the same, but now his abused body crawls away from me—he drags himself toward a door to the left he'll never make it to.

I follow at a leisurely pace.

For each step forward, I bring down the whip with precise strikes across his slim build: back, legs, and even the pads of his feet, all while ignoring his sad attempts at swaying my emotions. His tears and pleas mean jack shit to me; it's his blood I am after.

"No more. I've learned my lesson."

Each slash slowly releases his life's essence. Each pays one drop at a time for each pound he stole.

"You held a gun to the head of a Jameson employee." Another direct hit, this one down over the center of his spine, and he arches, a silent scream catching in his throat a second before losing control of his bodily function, once more. Jonathan throws up, the bile liquid escaping from both his mouth and the tear on each cheek. *Disgusting.* "You threatened his mum and twelve-year-old sister. You told him you'd put a bullet between the eyes of a minor if he didn't transfer half a million pounds into an offshore account in the Cayman Islands. Am I lying?"

"No." Jonathan's trembling, arms giving up as he falls forward. He's face down and mumbling, fingernails digging into the concrete, and that only serves to break each to the flesh. The meaty stumps leave tracks across the floor as he fails to escape.

His words—the low mutterings—reach my ears, and I know what they are. What they represent.

I let him pray.

Honor the one thing he grew up with; what his mum wouldn't forgive me for if I interrupted. They are devout Catholics, and I'm granting him mercy by letting him speak to his maker one final time.

After a few minutes, a shuddering breath escapes him. "Will you forgive me?"

"Already did."

"Will you end me, then?"

"Almost." Bending my knees, I lower my body beside his and place a hand on his shoulder, squeezing it, something I've done over a million times. "But before I do, I need you to answer one thing." His barely perceptible nod is agreement enough. "Why?"

Jonathan swallows hard, fat tears rolling down the corner of his untouched eye. "The truth?"

"Anything but, and I'll make your last breath excruciating."

His response is quick and just as bloody idiotic as I thought it'd be.

"Because I never thought you'd kill someone who's been like a brother to you."

"And that was your biggest mistake." My hand grips the back of his neck and I pull him up, forcing him into a painful kneeling position at my feet. Then I take a step back and the whip falls over Jonathan's left shoulder. Just lies there as I walk around him and say my own silent goodbye. *I'll see you again someday.* Stopping behind him, I bend and put my mouth near his ear while gripping the leather end hanging against his body. One end in each hand. "Your cockiness landed you here; I'd kill my own father if he betrayed the family."

His mouth opens, lips beginning to move but then snapping shut as I press the button on the handle. At once, two-inch blades—surgically sharp pieces of steel—pop out, and I pull them tight to his neck.

"No!" Bryce thrashes and tries to pull the whip away, but my grip is unmoving. Instead, I embed them deeper—each blade piercing his skin and cutting through as if it were butter. "Have mercy. Don't kill me like this!"

"All debt will be erased and your family protected." Those are my last words before I give one hard pull across his flesh and the blades slides through, sawing down to the bone without pause. His head falls back, and horrified vacant eyes stare back at me.

One second, you're here.

The next you're not.

A reality for those who let greed overtake their common sense.

A Jameson always collects.

CALLUM

THE BLOOD ON my hands is beginning to dry—cracking between my fingers with each flex of my hand on the steering wheel. The flakes, these minuscule fragments of what used to be Jonathan, are almost undetectable to the eye, but I see them fall onto my trousers and then the carpet of my Mercedes AMG G63 as I rush through nighttime traffic on my way to the family's pub.

Casper's waiting on me while the two men disposing of Jonathan's head and body take a more scenic route. That was his final penance. No funeral. No recognition. What remains of him is being disposed of in two pieces and in separate locations.

Stepping on the gas, I hit ninety miles an hour while my body thrums with endorphins. Killing is my high. The moment a person takes their last breath is unforgettable—feels almost as good as a warm cunt choking my cock.

It's a beautiful sensation that both calms and winds you up. My muscles are tense, yet my reactions are languid and fluid—almost serene as everything around me blurs into colorful lights and sounds. Picking up the lit cigarette laced with cannabis from my ashtray, I bring it to my lips and take in a deep inhale. I hold the smoke in my lungs and for a moment, I close my eyes and exhale slowly while the car maintains its course, opening only when the car gives a small beep alerting me to an object being too close to my right.

The vehicle is an older model BMW from the early nineties and has two arseholes revving up beside me unlike the rest of the calm traffic around us. Not these two, though. They're shouting while nearly hanging out the vehicle, waving hands to draw my attention, and I take in another deep drag instead. The wrapping paper burns quickly, the reddish glow almost touching my lips before I lower my window and toss it in their direction.

"You fucking wanker!" the driver shouts while his mate's mouth is open, yet no words come out. Especially after I flick on the lights so he can see me. His reaction is instantaneous: fear. The heady reaction brings a grin to my lips.

My mug is known. My reputation is all true.

However, the arsehole behind the wheel is slower, and it takes the backseat passenger forcing his face to stop moving for it to click. Then he pales while I simply stare, unmoving, not giving a flying fuck about ramming my car into anything or anyone.

They wanted my attention, and now they have it.

His eyes widen and the car swerves; a harsh yank to the right, away from me, causes two other cars to slam on the brakes. There's a lot of honking as I pass them while the idiots car stops in the middle of the road. *Pussies.*

From there, it takes me another ten minutes to reach the semi-empty parking lot, and I pull into my private spot. At this time of night, the place is closed to the public, but not those in our business. At night is when the dark souls roam and degenerate deals are made while someone does a line or two and a pretty girl entertains their boss.

The latter is always part of the visiting party's group. A mistress.

Never one of ours. We don't traffic or whore out.

We also don't touch.

It's the two rules my aunt demanded from her husband while he was the head of our family, and we've followed the same path out of respect.

When I walk in, though, the place is quiet except for the low riffs of a guitar playing—an old rock song—filling the space. Two tables are occupied with men that work for the family, and at the very back, a transporter from Ukraine is nursing an amber-colored drink. Just him. No associates and I raise a brow in question at our head guard, Jeffrey, while tossing him the keys to my car.

They know to clean and erase every trace of Bryce.

The shrug of his shoulders is barely perceptible, but I've known him long enough to read every subtle change or twitch. I flick my eyes to the visitor once more and then meet his eyes, and he nods at the silent command. *Watch him.*

I don't bother to acknowledge anyone else and walk through the clean, empty kitchen. The private door to Casper's office is open, and filtering through is the sound of music and chatter that sounds American. And I'm right as I stop at the entrance and my eyes focus on the screen.

We don't acknowledge each other. His eyes and mine are watching— struck by the same scene.

Two women, but it's one that stands out. Motherfuck, I can't look away.

My heart rate spikes up and a lick of heat flows through my veins, igniting every molecule in my over six-foot frame. I'm hard—furiously throbbing. *Who the fuck is she?*

The brunette is sitting with another woman, one I recognize as Casper's newest obsession and what's keeping him focused after the death of his mum. It was a senseless assassination that burns, and had he not found *her* —his end goal—London would be bathed in blood.

My own hands twitch to end her murderer's life.

The women are similar in height and hair color, but that's where the similarities die. No. Aurora Conte would never measure up to the reincarnation of Venus sitting at what looks like an American sports bar and sipping a pink drink with a sexy smile on her lips.

"Who?" This leaves me on a low growl, a rumbling that builds deep in my chest, and my cousin's eyes flick to mine for a brief second. In them, I find mirth and a bit of cockiness, a better demeanor than the pain-filled eyes of the last month. Moreover, whatever he sees in my face is enough to pull a low chuckle from him, and had he not been family, I would've given him a bunch of fives. *Arse.* "Answer me."

"Aren't you hostile tonight?"

"It's been a testy evening," I hear myself answer, but my attention is on the beauty on his screen. She's laughing now, head thrown back, while her tits shake in a low-cut top meant to tease—to destroy a man's self-control. "Name, and who's following?"

"Her name is Aliana Rubens—" If he said anything after, it doesn't matter. Not when said beauty stands from her chair and raises both hands, shaking her hips to the Latin beat playing in the background. Moreover, everything in my world stops. Nothing moves but her. Nothing exists but her gyrating form with arms up high, fingering her soft, long waves before dipping low.

Then back up again.

And I enjoy it, eyes traversing her short stature while taking in the flair of her hips in a pair of distressed jeans that seem to have been tailored for each sinuous curve. They sit low. Almost dangerously so, and I take account of every face in the background glancing her way. Some women, some men, and it doesn't matter if it's out of lust or envy; my hand itches to put a bullet between each pair of eyes.

Is this what jealousy feels like? Not that it makes much sense.

I don't know her. I'm a danger to her.

The sound of wood splintering registers a second later. I feel a few pieces of the now broken door trim embedded into my skin and then the few drops of blood that follow, and yet, I'm struck by her.

Watching her dance is foreplay.

Decadent. Sinful.

Another harsh jerk of my cock, and I feel the beads of pre-come at the tip roll down my engorged head. It's been a while for me since I've wanted a woman, and this one has my attention with a ferocity I've never experienced before. Never like this.

Another drop rolls down my length and it feels like a caress, like the tip of a soft tongue laving my heated flesh, and I bite down on my bottom lip to keep in the hiss fighting to slip through. Not that my cousin is paying attention to me—his eyes are on the woman he's claimed as his.

"Sit." His voice catches me off guard a minute later, a bottle of whiskey now on the table with two tumblers sitting atop his desk. When he got them, I have no idea, nor do I give a bloody fuck. I take the offered seat and drink, pouring him one as well before refocusing on the screen. Both women are standing and shimmying, laughing over God knows what, while my mind runs through different scenarios.

Because I will meet her.

Tomorrow. A few days from now.

She doesn't know I'm watching, but I'm taking in every sensual inch while placing a target on her head.

We have a meeting with Malcolm soon. I could...Aliana Rubens?

"Rubens?"

"Yeah." Casper nods, scratching his jaw covered with two days' worth of stubble. "Oldest out of three and the only girl."

"Who is she related to? The name is familiar."

"Why?"

My eyes snap to his, and my glare only makes the arse smirk. "That doesn't concern you, mate. Don't cross that line."

"Oi. Just giving you the same shit you give me."

"And yet you tell me to piss off just the same." Bringing the glass to my lips, I knock back its contents and pour another three fingers' worth. "Am I lying?"

"Negative."

"Then answer my questions. Who is she related to? Who's watching them?"

He clicks something on his mobile and the screen freezes, both girls' glasses mid-clink. Eyes on mine, Casper levels me with a serious look, and I meet his stare. We know each other, and the only time I back off is on business matters, but only if I agree. If he's wrong, he's wrong, and I don't hold back.

"She's not an easy lay."

"Answer me."

"Governor Rubens."

"Huh." I don't say anything more. That piece of shit isn't what he tells the American public, and I find it amusing. Always have. He's dirtier than some of the men he swears to prosecute and fails to each term. "Aren't we a few weeks from election season in the States?"

"They might be."

"Interesting."

"How so?"

"Because there's nothing a monster fears more than the devil pulling his strings." If he wants to ask, he doesn't. He has his secrets and I have mine; things that don't involve our business, and this is one of those instances.

He's crooked. Very dirty.

"And Alexander is there. He's my eyes."

"Good. He's loyal." Standing, I pull out my mobile and send a message to a good acquaintance of mine overseas. He'll have what I need. "Keep him there."

"I am." Pressing the play button, Casper's eyes turn back to Aurora. "Did you finish what you needed to tonight? Everything cleaned?"

"Yes." Aliana decides at that moment to press a quick kiss to Aurora's lips, and my groan isn't quiet. Neither is Casper's and I choose to leave, but not before drinking up the gorgeous doll on the screen a final time. *I want to bite her. Fucking mark her skin.* "Do we have anything pending stateside? I'll volunteer to attend."

I should be asking about the compromised wire. How Malcolm plans to make amends.

If we've had news on the cockroach hiding from us after killing my aunt—his mum.

Once again, I'm too struck by her to do anything but watch. My cock is hard for her—throbbing—while the coquettish little thing is ignorant of the dangerous web she's been caught in.

"Unless things change, two weeks. Malcolm's dealing with his family now."

Motherfuck, the tits on this goddess. "I'll be taking a few days off right after."

"Is that a request?"

"No." At my chuckle, he raises a brow, but I'm not deterred. He may be my boss, but I'm not afraid. I'm just as much of an arsehole. A Jameson. "That's a notice of intent without guilt."

"Aye. Are you staying or coming back for that time off?"

"Undecided." A lie, yet it's the answer I give before stepping out of the office and heading toward Jeffrey to collect my car. I don't care if they've had enough time to clean or not, there's something more important than a few drops of blood on a rug.

Our paths will cross and she'll fight, but I'm a man of my convictions.

My vow is unbreakable.

I'll be back for you, my Venus.

"Your allure is a mystery I will taste."

Aliana

LEAVING MY BEST friend with her father shouldn't be something to worry about, and yet it nags at me because they aren't the norm when it comes to paternal figures. With them, there were never any kissed scraped knees or congratulations for winning a spelling bee. Nada. Nothing but an icy indifference and a demand you give even if it breaks a piece of you each time.

Because we are commodities. Useful once at a certain age.

Mr. Cancio wants her to take over for him as the head of their dynasty, while mine wants total control of my life, my future, and the set of skills I acquired to survive in his world.

My best friend might not understand to what degree I sympathize with her dilemma, but I do. Better than she even knows herself, because being the child of a powerful man is a nightmare even if you don't carry his last name. That's her blessing, and one I wish were mine as well.

I am her in a lot of ways while privately worse off, because what I've done makes me everything she's not:

Dirty. A criminal.

Shaking off the negative thoughts, I walk past a man who looks at me from head to toe with a gleam in his eyes I'm all too familiar with. There's a seediness to his persona. The greed-fueled aura of a man ruled by darkness, and this isn't the first time I bump into him.

He works for Aurora's father. No one important, just a guard, and he's doing a poor job of watching this door while her father's right hand talks on the phone farther down the sidewalk.

"Evening, Miss Rubens," the guard says while giving me a half bow, eyes on my body the entire time. Not my face, but chest and then lower, causing me to shudder in disgust. I don't address him, and this causes the jerk to chuckle. "Did your parents teach you not to speak to strangers? Or did a cat catch your tongue?"

"You work for Cancio." My response is cold and flat. That of a woman who finds him beneath her standing, and one I've perfected over the years. The governor's daughter always conducts herself differently:

I can never entertain a man like him or anyone that isn't approved of by my parents.

The authoritative head of the house and his silent, submissive wife.

She does what he says, and I'm forced to do the same.

My sole reprieve from under his thumb is working at the Conte House, and it's because to the public, I'm the perfect daughter. Charitable. Humble. Hardworking. Between running the public relations part of the women's home and then teaching the computer literacy program three days a week, it doesn't leave much time to get into trouble. Add to that my college classes and breathing, some days are hard.

Not that anyone in my family cares. I'm a pawn the governor moves at his will.

"I know who your father is, sweetheart."

"Everyone does." Just as Aurora's father promised, a car pulls up to take me home then, and I'm thankful. "If you'll excuse me..."

He moves as if to open my door but pauses with his hand on the handle. His face is close to mine, breath on my cheek, and I cringe. "Does he know she's taking over?"

"Please move."

"How will it look to his constituents to have his daughter running around the city with a future mob boss?"

My eyes narrow, I meet his cocky grin with an icy glare. "My life is none of your business, and trust me, Cancio would agree that neither is his daughter's. Don't threaten me again."

"Will he hurt you?" he asks instead, his stare focused on my mouth now. "I could protect—"

Pig. But he isn't the first, nor will he be the last, to flirt or be pushy. Not in our world.

"And are you going to be there for me?" I'm watching him now from beneath long lashes, relaxing my previously stiff form. Men like him like that. To see a woman back down, but little does he know that they're nothing more than puppets against a quick smile or the thought of an easy lay. Pathetic, really. "Will you defend me?"

The guard licks his lips. "Yes."

"Should I bring that up while my father and your employer play a round of golf before Mr. Cancio heads back to Boston? Or what about at dinner tomorrow night over the first course?" This time, my sarcasm isn't missed and his eyes narrow, hand shooting out to grip my arm. I step out of reach, though, just as Cancio's right hand begins to walk our way. Another man that makes me feel uncomfortable. Something just isn't right about him. "Please move."

"You'll learn your—"

"Is there a problem, Santis?"

"No, Dominic. Just getting the door for Miss Rubens." There's no missing the hard grip he has on the handle nor the tightness in Santis's jaw, but he follows through and opens it for me before stepping aside. I don't wait and slip inside, closing the door before either tries to engage me again.

And yet, I don't miss the angry scowl on both their faces.

One looking toward the Town Car. The other watching him.

"Your parents' house or your apartment, Miss Rubens?" a voice I know asks, and at once, I let out the breath I didn't realize I'd been holding, my body semi-sinking back into the seat. Pierro has worked for the Cancio family for a long time—if Aurora's father is in town, so is he—and is the only person that my best friend will hug without a second thought. He's old, charming, and always respectful. He also engages the locks immediately. "Are you okay? Did they say something—"

"I'm fine, and my house, please." My smile is genuine, but I can't entirely remove the stiffness in my body. There's no hiding it, but thankfully he just nods while looking at me through the rearview mirror. "It's late, and I have an early morning tomorrow."

"As you wish." Pierro pulls off from the curb, but I can still feel Santis's eyes on me. Something about him puts me on edge more than Mr. Cancio or his right-hand man. "There are some chocolates back there, by the way. Your and Miss Conte's favorite."

"Have I ever told you that you're my favorite person, Pierro?"

"A time or two, and each involves chocolates."

"Just speaking the truth," I sing off-key, making the man chuckle while I find the offered treats near the opposite door. *Come to Momma.* They're from a shop back in Boston that does the best sweets in my opinion, and this box, their signature collection, is to die for. Grabbing a piece of dark chocolate with hazelnuts and a hint of orange, I pop it in my mouth and groan. Everything—all the stress I tend to carry—evaporates. My eyes close and the city becomes quiet; nothing matters. "I needed this."

"There's also a bottle of water in the pocket behind my seat."

Opening my eyes, I find the offered and reach for it. It's a little cooler than room temperature and I twist the cap, taking a small sip before grabbing another treat from the box. "You are a lifesaver and the best man to ever live."

"If only the missus thought so..."

I laugh at his reply, ignoring the vibrations coming from my wristlet. "Trust me, she does. It's just smarter to keep you humble."

"Women," he mutters, but his shoulders shake with amusement. "There's not much traffic tonight so we should reach your home soon. Do you need to stop somewhere before we do?"

"No. All I want right now is my bed." Pierro doesn't say anything else, taking the left turn at the light and then driving straight toward the area I live in. Just like Aurora, my home is in the Lincoln Park area and just a few blocks away from hers in a townhome community that my parents approve of solely because a few stuck-up acquaintances have children that live in the area.

My phone vibrates but I don't bother to look. There's only one person who'd contact me right now, and I'm sure he'll do so again once I'm safely inside. *I'm going to leave Chicago one day soon.* A throat clears then and I snap into focus, not having realized I'd zoned out. We're parked outside my place, the dark green door lit up while a large box from my favorite chip company sits atop the mat.

"Are you sure you're okay, Aliana?"

"I'm sure." My eyes meet his through the rearview, and while I can see he doesn't believe me, Pierro doesn't pry. Instead, he gets out and opens my door while offering a hand to help me out, which I take, gripping it while grabbing his gift with my empty one. Once outside, I give him a smile and place a chaste kiss on his cheek. "Thank you."

"I'll be in town until Mr. Cancio leaves. If you need anything, please let me know."

"Tell your wife that if I were older, I'd steal you away."

At my words, his grin widens and a small touch of pink stretches across his cheeks. "I'm the lucky one, Miss Rubens."

"And we'll agree to disagree." With one last smile, I leave him at the curb and take the small set of stairs that lead to my front door, pausing only long enough to grab the box and input my code before ducking inside. I'm smiling as I drop my wristlet, snack package, and my thin sweater before reaching for another small morsel of delight while my home phone begins to ring.

The generic landline's ringtone blares through my quiet home four times before the red light of the recorder signals my doom. Only two people have this number, and both reside in the same house while carrying the same last name: one as a control mechanism and the other because she follows his orders. Even if it means hurting her child.

They're both selfish; how they communicate with me when it's not a social call.

I know what it means. I dread what they'll ask of me.

Dropping the box of chocolates on the entry table, I toe off my shoes and then put my hair up in a high ponytail. *Not yet.* My kitchen is just to the left of the townhome's entrance past an arched entryway, and I walk to my fridge, grabbing the opened bottle of wine in there. It's still three-quarters full, and after popping the topper, I begin to pour myself what's left inside a huge glass Aurora gave me as a gag gift last year.

Am I taking my time in answering? Yes.

Will I get crap for it? Another yes.

"Screw it," I whisper before chugging the contents of the glass, not stopping to breathe until the last sweet drops sit on my tongue. The crisp note of fruit is refreshing, and so is the added warmth that sweeps my short frame as it mixes with my earlier drinks create a quick buzz that makes me smile. "Liquid courage for the win."

And no sooner had the last words passed my lips than there's a sudden pounding on my door. It's a firm knock, harder than needed, and I walk over, opening it without looking through the peephole.

"Why the fuck aren't you answering your phone, Aliana?"

"I just got home. Literally."

"Not good enough."

"Hello to you too, Father," I say, not that he acknowledges or even gives me a smile. Instead, he walks past me and looks at the empty glass with disdain. He also doesn't comment on the hint of annoyance in my tone. "Please, take a seat. Would you like anything?"

He does sit, crossing one leg at the knee while watching me, expression blank. "You know why I'm here."

"Couldn't this have waited until tomorrow's dinner?"

"No." It's hard—so hard—but I nod and take the chair opposite. I mimic him. "The buyer is waiting, and I need this resolved before the campaign for re-election kicks off at the end of the month. You'll be leaving soon."

"I have a job and my schooling. Getting up and disappearing on a whim isn't responsible."

"Neither is a political figure's daughter being best friends with a mafia princess and soon-to-be mafia boss."

"What?" My voice comes out shaky, my palms becoming sweaty. "Why would you say something like—"

"Do you really think of me as an idiot?" That's rhetorical, and I keep my lips shut because truthfully, I want to call him so much worse. My father is the kind of criminal that considers himself above others—untouchable. It's what all the men in my family believe, from the youngest adult to the oldest—it's a man's world, while it's the woman's place to dirty her hands for them. A life where public image is more important than the love or well-being of your child. "Cancio is in town and came to see me earlier today. He's donating a hefty sum to my re-election fund, so I turn a blind eye to his daughter's future endeavors..." Dad scratches his jaw, a dark gleam in his eyes "...and I agreed, with a catch."

A sinking feeling hits me, my earlier dinner threatening to make a reappearance. "A catch?"

"There are two things I need from him."

"Money?"

"Very astute of you." He uncrosses his leg and switches to the other. "I will get a monthly cut of all his illegal activity taking place in the state of Illinois."

"And?"

"I'm interested in doing business with someone he knows but has a dislike for me."

"Interested how?" Something isn't right. *God help me.*

"As a suitable husband for you."

"Husband." The word is thick on my tongue. Makes my skin crawl. "No. I'll refuse."

"Mateo hasn't agreed to that stipulation yet, but he will," my father says as if I hadn't spoken. "It'll be beneficial for us all. Someone to keep you in place."

"You can't do this. I'll never accept whoever this ass—" My face snaps to the side, the hard sting burning my cheek while he simply sits back. I taste blood in my mouth while heat scorches, throbs in time with my heart, and I swallow back my cry of pain. That would only make it worse. *Te odio. Hate you with every fiber of my being.*

"Watch your mouth, mi hija. You know the consequences of going against me."

Cradling my cheek, I bite back my retort because it's always the same. He threatens me with hurting my mother and younger siblings, and even though she deserves no pity from me, Diego Jr. and Sebastian will always have my protection. "Understood."

"Good," he says, softer this time, and I don't trust the tone. "You will do as you're told and go where I send you. No more arguing."

"Okay."

"Tell Aurora you're needed for a family emergency and plan to be gone for a few days."

"Anything else?" I want him gone. Loathe him.

"The information on the artifact will be sent to you via courier in a few days. Study it and prepare, Aliana; I won't allow a fuck-up on your behalf. That small statue is worth half a billion on the black market, and my buyer is desperate."

"So much so that you'd put my freedom in jeopardy?"

"So much so that I'd sell you if the offer had enough zeroes attached." With that, he stands and takes the few steps separating us, and before I can escape, his fingers grip my chin hard and tilt my face up. "You will not fail me, Daughter. Don't force me to hurt you."

Without waiting for a reply, my father walks out, and I finally let the tears fall. This is the shame I carry—the burden that no one knows about. And my biggest fear of all is that someday I'll be caught and live the rest of my life behind bars because no one will believe me.

CALLUM

Aliana Camila Rubens...

HER NAME IS the first thing I see after waking up.

It's on the screen of my mobile forty-eight hours after my eyes landed on her, causing my cock to swell and my stomach to clench. There's something about the little beauty that piques my interest, makes my body thrum with a heated excitement I've never encountered before...

Hunter versus prey.

Swiping a finger across the screen, I open the folder with a grin. I feel no shame while reading each line slowly, memorizing every detail about a slip of a woman I've yet to meet face to face. And yet, that doesn't diminish my interest in the little goddess.

Instead, it makes the yearning to see her again burn just a little brighter. Hotter.

Then again, it's her face that's accompanied me the last two days without pause. No matter where I've been and how much blood is on my hands, it's her I think about and what I'll do once she's in my grasp.

I want to hear her moans.

Watch her fall apart.

Feel her walls clench and milk my cock.

"What is it about you, Miss Rubens?" I ask myself before turning the page, but then pause and close my eyes while gripping my hard dick lazily with my unoccupied hand. I don't wank, just close my fist tight as I replay the way she danced while the people with her egged her on. Coquettish with the right hint of mischief that I find utterly sexy.

The mobile vibrates in my hand and my eyes snap open, Casper's name flashing across the top. We're meeting in a few hours, and I think I know what he'll ask of me. I know the chess-like moves he's starting to make within the organization. *I can almost understand him, too, but is it enough?*

Refocusing on the picture at the top, I'm starting to think his reasoning is indeed enough. It's one of Aliana with two other women at a beach, dressed in nothing but a pair of extremely distressed cutoffs and a bikini top, smiling at the camera. Her skin is sun-kissed, no makeup on her sweet face, and hair wavy from the salt water.

"*Motherfuck,*" I hiss out from clenched teeth, stroking down once and then twisting my wrist—tightening my hold further on the upward motion, and pausing. *One. Two. Three.* Then again, each piece of her I take in is a pump of my hand—my balls tighten, and I throb. Hurt.

Then stop.

I let myself twitch, a bead of pre-come rolling from the tip and onto my fingers as I bite my bottom lip.

There's an innocence to her that I find attractive, but it's the heat hidden underneath that draws me in. Even here, in a picture showing a relaxing outing with her mates, I see that *more*.

It's there. It calls to my own darkness.

My eyes take in the supple hips, how the button at her waistband is undone and exposing a hint of light green that matches the color of her swim top. The two minuscule triangles hold in enough to be decent, but not enough to calm the sudden lick of jealousy that snaps through me.

Each swell spills out at the sides and center; she's a lot more than a handful. Another harsh jerk forces my hips to pump. I fuck my hand as I make out the two beaded tips through the thin fabric, vowing to find out who was with her that day and kill any man who was present.

Kray was astute enough to send his female cousin out on this outing; they sent me separate emails pertaining to what they found. She took these photos—sent one where she's faking a selfie and Aliana can be seen in the background—while he pulled the background information.

Because for her I find myself being a possessive arsehole. It's sexist, and I have no shame.

No excuse. Not embarrassed over the fact either.

I want to be the only one that sees her like this. To enjoy her beauty.

My eyes roam lower, and I groan as a tiny jewel catches the sun's rays right at her belly button. It's small, highlighting her flat, toned stomach and the skin I want to mark. My teeth ache with an overwhelming desire to bite her.

She's bloody perfect. My cock swells in my hold and I jerk my wrist, taking myself to the edge before slowing down. There's something at her hip, showing just above the waist of those blasted shorts that causes every muscle in my body to tense. There's more to it, but the angle she stands at blocks my view and this both angers and excites.

"Christ." I know she's marked—the dark contrast highlighting the edge of a tattoo—and the lightest touch to my engorged head, feather-light across the slit, is enough to pull the come from my balls. Two long ropes shoot from the tip, coating my abdomen while the rest dribbles down my fingers and palm.

If this is how I react to a picture, I'm fucked.

Truly. Utterly. Fucked.

"This is how obsession starts," I mutter to myself, releasing myself and then tracing a come-soaked finger across the picture where her lips are. "We'll be meeting soon, Miss Rubens. Really soon."

Another twitch, and I close my eyes with a grin.

What she brings out of me makes no sense. My reactions aren't me, and yet I need more. To be closer. To feel those curious eyes on mine.

Maybe then the desire will wane, and I'll fuck her out of my system. One and done.

Lies.

Letting out a slow breath, I wipe my hand on the blanket near me and focus on the electronic file next, turning to the page with her personal information. Line by line, I memorize each stat for later use as any good stalker would.

Age: 21
Height: 5ft 3in
Weight: 125 lbs.
Blood Type: O Negative
Lives: Lincoln Park
Mobile Number: XXX-7174
Nationality: Spaniard and American

THERE ARE other details that I also take note of.

Aliana works with Aurora at the women's shelter—teaches too—and even with a heavy work week, she still attends the uni there, keeping a 90% overall. *Beauty and brains.* That's a heady cocktail that most men can't handle, but I'm above the rest. A woman should be both and never forced into one box to satisfy the needs of anyone around her. My aunt taught us this, God rest her soul, and it's also a lesson my mother failed at.

My mother's purpose in life is to travel and shop while pretending the money she spends isn't dripping in blood.

A note toward the bottom of the page makes me pause, and it's a unified concern by her professors over unaccounted absences without a note to excuse each—something the uni she attends is sweeping under the rug.

"Where are you going, Aliana?" *Or why?* The dates seem to all surround the latter part of the last two years, between July and October with one short trip over the New Year holiday. They are abrupt with no pattern, and it doesn't sit well in my gut. "What are you hiding?"

My informant attached a class schedule, and her days off coincide with my arrival in the states. *Perfect.*

There are a few other things about her family, but when we reach her father, his clean file makes me laugh. I know him. I've dealt with him once in the past while exchanging a beneficial favor, and the politicians in that family are sexist arses with no loyalty shared.

"How can she come from that rubbish?" This leaves me with more questions than answers, but I have to push it back until we land in America. It's the only way I'll concentrate, but it doesn't stop me from sending a message to the bloke that gathered the information.

Eyes on her at all times. ~Callum J.

A quick line, he responds to without pause no matter the time difference.

While the information on her was good, there's a gnawing feeling— demanding I dig deeper, see past what others want me to see. Knowing who her father is, it leaves a bitter taste in my mouth.

A man willing to prostitute women in exchange for donations isn't someone I trust.

A family led by misogynistic men, wankers with no real backbone, is one I'm repulsed by.

She doesn't belong there, and no matter how much this makes no sense and I don't understand this sudden obsession, I'm not fighting it. The only thing I do understand right now—what's been brewing since Casper spoke her name—is that I don't want him to taint her.

"YOU OKAY?" Casper asks, coming to stand beside me while our men and Malcolm's load a truck full of cocaine and stolen merchandise a few days later. Two days earlier than the original meet up, but it was opportune when the moment arose, and we were already in the US. My cousin has already tasted the product and accepted the generous donation. We're even now, could leave, but have been asked to remain and bear witness to the owner of Asher Holdings disciplining those involved. "You've been too quiet."

Casper's eyes and mine are on the men and one woman kneeling a few feet away. Some are crying, writhing, while some remain as still as statues, trying to keep themselves out of anyone's line of sight. *Motherfucking pussies.*

Malcolm is a mean son of a bitch when necessary, and I respect him for that. His beliefs align with mine: loyalty above everything.

You don't see.

You don't hear.

And you sure as fuck don't speak.

A lesson learned by his cousin who is now missing a tongue.

"Yes." We both know I'm taking some time off; I just haven't told him where I'm going. Not yet. To him, I'm either heading back home or slipping away while no one notices and it's best he leaves it at that. "Just enjoying the show."

There's a different kind of energy flowing through me, licking at my spine as the time draws near. I'm here as a witness and then gone, my evening to be occupied by a pretty little brunette that has no idea the devil exists. That I've laid a claim on her.

Because I'm back in Chicago.

Because I want a taste of every sensual inch of Aliana Rubens's small frame.

And I'm also not blind to Casper's own distractions. He hasn't asked me to take over yet—is still holding back, but the time will come. The wanker also knows I'll accept without hesitation. With honor.

"Still taking a small holiday?"

Momentarily, my eyes shift to him, and I arch a brow in question. "I am."

"Enjoy the time off."

"You do the same."

"I will." Casper squeezes my shoulder, a smirk on his face. "See you in a few days." He leaves after that, walking over to where Malcolm stands with a neutral expression on his face. No pity. No emotions. It's why the Jamesons and the bloke have become more than a business transaction over the years: he understands and lives by the same cold code.

They exchange words, not that I pay attention as I meet the eyes of the woman whimpering. She's afraid. Pale. *What did she touch to end up here?*

Two bullets dislodge from a gun, and I look toward the man holding this meeting. He's enraged but keeps the devil within on a tight leash, and yet I see the bloodlust. The desire to slowly kill each one of those he considers traitors.

The men—his guards who had been wearing hoods a minute ago—slumped over, a bullet to the neck and chest respectively. They tip toward the hysterical woman, and she subtly attempts to move closer to me until I remove the light sweatshirt I'm wearing so she can see the two Ruger's I have underneath in a leather holster around each shoulder.

I smile as the little glimmer of hope in her eyes dies. She wouldn't be here unless she's directly involved with our sabotaged wire transfer.

Blood pours from the dead guards' wounds, the cold concrete soaking up their life's essence while my cousin and Malcolm face the others on the floor.

The latter tosses something on the ground, and the younger of the two men kneeling gets paler. Shakes harder while Malcolm's cold eyes stare him down, unwavering, as he crouches to his level.

"If you ever lay a finger on her again…" Casper holds up his hand and motions for us to move. Jeffrey doesn't hesitate to follow orders while I watch just long enough for the butt of Malcolm's gun to break the bloke's hand before winking at the crying woman and exiting myself.

Just beside the loading area, I find the trucks with our men already behind the wheel. Jeffrey takes the one in the middle while I take the front, exiting the warehouse in relative silence while heading toward the port to secure storage before we move the electronics to a cargo ship heading to South America.

It takes a few hours, but we get it done. The hot equipment has already been sold and paid for, and I'm negotiating another shipment through emails with the buyer.

The mobile in my pocket vibrates again, the third message from the man watching Aliana. It's her location, a picture I requested, and status—

I'll only check once I'm inside my rental while these men head home to London.

"That's all of it," Jeffrey says, bringing a small towel to his face to wipe his forehead. "*Christ*, all this moving around has me feeling like a roast."

"It's a pretty warm evening." Another of the men hands me a bottle of water. I grab it with a nod of *thanks* and take a sip. "Sweep for anything left undone and head to the airstrip. The plane will be ready when you are."

"What about you?" Jeffrey's expression holds confusion. And he's not being nosy; I've known him long enough to see the wheels turning—calculating how he could be of assistance. "Do you need me to stay? You know I'm here for whatever has to be done."

A smirk spreads across my face, my hand gripping his shoulder and giving it a squeeze. "Not necessary. This is a solo mission, but there is one thing I'll need."

"Personal?"

"Extremely."

"Done, and please enjoy your time off, Mr. Jameson."

CALLUM

THE MOMENT I step outside the elevator and onto the rooftop lounge a few hours later, I'm met with a familiar scene from around the world. No matter the country, it's all the same. Bodies grinding, pulsing beats, the heated stares of strangers as you walk by, and then come the subtle whispers: *Who is that?*

Men and women.

They all look at me, not realizing that my hands will forever be stained with blood—a badge I wear proudly. I'm a killer. A criminal. And I've hurt many for the personal gain of myself and those who share my last name.

And yet, it's the over six-foot frame with dirty blond hair up in a small bun and light greenish eyes they focus on. It's the tattoos and the black designer trousers and long-sleeved vest I changed into along with the accent that lures them in. Because no one believes me to be anything but a businessman upon first impression, they don't see the devil within until close enough for me to execute without empathy.

A commoner walking down the street or inside a pub having a drink wouldn't think I'd easily burn them all alive if they crossed me. A costly mistake. If more people were aware of their surroundings, fewer innocents would die.

"Well, aren't you handsome." A woman in her mid-twenties with too much lip-gloss and mascara steps into my path. She's overly done from head to toe, the light pink in her bleached hair a bit nauseating, but it's the hand on my arm I'm repulsed by. "Where have you been hiding—"

Before she can finish, I've gripped her wrist, turned it just a bit, and removed it from my body. "Not interested."

"But—"

"Don't make me repeat myself, Miss." There's an air of arrogance to her, a slick remark sitting on her tongue, but she's smart enough to read the warning in my eyes. Without another word, she turns and walks away, her posture stiff while I search for my Venus.

The mobile in my pocket vibrates then and I pull it out, reading the text from Aliana's guard.

> She's at the bar with a few more people now.
> One male in particular seems interested. ~Kray

There are two bars in this place; I studied the layout he sent me earlier and I turn my head toward the smaller one. It's full. All men. A stag party judging by the stupid matching outfits and the one guy's tie with the word *groom* down the center.

The next one is on the other side of the roof, and the closer I get, the same sensation rushes through my veins. It's almost like I'm back inside Casper's office at the pub back home, watching—unable to fight this pull. It's tangible, this buzzing heat that forces me closer.

With each step, it's hotter.

A shiver rushes down my spine.

And it's when I spot a familiar head of dark hair that my cock swells to near the point of pain. Because there she is, the object of my lust, and the pictures I've received of her out and about until I came to Chicago didn't do her justice.

"Motherfuck," I hiss out through clenched teeth, unable to understand my reaction. How I'm unable to look away…

This delicate little morsel is a heady temptation. I memorize every delicate inch of her short frame, pausing to enjoy the swell of her breasts in a black sweater vest and then gaze lower, to the lithe thighs in a minuscule plaid skirt. Simply put, this woman is stunning and the more she ignores my heated stare, the more I'm intrigued.

A sudden presence beside me forces my hand to the gun at my waistband without taking my eyes off her, but his chuckle makes me pause. "It's me."

The cool metal is soothing in my grip, eases a bit of the heat snapping at my flesh, but I let go and readjust my jacket. "Never sneak up on me, mate."

"Understood."

"Good," I say, busy taking in how small she is—a delicate little goddess that I yearn to touch. Taste. Corrupt. "Who are the men?"

I could give a fuck about the women. Those two are insignificant to me.

"Those two…" from the corner of my eye I see him pointing in the general direction of two men beside the laughing girls "… are boyfriends of her classmates. This one, though, is not part of their group. He's crashing their outing, and Miss Rubens wasn't too pleased to see him. At least, the icy glare she sent him gave that impression."

"Hmmm." An amber-colored drink is offered by him and I take it, bringing it to my lips while I take account of the bodies around us. There are two guards on this floor, and they're not employed by the lounge. Big men with subtle earpieces and overly crisp suits, are out of the norm for a place filled with a college-age crowd. "They need to leave."

"By their own free will?"

"Doesn't matter to me." Taking another sip, I let this one settle on my tongue as the heady wooden notes calm me. I could empty my magazine in the arsehole's body, a tempting idea, but Aliana's first impression of me won't be tarnished by his dead body at her feet.

She can meet the demon within another night.

"There's a woman he likes to see— "

"Bring her," I answer without pause and beside me, he's nodding.

"She's already here. Has been for the last fifteen minutes."

"Is she under your employ?"

"No, but we're familiar with each other. This is all her doing."

"And those two?" I point toward the two blokes that don't belong here.

"The bodyguards are with her." *Why the protection to come see this arse?*

The woman in question—a tall, leggy blonde—walks by us, winking at Kray before strutting toward the bar. Her smile is wide, completely fake, as she wraps herself around the git while saying hello to everyone else.

He's pissed, while the smile on Aliana's face holds relief.

"You know what I'm going to ask for. I want everything on them." For a moment, I glance at Kray and find him watching the scene with anger. Jealousy burns in his dark eyes. "Are you okay?"

At six foot five and two hundred and forty pounds, he's a wall, Kray Timmons is an ex-MMA fighter turned private investigator due to his connections with me. I saved his little brother's life; the sixteen-year-old was caught at the wrong place, wrong time, and at the center of a dispute he had no business in.

So instead of taking his stepfather's words and pinning the kid with stealing and selling for his personal gain, I strangled his mother's handler until he confessed. I also let the brothers decide his fate and then made the body disappear.

Kray's loyalty has been infallible since then, and after breaking his leg in his last match a year ago, he became my eyes and ears here. My employee.

Because while Casper is the head of the beast, I'm the body.

A body that strikes to protect.

"Yes." It's a bit terse, but the look I give him is enough for his expression to quickly turn apologetic. He's angry with the woman hugging the arsehole that came to see Aliana. "It's not the first time I've seen him around, and I know one of the rat holes he crawls out from. You'll have it by tomorrow."

However, the scowl is back when he turns to watch them leave. The men in suits move in closer to the pair, and his clenched hands are proof of a history I give no fucks about as long as it doesn't interfere.

"Thank you," I say with a nod before walking toward the bar, my eyes set on her. I'm taking in her smooth tan skin, how the LED lighting bounces off her flesh while highlighting the sinful body she's swaying. There's a drink in her hand while she dances, nearly giggling as the unwanted arse is led away by the woman Timmons knows with the guards a few steps behind.

Who is she to Kray? But more importantly, who is this wanker to Aliana?

A question for another time as those gorgeous eyes meet mine from across the room, and pause. There's surprise in those sweet orbs and a small grin on her lips, but what I find bloody mouthwatering is the hint of pink that quickly blooms across her cheeks.

Her eyes roam my face and then lower, and I like the way they feel. Like a fucking delicious sweep of a finger down my skin, but I break the stare as I pause just beside her on an empty stool. Aliana watches me while the bartender comes over, a man who winks and smiles a little too wide. He's also older than everyone in this place.

"What can I get you?"

"Whiskey on the rocks." At my accent, there's a low gasp from my right. *Do you like accents, love?*

"Any preference?"

"Macallan. Twenty-five if you have it."

"Right away." He turns to grab a glass when the scent of peaches and vanilla infiltrates my senses. It's soft, fresh, and my cock throbs behind the zipper of my trousers. As the man pours my drink, I feel her eyes on me. And it's so motherfucking hard, but I bite back a smirk and instead keep watch through the mirror behind the bar. She's oblivious, and her curiosity in me is honest. "Here you go."

"Thanks, mate." Sliding a fifty across the bar, I turn to leave when I hear her.

"Is it any good?" *Motherfuck*, that sweet little voice is delicious.

I turn toward her. "Yes."

"Seems harsh to me." She shrugs, a small smile curling at the corner of her lips, and I want to lick the gloss off. "Plus, it smells awful."

"Let me guess..." I tilt my head toward the half-empty glass in her hand "...you like your drinks sweet?"

"Don't be judgy." Her glare is playful, and I enjoy the way she leans a little closer. How perky her tits look in the cashmere sweater. "I'm more of a citrus-with-a-hint-of-sweetness kind of girl."

"I'll be sure to keep that in mind."

"You do that."

"Saucy little thing, aren't you?"

She rolls her eyes at that and holds a dainty hand out toward me. "I'm Aliana, by the way."

"Aliana." It leaves me on a low rumble as I taste her name on my tongue. Softly, I grab her hand, moving a little closer before lifting it to my lips. I kiss her knuckles, her middle finger, and then turn it slightly to place my lips at her pulse point. My eyes never leave hers, cataloging every reaction, and I'm pleased by Aliana's soft gasp as her stare becomes slightly hooded. *Good girl.* "A pleasure to meet you, beautiful."

"Are you going to deny me your name?" She doesn't take her hand back. Doesn't chastise me for taking a few liberties. "Or do you want me to play the guessing game?"

"Ali?" One of the women she's with calls her name, but Miss Rubens doesn't acknowledge her past the minute shake of her head. I can feel her friends' stare, their curiosity, but more than that, I love her reluctance to break this little tit for tat. "We're heading to the dance floor. Will you be okay?"

Her concern for Aliana is the only reason I don't dismiss her myself.

"I'm fine. Text you in a bit."

"If you're—"

"I am." A hint of annoyance flashes across her expression, but it's soon replaced by a smirk matching my own. "Go have fun with your boyfriend. I'll be here."

"Okay." The four walk away while I take another sip of my drink, an action the beauty next to me watches, and when her small, pink tongue darts out to lick her bottom lip, I offer her a taste.

"Drink."

"Name first."

I chuckle at her demand, amused by the way her hand goes to her slightly cocked right hip. "Bossy too?"

"I can be," Aliana says, and the serious demeanor she tries to hold on to crumbles as a low giggle follows. "It's about the only thing I learned from my dad that's useful."

There's no missing the hint of animosity in her tone. It's quick, and evaporates the second the words slip past those plump lips.

"I'm sure you've learned a lot more than that."

"And I need you to quit stalling and tell me your name."

"Take a drink, and I will."

"Fine." She tries to take the glass from me, but I shake my head and tip it against her lips. They part, just a small opening, and she take a tiny sip. Not even a third of a shot, but I don't comment as I'm fascinated by the way she savors the warm notes of smoke and dried fruits before swallowing. "That's actually pretty good."

"I know." And because I can't stop my impulses when it comes to this woman, I lick the bloody rim where her lips touched. There's just the slightest bit of saliva there, and I hold back a groan at the small taste. "Perfect amount of heat to sweet with an earthy tone."

"Agreed." Her answer is a bit huskier. Her eyes, which I didn't notice until now, have small flecks of green within those brown orbs and seem a little darker. "It exceeded my expectations."

"One more." Taking a step closer, I offer her the last bit in the glass while leaning down until my lips are just against her ear. There's a shiver that runs through her body, goose bumps rise and spread while a groan reverberates through my chest. Sinful fucking woman. For a second or two, we remain still, just the rise and fall of our chests until I give her what she wants. "My name is Callum Jameson, my Venus. At your service."

Aliana

"YOU'RE LATE." Those are the first words to come out of my father's mouth the moment I enter their formal living room the Saturday after his last visit. No warmth. No asking how I've been since they'd canceled the last family dinner without a single explanation. "Where have you been?"

"In traffic." My reply is just as short, and his lips thin, but before he can respond, my mother walks back into the room with another woman right behind her. My cousin's wife. They're dressed in a similar fashion, conservative black dresses with delicate strands of pearl around their necks. There's also the matching updos, for my mother a tight bun high on her head while the other prefers it at the base. They're the epitome of Stepford wives, and the tray holding two drinks in my mother's hand finishes the ensemble.

Without acknowledging me, she walks over to Dad and hands him his drink. "Dinner will be served soon, dear."

"Thank you, Ada. Please set the table." He demands every meal to be catered to him: cooked, plated, and nearly fed to him.

"Of course. I'll be right back." As she speaks, my cousin's wife, Alicia, makes eye contact with me, and her disdain drips from every pore. I'm dressed in a simple pair of dress pants and a company shirt, having come from a meeting with a potential donor for the Conte House. And while normally Aurora handles these setups, I took over the pet project as it's the class I teach that would benefit the most.

"Do you have something to say, Alicia?"

"No."

"Then please refrain from looking at me in that manner or I'll be enticed to—"

"Why can't you ever act like the young lady I raised you to be?" My mom steps closer to Alicia, almost shielding her, and I chuckle. But what can I expect from her? She's used me as much as my father exploits me. My stealing has procured them both enough money to retire and buy more than one private island, while I don't get a dime. *She's just as guilty.*

A chuckle escapes me while my chest tightens. Not that I'll ever show them. "You raised me?"

"Of course, I—"

"Liars never make it into Heaven."

Her gasp is as fake as the tears that brim in her eyes. "How dare you speak to me like that."

"Because a fact doesn't change no matter how you plan to twist it. It always unfurls."

Alicia's husband, Jorge, walks into the room then. His face is tight, and his eyes are narrowed while the heavy scent of tobacco infiltrates the room. "Prima, watch your mouth or I'll be forced to knock it closed."

"Silence!" My father's sharp tone cuts through my cousin's threat, leaving it hanging mid-air without any weight to it. There's the anger in his eyes that catches me off guard. *Since when do you defend me?* "You don't threaten my daughter, Jorge. Know your place inside my home; you touch her, and I'll return the favor to your wife."

Both he and Alicia tense, faces becoming ashen. My cousin moves closer to her as if to act like a shield. "Uncle, how can you—"

"You don't threaten another man's property."

And there it is.

A word that cuts deep.

Destroys every bit of hope that for once, he'd be there for me.

Breathe in. Breathe out. Just eat and leave. A mantra I play on loop, forcing my emotions to the furthest recess of my mind where my heart can't dominate. Instead, ice fills my veins, and my expression mirrors the emotionless pit I become to survive near these people.

Because they're not my family. Never will be.

"My apologies, Tio. Won't happen again."

"Good." For a few minutes, everyone stands in place, unmoving, unblinking, until my father takes a sip of his drink and waves his hand in the air. The other occupants let out a quick sigh while I remain still; I don't trust them. "Please set the table and have our meal served in twenty minutes."

"Yes, dear," Mom says, voice meek while her hand grips Alicia firmly. As if worried for her. "We'll get to it right away."

They move toward the archways leading out and I follow, but the throat clearing makes me pause. My head turns in his direction, and his amused eyes are focused on me. "Not you."

"Okay." I acquiesce with a neutral expression, knowing what's coming and the small bit of leverage I have at the moment. He needs me, and without my help, they'd never pull off what he hopes to accomplish. "I'll stay, but he leaves."

"You're pushing it today, cousin. You don't have a say—"

Dad holds up a hand, and Jorge stops mid rant. "He'll leave."

"You can't be serious! She's in no position to demand anything."

"Am I not?" I arch a bitch brow and dare him to say something to piss his precious uncle off. *Wimp.* "You also forget I'm his daughter. Ruthlessness runs in our blood."

"Uncle Diego, do you hear her? How can you just sit there and not correct her behavior?"

"Like this." Before my cousin can move back, my father stands to his full height—towers over him while bringing down the not empty tumbler on his face. The sickening crunch is as loud as my gasp; the blood that now pours from the wound on my cousin's nose is disgusting. Dad hits him three times before stepping back, holding out the now-cracked glass for me to take. I do so, moving close and then retaking the few steps separating us quickly, while my father offers Jorge a handkerchief. "That's the last warning for tonight. Go home, son. I make the decisions here, not you, nor do you have any leverage over me. Keep that in mind, and this little incident won't happen again. Understood?"

"Yes."

"Good. Go eat and head home."

Holding the bridge of his nose with the fabric, he turns and does as asked, but not before sending me a hateful glare. His disdain for me is no secret nor is it a sweat off my brow. Jorge looks to my father for approval, wants to be his child, and has tried to one-up me all my life.

He has a seat at the city council.

He has an Ivy league education.

He does as he is told without question.

He's a sexist jerk that follows my father's ideology to a T.

"Take a seat, mi hija." Picking my battles is prudent. I won a small battle against the others, but not the war. So I do; I pick the chair furthest from him and sit with my head held high and shoulders straight. This makes him chuckle. "You are a lot like me. So stubborn."

"And yet, I'm the one risking everything."

"For the family, we all make certain sacrifices." His words pull a scoff from me which he ignores, choosing instead to stand and come sit beside me. "Name your price."

"W-what?"

"What do you want? I won't give you this opportunity again."

"My freedom."

"At the moment, I have to decline that request. You get one more." My stomach sinks; I knew he wouldn't give me the chance to back out. But what truly guts me is the menacing glint in his eyes, the victory smile on his lips. "Especially now that I've been offered something too beneficial in exchange for your hand in marriage."

My world stops.

All sound vanishes for a while. I have no idea how long, but I come back to the chanting of the word *no* over and over again. It's hoarse, so full of despair, and it takes me even longer to realize the person speaking is me.

There's wetness on my cheeks. My breathing is labored.

"Don't do this to me. This isn't the 1800s where women were traded for cattle," I manage to choke out while bringing my hand to my chest. I press down hard as if hoping to squash the sensation there. It's automatic, the distress and pain, and my breathing becomes labored.

"Breathe."

"You can't—"

"Breathe, dammit!" But I can't. Just the thought, thinking that I'd be trapped for the rest of my life—that my plans to move overseas in the next two years would vanish—caused my throat to close up. My body shakes. My vision blurs. "Last warning. Get a hold of yourself."

"Please." That's all I get out as his hand wraps around my throat and squeezes, forcing me from my panic and punching straight into fear. There's a difference in the two, a teetering edge that slams you back into reality where you can breathe but are being blocked not by your nervous system but by a physical presence.

"Calm yourself."

"Dad, stop."

"Are you ready to quit being childish?" My chest burns, the limited air he's allowing only reigniting the panic within me. I'm fighting it, trying to stay alert, but the tighter he holds me, the more it grows. Dad's face comes closer, his eyes staring straight into my wide ones. "I'm willing to listen to your reasoning, but you better have a very compelling reason as to why I shouldn't force this on you. Nod if you understand." I do, minute, but the movement is there. "We can shelve this conversation for now, but we will revisit. I'm only allowing you this respite because I need your head in the game and the artifact in my hands within the next ten days. Now, ask me for a favor, and I'll grant it."

He releases his hold and I cough, bringing a hand up to the tender skin. "What are you allowing?"

This is another way he controls me. I'm told what to ask for, but if I want to get out of the country and never return, I need him to think I'm being complacent. *After this job, I'll disappear. Maybe the Cancio family can hide me.*

"Money or a personal favor."

"Personal favor, then." I don't want his money. My response is immediate, though my tone is scratchy and my chest is still heaving.

"Ask."

"My brothers remain untouchable." Another cough leaves me and he stands, walking toward the water carafe atop the table next to the seat he'd occupied earlier. With the glass in his hand, Dad walks to me and holds it to my lips, urging me to drink. Begrudgingly I do, and with each second that passes, my body further calms. Not fully, but enough to control my panic. "Promise me. Not so much as a blemish on them."

Dad is pensive as he sits back in the chair beside me. He rubs his chin, eyes on mine, but then nods in agreement. "Done, until they turn eighteen or ask to be a part of my office."

They're twelve and fourteen now, which gives me a few years to breathe. That, and they're his golden children. His heirs. Their political careers are already set in stone, while neither care for the limelight.

Once they turn sixteen, I can take them with me.

"Then you have yourself a deal. I'll bring it back."

"I never had a doubt." His chuckle is loud, shakes him a bit. "Now, let's go eat. I'm sure your mother is wondering what's taking so long. She lives for these dinners."

"Can I go home instead? I'm not hungry."

"Sorry, kid." The fake remorse is another slap in the face, but I swallow it back. I just need to get through this and leave. I'll begin planning once I'm home. "Family dinners are sacred, and you know this."

"Of course." With a heavy sigh, I stand and make my way toward the entryway, and I'm almost through it when he speaks again. It's not what I'm expecting and not a single piece of me believes him, but the man knows how to hit low.

"Aliana, you might not believe me, but I do love you. You are my daughter."

"I know you do, in a very self-serving way," I whisper under my breath. Tears brim my eyes, but I blink them away before looking back from over my shoulder. "You just love money and power more."

PRESENT...

I'M FROZEN. Unable to so much as blink while he pulls back to stand at his full height.

Christ, out of all the men to flirt with. This isn't good.

Because I know him. Know men like him and those that he surrounds himself with.

Just like my father, Aurora's father, and plenty of other power-hungry jerks who step on others while maintaining full control of everyone and everything around them.

And yet, I'm not scared. I should be, but the feelings he's bringing to life are anything but. It also doesn't help that I've been drinking since leaving my parent's house after a disastrous dinner. I've been here for a while—after being home just long enough to shower/change and call two friends to meet me here. This now my personal area, rented by me with no plans of calling it a night any time soon.

My inhibitions are low. My desire to control any aspect of my life is a wrecking-ball-sized force I'm not willing to subdue tonight.

Not after being pushed into a panic attack.

Not after being choked into complacency.

But instead of pulling away, I take a step closer. I also find my fingers curling in the material of his shirt, stretching it, and all the while he watches with an expression that makes my cheeks heat up while he blindly places his glass on the bar top behind us.

It's want and amusement with just the right amount of cockiness.

This isn't an average man; I should leave.

My father would kill me if he knew I was here flirting with this man, the second-in-command to a family that has transatlantic criminal ties from here to London.

This I know for a fact. Because there's a fundamental survival instinct that a lot of people forfeit in their ignorant bliss, yet I don't.

I watch. I listen. I remember.

I want to lick each tattoo, starting from his neck and moving lower.

The blush spreads, skin tingling from my face to the top of my breasts.

He's dangerous. Turn around and go.

However, a low whimper escapes me instead when Callum cups my cheek with a gentle squeeze, his touch lighting me from within. "You are truly beautiful."

His accent alone incinerates any reason I have to leave.

His tone, that gravelly cadence, makes my thighs clench while the lace material covering my mound clings to my labia.

Dios mio, he's got trouble written all over him.

"Thank you," I say, voice low as unpleasant thoughts drifts across my processors: I'm a pickup. Just another woman in a bar with a random stranger, and I need to view it as he does. Like two people meeting and having fun. Nothing more. Nothing less. And yet, as I'm busy tracing a circle around his stomach, ignoring the way the muscles there clench while pursing my lips, I feel bothered by the thought. *Why does it taste so bitter? What is wrong with me?* "Now, is that the best pick-up line you have?"

Why am I even asking him this? He does not matter.

We will never be anything past what I'm allowing tonight.

Better yet, how strong were those drinks? Did Lynne order an extra shot for each?

CALLUM

I CAN ALMOST make out the thoughts swirling in her pretty little head. Her expressions are honest and open while being tinged with a heady hint of anger.

And the latter is something I find attractive on her.

It brings out a bit of the dormant claws I wish to feel break my skin. The sign of each aggressive thought is there in her body language. How she stiffens, pulls herself subconsciously a little closer while gripping—digging the blunt fingernails into my abdomen—while her lips curl up a little around the corner.

Bloody adorable.

Then, she ruins me when they turn into a pout.

She's Venus in human form. Perfection.

"Fucking delicious," I mutter low, not that she hears me either way. Aliana's thoughts are yo-yoing back and forth, at war with each other, but it's her fear of *what they would say* that is of no importance to me.

Fuck her father. Fuck what anyone thinks.

All I need is her smile and to watch that mouth wrap around my cock, and in that order. The rest we can figure out because this pull between us—the way my entire being is held captive by her—is something I won't deny myself.

I want all of her. Every bloody inch.

Because every part of this short, full-of-sass beauty calls to the part of me that's more beast than human. I'm a man who thirsts for blood, who tortures those who have done me or mine wrong, and that protective instinct is burning me alive with her proximity.

She has no idea of the target I'm placing on her head. Of the claim, but she will.

"Not even close, Miss."

"So that was—" Aliana's eyes narrow while releasing my dress shirt as if to step back, but I lay my hand over hers, trapping it there.

"Stop."

"Listen, Callum..." she begins and then trails off.

The way she says my name. *Motherfuck.*

A heated hiss escapes me, my entire body coiling tight in pleasure, and I bite down on my bottom lip to not scare her. There's a rumbling building in my chest, a growl I'm fighting back, but the now heavy-lidded eyes staring at me are my undoing.

"Say it again." Not a question, but a demand through gritted teeth. My need is too overwhelming to ask nicely.

"Say what?" *Lord help this girl because once I have her...* Especially with the way those dark eyes are watching me, a dangerous gaze that caresses my skin. She looks down, stopping at my Adam's apple, and licks her bottom lip with a slow sweep. Lower, and she bites the plump flesh while admiring my chest, belt, and then the thick bulge in my trousers.

Her gaze stops there, and a soft gasp escapes.

I flex behind the zipper of my trousers, fucking painful jerks as pre-come dribbles from the tip, staining my pants. An action she sees, and again her thighs move, clench for me.

Fucking temptress.

But before she can further test my control, I grip her waist and lift, holding her against me for a few seconds. Chest to chest. Her lips are a few centimeters from my own; my need to taste them is near perverse, but I don't. Not yet. Instead, I sit her down on the barstool I watched her occupy a short while ago.

Automatically her thighs spread for me, the fingers in my dress shirt tugging me closer. I step between them without pause, forcing them wider so my hips are cradled just an inch or two from her wetness.

I feel her heat through my trousers, though.

I have the perfect view of that sinful skirt pushed up, exposing the gusset of her underwear with the plump flesh of her pussy spilling out of the sides. There's a little bit of sheen on her flesh, her wetness, and I throw my head back with a groan.

This woman was made to tempt me. Chest expanding, I take in a deep breath and let it out slowly. Then again, and again, but nothing calms me. Instead, I'm lit with an unsatiated desire to lay Heaven down at her dainty feet before the demon inside breaks her apart with pleasure.

"Christ." Aliana's call for divine help is almost amusing. *Almost,* because no deity or man could pull me away, and as my eyes meet hers again a second later, I think that sinks in for her. I don't need to voice it. Not with the hunger in my eyes, nor the way my hands shake while tightening my hold on her hips. "Are you okay?"

Am I? Not in the motherfucking slightest.

My control is slipping, but I'm not questioning it.

"Say my name," I utter instead of answering her. Her chest rises, a slow, shuddering breath leaving her, and there's a low mumble of *fuck me* she thinks I don't hear but I do. For a few seconds, Aliana doesn't say anything. Her eyes are on mine, and the longer they meet, hers darken, the dark brown with hints of green disappear and eyelids drop to watch me from beneath long lashes. She's attracted to me, and it fills me with heat. Excitement. A want for more that's foreign. "Say. It."

"Callum," Aliana whispers, those supple lips molding over each letter, and I shiver—slam my body against hers while a hand moves to her back protectively. And having her like this, nearly wrapped around me, cements that need to not let go. "Callum, maybe we should—"

I cut her off with a soft, chaste kiss to her mouth. It's quick, but enough to pull a harsh flex of my hips against her heat. Her moan is low but throaty, and every molecule in my body throbs for her. Right fucking there; I feel her heat, a bit of wetness, and I want more.

To fuck and take and gorge, but not here.

A final thrust is all I give myself before pulling back, gripping her hand in mine before yanking her from the stool. Aliana stumbles right into me, a small yelp escaping before I have her turned around and facing the crowded lounge with her back to my front. No space between us as I pull the hem of her skirt back to cover what is mine. My lips are at the crown of her head.

"Will you do me the honor of a dance, love?" I say low, leaving a trail of kisses until I reach her temple. There I pause and breathe her in, pulling the sweet fragrance of peaches into my lungs. This calms me—I'm hard as fuck—while it ignites a fire at the same time. "I'll be on my best behavior *tonight*. Promise."

"What if that isn't what I want?" She's watching her friends dance not far from us. They're laughing, not an ounce of coordination between them, and oblivious to our observation. They forgot about her the moment whatever rapid-hand-movement-meets-booty-dropping routine they learned on a social media app began. "What if, for the first time in my life, I want to forget and be me?"

Be me.

Two words, and they stop me dead.

Be me.

Be me.

"You can always be yourself with me." *Something is dodgy.* The more the words turn in my mind, the more bloody scenarios become conclusions, and they all have to do with her father. Has he abused her? Or anyone in her family, for that matter?

I'd fucking skin them alive and feed them to my pet a piece at a time.

From what I can see, she doesn't have marks on her, but that means jack shit when things can be hidden underneath makeup or clothing. My hands twitch on her hips, the urge to strip her bare and check every inch is unbearable, but I grit my teeth and walk us toward the dancing crowd.

The music tonight is a mixture of the island beats with heavy bass, and I wrap an arm around her midsection, pulling her in closer. She's short even with heels on, and my cock nestles just above the curve of her arse, so I lift her off the ground and settle myself where I belong.

Her body is my home.

Motherfuck, I feel it deep within.

It's been there since I found myself entranced by a simple video, enamored by the mere sight of her.

A rightness that makes no sense and that I'm powerless to stop. *What is it about you that makes me want to bring the world to its knees in worship of you?*

More so when her hips begin to grind against me.

Aliana doesn't complain about being manhandled or how hard I am behind her. Instead, she works those thick hips harder. Even in my tight hold, she manages to massage my cock behind the zipper of my trousers for the next thirty minutes. Not once did she step away from me or demand to be put down.

She feels good. Too good.

One song flows into another, a dancehall rhythm taking over the crowd, and the girl in my arms loses all inhibitions. Back arching, she circles her hips, winding slowly with a little bounce against my thick length.

Had we been sitting down, she'd be riding my cock.

This little move is one I'll revisit. Bare. Sweaty. No barriers.

"You're playing a dangerous game tonight, Miss Rubens," I hiss between clenched teeth when her arms wrap around my neck and she fists the hair at the back of my head. She tugs and I feel it down to my balls, holding me prisoner to her every breath.

But then she stops.

Her hips cease all movement.

Craning her head back to look at me, she arches a brow. A little apprehension in her expression. "How do you know my last name? I didn't tell you."

Lowering my lips to her forehead, I kiss her there. "I know everything about you, love. You can thank my cousin for that."

"But why?"

"Because I'm very attracted to you." *Can't get you out of my head.*

"We just met." Aliana's eyebrows furrow in the most adorable way while a pout forms across that tempting mouth when I place her back on her feet. She doesn't like it and neither do I, but this is a conversation that is best had in private. "Where are we going?"

"I'm taking you home."

"Who says I want to go to your house?" Cheeky little thing.

"Never claimed you did." I nuzzle her temple. *Smells so sweet.* "That's why I'm driving to yours."

"How?" Aliana's fucking adorable as she rambles question after question. I also don't miss the fact she never said no.

My smirk turns cocky when I look back at her. I'm walking us toward the elevator, her small hand in my rough one. "With my car."

"Smartass." Smacking my arm, she rolls her eyes but keeps up. I'm gauging her body language, and so far she's at ease, making this easier than I expected. "I meant you don't know where I live. How can you take me home?"

"Because a Jameson always does his homework."

"What does that even mean, Callum?"

"Let me get you home, and I promise to explain." With a tug, I'm looking at her again after pressing the down button. "Any objection?"

"I shouldn't trust you."

"No, you shouldn't. And that's something we'll discuss after."

"Then why do I feel so comfortable with you?" The vulnerability in those words causes my heart to squeeze. "I'm not scared when you sound like a stalker."

"That's because I'd never hurt you. I can't." The door dings and I release her hand, stepping inside while giving her a choice. To choose to come with me. Warm brown eyes flicker between me and the crowd behind her then back again, before taking my offering. Soft, warm skin skims my palm while small fingers entwine with mine; one small pull, and she's in front of me as the doors close.

I press the ground button and she moves back, leaning against the wall, our hands disconnecting. Not liking the separation, I take my position in front of her while those plump lips spread into a sweet, wide smile. "You gave me a choice."

Not what I'm expecting, and I frown. "Of course, I did. You wouldn't have gotten far—want you too much—but I'd gain your trust and then all of you."

"Good answer," she says before fisting my shirt's collar and pulling my lips down to hers.

She ruined me since the first contact. With the tease of her desperation to feel me.

Her fate is now intertwined with mine.

There's no bloody going back.

Aliana

I T'S IMPULSIVE, AND crazy, and God knows I'm being irresponsible, but I had to. He gave me the one thing that no one ever does: a choice. The human right to pick and accept versus being given an ultimatum with the venom lacing of a threat.

I'm in charge of my time.

Of what I do.

"Fuck." It's a rumbled groan that rises from deep within his chest and vibrates against my mouth in the most erotic way. It's sinful, feels so good, and I can't stop myself from flicking his top lip and then bottom with the tip of my tongue.

They're so soft. Plump.

"Callum." It leaves me on a whimper he swallows, his tongue slipping inside my mouth to caress mine. Soft, then ardent, and then the way he's kissing me can only be described as famished. A hunger that matches my own, lit up like a match and I'm pushed back, his body caging me in.

One hand cups my face while the palm of the other slams against the metal wall, the sound of his raw hunger causing my pussy to clench. This kiss is everything you read about in books; a soul-destroying moment that exposes a weakness you didn't have before.

This is bad. So irresponsible.

A little voice says in the back of my head, and yet, I can't pull away. Just can't.

I'm not someone who sleeps around, much less right after meeting a man, but he makes me want to break every rule. To live. To be free.

"So sweet. Too good for me," he groans, right hand tilting my head slightly to his liking—angling me—before deepening the kiss. This is so much more and everything all at once. There's no fighting for dominance; Callum takes while I'm powerless against him—his touch—and holding on while I'm devoured like the sweetest treat.

Each groan pulls a shiver. Each curse is a rush of wetness where my need for him grows with every passing second.

Behind us, I hear the elevator ping and then its doors open, yet it's the throat clearing that brings us into the present.

"We should go." I'm boneless. Breathing hard. Helplessly watching his Adam's apple bob; the large dragon wrapped around his throat mesmerizes me with its haunting beauty. The style is beautiful; heavy on the black and grey, but it's the hints of color that create a striking piece.

Much like the ones lower. Ones, I hunger to discover.

"I know." Callum pecks me again, dragging his teeth over my bottom lip before turning around to glare at the person interrupting. "Move."

His tone is hard, a warning hiss for an impending strike if the person doesn't follow his demand. The two men, no older than twenty-five, do so quickly, shooting each other nervous looks while I'm being pulled out.

Not that Callum pays them any attention; instead, he's on his phone. "I'm exiting," is all he says before hanging up. The doorman sees us coming and quickly holds open the door, bidding us a good night right before we step through.

"You as well," we answer in unison, and I can't help but giggle. This night has been one giant rollercoaster, and I feel like a hot mess, but I can't deny that he makes me feel alive. That the sour mood I'd been in earlier tonight—the hopelessness I've been fighting—isn't heavy anymore. It's just not there.

Instead, I feel light and carefree.

I'm a woman making her own decisions no matter how dangerous they are.

A sleek sports car stops in front of us before we make it to the curb and a man steps out, tossing the keys at Callum. "I'll be off to the airport."

"See you soon." That's the extent of their conversation before I'm being picked up and placed inside of the car as if I were a doll. And once again, I don't protest his manhandling. *Why don't I protest this?* His large hand grips my seatbelt and buckles me in, and the clench of my thighs is answer enough.

This is sexy. I'm attracted to this behavior.

Attracted to what he's making me feel and what he represents: the ultimate flip-off to my family.

Or maybe, this is all because of him. A man with a bad reputation that's well deserved, yet with me is attentive. Almost soft. Contradictory.

I feel powerful next to him.

"You okay there, love? Need anything?" My face turns toward the driver's side where Callum is already behind the wheel and looking at me with a gentle smile. "I'll even make an exception and pick up some takeaway for you if you'd like."

"Takeaway? Exception?" I ask even though I know what he means. It's his reaction that I'm after, and I bite back a grin at the way his nose scrunches up. "Don't like greasy food and tasty calories?" Callum shudders, and it's the cutest thing. His disgust is clear to see and this time I can't fight my mirth, letting out a giggle. "Mr. Jameson, are you a food snob? Is that it?"

"Takeaway is how we say fast food, Miss Rubens." His mock glare only serves to amuse me further. "And to answer the latter, no. Not a food snob per se."

"Then?"

"I'm used to cooking all my meals, outside of family gatherings or businesses we own." His honesty is a bit unnerving, but I get it. In his life, trust is something not given freely. "But I'd make an exception for you. No questions asked."

Again, he gives me a choice. Placing my hand atop of his on the gear shift, I give it a small squeeze and leave it there. "Not needed, but thank you."

"Never thank me for trying to please you."

Those words hang heavy in the air, filling me with a sense of ease that thrills me. I'm comfortable with him, although it makes no sense.

I shouldn't be.

He's the kind of man I avoid.

Like Santis.

Like Giannis Martin tonight. He showed up without being invited—after I turned down his offer to go on a date two days ago—as if I was there for him. He's like all the others in my life; pushy, meddlesome, and thinks he knows what's best for me without asking for my input on my wants or needs.

An idiot I, unfortunately, see at school while moving from class to class and sometimes when I'm forced to play the dutiful daughter at events where family presence is necessary for my father's political career. He's the son of a lobbyist—my father knows his family—and is as self-right-eous as our fathers.

My parents approve of his interest, while I say no…

Find you a suitable husband.

A suitable husband.

Dad couldn't be talking about him?

No. Just no. I'd rather—

"What's wrong?" Callum's voice cuts through my thoughts, his warm fingers now intertwined with mine. They're warm, a little rough but soothing at the same time. "You seemed upset."

"I'm okay," I say, but he doesn't buy it. It's there in the tick of his jaw and furrow of his brows. "Just thinking about some family drama. Promise, nothing exciting."

He wouldn't care either way; this is a one-time thing. However, ruining the mood—these calm yet thrilling butterflies that have overtaken me since our eyes met—is unacceptable to my peace of mind.

"Are you sure?"

"Yes." Then I remember something else and I'm smiling, leaning a little closer as if to whisper a secret. "But your family dynamic is one I'm curious about. How do you know me?"

"My cousin." Our fingers flex, shifting the car into another gear. He switches lanes, driving around a five-mile-below-the-speed-limit van and punches the accelerator. The action pushes me back into my seat, adrenaline spiking as the city lights become a blur. *Did he hit 90?* "Relax. I've never been in an accident."

"Have you ever heard of cops? They'll pull you over and—"

"You're bloody sinful when you care."

"I don't."

My response is quick, earning me a throaty chuckle that ends in a smirk. He hit me with a twofer. "Of course, but to assuage you, we won't be pulled over."

"Why are you so sure?"

"It's a secret, love." I'm trying not to get excited over the term. Brits use it all the time and so do a lot of other countries, but I can't stop the way my heart rate picks up.

"That's not going to work here."

"No?" Callum asks, turning onto the expressway. "Care to elaborate?"

Slick bastard. "What does your cousin have to do with me? You're the first Jameson I've met, and you've now mentioned him twice."

"You know who I am." Not a question, and I nod. From my reaction when he told me his name, he knows I knew. There are a few families that span the globe who are notorious, and being the friend of a mafia princess —no matter how much Aurora hates it—does come with perks. As does being the daughter of a state governor; you know who to avoid at all costs. "How informed are you?"

"I'm a governor's daughter. It's drilled into my head to stay away from criminals, and your family does business here." It's not meant to be an insult, just the truth, and he nods for me to continue while that dangerous smirk remains in place. "Should your name not be on that list?"

"It belongs at the top."

"But that doesn't explain much."

"It does when my cousin is close to your best friend."

"Aurora?"

"Yes." The next exit is mine, and he gets off, driving straight before making a left, then a right. We're less than three minutes away. "They met in London."

"That little hoochie! He's who has her flustered and with her head in the clouds?"

"Casper would enjoy knowing that."

"But you won't spill."

"Is that so?" he says, brow raised and head tilted to the side. "How can you be so sure I won't tell?"

"Do you want to lose my trust?" The words are out of my mouth before I realize. I'm not even sure why I phrased it that way, but the sudden seriousness in his expression makes me pause. There's a hidden emotion there that I can't decipher, almost as if my words hit him deep, but instead of voicing his thoughts, he just pulls up in front of my little driveway. Shifting the gear shift to park, he lets the engine idle while his body turns toward mine. Well, as much as the car allows.

The man is the literal definition of tall, has a dark aura with dirty blond hair and eyes the color of a gem. A mixture of green with a hint of light blue. He's dangerous and exciting and maybe some regret if you let him break your heart.

One time. No emotions.

"I'd never do anything to make you not trust me. You have my word."

"Can I shoot you if you do?"

Jesus, help me. He grins this time, no cockiness, and his eyes crinkle just a bit at the corners. So boyish. "I'd let you empty an entire clip in me."

Those words don't sit well with me. No part of me wishes him harm.

"Don't say things like that."

"Why?"

"Just don't." For some reason, my heart clenches at just the mere thought. "Not again."

"Okay." Bringing a large hand to my face, he cups my jaw and slides his thumb over the edge of my mouth. "And I promise to keep my lips sealed."

"For now..."

"Until you say I can give him shit over it."

"Thank you." Then, because I can't help myself, I push his hand away just so I can smack his arm in excitement. This little nugget of gossip is too good. *I'm going to mess with her.* "Can't believe Roe's been hiding this from me. She's going to regret not telling me."

"Why?" His mirth is clear.

"Because I'm going to pick at it." Shrugging nonchalantly, I unbuckle myself as does he. "I'm going to annoy her with the sex-fest they had since she's keeping her lips sealed about the man's identity. Don't worry, I won't divulge what I know, but I will be pesky about it."

"Aurora must have her reasons."

"And I have mine." Turning in my seat to match his stare, I go back to being serious. Arms crossed over my chest, I narrow my eyes. "Which brings us back to how you know so much about me, Mr. Jameson? You know my name, address, and I don't believe in coincidences. You knew I was there tonight."

"I did." No shame or denying. "But I've already answered your question. I found you through Casper."

"I'm going to need a little more of an explanation here."

"We have eyes and ears in the states, and you just so happened to be in the frame when Casper was checking in on her."

"He's having her followed?"

"Protected."

"That's an invasion of—"

"His mother was killed while out shopping not long ago, Aliana." For a second, his voice breaks and the fresh pain is written across his expression. So unguarded. Open. Not at all what I am used to from the males in my family. "This is protocol, Venus. Everyone is guarded."

And it's that palpable sadness that stops whatever rebuttal sat on my tongue. I'm also not going to question the nickname.

"Okay."

He snorts. "That easy?"

"Not really, but it's been a long day and I would rather not end it in an argument."

"Noted." Unbuckling his seatbelt, Callum exits and rounds the car, stopping at my door. He's fast to open it, holding a hand out for me to take.

Which I do, letting his warm fingers pull me out and walk me up the stairs to the front door.

Stepping past him once we reach the entrance, I reach for my keys when a hand on my arm stops me. His touch is gentle yet firm, and then I'm being turned into his chest with one soft yank. I don't stumble. I give in, and when his lips slam into mine once again tonight, the low moan that escapes me is full of need.

They are firm and plush, and there's a hint of the drink he'd been sipping on; a heady concoction that I want more of and I take it, angling my head a bit, I return the kiss hungrily. A little sloppy with nips across his entire mouth before intertwining his tongue with mine.

My body feels as if struck by electricity.

My core clenches.

And I whine pathetically when he pulls back only to peck my chin, cheek, and lastly my forehead.

"Before you head inside, I need you to know this isn't a game for me."

"Uh huh." Breathing hard, I lick my bottom lip to catch a little bit of his saliva there. "Sure."

"I'll be back in the morning. Be ready by nine."

"If you say so."

"Bloody adorable." Callum's right hand grabs the back of my neck, his forehead pressing against my own. "I'm trying to behave here, Miss Rubens. Get inside, lock the door, and be ready for me at nine. We have a date."

"A date?" I ask, my mind still foggy from his kiss. His touch. His everything.

"Yes." Then his warmth is gone, and I'm left wanting it back. He's watching, waiting, and once my racing heart calms, I step inside my home and don't look back. *Why didn't he come inside? Did I misread things?*

Because he can't be serious.

We're not going on a date.

A thought that bothers me as I change clothes, brush my teeth, and then settle beneath my covers. Was I a game to him? Or worse, does he know my father?

"I can't see him again." *He'd ruin my plans to leave.*

CALLUM

I'VE BEEN THROBBING since I left her on that unworthy doorstep. Hard. Skin taut. Balls heavy and nothing will appease my hunger until she's pinned beneath me.

It's why after four hours of restless sleep, of imagining those pouty lips wrapped around my girth, sucking me in deep, that I made plans and got dressed. I promised a date and I will deliver, but while she sleeps, I watch her door while intermittently reading the notes Kray had on Giannis Martin and his connections to Aliana.

Most of it was rubbish. Things that I already knew, but I am intrigued by a pattern of unaccounted disappearances a few times a week. Same days. No deviation on the hours.

I also take account of Kray's neglect to add the woman Giannis left with inside this docket.

Which leaves me with two bloody conclusions…

"He's either being protective or she's covering her tracks." Which one doesn't matter. Before I get on a plane to London, he will atone for this oversight.

For now, I send Ezra an email with what I have on Giannis and ask him to cross check and then return my focus to the neighborhood's occupants. To each of Aliana's neighbors: an old lady three doors down, a couple to her right, a group of college kids, an empty townhouse, and then a man across the street who only comes and never stays longer than one night here and there.

No rhyme or reason.

No frontal picture of his face, as if he knows where the cameras are and avoids those angles.

But it's enough for me to deduce that the owner knows her. There's no other reason as to why someone would buy an expensive home under a fake alias and corporation as proof of income unless you're hiding your tracks. There's only a handful of criminals in this city worth a shit, and they all stay far away from the Jameson hold or Asher's nose.

Could one of them be bold enough to make this move and try pushing their product? Yes.

Has anything been attempted since they purchased this property? No.

Which leaves me to think someone is spying on her. But who, though?

An ex.

A family member.

Someone that shows up unannounced to an outing.

There's a vibration coming from my mobile alerting me to a text. Picking it up, I swipe my thumb across the screen.

> I'm a few feet from your vehicle with the breakfast you requested. ~Kray

Tossing my mobile aside, I exit a few seconds later and watch the large man carrying my breakfast approach. In his hands is a bag with baked goods and a tray with a cuppa for me, and whatever sweet concoction with a dash of coffee Aliana drinks. They're from a place near her school that she likes, a local bakery, and I know the gesture will be appreciated. I'm not hiding anything from her. She'll know I pulled a background check and that every single moment cataloged from her birth to the current date is accessible to me.

"You know, Jameson. This isn't in my job description," Kray says while I place the items on the roof of my rental. "I'm not a gopher."

"Yet you offered this morning, mate." Grabbing my cup, I take a sip of the breakfast tea: no sugar, splash of milk. My eyes are already back on her door from the driveway of my recently purchased empty townhome next to hers. Because money talks, walks, and has everyone bending over to take it up the arse if enough zeroes are attached. This purchase took me less time to accomplish than ordering at a restaurant. "Uber Eats would've worked just fine."

"So unappreciative, Jameson," he snorts, but then his amusement dies. "I don't think you'll like what I found, by the way. There's more to this than what I thought."

"So, the missing information I requested was a mistake?"

"I need a few more days for her. Please."

"Are you asking me as a mate or as the person paying you to do this?" He's quick to try and answer, but I shake my head causing him to pause. "Think before you speak, Timmons. One is a favor, the other an admittance to neglect and I'm giving you the option here to save your own arse."

"As my friend, Callum," Kray says the moment I'm done. No hesitation. "She's not a threat, I promise. We have history."

"Three days."

"Thank you."

"Your loyalty thus far has earned you the benefit of the doubt, don't disappoint me." That's the only warning I'll give him, and he knows it. If Aliana's hurt due to his idiocy, I'll kill them both. The threat hangs heavy in the air, yet he places a hand over his heart in acceptance of my terms. "Now, what did you find? Is it about the property with the phantom owner behind me?"

"Yes."

"Well?"

"Last night I pulled a few strings and traced the dummy company back to its owner, and you know him." My reply is a wave of the hand for him to keep going. I have a woman to wake up and feed. "It's Malcolm Asher."

Interesting, yet I'm not buying it. Something reeks of rubbish in this equation.

"Do you have the paperwork with you?"

"Yes."

"And you're sure he's the owner?"

"Not one bit."

My eyes leave her door and focus on him. The bloke's never lied to me yet. "What are your suspicions?"

"Someone's using his name to cover up whatever they're up to."

"Agreed." I scratch my jaw, my mind running through possibilities, planning how to rid Aliana of this arsehole that's too close for comfort. Either you're here for her, or you can involve her in the *wrong place, wrong time* scenario, which I don't appreciate. "A dead man walking."

"How deep do I go?"

"Until I have a name. No matter the cost."

Kray nods, mobile in hand as he shoots off a series of texts. "I'll have everything I find to you by tonight. No excuses."

"Good." The alarm on my mobile goes off then: it's ten a.m. and Miss Rubens needs a reminder to get dressed. I've already let her sleep an extra hour. "Expect a call from me."

"WHERE ARE WE GOING AGAIN?" Aliana asks from beside me between sips of my cuppa—the same cup of tea she teased me about since I didn't make it myself. *Such a bratty little thing.* More so when she just called me a pampered punk after I explained that a guard inspected our order.

Miss Rubens is the only person walking this earth that could get away with calling me that.

I'd shoot my own father if he'd made the same joke. Casper too.

But with her, I laugh and let it go. Love it, actually. The temptation. The foreplay.

I also let her steal my drink after she finished her sugar rush in a cup before walking out the door. The sinful little number she's wearing today had a lot to do with that decision.

A white bodysuit with a plunging neckline, and a pair of jeans that accentuate her hips and arse, while on her feet she has on a pair of nude wedge sandals. Her body is on full display, each bloody curve highlighted while my eyes keep coming back to the two little beads poking through her top. She isn't wearing a bra; her perky tits tempt me to nip each peak as they bounce in time with the car.

With each dip in the road, they strain against the cotton keeping them from me.

Each time I press the brake, a little more skin comes into view.

Motherfucking goddess of seduction.

"You'll know when we get there, sweetheart. Be patient."

"Patience is overrated." Her huff is cute, as is the way she licks her bottom lip to catch a drop of tea. "Besides, what if I'm underdressed? Or I'm wearing the wrong kind of shoes?"

"I wouldn't let you be uncomfortable, Miss Rubens. I'm prepared for all situations." It's the third time today I've said those words, the first time being seconds after she opened the door in nothing but a tank top and sleep shorts, looking rumpled and warm.

"Whatever it is, I'm not buying, nor do I care about saving the world at this time of day. Please come back during my non-sleep and on non-weekend hours."

"Good morning to you too, love." At my greeting, her head snapped up and a second later the door was slammed in my face. From inside, I could hear her grumbling and a few noises that made no sense, but I still found so attractive. What are you doing to me, Venus? *"Open the door, Aliana. We're going to be late, and I brought food."*

"Food?" she asks, voice low. Almost too low to hear, but I catch it and bite back a chuckle. I've never felt so relaxed around someone before. Not like this. *"Does the order come with any form of caffeine?"*

"It might."

"I need a yes or no answer, Mr. Jameson."

"You'll have to open the door and see for yourself, Miss Rubens."

"Not really." From the other side of the door, there's a snicker and even that sound makes my cock twitch. *"That's what peepholes and my Ring camera are for."*

"True. You could..."

"Why is there a but *in that pause?"*

"Because it's on you if the drink which you desire turns cold." I've never seen someone open a door so fast. A second later, she was tapping her small foot and holding a hand out with an expectant face. "Good morning, Miss Rubens. Ready to try this again?"

"My coffee, please."

"So polite." There's a flash of annoyance in her eyes, but that's dashed the second I hand over her cup and the bag of baked goods. Then, she's all smiles and stepping aside so I can enter while she swallows half the contents in the cup in one go. "I'll close the door."

"Sure," she says, but her attention is on the bag as she pulls out an orange and cranberry scone. For a few minutes, Aliana just looks at it before lifting her eyes to mine. "How did you know?"

"I have my ways."

"You were serious, weren't you? You've been watching me?"

"Yes, on both accounts." Closing the distance between us, I step beside her at the breakfast bar. "So eat, take a shower, and dress however you see fit. I'm taking you out, and there's no getting out of it."

"Who says?" The question loses all merit when a small smile curls at the edge of her lips.

"Me."

"Me who?"

"The man your mother warned you to avoid at all costs."

"We're here," I say, turning off the ignition after parking in the designated spot. It's an undisclosed building about a fifty-minute drive from Aliana's home; it's all red brick with one large glass door and the letter R above it in bright white neon. There's no one outside and only a car at the furthest end occupies the lot, but I send a quick text ahead of exiting. "Ready?"

"Is this where you kill people?" she asks as soon as I open her door, extending a hand for her to take. *Christ. This woman amuses me.* Aliana undoes her seatbelt and grabs my hand, letting me tug her out while looking around and seeing how isolated we are. The area we're in is affluent, private, and holds a business or two with a morally grey clientele. This building in particular is owned by a chef and is a private test kitchen, and he's been gracious enough to host us for a minimal fee. "Because if that's the case, I'm out. I've watched way too many CSI shows and know that buildings like this, isolated and empty, scream danger."

And yet, she walks beside me. There's a bit of trust there.

"First rule…" throwing an arm over her shoulders, I tug her with me to the boot of the car "… never believe your kidnapper or the person assaulting you. They'd never tell you the truth."

Not that I'm going to let anyone get close enough.

I'm going to enjoy dismembering anyone who touches a hair on her head.

My eyes go to the side of her neck on the left where a finger-sized bruise sits just below her ear, and I breathe in deeply and fight to find my calm and not demand answers—a name to engrave on the bullet they'll meet soon enough. *I will find out. They will pay in blood.*

But I don't voice my vow, dry swallowing the building ire at its sight. This is our first date, and I won't ruin it.

Then, there are her words about being free and having a choice. Her appreciation of me considering her wants or needs.

All this is starting to paint a picture full of utter shit I don't like, one I need to verify before I make her bury someone she cares for by mistake.

"So what do you suggest, then?"

"I'm going to give you one of my guns and teach you how to shoot. I never want you to be defenseless."

"Really?" The excitement in her voice is endearing. "I've always wanted to learn, but my father's a bit chauvinistic in that regard."

"I'm not him." Unlocking the trunk, I grab a zip-up hoodie and close it.

"I see that." Aliana clears her throat, looking down at my hand holding the sweatshirt. "Are you cold?"

"No, love." Bringing my lips to just below her ear, I kiss the fragrant skin there, exhaling roughly when she rewards me with a sweet sigh. "This is just in case you get cold in there. We'll be here a while, and I want you to be comfortable."

"What is in there?"

"Our first date." Goose bumps rise, a shiver of sensitivity across her processors when I nip her neck. I pull Aliana closer, walk toward the entrance with her body nestled against mine.

There's a man standing there now; he's in a chef's jacket and greeting us with a polite smile. "Welcome to Casa de Reyes, Mr. Jameson. We're delighted to have you both with us today."

"Holy shit." Aliana's whispered curse makes me laugh, while the chef and owner of this place bites the inside of his cheek to hold his own amusement in. "You brought me here to—"

"Yes, sweet girl. Today we will learn how to cook paella."

Aliana

I'M IN SHOCK.

Happy.

Swooning a little bit.

Just a smidge, but there's no stopping my reactions—the way my heart palpitates and body vibrates with excitement—with this surprise. It's sweet and thoughtful, and Lord help me, I'm wanting to throw myself at him and kiss those lips that are spread into a boyish grin.

He knows he did good. *He makes me forget the ugly. He makes me feel safe.*

I know I shouldn't be here. That he's the type of man—powerful like my father—I told myself I'd never so much as entertain, but I'm being pulled in by an uncontrollable hurricane and stepping away feels unnatural. Every instinct in my body, my heart and mind, agree that he's the epitome of danger, yet so much more beneath the expensive clothes and the gun he's not concealing in his car.

What is it about you, Callum? Why can't I say no?

Maybe it's because there's something special about someone taking the time to see you. To know your likes and dislikes—even if I know he's pulled information on me, I'm still touched. Being of Spaniard heritage is the only thing I have in common with my family on my father's side. They originally came to the US from the Northern area of Menorca. Fornells is a beautiful fishing village known for its lobster stew and glorious sunsets; I'd been a few times as a kid while my grandparents were alive, but now my father would rather focus on being seen in extravagant places—another social media attention-grabbing photo—than going to visit his parent's grave.

I'm proud of where my family is from.

Turning, I move to stand in front of him and rise to the tips of my toes. "This is very thoughtful, Mr. Jameson." My arms go around his neck, pulling him down just enough that I reach his chin with my lips. I breathe in his masculine scent: earthy and natural with just a hint of spice that most cedar-based colognes carry. *Smells so good.* "Some might even say sweet."

"I aim to please." His voice is husky, a low rumble that causes my walls to give an involuntary clench.

"You did."

"Always, my…*bloody fuck*," he hisses from between clenching teeth, his hands back on my hips with a tight hold. I'm biting his chin and then his jaw. "You're dangerous."

"I'm appreciative."

"And I'm thankful." Before I can nip his chin again, I'm turned to face the front of the building with his strong front against my back. His legs move mine forward, his hard length rubbing against my cheeks makes me blush.

It's impossible not to feel him; the bulge behind that zipper is thick and long. Has been hard every time I look down.

Why doesn't this bother me with him?

Anyone else I would've punched.

I have broken two noses before for much less.

"Welcome, welcome." Chef Reyes steps aside, his thick mustache twitching beneath his smile as we pass the entrance. "We've set up a small tapas selection for your enjoyment while we begin to prep. Is that all right?"

"Of course. Please lead the way," Callum answers after looking down at me and I nod. To be honest, I'm so excited about this. Paella is a dish I love but is scary to make. Especially when anything less than authentic is an insult to the country. I don't want a derivative or a likeness, no.

His warm hand is on the small of my back urging me forward, and I follow the chef up a spiral set of stairs near the middle of the first floor. The space is light and airy, all white furniture and walls with a splash of color from the few art pieces hanging on the painted brick.

The second floor is completely different, and it takes my breath away.

This floor is open with a wall of floor-to-ceiling windows that show-case the lake just a little beyond the end of this lot. There's a large terrace attached; it goes from one side to the other with one table near the center that is set for two.

"This is beautiful." There's no mistaking the excitement in my voice, and I turn my head toward Callum when he chuckles. "Don't poke fun. I really love this."

"I find you utterly adorable, Venus."

There's that name again.

Venus: the goddess of love, beauty, prosperity, fertility, and victory.

He's said it a few times now and I've chosen to ignore it, but the questions keep mounting the more time I spend with him. Callum Jameson is an enigma of a man, and the reputation that precedes him isn't matching up with the thoughtful and affectionate male who seems hell-bent on spending time with me.

Is that how he sees me? But more importantly, do I want him to?

"Venus?" I ask with an arched brow, trying to calm my racing heart down. *How can he unnerve me so easily?* My emotions are all over the place: confusion, to happiness, to unnerved, to this attraction that's palpable and dangerous. "Or is that what you call all—"

"Don't." Callum's tone is harsh, and I try to step away but he grips my hip before I can. My eyes dart around toward Chef Reyes, but he's nowhere to be seen and I find myself a little nervous. *Would he hurt me?*

"I'd shoot myself before I ever laid an angry hand on you."

"What?" It leaves me on a shaky whisper and I lick my lips, but that soon turns into a low moan. His hand on my hip is squeezing gently and pulling me a little closer while the other cups my cheek softly, almost reverently, and I rub my face against his palm. This is instinctual. Everything about the way I am with him feels that way: effortless. "What is all this?"

"A man spoiling his goddess. Simple as." Lowering his face, Callum tilts my chin up and brushes his lips across my mouth. Once. Twice. Then he bites down on the plump flesh of my bottom one before pulling back. "Can I do that, beautiful? Can I indulge you while cooking some good food and hopefully getting you a little drunk?"

I can't stop the laugh that bubbles out at that. *Cheeky bastard.* "I'm not a lightweight, I'll have you know. I'm really good friends with tequila, vodka, and rum."

"So, what you're saying is you're a lush, love?" He's fighting a smirk, and I have the sudden urge to flick his forehead. "That I'll need to lock my liquor cabinet in the future?"

"Who says I'll go anywhere near your cabinet?"

"You will." With one small peck to my lips, he guides me toward the large open kitchen where an island with two high-back barstools awaits us. Callum pulls one out for me to sit, and when I do, comfortably leaning back, he places his mouth against my ear. Each exhale is warm. The feeling of him against me is divine. "I call you my Venus because I've never seen such an honest beauty before, Miss Rubens. You're a little treasure. The literal definition of femininity and grace; what a man needs to conquer his demons."

His explanation brings goose bumps to my skin, a feverish shiver that flows through every limb while my heart gives a harsh thump inside my chest. Those words. *Christ*, he'll never know how much they mean to me. "Callum, I—"

"Shhh." I'm silenced by his thumb on my lips. "Let's shelve that conversation for later. For now, let's cook, eat, and enjoy the day out here. Nod if you agree." When I do as he asks, he moves back and then takes a seat next to mine. There's a bottle of white wine there that's chilled along with a small selection of covered tapas. "Thirsty?"

"Yes."

"Good girl." He pours me a glass first, sliding it closer, and waits for my approval. It's light and crisp, the fruity hint of apricots and lemon simply delicious. "Do you like this one? Or would you prefer something a little bolder?"

"Bolder is best saved for the after. Don't you think?"

"As you wish." Pouring himself a glass, he takes a few sips before setting it down and then uncovering the plates in front of us. There's one with what looks to be Manchego cheese and serrano ham with a few olives, the other has small meatballs, and the last is something called patatas brava, which I love. The potatoes are cut in cubes, fried, and then covered in a spicy cream sauce that I've tried to replicate but just can't ever get right. "Please, dig in. We'll be starting prep work here in the next thirty minutes or so."

"You're going to cut vegetables and proteins?"

Callum shrugs. "I told you before, I'm responsible for a lot of my meals."

"You seriously cook?"

"I do." Picking up a piece of bread, he sops up a bit of the ragu with the meatballs and pops it into his mouth. "My favorite's Indian food. I've got a mate I went to school with, and his family is from Jaipur. His mum taught me a few dishes, and I'm quite good; I can even make my own naan bread."

"Impressive." There are small plates in front of us and I grab two, sliding one over to him. "Fill yours, and let's sit outside. That view is spectacular, and I'm interested in hearing more about this cooking of yours. I'm a sucker for a well-made butter chicken or biryani."

"I'm going to enjoy spoiling you, sweet girl."

"You better." The words are out of my mouth before I can stop them. Idiotic. Irresponsible.

Because this, whatever we are, can't go past today. Not when I'm being forced to put my safety in danger and steal for my father's gain. Not when my family would never accept this.

They'd rather see me miserable than in the protective arms of a man that will destroy them.

They need me to be compliant and not untouchable. *Dad will go back on his word and hurt my brothers.*

I know my expression changed after that, but I'm glad Callum doesn't question it. He simply presses a button I hadn't noticed atop the counter and two women dressed in all black, like you see at restaurants, come over and take our food outside. They disappear just as fast as they appear, not that I have time to complain as I'm being picked up and carried outside only to be situated on his lap after the slick bastard settles in a chair.

"Eat, Aliana."

"Say please." My voice is low but he hears, and a chuckle meets my ears a few seconds later.

"Please."

"Thank you." Turning my head, I kiss his cheek. We sit like that for a while quietly, eating and sipping while watching the serene lake and the few birds that fly over it. Well, I ate all the potatoes while he gave me a look that screamed, *Are you seriously not going to share*? I stab the last two pieces with my fork and then raise it to his lips. "Would you like a bite?"

His eyes become hooded, and the thickness beneath my ass gives a hard jerk. And I won't deny that I gyrate just a bit, teasing him further, and the harsh hiss that escapes him is worth it.

The proof of his desire is raw and palpable.

I caused that sound. I made him throb.

For *me*. Because he wants *me*.

"Careful, sweetheart." His voice is deeper, accent more pronounced. "I'm trying to behave, but you're making it very hard on this hungry chap. Don't complain after if I bite."

"And how often do you *bite*?" I ask, because curiosity is a nagging whore. I've thought about it, how often he gets around, and the idea of him with another woman doesn't sit well with me. And while I'm not a virgin, self-love and a one-time mistake makes me a little self-conscious. "Because I'm squeaky clean and a solo type of gal. Have been for a while."

"Not as often as you might think, and I've had months with the company of my hand." He shrugs. "This type of life isn't easy, Aliana. Most women see me as a conquest with a thick wallet."

"I could care less about your money."

"I know. It's one of the things I enjoy about you."

"That I'm cheap?"

"No." A bark of laughter escapes him, shakes his shoulders. "It's how at ease I am with you. There are no pretenses with you."

"Well, a little nibble never hurt anyone. Just for future reference." Again, the words spill out before I can stop them.

"You're trouble, my Venus."

Every cell in my body vibrates when he calls me that, but this time, the meaning behind it sets my heart into a palpitating cadence I can't control. Then, there's the goose bumps and the embarrassing sigh that wants to escape, and almost does when a throat clears, and we both look toward the intruder.

"We're ready to begin when you are, Mr. Jameson," Chef Reyes says, staring straight ahead instead, giving us privacy. "Everything has been set out per your wishes, and your aprons are at each station."

"Cheers."

When the chef walks away after nodding, I flick my eyes back to Callum who's busy staring at me. Heat blooms across my cheeks, but I ignore it and raise a brow. "Cheers?"

"It's a universal answer, love. It can mean just about anything."

"Good to know."

"Why?"

"Mind your business, Mr. Jameson. A woman has to have some secrets." Jumping off his lap, I fix my top a bit and walk inside, his heavy footfalls following close behind. Almost touching. The heat from his body licks at mine. *I'm playing with fire. So stupid.* "Now, where do you want me?"

He sidles up next to me, his arm brushing against mine. I shiver, and he smirks. "That's a bloody dangerous question."

"Am I at the veggie station or the protein?" It comes out a little breathless, and I cross my arms to cover up the way my nipples pebbled—how tight each bud is. "By the way, can I—"

"Vegetables, and yes." Voice gruff, he leans over and picks up the hoodie he's brought for me from a little further down the counter. The other people, the chef and now one assistant, are not far from us, waiting. Both males. Undoing the zipper, Callum walks behind me and places the sweater over my shoulders, turning me around to face him so I can slip an arm into each sleeve. Eyes hungry, he looks at each hard tip and then swipes his tongue over his bottom lip. "No one sees those but me."

"Very possessive of you, don't you think?"

"You have no idea." Before I can protest, he dips down and steals a harsh, yet quick kiss before pulling the zipper halfway up. "You look simply mouthwatering in my clothes."

I laugh at that. Dear God, I'm swimming in his hooded sweatshirt. Looks more like a no-shape dress, almost a winter-style muumuu on me. "I'm sure I look smashing."

"More than." Callum stands to his full height and places a hand on my shoulder, turning me around to face the others. "We're ready to begin."

And that's what we do. For the next thirty minutes, we watch and then follow instructions, each working with one of the cooks. I'm with Chef Reyes, while Callum works with a guy who seems scared of his own shadow. It's quite amusing, really.

"Good job, Miss Rubens. You're a natural in the kitchen." We finished prepping the vegetables, bringing them over to the large paellera where Callum was busily browning the rabbit and chicken, all the seafood set aside for now.

At the chef's praise, I smile. "My abuela taught me everything I know. Best cook in the area she lived in while alive."

"Really? Que parte de España?" he asks, his Spanish accent becoming thicker, smile widening. "I'm from Valencia myself."

"Fornell's in Menorca."

"What a small world."

"It is." We stop near the hot pan, placing the tray down with all our diced vegetables. "You ready to get out of my way, Mr. Jameson? You're taking too long."

"Brat." One by one, he pulls out the meat and places it in a large glass dish while handing over a metal spoon the likes of which I've seen before. My paternal grandmother had a few and never used anything else while cooking. This was her all-in-one kitchen multi-tool. "Now I'm hungry. Hurry up and feed me, woman."

His playfulness makes me laugh while the other two men hide their chuckles behind a sip of wine. We've gone through a few bottles now and I'm a tiny bit tipsy, but I've never had so much fun.

No pretenses. No pushiness.

And while the chef instructs, I take over the cooking and put the rest of the dish together with Callum at my side. Handing me items. Giving me a sip or three from his own glass. By the time we finish, I am relaxed, hungry, and more than ready to be alone with him.

CALLUM

"I 'M SORRY IF I ruined the rest of your plans," she says from beside me, head resting on my shoulder as I drive back to her place after having spent the rest of the afternoon sitting out on the large balcony at R's eating and drinking. Just being while watching the sun rise to its highest peak and then begin to set.

And while it's still somewhat early, only a little past seven, we're heading back to her home for something she likes to call Netflix and only chill. *She's bloody adorable.*

Aliana likes to pretend she's not as affected by me as I am her, a lie she's feeding herself to not feel so out of control, but the truth is there's no denying that she's my perfect catastrophe while I'm hers.

Something brought us together, and I'm no longer questioning my sanity. Not after the last twenty-four hours in her presence. She calms the demon within me. He's a playful beast for her.

"To be honest, I much prefer your idea." At my words, she sighs and nods. There are so many questions floating around that beautiful head. So many doubts, but I plan to shut them all down. This is right. We are right.

"Anything you want to watch in particular? Any sweets or nibbles we need to pick up?"

"Sweets or nibbles?" Her lips quirk. She's loving the accent, the differences in her English to mine. "You mean junk food?"

"Aye."

"You're Irish now? Or a pirate?"

The road is empty near her home, and I press the brake before attacking, digging my fingers into her sides. Loud giggles fill the inside of my rental, her hands trying to fight me off and failing. "You love taking the piss, love? You think yourself a comedian now?"

"Oh God," she yells out, trying to push me back, but I don't stop. Those two words cause me to throb, fucking jerk behind the zipper of my trousers while she's unaware of the cruel punishment she's submitted me to. I want her crying out beneath me, to hear her beg God for mercy while I give her none. "Please....please!"

"Apologize, love."

"No!" My fingers dig in deeper, especially when I discover that right above her hips makes her squeal. I focus on that area until tears run down her flushed cheeks and the word *sorry* becomes a mantra. "No more."

"Then don't be cheeky." Her warm eyes narrow at my wink, but she settles back when I put the car in drive and continue toward her house. "And to answer your question, I use it from time to time. When the family votes, *aye* means yes."

"Gotcha." Still out of breath, Aliana reaches over and flicks my ear hard. "You're still a jerk for that, by the way."

"My apologies." I'm anything but.

"Not good enough." Arms crossed over her chest, I look over to catch her lips pursed in thought. *Fuck, I want to bite them.* "You'll need to make it up to me."

I swallow hard, forcing my eyes back to the road. "Name it, and it's yours." It takes her all of two seconds to snort then fight to contain her amusement. "How painful is this going to be, Miss Rubens? Can I buy my way out?"

"No, and excruciating."

"What if I—"

"No."

"No?" Pulling into her driveway, I put the car in park and cut the engine. "Are you sure you want to say no to me?"

"Positive." Her gorgeous brown eyes sparkle in the dark, the little bit of streetlight streaming in through her side bringing out their warmth. "You will head inside, eat what I give you, and not a single complaint."

"Are you giving me orders, love?"

"Yes." No hesitation, but what I enjoy the most is the look of surprise on her face. The shock, yet she doesn't waiver or cower from me, and I'd sit through a hundred corny movies to see the silly grin on her face all day.

"As you wish. Do your worst." *Someday I'll repay you for this with my tongue between those thighs.*

I LEAVE her primly asleep on her bed—after being carried—before we reach the midway point of *The Little Mermaid*. She was snoring a bit, stretched out on the couch she slowly overtook while I played with her hair. The soft strands felt like silk on my fingertips, but it's the satisfied groans that had beads of pre-come falling from the tip of my cock and rolling down the length.

Unlocking the front door to the townhome beside Aliana's, I walk over to the Ziploc box sitting atop the kitchen island. It's there along with a thick manila envelope, a cheeky welcome basket that makes me snort, and the instructions to change the front-door passcode to my temporary residence.

Kray's been in and out all day, the security app on my cell alerting me each time he entered, allowing the furniture company access to set up the few things purchased. Couch, dining table, and a king-sized bed are all I need. My plans don't account for staying long, but this place will come in handy and when you have the money, anything is accessible within the timeframe you allow.

Pulling out the set of keys I took from Aliana, I remove the one I need and slip it inside a small plastic bag. Timmons is already at the door per my instructions silently waiting, and I toss the item his way.

He catches it, giving me a nod. "This will take thirty at the most. The shop is a little far."

"No worries. I'll be here."

"Will you be needing me after?"

"No." I know what he wants, and she should be easy for him to locate. "Handle what you need to. I'll call you when I'm ready to discuss her protection detail."

"Will do. My phone is always on if you need me." He leaves, the door closing behind him, and I'm already at the fridge, grabbing a cold lager and popping the top. The first sip is refreshing, almost enough to cool the simmering heat left behind from her skin on mine.

It doesn't, though.

I'm starting to think nothing will.

There's a TV in the living room and I turn it on, switching over to the app with the feed I'll need, which leads me to the Airplay setting on my iPhone. I left three gifts inside her home, an invasion of privacy I don't regret.

Her words, the genuine reactions every time I give her a choice, don't sit well with me. It nags—like a slowly penetrating blade—piercing my skin until a wound appears that will not close.

If someone is hurting her, I will kill them.

Without a second thought. No empathy.

My beautiful girl deserves to smile more. I've claimed her. There's no going back.

I'm a man of my word and convictions; Aliana Rubens is mine and will be.

"She'll catch up soon enough." Placing the bottle down atop the granite, I open the file and read. It only takes a few lines for things to begin clicking into place, and my vision turns red. Anger burns through me just as a light across the street turns on, bringing a smile to my lips.

A man should never hunt when he's unprepared. Being comfortable makes you weak.

And while I want to empty a clip in his head, I have better plans for Mr. Martin.

His shadow moves across the window while my lights go out. He sits where I can make out his body, and I can easily shoot him from here without him noticing the man taking in his every move.

I have a silencer. I have enough bullets to repaint the inside of that home with his blood.

"Your time is almost up."

MALCOLM AND JAVIER are waiting for me at the front door of the Asher estate when I enter his driveway. It's a little after one in the morning and past the customary visiting hour, but this matter couldn't wait. Not when my concerns for Aliana continue to grow, and after this visit, I have one more person to see.

I also can't show up at Asher Holdings with the feds looking into our moves.

Casper and I aren't "here." There are no tracks leading to our entry or exit.

They're both looking a little haggard with a few specks of blood on their clothes, but the identical business-like grins on their faces say they know why I'm here. Truth is, though, they don't. They'd never guess the trouble I'll bring to their doorstep if I'm pushed the wrong way.

Friendships won't matter this time.

With a nod and no words exchanged, we walk inside and straight to his home office, and I understand why when I catch a glimpse of a woman laughing down the opposite hall with Mariah. She's young, reminds me a bit of Aurora, but I know she's not. My cousin hasn't let his girl out of his sight since we parted ways.

"Callum, it's good to see you," Malcolm says after Javi closes the door, extending a hand for me to shake. "I didn't know you were still in town. Everything okay?"

"Oi, mate..." I roll my eyes before pulling him in for a hug. "...take that formal crap and shove it."

"I'll take note and add it to his file," Javier says from behind me, moving to sit in a chair across from Asher's desk. "Doubt he'd listen, though."

"You two are a pain."

"A needed one," I counter, and then pull back to sit in the other unoccupied seat. The amusement drops from my face the moment I sit and the other two men take notice, mimicking my body language. "I'm heading back to London soon, but I have something pressing to take care of first."

"I see." Malcolm walks to the bar inside his home office, lifting up a crystal decanter with what I'm sure is gin. "Drink first or after?"

"First, but not that shit." At my response, he laughs, presenting me with a bottle of whiskey from the shelf beneath, and I nod. "Better, and bring it over."

"Shot or?"

"Better go with the full bottle just in case."

"That bad?" Malcolm's brows furrow, he casts a quick hard glance at Javi.

I shrug. The way this conversation will go depends on his answer. "Not per se."

"Are you here to discuss the financial issue we—"

"No."

That surprises Malcolm, his head tilts to the side while he scratches his chin. "Then?"

"I'm here to discuss your business agreement with Diego Rubens and Rigo Martin."

"You know I don't discuss banking between clients." He places the bottle down with two empty tumblers, one for myself, and the other for Javier, before taking a seat. His expression gives nothing away. "That's against the NDA we both sign."

"I could give a bloody fuck about money right now."

Malcolm doesn't react to the anger in my tone. "What's going on, Callum? What did they do?"

"My apologies." I take in a deep breath and calm myself. He's considered family, and I need to remember that before I do something I can't take back. At least, not until I know how deep he's involved. "But Malcolm, I need the truth from you. I need your word."

He nods. "Ask me what you must."

"Do you or do you not own a townhome in the Lincoln area across the street from Rubens's daughter?"

"No." No hesitation. His posture is calm.

"I believe you, but…" grabbing the whiskey, I pour three fingers' worth for myself and Javier. "…why is it traced back to you?"

Like a light being switched on, he's furious. His anger runs as hot as mine. "Please explain."

"A bullshit corporation was set up with your name as the sole owner. They purchased a home where one of my men is monitoring someone under my protection."

"Who's under your protection?"

I raise my glass in appreciation before taking a deep sip. "The governor's daughter."

Understanding flashes across his eyes, but he keeps a controlled expression. I see it, though. There's anger in the twitch of his jaw and the tense way in which he grips his drink, one he throws back before placing the glass down with care. "Is she okay?"

"Yes."

Javier gets up then, walking over to a cabinet behind us, and opens the bottom drawer. Without a word, he walks back and places a single sheet of paper down in front of me.

"I had no knowledge they'd done this, and I apologize for my ignorance on this issue."

"My anger isn't directed at you, but her safety is my main concern." Both men nod in understanding, they also share another look. "My belief is that either the governor is behind this or Martin, and while the end game is still unknown, it won't be for much longer.

"How serious are you about this subject?"

"Enough for me to consider putting a bullet between your eyes had I thought you to be involved."

His lips twitch with a smirk. "Fair enough. I'd do the same."

"So, you understand I'll do whatever needs to be done."

"Yes." Nodding toward the face-down sheet of paper, he taps the wooden desktop. "Rubens banks with me, and the other man hasn't stepped foot in any of my banking institutions in a year at least. Cleared everything, moved it offshore, and has been laying low from my understanding."

"Why low?"

"He owes someone a lot of money."

"Who?" I ask. There's no one in the city that moves higher quantities than my family, even with our headquarters out of the country.

"A loan shark with a hard-on for taking over, but he's made no move yet. Casper knows this; they've had words in the past."

The name comes to mind at once, and I also recall the way I personally killed the right hand to their boss. "The Gaspar family?"

"That's the one."

Hmmm. "Not too surprised. Those wankers are too hardheaded for their own good."

"They are. They've also been warned, so do what you must."

"Aye." For a moment he's quiet, while my mind is running a hundred miles a minute. There's more here than meets the eye, and I don't trust any of the players. Gaspar and Rubens shouldn't be on speaking terms, much less, after the latter used his father once as a piggyback bust to claim victory over his opponent when he came into office.

"I move all of Rubens's money, you know." Malcolm's voice pulls me out of my thoughts, but those words make me smile. "All of it."

"With stipulations, I presume?"

"Plenty, and I believe a few here have been broken. Thank you for bringing it to my attention."

"Of course." Throwing the rest of the spirit back, I place my tumbler down and relax a bit, leg crossed at the knee. "I'll respect your NDA, but I want the rest. Addresses, mobiles, where they eat and shit. We both know you have this information., Malcolm."

"Already in front of you."

I don't turn the sheet over, but I do grab it and after folding the paper, I place it inside the right pocket of my trousers. "Cheers. It's much appreciated."

"If you need any assistance—"

"I know." There's an understanding between us; a man must protect at all costs what's his. Malcolm has done so with his woman. My cousin will shift his life for his, a conversation I know is coming.

"But there is one request I ask you to adhere to for my assistance on the matter."

"This is your playground, not mine. The guest is always courteous to the host."

"Rigo Martin is mine to deal with."

"As long as you understand the others are solely at my mercy."

"Understood."

"Good." *This isn't the first time I've dealt with greedy politicians with White House or Parliament dreams.*

CALLUM

"**W**HAT THE FUCK?" Giannis wakes up sputtering, the ice-cold water running down his front while he startles on the chair he'd fallen asleep on. *Two p.m. and taking a nap, fucking waste of sperm.* He's not strapped down. He's untouched so far, completely unaware of the man sitting across from him in a plastic chair with a folded table to his right. My Ruger with a silencer is visible on the table; it's all black and heavy, with a full magazine. Each bullet has his name on it, but the discharge will all depend on him. "This shit isn't funny!"

"No. None of this is amusing to me." At my response, his eyes fully open and focus on me. His blue eyes widen, and his mouth drops open while consecutive bouts of shivers begin. "Who are you?"

"The bloody boogie man." Lifting my hand, I tap the small table and he flinches. He's a small bloke. No real muscle. No balls. "And I'm here to either kill you or watch you become my bitch."

"I haven't done anything. Please—"

"Speak when spoken to and we'll get along..." he exhales before I'm done "...for now." Immediately, he scrambles back, falling off the arm of the chair. Not that he gets far as Kray steps into his line of sight. "If it's money you want, my father has more than enough to pay you twice over even if the ass refuses to pay his debts." The last parts were mumbled, but I hear him loud and clear. *Rigo owes money, but I wonder how many times this git has been threatened because of him.* "Call him and demand a high amount. Just don't kill me."

"Who is Aliana Rubens to you, Mr. Martin?" At her name, he becomes paler. Sweat begins to bead on his forehead, his chest rising and falling rapidly. His mouth opens and closes, but no words come out. "Speak up, Giannis. I asked you a question."

Martin swallows hard, his shaking a little worse now. "You're a Gaspar?" My eyes meet Kray's for a second; he immediately pulls out his mobile and steps outside. The man on the floor lets out a whimper, and I look at him again. His fear is heady, but more than that, he's confused. "Dad has an agreement with your boss. And I only moved here because it's a nice neigh—"

"No. I'm not."

His low *shit* almost makes me smile. Almost. "W-who are you?"

"Callum Jameson."

"Oh fuck."

"Answer my earlier question, you arse." Leaning forward, I let my hands hang between my legs. "How do you know Aliana Rubens?"

"Our fathers." Giannis is shaking, a small pool of wetness now on the front of his joggers. *Disgusting.* "We grew up together. Our families have run in the same social circles since we were in middle school."

"And?"

"A-And they always expected us to be close."

Fucking choir boy is testing my patience with his stuttering. Before he can scream, I grab my gun and dislodge two bullets to the right of his head. They break through the drywall and wood beneath, leaving circular open-ings where a bit of sunlight filters through. "This is your last warning. The full story, or the next time I fire it will be aimed at your knee. Understood?"

"Yes."

I place the gun down. "Carry on."

Giannis licks his dry lips, swallowing hard while trying to control the uncontrollable twitching of his body. "Before I start, I'm begging you not to hurt her. She's been pulled in every direction all her life and doesn't deserve to end up in the middle of the crap her family pulls."

"Agreed."

"You do?" The cracking of his voice is amusing, yet I don't answer. Instead, I wave a hand for him to continue. I'll be heading back to London soon, but before I step foot on the plane, protection for her needs to be in place. "Because men like you don't—"

"Be very careful how you finish that sentence."

"I mean no disrespect, Mr. Jameson," he says, eyeing the gun without blinking. "Please know that, but with the type of men who seem to follow us or show up randomly at our fathers offices, we can't trust anyone. It's an expectation that scares the fuck out of me."

"The men?"

"The Gaspar family."

Again, that family. Two different people that mention them.

Twice that I'm made aware of how little respect they have for our territory if they're harassing people here.

"This is the last time I'll ask you this, kid. I want the full story." Giannis takes in a deep breath and then lets it out slowly. He looks to be giving himself a mental pep talk, one that is taking too long. "The clock is ticking."

"We met in school after our fathers became close. Dinners, fundraisers, even the occasional BBQ while they talked politics and money with the donors at these functions. And because we were stuck there, we hung out. Nothing more. Our parents saw that, though, and a passing hello became a forced conversation or *you two don't move from here* while they socialized. It just became our thing."

"Keep going." My hand closest to the gun twitches, and he shrinks back. His fear overwhelms the room in a way that soothes the need within me to spill his blood. "And get to the point. My patience only lasts but so long."

"They wanted us together at first." *At first?* "Her father wants my father's connections while my father wanted an insider to push his employer's agenda, and through marriage they'd forge the bond. No one asked if we so much as tolerated each other; we were not given a choice."

That word again: choice. *What else have they taken from you, beautiful?*

"Why at first?"

"Because I don't see her that way, and our fathers made a very costly mistake."

"What way? What bloody mistake?"

"The latter is more important than how I see her." He stands to retake his seat, watching me as he does and then leans back. He looks knackered, nothing like the cocky arse inside the lounge a few days ago. "Because this involves money my father owes the Gaspar family while Mr. Rubens incarcerated their old boss. The Gaspars want blood and retribution, and right now, I'm here to watch out for her. She may think I'm an asshole, but I stay close to try and dissuade them as much as I can. My father still has hope that she'll be the one."

Then it clicks.

"You made the fake corporation to buy this place?" He nods in answer, head down and not meeting my eyes. "On your own?" Another barely visible nod. "Why the fuck would you cross a man like Malcolm Asher? Did you really believe no one would notice?"

"Because I fear for her safety more than mine." Those words immediately calm the raging ire flowing through my veins. I'm looking at him differently, putting together puzzle pieces that will ultimately rain blood down on the streets of this city. "And without many choices, I picked one of two names they will not cross. It's all I could do to help."

"Asher and who else?" I ask when he doesn't divulge, and only when another bullet dislodges, this time near his sock-clad feet, does he look up. A horror-filled expression overtakes his features, yet there's a hint of determination in his eyes that I admire. Most men wouldn't meet my stare head on unless it's for someone they care about. "Why are you so protective?"

"Asher and the Jamesons. They want no problems with you." Tears brim in his eyes then, and he gives me a forced smile. "I'm a shithead most of the time and can be very self-absorbed, but I don't want her hurt. And while I don't see her in a romantic light—I just can't—I'm begging you not to hurt her."

"You have my word that I won't."

He lets out a ragged breath. "Thank you, Mr. Jameson."

"What are you not telling me?"

That makes him pause, a small bit of blush staining his cheeks. "The reason I'm not attracted to Aliana is because I'm in love with someone else. I see her more like a cousin or annoying sibling when she's being hardheaded, but nothing romantic." At my raised brow, he lets out a small chuckle, but it's done out of nervousness. "I have a boyfriend, sir. I'm in love with my soulmate."

And just like that, he's been born again.

I won't kill him if he's telling the truth.

At least not today. He can be of use. He's going to become my eyes and ears on the inside.

"MEETING THE DAY AFTER TOMORROW," Casper says the moment I answer my mobile after exiting the townhome where Giannis has been hiding. It's a little late, just after six in the evening, and my girl is finally home from work. I left him to get himself sorted; he's to expect my call within the next twenty-four hours to come clean to Aliana. Because what he said, and my own conclusions have left a bitter taste in my mouth; my little Venus being anything but happy doesn't sit well with me. Fucking infuriates me, and I've accepted the fact that I'll kill to protect her. May the universe have mercy on anyone who makes her so much as frown. "We have a lead."

"Time and place." My plan has always been to catch a very late flight out. I'm not leaving without a taste of her natural sweetness.

"Early afternoon and my home."

"I'll be back in London by—"

"You're still in Chicago?" His surprised tone any other day would've had me giving him shit, but I'm not in the mood. Right now, he's not my boss or cousin and being polite isn't on my list of priorities.

For the most part, we never go completely off the grid, the locators on our mobiles always stay active, but this once, I didn't follow protocol. I want no one near her until things are settled between us.

"Yes."

"In Lincoln or a few states down south, Callum?" *Tosser.*

"That doesn't concern you, mate." His response to my dry retort is a snort. *Bastard knows exactly where I am now.* "Are you heading home tonight or tomorrow?"

"Tomorrow."

"Fancy catching a flight home together? I feel like we have a conversation pending."

"We do," Casper says. For a beat, the silence stretches between us. Changes are coming and it's inevitable, and while I'm not angry at him for wanting what he does, no more waiting. My own immediate plans have changed, and I have Aliana to account for in the equation now. "The plane will be ready to take off a little after midnight."

"I'll be there."

"Be safe."

"But not too much," I finish for him before hanging up, pocketing my mobile and then pressing her doorbell. There's a bit of movement from inside, what sounds like something falling before a rush of feet stops on the other side of this door.

And fuck me if I don't feel those warm eyes watching me through the peephole.

There's just something about her. This connection doesn't break or wilt, and the more I'm blessed by her presence, the more I crave it. Want to devour and then cuddle, taking her with me everywhere I go.

Things need to get settled first. A reminder that sits like acid on my tongue.

I owe it to my family to avenge my aunt's death. I can't bring her into the middle of a blood-filled hurricane, my world, until I guarantee our enemies are dead.

My wife will fear no one. "Fuck me," I mumble, surprised by that last train of thought, but I'm not opposed to it. No fear. No questions. No second thoughts. "My beautiful little Venus."

Cock hard, I reach down and adjust it, but not quick enough as my grip tightens to just shy of pain. I hear her. This beautiful little hiccupping breath through the camera's speaker, and I was wrong; she's watching me through the Ring app like a naughty girl. I'm also sure Aliana has no idea she's pressed the talk button on her screen.

"Open the door, Miss Rubens." Another sound. This one a low, an almost indiscernible sigh, and I groan. No shame. I want her to hear me. Know that I hunger for every single inch of her. "I'm here to claim the morning kiss I didn't get this morning."

"Kiss?" The tiny whimper makes me bite my lip. "Who said I owe you a kiss?"

"I do."

"That's very demanding of you even if I'm not opposed to it."

"Not going to deny that I can be a dictating bastard, Venus. Now open up." The lock disengages, but Aliana doesn't open the door. Instead, I hear the shuffle of her feet walking away through the speaker of her alarm. "So be it."

I have her door open and locked within a few seconds, my heavy footfalls following the path to her bedroom. I'm not going to waste my time searching for her; she's either there or will come to me.

The half-open door lets me see inside the dark room. And there is the object of my obsession; Aliana is on her bed atop the strewn covers with an arm thrown over her eyes. Her chest rises and falls rapidly, each sinuous curve highlighted by the last streams of daylight coming between the window drapes where one small bit where it's parted, and I'm bloody thankful for that ray.

My mouth waters, eyes devouring the glimpse of skin beneath the threadbare light pink lounge set she's wearing. Just a tank top and shorts, nothing over the top, yet minuscule and tight. *Christ, she's beautiful. Looks so warm and comfortable.*

"Are you going to take that kiss now?" Aliana says without looking at me, tone breathy. *She wants it just as much.* A heady realization that makes my cock swell to the point of pain.

"I will." Not saying anything else, I slip through the opening and then close the door, leaning against to simply watch. For a minute or two, silence turns into heavy breathing while her lithe body squirms under my gaze. Her nipples pebble. Her thighs press together. "Just let me enjoy you like this a little more."

A shiver runs through her at my words, and a stuttering breath gets caught in her chest. "Okay."

"Good girl." In the dark with limited lighting, I take her in. My eyes have adjusted, loving the softness—how natural her position is without a single ounce of tension in it. From her small toes with a light purple coloring on them to the lush curve of her hip, I memorize each dip. From her tiny waist to the ample swell of her chest, I take count of each area I plan to kiss before heading back to London.

Pushing off the wall, I walk across the room and pause at her bed with a knee atop the mattress. It dips under my weight, the movement causing her to tense. She's not afraid. This, that reaction, is all anticipation.

A want that mirrors mine. *My girl.*

My plan was to get on the plane tomorrow with her juices still drying on my lips, but I'm not going to turn this gift away. Now, she'll be my dinner and then breakfast with the potential to become a snack at any given moment until I walk out of her home.

"Callum, I'm—"

"Can I touch you?" I'm not a man that asks for permission in any other area of my life, but I want hers. Crave it.

"*Fuck,*" she mutters under her breath, but I hear. I also don't miss the way her tiny hand reaches out for me, and I want her to grab me. To pull me closer. "Please."

"Please what, gorgeous. Tell me."

Fingers wrap around mine, skin so soft, and she gives a tiny tug while meeting my hungry gaze. "Lay with me."

Without a word, I do as she asks and crawl in beside her. On my side, my face next to hers, I close my eyes and inhale deeply. Motherfuck, she smells bloody good: sweet and all woman with just a faint hint of peaches that lingers all around her.

"Are you tired, sweetheart," I say, skimming a finger of my free hand from her elbow to shoulder. She shivers, moves a little closer, and I bite back a grin. Instead, I focus on the feel of her near while I continue my exploration. I'm keeping my touch innocent; I hunger for her consent.

She's not a woman to throw herself at a man or a one-time deal for me. No.

I want her again and again and again. The ferocity in which I crave this small woman is near painful, and only the taste of her on my tongue will satiate the beast within that demands I make her mine.

Because this is what being in her mere presence brings forth. A yearning.

She's driving me fucking insane.

Her head turns in my direction, a bashful grin stretched across her lips. There's also a slight blush at the apple of her cheeks that I find delicious. "Not at all."

"You sure? You seem ready for an after-work nap."

"My shower was relaxing." Slim fingers twitch, her grip tightening. "I feel peaceful."

"That's good." *Motherfuck,* a throaty little mewl escapes when I skim my fingers across her collarbones. "But you still haven't answered my question, love. Do you want my touch, or is this too soon for you?"

CALLUM

"**I** WANT IT."

"That's my good girl." The fingers on her collarbone travel lower, just to the edge of her top, and slip beneath the soft fabric. Not low, but just under the trim while my eyes watch her every reaction. Those sweet brown eyes close for a brief second, her lips parting on a sigh while a lovely vibration runs through every limb. "Thank you for the honor."

"Christ, I love your accent," she whines after a minute or two, not liking my standstill position on her skin. "It's quickly becoming a weakness."

"Is it, now?" My lips are at her temple, leaving tiny open-mouthed kisses on my way to her neck, inhaling deep to brand my lungs with her scent. I pause at her ear, though, nipping the sensitive flesh there, and enjoy the sight of goose bumps rising—the way her body arches into my touch. "Even coming from a bastard who has no right to want something so pure."

"You're not a bastard."

My rough exhale against her neck makes her whimper. "I've done things with these hands, Aliana." With a painful slowness, I caress the swell of her right breast and then the left. Once, twice—moving lower with each pass. "I've worn my enemies' blood with pride, my Venus, and yet, nothing would give me more pleasure than a single taste of the sweetness between your thighs. The need is near maddening."

"I feel this..." she trails off, but there's no fear in her eyes. No disgust. If anything, they become darker. Heavy-lidded. "Callum, this is—"

"Did that make you change your mind?" I know she hasn't. It's there in the way she keeps her hold on my other hand tight. How she's making sure there isn't a single inch of space between her side and my body. "Do you want me to move?"

"No," she hisses out; the urgency in her tone would shock anyone else, but not me. Not when I understand it. Not when I feel it too—just as much if not more—and have accepted whatever consequences come from this.

I'll take on the world just to feel her like this. To have her laid out like the perfect meal.

This between us is fast and unpredictable, but palpable and real. And I want it.

All of it. Her.

"Then relax for me, sweetheart. Let me make you feel good."

"Please, Callum. I dreamed of you last night and—" I cut her off, taking her lips in a hungry kiss while positioning myself to hover above her. Her thigh's part, lifting a bit to urge me closer while I maintain my distance. I'm not going to fuck her today. I'd never do that to her when I'm getting on a plane tomorrow night; she'll be safer here until things settle down in London.

Then, I'm going to bring her home.

I'm going to make her my queen.

She releases a little mewl from the back of her throat, so much like the one a short while ago by her front door, and I can't control the rumbled groan that builds in my chest. It's deep and almost angry, spilling between her lips when I press mine a little harder. I take her mouth with every bit of the passion that's been building since the day I saw her on Casper's screen, while a hand slips beneath her head to grip long, soft tresses. The tighter my hold, the more she arches into me, swiping her tongue across mine in a sensual cadence that I throb to.

My cock jerks, seeking out her warmth, and fuck me—I want to take. To leave her a dirty mess, but not today. Today will be about her.

Next time…

I'll be selfish.

Pulling my mouth from hers, I sit back and grip the bottom of her top, nearly ripping it in my haste to take it off. Her tits spill out, giving a small jiggle from the movement while the fabric lands somewhere on the floor. They're perky. More than a handful of perfection that sit high on her chest while the pebbled tips tighten further under my heated gaze.

I don't touch them for now, turning my focus to the next offending obstacle: her shorts.

I'm rough in my need to see all of her. The fabric gives a small groan, splitting on the right side while my hands drag them down shapely thighs and off the end of her feet where they'll lay in tatters.

"Son of a bitch," I hiss out, the sight of her bare and so wet is almost too much. It brings forth a haze of lust I can't control. Every molecule in my DNA throbs within me; I'm hard while my mouth salivates—desires to catch the drops of wetness sliding from her tiny entrance and down toward her arse. "I'm going to taste you, sweet girl," I groan, licking my bottom lip while flicking my eyes from her cunt to her sultry brown eyes. "Not a single inch of you will be left untouched. You will never forget the feel of my tongue or the bite of my teeth. How hard I made you come."

"Callum, please. Please touch me." Her cry settles on the tip of my cock like a shock of electricity, and I give in. My mouth brutally reclaims hers. Teeth clashing, tongues intertwining, but it's the sting of her teeth embedding into my bottom lip that breaks the last of my resolve.

I pull back, gripping her neck while I trace a path down her chest with my tongue. Loving the skin, leaving little indents of my teeth until I reach her right nipple and nuzzle it. It's soft; the perfect little dusky rose bead against my skin, but it feels better between my lips.

Suckling, I squeeze her left breast, weigh it in my palm before pinching the tip. It throbs under the harsh treatment, but my girl only moans, thighs trying to pull me in against her slick heat.

Aliana flushes, the tantalizing pink growing from her cheeks to the swell of each breast, and I smirk against her warm flesh.

Releasing her, I move across from one tip to the other. Bite. Lick. Sucking hard enough to sting before pulling back. "How sensitive are you, my Venus?" Not that I give her a chance to answer, testing her limits myself with one sharp smack to the slope of each breast, catching her nipples.

And the immediate scream that follows isn't of pain, but of need. Of want.

Her muscles lock, a hiss catching between small teeth before beads of sweat begin to spread. I lick the path from her sternum to belly button, savoring each salty drop before tugging at the small piercing there with my teeth.

Aliana hisses, while I smirk. "Something wrong, Miss Rubens?"

"Yes."

"Then speak." Another bite, this time on the area between her abdomen and mound. There I pause, resting my chin while she squirms. Trembles for me. And while she gathers her thoughts, vocalizes her needs, I begin to trace the lines of a beautiful tattoo adorning the space/skin from hip to just below her breast with a tip of a finger.

It's a black and grey vine curving along her skin, its thorns embedding in her flesh while roses bloom where each puncture would be. They grow from the representation of blood, hers, giving life to each flower that grows in the same color. Vibrant reds in different tones, yet striking against her lightly tanned complexion.

"Enchanting." I follow my digit with my lips and tongue, tracing from the top to bottom and then nipping her hip. Her scent is so sweet, decadent, and I inhale deeply. "You're a treasure worth savoring, Aliana. Worshipping."

A gasp escapes her, hips rising off the bed. An offering. A silent demand to touch where she needs me most.

My eyes leave hers. Slowly, I take in her hard nipples, the contracting of her flat stomach, and then the way her hands clench at her sides, gripping the sheet tight. The fine mist of her sweat, wetness, and that mind-fucking smell of peaches is all around me. Enhanced. Drowning me.

But nothing. Not a bloody thing compares to the pink of her cunt and the wetness that clings to her bare lips when I settle right over it. My breathing is hard, every muscle tight.

Aliana whines, the sound almost angry before slim fingers grip my hair. She pulls, forcing my eyes from her pussy to her face. "No more waiting. I need—"

"Only me," I growl before my lips graze her clit. The soft touch makes her shake, nearly pulling my hair from its root, but I pay no mind. She could leave bald spots for all I care. All that matters is the softness, her natural scent, and the hungriness in which I lick her from tiny entrance to clit, sucking the small bundle of nerves between my teeth as a deep groan reverberates through every inch of me.

One taste. A barely there touch.

I'm gone.

I feel like an animal salivating over its prey, and I feast on her like one too.

Nothing about the way I eat her cunt is gentle or sweet; I give into every baser instinct.

"Oh God. So good." Her moan is like lightning to my senses. It settles over my flesh and spreads before snapping against the tip of my hardness. I can feel each bead of pre-come as it stains my trousers with each jerk against the fabric. No underpants. Nothing but a single piece of clothing is keeping me from her slick heat. "Never...good...more."

Each word is a choked breath, her hips rolling against my mouth in search of more. And I give it to her because it's my duty to do so. With the flat of my tongue, I part her lips and catch the rush of wetness that seeps from her entrance in a nirvanic rivulet.

"Son of a bitch," I snarl against her swollen flesh, my tongue working her harder. I'm lost to her taste while slipping a finger inside to the first knuckle. *Christ,* she's tight. Her walls are snug around my digit, clenching to pull me in deeper, but I don't.

I keep my strokes shallow. Just caressing her entrance.

However, my lips suck her clit harshly, and I'm rewarded with the shaking of her thighs on either side of my head while her back arches off the mattress. Her hands are no longer in my hair but gripping her breasts, squeezing the firm globes while undulating against me.

My finger slips in deeper and then out, alternating between the suckling of her clit and labia. Her juices coat my mouth and chin, her tight walls begging for my cock while I finger fuck her with precise pumps that rub against that beautiful little patch of rough flesh that swells with each touch.

"Come for me, Venus. Feed me what is mine."

"I'm close." Aliana pinches her nipples, but it's not hard enough. Not how I would.

I push them off her tits. "Hands up and don't move them, love."

"Callum, please. Just…oh *fuck*!" she screams out as I squeeze a nipple, pulling on the tip while my teeth scrape across her trembling bundle. It throbs, swells against my harsh licks and alternate sucks—her wetness seeping onto my wrist, but it's the next time I bury two fingers deep and press against her spot that she loses control.

Aliana's muscles contract, orgasm slamming into her with force as her eyes roll back and mouth drops open, but no sound comes out. Instead, I'm rewarded with the sight of her lost in pleasure and her natural saccharine sweetness on my tongue.

I don't stop eating her until she calms and a satiated smile curves her lips. And even then, I take a few more licks before crawling up her body while leaving tiny kisses on her exposed, sensitive skin. Lip caught between her teeth, Aliana welcomes me and then moves without hesitation to cuddle into my chest when I lie facing up. My arms go around her, my lips at the crown of her head, and I find myself wanting this for more than today.

Yes, we need to talk and discuss our relationship.

Yes, she needs to meet the people I'm leaving to watch over her.

However, what I do is close my eyes and relax with her tucked in close. We'll get up in a minute or twenty, I'll order in dinner for us, but first I need her like this, so supple and warm and letting out a content sigh each time my hands rub up and down her back.

It further cements that we aren't done. Not having this is something my male instincts rebel against.

If Casper doesn't speak up, I will.

He needs to be here with Aurora, and I need my Venus home in London and standing to my right.

CALLUM

"**A**RE YOU BEING honest right now?" Aliana asks, eyes narrowed while darting between myself and the man beside me and opposite of her the following afternoon. We've been sitting in her living room for thirty minutes now—she'd gone in to work for just a half day—and it's been six hours since I woke her up with my face between her thighs. I'd licked every drop of her sweetness, made her coffee with a bagel, and then told her I'd be leaving tonight. The immediate sadness that flashed through those lovely orbs cut me deep. I don't want to leave her, but the sooner I go, the sooner I'm back to escort her home.

Because she belongs with me. She's my better half.

The Martin kid swallows hard. "I am."

"Jesus, Giannis. Why didn't you say anything before?" It's not lost on me that she hasn't given Kray more than a passing glance, not the least bit affronted by his presence in her home, at least, that's because she doesn't know he'll be her shadow while I'm gone. *That's a conversation best had in private. I'm not taking no for an answer.* However, the kid she's known since middle school—*he's* another matter. That's her focus. There's confusion, a bit of anger, and now sadness. "For crap's sake, we've known each other for years, and it would've made things easier between us. At the least, I wouldn't have been so rude to you."

"I'm not blaming you for that. I was pushy."

"But still."

"It's not that I didn't, Ali. I just couldn't." Giannis flicks a quick look toward a sitting Kray who's listening with a neutral expression. The bloke already sent me an email this morning with the header: *Her name is Lindsey Blackheart*, but I haven't cared to open it. His reactions right now are speaking louder than words on a screen. "Too many factors stood in the way. People who asked me to keep it quiet; one of them being a good friend and the other my father—"

"He knows?"

"That I'm gay?" She nods and he shrugs, body language showing heavy exhaustion. "They *all* do."

"What a mess." That's it. She hasn't yelled or ranted. Instead, she's looked at me for confirmation, and my nod seems to be enough each time. Aliana grabs her can of pop and sits back in her large accent chair, taking a few sips, while the matching one is occupied by Kray. He's on his mobile checking the addresses I gave him for Rubens and the Martin family, but when Giannis confessed, I didn't miss the sudden drop in his tense posture. Not in surprise, but as if this is a confirmation he needed. *Interesting indeed.* "Wait a minute. Time-out." The adorable girl even holds her hand up in the universal sign for stop. "What about the chick from the other night? The one you went home with?"

Thank you, gorgeous. But then again, I wasn't going to ask. I'm a person who watches, lets those around him hang themselves, and these two are protective over the woman but for different reasons.

"Umm." Giannis rubs the back of his neck, ears turning pink while Kray pauses and looks up. His eyes are hard on the git, silently demanding that Martin tell the truth. "About her..."

"Speak up, bloke. Don't dig yourself a hole you won't get out of."

It's not a suggestion, but a demand he adheres to. Giannis takes in a deep breath and lets it out slowly. "Lindsey knows my boyfriend. They're cousins, actually, and she's around to help buffer for us. He was one of the men that came in with her to the bar; they all work together."

A loud, boisterous laugh pulls our attention toward the guard. He's smiling, slapping his knee while sitting forward in the green velvet chair with gold trim that's not large enough to contain him properly. *Dwarfs my perfect girl, though.* "That woman is a genius little troublemaker."

"Oi. You okay there, mate?" Had this meeting been formal, two lashes from my whip would've reprimanded his outburst. Kray sobers immediately at my harsh glare, but his relief at their non-intimate connection is notice-able. *She's his.* "Is there something you want to share with the rest of us?"

"Please forgive my interruption."

I nod. "Carry on, Giannis. Finish explaining."

"Dwayne is my everything." Hands in front of him, he wrings them together nervously. "We've been together for eight months now, and we met through her. By pure divine luck, to be honest, I caught a flat and she happened to be driving down the road. Lindsey offered to help, and then called him when she realized her kit wasn't in the trunk."

"So, he changed your tire?" Aliana is smiling now, a genuine, silly grin, and my chest clenches at the gorgeous sight. "That's how he swept you off your feet?"

"And gave me his number."

"You meet up with Lindsey and her cousin outside the city limits every Monday, Wednesday, and on the weekends. Correct?" Kray interjects, and Giannis blushes a bit but doesn't deny it. "I could've helped her. She had no need to lie."

"The better question is why did they pull you out of the bar?" All eyes turn toward my girl, and I'm proud of her for being observant. The answer to her question is the one that matters. "What was the urgency, because she was adamant on you leaving."

"Your cousin was in the building with his newest flavor of the month. I cut them off in the elevator before they made it upstairs." The rosiness in her cheeks disappears at his words and she becomes pallid, eyes wide. "We cut off Jorge and invited him to join us at another club. He didn't see or know you were there."

"Thank you." Her voice is shaky, uncertain. "This is such a clusterfuck."

"This is my truth, Ali. What I'm doing to help—"

"Giannis, what do you...no." She's shaking her head from side to side. "No. You can't get involved."

"I already am." They share a look I don't miss, nor can I ignore the heavy implication.

"Venus," I say, pulling her attention toward me, hating the worry in her expression. "What is going on with your family?"

"Don't ask me that." Head shaking from side to side, she stands and walks into her kitchen. The other two remain seated, but stand once I point at the door. In the background, I hear the slam of kitchen cabinets and a muffled curse that worries me.

"Get out. I'll see you before I leave with instructions."

"I'll be near. My brother has a baseball game tonight." Kray steps beside me, carefully placing a hand on my shoulder. It's a friendly gesture. "Are we okay? Everything he said is true and can be found in the email I sent you. I love her and don't want to see her get hurt."

"We are." That's the only reason I'm calm. I'm doing the same for Aliana. "But fuck up again, and I won't be so forgiving. Don't make me doubt you."

"Thank you."

Timmons walks out without another word, and I turn my face toward the other man. He's running a rough hand down his face, eyes shifting toward the kitchen. "Something you want to say?"

"My family's having dinner tonight, but I can get out if you—"

I level him with a hard stare; it's not friendly. "You will go and pretend nothing has changed. Understood?"

"Yes."

"You will also be spending more time across the street until I return." There's no doubt in my mind that he's aware of what's going on with her, but I'm going to give her the chance to be honest with me. To trust me before I act out of reflex and not fact.

"Okay."

"I expect a report every night when I call. No exceptions."

"Yes, sir."

"Good. Now leave." The front door hasn't fully closed when I enter her kitchen, leaning against the doorframe to watch her. She's wiping down cabinet doors while muttering under her breath, ignoring my presence. "Talk to me, love. What upset you?"

Venus doesn't pause in her cleaning but tilts her head to let me know she heard me. "Too much at once. This is all so overwhelming."

"I can understand that, but—"

"Why is there a *but* in there?"

"Look at me." She doesn't, and I push off the wall to walk over, taking the dishrag from her hand and settling that, and bottle atop the counter. There's a small whine of protest and I get a dirty look when she looks up, but at least I have her full attention. "Much better."

"You're not going to let this go?"

"No." A single tug to her arm and she's standing upright, both hands on her hips. I lift her small frame, loving the way she immediately wraps those pretty thighs around my waist. She's so warm and soft, melts into me, and I walk us back toward the bedroom.

Her bed is still unmade. The room still holds a small hint of her earlier release.

Lying us down in the center, I remove her top and mine, rolling onto my back before pulling her in close. I need to feel her skin to skin. Aliana doesn't complain, her willing body burrowing closer until half her lithe curves cover my harsher planes. It's perfection.

To feel her like this is my version of heaven.

We don't talk. I have a feeling she needs this. To just enjoy the silence, and I'll be whatever she needs, whenever it's needed, until I have her full trust.

That's not to be mistaken with sainthood. My moves in the shadows will always be dark.

"I know you mean well," is the first thing she says after a while. Her fingers are busy tracing the lines of the Jameson name across my abdomen in Old English and leaving behind a trail of heat over every inch she touches. It's maddening, but at the same time absolutely fascinating how enraptured I become in her presence. "So please understand when I ask that you give me time. We just met, Callum. Literally. I'm still trying to wrap my head around you and this..." pushing off my chest, she points a finger between myself and her "...attraction I don't understand and can't help. My life is complicated enough as is, and all I need is time to assimilate you, Giannis, and the meathead you have lingering around like a guard."

The teasing tone and sassy grin on her makes me chuckle. "Caught on to that, did you?"

"Hard not to." Aliana snorts, then rolls her eyes. "The guy is a fridge."

"So dramatic."

"So is avoiding an admittance," she counters, and I roll us over, my body pinning hers to the mattress. "Hey! No fair."

Running my nose against hers, I nip her top lip. "I'll give you time, Venus, but he stays. I'll be gone a little bit, but I need eyes and ears here to make sure you're okay. That's not up for negotiation."

"You're being extra." Even her huff is cute. "We just met, and a security detail should come after a three-month relationship, not the first weekend."

Not a no. Not denying that we are more than a passing hookup.

"Three days was my limit." I run the pad of my fingers down her side and to the edge of her tights, slipping a finger beneath the waist to feel the warmth of her skin there. "I need you safe. My world is dangerous, sweetheart, and I can't take chances where you're concerned."

"Part time." Voice low. A bit husky. "Actually, more like a trial basis, and I choose the events he's allowed to come to."

"Full time, and you don't complain."

"Three times a week, and I'll FaceTime you on the other days to give you a day-by-day breakdown. It'll be boring, I must warn you. I'm not that interesting between work and school." She arches her back, pressing her chest against my mouth. Goose bumps rise across her skin and her thighs cradle mine, my trouser-covered-cock against her yoga-pant-covered heat. "I'll even throw in the occasional picture."

"Naughty?" I growl, flexing against her once. The thin lace bralette she's wearing is black and covers nothing. Her nipples are hard, her flesh spilling out. "Are you trying to bribe me, Miss Rubens?"

"It can be if you agree to my terms." Her attempt at distracting me is charming, but all it does is make me want her even more. To be around every second of her day.

"Love, I was going to demand that either way." I lick a path from one pebbled tip to the other, lightly biting on the right one. "I'll give you time, but my sanity needs this. Agree."

"Not fair."

"Nothing in life worth a damn ever is." This time I blow across the tender flesh, my hands moving lower to the waistband of her bottoms. They're easy to remove, more so when she whines and lifts her hips when I tease her nipples, but once they're off, I pause. It's easy to become lost in her body, but Aliana needs to understand what I'm asking of her.

"Why'd you stop?"

"When I walk out of here tomorrow, I'm no longer the man you have at your mercy, Aliana. I'm a murderer. A criminal." It's the truth, and I won't lie to her. I'm exposing myself so she sees that I'm serious, that she can trust me. "I'm going home to London to help my cousin kill every single man involved in the murder of my aunt. I'm going home to make changes, eliminate every single threat, and then I'll be bringing you home. You, my stubborn beauty, are important to me and I want you safe. So can you please do this for me? Don't give them a tough time, and let me know if something is wrong."

Tears brim in her eyes, and she nods. "After my trip."

"What trip?"

"Give me this, and I'll accept this without further argument."

"What trip?"

Lifting a hand, she cups my face and brings it to hers. Lays a tiny peck across my lips. "Trust in me the same way you're asking me to trust you."

"Okay." This time I kiss her, dragging my teeth across her bottom lip. "Will you be safe?"

"It's a family retreat. I promise to be careful while vacationing."

"Aye."

"Thank you." Relief sweeps across her expression, but I'm not letting this go. I'll find out what she's hiding soon enough, but Kray will remain on duty, just not out in the open. At least, until she gets back. "I appreciate it."

"Then show me, my Venus."

"How," she moans low, a keening sound as I drag my lips down the column of her throat and to the valley between her breasts. I lick and suck the skin there, the lovely shade of bruising complementing her tanned skin tone. "What can I do to show my—"

"Feed me." A grunt. My chest rumbles as I hold back my need to dominate and own. To demand she be honest and then take her away from whatever problems she has. Because I know they are there; the clues laid out so far create a picture that would lead to the destruction of her family, but before I make her an orphan, I need concrete proof. I'd hate to be wrong and eradicate someone she loves. "I need you to shimmy out of your knickers, arch your back, then spread your pussy lips and present me my meal."

"Oh *fuck*."

"Soon, Aliana. I'll claim you soon, but today I want to taste your pleasure."

Aliana

I'M AN IDIOT. Completely and utterly moronic, but smiling like the hussy this man is turning me into. *If only I could say no.* But I can't, and every time those piercing, gem-like eyes ask me for something or need an answer, I end up agreeing while letting down every single one of my walls.

Dios mio, ayudame. This position I've put myself in will cost me. I know it will.

My father will never allow this, but I also can't stop the small bloom of hope taking place in my chest, burrowing deep and holding on for dear life after Callum shared his plans.

He wants to take me home. To London.

Somewhere far from Chicago and all that I know, but with him I'd do so happily and without a second thought, knowing this could blow up in my face in so many tragic ways.

That man is the perfect heartbreak waiting to happen.

He'd tear me apart, something I'm no longer able to stop if he walked away.

I already care too much.

So much can go wrong.

What about returning to Spain?

That had been my original plan, but after hearing his, it doesn't hold the same appeal.

Nothing else does. And perhaps I'll feel differently tomorrow, but in the afterglow of his touch, I want to follow him. Because a part of me, the scared and disillusioned fragment of my soul, wants it—craves his words to be true.

Which makes no sense. But then again, nothing of the last few days does.

"How did I let myself get caught up in such a mess?" I want to feel whole again. I want to trust him. "Things that sound too good to be true usually are." My low muttering is accompanied by a hiss, my thigh muscles protesting as I stand on the tips of my toes to grab a glass from the cupboard. This is the aftereffect of being kept on my back, legs spread wide while he worshipped me for hours.

Mouth. Fingers. But never his cock.

And damn him, I wanted the latter. Begged for it, but Callum denied my request each time.

"Oh God," I moan, body thrumming as the aftershocks of my last orgasm still ring through me. Not that the man between my thighs cares. If anything, the last two weren't enough. Another long lick with the flat of his tongue and I close my eyes, fighting instincts that contradict each other. Push him away. Pull him closer. More. Stop. "Callum, come here. Please, just come up here."

"No." A growl, the vibrations of the simple word running through me like a live current. From the tip of my toes to the last strand of hair on my head, I feel it. Pulsing. Pushing me. "Need you to give me another, Venus. One more."

"Too much."

"Never bloody enough."

Back arching, I scream as his teeth scrape over my throbbing clit. It hurts a bit; a painful pleasure seizes every nerve ending and lights me on fire. "Please. Please, I need to feel you inside me...son of a—"

"I'll never fuck you and leave, Aliana." He bites my thigh, teeth digging in. This shuts me up. My mouth is open in a silent scream, body shaking as another orgasm is ripped from me with nothing more than a harsh nip. With my flesh between his teeth, his hooded eyes watch me come apart, his cheek nuzzling my tender pussy as uncontrollable tremors rock me. I pulse. I cry a bit, but then my breath gets caught in my throat and nothing matters more than the sight of this man gripping his cock. "Please tell me you understand."

"Callum, I—"

Muscles straining, he braces himself with one arm on the mattress, his body leaning over mine. "Answer me, Venus. Tell me you understand," he hisses, teeth gritted tight as he jerks off at the juncture of my thighs. He's thick, the head almost angry while his pace is punishing.

I've lost all ability to speak. I'm lost to the perfect picture of masculinity he paints.

I'm following each movement hungrily, my core clenching involuntarily, and another rough spasm shakes me. "Fuck me."

Pace quickening, Callum's eyes travel from my wet core to my eyes. "Beautiful." His stare is hooded, so hungry. Those gem-colored eyes stay on mine as the first rope of warm come lands across my labia and clit, dripping down to my ass and then the sheets. They don't waver when the next two make a mess of my mound and stomach. Instead, they darken even more as he rubs the tip against my skin, spreading his release all over me.

I'm a mess. My pussy still throbs.

"Why?"

"Tell me you understand why I denied us both what we need?" he counters, and I want to tell him that I do, but that would be a lie. Rejection suddenly floods me, and I look away, my eyes tearing up for a different reason. Maybe I'm being too desperate? *"Stop that."*

Callum's hovering over me now, lips almost touching mine as I meet his hard stare. He's a total contradiction to the man that watched me come a minute ago and then marked me with his release. I try to move away, to slide out from beneath him, but his weight drops, and I find myself pinned to the bed.

"Please move."

"No." Two warm hands cup my face and hold me so I can't look away. "Don't shut me out, Aliana."

"It's okay."

"No, baby. It's not." With a pained groan, he lowers his mouth to mine and kisses me slowly. So tenderly. The way Callum takes my lips this time is what every woman dreams of, and I didn't know I've been missing for so long. It's raw, shakes me to the core, and the taste of my release on his sweet lips quickly becomes something I'll crave until the day I die. It's the tangible proof of his hunger for me. A peck and then nibble to my bottom lip and he pulls back, smiling down at me. "Never think that I'm rejecting you, love. I couldn't, but I am postponing the inevitable when in a few hours I'll be gone. There's no way I'd be able to leave if I do, and taking you back with me until our enemies are removed; I can't put you in danger like that. So please, sweetheart. Be patient. Wait for me."

Wait for me.

He said those same words a few days ago when he walked out after a final kiss and the exchange of our phone numbers. Formally, anyway. I know he's had mine since pulling information on me, and it doesn't bother me in the least.

The sudden hard knock on my front door pulls me back into the present and away from the memory of his touch. They're not pounding, but the noise is loud, and I cautiously make my way over.

I'm not expecting anyone.

Standing up onto the tips of my toes, I look through the peephole and find a man I've never seen before standing on the other side. He's tall, his face impassive, and in his hand is some sort of envelope.

I don't open the door. Instead, I take quiet steps back until I'm back in the kitchen and can grab my cell.

With shaky fingers, I press the security camera app and go to live feed. His retreating form is what I find, and the envelope is no longer in his hand.

"What the hell?" For the next ten minutes I keep watch through my phone, not moving from my spot until I'm sure no one is outside, and then I rush to check the outside of my door. With each step closer, dread fills my stomach and my nerves pick up. And I'm right in doing so, because there lying atop my floor mat is a padded manila casing with my name written across the front in a penmanship I'd know anywhere.

Moreover, my suspicions are confirmed when I open it and read the first page.

This slice of reality slams into me with a vengeance. Brutally. Unforgiving.

There's no future with Callum. There's no reason to entertain him or any offer he makes when this is my life.

I'm a puppet on a string.

How can I withhold this from him and my newly appointed guard long term while keeping my father happy and at bay?

I can't juggle this.

I can't live multiple lives.

You leave in seventy-two hours. Disappoint me, and you know the price.

CALLUM

"**W**E'RE BEHIND SCHEDULE."

Casper's head snaps in my direction at the sound of my voice, a shitty grin on his face. He has a small carry-on over his left shoulder and a large love bite on the left side of his neck. Our plane is ready, the pilot is on standby, but we won't be getting on it until much later. *I'm not leaving this up to him.* "By four minutes, you arse. If I'm late, it's acceptable."

Pushing off the wall beside the door he walked through, I clap his shoulder. "To me, it's not."

At once, his amusement drops and the bag in his hand is tossed to a male crew member standing at the ready to assist a few feet away. The lad catches it, rushing away to stow it while Kray's car pulls up and idles.

Before we leave the States, there are two personal messages I'll be delivering.

"What's wrong?" This is the head of the family I know and have trusted all my life.

"Gaspar."

"What the fuck did that cunt do? Is he pushing product here?"

"Worse." Tilting my head in Kray's direction, I motion for him to follow me. We don't talk while we walk, and when the door closes and the SUV drives off the private airstrip, I look over. "I'm going to ask you a series of questions, and I want your honest answer, Casper. Not as my boss, but as my family. Can you set your ego aside and do that?"

"What the fuck?" An angry hiss. "Of course, I can."

"Good." Turning my head, I lean forward and tap the back of Kray's seat. "Pull up to the end of the road and step outside."

"Understood," Timmons says, following my instructions and stopping near a small cluster of trees and then exits, holding his mobile up to let me know he'll wait for my text to come back.

When his back is a few feet away, Casper clears his throat. "Talk to me. What's going on?"

"Are you moving to Chicago?"

For a few beats he's quiet, his face unreadable, but a nod follows. "Yes. For a little bit, at least."

"Fuck does that mean? When were you going to tell me?" My tone comes out a bit accusatory, although I'm not mad—more like annoyed with his current lack of communication. We've always had each other's backs, I respect him, and having to deduce clues and decipher his head space shouldn't be how we work. Because even if he moves to Japan or the South Pole, we're family. He will always be a Jameson. "What are you planning?"

"I want Boston." No further explanation. Just throws that out.

It's also not something I saw coming, and I scrunch my nose in question. He's never expressed a need to take over another state in the US. "Now isn't the time for riddles, cousin. Speak up."

"You sound like a boss."

"That's because I am." I'm not going to pussyfoot around this subject anymore.

"I haven't stepped down."

"You will."

His reply to that is a smirk and another nod. Acceptance. "Gem's father wants her to take over Boston, and she will. By my side."

"Are you with her for—"

"You fucking taking the piss?" Callum says, his tone acerbic. "I love that woman."

"Good."

"Good?"

"Yes, good. I'd hate to break that ugly mug of yours for being a cunt."

Usually, something like that would make him laugh or flip me off, but instead, his eyes narrow and lips thin. "Since when do you care who I see or don't? Or if I'm using—"

"You hurt Aurora, and that affects Aliana." Shrugging, I begin to undo the button of my right sleeve and roll it up to my elbow, then repeat with the other. "I won't allow that."

It clicks where I've been, and his hand comes up to scratch his jaw. The tosser hasn't shaved in days, it seems. "My offer is to help her. She can take it or leave it, but I'd still move here for her."

"You don't think she'll relocate to the U.K.?"

"Not when the Conte House is here. She'd never abandon her mother's legacy."

"She'd still be leaving Chicago." *Aliana didn't reject my desire to move across the ocean with me. My Venus smiled, more than likely unaware of the act, but she did, and that's all that matters.*

"We're talking from a few states away to across the ocean. It'd be easier to relocate the office here and just expand locations, something I know she wants to do."

"That's very true." My mobile buzzes in my trouser pocket, but I ignore it for now. "Think she'll turn down his offer?"

"No. She won't." Casper closes his eyes and leans his head back. A small frown on his face. "That woman has a huge, yet fragile heart, and it bites her in the arse at times. This is one of those instances, and her father is close to having her cave."

"You think he'll go for it?"

The smirk is back as he shrugs while looking at me through slits. "Fucker has no choice."

At that, I throw my head back and laugh. He means it. He'd kill him if he had to for Aurora. Sobering a bit, I hold a fist out for him, which he bumps with his. It's a gesture we've always done over the years right before celebrating or eliminating an enemy. "When do you want to make the announcement? Our clientele needs to be informed of the change in management, Casper. I'm not you, and things will run a bit differently."

"They all know and have dealt with you in the past."

"You still had the final call. Not anymore."

He's pensive for a moment, a flash of pain crossing his features. "As soon as I've burned Mum's killer alive."

"Aye." That's more than fair. I would've insisted on it. "Now, as for our visit—"

"Gaspar's meeting with Rubens, isn't he?"

"He is."

"Personal or business, Callum?"

"Personal."

"Then let's go ruin their night, boss."

———

THE LEADER of the Gaspar family is sitting in a booth inside of a seedy strip club across town. He's unaware, body relaxed, while a dancer gyrates atop the table like a perverse buffet. Men sit and watch, point and make lewd gestures, while ignoring the three men walking inside and taking over a table near theirs.

Then again, it's dark in here with the harsh strobe light highlighting specific areas: the stage, and two high, circular platforms that have a pole at the center and are only big enough to hold two people at the most. Then, there's the tobacco smoke and the lines of blow in plain sight.

Most of the men here surround the stage, tipping the girls, while a few sit to the side with a dancer on their lap and with wandering hands.

My eyes shift around the room, and I find a few more of his men spread throughout, not really paying attention. They're busy celebrating something, the ends of their noses powdery white while their pupils are blown wide. Stumbling. Laughing. Fucking twats.

All out in the open, no fucks given. However, their unprofessionalism works in my favor.

"Spread them cheeks, sweetheart. Show me how loose you are for me?" Flavio says, his stubby finger running up the young woman's leg while she dances with her eyes closed. The smile on her face is fake, forced, and highlighted by the mirror above where they sit, but none seem to care. They ignore. *Sick fucks.*

I point to the emergency exit near the restrooms and Kray stands, quickly taking position and blocking with his weapon drawn. The bouncers here won't be an issue. We've already taken care of them, knocked unconscious by the front door and then dragged off to the side of the building.

"I can handle those by the stage," Casper says. In his hands are two loaded Rugers like mine, but his are from a limited addition line. Mine are all black, the silencer matching the murdered-out powder coat finish. "You ready?"

"Always." We share a look and wait. Watch as those around us become more inebriated, uncoordinated, while laughing at the implication of their boss's words. His hands are higher up the dancer's thighs, almost to her core when the first shots are fired. Then, there is chaos.

Blood splashes the front of a waitress at the center of the room, and the man she'd been serving while pushing his hands away is dead upon impact: neck wound with a head thrown back by the force. Her scream is the first to rend the air, but quickly a symphony of fear overtakes the room as panic and confusion—the flight or fight instinct—takes over and like roaches, bodies begin to scatter.

Many fall, pushing against each other as they fight to get out while the second and third bullet rips through the wall near Flavio's head. His men stand, eyes darting around the room while missing the two men standing a few feet away with their guns drawn.

They're too high. Too unprepared. Yelling at each other while their unfocused eyes dart around the room in search of the threat. Not once do they look at us; they glance over and then focus on the other side of the stage as if the perpetrator is using the elevated platform as coverage.

Having men like these is a costly mistake for someone who is hell-bent on making enemies. Because in this world, you never let your guard down. You don't stop questioning every single person that walks into the room you occupy, and you never get plastered while on the job. Losing the awareness of your surroundings is dangerous: a death sentence.

A lesson this family needs to learn.

From his place by the emergency exit, Kray fires three consecutive times, and more bodies fall. The women huddled against a wall all cry, shaking, but he raises the gun to his lips and taps it once. *Silence.*

They quiet down, still whimpering a bit, but calm down enough to walk when he steps aside and lets them scramble out the door.

"The fuck!" Flavio screams, shoving the poor scared woman and table out of the way, knocking her hard onto the ground while those around him crowd in a protective way. Casper shoots again, hits one of the enforcers in the knee, tripping him, and the man's sheer size alone knocks the two beside him to the ground. "Fire back! Find who's shooting!"

Six left.

"Bloody idiots," my cousin sneers, lip curling in disgust while I aim at the arm of Gaspar's right-hand man. I'd studied his profile earlier today, a young wannabe playboy related to the man I killed last time we had words. I killed the last right hand arsehole, and I'll prove just how easily I can do so again. "It's insulting to the human species."

"Agreed." Another shot, this one to the opposite arm. He falls back on impact, yelling some form of a curse that makes no sense when I step forward. "Oi. Your men are too slow, mate. You're bloody sitting ducks."

"Who the fuck are you?"

"Callum, what are you doing here?" Flavio, and some bloke who's too green in the gills, speak in unison. One with fear. One with cockiness.

The latter of the two slumps over with a bullet to his head before I respond, my silencer muting the sound. "Muzzle your pets, Gaspar. My patience is running thin tonight."

A flash of fear crosses his face, but he schools his features quickly. "Is Casper aware of the trouble you're causing tonight? There are codes in place, Jameson. You're starting a conflict between our—"

"Silence." Casper steps in beside me, his face impassive. "I'm not his boss. Callum makes his own calls."

You can see the confusion on his face and the utter look of loss on what's left of his men. Their expression says it all.

No one else is here. The music, a heavy-based beat, plays in the background while the lights continue to highlight how easily we ruined their night. How easy they are to kill.

"Sit, Flavio." I point my gun to the area he'd been enjoying himself in before. The dancer he'd been touching is on the ground, though. She's not unconscious but is shaking in fear, and I look over at Kray. "Get her cleaned up and out."

"Yes, sir." Without another word, he walks over and kneels next to the woman. He says something and she nods, quickly gripping his hand, and then stands on trembling legs.

"Tip her."

"Callum, this is—"

"Tip her, or I shoot you. Your choice."

Flavio nods, lips in a tight line while pulling out a wad of cash. He tosses a hundred-dollar bill at the floor by her feet. "Here."

"All of it, and if you toss it, I'll make you pick it up with your teeth. She's not a dog."

"It's okay, sir," the woman says, looking toward Gaspar with that forced grin back in place. "He doesn't owe me anything."

Ignoring her, I tilt my head to the side with the barrel of my gun pointing at the same man I've already shot twice. His second-in-command is bleeding, gritting his teeth as the pain begins to settle and his body shakes. "All. Of. It." Flavio heeds my warning as Casper grabs two chairs from a nearby table and brings them over. One for me. One for him. The large stack of bills is exchanged under my watch and then Kray takes her away, walking her to the back to collect her things and then out the front door. "Now sit."

Cautiously, one of the men with him rights the table and then steps back.

"Callum, what's the meaning of this?" Flavio asks, his anger and embarrassment is palpable. He feels disrespected in front of his men, something that no boss can ever allow. Once you show weakness, no one will follow you. "You're in my territory and I can—"

"Can what, mate? What the fuck can you do?" I take my seat casually, and Casper does the same. He's quiet, while I enjoy watching the maggot not worth a shit try and keep his composure.

It won't work. Gaspar will make a mistake.

His men will pay the price.

He takes in a deep breath and sits across from us, hands atop the old table. "Why are you here?"

"Because you seem to need a reminder on how this business works. On how to stay in your lane." Someone scoffs as Kray reenters the room and walks toward me, the woman now gone. My guard hears it, head snapping to the side with a gun against the man's temple before the already injured git could react. "What's your deal with Rubens?"

Flavio swallows hard, throat bobbing harshly, but recovers quickly, expression neutral, while those around him are anything but. "I don't know what you're talking about."

"Are you sure you want to take that route, lad? My patience is bloody thin as it is."

"I haven't done anything to warrant this level of disrespect, Jameson. You're in my home, my country, and…son of a bitch!" he yells out, hand gripping his ear where my bullet took out a small chunk. Blood seeps through his fingers, the left side of his clothing now ruined.

"Watch it, Flavio. I'd hate to think you truly meant that insult." One of his men twitches, his hand moving toward his belt, but before he can take his next intake of air, Casper's gun remedies his idiocy. He's not dead, but a bullet to the abdomen can do a lot of damage and if not treated immediately, it'd become irreparable. "And you wouldn't be stupid enough to do so. Would you?"

"No." Voice low, he looks at the men beside him. Not one of them is fit for the job, in my opinion, but I'm almost embarrassed for him. I'd feel bad had he not been stupid enough to be intertwined with Rubens's and Aliana's safety.

People like him have no word. No code.

He's an animal that needs to come to heel or be put down for his insubordination.

"Last time we met, Flavio, do you remember what I said to you before walking out the door?"

"That you'd kill my—"

"Louder," I hiss out, my own weapon on the table. My finger is on the trigger as it lays on its side, its muzzle pointing at his heart. "What did I tell you before walking out?"

"That you'd kill my men and then force me to eat them before ending my pathetic life."

"And yet you try to gain territory when we've been generous." My eyes scan the room, finding product on nearly every table. A waste. The color is also off; it's cheap and cut wrong. Shaking my head, I level him with a hard look. "You try to befriend a politician to what end? What is he offering?"

"Nothing. It's a monetary—"

"The truth, arsehole."

"A truce."

"A truce?" I ask while Casper scoffs beside me. "Fuck do you have to gain from that?"

"Immunity." Flavio's explanation sounds plausible, and any other day I'd give him the benefit of the doubt, but Giannis wouldn't be so afraid if it were that simple. The way his hands shake is also telling. *Wanker is scared.* "We'd be left to do business without harassment or possible jail time in the future if caught mid-transaction. Just that. Nothing else."

"Bullshit." There's only one man left in his circle that hasn't spilled blood, and I bring the count down to zero before his next blink. All of the men sitting or surrounding their boss have now paid for his greed. They groan, some trembling where they stand at the ready to die for Flavio. Admirable, but he's not deserving of their loyalty. "But I'm going to let it slide…" Flavio exhales roughly while the man now on the floor cries out in pain "…for now."

"I swear it's the truth."

"And I don't give a flying fuck either way."

"Callum, Casper…this hostility between us isn't necessary. I can talk to Rubens; we can all prosper from my alliance. Think about it."

"There's nothing for me to think about, Gaspar." Sitting forward, I level him with a hard stare. He's sweating; the fear pours out of him. "You will stop whatever it is that you have with Rubens and Martin. No more meetings. No more threats."

"Listen, Callum. I don't know what the problem is, but you can't—"

"I can and will." Lifting my right hand, I empty every bullet left in the wall just two inches from Flavio's head. The gun in my left hand still has ammo, and he sees the intent. The next time my Ruger discharges, the target is his skull. "The next time I visit over this, I'm going to burn you each alive and then feed your cooked meat to my pet; I'll ship him over from his cushy home in one of my London properties just for this meal. This is your only warning, Flavio. Stay away from the Rubens and Martin family. All of them. Understood?"

He nods. "Yes."

"Any Gaspar found to be trespassing my order will be put down. Understood?"

"Yes."

"You don't speak to their families, employees, or the person who makes their coffee at the local deli. Not so much as a bloody nod in their direction." My eyes shift to all the men one by one, not moving onto the next until they nod. "Heed my warning. I won't hesitate to kill you."

Aliana

"WE DESERVE A gold medal after the last few days," I say, sighing as the warm water of the pedicure bowl pulses with massaging jets. We're in pamper mode today—activated and unreachable while taking a much-needed break. It's been a week now since both men left, since my father canceled my trip again—no notice or explanation, just a text telling me to hold off until further notice. It's also been seven days since all hell broke loose and we got an influx of women that left us scrambling to accommodate and protect, leaving me no time to wonder why the sudden change in plans.

Two of the new residents had a drug addiction, while the other three were running from abusive men that had no qualms about threatening us, but one took it the extra mile. That one didn't care, charging in with a weapon drawn while trying to intimidate by looking to hurt us or the building his ex was seeking sanctuary inside of.

The visit lasted a few minutes at the most, tense seconds where Aurora pulled out her gun while I doused his face with pepper spray before he could shoot, or worse.

"*Bring her out,*" the man screams; a tall jerk with twitchy movements and the nauseating scent of garbage all around him. He's unkempt. His expression is of pure rage while holding an old pistol in his grip. Arm down and shaking, he stormed inside, scaring the two assistants helping with the dietary changes needed for a seven-year-old with a peanut allergy. "*Where is my wife?*"

"*Sir, you need to put your weapon away, or we will be obligated to call the police.*" Aurora moves in front of the two shaking women while I gently push them toward the office. We've gone over drills with the staff and those who live here, practice these at least once a month, but when fear kicks in, you can't predict how a person will react. "*Put it away, and we'll go to my office and speak calmly—*"

"*Shut the fuck up, bitch. Bring me my wife, or I'll shoot every single one of you.*"

"*Last warning,*" Aurora says, tone neutral while her hand opens the drawer of the desk right beside her. The man looks down at it, but before he can see her reach for her weapon, I push a high stack of papers onto the ground; it flutters in the space between us and him. It's just enough of a distraction for Aurora to grab her gun and aim at his chest, while the other women lock the door to her office. "*You didn't listen. This is private property, and I want you out.*"

"*I'm not leaving without her. I'd rather burn this entire place to the ground.*"

"*Get out,*" I hiss, while Aurora clicks the safety off. The man's eyes flash with fear, but soon that's gone. That miniscule second reasserts his careless way of thinking, and it also gives me a chance to pull out the pepper spray I keep on myself, finger ready to dress down.

"*No.*" He takes a step forward in my direction, but I'm already spraying. I empty the bottle, focusing on his left eye that is partially uncovered through spread fingers, and then step back.

"*You whore!*" the man screams, stumbling back and falling as the papers cause him to slide. His body crashes hard, the gun slipping out of his hand and ending against the opposite wall. "*The fuck is this shit? It burns!*"

"*That was a warning, sir. Get up, and get out.*" No sooner do those *words pass through Aurora's lips than we hear police sirens. They are close. The office is at the front of the compound, not far from the parking lot and main road. The closer they get, the more he panics and scrambles to get up, only to fall once more, hitting his face this time as he's having a hard time keeping his eyes open. "And we will be pressing charges. See you in court."*

With difficulty, he pushes himself up and stands. He's facing us, but not really focused. "I'll be back. This isn't the end, and my slut of a wife will pay for this."

After that, he left, body stumbling into the wall beside the door before managing to exit, still screaming, insulting us, and then not a single trace left for the cops to find.

None of our cameras caught sight of him past the front door. He disappeared.

No blood. No body. Nada.

These occurrences aren't really the norm with us. Most men don't want cops involved or looking their way and approach the women in a softer manner. Some fall for the fake repentance, some don't, but we defend ourselves either way. This also makes me think that Aurora's still being watched.

Or is it me?

Callum gave me his word—that he'd respect my wishes for a few weeks, but did he?

But more importantly, I'm not upset if he hasn't. The last seven days while stressful, have been pleasant in a way I'm not used to. My father has left me alone since that text, and no more harassing crap from Giannis as I know the truth and our friendship grows. Instead, I'm coming and going with more ease, and I don't want to go back to the way it was before.

"Amen, chica." Aurora cranes her neck back and closes her eyes. "I was seconds away from turning to a life of heavy drinking and a full-time hermit career."

At that I snort, ignoring the vibrations inside of my pants pocket. It's a little after three in the afternoon and I know it's Callum, but I don't want to draw attention to myself. If she hasn't told me about Casper, then I'm keeping Callum a secret.

Besides, it's kind of fun. The secret messages and the naughty phone calls. The picture of him shirtless and joggers pushed below mid-thigh while he gripped his cock; a picture now forever inside a private folder locked under a passcode.

"Aye." It slips out, and my cheeks burn. *What the hell?* "I hear ya."

"You a pirate now?" A spa worker comes over with another mimosa on a tray and we each take one, smiling at the girl. When she leaves, my best friend looks over with a raised brow. "Have you been watching *Pirates of the Caribbean* again? Your obsession with the male actors in those movies is highly—"

"Shut it, and guilty."

"You look guilty."

"So do you, bestie." I waggle my brows. "I'm still waiting for the play by play of lover boy's trip here. When are you going to spill?"

"I already did." She rolls her eyes, and I want to flick her forehead. "You know he came, and we spent a few days together. We went out on dates, ate, and there was plenty of the good stuff I'm not sharing about."

"How can I live vicariously through you if you deny me the juicy details?"

"How about you tell me about Giannis instead? Is he still following you around like a lost puppy?"

Immediately, I want to defend him—correct her—but that wouldn't help the low profile we've decided to maintain. Giannis came to me after Callum left and we talked; he explained himself and the situation fully, and I'm so grateful to have him in my corner.

I've also seen pictures of him with the boyfriend. The goofy smiles they both wear when together, and if I can help make things easier on him, then why not? We are two people stuck in a tough position and deserve a break. To be happy.

"You know it. I'm almost tempted to say *yes* just to get it over with." The lie feels wrong, but I can't tell her what's going on. The less people involved, the better, and besides, if her father plans to help mine in finding me a "suitable" husband, things will be out in the open soon enough.

Do I want to be responsible for another fight between them? No.

Do I want to kill the glow that surrounds her amid a Casper Jameson romance? No.

So, while the nail technicians come over and we hand them the chosen colors, I giggle. While they scrub, file, and then massage our feet, I do what I do best and pretend nothing is wrong.

She's oblivious, but I'm not mad because hiding my truth is what I've been taught to do. Someday she'll know, and she'll be mad at me for not asking for help, but until then, I want to enjoy the peace and quiet.

"I'd pay good money to see the look on his face if you do. He'd probably pee his pants." She laughs, pulling out her phone after it pings in her small bag. Her eyes brighten while reading a text. Smile wide and cheeks with just a hint of pink, she quickly begins to write back, oblivious to my movements.

Because I check my cellphone too, a small smile fighting to curl at the edge of my lips. I don't, though, biting it back even though my heart is racing, and my skin breaks out in goosebumps.

> I miss you, my Venus. ~Callum J.

Five words. So simple and yet, I feel each one down to my bones. They make me happy. Make me want to giggle and be all high-pitched squeals, but I can't.

Aurora has enough on her plate, the mess with her father and his demands for her to take over weighing heavy on her shoulders. I also don't know how she'd feel about me seeing Casper's cousin. Would it bother her?

I'm keeping so much from her already.

I hope that on the day all my truths come out, she forgives me.

"CLEAN SHEETS and shaved legs for the win." I sigh, snuggling deeper into the bed after another long day. Yeah, we took a break in the afternoon, but that was cut short mid-lunch when the receptionist at the Conte House called with an urgent new case. This one came with a police escort and two signed court orders that say her ex-boyfriend isn't allowed within a hundred feet of her and their son. No excuses.

That led to more paperwork, room placement, and then a long meeting with them while Aurora explained the ins and outs—rules—while I worked in a curricular activity for both. Schooling for the twelve-year-old, job training for her, and then medical and mental health visits for both.

I'm not sure the extent of what they've gone through, but one look into her empty eyes spoke louder than the screams of a thousand angry souls. And while I usually handle the public relations side of the house and the few classes I teach a week, I sat down and helped a tired Aurora with what I could before walking out the front doors a little after seven p.m.

I'm hungry, but too tired to make anything.

I'm sleepy, yet awake and wanting something. Him.

I miss him.

Grabbing my phone from the nightstand, I open our last text exchange and read them. His last reply was over twenty-four hours ago, a corny joke that made me laugh until my eyes watered. It involved a bike, being tired, and the mother of a dad joke delivery that morphed into a catastrophe of comedic genius.

His timing killed me. I'd been running late, rushing to my car when it came through, and I laughed so hard my phone slipped and skidded across the ground, earning itself a nice scratch across the screen.

> You should be arrested for this joke. ~Venus

I changed my handle to his nickname before hitting send. Couldn't help myself.

Before I'm able to place the device down, though, it rings, and I'm surprised. It's so late in London. Pressing the green button, I smile as a tired-looking Callum smirks back at me.

"I'll have you know I'm very funny. Have been approached several times to run my own big network special."

"Is that so?"

"Aye." At my snort, he rolls his eyes and then sighs. His finger traces across the screen. "You're so beautiful, Venus."

My cheeks heat up, and my heart races. That same fluttering energy fills my stomach, and it's like he's here all over again. "Thank you."

"You look so soft and warm, love. Are you in bed?" That's when I notice he's in an office of some sort; a large screen hangs behind him while a half empty bottle of dark liquor sits just to his right. "Let me see you."

"I am," I say, sitting up against my pillows. My back arches a bit as I situate myself, and the thin cotton of my shirt stretches—exposes just how hard my nipples are. The mere sound of his voice does wicked things to me; I'm wet and achy with that growing need he incites. Just like when he was here. When I had his touch, his mouth on my skin. "How do you want me?"

"Don't tease me, sweetheart." His groan is loud, and I shiver. "It's been a long day, and I'm nowhere near done. Take pity on a lad and show me a little skin."

"Have you missed me?" At my counter, he gives me a lecherous look. "PG-13 miss me, not rated MA, Mr. Jameson."

"I have. More than you could ever imagine." There's amusement in his tone, but it's the heated look that makes me simper. A low, keening mewl escapes my lips, my skin breaking out in goose bumps while he watches. Licks his lips. "And you…did you miss me? My touch?"

"Both." It's my truth, and his expression softens a bit. *A sweet hunger.* He's older than me, in his late twenties, but the boyish looks and the way his gaze sweeps across the screen should be considered illegal. "Has anyone told you you're quite charming? It's nearly impossible to not be drawn to you."

"And you're simply captivating." Callum pours himself a drink, grabbing a glass from somewhere within arm's reach while not standing from his seat. It's a few fingers' worth, no ice or soda to mix. "I can't stop thinking about you, Aliana." He takes a sip and holds it. Savors it. "All day. All night."

"I'm stuck in the same cycle." Because I am. Morning, noon, and night; this man is on my mind and refusing to give me a single moment of reprieve from the promises he made. "Yet you're far, and I'm here."

"This separation is temporary."

"What do you consider temporary?" I pull the phone further from my face and tilt it, giving him a better view of my body from my mouth to the edge of my panties. Then a little lower, where I shimmy my bedsheet down to lay over my mid thighs, pausing at the juncture where he can see me. There's no hiding the small patch of wetness there nor the small lift of my hips. His groans fuel me, make me want to be bolder, but I want the answer to my question more. Not keeping the focus there for long, I pull it back, drag the camera view up slowly until he can see my eyes again. "I'm still waiting for your answer, sir."

"You're a naughty little thing."

"And you do this to me."

"Everything I told you was true." Callum lets out a rough breath then. The desire is still there, but I'm transfixed by his gem-like stare that's so honest and open. "I want your home to be London, Aliana. Beside me." Before I can answer, though, someone comes into the room after knocking once; their words aren't clear, and after Callum nods, you can hear the door close. His face is tense now, a complete contradiction from the man who a minute ago confessed to missing me. Wanting me with him. "My apologies, love. Casper's looking for me."

"Is everything okay? Is this about your aunt?"

His head bows slightly in affirmation. "It will be soon."

He's going out to work. To possibly kill.

"You need to go, don't you." Not a question and he nods, knocking back what's left of his drink. Whatever he's about to do isn't something I want the details on, but I worry. It builds, creates this uncomfortable feeling in my chest that begins to eat at me. I'm in too deep and care too much. *Diosito, please watch out for him.* "I need you safe, Callum. Promise me you will not get hurt."

"You have my word." For a second, neither of us speak. We watch until there's another knock and he sighs, the sound heavy, and it settles across my body like a warm blanket. It's a sound of remorse and need, and I feel the heaviness in my bones. *I don't judge you. I can't.* "You're embedded deep, Venus. So motherfucking deep, and I don't want it to change because every part of me needs you."

CALLUM

"**H**IJO DE PUTA, I'm going to...*fuck*!" Felix De La Vega screams two weeks later, the gun he'd been clutching—hand shaking while reality sets in—is now on the floor. One bullet from my Ruger, that's all it takes, and I chuckle at his idiotic expression.

Fear and loss; he reeks of it. *Pathetic cunt.*

He's a nobody. A bloody middleman that made himself available to my aunt's killer by facilitating a hitman while gaining a pretty penny for the connection. His hands are tinged with her blood, and we have plans for him.

"Oi, my apologies, bro. My finger slipped."

Casper chuckles a few steps from me; his amusement rivals mine. "I'm going to start calling you *butterfingers*."

"I'm not that bad." I shrug, not the least bit repentant for the slip. If it were up to me, I'd do worse, but being a patient killer has its benefits. No one can say I'm anything but thoughtful and accommodating, and I take repayment in their screams shortly after.

While he prays, I'll peel his skin back.

While he cries, I'll feed it to him.

"You only have a few seconds left, Felix." Casper's mood changes then, his body language aggressive—from relaxed to a volcanic rush of ire that makes the man bleeding from the hole in his hand shake. He eyes my cousin, the tick in his jaw more pronounced now with each beat of the clock.

"Who are you?" Felix screams, but we all see his intent. The man's a runner, taking a few steps back and turning his hip toward the halls behind him. His Ocean City home in New Jersey is big, has plenty of places to hide, but he won't get far. "What do you want?"

"Your head on my mantle." At Casper's words, he takes off as bullets rain through the house from each of our guns. A door slams closed, and I pull out my empty clip, replacing it with a full magazine.

"Don't shoot to kill. We have a deal."

"We do, Callum." Green eyes meet mine; the silent promise is all I need. Because we might be bastards—arseholes—but we've never taken back our word. There's always been a certain level of respect between us, even when he was the boss, and I trust him with my life. "Watch the exits. I'll be back with a gift."

With that he takes off upstairs while Archie, one of our new guards and a close friend to Jeffrey, heads toward the back.

My gait is slow toward the front of the home.

Two things stick out the moment I cross his threshold: the area is quiet, and it's warm. Sun high and no clouds, I turn my face from right to left and pick up no movement. No police sirens. No one walking down the street and no passing cars.

From the open door I can make out a bit of shouting, the heated, hushed words of desperation, but it's the sound of a gun going off that makes me smile.

Then again.

Two, and I cock my head to the side. Immediately, Felix's screams fill the silent afternoon with a pain-filled cadence that I quite enjoy. Loud, full of misery, but most importantly, it gets closer. And closer.

Their feet are heavy on the stairs, his whimpers rending the air until both stop at the foyer.

Casper's eyes meet mine. So much anger in them. So much pain. "He's being gracious and accepting our offer to ride with."

"What a courteous tosser." The man in question groans, his body landing at my feet after a small push from my cousin. He has a bullet wound to his knee and hand while a few bruises are beginning to form on his face. *Casper went easy on him.* "Do you need anything before we go?"

"Please don't do this. I'll…I'll tell you everything." His wounds are bleeding, but the flow isn't excessive. Not enough to need any wrappings.

Crouching to his level, I tap the muzzle of my gun on his lips. Push the dark metal past his lips just a bit, not even past his teeth, and Felix gags. A few tears spill down his dirty cheeks. "Oh, I know you'll talk, Mr. De La Vega. And I'm going to enjoy every bloody scream as you tell it."

That's the last thing he hears; I pull out the gun and whip him across the face with it. His unconscious form topples over, blood covering his face as Archie comes around the corner, rushing over and dragging him to our vehicle. De La Vega is put in the trunk while we exit the property without another word.

It's time to play.

"Wake up, arsehole," I growl out, landing a swift kick to Felix's midsection. He's tied up, hands up on a high water pipe with his feet dangling just a smidge off the ground inside of a borrowed property not too far from Felix's home. We've let him sleep for the last five hours, gave him time to calm down after the small panic attack at his house. It's almost funny how quickly a person can go from *do you know who I am* to *please don't hurt me.*

In that time, while he slumbered, we've gone through every last connection he has in the US and back in the Dominican Republic. His ex-wife has been notified of his death; his money transferred to her account along with the two properties he's purposely screwed her out of.

How can a man vow to love a woman, marry her, and then leave her with kids for another?

How can a man abandon his children and leave them to live in squalor while his whore travels the world on money that belongs to their mum?

That's why he's here now.

Greed. Cockiness. Stupidity.

Felix groans, his body swaying a bit from the blow. "W-what's going…*fuck*!" he screams, the next blow from my boot landing on his ribs. It's hard enough to crack a rib, and the way he tries to fold into the pain is a good sign of just that, but this is just the beginning.

He dodged up. Touched a woman that to the Jameson's was sacred.

"The next time I strike, I'll use my knife. Wake up." Casper tosses a sleek blade in my direction, and I catch it, a butterfly version, and flip it open. The clean metal glints in the sunlight filtering through the glass panels used to make up the building's roof. "You have five seconds to open your eyes."

They snap open at once, and he winces from the earlier strike across his face. The area is swollen and a nasty shade of purple. He tries to move his head back, away from me, but I don't take it personally as I'm sure it has something to do with the cold tip running down his cheek. From temple to jaw, I leave a shallow cut that brims red, but only a few small drops fall.

There's fear in his eyes. Petrified with a good mixture of horror that seeps from the cunt's every pore. *Pathetic.*

"Nice of you to join us," I say as I embed the very tip into his skin, just an inch. "Now, are you ready to play?"

"Who are you?" He's asking me, yet his eyes are on Casper; I look over at the latter and find him sitting atop a few boxes. His posture seems relaxed, but I know better. Can read him like no one else, and I'm not the least bit surprised to find Casper's gun on his thigh and his finger on the trigger.

"Oi."

"Callum."

"We made a deal to play nice." As I say this, I push in another inch of my blade. "We need him to talk."

"Agreed." Casper shoots him once, on his thigh this time. "Please ignore me."

"Thank you." With my attention back on Felix, I pull the knife out and wipe the bloody metal across his bare chest before dropping it. I'll be going a different route today. "I'm ready for that story now. Why did you do it?"

"You're Callum Jameson?"

"I am."

"And he's Casper Jameson." Not a question, but I nod in confirmation. "Dios mio ayudame. Que hice."

"You helped an innocent woman die. You have his mum's blood on your hands." Leaning closer so we're at eye level, I pat his bloody cheek. "God will not save you, De La Vega. He's gifted you to us; we are your penance."

Tears flow down his cheeks, body shaking, but I stand back and let him have his moment.

I take a seat next to Casper and accept the cold bottle of water Archie offers me. "Thanks, mate." He doesn't reply, just gives a subtle nod, and retakes his position. "Any news on the wanker?"

"Ezra's working on it. Last known location was in South America, but I know he's not there now. No man running would be stupid enough to stay in one place for long."

"Caribbean or—"

"We already know he lives there, but don't know which island yet. My guess is one not too far from the US."

Nodding, I empty half the bottle in two deep pulls. "That gives us a few choices, starting with those closest to Florida."

"It does."

He gives me a pensive look, and I raise a brow. "Something you want to say?"

"You okay, Callum?" His question catches me off guard and I frown, not getting it. "You've been a bit quiet lately. Since Chicago."

"I'm fine."

"Are you? Is there something I need to know?"

"I'm fine." I make a move to stand, but Casper puts a hand on my fore-arm, and I pause. Look down at him. "Bro, I promise I'm okay. Trust me... nothing I can't handle."

"Mum would be proud of you," he says instead of prying further, and a knot forms in my throat. For as much shit as we give each other, we know the other, and his mother was like my own. She was there when my mum decided that vacationing—or for my father, work—was more important than raising me. And while I don't hold anything against them, my loyalty lies with Casper's parents.

His mum's passing hit me hard. Still hurts.

And just like her son, I've made a private vow to avenge her death.

The doorbell rings suddenly, making me pause inside my aunt's kitchen, the sound loud—seems to reverberate throughout every square inch of their massive estate. My aunt is out in the shops picking up an order while my uncle's footsteps walk toward the front door.

No one from the house's security team rang. No one's expected to drop by, either.

"Wait two minutes before opening," I call out to my uncle, knowing he heard by the two taps on the wall closest to him. It's not too loud, not enough to be heard by whoever's waiting by the front door, but it does give me a moment. Opening the drawer beside the fridge, I grab the Glock inside and head toward the French doors.

This exit leads to the garden, and past that is a swimming pool and a small cottage my aunt claims as her woman cave. *I'm quick to rush around the side of the home, keeping alert for any movement, but there's none when I reach the front.*

What I find is one of our guards, his face pained and eyes red-rimmed. A sinking feeling settles over me, my heart clenching, but I manage to walk over and use the key code to unlock the door.

Then it's the four of us, my father, who'd been inside his brother's office, joining us. He's the reason my aunt went out alone today, needing to discuss some half-arsed crap or other that will never go anywhere. His brother's no longer in charge, and Casper feels like I do; we don't live in the past—this family is run by young blood and new ways.

Dad's eyes meet mine then, and his expression mirrors; something isn't right. It's a heavy cloaking aura that suffocates, and I shift to look at the man. "Speak."

"I'm so sorry, Mr. Jameson. So sorry." He's not speaking to me or Dad. His eyes are on my uncle, and when it clicks, the world beneath his feet disappears. I've never seen a strong man crumble like this before.

It's heartbreaking.

This has nothing to do with Casper. The wanker is off with Aurora, and had something happened, the call would've come via Jeffrey or Ezra. That leaves one other person. Motherfuck. No. *At once, my chest squeezes painfully tight, and my eyes close. This can't be happening.*

Words fail me. I can't voice the questions running through my head.

My uncle's legs give out and a fist comes up to his mouth, body shaking as a sob catches in his throat. "Where's my wife?" How he manages to ask this, I have no clue, but he does. Voice cracking, he stumbles toward the guard and grips the man's long-sleeved vest. One tug, and he's face to face with Jameson senior, with his glare—eyes red while his body language is pleading. "Where is she? What happened?"

"I'm so sorry, sir. Mrs. Jameson's vehicle was attacked, and she's been taken to the A&E with multiple gunshot wounds."

"Get the car," my father shouts, moving to help his brother close the door and walk down the few steps onto the circular drive. I'm on autopilot. I can't get past the feelings coursing through my veins. This is something I've never experienced before: fear. A choking, bloody helplessness.

Not for me, but for her. Her husband. Her son.

And I vow to do what I must to keep my family standing no matter what the future brings.

I'm pulled from the memory by a choking cough. Bloody spittle flies out of Felix's mouth, landing on the cold concrete below his feet.

He looks tired, his wounds a nasty red.

"Something you want to say?" I ask, looking toward Archie and giving him the signal to drop the lever. He does so. De La Vega's body drops to the ground and his ankle turns at an awkward angle. It's dislocated, and the accompanying scream is almost as satisfying as Aliana's taste. Almost. "Speak."

"We can come to an agreement." Gritting his teeth, he twists in pain while finding a position to sit in. Sweat beads at his brow, and his chest heaves. "Please. I can help you."

"How can you help us?"

"I can tell you what I know."

"And what is that?"

"I'm the one who—"

"How well do you know Mauricio Hernandez?"

"In passing." Felix swallows hard, his hands fisting on his lap. "I know someone he does, and vice versa."

"Is that true, Casper?" I ask, feigning stupidity. Even before picking up this sack of shit, we knew of his involvement and how well he knows the hitman.

"Negative. Not what he said earlier."

"So I'm dealing with a liar, then?"

"Aye."

"All right." Turning my face toward my cousin, I point toward the black bag near him. "Toss that my way…" he does, and I catch it with one hand "…And Archie, we'll be needing the bench now. Go ahead and set it up near the back."

CALLUM

"**W**HAT ARE YOU going to do to me?" Felix asks, his body dragging backwards, and I make no move to follow him. He *will* come. He *will* accept his judgment. "Please, let's be reasonable. We can work something out."

"Come here."

"Callum—"

"If any of us have to grab you, it will be worse." Taking the item out of the black bag, I test the weight in my hand and check the leather used. It's not like mine back home. No. This one doesn't have the added touch of a madman, but it'll inflict plenty of pain.

One snap of my wrist and it unfurls, the whip snapping against the dirty concrete. The sound is loud, meant to spike his fear, and Felix throws up. Hunching over, he empties his stomach and I scrunch up my nose. *Disgusting.*

"Would you like me to fetch him, Mr. Jameson?" Archie asks, coming back inside. He wipes his brow and eyes the man with a mixture of pity for the lad and ire. Every person in our organization, from the tenured to the newest guard, has felt the death of Aunt Penelope. "Ezra called to make sure we are on schedule, and he's waiting for the signal."

"He worries a lot." Casper's traded the gun in his lap for one of his Karambits. "Send him a message with new airport ETA. An extra two hours today should be enough."

"Yes, sir."

Turning back to the man on his arse, I see he's still trying to crab crawl back and failing. His dodged-up knee, thigh, and hand are an impediment he can't escape. "Last chance, De La Vega." A warning he doesn't heed, and I flick my eyes to an eager Casper. "You get two shots."

"How magnanimous of you."

"I try, you arse."

The wanker doesn't answer; he's too busy looking at the man. For a few minutes neither moves, my cousin waiting, and when Felix whimpers, the Karambit breaks through the air and slices a clean cut across his left shoulder before landing on the ground.

Because that's the beauty of that knife: it's bloody sharp. The skin parts, the flesh having given way, and what's left is a deep gash that bleeds at a high rate.

"That's one." I'm admiring his work, ignoring the way Felix screams and writhes before picking up the knife. It's in his grip, but the twat doesn't know how to place his fingers, much less how to angle the blade for a more accurate slice.

"All I'm going to take."

"You sure?"

"Positive."

Blood loss is a bitch and Felix is beginning to show a bit of fatigue, the Karambit slipping through his loose grip. He's bled quite a bit from each wound, and when he attempts to stand with his uninjured hand extending the knife out, it doesn't last. Instead, he stumbles, and Archie comes back in time to grab him.

Felix thrashes, tries to fight back, but is quickly outmaneuvered and taken to a deviant little section Casper's acquaintance keeps here. Every apparatus back here is for discipline, to keep the recipient in place, and I chose the bench to start.

His body's bare except for the pair of boxers we've left on him. His feet are stepping on an array of broken glass that's kept inside of a built-in wooden box for added punishment.

He shuffles, tries to push the shards aside to save the bottom of his feet, but the first strike of my whip remedies that. It slices through the air, connecting with his back while leaving a sharp welt behind that quickly blisters.

"Fuck!" he screams, fighting his bonds, back arching yet the limited space keeps him in place. The blubbering starts at once, and it's disappointing. "Don't. I'll do…no!"

The second lash strikes from his right shoulder to the middle of his spine, this one breaking the skin, and the surrounding flesh turns red. "Why did you do it?"

"No more."

"Why did you do it?" I ask again, gifting him the third and fourth before delivering the fifth over the back of his thigh. The sounds coming from the man's throat are horror-filled and full of pain, loud and a little soothing to me. "If I have to ask again, I'm going to play the eye removal game. Count each strike across your face until I hit the orb at just the right angle to make you lose it. Your choice."

"I'll talk," leaves him on a pathetic whimper.

"Then do so." This time, the whip's tip hits his injured shoulder. "Convince me you're worth one more day."

"Mauricio is in the Caribbean but moves around a lot. He has homes in Jamaica, Puerto Rico, Dominican Republic, and Cuba. There's also Guatemala, Honduras, and Belize. That's just to name a few." He swallows hard, his teeth chattering as the pain peaks. "H-he's been a hitman since his early twenties and is smart, too smart to get caught easily."

"When did you meet, and where?"

"I need water." Each word is spoken between clenching teeth, but the way his body shakes is an indicator that he's breaking. He'll either pass out or lose control of his bodily functions. "My throat."

And to keep him alert, I flick my wrist and the leather snaps across his right flank. "Answer the question, lad. Don't test my patience."

His head nods, legs shaking. "We met in Miami while I was on vacation. He was close to a trafficker there."

"Who?"

"The Villegas, but they're all dead. Killed by the reigning family now: the De Leon's."

"Okay." Tilting my head toward Archie, I signal to the bottle at his feet. It's hot, has been sitting in the sun all day prior to this, but it's water. "Hold it up to his lips." Archie does so, and when that first sip lands on his tongue, Felix gags. He tries to reject it, but I nod, and Archie lets the entire one-liter tip and pour onto his mouth or face. "Thank you."

"Of course, sir."

"Felix, thank you for the information so far."

"I'll do anything."

"I'm sure you would, but finish answering my earlier question. Why?"

From the corner of my eye, I catch Casper move closer. In his hand, he has his favorite toy once more. He's worse than I am with my whip. "Go ahead."

Quietly, he gets behind Felix and waits. The man is unaware, or maybe he isn't. Doesn't matter as a few tense seconds later, he begins to speak. "They offered me a lot of money to do so. More than Mauricio and I have ever been offered for one job, and we took it without pause."

"How much was your cut?" I ask, placing the whip down just long enough to take my vest off and crack my neck.

"Half a million."

"And that was worth a woman's life?"

"It was never supposed to be his mama. His father or uncle, but not his mother."

"Then why protect Mauricio Hernandez?" Casper's voice tone is cold. His muscles flex, coiling as if he were an animal ready to strike. "Answer me."

"I didn't   "

"Liar," my cousin snaps, gripping the back of Felix's head, hair in a tight grip while he digs the tip of his Karambit down his back in a long and straight line. Then, he creates a half circle on the top of the line, the corners touching and turning his mark into a large letter 'P'—his mother's initial.

"You hid him. You bought his plane ticket out and brought in others to help him escape our wrath."

"N-no. I-I swear…I-I didn't."

My cousin lets him go and steps back. "Enjoy yourself."

"Thanks, brother." A tsking sound escapes me while Felix blubbers and begs. His cries and pleas fall on deaf ears. "Liars never make it into the kingdom of heaven."

I show no more mercy.

We knew his moves, motives, and connections.

We just wanted him to voice it out loud. To be a man and admit it.

This time as the whip's leather snaps against his back, I don't pause or let him breathe. Each strike is brutal, cutting and breaking flesh as his life's essence splatters after each precise lash. Some lands on my skin, some on the ground and the equipment within. There's no counting or spoken words inside the room as his screams of pure agony go from loud to unintelligible blubbers—from begging to silence as he loses consciousness and Felix's body goes limp.

He's a mess. Broken. Bloodied.

The last two from my whip land at the back of his head, and when it bounces, just a slight rebound that leaves behind a thick welt on the shaved bottom half of his skull, I step back.

It's a disgusting scene to most. The torn flesh and rivulets of red that flow down and to the ground, creating a puddle at his feet.

To me, though, it's poetic. He deserves so much more, but I know this isn't enough for my cousin, and I have a gift of my own.

I turn my gaze to Archie. "Get him cleaned up and as stable as possible before we leave."

"Leave? Where are you—"

"Alexander's on his way to finish this, cousin." His smile widens and nods in approval. Alexander is Aurora's bodyguard for a reason, and it's his brutality that's kept him under our employ for so long. He has no boundaries nor empathy, and he'll give De La Vega an ending he deserves. "And don't worry about Gem. I moved someone there already, and Archie will be in charge until Alexander returns."

"Thank you."

"None needed." Walking to him, I clasp his shoulder and squeeze. "Just don't forget to videotape it. We've got plans for it."

"We do?"

"We do."

CASPER NEVER ASKED me why I took off or where I was off to, but I do send a text when I land.

Twenty-four hours. ~Callum J.

His response is just as fast, and nothing more than *okay* before I pocket my mobile. I'm turning my locator off, but the device will stay on until I'm back in the air and across international waters just in case something goes wrong.

No one but Ezra knows where I'm at or why, but he'll erase every proof of our—my—being on US soil before sending a second plane for my private use. I'd left Casper with the other. The government doesn't need that kind of information, not while investigating that bullshit wire fraud case, and Malcolm helped by letting me use his private jet and airstrip to land in Chicago after cleaning off Felix's filth in the meantime.

He's also moved our money again. Every cent. Something that gives security to our suppliers back home.

The tarmac is empty when I arrive, except for Kray who waits outside his large SUV. Once I'm close, he pushes off and holds out a hand. "Good to have you back," he says, and I take it, shaking it quickly before tilting my head toward the car.

It's been a few weeks since I've seen Aliana. A day feels like too many, and although she understands that duty binds me this once, I need to see her. The daily reports that Giannis turns in are shit in comparison to being near her.

They don't fill that void, this ever-growing need that I can't contain.

"Aliana's home tonight. It's been a busy time at the center, and she seems exhausted." This I knew; Giannis has told me as much. Seems the last few weeks they've had an influx at the Conte House, and she's been working late to help Aurora. "Is there anywhere you want to stop first, or…?"

"Straight to her house."

"Done." After a minute, he begins to thump his fingers on the steering wheel, and I know why. I'm waiting for what I know is coming. Kray settles after a minute, exhaling roughly. "I'm sorry, Callum. I let you down."

"Am I angry? Yes," I say, resting my head back with eyes closed. "However, they were at work. They take risks every day to help women in need, and I understand that. You stepped in and removed him the moment you realized what was happening."

Kray chuckles and I raise a brow. "Miss Rubens emptied a can of mase on his face. Direct hit."

"That's my girl."

"I was on my way in when he ran out and into me. Those women are exemplary—tough."

"But…"

"It won't happen again. I'm working on an idea to have someone on the inside."

"Smart. Let me know when you have the specifics."

We don't talk the rest of the way. With each turn the vehicle takes and the closer to her home we get, my body thrums. It's a different kind of energy. Just as pleasurable as taking a life, but with the memory of her taste still lingering in my mind, I'm throbbing.

Hungry. Pulsing.

A heady feeling that almost compares to taking a life, and yet, this one is more. It's everything.

The street where her townhome sits looms close, and I notice Giannis outside when I pull up. He doesn't say anything when I exit, but simply nods and then gets into a vehicle with a man I recognize as his better half. They drive away, and Kray does the same.

I want no one around.

No interruptions.

There are twenty-four hours between this trip and my return to England, and I just want her.

I'm at her door before both cars turn right at the stop sign down the street, my fist pounding on her door. Five hard knocks, and nothing. No sound. But when I raise my fist once more, I hear that melodic voice.

"I'm coming!" my Venus yells, her feet stomping toward the door before yanking it open. "Giannis, for the love of God, I just want a quiet night and—" Aliana stops abruptly after I clear my throat. She's in a cute romper set with a towel wrapped in her hair, a warm flush covering her peach scented skin, and staring at me with wide eyes and plush lips in the perfect shape of an "O."

"I've missed you too, love."

Aliana

HE'S HERE , and it feels like I can breathe again—like what's been missing since he left has been returned and the world feels a little calmer. Safer. For me, at least.

I've been left to my own devices since he left, and I've wondered if he has something to do with it. *Do they know about him?* My family has been quiet; even Dad's campaign manager has excused me from any of his recent events—a first, and I appreciate it heavily. He's not in full-swing campaigning yet, just a brief base-run affair for the people who only care about money and the status quo.

Those men whose wives get younger every three years.

Those men that spend millions of taxpayer money to front their travel expenses and dirty secrets inside of hotel rooms.

Because I've seen things. Hear things.

My father has never hidden his cheating or how beneath him he feels the female species is.

"What are you—" I'm unable to finish as his lips meet mine and I find myself being pushed inside, the door slamming behind us. His groan reverberates through me like a sinful caress. His touch sears my skin, and I want to bleed for him.

But that's what he does. I go from nothing to everything right before the floor is swept out from beneath my feet each time he's near.

"I needed this," he growls against my lips, body forcing mine deeper into my apartment. Callum doesn't pause or say anything else. He's on a mission, and I won't stop him. Can't, because it's been obvious for the past few days that I've *missed* this too.

He's deep under my skin.

Strong fingers grip the back of my towel and he pulls, forcing my newly cut strands to sweep across my shoulders. This makes him pause, and I become nervous when he closes his eyes and then buries his head in my neck. *Does he hate it?*

"Fuck, Aliana." Callum's groan brings goose bumps across my skin, the heat of his breath on my skin making me shiver. He's breathing hard, holding me close while his lips sweep across softly. "I'm almost afraid to look, beautiful. I don't think I'll survive it."

"It'll grow back. A few months and it'll be like...*shit!*" I yelp, suddenly airborne as he stalks toward the back of my house where my bedroom and bathroom are with my body over his shoulder. A warm hand holds me in place with a firm grip on the back of my bare thigh—squeezing and caressing between steps. "What are you doing?"

"Proving a point." Callum doesn't turn toward my room. Instead, he enters the large bathroom and sets me down in front of the vanity. I'm turned, our eyes meeting in the mirror while he runs his fingers down my slightly curled, dark locks. The strands are still humid, barely towel dry, and the look on his face is of a man transfixed—mesmerized.

"Beautiful." Voice low and gravelly, Callum pushes one piece behind my ear and then twirls another. "How is it possible for one woman to be this stunning. I loved your long hair, my Venus, but this little shoulder length cut frames your face in the most sinful way. It's fun and sweet, and the only thing I want to do is bend you over this sink and bury myself deep. So deep that you'll spend the next few weeks feeling me every time you so much as inhale."

"You like it?" It's breathy, my body thrumming at his words.

"I fucking love." Pressing his back against mine, he lets me feel just how much he does. How hard he is for me, and every cell in my body vibrates for him. "You look so sweet and tempting, Miss Rubens. Like the perfect little doll."

"A doll?"

"Aye." From behind, he kisses the crown of my head and then lower until placing his lips at my temple. "Every inch of you is perfection, Aliana. How can you ever question that?" Then, he inhales deep and groans, his hands gripping the edge of my sleep top before slowly lifting it up. My stomach is exposed, the soft cotton stopping just below my breasts. "Your curves are decadent, while your scent is enough to bring any man to his knees. So sweet."

"Callum, I—"

I'm cut off with a quick nip to my ear. "Just listen, baby girl. Let me tell you what I see."

"Okay."

"Good girl." Callum steps back just enough to pull my top over my head and then he's back, skin on skin, my back to his chest. "When I look at you, Venus, I see a future I'd never wanted before. I see holidays all over the world. I see candlelit dinners." Strong fingers undo the delicate bow at my waist before pushing my bottoms down. They fall to my feet, leaving me bare to his eyes. No underwear. No barriers. There's lust in those eyes when they meet mine again, but something else pushes forward—an emotion that I don't understand but find myself wanting to. "I see a woman who's sweet and pure with a body I want to worship for years to come. You, my perfect girl, are a gift I plan to cherish, and you have a heart I'll nurture. You deserve the world, Aliana, and I'll give it to you. I'll help you see what everyone else does when they look at you."

"And what's that?" I whisper shakily, my eyes misting. "How do others see me?"

"A smart, gorgeous, and goal-oriented young woman that doesn't need a man to give her value, but when she allows one to stand beside her, he'll be the envy of every bloody bastard alive. They see a woman full of so much love and loyalty. They see a woman who deserves to have the world bow at her feet, and one day, I plan to make that a reality."

"Thank you." Those words fill my heart and warm my soul. To have someone like him see me like this… *Jesus*. With him, I feel like someone and not a commodity. "That means a lot."

"That's not enough for how special you are." Placing one last kiss, this time on my cheek, he steps back and holds out a hand. "Come take a shower with me."

I just took one and the proof still lingers in my hair, but I place my palm in his and let him lead me toward the shower where he turns the lever and waits a second for it to heat. Within seconds, a little steam begins to rise and he checks how hot, humming in the back of his throat when he approves.

Then he leads me in, body behind mine. I'm under the spray while he fingers the wet strands, pushing them back so the ends all meet at the center. His warmth rivals the water, his hands massaging my back and then spreading out.

"That feels good."

"And you are my heaven. My calm." Callum reaches for my bottle of shampoo and adds a generous amount to his palm. He rubs them together, creates a little lather, and then runs those talented fingers across my hair and scalp. From the very top to the last strand, he washes it slowly and with firm strokes that feel so good.

I'm lax. Had I not been leaning against him, I'm sure my body would be slumped against a wall. As it is, my legs feel weak and when he gives a gentle push so I'm standing directly under the rain shower attachment, I pull him with me. Reaching back, I grip his hip and keep him close, give a subtle gyration against the hardness digging into my lower back.

"Behave, love. Let me take care of you." A recurring theme. Each time it's about me, but I want to touch him too. To make him feel what I do, but when I try, I'm rebuffed by strong hands and my peach shower gel that he uses to rub my chest. From shoulders to breasts and back again, he massages my skin with firm strokes and then quick smacks to the tip of each tit. My nipples are hard, and each slap borders on pleasurable pain. "And trust me, Aliana, I'm doing this for selfish reasons. All I want is to touch you. To feel you bend under my fingertips."

"Feel the same," I whimper, the keening sound a mixture of frustration and bliss.

Hands wandering lower, he washes my midsection. Pays extra attention to my tattoo and piercing, fingering the new belly-button ring I bought with a jewel in the same tone as his eyes. If he's put it together, he doesn't say, but when Callum gives the metal a small tug, I push back harder. Grind myself against his cock; a torture, since I want to feel him stretch me.

To make me his.

"Do you dream of me every night?" One of his large hands cups my core, and I stop all movement. Whine in his hold. "Do you make this pretty little cunt come with my name on your sweet lips?"

"Yes." Another truth I can't deny. These last few days, no matter how tired I am, he's the last thing I see when I close my eyes, and not coming is an impossibility. "I touch myself to thoughts of you. To the memory of your mouth between my thighs."

"Motherfuck, love." A single digit parts my labia, the proof of my desire coating its tip. It's not the water, but him. All because of him. The eyes, tattoos, and raw hunger that possesses me even when he's not here. I'm powerless. "Such a good girl. All soaked for me. Ready for me."

The heel of his palm massages my clit, touch firm, and I moan. Loud and drawn out, the quickness in which he slips two fingers inside and pumps them savagely leaving me teetering on the edge before I can regain rational thought. I'm on the tips of my toes, hands on the wall now while he curves over my back, pumping two fingers deep and then pulling them out.

In and out. In and out.

Then they're gone, and I'm left gasping—groaning as my walls clench in need of him.

"Turn around."

"I can't move."

"You will." There's a sound that greets my ears above the water and my entire frame pauses. It's skin on skin, repetitive, and my mouth waters. My core throbs. "Turn for me."

"Please."

Faster. He's groaning low. "Now," Callum grits out and I force myself to function. Will myself to confirm my suspicions and seeing this specimen of a man pumping his cock into a tight fist is enough to break me. My knees buckle. I kneel before him and take the head between my lips and moan. He's warm and hard and the heady *fuck* that escapes in that deep voice is sinful. Worth the discomfort of the tiles digging into my knees.

I move his hand aside and take in another inch. Then another, bobbing my head along his thick length before pulling back with a string of spit connecting us. "Are you going to *behave* now and let me touch you? Let me feel your weight on my tongue?"

"You have sixty seconds."

"And what happens after," I ask right before flicking the tip with my tongue. "Will you punish me?"

"Fifty."

"That's not fair."

"Fifty-two."

With my eyes on his, I take him down to the back of my throat and swallow. His eyes narrow, hands clenching at his sides while I flick the tip of my tongue against the base of his length once, twice, and then pull back. This time, though, I pause at the engorged head and suck, hollowing my cheeks until I get what I want.

"Fuck, love. You have such a pretty little mouth," he growls. The sound is deep and reverberates through his chest, and I feel it all the way down to my core. My walls pulse—they grip at nothing. I want him. "Lips stretched. Full of me."

"More."

"You want more?" One of his large hands grips the back of my head, fisting the wet strands there. "Want me to fuck you?"

"Please."

"Then take what I give you." His hips snap forward and he strokes deep, not stopping until my lips touch the base and then he stays there, savoring the feel of my throat choking him. Callum groans deeply, shivers, and then pulls out and in. With each pump, the dark look in his eyes is hot. Exhilarating, and I let out a long moan at the sight. "You like this, don't you? To be used by me?"

All I can do is nod. Suck harder.

I'm not a virgin. I'm not someone who sleeps around or needs a man to get off.

But this, him…*he* brings out my inner whore.

I want to please him. Watch him lose control.

"Give me all of you, Callum."

For some reason, those words snap him back and he pulls out abruptly. The look on his face is feral, aroused and angry, but before I can ask *what's wrong*, I'm up, feet off the ground.

He's holding my weight and core right over his hard cock, labia against the heated flesh. My wetness coats him, my right thigh lifting a bit to open myself up a little more before closing.

I trap him against me, my thighs tightening.

This also reminds me of the night we met, how he lifted my body off the ground and held me while I gyrated against him, my ass to his thickness. Now it's my slick flesh that rubs him. *He feels so good.*

"All I wanted was to hold you all night. To rest, because I'm tired, Venus. So tired," he says, voice deep and low. Almost a growl. "I've missed my girl. Missed her smile. Her fresh peach scent." And I no longer argue those words. *He's right. I'm his.* With one hand, he grips my right asscheek, flexing his cock between my lips and they part, spreading to let him slide through. From clit to entrance and then poking out from the curve of my cheeks, I feel him. I'm nearly overwhelmed by his size and girth; I know he'll stretch me to the point of pain. Because Callum is bigger than my one rebellious mistake and the toys I have inside the drawer beside my bed. "Since I left, all I could think of was coming back to you. To have you beside me again."

"Me too." I'd leave with him today if he asked. No hesitation.

"But more than that, I hate that all I get is a few hours before I'm back on a plane."

"It's more than I thought I'd get," I whisper back, the heated rush of lust receding a bit. It still lingers in the background, simmering, but it's his sincerity that takes the forefront. To hear him, to experience his need, is heavenly. This between us isn't easy. Hell, my circumstances are a mess, but I'll wait. Find a way to be with him. *I was leaving for Europe soon anyway. That alone is a sign.* "We knew it wouldn't be an overnight fix, Callum. I'm willing to wait."

"I know, but the guilt still sits heavy with me. It's a feeling I'm not used to."

"Why guilt? You've done nothing wrong."

"That's the thing; I should be here. Always with you." His lips slant over mine the moment the last words slip through his plump lips. This kiss is less hurried and more worshipping, a slow overtaking of my senses, and I can't stop the gentle roll of my hips. Cock hard and tight against my slick pussy, I do it again and again, earning a hiss that I taste.

It's need and lust and an emotion that I'm not ready to decipher. The implication alone would be the end of me.

So instead, I give in and close the world out. I kiss him back just as eagerly, entwining our tongues and savoring a taste uniquely his. There's a hint of whiskey and smoke, but not cigarette. This is earthier. Attractive. Drawing back, I bite his lips, dragging my teeth down the abused flesh.

His grip on me tightens, and I cry out as pleasure spreads through my body. That small jerk, how the thick flesh drags across my clit, has me gasping for breath. I'm wound tight. I'm in need, and he knows this.

Revels in it.

"That's my Venus. Work me between those soft lips…" his exhale is rough, his touch a bit savage the next time I circle my hips "…I want to feel you come on me. I want to watch you lose control."

"Oh God," I whimper, picking up speed—rubbing my sensitive flesh over the hard flesh. It's all I can do with the limited movement he allows, and I press harder. Hump a little faster, my movements jerky and uncoordinated, but the rush of pleasure right within my grasp is all I can focus on.

It's right there.

He thrusts against me, and my eyes roll back.

Another pump and my fingernails dig into his shoulders, breaking the skin, and I use the anchor as leverage and bear down. I feel every ridge and vein, how he throbs and then his desperation to come undone.

"Motherfuck, baby girl. That's it…fucking feel you."

"Come with me." Eyes on his, I bite down hard on his chin. Gem-like eyes blaze at the move, and his cock slides across my pussy angrily before the resounding smack over my left asscheek makes me freeze. Pain blooms over my flesh, sharp and wicked, but then I'm coming hard and nothing else matters but the euphoria burning through my veins.

I hear his grunt in the background, feel the second spank, but it only serves to prolong my pleasure.

I'm jittery and breathless and dirty. I'm tender and achy and watching him the same way he's looking at me.

In awe.

In salvation.

In need.

His cock jerks between my thighs and his come coats my skin, running down my leg and then mixing with the water below us. It's a glorious feeling. We are right together.

After a few minutes, I let my eyes close and rest my head in the crook of his neck. My body is lax, and the exhaustion of the last few days hits me hard.

Callum cleans us up as best he can because I refuse to let him go. Instead, he lifts me higher and wraps my legs around his waist, gaining the room needed to wash me gently. He doesn't linger in the bathroom. My droopy body knows we are moving, and I feel the warmth of a towel across my back before he whispers, "Rest, I got you."

And I do. I'm out before we make it to the bed.

CALLUM

"**I** NEED YOU to wake up, sweetheart," I whisper in her ear, the clock on her bedside table reading six in the morning. I'll be leaving soon. My flight's scheduled for eight, but I want to spend a little more time with her.

Last night was amazing. Each time I'm near her brings me a sense of calm and happiness I've never experienced before. Yet, it also brings a level of guilt that eats at me like an infectious wound.

Leaving her doesn't sit right with me. I don't like the separation.

Aliana stirs but doesn't open her eyes. If anything, she tries to burrow in deeper, and I chuckle. She's bloody adorable—this beautiful little doll that I wish I could carry with me everywhere. I find myself being obsessive with her—wondering how she is and if she's eating or sleeping enough, something the bags under her eyes last night showed me she wasn't.

Giannis and Kray have explained that the Conte House has been busy, more so than normal, and long days have sometimes become longer nights. I'm also aware of the man that threatened to shoot the girls, and he's currently on his way to my plane after being held a couple of weeks in isolation.

He's been fed. He's been given one bathroom break a day.

I've been the model host.

"Baby, I need you to open those warm eyes for me."

"Don't wanna." She's pouting against my skin, lifting the sheet higher to attempt to hide. One second, she's half over me, leg across my hip, but on her next intake of breath, Aliana's on her back. I'm hovering, my hips cradled between her thighs—her lack of startling is an indicator that she's been playing possum the whole time, and I arch a brow. "Don't give me that look. You're warm and cozy."

"Every time it gets harder to leave."

"What time is your flight?" she asks, but her expressions are so unguarded. Open. I notice each: the sadness that flashes, and then the fake smile as if nothing bothers her. Her bravery and the hint of pain that's always there, lingering, even when she's laughing. *I'm going to uncover your every secret, my Venus. I want to take the weight you carry and make it mine.* "Do you need me to take you?"

"The only thing I want is to spend a few extra minutes with you."

"Okay." Aliana stretches, her naked flesh so bloody soft and sweet. She opens her arms, telling me without words to lower myself, and I do, covering her small form with my larger one. My lips are against her neck, taking her scent into my lungs and tattooing its genetic makeup on my DNA. "God, I need this too."

"Soon, sweetheart. Soon you'll be with me in London."

"You mean that? You want me to move across—"

Pulling back just enough so she can see my face, I stare into her eyes. That slight hesitation in her question—voice—shouldn't be there. "If I could take you today, I would without a single hesitation. But I will. We've taken care of everyone but the man who shot her. I left Casper yesterday to handle the facilitator to come be with you, but I do have to go home now and handle work. We're so close, baby. Just please be patient with me."

"I could never fault you for what's happening."

"Thank you." Retaking my place on her neck, I place a chaste kiss there. "By the way, when's your family holiday?"

"You remember that?"

"I do."

She hums for a second, her fingernails scraping down my back. I don't miss the way she tenses, but I'm not going to call her out on it. Not today. "Dad hasn't said anything yet, but I think in a week or two."

"You sure?" She's hiding something, and I will find out what.

"I'll ask and get back to you. Just give me a few days."

"Aye, love." The rhythmic way she touches me is soothing. Almost lulls me, and I go to move and lie beside her, keep from crushing her, but Aliana makes a noise of complaint in the back of her throat. "I just want you to be comfortable."

"I already am." She pulls me closer; her leg hooks mine behind the knee to keep me in place. Silence fills the room after that. We just lay while the early morning rays filter into the room, and my second alarm goes off. This is a text, the ringtone belonging to Kray, and it means he's waiting outside. "Already?"

"Unfortunately, yes."

"Hey, Callum?" she asks, but I don't move from my place at the crook of her neck. Instead, I close my eyes and nod, drowning myself in her warmth for another minute. "When will I see you again?"

"Soon."

"Can I get a timeframe?"

"I'd like to have that second date in two weeks, Miss Rubens. Do you accept?"

"Aye." Her attempt at my accent is atrocious, yet lovely

She has me by the balls and doesn't even know it.

***

WE ARRIVE at the airstrip two hours behind schedule, but fuck it, I couldn't leave her yet. Not when she was all warm and sweet and clinging to me while her mouth lied. Aliana says she's okay, understanding and unaffected, but I see her.

All of her.

But it's not just our situation. Something or someone here upsets her.

We need to talk. ~Callum J.

Pocketing my mobile after messaging Giannis, I exit the vehicle to an already waiting Kray while ignoring the responding buzz of a message. He's become someone I trust, reliable, and soon enough he'll have a decision to make.

"Thank you for the change of clothes and accessories, mate." I'm pulling the Glock provided out of the small case it came with and checking the magazine. It pops out and in easily enough, but I'm not one for deviate from my norm and my Ruger is predictable. Its accuracy is unparalleled, something not needed right now. "I'll leave the latter for you to dispose of."

"Will do."

"You can also bring her on."

The look of surprise on his face is almost comical. "What? How—"

"The Jamesons are good at what they do, my friend. We have eyes and ears everywhere." The meaning behind those words dawns on him and he nods, accepting that a life around my family means no privacy. We take no chances. "I won't hide who she is or what from Aliana, but Lindsey could keep close during the day without drawing too much attention. I'll video call you this week to discuss further, but I agree with it so far."

"Thank you, Callum." He steps back, and I walk toward the jet where a man waits for me. On his knees and on the left—away from the stairs—the arsehole that tried to hurt Aurora and Aliana at work waits while the flight crew looks straight ahead. "I'll personally handle this cleanup. No one will get this close to her again."

"You make sure of that."

From pilot to attendant, they stand side by side and I don't pause to acknowledge anyone.

I pull the trigger. And again.

Bullet after bullet empties into the man's head, and he drops sideways as the gun meets the tarmac.

"No one threatens Aliana."

"Yes, sir."

No one moves as I enter the plane and sit.

No one talks to me as they finish prep and then take off.

"GOOD TO HAVE YOU BACK, SIR," Jeffrey says, greeting me at the family's private airstrip. His hand's outstretched at the bottom of the jet's steps, a cuppa in his other from my favorite shop. It's for me, and after a quick shake, I take a hearty sip. "Miss Langley sends her regards."

"Cheers, mate."

"There's also a bag of biscuits in the car."

I nod, smiling. That woman is something else. "Did the old bat flirt?"

"Of course. It's what she does at the ripe old age of eighty." His laugh is loud, catching the attention of the flight crew beginning their clean-up procedure. "Says it keeps her young."

"As long as she makes me this, I give no bloody fucks." I make my way toward the black Lincoln he's driving but notice he's not behind me. "Something wrong?"

"Did you not bring a bag?"

"Casper has it. I had a secondary stop to make."

"Understood." That's what I like about Jeffrey. He doesn't pry. Doesn't meddle, and it also shows me Ezra continues to be loyal. He's the only one that knew of my stop in Chicago, although the reasons elude him too. "By the way, your father and uncle are at Sr.'s home. They're both living there now."

"Since when?"

"About a week ago."

"Interesting."

"Your mum doesn't think so." He's not being disrespectful. That's a warning of the situation I could be walking in to.

"How bad?" My tea is getting cool, and I drink half the contents in a few deep sips. "She still around?"

"Yes, sir."

"Great." I walk toward his vehicle and slide into the passenger side, Jeffrey just a few steps behind me. Once inside, he's quick to put the already running car in drive and exit the airstrip. "Head to my uncle's house first and then take the rest of the day off. I want no one inside, just leave two guards on the grounds, and we'll talk tomorrow."

"As you wish." Traffic isn't too bad today, just a few slow drivers that don't understand the *move the fuck over* policies of the road, but within thirty minutes, we're pulling into the long driveway where sure enough, my father's car is present. Jeffrey parks behind him, car idling. "What time do you need me tomorrow?"

"Ten."

"Here?"

I shake my head, hand on the door handle. "My penthouse overlooking Parliament. We have a lot to discuss."

"Of course, Callum. And if you need me—"

"Take the day off, mate. You never stop."

He laughs at that, his age showing in the crinkles around his eyes. "Old habits."

"Old being the operative word," I deadpan before getting out and closing the door, his laughter following me up the steps to a grand manor that seems cold and empty now. My aunt's flowers haven't been taken care of and the wreath at the door is faded and old, something she'd never allow if alive. "She'd be pissed at the sight of this."

The front door is unlocked, and I step inside, listening for noise. And it doesn't take me long to find the two old men whose ruckus makes my ears bleed. They're in the kitchen and arguing about something—more than likely politics—and sharing a bottle of whiskey without any glasses.

"Oi, isn't this a sight."

"My son returns." Dad stands, then sits, a little on the wobbly side. "Where have you been?"

"None of your business." Looking at the man beside him, I walk over and squeeze his shoulder. "You okay, old man?"

"Day at a time."

"That's all you can do." Grabbing the bottle, I walk over to the sink and pour it down the drain. "But this isn't going to help. You need food, a shower, and then we need to talk."

"My son made up his mind?"

"He did." There's a pod in the coffee maker and I press the start button, grabbing two cups from the cabinet above the machine. And while it brews, I grab the fresh bagels and cream cheese, popping the bread into the toaster. "Where's the house staff? Why are you two having a liquor-filled breakfast?"

Casper's dad nods, scratching at his unshaven jaw. "She'll be good for him. Has given him purpose."

"The staff?"

"Gave them the week off. It's been a loud one."

"What the bloody hell are you two going on about?" Dad asks, but I pay him no mind. Our dynamic has always been strained—like associates rather than father and son. "Who will be good for who? Who is *she*?"

"My son is taking over Boston, and my nephew is now the head if this family."

"Since when? Why am I just finding out now?"

"Because you have no say." Both turn to look at me, one with pride and my father with surprise. "That conversation was between Casper and me, the two who matter." The ceramic mug in my hand shatters upon sudden impact, the shards flying through the air and across the quartz counter. A piece slices across my knuckles, the blood pooling beneath my fingers. "We ran this syndicate for the last five years. We bathed London in the blood of our enemies while you spent your time between golf games and drinking with members of the house."

In the background, I hear the toaster pop and the coffee machine beep, but fuck it all—I couldn't care less. What this arse has implied won't be swept under the rug. Fuck him. Not this time.

"Callum, I think we should—"

"Stop protecting him from me," I seethe, flicking my heated gaze to my uncle. "You always step in, saving him from hearing the shit he doesn't want to hear. He was a horrible father, a messy right hand to you, and always unable to admit his wrongs. He's as bad as Mum, but at least her excuse is being absent and not just the self-centered nature neither grew out of."

My uncle tries to interject again, but Dad holds his hands up. "Let it be. He's right." There's no hiding the surprise on my face at that. He's not a man to ever admit his wrongs. "I've been an arse all these years, have missed a lot, but let me be clear here, son. Not once have I doubted you or implied that you're not capable of running this family. On the contrary. I know you'll do better than those before you."

I relax my stance and take the offered towel from his brother. "Then what did you mean?"

"I'm a member of this family, Callum. That's what I meant." Dad walks over and puts a hand on my shoulder, his expression softer than I've ever seen. "I'd like to be kept up to date, not shoved aside. That's it."

"Fair enough."

"You also need to know one more thing, lad." When I don't answer, he gives me a sad smile. "I've never…not once, doubted you or what you're capable of. You've always been bloody brilliant and responsible, you excel where I lack, and I'm proud of you."

"Thank you."

"Don't. I'm a shit parent, if you don't already know this."

"Speaking of parent," I say, changing the subject. That, and I need to move this along and get my hand stitched up. "Where is she?"

"At the house, fuming." Dad lets out a loud, long sigh. The sound heavy and full of exhaustion. "It's over. I've given her the divorce papers."

Motherfuck. "Great. I'm sure she'll call me to complain soon enough."

"And I apologize for that ahead of time."

Aliana

"SOCKS. I NEED SOCKS," I grumble under my breath, heading toward my small laundry room. I've done nothing but wash, fold, and arrange for the last two days—since getting the news— and my closet has never been so clean. I'm not a neat freak or anal over what goes where, but right now, I rival professional organizers. "Socks. Must get socks."

This is a coping mechanism, a way to distract myself from the inevitable. I know this. I'm not unaware of my faults and the role I play in this mess.

I'm leaving.

I'm doing this, even though every fiber of my being hates it.

I've lied to my friend. I have no choice but to lie to him, a phone call I'm dreading.

"Today." I'll call him today and just get this over with.

In a small way, I find reprieve in our long-distance relationship. The weeks without him near have made the lies a little easier to say—the phone calls and video-chats hide more than just a person's true feelings. He didn't see my reaction after having no contact with my family for months. He didn't see how physically sick I became after the instructions were delivered.

A knock on the door of my small office at the women's home makes me look up from the new software I'm thinking of adding to our budget. It's nothing fancy or difficult to navigate, but definitely one you need if looking to land any office job.

"Can I help you?" The man standing there looks vaguely familiar, but I can't pinpoint him.

"Miss Rubens?" he asks, voice rough as if he's smoked his entire life.

"That's me." Discreetly, I bring a hand to my waist and the new bottle of pepper spray there. It's a new brand and promises near blindness upon contact. "And again. How can I help you?"

In his hand he holds a stapled sheet of paper and envelope. "I'm here to deliver this. Can you please sign for me?"

"Sure." I'm not expecting anything, and he just doesn't fit the bill of a courier. This man is in a cheap suit and is wearing too much cheap cologne. His hair is slicked back and face unshaven. "What is it?"

"It's from Governor Rubens's office." Five words that ruin my day. My stomach plummets and hands begin to sweat as he brings the envelope over.

I thought he was leaving me alone. I thought I was free.

Hastily, I sign my name, the man leaves, and I'm stuck with the manila bomb sitting atop the desk.

Just get it over with. *Tearing into the package, I'm greeted by the sight of airplane tickets, a fake itinerary, and a note that says:*

My Beautiful daughter,

You work too hard and deserve a break. There's more to life than the hustle and bustle of an office or school, Aliana. Please accept this early birthday present from your mother and no complaining sweetheart. It's done, and we've booked you an all—inclusive package with six days of fun in the sun and relaxation.

You leave in five days!

Have fun,

Your loving parents.

But worse than that is the picture I find folded within the itinerary of my father with an arm thrown over my brother's shoulders. A knot forms in my throat. This is a silent threat. The picture depicts a loving family, a dad and his two boys, but I see the evil in his eyes. I take in the way my brothers are tense and…

The ringing of my cell in another room pulls me from those depressive thoughts—how easily they use and manipulate me while always saving face for the public. To an outsider, they seem like loving, caring, and generous parents. Doting and sweet, but I know better, and my father does everything in a way that saves his own behind.

He'll gamble mine, but never his. He'll hurt them to make me bend.

Rushing out, I toss my basket atop the dryer. It's Aurora's ringtone and I manage to pick up on the fourth ring, slightly out of breath and stomach in knots. "Yolo!" I half wheeze, half chuckle. "You back to the land of the living?"

"I am," she laughs, whatever music she'd been listening to dimming down a bit. She's been a bit under the weather the last few days, not coming into the Conte House. Thank God it's been manageable, the women who've been there the longest stepping up to help the newbies acclimate to the rules and daily routine.

Everyone has a chore or job: from cooking, to cleaning, to daycare, and that has nothing to do with the classes we offer. And while most don't like the tight structure at first, they love it soon enough when it cements bonds with those around them. Friendships. Understanding.

They no longer feel alone or misunderstood.

"I'll be back in the office tomorrow. We need to go over the new class schedule before you leave, and that software you mentioned. Sorry about that, by the way. This bug came out of nowhere."

"Only you would apologize for being sick."

"Shut up." Roe snorts, then smacks her lips as if tasting something sour. "God, this stuff is awful."

"What are you eating?"

"Drinking." A groan of disgust comes through the line. A little gagging. "Kombucha is just not for me. Dear Lord, just say no."

"Who told you to put that in your mouth?" I've had that experience. That's one of those drinks that you either love or hate, and there is no in between. I get that the benefits outweigh the taste, but I'm a chicken and avoid it at all costs. "You should know better."

"Just a friend." The way she says *friend* makes me smirk. *Why are you hiding him, doofus?*

"Does this 'friend' have a name?"

"The person does, but my lips are sealed."

"Why is that?" A text comes in, the small device in my hand vibrating. I pull back to look, and a smile stretches across my lips.

> We're going on a vacation soon. Just you and me. ~Callum J.

I'm not thinking of Aurora when I begin to type, ignoring her voice in the background.

> Where to? Somewhere sunny and with a private beach I can skinny dip in? ~Venus

A few moments after I hit send, two things happen at the same time...

Aurora's face greets me through the FaceTime setting, switching over without me knowing.

Callum texts back, and I open it like an idiot, face flaming red when I'm greeted by a glistening-from-the-shower, thick cock.

My mouth waters. Her eyes narrow.

"You're hiding something," Roe sings, arching a brow from her kitchen, the phone propped up against something. But more importantly, that look is daring me to deny her. Funny, she says I'm a dog with a bone when I want to know something, and yet, I've left her alone. *I've been too busy losing myself in Callum.* "Spill."

"No, I'm not."

"Yes, you are."

Matching her stare, I mock-glare. "So, what does that make you?"

"Too nosy for her own good when I've been a shitty friend lately." Her voice is contrite and face sheepish—sad. It's not what I expected either, nor is it right. She has no reason to feel like this. Not at all.

"Stop it, chica," I say, flicking the camera as if it were her head. "You've done nothing to feel like that. We've been busy and life is a hormonal bitch at the moment, but a shitty friend you are not."

"Feels that way."

"Then so am I, if you look at it from that perspective. I should be burned at the stake."

Aurora rolls her eyes. "Always need to one up me. So extra."

"Who else will keep you in check?" Taking the device with me, I make my way back to the laundry room and lean it against the large detergent pod container. "But if you want to make it up to me..."

She snorts, the tightness around her eyes disappearing. "Lunch tomorrow?"

"Yup. I'm in the mood for Thai."

"Done." While I pull out my small load, she takes another sip of her fermented drink, grimacing after she swallows. "By the way, where are you guys going this time? Did the governor tell you, or does he just expect you to show up?"

"What do you think?"

"The latter."

"Word." With my hip, I close the dryer and walk out with her lying atop my clean ankle socks. "That's how the dependable man of the people always behaves. We are his sheep."

"He's so much like my father. Exhausting."

"How is dear Papa Cancio?" My luggage is atop the bed, empty, but there. I have my clothes all in piles and separated by types. *I'd rather go on vacation with Callum.* "Is he still expecting you to take over?"

"He is."

"And?" I ask, looking back at the screen to find her head tilted, studying me. "What?"

"You can't hide your emotions, Ali. Not from me."

"Why do you say that?" My voice comes out an octave higher. My hands are a little shaky and I dig them into the laundry, pretending to be looking for something.

"Maybe it's because in the span of this conversation, you've gone from smiling and blushing to sadness and then a one-eighty into irritation, only to turn back around and end at longing."

"You're seeing something that isn't there."

"Or something's going on with you." She taps her lips with her middle finger, and I can't help but snort. So immature, but it does help loosen a bit of my tension. "Something you don't want to share."

"Like you and mystery man?"

"Do you have one of your own? Because I know you, Rubens, and you're being weirder than normal."

"And if I do?" Better to give her something than continue evading. This way, she understands. "What if it's really new and I'm just feeling him out? What if he's knocked me on my butt, but I'm not ready for the intros and—"

My best friend holds up her hands. "I get it."

"Do you?"

"I do." For a beat, we're both silent but then she sighs, and I scrunch up my face in question. "I'm being an ass when you've been patient with me...aren't I? It's not like I'm sharing."

"No. You're not, but I'll be here when you're ready."

"And I'll do the same."

"Deal."

CALLUM

IT'S BEEN TWO months since I last touched her. Showed up unannounced and tasted her.

Sixty-one days since I've had to live off FaceTime and phone calls. Where I spend all day waiting for our nightly routine where I log into the cameras in her home and watch her sleep. My obsession knows no bounds. My need is near maddening.

Because since taking over, I've had one truth smack me in the face over and over. No matter where I am, who I'm dealing with, or while joining Casper on this search, I always have her on my mind.

Her place is beside me. She's my home, and I am hers.

It's one of the reasons I'd been so calm while flying into Cuban soil. We're here to put an end to the manhunt—I'm quiet and alert, talking only when necessary, and my bloodthirst is high.

The man inside is more than my aunt's killer; he's an obstacle that needs to be removed.

Where the fuck am I?

Let me go, cabron!

I'm going to kill you.

Mauricio Hernandez is a loud one, yelling and threatening from his place inside of the De Leon compound in Cuba. He's been here a few days now, a place where those who enter do not escape, and I admire the colonial facade and isolated structures.

No one to hear you for miles.

No one here will lift a finger against this family.

The doors are closed to the main area, and a quiet Casper opens them without pause.

Archie will stay outside with the De Leon guards, awaiting orders, while Ivan, the second-in-command and youngest son, walks beside me in silence. He's a lot like me in a way: easygoing until you touch one of ours. And the putrid twat inside did just that.

All the women in crime families are sacred. Untouchable, but to kill a mum?

That's an instant death sentence.

My nostrils flare as I step inside. The stench is rotten—disgusting—but it only makes the demon within me happy. Because I know the smells will match the almost corpse tied up and awaiting trial.

Bright lights turn on, and the noise level rises. Animals—large hogs— make their presence known within empty cells. Each door is open, the inhabitants quiet and watching now, while surrounding the lone figure at the center. I'm pleased with the hospitality he's been shown.

Dirt-caked blood on bruised skin, a dislocated shoulder taking the brunt of his weight from his restrained position.

For a second, I close my eyes and breathe in deeply. Ire pulses through my veins. Heat licks at my flesh.

I've come to accept a long time ago that I crave moments like this. I need the violence, but today it's more. It's personal while signaling a rebirth.

Casper's and mine. Two different paths, two syndicates to run, and yet, we'll always be intertwined by more than familial ties because of the women we love.

Because I do. It's been there the entire time.

No hiding. No denying. The moment she sassed me inside that lounge, she owned me.

Burn him alive if you must, Callum. Just take me
away when you're done. ~Venus

Her text from this morning replays in my mind then, and I can almost hear Aliana's sweet voice utter her plea. Her need. *Something is off with her.* I notice it each time we talk now.

It's been that way since finding out she's going on holiday with her family. As if she hates the idea. No excitement. No funny quip or mention of the things she'll be doing while at some all-inclusive resort in Mexico.

Something that further cements she needs me as much as I breathe for her.

"I will, sweet girl." No one hears my words, and I open my eyes to meet Mauricio's.

He's dirty. Smells like utter shit. An old cunt with a big mouth.

"Who the fuck—"

"Evening," Casper says, tone even and calm. Mauricio's eyes turn to look at him, squinting due to the bright lights before looking at me again. He does this a few times. Back and forth before pausing on my cousin.

We're both dressed similarly; all black and wearing the damn suspenders I hate, but his mum thought they were dashing. And like him, I carry with me a piece of jewelry she had blessed when we were young—his by the Pope, and mine by a Buddhist monk.

He has a chain, while I have a bracelet with an attached medallion: a Greek warrior's helmet on the front.

"Who are you?" he asks again. "Why am I here?"

"Why *is* he here?" Casper repeats, looking back at me, then Ivan. His eyes hold a feral tint I'm sure reflected in my own, but we're not here for a quick death. Hernandez will hurt. Bleed. "The man's asking why he's here?"

"Poor lad," I answer in the same tone, my rage barely controlled as I walk over. In my hand, I have the package Ivan gave me when we arrived. "This is a horrible predicament to find yourself in."

Ivan steps into the light then, placing a chair in Mauricio's line of sight, then steps back. "It is."

"You!" the arsehole yells, fighting his restraints. His eyes are narrowed at Ivan. *So much hate.* "You were at the bar—"

"Yes. I was. And it was an interesting night, indeed. Many stories shared over a bottle of Havana Club. Do you remember that?" The doors to this room slam shut, locks engaging before Ivan hits the button at the center of the remote in his hand. At once, the lights dim making it easier for the piece of shit to get a better look. No more squinting. "Remember the story you shared of your recent time in London?"

"I don't remember."

"I'm going to give you a minute to go through your memories, Mr. Hernandez." Casper cracks his neck, then shakes out his arms. "Use your time wisely."

"You have the wrong man," he says without pause. His body glistens with sweat, more than when we came in. A natural reaction to fear; his choking is a pulsing wave permeating every inch of this personal jail. "I'm innocent."

The wanker gave himself away.

If you've done no wrong, there's no reason to defend yourself.

"I haven't accused you of anything yet, mate." Casper looks toward Ivan. "Have you?"

"Not at all."

"And you?"

My response is a snort. "I haven't said a word."

"See?" My cousin does a 360-degree turn, arms out wide. "No accusations. However, I do believe you have a story to tell us."

"I'm not him."

At that moment, Ivan turns, and I follow him toward the last cell. This one doesn't have an animal inhabitant but is full of useful items: a collection of knives in various sizes, ropes and chains, and two hospital beds that have seen better days. Both are rusted, and I'm not sure if the stains aren't blood.

We move the latter of the two farther back and pull out an old, creaky cart.

The laptop and camera on top of it are new, and it'll serve two purposes. We have a special movie-time feature, and my uncle deserves to watch his last moments.

This was too short notice for him to come.

"Motherfucker!" Mauricio suddenly yells out, and I smirk. *Fucker didn't wait.* Not that I blame him. This is his kill. "Stop! This is a mistake."

We stop with the cart a few feet from the now wounded arse, the blood coming from the back of his leg.

Casper's Karambit drips with blood.

The large swine squeal.

My eyes meet Ivan's and I nod. He's quick to press the button for the cells and they close, locking in all of the pigs but two.

Those two roam close. They're curious, the scent of blood creating a frenzy, and soon hunger will follow.

Because pigs can be cannibals. Cases have been reported of bodies being consumed, leaving only the bones behind.

"I'm going to ask you once more, Hernandez." Casper crosses his arms, his expression neutral. Yet, I notice the twitch of his fingers around the knife's handle. "Tell me the story you shared with my friend, here. Last chance."

"He's lying!" Mauricio's struggles intensify against his bonds, thrashing—shaking. "I was just at the bar celebrating my wedding anniversary."

"Really?" Ivan shakes his head, eyes hard on him from his position by the laptop. He's hooking everything up. "Because there was no one with you but the prostitute you bought for the night. And don't worry; I left her every single cent you had in your wallet back at the cheap hotel you were hiding in. Those two hundred thousand in cash will be used by her family and friends to survive and have a better life."

"You piece of shit. I will kill you!"

Ivan just stares. "That's a mighty big threat from an innocent man."

"Do you know who I am? I will...*fuck*!" My cousin strikes, this cut running from knee to mid-thigh. It's deep, bleeding heavily, and the floor beneath him soon has a puddle. This gets the animal's attention.

One gets curious. Snaps his teeth.

"Feel like telling me that story now? Come one, Mauricio. Let's reminisce."

His silence feels like a slap in the face. He's ignoring the man whose mum he killed. Denying his past instead of accepting his reality like a man. *Fucking pussy.*

"Maybe he just needs a little help getting there. Something to remember?" I walk over, my steps unhurried as I pick up a bottle of rum. It's open, half gone, but has enough left for me to get my point across. "Right, friend?"

Immediately his eyes widen, and he arches back, digging the rope into his wrists. "Don't. Please don't…I'll talk."

"So you do remember?" And like the arsehole I am, I pour a wee bit of the alcohol onto his leg. Not on the cut, but close enough that he screams like the twat he is.

"Don't do this."

"Do what?" A little more, this time a few drops slip onto the wound, and he cries out. Full-on blubbering mess. "Repeat that?"

"I'll tell you what you want to know. Just let me walk out of here alive —promise not to kill me."

"But first, let's start with a slide show. A beautiful message from a friend?" Casper nods in approval, while Ivan turns on the computer. The guest of honor is quiet, though, and I add another few drops over the last. "What do you think, Hernandez?"

"Yes."

The cart is moved closer, touching his body. Rust smears across his dirty flesh, a streak Casper follows with the tip of his blade. A shallow cut, but if you were to believe the sounds coming from Hernandez, you'd think we tore a limb off.

"Where are they?" Casper grits out, his lip curling over his teeth. I know he's hurting. All of this cuts deep.

His mum will never get to meet Aurora.

My aunt will never get to embarrass me in front of Aliana.

I point at the app, and he stalks over, pressing play before standing back. We all do.

Let him see how far our depravity goes. Let him see his friend, Felix Vega, take his last breath.

Because I was right in sending in Alexander when I did.

Mauricio should've never accepted the job. Neither should've.

Felix received a punishment—was tortured by one of the best in the business. Burns. Strikes. Cuts. Alexander is brutal, and he took pleasure in cutting the man's cock off an inch at a time. Then his balls. Slowly, bleeding him and then patching up enough to stave off his death before doing it again.

He broke his mind. His will to live.

And then when Felix takes the gun Casper gave him and pulls the trigger, blowing his brains out; it's all documented. It plays once and then again. Every brutal moment. Every scream reverberates inside the large room.

"I'm sorry."

That's my cue and I'm quick to flip from video to Skype, my uncle coming onto the screen a few seconds later. He nods at us, but no one speaks.

"So, you do know who I am?"

"Yes. I studied your picture and file for two weeks before the hit took place."

"Who sent you?" No answer. Mauricio's lips press tight.

That shit pisses me off, and I grab the bottle, jamming the nozzle into his thigh. Tip it over. "Answer him!"

Screams rend the air, the wail painful to the ear. It also riles up the animals. They bang against the cages, squeaking and grunting, while the two on the loose come closer.

They shuffle at the floor by his feet. They snap at the air.

Ivan pushes them back with a metal pole.

"This will only work for so long, Hernandez." Casper taps his cheek with a bloody hand. "Tell me their real names and not the bullshit Felix gave me."

"No one knows their real names, and I didn't care enough to ask."

"Tell me what you know. All of it."

"Nico and Antonella are the children of Giada Savino. These three hate Matteo Cancio for something that happened between their father and the Boston mob boss a very long time ago. They never told me what, but from what Felix said, it all started a year after Aurora, Cancio's daughter, was born."

We're not surprised by this. Aurora's family is somehow involved; they're the catalyst, while we're the combustion.

"Matteo wasn't in charge then."

"The father, Matteo Cancio Sr., was."

"Okay." Casper tosses his knife onto the cart while I hand over what's left the liquor bottle. He brings it to the injured man's lips. "Drink. It'll help."

"Just kill me."

"I will, but I need something first."

Mauricio takes the offered drink, swallowing a heavy shot. "You want to talk about your mother?"

"She wasn't your intended target." Not a question, and Hernandez nods. "Then why shoot an innocent woman?"

"They doubled the offer." Another shot, this time a wee bit falls into his wound, and he hisses. "Those are a bitch. Hurt like hell."

"That's the point." I take the bottle back from my cousin, pouring the rest onto the floor. "Now, about the money?"

"I was supposed to receive the other half a mil next week to an account I have in Guatemala City. The national bank doesn't ask questions and after slipping the manager a couple of bucks, he speeds the process up personally."

"What day next week?"

"Wednesday."

"Thank you for your cooperation." With that, Casper pulls out his gun and shoots him four times in the upper torso. Mauricio groans, eyes rolling back, and I use Casper's knife to cut him down.

He lands on the cold, hard floor with a thud. The sound and his blood draw the roaming swine closer, and closer, while we walk away.

Once at the exit, Ivan lets them all out.

Hungry, feral animals.

It doesn't take them long to attack, and his horror-filled screams are beautiful. A soothing balm to my soul.

His ending is justified.

A man without honor deserves to be pig food.

CALLUM

I'M FRESH OUT of the shower, towel drying my hair, when my mobile goes off. It rings twice and goes to voicemail, but within seconds someone's calling again. Walking to the dresser where I left it, I notice the screen is lit up with ten missed calls, eight texts, and three voicemails.

"What the fuck?" Unlocking the device, I scroll through the list and they're all from Giannis.

That puts me on alert, and I quickly log into the cameras in Aliana's home, finding her walking through the living room toward her room holding a laundry basket. She's talking to someone, laughing, but before I can turn the speakers on, Giannis's name flashes across my screen.

I press answer, and all I hear is a muttered, *finally.* "Callum? You there?"

"Yes." Tone annoyed, I snap at the interruption. My need to know who she's giggling with claws at me. "What's with the calls and messages?"

"I shouldn't be telling you this," he starts, voice a bit shaky, and I pause. He's not one to reach out outside of his reporting, and even then, I can tell he wants to get off the phone quickly. I intimidate him. "She's left me with no choice, though. Stubborn woman."

"Get to the point." Tossing the towel still in my hand and the one around my waist onto the bed, I grab the plain grey pajama bottoms and slip them on sans underwear. It's a warm night out, the windows are open, and a soft breeze comes in off the coast that isn't far from here. Between that and the ceiling fan above my head, I find it rather comfortable. "You're rambling is rather off-putting."

"Callum, before I begin, please know that I told her to tell you. I've been arguing with her over this for the last few days and—"

"What the bloody fuck is going on with Aliana?" My breathing is harsh, my grip on my mobile causing the plastic to strain. "Straight to the point. No more bullshit."

"Her father is sending her to Brazil on an errand by herself."

"Come again?" I must've heard wrong. Because that's not what my sweet Venus told me.

TWO DAYS AGO...

Hey, you got a minute? ~Venus

Her text comes through while I'm sitting in on a meeting with our gun supplier, giving him the courtesy of knowing there's been a change in power. Not because we have to, but because he's worked with our family for a long time, and we consider him a friend. Or at least, his father was. This bloke I find to be an obnoxious twit with the personality of a potato.

In a meeting. What's up? ~Callum J.

Three dots appear on the screen and then disappear. Start up again and then nothing.

Are you okay? ~Callum J.

A throat clears and I look up, meeting Alfie's eyes. "Are you listening to me?"

His tone doesn't sit well with me, and I lean back, drumming my fingers on the table. "No. I'm not."

"And this is who you chose to take Casper's place?" he questions my uncle and father, that haughty arrogance coming through again, and I exhale roughly. It's been a busy few weeks between my stepping up while Casper searched and killed the man who shot his mum. I'm constantly traveling to where he is if I'm needed, and also dividing the men between who I will keep, and who will be moving abroad.

Most know what's going on, but the announcement's been pushed back for a reason.

I want to go through each person on our roster, from vendor to buyer to the fucking arse that delivers the morning paper.

My uncle vetted his people.

Casper vetted his crew.

I will decide mine.

Of the four people in the room, two move one hand beneath the table at his blatant disrespect while I look at the last message that came in.

> I'm fine, just need to talk when you get a chance.
> ~Venus.

> Give me ten. ~Callum J.

Placing my mobile face down atop the table, I meet my father's eyes and then look at the door. He gets it and stands, walking to it and then locks it while my uncle glares at the git. This makes Alfie nervous, and he shifts in his seat while the man beside him pales.

I feel for the bloke. He truly seems like he abhors his job.

"You're fired." At those two words, his head snaps in my direction, eyes wide. He tries to say something, to protest, but I hold a hand up. The same one that now holds my gun. "Our contract is now void, Mr. Buford."

"You can't do that," he gasps, looking toward the older men inside the room for support. There's none there, and Alfie swallows hard at the other weapons placed upon the table. "We've been in business for so long. Your cousin wouldn't agree—"

"It's my word you should concern yourself with." Relaxing back in my chair, I tsk. "Please hand me the folder to your right." Casper's father slides it across the table to me, his stare never wavering on the man who has no business being the head of a respected trafficking ring. When his father was alive, Sr. made sure to anticipate needs, adjust pricing to market demand, and compete with a quality rivaling that of the American and the British army.

This man is a joke.

Useless.

"Please think this through. No one can supply what I can."

"Wrong." I open the file and grab the top sheet, skimming down, and then passing it along.

"What's this?" Instead of answering, I point to it and wait. Alfie's eyes lower and read, face pinching tight while the paper in his hand crumbles. "How could you do this? We have an agreement—"

He doesn't get to finish. My finger's quicker than his reactions, and I shoot once, the bullet going through his arm and embedding itself into the wall behind him. "This has been a long time coming, in my opinion. You've relied too much on your father's legacy to keep up with the demands of loyal clients. The last three deliveries have been rubbish, your attitude obnoxious, and quite frankly, I can't see myself continuing this working relationship without slitting your throat."

"Callum, I—"

"It's Mr. Jameson to you." Pushing my chair back, I stand and lean over the table. "We're done, and as you can see," I hiss, hand slamming atop the new contract I signed yesterday with a Spaniard bloke who brings more to the table than guns. "I already made my decision. Leave with pride, or inside of a body bag. The choice is yours."

With that, I pick up my mobile and walk out of what is now my office. My father and uncle will see them out, while I have a more pressing matter to attend to. I press the number one on my mobile and her name flashes across the screen, ringing twice before her light breathing comes across the line.

The pub is not busy at the moment as I exit the establishment and pull out a joint. I light it up and take a deep drag, warming my lungs with the earthy smoke. It's soothing. My body calms.

"Talk to me, Venus. Everything okay?"

Whatever she hears in my voice makes her giggle, and fuck, I'm hard at once. Throb. "I'm fine, silly. Just have some news."

"Oh yeah? You coming to visit me?"

"I wish," she mutters low, but I hear. I also don't question it. "This is actually about our family vacation, Mr. Jameson. We have a date."

"When you call me Mr. Jameson..." reaching down, I adjust myself, squeezing a bit "...the only thing I want to do is bend you over my knee, love. I want to make that gorgeous arse a pretty shade of pink."

"Promise?"

"Naughty little thing."

My response makes her laugh again. The sound so sweet. "Behave. You're far away and my hand needs a break."

Fuck. That image is dangerous. For me. For her. *I'd break her.*

It's been too long since I've had her. Touched her.

"Tempting me—"

"We're heading to Bora Bora for a week," Aliana interrupts, her tone a bit nervous. The change in her lilt is minor, but almost as if she's embarrassed. *Cute*. "The entire Rubens family is going."

"You excited?" Another deep pull of my spliff, deeper inhale this time, and I hold it in for a few seconds before exhaling slowly. "Packed yet?"

"Sure."

Not the answer I'm expecting and my brows furrow. "Do you not want to go?"

"I do, but I'll miss you."

PRESENT...

"Are you sure about this?" I ask Giannis.

"Yes." He lets out a grumbled groan. "I told her to tell you. To ask for help."

"What the fuck is going on?" When it comes to my Venus, I have no patience. I'm trying hard to remember that he came to me, that he's worried, but rationality isn't my strongest suit with those I consider mine. "Where is she now?"

"Please don't kill me, but I can't tell you. I've broken her trust enough with this call."

"Then why tell me?"

"Because no one else can protect her."

Exhaling, I run a tired hand across my face. "Get me her itinerary and include yourself on this trip. Do whatever the fuck you must, but where she goes, you go. Understood?"

"Already done. I convinced her father she needs help."

"Good." My tone is cold. Angry.

"Please don't be mad at her. This really is out of her hands...it's her story to tell."

"Too late." An email comes in and I pull the mobile away, checking. It's from Giannis with confirmed days, airfare, and the place booked for their stay. Ezra will change this. She'll go to my home there. "I'll take care of everything. Your job is to get on the plane with her and find alternative lodging for the days following your arrival; I'll cover the cost. She's mine to deal with."

Aliana

I HATE LYING TO HIM.

It eats at me. Makes me feel like utter crap, but I have no choice. Yet, as I land in Brazil with Giannis in the seat to my right, I wish it were Callum beside me. That I'd been strong enough to tell him what's going on, the threats and illegal deals I'm forced to be a part of.

"You can always call him," Giannis leans over and whispers before undoing his seatbelt. Those around us pay no mind, though, too busy opening the overhead compartments and grabbing their carry-on luggage. "He can help you, Ali. Hell, if you don't want to explain, I will. This is fucked up."

This is fucked up. I know. I've been repeating those same words for the last few years while trying to find an explanation for the way my father treats me. Uses me.

"He has enough on his plate. What they did to his aunt…" my voice trails off, the memory of his face—expression—while he asked me to accept the protection of the man he called Kray, broke my heart. So much pain. His eyes, those beautiful, gem-like eyes, showed me in that moment the kind of man he truly is.

Caring. Passionate. Loyal.

Categories I'd never thought he'd be a part of. Because in my ignorance, I wrote him off the moment he introduced himself, and yet, walking away has been impossible. I can't.

Callum is everything the men in my family wish they could be, and so much more. His power doesn't dominate him. His money doesn't define him.

I'm falling for him. My truth. Undeniably.

"I'm screwed." Those two words, my tone, they say everything I can't. And weirdly enough, Giannis understands. He nods, making no move to stand as those around us disembark. And we don't, not until every person exits and the flight attendants congregate at the front.

He's first to stand and grab our bags. The two carry-on's we brought have just the basics while what we'll need for the job was shipped to the house the governor rented days ago. My father's been planning this for a while, longer than I suspect, and he'd given me enough freedom to mess with my head.

It doesn't take long to get off the plane or out of the airport. Giannis handled this part of the arrangements, renting us a fun convertible for our time in the country. Not that we'd get to enjoy any of it; we can't be seen or draw attention to ourselves, but the drive out to the private property in Rio will be amazing.

Maybe I can come with Callum one day.

"If he's around that long," I mutter low, grateful that Giannis is too busy hooking up the Bluetooth system to his phone. The last thing I want right now is another lecture. To be told I'm an idiot.

Because I am. I should've told him. Asked for his help.

"Are you hungry, Ali?" Giannis asks, pulling me back from my thoughts. "You haven't eaten much in the last few days."

"How would you know that?"

"That's a dumb question, and you know it."

"Shut it." And because I'm not ready to get into that conversation, the implications of him watching me because of Callum, I slap his shoulder with a giggle. "By the way, I can't believe our fathers bought the whole, *I'm trying to make sure she doesn't fuck up*, spiel you gave them. It was almost insulting how easily they gave in to you coming with me."

"Don't take it personally. They're both arseholes." His butchered British accent at the end makes me miss Callum. Even when cursing, he sounds so proper it's sexy. "My boyfriend, on the other hand…"

"Is he here?"

"Look behind you." And sure enough, there he is in a mid-sized SUV just one car behind ours. The tall man looks cramped behind the wheel, his posture stiff and aware, but more importantly, he is here for Giannis. In case anything goes wrong.

Why am I so jealous of that? Why didn't I just speak up when I had the chance?

I'm quiet and lost inside my head for the rest of the ride. I know my friend means well, that his attempts at pointing out landmarks and the beauty around us is an attempt at distracting me, but nothing works. The closer to the house we get, the gloomier I become.

My mood stinks. My body language is one of sulking.

And when we pull into the huge private beachfront property and Giannis parks, getting out to grab our bags and open the front door, I can't help but shed a tear. Then another. I'm quick to wipe them away, but the evidence is there for anyone who looks my way.

I shouldn't be here to steal an artifact for my father. I shouldn't be here and possibly go to jail if anything goes wrong.

But more importantly, Giannis isn't who I want with me if things get rough.

He's not who I trust blindly.

He's not Callum.

He's not the man I've fallen in love with.

THE NEXT DAY, I feel like a zombie. I'm going through the motions while the world around me moves—it shifts and carries on. Giannis tried to talk to me a few times, to get me out of this funk, but nothing works and after a while, he too gives up until it's time to go.

Which brings me to the present…

The outside of this building is intimidating and highly secured. There are guards everywhere: walking, posted, and a few snipers on the south end with their eyes on the main entrance. Their job is to not let anyone in or out, much less lose one of the pieces inside.

The official who runs this department is smart; the secretary of state or equivalent of, and his job is to keep certain items under lock and key. This could destroy the country's wealth, and the hold the government has over its citizens.

What my father's client wants with the artifact, I don't know, but its black-market price is exuberant. I've done my own research. I'm half tempted to run away with it and make a new life for myself, far from all I know.

No family. No restrictions.

What about Callum? "Focus," I grit out from between clenching teeth and Giannis looks over, nose scrunched up in question. "We need to focus. No mistakes."

"Got it."

The plans provided showed me three possible entry points, and I chose the heavily guarded one. Why? Because no one thinks you'll attempt a crime under the heavy watch of national police. Where the danger lies. A mistake many make, but I've learned over the years that the best way to hide is in plain sight while drawing innocent attention.

That's why I'm stumbling, giggling while walking by the back entrance with my sandals dangling from a finger and phone in the other hand. They see me but think nothing of the gringa taking pictures—selfies with an exaggerated pout and low-cut top.

Then, there's the man beside me in full military gear.

Their colors. Their medals on the breast pocket.

Some salute and he returns the gesture, giving two a nod before bending to lay a kiss below my ear. My giggles turn louder, I smack his chest, and I hear the chuckle from the guard closest to us.

To them, I'm just another tourist, drunk and out for a good time.

Like so many, we're curious and looking to live a little dangerously. Like so many, I'm letting my hair down, and they enjoy the show.

We walk past them after a few more pictures, him dragging me away with an arm tight around my waist until their attention goes back to the front. Straight ahead, where we left a present earlier.

The first small explosive goes off after ten minutes, and the heavy footfalls of soldiers are heard. They shout orders in Portuguese, and the snipers change positions, their scopes looking for the slightest movement in the general vicinity of the first bomb.

Not a real one, but the sound is loud and one I hate from every 4th of July celebration my father makes us attend. It doesn't have rays of colors light up the sky or the blinking of twinkling starburst. No, this one sounds like a machine gun, but ten times as loud.

The second goes off and someone shoots, a man on the ground talking through a walkie-talkie and demanding to know if those on the roof see anything.

This is when I enter through the unlocked door that three soldiers hovered by a few minutes ago.

Giannis is quiet beside me, his steps matching mine, and we duck behind another small building and keep to the shadows until the office I need comes into view. The keypad outside is the sole illumination after pressing the frequency blocker my father provided, a gift from the buyer to ensure our faces aren't seen.

Not that I trust it, but I warned him I'd talk if caught. If the equipment he gave fails, I'm not protecting anyone.

"Code?" I ask Giannis without looking over, my eyes on the device as I slip on gloves. "Five and counting."

He understands what I mean and follows suit, latex now covering his hands. The holiday-themed explosives are spread and the next two go off not far from the first, leaving us a short window before all is confirmed and they return to their post.

"1982." Voice low, he moves a little closer while I punch in the numbers. It pings green and the door disengages, the audible click loud, yet doesn't draw attention. "Get in."

"Hit the next explosive."

"Two minutes."

For someone who's never done this before, Giannis is a great help. I don't feel alone and breathe a little easier while scrambling the signal again, making sure we have no surprises inside. However, nothing takes the pressure off like seeing the jade statue inside of the glass containment, it's enclosure small and unprotected.

At least, I think so until a small red dot captures my attention. The minuscule circle glints off a metallic rim at the back, its beacon bouncing off and landing on the artifact's head.

"Second alarm?" he asks, stopping beside me.

"Yeah."

"Can you undo it?"

"This one has a remote. We just need to find it." How do I know? Because I've seen it before inside of Dad's office at the Thompson Center. The door to the left of his desk leads to a small room where they file and keep certain documents, things that the public doesn't need to see, and I was there the day it was installed.

Same small bead of light bouncing off metal. Same two wires poking out of a small hole, an open conduit, meant to deter if touched. The remote that turns it on or off is never far from the receiver, and as I turn my head and look around, I find a small stack of books that seem out of place.

A young adult series based on a vampiric love story doesn't seem like something the owner of this office reads. Nothing on his dossier—the fifty-page life story with everything from his breakfast routine, the seedy establishments he visits on the regular, or the three mistresses he keeps—hint at him being an avid romance reader.

Walking closer, I ignore Giannis's questioning look and stop in front of the books. To an outsider, they seem normal, the outside worn down from use. However, not so much when you're close. From my vantage point a few feet away, I can tell they're fake but painted to appear realistic.

"Bingo," I whisper, looking around to detect a secondary alarm, but after finding none, I pick up the small box and find exactly what I want below. The device is small, no bigger than a candy bar and with two buttons at the center.

"How did you—"

"Later," I cut him off, pressing the right circle while holding my breath. I'm going off of a memory here, what I overheard the installation company explain to a pompous governor who ignored his child being there, and when nothing goes off, I let out a rough exhale. "Christ, I'm going to need a lot of liquor tonight."

"You and me both, girl. This shit is heart attack inducing."

A whirling sound fills the room, a low buzz, before the display goes dark and the glass door unlocks. We look at each other, both smiling before rushing across the room and exchanging the pieces.

One jade, the other cheap ceramic painted green.

Within seconds we've made the switch and closed the display, re-engaging the lock. The remote is put back, the room given a quick glance over before we try to exit.

Try, because standing outside the room the moment Giannis peeks out is a man dressed in a soldier's uniform. He's tall, way over six feet, and the scowl on his face has me nearly stumbling back. He looks at us and the small backpack on my shoulder before stepping aside.

We don't move, though. Too scared.

"Leave before you are caught," he hisses, hand on his gun, and it's the heavy Spanish accent that makes the air catch in my throat. Not that I'm given much time to ask him anything; Giannis all but drags me from the room before I can ask who he is.

Did my father send him?

Why is he helping?

The man moves past us, his weapon drawn high while there seems to be a war zone not far from us. Many shouts, some gunfire, and all while the stranger walks us to the exit and tilts his head at the door.

"No one will follow you. Get out." That's the last thing he says before running back in the direction of the chaos, his large body disappearing behind a building. *What the hell was that?*

"You heard him. Let's go!"

I nod, my eyes meeting a scared Giannis. "Run."

Aliana

OR THE LAST forty-eight hours, I've been on edge.

Worrying. Watching the news.

And nothing.

Not a single news story has broken out, nor has there been sight of the man who helped us escape.

He's the most predominant thought in my mind. Why did he help? Why not take it for himself?

That statue is worth a lot. By my research, more than the national debt of a small country.

So again, why help?

The only answer that makes sense is that my father hired him. Bought the soldier off to make sure we didn't screw up.

A knock at the door pulls my attention from those thoughts and I freeze, fear taking over, until I remember that Giannis went out with his boyfriend and left the key behind. Looking through the window beside the door, I catch sight of a white shirt and dark green shorts and smile. *Yup, Giannis.*

"You should've taken the key, doofus!" I call out, bare feet padding over the few remaining steps. The heavy door has a large metal handle on this side, and after turning the lock, I pull it open. My mouth opens as the man turns around and then I'm choking, nervousness settling in deep. "Callum?"

"Aliana."

One word, and I'm swallowing hard—chest rising rapidly while taking him in. From head to loafers, I watch him through wide eyes and trembling hands. I'm nervous, but happy, and at the same time a heated flash of fear runs down my veins and settles in my chest.

"How? What?" Not the most eloquent response, but my mind and heart have shut down. His presence hits me in the chest like a wrecking ball.

Oh, God. Does he know?

"Are you going to let me into my home, Venus?"

"Your what?" I wave a hand between us back and forth a few times before it drops, and I tilt my head to the side. I'm lost. So unsure of every-thing. And to make it worse, he's looking at me as if I'm the most amusing thing he's ever seen.

Hip jutting out, I put a hand there and narrow my eyes. Something isn't right.

Gem-colored orbs drop from my face to my hip; he bites his bottom lip. "You look beautiful, sweetheart."

"How did you find me?" I ask instead, although my cheeks stain pink.

Callum doesn't answer, but he does hold a finger up and turns it in a silent demand for me to twirl. When I don't move, he gives me a little grin. "Please."

The short, white cotton dress I'm wearing clings to me, molds to my every curve and when I turn for him, it rises just a little higher on my thighs. With a halter-style top, I didn't bother to wear a bra. A mistake now.

My breasts spill a little over the edge while my nipples are hard, pebbled tight and pushing against the soft fabric of the dress. His hooded eyes linger there for a minute before going lower and down the flat of my stomach to the width of my hips and then bare legs.

He even watches the way my white-painted toes wiggle against the travertine flooring with hunger.

How he watches me—devours me where I stand—makes me nervous. Fills me with anxiety, but more than that, it creates a palpable need in me. Those few seconds of silence make me shiver where I stand, and the thick outline of his cock becomes more pronounced. It jerks, and his name slips through my lips on a little moan.

Callum takes another step in my direction and lifts his hand to my cheek, cupping it while his thumb rubs my cheek. "I'd like to enter my home, please."

"Oh!" That snaps me out of it, and I scramble back, nearly tripping, and his hands shoot out to catch me. One hard yank, and I'm against his every muscle, can feel them move, holding me tight as his arm goes around my waist and I'm lifted off the ground. "What're you—"

"Let's head inside first."

"Okay." What else can I say when he's looking at me like I'm everything? Like he revolves around me, and it's more than likely wishful thinking on my part, but I indulge in the feeling and let him. I settle my head in the crook of his neck and breathe him in as the door closes behind us and his loafer-covered feet walk past the foyer and straight to the back deck with views of the ocean a short distance from the sliding glass door.

The view is pristine. His hold is the sweetest torture, but all I can focus on is the happiness seeing him brings.

My earlier concerns over getting caught are gone. I know he wouldn't let anything happen to me. *He'll protect us.*

Callum takes a seat at the edge of a large hammock while balancing me in his hold, hoisting me a little higher on his hip so he can lay back with my body over his. It's a little awkward at first, I'm gripping him hard and afraid we're going to fall, but a low *relax* and another short shift and I find myself nestled against his warm body.

We stay like that for a while.

Lying in silence with the soft breeze off the ocean flowing around us, my body slowly gives in to the fatigue that's been building since before this trip. I know we need to talk, all the questions I need to ask, but as his hand sweeps up and down my back and his lips press against my forehead, I close my eyes.

Each slow swing settles me. His earthy scent soothes me.

"You're in so much trouble, love." That's the last thing I hear before going under, but I'm too tired to fight the heavy blanket of sleep knocking me unconscious.

I'M PULLED from sleep by the scent of food. I don't know what time it is or how I got on the hammock, until Callum's low timbre greets my ears from somewhere to my left. He's not beside me anymore and I peek out carefully, barely opening my eyes, but he sees.

Standing at the large outdoor kitchen and without a shirt is Callum with a phone between his ear and neck while holding a pair of grilling tongs. The sizzling of meat permeates the air with a delicious aroma, just like the view of him flipping what looks to be steak before stepping back.

Wide awake and biting my lip, I look away just long enough to catch the setting sun. *Jesus, how long was I asleep?* It was barely midday when Callum took me by surprise, but now it looks to be easily six in the evening.

"You've been out for a little over five hours," he says from beside the hammock, and I jump, almost falling down. Callum rights me, gripping my arm with one hand and the fabric with the other and pulls me in close. "Careful. The dismount can be tricky for a first timer."

"Thank you."

He nods, bending a bit at the knees once he's sure I won't fall. "Let me help you out."

"Please." Not because I can't get out by myself, but I want his touch. Crave it.

"Arm over my shoulder, love." I do as he asks and strong hands lift me out, turning with me in his hold to walk back toward the outdoor kitchen/dining area. The table there is set for two—plates and silverware with a small crystal vase holding a delicate white flower inside. I've seen that flower around the property; his garden is full of them.

His garden. His house.

He has to know.

"Thank you for letting me sleep for so long. I've been exhausted."

"I bet." There's a slight hardening to his eyes, but it doesn't last long and he doesn't elaborate. And I'm glad. I'm not ready to have the *who, what, when, and how the hell* conversation. "There's also a bit of selfishness in why I let you sleep for so long."

"There is?" I squeak a bit and he laughs, full on and loud before settling back with that smirk that does things to me. "Why?"

"Because I want you well rested tonight." The implication is there while the heat of his stare holds me captive, and all I can do is let out a shuddering breath. There's no fear or nerves, more of a building anticipation of what's to come, and for now, I'm pushing away all thoughts of the reasons we're both here.

I know we'll discuss it. That he's going to be mad.

But for now, I want to enjoy this because he might leave after knowing what I did.

Or did he send the man there to protect me? That thought strikes me like a lightning bolt where I sit and my head tilts, analyzing him from head to bare feet.

Would he do that? Does he care enough to?

Or, more importantly, how did he know? Because he does, of that I have no doubt now.

"How did—"

"Hungry?" he interrupts, and as if on cue, my stomach rumbles. I haven't eaten since yesterday morning, too nervous to do so. "I made a mixed grill churrasco for tonight with picanha, and some chicken in case you prefer that. The sides aren't extravagant: salad, sweet potato fries, fried banana, and cheese bread I picked up while you slept. There's a lady in a market a mile down the road that makes the best I've had."

"You went through a lot of trouble."

"I'm spoiling you tonight." *Tonight*. Tomorrow, I'm screwed. "Do I bring everything to the table, or do you prefer I serve you just what you want?"

"Let's bring it all over." Standing from the seat he placed me on, I walk over. My hands are shaking. My stomach is in knots. Callum notices right away and brings me in close with an arm around my waist when I reach the extravagant kitchen. It has everything from a grill to burners to a roaster, and that's just to cook; the fridge alone is larger than the one I have at home.

"Relax."

"I am." Lies.

"Aliana," he says lowly, an angry tinge to his tone that makes me freeze, "don't make a habit of lying to me. That's one of two offenses I won't forgive. You already used your freebie here, love. Understood?"

"Yes."

"Good girl." He kisses the crown of my head and then down to my temple, exhaling roughly against my skin. "Lying and cheating are my limits. I'd hate to look at you differently one day, when I know you are neither of those things. I'm not mad at you right now, but we will discuss why we're both in Brazil and it's not because we took a holiday."

"Okay."

I'm still tense and he loosens his hold, moving his face back so he can meet my eyes. "I'd never hurt you, nor will I take my anger at the situation out on you. This isn't your fault, but in the future, trust is key. You getting hurt is unacceptable to me."

"I'm sorry."

"I know." His expression relaxes, and so do I. "Now, let's eat. I'm not a fan of cold food."

"That makes two of us." And because karma deems this the perfect time to embarrass me, my stomach grumbles once again, causing him to let out a loud laugh. Like this, carefree and calm, he's simply the most handsome man I've ever seen.

"I CAN'T EAT ANOTHER BITE," I moan, pushing my plate away before picking up the glass of red wine he brought out with the bread. The taste is drier than something I'd pick for myself, but paired with the meal, it balances and leaves the pleasant taste of fruit and spice after each sip. "This was amazing."

"Glad you approve." Callum eats the last bite of fried banana and mimics my pose, relaxing in his seat. He's across from me, watching with a grin that hints at a sinful promise, and I squirm. Between the full stomach and three glasses of wine, I'm relaxed and aware.

Of his every inhale.

Of the way his fingers twitch atop the table.

"Dessert will have to wait, though."

"Who said anything about dessert?"

"I did." I remember the sweet treat on the kitchen island, waiting to be eaten. "I'm a huge sucker for a well-made flan."

"That's mine."

"You mean *ours*."

"No."

"Yes."

"So bratty," he grumbles, the mock glare only serving to make me laugh. However, that laugh turns into a shriek when he stands abruptly, chair flying back, and lunges in my direction.

I'm out of my seat just as fast and running, heart thumping harshly inside my chest with a devilish Brit at my heels.

The beach isn't far off the large deck, and I take the small staircase down, my feet sinking a bit when I hit the sand. At first I wobble, squeaking a bit, but right myself before he can touch me.

His fingers barely skim the back of my arm

His breath warms the back of my neck.

"No!"

"Run, love." That hungry timbre causes my walls to clench, and my nipples to throb. "I love a good chase."

"Have fun trying!" I yell back, pushing my legs to go faster. My eyes are fixed on the water's edge; I'm going to dive in and swim a bit out but stop when my feet touch something soft.

Looking down, I'm standing on a large blanket surrounded by lit torches and a small speaker. The notes coming through it are soft, sounds like Bossa Nova, and I'm gasping—not understanding.

"Told you I'd catch you," Callum croons low, his arms wrapping around me from behind. "Now, I think you owe me a reward."

"Callum, what's—"

"Dance with me."

CALLUM

SHE'S SOFT IN my arms. Pliant and sweet, and I pull her in closer. With her back to my front, I sway us in tune with the sensual cadence of the music playing. This feels good; having her lithe body move against me is a sinful experience that both sends you to heaven while condemning you to hell.

Heaven for her beautiful soul.

Hell for the wrath our world will face after we leave Brazil.

I've bloody condemned us both.

The music changes and a well-known song begins to play. It's the original version, the words sung in Portuguese about a beautiful girl walking by and I can't help but compare the woman in my arms to her.

Everyone she passes turns their head. You can't help but to feel enamored with her mere presence.

Twirling her about, I extend my arm all the way and then curl it back, this time bringing us chest to chest. I hold her closer. My face lowers to hers and I can't stop myself from skimming that mouth—from tasting the little keening sound that escapes her. "I need you, my Venus. Can I keep you?"

Not that she has much of a choice since I'll chase her to the ends of the earth if I have to. I'll spend my life convincing this treasure that the only man who can cherish her perfection is the man holding her.

Only me. Always me.

"Callum, I…" I don't hear anything else. Not after the breathy way she said my name and the subtle shift in her thighs, the rising pink on her cheeks at my question and all its implications.

How can such a simple request bring out the most delicious responses in her?

So decadent. So inviting.

It seals her fate and mine. There is no going back for either of us.

She's mine. In this life and every reincarnation, we're granted.

Fuck the past, her family, and the circumstances keeping us apart. The bad timing.

Whatever deity my Venus believes in screwed her with a man like me, but I'd never let her go. What we are—this insanity—I have no doubt that it'll always be.

This heat. The throbbing fucking yearning to always be near her is all-consuming—it dominates my senses—and nothing short of my cock buried deep within her tight walls will ever be enough. I crave the connection. I need her—just her.

No more waiting.

Cupping the back of her neck with one hand, I skim my lips up her throat, tipping her body back to gain better access. We don't stop swaying, touching, but her needy moan is my undoing when I nip her collarbone.

That sound is precious. I want more of it.

Standing us both upright, I lay my forehead against hers. "You haven't answered me, love."

"You already know my response," she whispers immediately, looking up at me from beneath long lashes.

"Do I?"

"Yes."

"Say it, Aliana. I need to hear the words."

"I'm yours."

Before she can take her next breath, my mouth slants over hers in a possessive kiss. This kiss isn't gentle. It can't be. Those two words have destroyed the last bit of sanity within me and bound my body at her feet.

I need to possess her just as she does me.

"Fuck, sweetheart. Can't get enough." Aliana's mouth parts on a moan at my confession while my grip on her neck tightens; I tilt her head back while my tongue slips inside and explores the unique taste that is solely hers. Madness grows within. My hunger is uncontrollable, and I revel in the little sounds she makes when I nip her plump lips or the breathy sigh when our tongues touch.

Everything about her was designed by God himself to bring a man like me to his knees. Her unexplainably divine taste sets every molecule of my DNA ablaze.

I'm hard. Throbbing.

Dragging my teeth down her plush bottom lip, I pull back. Her breathing matches mine, labored, and we wear matching grins. "Feel like taking a little dip with me?"

"Yeah."

"Good girl." One last bite to the abused flesh and I release her, taking a step while those hypnotizing brown eyes stay on me. She watches me toe off my shoes and then remove my vest top and shorts, letting them land somewhere beside me. I'm naked. Nothing covering my body, and I love the way she watches.

Hooded eyes. Lip caught between her teeth. Chest rising rapidly.

"Strip for me."

"W-what?" Her blush is endearing, but right now I want to explore the side of her that's equating me to her next meal, that hungry little minx I see beneath the surface but has never been given the chance to play. To be herself.

"You heard me, sweetheart." Turning my back to her, I move down toward the water. "Strip."

I don't wait for her. Instead, I step into the warm ocean behind my home in Rio and let the waves lap at my feet. There's shuffling behind me, a very low curse or two, but then she's standing beside me and reaching for my hand.

"I trust you." The words are spoken so low I almost miss them, and each syllable makes me feel a hundred feet tall. An arsehole like me doesn't deserve her, but I'll worship this woman like no one can or will ever get the chance to.

"And I promise to always be worthy of such a gift."

"Then show me, Callum. Show me what it means to be yours."

Without another word, I bring her hand to my lips and place a chaste kiss across every knuckle and tip of her fingers before walking us into the ocean. The waves are slow tonight, just a gentle rocking that moves—pushes us—against the current and the deeper we go, the closer to me she gets.

We wade through until the water laps across her hard nipples, the tight peaks highlighted by the moon.

"So fucking beautiful." Even in the moonlight, I can make out the light contrast of pink across her cheeks. "Don't be embarrassed, my Venus. You're above everything and everyone; the world will always bow at your feet."

"You make me feel that way." One tug and she's back against me, but this time with her legs around my waist. Her pussy is right against my thickness—she's rubbing herself. "Make me feel alive."

"I'm going to give you the world."

"All I need is you." Two warm hands cup my face, her lips hovering on mine. Her smile is sweet, but it's the glassiness in her eyes that makes me pause. I don't like it. Her tears cut me, but before I can ask, I'm silenced with a kiss that robs me of my senses. All I feel, hear, and understand is her. Her body. Her noises.

"Motherfuck, sweet girl."

"Always you," Aliana moans low, shifting in my hold. Her pussy slides against me, and on the second grind, her tiny entrance nuzzles the head of my cock. She's slick, and it's not the water. "I need you to know that…"

"Tell me."

"I love you."

Three words. Eight letters.

They undo me. They express so much and not enough.

Moving a hand to her hip, I keep her poised above me, the tip of my cock just within her entrance while fisting her shorter hair. The soft strands give me a good grip, and I tilt her head slightly.

Our eyes meet, green on soulful brown. "There are three things I need you to understand, Aliana. You agree, and I'll fuck you like the perfect doll you are." She nods, her bottom lip trembling, her hips trying to gyrate. "First; no more lies or secrets. Don't ever put yourself in danger like this again…*understood*?"

"Yes."

"Two; I need you with me."

She's nodding, yet her lips frown a bit. "I'll need a little time."

"Fair enough, but it will be soon."

"Really? You'll wait for me to settle everything?"

"Aye."

"Thank you," she breathes out, her legs around my waist flexing. That pretty little mouth smiling is dangerous for my sanity—showcases just how innocent she is. *My life now revolves around your happiness.* "It won't be long. Promise."

"Good girl."

"And number three?" Her tone is sweet, but I notice the subtle winding of her body. She tries to rub herself against my swollen head. *Or maybe she's the devil disguised in the one form meant to subdue me.* Aliana can go from angel to seductress without effort. As simple as breathing, and I'll reward her.

I want to hear her.

"And three…" I snap my hips and in one fluid motion bury myself deep. One thrust and we are flush, her cunt spasming around me while a throaty moan slips past parted lips. Wet. Fucking. Heat. She's tight and soft, and my cock swells to almost the point of pain. "*Christ,* I love you."

Her eyes close, a lone tear falling down her cheek. "Look at me."

"You…I—"

"Look at me, Aliana," I growl, pulling out slowly—dragging every ridge and inch against her pulsing walls. "Open those gorgeous eyes and see me." They open, hooded and full of desire. "There's my perfect girl." I drive back in and then out. And again, all while holding her stare. Our rhythm is slow, drawing out our pleasure. "The last thing I need you to know is that you've owned me since the night we met. You're an obsession, my need to breathe, and the one thing that's always right in my world. I love you, Miss Rubens. I'm yours."

"Oh God," her walls constrict, her hands finding purchase in my hair while I fuck her nice and slow. The water laps around us, her body so needy, and I make sure every stroke rubs her clit against my pelvis. "I've needed this. You."

"You have me."

"No. More." It's a whimper; she's thrashing in my hold now. "Love me fully and without holding back."

"Are you sure?"

"Please." Again she clenches, and I hiss, my fingers tightening on her hips, digging in hard enough to leave a small smattering of bruises behind visible in the morning. Another mark, and a rush of pleasure strikes down my spine. My next thrust is harder, forces her body out of the water. "*Fuck*, just like that. Callum, I need you to let go and make me whole."

I nip her lip for that, breathing hard. What she's offering is...*Christ*. "Our first time should—"

"Be what we both need. I won't break."

"I love you, beautiful."

"I love you, too."

No further words are exchanged as I carry her out of the water, her warm body wrapped around mine. Cock deep, I pause every few steps to bounce her a few times. Just to take the bloody edge off.

The blanket I'd put out for us to talk on is my target. The soft material will protect her from the sand below, because she's going to get exactly what she asked for. I want to claim her like an animal.

"Are you sure?" I ask a final time, and I receive another of her sweet grins while her hands wander across my shoulders and to the middle of my back where she sinks her nails in. It stings a bit, the cutting grip, but that only enhances the pleasure her pussy gives with each rhythmic pulse. I pull out, gritting my teeth as I try to fight back my natural impulse, that testosterone-fueled need to make her forget everything but me. My touch. My lips. My cock. "Say it. Tell me what you need."

"You. Only you."

"Fuck, baby girl," I growl, slamming back inside her tight cunt. She's gripping me, nearly choking my cock while goose bumps break out across her sun-kissed skin—while sweat and water drip down each muscled plane of my body as I fuck an imprint of my girth into her walls.

This perfect girl is my fantasy come to life. A distraction I welcome and crave; God himself couldn't pull me from tasting—chasing this piece of forbidden fruit served on a golden platter—and claiming her for myself.

She's beautiful and delicate; no taller than five foot one with raven locks and brown eyes with just a hint of green in the irises that watch me beneath long lashes. Those hooded orbs look at me with hunger—a starving need that pushes my own desire to a near manic state. Each thrust pushes her deeper into the blanket on the sand, the salty mist of the sea cooling our heated skin.

My Venus is too sweet for an arsehole like me. But fuck us both if I'm not riding her rougher than I should. Her cherry-red lips part, but no sound follows. Her chest rises rapidly while those sinful thighs around my waist tremble.

"You feel so good, love. Too good." At my words she cries out, her back arching and I take the invitation, wrapping my lips around her right nipple and nipping the budded flesh. It throbs against my tongue, her soft skin breaking out in goose bumps. "The perfect mixture of dirty and sweet."

I punctuate the last word with another hard thrust, but no matter the force, she follows my lead, grinding against me. Thrust for thrust. Bathing my cock in her juices, the wetness sliding from the tip to base and then down to my balls. I can feel each drip. I smell us, and the heady scent mixed with the soft ocean breeze is intoxicating.

There's no cooling the inferno this woman writhing against me has created.

There's no ignoring the curves pinned beneath me. How good she feels, and I'm powerless to stop or gather a single rational thought. Not a bloody one.

But then again, this is a problem of her making from the moment our eyes met.

"You wanted this. You wanted me," I hiss out, neck straining as another rush of wetness slides down my length. "Fuck, you dirty girl. I can feel how much you like this."

"Please." Lightning strikes somewhere behind us, and a light drizzle begins to fall from the sky, however, all I can give a single fuck about at this moment is her moans and the way she claws at my flesh. Trying to pull me closer. Rubbing her tits against my chest while the walls of her pussy massage my length. *Motherfuck*, she feels good. "Callum, I'm so close." Her whimper sends a shiver down my spine; I close my eyes as a rough groan rumbles up my chest. "Please...I need—"

"I know." It's the only thing I understand at the moment. Her need to come becomes one with her need for me, and together it creates a heady feeling I revel in. "Just feel me, gorgeous. Let go."

Those thighs cradling me tremble—tighten—and I respond with another brutal snap of my hips before pulling back just enough so the bulbous tip rests against her tight entrance. From tiny hole to clit, I rub the length up and down her pussy twice, before sinking in to the hilt. Then again, I do this until she's angry and glaring, trying to keep me inside with the use of her legs.

Legs that now cross at the ankle at the base of my spine.

"Why are you—"

"Silence." Her heavy-lidded eyes widen, the warm brown irises focusing on me while small tremors rock her body. Not in fear, but want. In a desperation that makes me shiver. "We're going to play a quick game of questions, and for each honest answer I'll give you a reward."

"Are you insane?"

"Yes." And just because I need to watch those eyes roll back, I grab her hands and place them over her head while my hips punch forward. For the count of thirty seconds, I fuck her harder than I should, the sound of skin slapping merging with the night, and right when her mouth opens on a silent scream, I pull out. She's on the precipice, hanging between frustration and nirvana. "First question—"

"My father." Her chest heaves and eyes close. "I'm here because of my father and the money the statue is worth."

"Good girl." Leaning down, I kiss her mouth softly while grinding down against her clit. "Second question: why you?"

Aliana's back arches, hip fighting my hold. I'm keeping her on the edge, but not giving her what she needs. "He trained me to steal because I'm small enough to hide well."

Her response infuriates me, but I keep my ire in check. It's not directed at her, and she won't pay for the arsehole's idiocy. He'll pay with his life. Everyone involved will bleed at her feet.

"Third: why are you doing it?"

"Because he's threatening two people I love."

"Thank you," I growl out before pulling back, flipping her onto all fours, and burying myself deep. She screams at the sudden movement, but that quickly becomes a whimper when I grip her hair, curling the short strands around my fingers. Then, her arse rises higher as my other hand takes possession of her hip. I'm yanking her against me on every thrust, forcing my cock so deep she's clawing at the blanket while her cries fill the night. "I'm here now, Aliana."

"I trust you."

"And I'll live for you." Each punishing stroke brings her closer to the edge, but my beauty needs more. A little harder, and I lower my body over her—fuck her into the blanket with the shoreline a few feet away. "Come for me."

My hand slips between us, my cock pounding hard, but when a single digit grazes her clit, she tenses. From head to toe, she doesn't move, her breath caught in her throat.

I pump harder, feeling the plump globes of her arse jiggle while a low whine builds. Another harsh tremor overtakes her form and I take in the goose bumps on her skin and the glistening of sweat, the way her hair sticks to the side of her face.

She's never looked more beautiful. *Mine.*

"Baby, I—"

"Come for me." With my lips at her ear, I nuzzle just below as two fingers press on her trembling bundle of nerves. She curses, strains against me, but when my teeth clamp down on her neck and hold, she comes. Wave after wave passes through, and I feel her pleasure as if it were my own. Her walls milk me. Pull me in deeper. "Fuck, sweetheart. Your pussy feels so good."

"*God.*" It's a short gasp, she shudders and cries, her hips pumping against mine, but when she whispers a keening, *I love you* there's no holding back.

"Son of a bitch," I hiss and let go of her neck, my hips flush to her asscheeks. I'm held captive, unable to so much as breathe, while she pulls every last drop from my cock with nothing but the never-ending after-shocks of her own orgasm. "Just like that, Venus. You beautiful little treasure."

She doesn't respond. My girl looks so tired.

Instead, I cuddle up close while turning us slightly, my cock resting deep within her walls. We're a mess; sweaty and breathing hard but stay like that until her breathing evens out. And I close my eyes too, not to sleep but to enjoy her just like this.

No outside world.

No commitments.

No familial ties.

I need you home with me, Venus.

CALLUM

"**A**GAIN, ALIANA. Aim for the middle."

"It's harder than it looks," she grumbles two days later while staring at the target set up near the back of our property. *What's mine is hers.* Forty-eight hours where I kept her my prisoner, my personal toy—where I pulled orgasm after orgasm from her lithe body, and then licked every drop. Her pussy is the sweetest fruit, and I can't help but want more. All of her. "Quit laughing!"

"Breathe."

"You breathe." Her attitude is quite adorable, but she's too tense—afraid and avoiding the giant elephant in the room as if it were the plague reborn. I haven't asked about the theft after that first night; I've let her stew in her thoughts while silently letting her know I'm here when she's ready.

The tick of the clock is her enemy, though. Tomorrow we leave, and I'm adamant about two things with a bonus stipulation: I'm going to destroy her father, and she has a month to settle her affairs stateside while not complaining about the added security.

This isn't up for negotiation.

We ran through that road already: where I gave in, and it got her here.

So much could've gone wrong had Giannis not spoken to me. Moreover, had I not sent in Giannis's boyfriend and Kray, they would've been caught and dumped inside of a Brazilian jail cell where so much could've gone wrong before I'd been notified.

That piece of shit she calls *Dad*, wouldn't have done anything to help her. Of that, I am one hundred percent sure.

For his part, though, Mr. Martin kept his expression neutral when his boyfriend helped them get out unseen—or worse, arrested. Aliana didn't recognize him or Kray standing guard not too far from them while paid rioters distracted the military guards that night.

"Again."

"Why is it so easy on TV?" She squints her right eye, trying to focus. "What aren't you teaching me?"

I take a step forward, and she freezes.

Silly girl doesn't understand that I'm not mad at her. Never her.

My ire is directed at her father and his pig-shit schemes involving Aliana.

"Relax." Moving in behind her, I raise her arms a little higher and then anchor a hand at her hip, showing her how to keep a better center of gravity. Because while shooting is an art form, making the gun an extension of you is important. The more you tense up, the harder your reaction will be to the recoil.

There's a difference between locking your arms and being afraid.

"Easy for you to say," she complains, but lets me manipulate her into position. We stay like that for a few seconds, letting her get used to the weight and feel of the custom Glock in her hands. "Can you count me down?"

"Aye."

"Start at five."

"Five." She exhales roughly. "Four." She stretches her neck from side to side. "Three. Two." Aliana locks her arms and nods. "One."

Her finger on the trigger pulls, unloading the first and then second shot, each one missing the center target, but she does hit the paper. The next one moves into the man's torso, just barely hits his left side, but that shot is better than anything she's done today.

"Good. Now pay attention to that last shot, do you see how close you are to the chest area?

"Yeah."

"So what do you need to do to fix that?"

"Adjust my aim?"

"Are you asking me?"

"No." Her voice is firm, more secure, and I hide my smile behind a kiss to the back of her head. "I need to adjust and refocus."

"Correct." I drop my hold on her and take a few steps back. "You got this."

"I got this." Aliana tilts her head a bit to the side and shifts, a minute movement, before retaking the position I taught her. This time, I admire her posture and countdown to her next shot. It takes twenty-seven seconds for the finger on the trigger to jerk, firing off a shot that hits the target right at the center of his chest. "Oh my God!"

"Good girl." Her head snaps in my direction. The grin on her face is wide and holds so much pride. "That was an amazing shot, love."

"I did it." So much awe in her voice.

"You did."

"Again?" My answer to her question is a nod, and she turns, retaking her position, but this time for fun. She won her reward, and I waited patiently for her to finish—emptying the clip—before taking the gun and placing it on the ground.

I have her in my arms before my Venus can run, her legs around my waist and my mouth on hers before she can squeal.

The lightweight dress she's wearing gives me easy access, and so does the lack of knickers. Within seconds I have her back against a large tree, my swim shorts hanging mid-thigh, and my cock poised at her entrance.

She's wet. So slick

I drag my teeth down her chin and to the base of her throat. "You did so good, my Venus. So proud of you."

"Thank you," she whimpers, arching back to give me better access. She's trying hard to move against me, but I keep her movements limited.

There's no space between her body and mine. Not that I make her wait long; I quickly bury myself deep and reclaim her lips. "Baby."

That's her new thing. She's been calling me that since the first night, and I like it more than I should. It's quickly becoming an obsession; see how many times a day I can get her to call me that.

"Just feel me, sweetheart." My hips punch upward, bouncing her on my cock while I slip a hand behind her back to protect her from the bark. This is rough and fast, my punishing strokes not giving her a second of respite —bringing her to the edge quickly with one of her weaknesses.

She likes to be taken. To be manhandled and fucked rough, to be used for my pleasure.

A vicious circle.

I love to watch her break, apart and she enjoys my pleasure in the act.

"So tight, Venus. Precious little cunt," I growl, forcing myself deeper with each stroke. And she takes it with a smile, that sexy grin that tells me she's close and so fucking sensitive—her walls clenching.

Bringing a hand to her dress, I yank on the top and bare her breasts to me. They jiggle with each stroke, the tight tips a dusky rose that make my mouth water. Lowering my head, I suck one between my teeth and flick my tongue, timing each tease with my strokes before biting down.

"Oh my fuck!" she yells out suddenly, caught off guard by the sudden pleasurable pain. Her orgasm is hard and fast, striking me like lightning, and pulls the come from me without mercy.

"Bloody hell." Another deep stroke, and I hold myself deep inside her. I don't care if she gets pregnant. The bastard side of me wants that too. To have all of her. To see her grow round with my child.

Is it wrong? I give no fucks.

Is it too soon? Don't care.

Once that thought takes root, I see it behind closed lids. Again, I pull out and slam back in, and it's almost too much. *Christ.* The things she makes me want—all of this wasn't in the cards for me, but now I'd kill anyone who tries to break what God himself can't.

Slowly, I regain my composure. My breathing returns to normal, and I open my eyes to see her soft face smiling at me.

"Hi."

"Hello, love." Aliana's hair sticks to her, and I push it back, caressing the soft skin of her cheek. "Want to shoot some more or go relax in the pool?"

"How about we relax in the pool for a bit and later come back for another lesson?"

"You look like there's something else you want to say."

A lovely shade of pink grazes her cheeks. "There is."

"Go ahead, sweetheart. You can tell me anything."

Aliana takes in a deep breath and lets it out slowly, her shoulders straightening back. "I know I messed up by not coming to you, but I promise it won't happen again. Being with you makes me happy, Callum. Truly happy, and I don't want to lose this over a family that doesn't care about me."

"I'm not going anywhere, but I do appreciate those words." I peck her mouth softly. "Am I angry? Yes…" she goes to say something, but I nip her bottom lip and shake my head "…but not at you. What your father did is not something I'll let go of. I'm warning you now that he will face my wrath, but I do it because I love you. What he did is unforgivable."

"I'll accept whatever your terms are for going home, but I need time. There's my job and school and lastly, my biggest worry—"

"Your brothers?"

"Yes."

"Has he hurt them?"

"Once." Aliana's eyes gleam with unshed tears, and that hits me in the chest. *He'll pay for those tears.* "Dad closed them in the basement of the house for a week. They were ten and twelve at the time, and all because I refused to sneak into another politician's office and take a file he wanted."

My poor girl.

"I'll get them out of the country too."

At once, those brown eyes widen. "You will?"

"Aye."

"I'm so lucky to have met you, Callum. I'm so grateful—"

"Never thank me for taking care of what's mine, love. I'm honored to do so until my last breath."

"How about we grow old together instead?"

"You have my word." And then I kiss her, slow and sweet, while my cock hardens inside her soft heat.

"Again?" She giggles, yet I don't miss the clenching of her walls, or the slight flush traveling from her face to the top of her breasts.

"Always."

"THANK YOU FOR COMING TODAY," I say a week after Brazil, entering the room and taking my seat at the head of the table. It's weird in a way to have Casper to my right, but he's made up his mind and his sights are set on Boston with a feisty brunette currently giving him the cold shoulder. My father and his are also in on this meeting as is Archie, who'll be staying to work as my third-in-command. The job of my right is going to someone else, someone stateside at the moment. "I know this is short notice, but I'd like to set my plans in motion before the end of the month."

"No problem at all," Mauro Collado says, extending a hand from across the table. His grip is strong and expression neutral, not scared, but I notice the way he takes in the room. Everyone's position. "We are excited for this new venture."

"We?" Casper asks, brows furrowed.

"My brothers are also a part of the operation, Mr. Jameson." He chuckles a bit as if remembering something humorous. "I'm the brains, while they're a bit trigger happy."

"Good to know in case I ever need some hired assistance."

"They'd take it as an honor, Mr.—"

"Cut that out, mate. I'm Callum to you, and he's Casper."

"Understood. Gracias." He has a woman to his right, very serious and leaning toward him. I catch the glint of a ring on her hand. *She's the wife*. "The file, mi amor?" Without answering, she slides it over and he hands it to me.

At this point, it's all a formality to the people inside the room, but it doesn't change my plans.

"Do you have copies?"

"I'm sorry, I—"

"It's okay." Archie anticipates and holds a hand out to me; I pass the file and he rushes over to the copier inside the room. While he's there, I pour myself a cuppa and offer one to the others around the table. "Please, help yourselves."

"We need one of those." Collado takes the carafe and serves his wife and then himself, fixing each cup to their liking. Casper follows after, his like mine without sugar, and then sits back.

I can almost see the questions swirling in his head. He's looking at the new office inside of the three-story warehouse with construction workers just outside these doors outfitting the space. There will be a showroom, a testing facility, and then this floor which overlooks everything and will be used as office space.

One for myself.

The other for sales staff.

"You've been busy," my cousin says after a while, his smirk in place. "Holding out, too."

"Just a different perspective, is all."

"Here you go, sir." Archie places the main copy in front of me and then goes around the table handing one out to each person sitting around the conference table.

"Thanks, mate." Everyone but the Collados and I look at the contract. A few times, the three other Jameson heads snap up and look at me, their smiles growing wider the closer to the bottom they get. This isn't a complicated agreement; Mauro is the supplier while I'll distribute with a seventy/thirty split that suits us both. I'm going to showcase each piece and meet with different nations on a mass production end goal.

I take on the more dangerous side, so I take the heavier cut.

But more important than money, everything is done above board and legal.

No hiding. No small-time sales. No random searches.

I want it all.

I'm going to supply armies before they go to war. I'm going to play devil's advocate.

I'll design and he builds each piece; the new production location is being kept under wraps from the public and on a small private island off the coast of Spain.

"Are you shitting me?" That's the first thing Casper says after putting his copy down. He's sitting back, relaxed, but I see the interest. "That's quite an ambitious goal."

"Aye." I mimic his relaxed posture, bringing the cup to my lips for a sip. "But doable and very profitable while everything else stays the same. The drugs and hot electronics will continue to run through the UK via containers and into the Port of Miami, the latter of which will still be heading to Central and South America—our agreement with Thiago stands. The clientele he brings to the table is very valuable."

"And you've already contacted a British general?"

"I have. They're interested in what I have to offer after sending an email with the schematics and video demonstration."

"All in favor," Casper calls out, not that it matters as this is a done deal, but it's to prove a point.

All three Jamesons look at me with pride. "Aye."

I nod and then look over at Archie. "Please bring in the suitcase."

"Yes, sir."

"We are very happy to do business with you, Callum. We've brought you a gift to celebrate."

At Mauro's words, my eyes snap to his and I tilt my head. "I do enjoy gifts."

He laughs, and the others in the room follow suit. His wife, though, lifts up a large purse from beside her and pulls out a box. Nothing too big, but the wrapping is cheeky with a *Happy Birthday* theme. Mauro holds it out to me. "We, my family and I, hope you enjoy this."

"Thank you." Taking the box, I undo the wrapping and open the top. What lays inside, nestled within a soft piece of fabric, is a thing of beauty. The two guns inside are all black, heavy but when picked up and examined, the detail is on the powder coat finish. Desert Eagles with tiger stripes, the two tones of black—shiny and matte—working together flawlessly. "This is beautiful. How did you know?"

"That you like big cats?"

"Yes."

"You mentioned feeding a tiger the first time we talked, and I ran with the idea."

"I'm touched." Picking up one in each hand, I test their weight and grip. "Very sleek and comfortable. This is a fine piece."

"Aye," Casper agrees and holds his palm out. "I'm almost jealous."

"Wanker." Handing over one, I let my father and uncle check out the other. Archie walks in then with my own gift. He places the case in front of Mauro. "That's the agreed amount, and an extra ten percent to enjoy a weekend on us at the hotel I've booked in Monte Carlo."

"Thank you, Callum."

"Here's to a lucrative business venture, partner."

Aliana

"**Y**OU'RE LATE," my father greets, the second I step foot inside his office. That seems to be the way he breaks the ice each time we see each other, and yet, it's his instructions I've been following. After coming home from Brazil, leaving Callum, he refused to see me until now. *Just in case you're being followed*, he claimed over the phone while demanding I send him pictures of the statue beside a newspaper showing the current date.

That's how he's kept me for three weeks.

On edge. Always wondering.

And I've never been more thankful for the protection Callum put on me. For the man who comes to Chicago once a week to spend the day, to spoil me, while helping me sort through my priorities. So far, we have a few plans in place. My conversation with Aurora is coming soon, and he knows this one will be tough for me.

She's my best friend. My constant for so many years.

I'll be patient, but I'm not waiting six months, Aliana.

Kray and Giannis seem to always be around, but the one who's made the difference for me is Lindsey. We bumped into each other at my favorite breakfast spot before work, both picking up an order of coffee and an egg, bacon, and avocado sandwich.

"You know, a dash of hot sauce on that gives it a better kick than black pepper," I said, not realizing who she was. We were by the pickup counter, side by side, when she turned her head and gave me a bright smile. "You?"

"Me." Her shoulders shook a bit from giggling. "Hi, I'm the extra Mr. Jameson requested."

"You're a personal guard?"

"Among other things, and for the right person, yes."

My brows furrowed, not liking the implication. "What's that supposed to mean?"

"Just that you're important to Giannis, and he means everything to my cousin. Then, we have my personal headache that's your main security, Kray, and then his boss. That's three people watching out for you, and with good reason, I hear."

"I'm not useless."

"Not at all. I heard through the grapevine you have a decent shot, just needs some fine tuning." Lindsey placed her hand on my shoulder, giving it a light squeeze. "Just to stay limber, of course."

The thought of going to a range and shooting made me grin, but then it dropped. Callum took my Glock after each lesson and didn't hand it over before we left. "I don't have my—"

"That's because I have it. Mr. Jameson had a last-minute adjustment made to it."

"You're serious?"

"As a heart attack."

"That would be amazing. I didn't think I'd enjoy it as much, but once I broke through the mental fog, it all clicked." Unwrapping my sandwich, I grabbed the homemade chili pepper sauce and put on more than I should. And while I didn't usually eat super spicy, this one was like crack for me. "That, and I like knowing I can protect myself. Precautions never hurt."

"Agreed." Lindsey wiggled her fingers and I handed over the bottle, smirking when she poured more than me. "What about today after work? I know a place that's open late."

"Sounds good."

"Good. Then let's go."

I arched a brow. "Go where?"

*"To the Conte House, silly. I'm the new self-defense class instructor."
At my perplexed look, she shrugged. "The old instructor was paid hand-somely to take a sabbatical so I could step in. I 'work' for the same
company."*

"Well, shit."

*"Exactly. So let's go." Packing her items back inside a brown bag, she
nodded at my sandwich. "Can't be late on my first day."*

"How have you been, daughter? Had a good vacation?" Dad's voice
snaps me back from the memory, and it's hard, but I hold in my glare,
focusing just past his head so he doesn't see the hatred that brews within
me. Because I do; I hate him. "Did you take any pictures? The place I
booked was…"

My attention isn't on his words. Instead, I take in the dark room with
the moon glinting through the floor-to-ceiling windows. The sole source of
light is coming from a desk lamp near a turned-off computer and his cigar.

There's a small sitting area behind me and to the left, while the wall
right across has built-in shelves filled to the brim with books he's never
probably heard of. A bar with the kind of alcohol he drinks is there, too, the
glasses cleaned three times a day by his personal assistant.

"…are you listening to me?" His terse tone pulls my attention to him,
and I meet his eyes for the first time since stepping inside the room. He
looks tired and stressed, hair mussed, and tie undone while sweat dots his
forehead. "I asked you a question."

"Repeat, please."

"I said, did you run into any problems?" Exasperated, he levels me with
a glare. "Giannis wasn't very forthcoming on your time in Brazil."

"Does it matter?"

At my counter, my father slams a hand atop his desk. "Cut the fucking
attitude, kid. When I ask a question, I expect an answer. Keep testing me.
You know the consequences better than anyone."

"That's not necessary." Another voice, male, fills the room, and my
head snaps to the dark corner of the sitting area. With little to no lighting,

it's hard to make out the tall form sitting there, but the light at the end of a cigar is bright red. "She's done her part. Surpassed my expectations, to be honest."

Uneasiness settles over me. My stomach drops, and I can't stop the shaking of my hands.

"Mr. Gaspar, with all due respect, how I discipline—"

"She's not yours anymore." His words are spoken low, with ease, but the heavy implications fill me with dread and all I want to do is run out. Kray is in the building along with Lindsey, waiting for me in the main lobby, with the excuse that we're heading to dinner right after. At once, I put my hand inside my pants pocket, and find the number *3* on the old prepaid phone Lindsey insists I carry with me now. "Isn't she?"

Because it's easier to find a number in button form than on a screen from inside a purse or pocket. And now, I see how right she is. I press and after fifteen seconds, hang up, and then again, following the same pattern.

"No. I guess not, my apologies." Dad's expression is cold, unaffected. He's speaking about me as if I were an item and not his child. "But for today, I need her cooperation in the exchange. That statue has a buyer, and we made an agreement to split the profit to appease Rigo's debt."

"I don't care about the profit and consider the debt canceled. She's already proved her worth." The man moves in his seat and a second later, another lamp is turned on. It illuminates him, bathing him in a soft yellow glow, which presents just enough of his profile for me to make out his features. He seems very familiar to me. *Where have I seen him?* "My plans are larger than the bullshit statue she's been carrying around for you. This was just a preview of what she's capable of, and my wife did more than satisfy my curiosity."

"Wife?" I ask, swallowing back the bile rising. This—he can't be serious.

No. No. No. No!

"Yes, princess. We're betrothed."

My reaction to that is instantaneous; I take the artifact out of my bag and slam it atop my father's desk, glaring at him. If the damned thing cracked, I have no clue nor do I care, but my ire is mounting and for the first time, I understand how Callum can kill without remorse.

And while I don't consider myself to be a violent person and choose to pacify and de-escalate always, right now that's all out the window when all I can taste is the bitter edge of betrayal. This is a hard pill to swallow, and had I brought my Glock, I would've shot my father.

Of that I have no doubt. Right between the eyes.

"I will not marry him."

"You don't have a choice!" Dad thunders. The tumbler with a few fingers' worth of amber liquid flies past my head. It shatters upon impact, the picture frame it hit breaking too. "This isn't up for negotiation, Aliana. You will marry Mr. Gaspar or else—"

"I'm already seeing someone."

"Who?" the man asks, voice ice cold.

Before I can respond, the door is opened, and Kray walks inside. He doesn't give either of them any attention, his sole focus on me, gun drawn. "You ready to go, Miss Rubens?"

"Who the fuck are you?" comes from the governor. That man is no longer my father.

Kray's eyes turn hard; he's now looking at my father. "Callum Jameson sends his regards."

That's it. That's all he says before ushering me out while I avoid the two heated gazes on me.

They remain quiet. My guard's words still hang heavy in the air.

Callum staked his claim.

———

"Tell me again why I'm going with you to look at bridesmaid dresses?" I ask London while her cousin snickers beside me. We've been to three stores today, and we haven't stopped for food. They literally drag me from bed, stuff me in clothes, and make me try on dresses while my best friend's newly found cousin picks one.

Mind you, I'm not in the wedding. I'll be a guest, not because she didn't ask me to be, but because they decided to keep the numbers very small; Mariah and Aurora for London, while Javier and Casper, even though my best friend doesn't know this tiny detail.

Not like she's shared info on him either.

"Because it's easier to be objective on someone else's body." London walks around me, studying the red dress I'm in. It's an empire waist with an off-the-shoulder neckline that ends just below the knee. Very form fitting and classy, but also plain. "I feel like we're getting close, but no dice yet. Can you try the eggplant one next, please?"

My stomach is eating itself; I'm annoyed with her, but she's too sweet to get mad at. Grumbling, I take off toward the changing room while they discuss something between them.

Reaching for the zipper on my right, I lower it and slip off the garment. The hanger is next, and I place everything neatly for the salesgirl when my phone rings with *his* tone. I'm quick to pick it up before they hear or ask, moving further back into the changing area.

This area is private; a large space where you normally have someone helping you change into their gowns, but with London's selection being less extravagant, I've been given free reign. Which works, because he's Facetiming me.

"Hello, love," he says the moment I answer, that grin I love in place. Callum looks a bit tired, and I know it has to do with the new business venture the Jamesons are taking on. The last few weeks have been busy for him with extensive travel from London to Spain to Chicago, the latter for me. "Having fun?"

"No," I pout, angling the camera so he can see how little I have on. I'm in a nude, strapless bra and tiny hipsters which leave my cheeks bare. "I'm hungry, sleepy, and ready to start the next season of our show."

That's another thing we've been doing since our time is limited at the moment—something that is wearing heavy on him and me.

I'm still here while he's home, because that's what London is to me now, and while he comes to see me as often as possible—at the least a day a week—I promised Aurora I wouldn't leave yet. Not until after London's wedding, since her mind is on Boston and her cousin will take over the Chicago office. At least, until Roe's brother is older, and the kid wants to take over.

To me, it sounds like she's avoiding.

She's dodging Casper and his calls. His every attempt at communication.

"Fuck, Venus. This is a cruel punishment."

"Would you prefer me taking the view away?"

"I'd rather saw my arm off than miss this."

"That's overdramatic."

He shrugs, not the least bit embarrassed. "I stand by my truth."

"You're too cute sometimes." Callum tries to argue, but I hold a hand up and he quiets down. *Huh, so that does work.* I've seen him do it before, and those around him tend to zip it when he does. "But I wanted to discuss our show. How deep are you into the fourth season?"

We've become addicted to a horror show based in America with storylines that seem to always intertwine with a previous season. It's addicting, and our thing. We try to watch an episode together every night it's possible, and two or three when he's here between my being bent over and displayed for him.

"It's good…isn't it? And I haven't watched any without you."

"Bloody brilliant, you smart lad." My British accent sucks, and a second later he's laughing so hard, Callum snorts. "I heard that."

My sing-song mocking makes him stop, fake glare in place now. "You heard nothing."

"Yes, I did. You snorted!"

"Prove it."

"Maybe I—"

"Who you talking to, chick," Aurora asks, and my eyes widen while Callum rolls his eyes. "You've been in here a while."

"Be right out. It's Giannis."

"Giannis?" Callum gives me an almost insulted expression.

"Since when are you so close to him?" Aurora taps her fingers on the door. "You two dating?"

"No."

"Okay…" she drags out the word while Callum tries hard not to laugh "…well, I just wanted to tell you that London needs to see the eggplant dress within the next few minutes. Malcolm's on his way to steal her away for a late lunch. And yes, before you ask, I know you're hungry and getting bitchy. I'll stuff you full the second we get out of here."

"You freaking better. Your treat, too."

"Deal, but hurry up." Her feet move away from the dressing room, the sound becoming fainter and fainter until I hear nothing at all.

Leaning against the wall, I let out a sigh. "That was close."

"Tell her the only stuffing you take is from my cock."

It's my turn to snort. "Seriously?"

"Yes. My cock and nothing else."

"So possessive," I hiss low, before blowing him a kiss. "Call you later?"

"Aye. Behave."

Aliana

DESTINY HAS A way of showing you it can't be tampered with. You will end right where you're meant to be, and I've never been more sure of this than I am now.

The traditional wedding march fills the church and guests stand, watching a beautiful woman walk toward her future, but they're not the ones I'm focused on.

No, right now I'm watching my best friend smile and shiver as a man with a familial resemblance to Callum mouths words I can't quite make out. Anyone with a pulse can feel the electricity that flows between them.

He's her person. Her lobster.

Stubborn woman. How could she try and fight that?

"They're being fresh," Callum chuckles from his seat beside mine just one pew behind Malcolm's closest family members. Another sign that fate is a persistent, all-knowing bitch. Without our knowledge, London sat us next to each other, and it's been a blessing and a curse. I'm happy, but keeping my true emotions hidden is nearly impossible when the man I love is currently running his pointer finger across my wrist, his touch gentle.

He smells so good; I'm fighting every instinct in me to lean over and kiss him.

"My guess is they kissed and made up."

"Why do you say that, love?"

London walks past us, her eyes on the man waiting for her. Malcolm sees no one but his bride. It's there in the way he walks forward before she makes it to the end of the aisle and kisses her without shame or pause. Not caring for tradition or what the priest has to say, a man who's watching them with amusement and not rebuke.

"Because I caught the sight of a hickey on her neck right before she met my questioning stare, which she's avoiding. That, and the way she shivered when he kissed her hand before taking their respective places."

"Observant little thing."

"For years, watching is all I did."

"Not anymore."

Turning my head, I meet his warm eyes and nod. "I don't need to when you've brought me back to life."

The priest chooses that moment to start the ceremony, and I face forward once again. His sermon is about love and acceptance. About opening your heart and letting go of what ails you in order to welcome what heals.

His words resonate with me.

There's so much I want to do with my life, so much to see and enjoy, but to move forward, I need to let go. My leaving Chicago is inevitable, my being with Callum is destiny, but to move past the pain I've buried deep, I need to find closure.

I'm going to speak with my parents.

Something the man beside me will not be happy about, but I need it. Their lack of communication lately—since the day in Dad's office— while welcomed—has left me thinking. I've questioned so much. Him. Her. And how a parent could not care or hurt those they brought into the world for personal gain?

I also miss my brothers. The most I've gotten out of the two in the last few months is a message here or there with a *hello* and *we're good.*

"You okay?" Callum whispers beside me, his breath tickling my neck, and I smile. Hold back a giggle. "That serious expression on your face doesn't sit right with me. You're too pretty to frown."

"I'm okay. Promise."

"Swear?"

"I do."

"Good, because I do too."

His words had their desired effect and I blush, warm heat with this incorrigible need to smile, and I do. Ignoring the world around us and the two people saying their vows, I look over and give in to my desires:

I kiss his chin and then lay my head on his shoulder while his arm wraps around my waist, pulling me in closer. Touching. Keeping me warm. *Now, I'm home.*

"MY GORGEOUS GIRL," Callum croons as we sway to the music a few hours later. Most of the guests are drunk, overfed, or heading home at this point. No one's paying us a lick of attention in our corner of the room.

Malcolm and London didn't stay long themselves, and Aurora never made it to the reception.

Now, it's just us while Malcolm's family says goodbye to those walking out of the reception hall inside of Chicago's most coveted hotel. I'm tired and could eat, but leaving Callum's arms isn't something I want to do, no matter how much my feet hurt in these heels or how tight my dress is.

No one can pull me away.

"You like?" Fishing for compliments never hurt anyone, and I give him a shy smile.

"Don't give me that bashful look." He spins me out, twirling me fast twice before pulling me back in. "You and I both know you look simply ravishing."

"Say that word again? Slowly this time."

His chuckle is warm against my temple. "I quite enjoy using my accent to tempt you."

"Tempt me how?"

"You feel like getting out of here?" Another turn, and this time when I come back into his embrace, I'm tipped back. He rights me, smirk on his lips. "We're overdue for another date."

"Hmmm." I purse my lips in contemplation, making the cocky man wait. Callum doesn't like that and pokes my side with his finger. It makes me laugh, the sound a little loud, and I blush. "You suck."

"Your answer, Miss Rubens."

"Yeah."

"Good girl." Callum all but drags me out of the room using a back entrance. It leads to a long hallway that holds back-up chairs and a secondary entrance for the kitchen staff before curving left. No one's here and we walk right through, following the signs that lead to different sections of the hotel that are for staff only.

The last door we encounter, though, this one says valet parking.

"You have a car here?" I ask, following him out into the cooler night air. This time of year is enjoyable, not too cold or warm out, but the nights can nip at you. Especially in my strapless, emerald bodycon dress with a little ruching at the waist. The length is modest at just below the knees, while the fit accentuates my every curve, which the man currently keeping a firm grip on my hand has been enjoying all evening.

"A rental." I shiver and Callum removes his jacket, draping it across my shoulders. "Better, or would you rather we stop at your place so you can change?"

"I'll be fine, but you might need to carry me or buy me flip flops."

"It will be my pleasure."

"Oh, I'm sure." My eyes look toward the entrance, and an idea comes to mind. "I'll be right back."

"Where are you going?" The two men working the valet area turn toward us, the older of the two looking to reprimand, but his co-worker saves him with an elbow to the side. "Wait for me. I'll go with you."

"No need, I'm just going to the restroom right quick. Give me five."

"Okay. I'll be here." Leaning over, he pecks my lips before turning to face the two men. "Here's the ticket. Heavy tip if it's back quickly."

The younger man jumps from his seat inside the small two-person kiosk. "Yes, sir."

I leave him there and head inside, rushing to the in-house mini-store and grabbing three things before Callum comes to investigate: hotel moniker on the joggers and shirt while the flip flops are plain black. Not the sexiest outfit, but it'll do in a crunch like this.

After paying, I rush to the bathroom not far from the reception desk and nearly rip my clothes off in my haste. It feels like heaven to take them off, especially the shoes, and I nearly shove the expensive garments in the bag the attendant gave me. There's a knock on the door while I'm shimmying into the bottoms, which becomes a little harder while I tug down the shirt.

"That man is so impatient." My hair's been down all evening in soft waves down my back and I open the small clutch with me tonight and dig through for a hair tie. "Bingo!"

Quickly, I tie my hair up, check for smudges in my simple makeup, and walk out. He's standing there when I exit, and the look on his face is comical. Callum does a double take, then narrows his eyes. From head to toe, I'm inspected as he reaches for the bag with my dress and shoes inside.

"How do you look even more beautiful like this?" Not the question I'm expecting, and I giggle because words fail me. The compliments and attention and the way he's always watching is enough to drive any woman mute, but for me, it's the lack of control of my impulses.

Right now, I want to kiss him stupid outside of the hotel bathroom, but can't. One kiss wouldn't be enough for me. With him, it never is.

"You ready?" I ask instead, trying to walk past him, but Callum isn't a man to be denied. And secretly, this thrills me. His grip on my arm isn't tight yet unyielding, and I find myself being pushed against the wall by a very amused man.

Lowering his face to mine, he pauses just a few inches from my mouth. "Did you really think I'd let you walk out of this hall without stealing a kiss?"

"We can't."

"Says who?" There's no playfulness now. This is a man determined. "Who the fuck is going to stop me from showing the woman I love how important she is to me? Who's the arsehole stupid enough to try?"

"No one."

"Correct." A little closer now, he skims across once. "I'm not hiding us. That's a disservice to you and our relationship, and I won't stand for it."

"Then why sneak out of the ballroom?" Up until this moment, I didn't realize this bothered me. Yeah, it's fun to rush through long corridors with a man unafraid of the devil himself, but walking out together would've been fun too. *Is it all on him, though? I've been watching myself all night and keeping things as innocent as possible.* "Sorry, that's not entirely on you either. I've been—"

"Aliana, I do what makes you feel comfortable. My claim on you has already been established; if someone knows or doesn't, that's irrelevant to me." This time I get a peck. Small, but it sets me ablaze with want. "That, and I didn't feel like talking to anyone. We'd still be doing the bloody goodbyes that never end with Mariah and Javier, or agreeing to head out somewhere because that woman can convince a monk to snort a line or two."

"Tell me about it. She convinced me to join her for a spa day next week."

"What's so bad about that?" He looks genuinely perplexed.

"I'm going for a Brazilian."

"What day?" And just like that, he turns boyish. Almost giddy. "I'll take the day off and fly in—"

"Let's go on our date, and if you behave, I'll tell you before bed.

"Fucking trouble," Callum grumbles before kissing me. One arm wrapped around my waist, the other now cradling my neck, he slants his mouth over mine in a needy and possessive kiss. I taste the whiskey he's been drinking with a hint of cigar from when Javier pulled him outside earlier tonight. I taste him, that uniqueness that makes me weak in the knees, my lips moving as eagerly against his onslaught.

This man owns me. Knows it.

"Do we need this date?" I nip his bottom lip harshly, and I love the way his eyes flash with fire, a warning I won't heed. There's something so sexy about a man who loses control and worships you until there's nothing left but a satiated body and a sleepy grin. "We could—"

Abruptly, he releases his hold on me before taking a step back toward the opposite wall. The lack of physical contact sucks; I don't like it and neither does Callum, as a second later he picks up my hand, sliding his thumb across my knuckles. "Spending this time with you is something I need, too. I miss you, Venus. I'm ready for you to come home, but I promised to be patient while you settle your affairs and now help Aurora."

Could he be any more perfect? Those words mean more than any gift or orgasm. He wants me. To just be with me, and this time, I'm the one who kisses him. It's quick and fast, my body pressing against his on the wall, but before his arms cage me in, I pull back.

"I'm ready to leave, too." I place a tiny kiss to his chin, and then Adam's apple. "This is just until London gets back, or Aurora decides that she's staying after all."

"Because they fixed their shit?" Voice hoarse and hair a little disheveled, he's the epitome of sex and the promise of depravity.

"Yes."

"Let's hope."

"Now, that date?"

"You cheeky little thing, you." Callum winks before turning to walk away, giving my hand still in his a small tug. I follow him out the small hallway and out to the quiet lobby where a guest or two still lingers, but we don't stop to talk to anyone. Instead, we make it to the car and after making sure I'm in, he walks to his side and slides in behind the wheel.

I don't know where we're going as he peels out.

I also find myself not caring.

As I study his profile in the dim lighting and the city zooms by my window, I realize something:

This is a man I'd follow to the ends of the earth. This goes beyond fun or love. We are much deeper than that. The tether that keeps us together vibrates between us; I can almost physically feel it, and it's not something I'm going to give up for anyone.

I need to tell Aurora. I need to move to London.

"SWEETHEART," I hear his voice, but it's not coming from the side he slept on last night. No. This is a few inches from my face, and it's confirmed when he caresses my cheek. "I need you to wake up for a minute or two, please."

I whimper but do as he asks while pouting. A pout he nips at. "Where are you going?"

Callum is dressed, albeit casually, but it's late out. Then it dawns on me; this is business, and I sit up, almost knocking into his forehead. "Is everything okay?"

"It is, love. I'm just meeting with Casper and Aurora at a hotel nearby."

Shifting my eyes to my bedside clock, I take in the time and look back at him with a raised brow. "You do realize it's a little after two in the morning, right? Most people are sleeping at this time."

We came home about two hours ago after spending most of the night on a private yacht cruising slowly out of Navy Pier. Lake Michigan is cool at night most days, but today the slight chill was pleasant, especially when Callum kept me close. We sat at the back of the boat with a blanket and a pint of ice cream, talking and joking. Extravagant but simple. Perfect for us.

Best date to date, and I don't know how he'll ever top it.

No one around. No guards or interruptions.

I find myself liking his version of spoiling quite a bit.

"Not for a criminal." At his words, I snap out of my memory fog and glare. "Relax, tiger. I'm just stating a fact."

"Don't call yourself that." Accurate or not, I hate the title. I view him more as a loving man, my man who has a short leash on his temper when his family is wronged. When it comes to my safety.

"Aliana, the truth is the truth no matter how we disguise it." My answer to that is to flick his forehead hard, which he doesn't like. One minute he's daring me to do it again with his eyes, and the next, I'm on my back with his hands digging into my sides. He's tickling the hell out of me; knows my weakness and uses it against me without shame. "Say sorry."

"No." I kick, squirm, and bite his arms—he's unyielding. "Stop it!"

"Say sorry."

"You'll pay for this," I say, choking on a laugh when he finds my sweet spot. The area just above my hip bones are sensitive, the one place I laugh so hard I cry. "Oh fuck!"

"Say. Sorry."

"Sorry!"

"Good girl." Lowering his body fully on mine, he kisses the few tears that fell and then the tip of my nose and lastly, places a chaste one on my lips. "I'll be back by midday tomorrow to take you out for lunch and then, I want you to meet Casper." Before I can respond, he places a finger over my lips. "Just him, no Aurora as I'll let you handle that, but I want him to know about us and who you are to me. He's my cousin—brother—and we don't hide things from each other."

"Okay." I wasn't going to deny him. Not after his mini speech last night.

Callum is right.

My father knows, and I'm sure the rest of my family does as well.

There's no need to hide, nor am I ashamed of who he is. I'm actually proud.

It's time everyone else finds out, too.

"Thank you. I'll set that up during our meeting."

"And then you'll come back?"

"I will." Lifting the sheet covering my naked body, he bites his lips while those gem-colored eyes traverse my frame. Every curve. My tattoos. He watches me with hunger before dropping the bedsheet, standing, and digging his clenching hands inside the front pockets of his pants. "You have any plans of your own?"

"There might be a nice warm bath involved and a few naughty kisses, too."

"I'll be here." With one last heated look, he turns and leaves, but before crossing the threshold, he pauses and tilts his head. "I'm going to suggest you sleep in late and enjoy the quiet, because once I get back, your screams will fill every inch of this home while your come bathes my cock."

Aliana

A POUNDING ON my front door wakes me up God knows what time later. It's bright out, the high beams of light filtering through the side of my curtain and illuminating the room. The next thing I realize is that Callum isn't back, and an unsettled feeling crawls under my skin.

Another knock, louder this time.

"Who the hell could be..." I trail off, scrambling off the bed as the worst-case scenario plays out in my head. There's a small stack of loungewear on a chair in the corner, and I grab whatever is at the top before running out of the room. "I'm coming!"

This time the knocking is less loud, but still as persistent. "Hurry up."

I almost trip over the bag with my clothes. *How did that end up in here?* Not that I stop to pick it up or try to remember. I stumble-jog with a little jumping thrown in as I find my balance before throwing the door open. Giannis is there, hand poised to knock again and grinning.

What the hell?

"Who's hurt?" I ask, my hand shooting out to grab his shirt. "Where's Callum?"

"That man is more than fine, but busy at the moment. It's why I'm here." I've never gone from worry to annoyance so quick in my life. "Lose the grip, Ali. I really like this shirt, and so does Dwayne. He bought it for me."

"Why are you here?" Each word is spoken slowly while I release my hold and step back, hand on the doorknob so I can slam it in his face. "Why knock like that and scare a few years off my life?"

"Callum said you might be sleeping, so I wanted to make sure you heard."

Closing my eyes, I take in a deep breath and let it out slowly. *Choking him would be bad. He's been there for me.* Looking at him again, I nod and take it as that. He's an idiot sometimes. "Okay. And why are you here to wake me up?"

"Because your boy toy said to do so. We're getting a mani-pedi!"

Sweet man. *I bet this has to do with me hating the green on my toes to match my dress last night.*

"WHAT DO you think of purple for my toes?" Giannis asks two hours later, sipping on a coffee while the nail tech files his nails. "It's my favorite color."

"Depends on the shade, but I much prefer white on feet. I haven't seen a single person it doesn't look good on."

"True, but Dwayne likes bright colors."

"What about teal?"

"Teal could work." He's pensive for a moment, then takes out his phone and sends out a text. It chimes back within seconds, and Giannis's smile is sweet. The way his eyes brighten is adorable. "He approves, just asks that it's on the darker spectrum than pastel."

The lady doing his nails stops and looks at him. "I have the perfect shade. Just came in a few days ago."

"Perfect. I'd..."

The cell in my wristlet alerts me to a text message and I take it out, opening the app. It's from Callum, and I frown.

> I'm sorry. Still with Casper. Impromptu business
> meeting with his father on a video call.
> ~Callum J.

I don't like it, but I'm not mad. He needs to talk to them and in the meantime, I'll spend a little time getting pretty for him.

Before I can tell him that, though, I get another text.

> I miss you. I'd rather be taking that bath with you
> now than listening to these two talk. ~Callum J.

My fingers fly across the keyboard on the screen.

> Raincheck for later, Mr. Jameson? And by the
> way, thank you for the lovely surprise. Although,
> if you ever send him to wake me up again, I will
> shoot you. ;) ~Venus

Three dots appear. Then pause. Appear again. And pause.

> So violent, my Venus? I'm hurt. ~Callum J.

> You will be if he ever pounds on my door like a
> maniac again. Idiot scared me half to death.
> ~Venus

> Do you need me to scare him? I can make him
> pee his trouser's in penance. ~Callum J.

Laughter bubbles out, loud at that, and Giannis looks over at me with a cautious expression. More so when the more I look at him, the harder I laugh. There's no doubt in my mind that Callum would do it, scare the hell out of him, but I'm not *that* mean.

> Not this time, but if he ever does it again...
> ~Venus

> Noted. ~Callum J.

"Why do I get the feeling that my life's been threatened?" Giannis asks, leaning over to try and read the message thread. My response is to flick his nose. "Ouch! That stung."

"Then don't be nosy." The nail tech finishes massaging my feet and cleans the nail bed in prep for polish. She holds up two bottles: one that is just stark white, while the other has a bit of gold glitter to it. "Always go with the sparkly."

"Good choice."

Turning my face toward Giannis, I raise a brow. "What's next on the agenda? Nails will be done in the next ten minutes, and I'm getting hungry."

"Lunch? There's that new gastro pub on South Port."

"Works for me. I'd kill for a burger and beer."

"Let's do it, then."

> Heading to lunch with Giannis next. Want me to
> send something over? ~Venus

I watch the screen for a few minutes, but no reply comes through.

Unusual, but I don't pay much attention to it. He's with his family and they need to talk.

He'll get back to me the second he can.

> Is everything okay? ~Venus

THAT'S the last message I sent Callum around four in the morning, fifteen minutes before sleep pulled me under. We didn't talk again after our exchange while I was getting my nails done. Not so much as a smoke signal from him, and the more time passed, the worry grew.

And grew.

It grew to the point that I called Aurora under the pretense of returning her calls from the day before. Not that she gave me much to go on; Aurora's attention was on her guest, not us, and after a few minutes of stilted conversation, she promised to call in an hour or two.

She didn't. Hasn't.

So, I sent him another text. No answer.

Another one around ten at night. Nothing.

Watching my phone's screen became a necessity, and I did so, until I couldn't stave off my sleep. That's why I'm uncoordinated when my doorbell rings and the app chimes through the kitchen's hub and then my phone. The time right now is irrelevant to me, and as if in déjà vu, I once again scramble and rush to the door, not worrying about how I look.

All I want is to see him. To know he's okay before I punch him for scaring me like this.

However, the person on the other side is not someone I expected to see today.

I don't want to see him.

"What are you doing here?"

"Is that how you say hello to your father?" He's looking at me with disdain, something that makes him grimace as his face has been at the end of someone's fury. Black eye. Busted lip. His clothes are disheveled and he smells a bit, as if he forgot to put on deodorant and spent a few hours under the hot sun. "Well?"

"Why are you here?" My ponytail sometime during the night became undone, and I take the tie out and twist my shorter locks into a low bun. "We have nothing to say to each other."

"That's where you're wrong." Pushing past me, he enters my home und heads straight for the fridge. Inside he finds a frozen bag of peas and after removing his jacket and rolling up his dirty sleeves, he puts the cold vegetables against his face. "Fuck, this shit hurts."

"Again, why are you here?" My phone is on the counter, and I press number one this time, Callum's digits. Lindsey and Kray are out of town for a few days, taking advantage of Callum being here, to spend some time alone. Lowering the volume, I wait for the connect sign to come on, but nothing.

It never connects. As if he's out of service range.

What the hell is going on?

I try Giannis next. The same. No call goes through.

"If you're calling Mr. Jameson, he's busy at the moment."

"Busy?"

"Are you deaf now as well? What part are you not—"

"Get out."

Ignoring my request, Dad walks to my sofa and sits back, looking at me with humor in his eyes. "Tell me, hija. Why aren't you at work today?"

"That's not your concern."

"Are you ill?"

"Leave."

"Is that why you weren't there for Aurora? Your best friend?" The blood in my veins freezes at his words. Literally turns to ice. It's almost as if my body shuts down and time slows; I sit down in the nearest chair, hands shaking as panic seizes my body. "You don't know, do you? This is priceless."

"What do you—"

"Aurora's gone missing, Aliana. Taken right outside of the Conte House, and she's God knows where now. Not that I care." He shrugs before stretching his jaw, wincing a bit. Whoever did this to him got him good—I'd thank them if I could function. *Is this why Callum has gone missing? But why not tell me himself?* "Better for me if the little bitch and her new family are far from you. The Jamesons have cost me enough trouble with the Gaspar's boss."

"How can you be so cold?" Tears fall from my eyes and my chest aches, the pain intensifying. "You disgust me."

"I'd watch that mouth if I were you. The Gaspar men don't tolerate that in their women. Then again, maybe that's what you need. Someone to smack the rebellion out of you."

"Leave," I say, voice low and shaky. "Leave, and don't come back."

"Fine. Have it your way." My father stands and after tossing the soiled pack of peas on the floor by my feet, he grabs his jacket and slips it on. He fixes his lapel, buttons the front, and walks over with the calmness of a monk. For a moment or two, he stands there silently; I feel his angry gaze on me, but then two fingers appear in my line of sight and my face is tipped upward.

The asshole smiles down at me, happy in my misery.

"I wish you weren't my father."

"And yet, you're stuck." Those same two fingers tap my cheek hard. "You will marry Flavio Gaspar and save your family, Aliana Camila Rubens. You will not fight me on this. You will spread your legs when he wishes. And you will continue to steal what we decide."

"So that he doesn't kill you? What does he know that you don't want getting out?" I strain my head back in time and he misses, the slap meant for my face catching nothing but air. He tries again, but my front door slams open and Giannis rushes in with Dwayne in tow.

"I was just leaving."

"You do that, Mr. Rubens," Giannis steps between us, and I catch sight of a small line of stitches over his right eyebrow. There's also a wrap around his wrist. *Did someone come after him, too?* "Your driver is waiting outside."

"Listen to him. Leave." Dwayne takes a step closer to me as well. "It's the smart move, and you know it."

"Of course. I'll be on my way." Dad eyes Dwayne and rethinks his attempt to lean down and kiss my cheek. Any other time, it'd be funny to watch him bend and stand like a scared puppet, but I'm shaking hard in my seat, gripping each armrest tightly. "We'll be in touch, Aliana. Just remember what I said: you are a Rubens, and the weight of making amends lies on your shoulders alone."

The door closes after him a few seconds later. We remain quiet.

That is, until I get up and run to the bathroom, emptying the liquid in my stomach. I'm dry heaving so bad, crying, and the bitter taste of bile only makes it worse.

"Tell me it's a lie," I whimper, begging Giannis. "Tell me he's just a lying piece of garbage."

"I'm sorry, Ali." Giannis holds my hair back from my face with his uninjured hand. "We heard, and once the doctor gave me the okay, I came right over."

It took a while for the nausea to abate and my stomach to stop clenching as if still heaving, but it did, and I stand on shaky legs. He helps me a bit, and I walk over to the sink after flushing the toilet to brush my teeth.

"What happened to you?" I'm watching him through the mirror, my body leaning heavily on the cabinet. The tears won't stop. The tightness in my chest won't lessen any time soon.

Giannis chuckles a bit, rubbing the back of his neck with his other hand. "Small fender-bender. I'm fine."

"You sure?"

"Yes."

"Okay." I'm still a bit queasy but manage to get a grip on myself and walk out of the room. The living room is empty, Dwayne nowhere to be seen. "Where's—"

"Making sure your dad left."

"Thanks."

"She's going to be okay. They'll find her."

"They?" *Please tell me Casper and Callum know where she is.*

"The Jameson family," he whispers, pulling me into a tight hug. Tears fill my eyes, relief settling into my bones. "They know where she is, Ali. They'll bring her home."

CALLUM

"ARE YOU SURE, Ezra?" I ask, reading the urgent email he sent me fifteen minutes ago. I'm still in the underground parking lot of the hotel where Casper and Aurora are staying; she knows where he stands, what he's offering, and Miss Cancio accepted with grace and a few terms of her own.

Did I give them shit? Yes.

But the woman has a quick wit, sassiness that reminds me of Aliana, and put me—and all the Jameson men—in our place. She'll do bloody well. Keep Casper on his toes.

"Boss, I'm sure." The clicking of a keyboard is heard in the background, several alerts pinging in different tones and ranges in volume. "The man's real name is Santis Gaspar and he's the youngest son of Cornelio Gaspar who's currently in ADX Florence serving a two-hundred-year sentence."

"Someone threw the book at the cunt." I'm going through each document with everything from passports, real and fake ID's, and then family photos dating as far back as the arseholes first birthday to as recent as a month ago.

"They did. Wanker's arrest was over tax evasion, but while inside, they pinned everything the city of Chicago could within the statute of limitations, from money laundering to the killing of two CPD officers, and then the added charge of distribution of heroin. This came on the heels of Governor Ruben's election. His prosecution of a known drug trafficker made him a man of the people and a champion for the city."

"And now they're getting paybacks from Rubens."

"Yes." Another email comes in and I open it, my ire growing the more I stare at the photo of Rubens celebrating with Gaspar and Martin. The date is from a few days after Aliana delivered the fucking statue and walked out shaking.

I've let this go on long enough.

I'm going to break each skull with that blasted fucking artifact.

An artifact I bought and will be getting a full refund for very soon.

"Does Casper know about Santis? Does Cancio know he has a rat in his organization?"

"No. I'm preparing the docs for Casper now."

"Send them to me and I'll forward it in the morning. He's busy at the moment."

"Will do." He doesn't say anything else, and I almost disconnect when he clears his throat. "There's one more thing, Callum. I was going to explain this to Casper, but you need to know as well. Santis has gone missing, two days now, and from my investigation into every soldier in that organization, he's close to Dominic."

"As in Cancio's right hand?"

"Correct." There's no bond with any of the other men, no drinking a pint after work or socializing. He talks to Dominic and no one else, the latter of which hired and promoted him to his current rank as head bodyguard for Aurora's father."

"Does he know them?"

"He's shown interest in one."

"Which one?" I grit my teeth, knowing the answer already. Dominic wants Aurora, and that leaves my Venus. "Who's your informant?"

"Pierro, sir. He's Cancio's driver, and both women like him."

"And?"

"And he's confirmed that Santis makes Aliana uncomfortable."

"Thank you." Tossing my mobile on the seat next to me, I back out of the parking spot and then garage, taking a sharp turn and driving straight until I reach the interstate. "I fucking warned them."

***

THE STRIP CLUB is empty tonight, no cars outside of three that occupy the spaces closest to the front door, and I park in front of it.

I have no backup with me. It won't be needed, and after grabbing my Ruger and extra magazine from the glove compartment, I put the latter inside of my trouser pocket.

I'm calm as I exit my vehicle and walk up to the door; a solid kick and it slams open, the wood damaging the plaster. Two men rush forward then, hands on their weapons, and they're dead before either can fully react.

A bullet to one head, the other to the neck.

"What the fuck is...Callum?" Flavio Gaspar's imbecilic second-in-command pales, his body moving backward. Probably remembering the damage inflicted the last time we met. "We didn't know you were in town. Flavio would've... *son of a bitch!*" His gun now lays on the dirty ground while blood drips from the wound on his wrist. "Why the hostility," he grits out, eyes darting behind him. There's movement back there, more than one person. "Let's talk this out. Whatever you're here for—"

"Open the curtain."

"This isn't a good time."

"You sure?" At his nod, I shoot him two more times. Thigh and shoulder; he'll bleed but won't die *yet*. "Is that still your answer?"

"No."

"Good boy." I point at the curtain. "Open it."

Whimpering, he does as I ask. The sound is pathetic, almost comical, but what I find as he pushes the fabric aside infuriates me. There are five women, no older than twenty and naked, some with a few bruises on their faces.

These are not their dancers from the other night.

With how they're being treated, I'd say forced prostitution, and I can't allow that.

"You sick fuck," I snarl, biting back my action for a moment when some of the girls scream in fear. Exhaling roughly, I lower my gun and then face them. "Grab your clothes, get dressed, and head outside. Please wait for me. My family will help you with whatever you may need."

"Why are you doing this?" One of them, a short blonde, asks. She's shaking. Her left eye is almost swollen shut. "We were tricked like this once before."

Before? The bloody fuck?

"How long have you been held against your will?"

"A month," she says, tears falling down her cheeks.

"Shut the fuck up, Jenna, or I'll—" The twat doesn't get to finish, not when the next bullet enters and exits through his hip. I'm sure the bone shattering has something to do with his scream of pain and the way he crumbles to the ground like a broken puppet.

"Threaten them again, and the next one will be on the tiny prick you try to pass for a cock."

"Callum, we can talk this out," he gasps, pain radiating across his features.

"No." Pulling out my mobile, I text Lindsey and Kray. They're off, but together, and I need them here fast.

> Situation with women held against their will.
> Going to need help with clean up and delivery to
> the Conte House. 3 dead and 5 innocents. ~
> Callum J.

Kray is the first to respond.

> Where? Medical attention? ~Kray

Flavio's right-hand man drags himself toward the blonde, more than likely seeking to use her as cover, but I walk over and place my boot on his chest. Press down hard enough that it hurts, and his wounds bleed profusely.

A text comes in, and I look down at my mobile.

"I have someone coming that will help you," I keep my voice low and unthreatening. They still cower back, and I don't blame them. God knows what these arseholes have done to them. "Lindsey works for the Conte House—"

"I know that place." A brunette, tall and gangly, steps forward. "They helped my sister escape an abusive husband. You know them?"

"My girlfriend works there. Her name is Aliana."

"She's not your girlfriend. She belongs to…" You can't understand garbled speech when the person is choking on his own teeth.

"Aliana, I know her! She teaches and helps in the office."

"That's her."

"I trust you. Where do we go?"

"Grab clothes, yours or not, and cover up. They'll be here to help you soon." When she steps forward to go, the others follow with a look of pure relief but before they exit, I ask for a final favor. "Do not leave, but keep out of this area. Wait in the dressing room with the door locked if that makes you feel better, but stay away. This is a conversation you do not need to witness. Understood?"

"Yes," they answer in unison.

Before the last girl closes the door to the dancer's dressing room, I turn and meet the scared eyes of a man who has a few minutes left to live at best. "You want to know what the saddest part for you is?" He tries to answer my question, but instead spits out blood with fragments of teeth.

His lips and gums are a bloody mess, the cuts very deep. "Don't hurt your-self, lad. I couldn't give a flying fuck if you want to know either way."

"P-please." *Pathetic.*

"I warned your boss. I made my demands very clear."

Another cough, his face etched with pain. "Don't."

"Flavio didn't listen, he didn't stay away from her, and now I'm going to show him just how deep my reach goes."

"Callum—"

"You're a lackey with no real worth. I'm going to kill you, and I still don't even know your name." Standing over him, I aim my gun at his head and empty every last bullet in the clip and then exchange the empty one for the full one. His head is unrecognizable, what's left is disgusting, and yet I empty that magazine in him too.

A real man doesn't hurt or force a woman. A real man doesn't follow a weak leader.

There's silence as I walk out of the strip club, spliff in hand and a cloud of weed smoke behind me. I'm a mess, and those women inside have seen enough horror to last a lifetime.

Kray and Lindsey pull up a few minutes later. They take one look at me and share an amused look.

"Disposal or a delivery?" Kray walks to the boot of his car, finger on the key fob.

"Freeze him. This is personal." I take in a deep drag and hold it, before letting the smoke exit through my nose. "As my second, you're going to need more men with you. Assert yourself."

He takes it for what it is. That was his interview and promotion. "Done."

"And the women?" Lindsey has some first-aid items in hand. "What of them?"

"Whatever they need, make it happen. I'll assume the cost." Pointing at one of the water bottles, she tosses it, and I catch. "There's another stop I need to make tonight before going back to Aliana's. There's a rat, and I'm going to find him."

"Need help?" Kray offers.

"Not for this one."

FORTY-EIGHT HOURS AGO...

WE'VE GONE from Miami to Chicago and now Vegas in less than twenty-four hours, and a few things are weighing heavy on my mind:

I didn't find Santis.

I didn't see this attack coming.

I didn't have time to call Aliana.

The latter one stings the worst. I'm not trying to ghost her, to avoid her, but right now Casper needs me, and I will do whatever it takes to help him save Aurora. For him. For my Venus.

Aurora is her best friend, and she has to be worried sick.

How could her father not realize his right hand's intentions? His lack of background checks on the people he employs is concerning. Lazy, if I'm being honest.

"I'll be home soon, love," I whisper lowly, not that anyone can hear as I shoot the lock and then kick the doors to the run-down wedding chapel open. They slam against the wall, yet no movement comes from the inside. Quietly, we make our way in, Casper at the front, and he pauses when the view of an older gentleman playing the organ comes into our line of sight.

There are people inside, some drinking cheap stout while others watch as if this were one of the soaps my aunt loved to watch when we were lads.

A woman begins to walk down the aisle, all but dragging Aurora behind her, and I want to shoot the cunt. This is her stepmother; a cow of a woman with no heart or conscience.

"Don't do this, Samantha. Let me go!"

"Shut the fuck up, brat. I should've had you disposed of years ago."

None of the people watching do a thing.

They will now.

Casper raises his gun and shoots the man pretending to be a preacher. He falls to the ground, a puddle of blood around him, and they all scatter like insects. They don't get far, and I take great pleasure in watching bullets descend on the crowd of nobodies as we pick them off one by one.

It almost reminds me of a video game I used to play in my teenage years.

To my right, the De Leon brothers take care of the organ player and the lady with fake flowers, while I shoot a tweaker in the neck. They came with us from Miami no questions asked, and I trust both with my life. Bodies fall all around me, blood staining my clothes, but it's one particular son of a bitch that catches my attention.

Amid chaos, Santis Gaspar tries to sneak out of the room. *Fucking twat. This is where he's been hiding.*

I don't aim to kill. Not this time.

Instead, I fire low, shattering both kneecaps and causing the arse to tumble. His head smashes into a tall mirror, and his body sags. He's knocked out cold, unmoving, and when Thiago raises his gun beside me to finish the job, I shake my head.

"He's mine." Yet I don't fire again. Instead, I plan. My mind goes through ways to get him back to Chicago for the time being, until I'm ready to deal with him.

"Did you forget how to shoot?"

"Oi, that's insulting." I chuckle, killing a man just to the left of Aurora's stepmum. "His is a long-term care treatment, and I need to fly his *live* body out of Vegas."

The man scratches his jaw, pursing his lips. "If you pick him up in Miami, I'll take him outside now and dump him in a trunk?"

"I owe you."

"Family never owes." He walks away then, and I turn my attention back to the old cunt now screaming, crying over someone who's dead on the floor while the idiot holding Aurora backs himself into a corner. They know they're fucked, and I watch, amused, when that moment of clarity hits.

Aurora's mother takes off running in a ridiculous pair of high heels, and the act alone is almost insulting. Almost, because the moment Ivan De Leon goes after her, she teeters.

A few stragglers attempt to crawl away, and while the others are occupied, I make quick work of those groaning while covering Thiago, who drags an unconscious Santis out the door. If Casper saw him, I'll explain later, but right now the son of a bitch is too valuable to kill.

The last body still twitching is that of a heavier set man who'd been drinking from a paper bag. Three bullets to the chest, and he's still complaining; one bullet to the head ends that. Then, those inside turn to watch my cousin as he walks toward his Gem and a shitting himself Dominic.

"Let her go."

"I'll kill her."

"No, you won't." His eyes meet Aurora's, and the bloody tosser smiles at his woman. "Close your eyes and walk toward the sound of my voice, sweetheart. Trust me, baby. Nothing will happen to you."

"He's got a gun to my back," she says lowly. A tremble to her voice.

"He'll die before a single bullet dislodges from his gun. They will all make sure of that."

"I'm right here, you piece of shit."

"Nico!" Samantha's screech fills the room; she's fighting Ivan's tight grip. He all but drags her back, clothes ripped and one shoe missing. "Baby, help!"

"Mom!" Dominic yells out, pulling the gun away from Aurora. Big mistake, because a second later, Aurora ducks just as we raise our guns and empty what's left bullet wise in his torso.

His body jolts with the onslaught, blood splattering across the room. He's lifeless when he hits the ground, disfigured and with a wailing mum as the only being to mourn him.

A woman who will spend the rest of her life replaying that image as a penance.

Dominic broke a sacred rule in our business: loyalty above all. You don't turn on the organization, your boss, and his family.

Aurora is in Casper's arms before I look over, talking to him lowly while the rest of us walk out and give them a moment. They'll come out when ready, and we'll burn the place down to the ground with the bodies inside. Fuck them all.

Thiago meets my gaze when I walk over to the car, and I accept a towel Ivan's holding out. "Are we good?"

"Yeah, we'll be heading back right away. I have my own woman to reclaim."

"If she lets you," his brother teases, but Thiago doesn't fall for the bait. His story with Luna is a bit complicated, but that's a mess of his own doing.

"I'll be by soon for a pickup. We'll be in touch."

"Dale, I got you." Thiago gives me a hug first and then Ivan, both standing back when my cousin and his girl walk out. They're smiling. Happy. And I find myself in a rush to head back to Chicago for the sweet girl I left behind.

To explain. To ask for forgiveness.

Not talking to her isn't something I can do again.

Not even for an emergency.

PRESENT...

I KNOCK on her door and wait. Not that it takes long as the padding of her feet rushing toward me is heard through the thick wood a few seconds before the object of my adoration all but yanks the door open.

Then she's there, and I'm breathing again, exhaling roughly as the heaviness of the last few days hits me in the chest.

One second, she's looking at me through teary eyes, a fist raised to her mouth, and in the next, my arms are full of my sweet girl. Aliana's shaking, her tears gutting me, but I understand she needs to let this out. It's been a rough few days.

"Is she?"

"Safe with Casper and very happy at the moment."

"Oh, thank God!"

"Please stop crying, sweetheart. It cuts to see you like this."

Aliana

"*PLEASE STOP crying, sweetheart. It cuts to see you like this.*"

That only makes me cry harder.

Between his disappearing act, my father, and constantly throwing up these last few days…I've been a hot mess. My panic is high and my tolerance for stress is at an all-time low. I'm tired and just not myself, but I know it's not because I'm pregnant. The test Giannis made me take came back negative, and a quick trip to the doctor confirmed it to be anxiety related.

"It's been a crappy few days, Callum." I sniff, burrowing my face in his neck and tightening the hold of my legs around his waist. "Very crappy."

"I'm sorry, Aliana. Truly, I am." He walks us over to the couch and sits with me wrapped around him. *I don't have plans to let go any time soon, either.* "Will you please look at me?"

With a small whine, I pull back and sit up. Meet his soft gaze. "Before you begin, I don't want specifics. No gruesome details, a gloss over works more than fine for me. All that matters is that you guys saved her and she's happy."

"Dominic—"

"Doesn't he work for Mr. Cancio?"

"Aye. Dirty fuck kidnapped Aurora with the help of her stepmum."

"Why?" *He's always been a bit creepy. Just like the other man.*

"Greed. Power. Corruption." His shoulder's shrug, but then again, in his world, all that is normal. "Which is why I'm taking you with me in two weeks. Aurora and London will be back by then, and we'll head home. For now, I'll be working from here and flying back every few days to oversee the progress on the Jameson Arms."

"You don't need to—"

"Yes, I do," he cuts me off before giving me a kiss. It's tender, so soft, and I melt against him. My clothing feels constrictive even though I'm just wearing one of his oversized shirts and some panties, something, he notices and confirms when he lifts the back and grips a cheek in each hand. "Fuck, baby girl. I shouldn't be trying to—"

It's my turn to cut him off, and I do by biting his chin. "I'm thankful you helped them, Callum. I can't be mad at that. Never that." Another nip, this one to his bottom lip. "I'm more upset by other things that happened while you were gone, things we'll talk about after."

"After?" He smirks, but I still see the lingering guilt in his eyes, and I hate it. As much as he dislikes my tears, it hurts to see him down. To me, he's a hero. End of. "What could we possibly do but talk right now?"

Rising myself slightly, I move my panties aside and show him my bare pussy. Just a small landing strip neatly trimmed above my clit. "You could be stretching me. I want to feel every inch of you buried deep."

"Are you sure?"

"Nothing makes more sense than reconnecting with you." It's the truth. The last few days were horrible, I have so much to tell him, but right now I need this. Need him.

"Want to go to your—"

"No. Right here." Reaching down, I undo the button of his jeans and lower the zipper. His hips lift and so do mine, and I hover over him, bending a bit at the waist to help him lower his pants. Cock hard and throbbing, Callum grips himself once he's out, pumping his hands twice while I push my panties aside. "I want you just like this."

"Then come sit on my cock, beautiful. Lower that warm cunt and squeeze me tight."

"My pleasure." Pushing his hand away, I replace it with mine and rub the head along my slit from clit to entrance and back again, twice, and then slip the first few inches inside. Just an inch or two, and then I circle my hips, letting him slip in and out a few times while watching his frustration mount.

His hands clench at his sides. His nostrils flare.

"Aliana," he warns, lifting his hips, but I follow and evade. *Not yet.* "Don't be cruel, love. I've missed you too much."

"You know I love you, Callum."

"Aye. Just like I breathe for you."

"Then I want you to know that I'm ready to start my life with you." Before he can respond, I drop my weight and take him in deep, body flush with his. At once he twitches, throbs, and I close my eyes to savor the moment. "I've missed this connection. I can't go so long without it."

"Never again. I promise," Callum grunts, meeting me thrust for slow thrust while his hands grip my asscheeks. Tight grip in each hand. We keep a steady rhythm, his touch controlling my movements while his cock drives in deep from beneath me. "This is my heaven. Where I find peace."

"I'm yours." Leaning my forehead against his, I stare into his eyes. Breathe in the delicious scent of his skin while those hands on my skin squeeze and push down harder, my body bouncing slightly. "Always yours."

"Mine." It's a growl. His chest rises and falls faster, as does mine, and I'm teetering on the edge. Almost there. "Let me feel you, beautiful. Fuck, just like that."

"Oh, my damn." Every inch of my body tingles; I'm shaking.

"Come." A command that Callum follows with a sharp smack to my right asscheek and I clench, muscles locking tight, and a cry leaves the back of my throat. I'm caught off guard by the sudden roll of pleasure, how quickly I heat for him, and I'm left gripping his shoulder and bouncing hard when he whispers my name. So low. So soft.

My name is on his tongue as he comes inside me.

Destroying me. It's not the first time he's done so, either. And yet, it doesn't stop me from seeking the feeling again and again.

Becoming a mother doesn't scare me.

Even if it's too soon. To be honest, I was disappointed at the negative result.

I want everything with him.

———

"Do we really need to come here?" I ask Callum, stepping inside of an elevator I'm all too familiar with. We're a few floors from my father's office heading to speak to him, and to be honest, I'd rather the man beside me have done so by himself.

To say he's furious is an understatement.

He knows about the stunt my father pulled. He knows every word he said.

I'm also done with the games my family plays; always willing to threaten my brothers while risking my life and freedom.

"It is. Trust me." The elevator opens and we walk through, heading toward a closed door while ignoring his secretary and assistant. He has both; one is a doormat while the other is there to look pretty. One glare from him, though, and both women go mute. "Behind me, sweetheart. I need you to do as I ask and trust me."

"With my life." And when he barges in without knocking, I follow a few seconds later, closing the door so we're not interrupted. "Gentlemen. What a surprise."

"What's the meaning of this? Get the..." My father doesn't finish his sentence, eyes wide when Callum pulls out two large guns, one pointed at his head and the other at who my father called Gaspar. Both watch him with trepidation. Fear.

But it's the third occupant inside the room who I find amusing at the moment. Rigo Martin sits across from Gaspar, no gun aimed in his direction, and yet, he's shaking hard enough for his teeth to rattle. He's pale, looking between my father and the man across from him for help, and nothing like the boisterous, pompous jerk he usually is.

"Aliana, love?"

"Yes." Dad chokes at Callum's term of endearment. The severity of the situation is dawning on him.

"Do you want me to kill the governor? Say yes, and I'll pull the trigger right now." I don't answer right away. To be honest, I've wished so many times for someone to do just that. To end it all and release me from this burden. "His pathetic life is in your hands."

"Mi hija, answer him!" Dad yells, and it doesn't help his case. If anything, it annoys me. "How can you let him do this?"

"You don't get to speak to her." And while I decide, my boyfriend looks down at the phone in my hand and nods. "Toss it at the arse on the couch, please."

Once I do, the man with dark, leering eyes picks it up, grip tight. "This is all a big misunderstanding, Jameson. We're all friends here."

"Press play, Flavio. I warned you."

"Callum, I—"

"Press. Play."

"I know what you did. I don't need to—"

"Press play, or it'll be your brain matter the janitor peels from the ceiling. Your choice."

In this moment, I see the man everyone fears. The brutal killer and shrewd mob boss.

And yet, I feel no trepidation at his side. *Does that make me crazy? Or just as bad?*

Flavio, as Callum calls him, hits the button and a clip begins to play. The sound is off, for that I'm thankful, but his expression says it all. He's horrified. Looks a little sick. "I've seen enough."

"Have you?"

"Yes."

"Then I suggest you walk out and don't look back. Final warning." Flavio stands, dropping the old cell phone beside him, and walks toward the door. We step aside, my body covered by Callum's, but before Flavio can place a hand on the handle, the man beside me clears his throat. "I'm letting you walk out alive because Aliana's here—you owe your life to her, arsehole. However, you come within a thousand feet of her again and what I did to *him* will seem like a gentle pat on the back. Understood?"

"I do."

"Then go and give him a proper burial. He's been delivered to your home." Callum's message is there. He knows where Gaspar lives. The door closes after him, and we turn to look at my father and Rigo who sit as still as statues in opposites sides of the room.

Both guns are on my father, though.

"Your answer, Venus."

"As much as it would make my life easier, no. The answer is no," I say and Dad exhales roughly, shoulder slumping in relief. "But not out of love. That, I need to make sure you understand." My eyes are on the man I no longer see as a father. Not after how easily he threatens, hits, or sells me to save his own skin. Parents should protect and love, two things the man sitting behind a desk is incapable of. "I do this for the two boys you couldn't care less about. They deserve better than you, an absent father and a vain mother, but I can't in good conscience be the reason they bury a parent at such a young age."

"Aliana, you can't mean that. I've always been there." His indignation is almost amusing. His acting, though, leaves a lot to be desired. "You kids are my life."

"Bullshit, and we both know that." Callum walks over to the chairs across from my father and motions for me to sit. His guns are still out but lowered. "You don't give a bloody fuck about her well-being or happiness, and I can only imagine what your sons put up with. Which is why you're going to be doing a series of tasks to prove how unselfish you can be... isn't that right, Governor Rubens?"

"Yes." He swallows hard before picking up the pen beside a notepad.

"First, you will be sending both to study abroad. You have two choices: London or Sweden." My eyes widen, a smile curling at my lips. This beautiful man. *Christ, I love you.* Dad writes it down, his teeth gritting, but I'll give him brownie points for nodding. "Second, you will end whatever business dealings you have pending with the Gaspar family. I don't want them near you or the entire Ruben/Martin idiocy. And trust, I will find out if you do."

"Of course."

"And lastly…" Callum moves quickly. I don't see it coming until he slams the butt of the gun on my father's hand. He does this four times, and only stops because the unmistakable crunch of bone is heard. For his part, the governor bites down hard on his lip and keeps most sounds to a minimum—a low cry here or there while looking at me for help. No part of me wants to. This is his bed. "Lastly, you ever look at her wrong. Put your hands on her. Or use Aliana to do your dirty work again, and I will gut you like the spineless cunt you are. Nothing, and I mean not a bloody fucking thing, will stop me from ripping you open from neck to dick before throwing you in Lake Michigan and watching the fish pick you apart. Nod if you understand."

He does, and my boyfriend puts his guns away before grabbing my hand and leading me out of the room. I don't say anything. I don't look back either.

This is closure for me. I'm ready to start a new life.

We're almost to the door, though, when Callum stops to look at a scared Rigo. "Stay in your lane, Mr. Martin. I have eyes and ears everywhere, and I am everything you heard me to be."

THERE'S a certain beauty in life when you're happy.

Things seem brighter. People appear nicer. And friendships morph and adjust, creating something special.

Like mine and Aurora's. It's been a few months since her kidnapping, eloping, and then taking over Boston with Casper by her side. They're domesticated now, living and working between Chicago and Boston, while plans evolve and their family grows.

For the first time, I can say that she's living and not just maintaining her mother's dream.

I've been to the grounds where Conte House #2 is being built in Boston, and the area is huge and will easily double the size of Chicago. This one will also have a few things that we don't have back home; the expansion of an on-site school for the elementary-aged-kids is one of them.

That, in and of itself, will help the anxiety mothers go through when their children are off to class. Older kids understand the situation and will defy the abuser's attempt to pull them out of school, while the younger one recognizes a parent or someone close to their mother and can be swayed with something as simple as candy.

We've seen it. It's sickening the lengths an abuser will go to in order to hurt someone.

Then, there's the original women's home. My second home.

I've spent so many years of my life working there, helping in the day-to-day planning, but my heart just isn't there anymore. London's is, though. She's such an amazing woman and has plans to expand the location, too, but I don't see myself in those plans. Not because they don't want me to be, but because the moment I felt secure in her reins, I asked for time off.

No return date. No plans to do so at the moment either.

I came to London, and I found *my* home.

This is where I live and breathe, especially, with my brothers nearby at a school a short car ride from Callum's penthouse in the city, where we stay most days.

For their part, my parents have left us alone. No news is the best news in my opinion.

"Miss, your order is ready," an older lady, who has a crush on Callum, taps the counter and I smile. Beside me, Lindsey snickers; she finds the stink eye I'm getting hilarious. *I need a new guard.* "Do hurry with those, ma'am. Mr. Jameson is very particular about his afternoon cuppa."

"Of course. Right away." Grabbing my items, I keep a straight face until we step outside and then I lose it. Laugh so hard that it starts a domino effect we can't stop. I laugh, she laughs, and it goes round and round until a throat clears behind me.

When I turn around, a sickening feeling turns my stomach.

"Hello, prima."

"Jorge, what are you doing here?" Beside me Lindsey moves slightly, the glint of her gun visible, but I shake my head when a group of kids who appear to be on a field trip walk by with some nuns. "Please leave."

"I can't do that." He shows his own piece, a heavy caliber revolver. "You're coming with me. You both are."

"No. We're not," Lindsey hisses, but then stumbles a bit. My head turns and I notice Alicia for the first time. In her hand is a syringe, the end dripping with some kind of liquid. But when my guard loses strength in her legs, she's caught by two other people. These men I've never seen before, but worst of all, the way they crowd around us makes it hard for anyone to notice what's happening.

They hold her up while I turn horrified eyes at Jorge. "What do you want? What did you inject her with?"

He shrugs uncaringly. "Your mother simply wants to have a word, and she'll live. A mild sedative never hurt anyone. Besides, your brothers survived it. You all will."

"My brothers? What the…you *bastard*!"

The pinch was sudden; I didn't pay attention to Alicia's movements. She smiles at me as the sedative begins to work, my legs feeling weak first and then my tongue is heavy while black dots fill my vision. "He is a *bastard*, Aliana. You've always been too stupid to realize what was happening right under your nose."

"What's that…?"

CALLUM

NINETY DAYS. THREE MONTHS.

That's how long my Venus has been missing, and no one can find a single trace of Aliana. It's as if the ground has swallowed her, hiding all remnants of her existence, and those around me are paying for the volatile ramifications of my failure. Because this is on me.

She was in my city. My motherfucking country.

Then, there's the disappearance of her guard, brothers, and the rest of that sack-of-shit family. *I should've killed them all, even if it meant she'd be angry at me.* That's where I dodged up. I take full responsibility for not chopping the head off the snake before burning the nest with the other members inside.

"Callum, I think I found something. Or better yet—someone," Ezra says from the other side of my office inside the pub. He's been here since she was taken, working tirelessly to find her, but all leads so far have been dead ends. "This is Jorge Rubens, is it not?"

My eyes shift to the man on the screen and sure enough, that's one of the arseholes. *I'm just missing Rubens, Martin, and Gaspar.* "Where is he?"

Before Ezra can answer, Giannis comes to stand beside me. I look over and find his eyes narrowed and lips in a thin line. "I know exactly where he is."

"You do?"

"Yup." His head tilts, studying the screen. "That's their grandmother's home in Fornells. That son of a bitch has been in Spain this whole time." He's angry. Has been furious since she disappeared. And I understand him. I feel the same gnawing guilt.

This sense of responsibility because she was there to pick up a drink for me before we could meet up with him. The three wanted to visit some shops in the area and I volunteered to accompany them, be the added protection because a repeat of what happened to my aunt isn't something I can live with.

And yet, to me this is worse.

I don't know how she is.

If she's hurt.

"How soon can we be there?" Kray pushes off the wall. He's kept a solid grip on his emotions for now, but I do pity the bloke that receives the brunt of it once he unleashes.

"In two hours." Ezra moves the mouse, clicking on another webpage. This one is a database; he's running Aliana's picture through it. "I'll have everything ready to go and will call you with any news."

"Thanks, mate." I give his shoulder a squeeze and look at the others. Archie, Kray, Dwayne, and Giannis await my orders. "You have five minutes to grab whatever you need; the vault is open."

FORNELLS IS BEAUTIFUL, a quaint village in a bay north of the Balearic Island of Menorca, Spain. The population is small. Everyone knows everyone. And this couldn't be more apparent when we disembark the boat chartered to bring us over.

The locals stare.

They murmur.

Yet, it's a small boy no older than eleven that approaches when we make it to the village center. He's sweaty and is missing a few teeth, but I appreciate his bravado. "Are you here to take the idiot home?"

The others laugh at his description of who I'm certain is Jorge Rubens.

"That depends on the idiota?" I ask, and his eyes narrow. Behind him, a worried man—by resemblance, I deduce he's the father—walks over.

"Forgive my son. Lino can be too outspoken at times."

"Nothing to forgive. The bloke he's referring to *is* a pest." At my words, his shoulders relax a bit. "Now, can you please point us in his direction. We need to clean him up and get him home. His mother is worried sick."

"Of course." He's not buying it, and he's a smart man for doing so. "I'll take you to my family's small bar."

"Gracias."

"De nada. Just take him and don't let him come back," the boy interjects, and I laugh for the first time in months.

"You're something else, kid."

"That's what my mama says, too." Lino begins to walk toward a small building not far from where we stand, but before he steps inside, he motions for us to follow.

No one else in town says anything. They watch us. Untrusting.

"Keep your eyes open, and any member of the family is to be taken in."

"Yes, sir," all four answer, voice low. If Lino's father heard my instructions, he pretends otherwise, and we walk inside the establishment to find quite a scene.

Jorge Rubens is here and drunk off his arse.

He's stumbling, trying to find rhythm in a flamenco beat playing in the background and doing a piss poor job. There are bottles occupying three of the eight tables inside, all empty and some broken from being slammed down too hard. Then, there's what looks to be vomit on the floor in various spots.

It's a disgusting sight.

"Hello, Jorge." At the sound of my voice, he freezes and his face whips around toward me. It's almost funny how quickly he sobers up a bit, face paling when he takes in the others behind me. "You've created quite the problem for yourself? Yes?"

"Jameson, what are—"

"Silence." The two other patrons leave the bar while I turn my head to Lino and his father. "Please take your family and go. I will pay you for the damages incurred, but this won't be gentle."

The father swallows hard, his eyes flicking between me and the nuisance. "Understood."

Lino, though, has other plans and tries to resist when his dad ushers him out. "But, Papa!"

"Listen to your dad, kid. Help him take care of your mum." At the mention of his mum, his chest puffs out and he nods. Takes off in the direction of the back, while I move my attention back to the scum pissing on himself. "Get him a change of clothes and on the boat. We have somewhere to be before sundown."

"HIJO DE PUTA!" Jorge screams. The boiling hot water dripping from his naked torso has taken most of his skin off, the top layer anyway. He's in pain. Bleeding in some parts. "Please. No mas…I can't take…*fuck*! I'll talk."

"Mate, you really suck at this whole torture thing." Those standing against the wall inside the pub back in London all chuckle. We've been at this for ten minutes now; we allowed him a nice nap since returning, but the man makes this too easy for his position on floor. "You're supposed to let me ask the question first."

"I know where Aliana and her brothers are."

"I'm sure you do."

"Isn't that what you want?"

"It is." I hold a hand out, and Archie places my whip at the center of my palm. Its weight feels good. This weapon is an extension of me, and I let the leather unfurl and crack it once against the cold concrete. I press the button to release the blades, and the audible click sends a shiver through Jorge. "But I need to know the full story before I pass judgment."

"She's in Nicaragua. So is the woman, Lindsey, and the boys." Jorge licks his cracked lips. "They're not hurt, but that's because Aliana will be stealing something very valuable in three days." *Three days. Day after Valentine's Day.* Instead of celebrating with me, they'll be putting her life at risk for their personal gain. *I won't allow that.* "That's what kept them safe, for now. They need her compliant, and my mother—"

"Your mother is dead," Giannis interrupts, his lips curled up in disgust. Normally, I'd shoot someone for doing what he just did, but he has permission to do so if the wanker is lying. "You forget I went to the funeral."

"That woman wasn't my mother."

"Then who the fuck is…" Giannis trails off and his eyes widen. The look on his face is almost comical. *Almost*, because I'm clueing into what he's hinting at and it's sickening. "You mean to tell me Ada Rubens is your mother?"

"She is. She also killed Aliana's father, and he's not her first victim."

"Governor Rubens?" He nods at my question. "What else has she done? Why is she holding Aliana and her siblings?" You have to be one mentally fucked individual to hurt your own kid. Then a thought occurs. "Is she even their mother?"

Because at this point, nothing would surprise me.

"She is."

"But?"

"But she loves money and her freedom more. That's why she killed my father all those years ago, the governor's ambitions were similar to hers. However," he coughs, then rubs at the skin of his chest which is a mistake. His hiss is loud. "Fucking shit."

"However, what?"

Jorge's face is pinched tight with pain. "She does have a weakness."

"Which is?"

"Rigo Martin."

Rigo's son is in the room, and the look on his face says it all. There's hurt and betrayal, but more than that, I see hatred and a thirst for vengeance that rivals my own.

"I want every last detail of your mum's plan, Jorge." Flicking my wrist forward, I strike across his blistered chest twice and then watch the skin part where the blade sliced through. He screams, snot and tears mixing together at the bow of his upper lip before sliding lower. *Disgusting.* "I want her location, and that of your wife, because I know she's involved, too."

"Yes." A whimper.

"You will also call your mum and tell her you're taking a holiday somewhere you've always wanted to visit."

"Yes."

"And Jorge…" bloodshot pupils stare back at me, the pain on his features prominent "…I'm going to thank you ahead of time for your cooperation. Now, please try and relax. It's going to be a long day."

CALLUM

I'M OUTSIDE THE penthouse door, leaning against a wall, when Casper steps out. My eyes are on my cell, reading my last text exchange with Aliana three months ago. It was a silly argument over a TV show character's death, and she'd been pissed by my nonchalance. But that's one of the things I love about her; she's passionate in every aspect of her life, even something as mundane as a television series. "Took you long enough, mate."

"You consider this late?" At his reply, my eyes snap to his. His are on my mobile, trying to catch a glimpse of the photo of her flipping me off, but before he can make her out, I pocket the device. He'll know soon enough. The world will.

I never wanted to hide us but did so because Aliana wasn't ready.

And when she was taken, Casper was busy. Our conversations have been stilted at best, but I understand more than anyone what the safety of the woman you love means to you. He dismantled and rebuilt the Boston syndicate, eliminating every single threat to the Cancio name, and then handed their heads to Aurora and her father on a silver platter.

I can't fault him for that.

"I can always head back inside and slip beneath the covers and violate—"

"Shut it," I snap, a shudder of disgust running through me. *Disgusting arse.* "Aurora's like a sister, you wanker. I don't need to hear that shit."

"Noted." Casper's chuckle grates on my nerves, but I've missed the condescending sound just as much. *Aliana has made me soft.* He checks his pocket, taking account of all placements, and then adjusts the custom gun holsters I got him last Christmas. "Lead the way."

"You told her where to meet up with your dad in case of...?"

"Gem knows everything." There are no secrets between them; she's aware in the same capacity Aliana will be. A way of thinking we share.

Nodding, I turn toward the elevator and press the down button before pulling out a small remote. I toss it at him. "This is for the cameras on this floor. You have them blocked, no?"

He takes it, turning the fob in his hand. "The hotel's security is circulating the feed from last night; I paid them handsomely for their discretion and compliance. Inside, though, my own devices are on. Everything is being recorded."

A snort escapes me at that. "Did this compliance come with a threat attached?"

"Would I be me if it didn't?"

"Touché." Tilting my head at the device, I send him a meaningful look. This is part of the *just in case* precautions. "That will send you a direct feed of this door. Add it to the app dashboard that Ezra set up on your mobile... it's my Valentine's gift to you."

"Very thoughtful, *love.*"

"Piss off." The elevator signals its arrival, and I flip him off before stepping inside the now open doors. We're heading toward the parking level where my men wait inside of a black Range Rover with dark windows.

Once inside the vehicles, no one talks. Casper's attaching the new security system to his app while I go over every detail Jorge shared before taking his last painful breath. Because I beat him—brought him to the brink of death multiple times in the last seventy-two hours, only to start all over again.

He bled for his sins. He told me something very interesting about the item they want Aliana to steal.

Countries have secrets.

Many countries pay handsomely to hide them on foreign soil in hopes of no one ever finding proof of their dirty deeds. The United Kingdom and Spain are two of those countries; interchanging classified information to avoid anarchy amongst their people.

There's money involved in that. A lot of it.

Power too.

The drive to the port isn't long, and when it comes into view, I hand Casper a small stack of papers. My driver passes the parking lot and drives straight through; he knows where to go, while the others stay alert. These are men my cousin isn't too familiar with; the other Collado brothers being two of them.

Contract killers from Spain I've hired on a long-term basis, something they were pleased with since Mauro is my weapons supplier. We're keeping it all in the family. And with them, once a contract is signed, nothing will break it.

"Read it and tell me what you see," I say, my tone leaving no room for jokes at the moment. Right now, he's not my cousin. I'm in charge.

Nothing will fuck up a job more than lack of focus.

"Okay." His eyes scan the top sheet with the artifact's picture and estimated worth in both legal avenues and the black market. The numbers are high. Ostentatiously, which could mean one of two things: others know what's hidden inside, or it's a set up by Interpol.

The second sheet holds the schematic, weight, number of people working the dock tonight, and the container ship's number. Then, he flips to the last and his brows furrow. I know what he's looking at—it's a picture of the thief. My Aliana.

They show a thin person wearing all black with a demon's mask covering her face. However, there are two things you can't hide from me; the brown hair even if the length is off—and the small tattoo she got while in London of a black whip on her wrist.

It's her idea of a corny joke. She holds the whip in our relationship.

Funny thing is, she does. That woman owns me.

The next picture is of a man I don't recognize, and he's not a part of their family either. He's either someone they know in Nicaragua or was brought in to do a job. These images came from a small memory drive on Jorge's keys Giannis went through and saved what was important, before demanding to know what they'd done to her. *He's grown on me, to say the least.*

What came out of Jorge's mouth next is why I lost one of my favorite hunting knives that day. I drove the blade so hard into his skull that the handle broke and we had to bring in a butcher to remove it.

"Two different people here. A couple?"

"Possibly." *No.* My jaw clenches, leg shaking. He knows my tells. "Don't give me that look, Casper. I need your help to confirm my suspicions."

"Okay. You know the risks attached to your request."

"I can't let her get hurt." Once those six words are out, I know they change everything. He'll do for me what I did for him. "I'm asking as your best mate. If she's involved…if she's *really* here today, I need to get her the fuck out."

"Done." Papers down, he holds up both hands. "The right one means in and out without incident. The left is we tear the bloody place apart and walk out with everything, and this time it includes the artifact they are here to steal."

"This one depends."

"On the *why*?"

"On what it means to her." If she wants me to break it into a million pieces, I'll do so happily. If she wants to live dangerously by my side, I'll marry her tomorrow. "You in?"

"I'd never let you go in alone, wanker." The car stops behind a stack of old containers for shipping overseas the area seems empty, devoid of security, but we know better. Casper spots a flashlight skimming along the ground; he rolls down his window and aims in their direction. "Ours, or not?"

A low whistle rends the air, and I snort. "Ours. It's Archie."

"He's a good lad."

"A little psychotic too." All doors open and we step out. The smell of salt in the air is crisp, as is the wind coming off the water.

Archie stops before us, hands full of uniforms similar to what he's wearing. "Good to see you, Mr. Jameson." Casper shakes his hand while I take a port overall for myself. These are customary for all employees working the unloading zone. "It's a busy night and all hands are on deck— bobbies and every other department they could swing this way. Bloody bastards are watching every entry point for movement, but they missed this section due to it not being used and the museum's director wanting them to surround the piece until it's inside the armored car waiting to transfer."

"How many in total out there?" my cousin asks, slipping on his own uniform.

"About fifty, and twenty of them work for us. Those handling are all under payroll." Archie looks at his watch and then back at me. "You two will walk toward the armored truck, slide your ID, and pretend to go to the bathroom to clean up afterward."

"We have our change in the truck?" I'm smearing mechanic's grease across my face, making sure to look dingy before handing over the tub to Casper. Our hands are filthy now and our faces have enough to dissuade others from looking our way, especially when we put on hats with the company's logo.

"Yes, sir. Everything is there."

"Good job, mate." Turning to look at the brothers, I give them a pointed look. There can be no fuckups here. If Aliana gets hurt because of someone's stupidity, their families will pay. "Everyone knows where to meet after. Be there by five, or we come looking. No one will be left behind. Understood?"

"Yes."

"Go on."

"We are taking the truck?" Casper claps me on the shoulder. He knows I'm worried. Knows how this feels.

Nothing will make this right until I have her in my arms again.

"Yes."

"You're banking on her being inside."

Not a question, but I nod anyway. "She's smart. Way smarter than me, and I know that stealing this from beneath the watchful eyes of Scotland Yard and Interpol won't be easy, but sneaking onto an isolated truck isn't impossible. We know this. They'll watch and track all movement while outside, but once inside behind a locked door, they always become sloppy."

"Underneath the truck?"

"Or above."

"We'll help her, bro. You know I'm here for you."

I'm not the biggest sentimental bloke with my family, but in that moment, I turn and give my cousin a quick hug. It catches him off guard, but he squeezes me just as hard before we pull apart. "Thank you, and I apologize ahead of time. It'll all make sense soon, and I understand now your reaction when it came to Aurora. I wouldn't hesitate to kill for her, and if shit goes south, I'll give my life for hers."

"It won't come to that. Trust me."

We bump fists, and then it's all work. No more jokes. No talking.

We walk toward our destination while the commotion on the dock grows in crescendo. Dock workers yell out, and heavy machinery is being used to lift the crate. Every employee is watching that wooden box as if it were the holy grail while ignoring the two men who don't belong there.

Shouts to be careful fill the night's sky.

Loud noises follow as machinery lowers and then opens it.

And all while Casper slides in the keycard through the reader, making sure to avoid touching anything. He uses a handkerchief to open the door, and just before we step through, there's a loud cheer from the unloading zone.

The metal door closes, and all noises cease, especially the low whining noise from the cameras as they move to follow our movement. We don't look up while I press the scrambler to fuck with the signal, making it impossible for photo detection to play a part in the case when it's discovered we have it.

The truck is right where Archie said it would be, and we open the cab to find our bulletproof vests and jackets, the holster that these drivers wear, and two badges. Each has a fake name, company IDs, and a pack of gum in mine that Casper raises an eyebrow to.

"It's her favorite candy and trust me, she'll freak out. I thought it might make her smile."

Changing takes seconds, and I jump into the cabin and grab the set of keys along with the lock from the glovebox. I switch the originals to ours before coming back to where I wait.

After a minute, we hear a small thump and low curse. The noise is easily hidden behind the commotions the loading crew makes and the orders being shouted out by the museum director.

"Where are the men driving the decoy?" she suddenly yells out, and the Collado brothers walk forward, changed and with a set of papers in hand. They are dressed like us, and the older of the two makes eye contact through the side mirror as dock employees secure and lock up the artifact. "You two need to split up at the designated intersection. The maps are in the truck."

"Yes, ma'am," they answer in unison.

"Thank you, gentlemen." There's a hint of a fluster in her voice. It's softer and husky.

"Of course." This time it's the younger of the two who answers, amusement coloring his tone while from my view, his brother's eyes become hard. *The hell?* Within minutes, two other engines roar to life and Casper turns the ignition, waiting for the signal to back out and go.

"You okay?" he asks, his face holding concern. My knee bounces and my jaw ticks.

"Two of them.," is all I can manage through gritting teeth, my eyes on the live feed from inside. Again, two figures. The male and the female; she's doing all the work, though. Prying the container open with a crowbar to make sure they're in the right truck. "They came in from the top, and their hope is to be out before we leave. There's a beam above the truck they could climb out onto, and then escape through a window just below the roof line."

"Electrical?"

"They haven't noticed it yet." As soon as I say this, the man moves to open the exit latch they used to get in and quickly snatches his hand back.

All movement stops then for a moment, shock on their faces before they begin to communicate lowly. They're murmuring to themselves while she waves her hand in a frantic motion.

Bang. Bang. Bang.

"Seatbelt, and keep your eyes down." Casper pulls back and out, following the instructions on the pre-set GPS they provided. We're heading toward the A13 and we'll deviate paths at the second roundabout, where the Collado brothers will go to a warehouse twenty minutes out and dump these trucks there before blowing each up.

No evidence left behind.

The direction has us driving the main road that connects east and central London, but we'll disappear at Limehouse Link Tunnel. That's where our connection will cease and so will all the cameras in this area, not one being able to tail our direction.

And that's what we do until reaching an open field out in the middle of nowhere.

That's as long as I can take it, and the second Casper puts the truck in park, I'm rushing toward the back. There are no houses here. No witnesses. My hands shake as I input the code on my lock, and when it beeps, I all but yank the entire thing off its hinges in my rush to see her.

It's been fucking months.

Brutal and agonizing days where I thought she might be dead.

The doors bang open, and inside two people stand with fear in their eyes. But it's hers I'm focused on, the pure relief that pours out of her slim body and she sways—grips onto the wooden box to right herself at the sight of me.

"Aliana, come here." My tone is gravelly. I'm at my limit of patience. "Baby, please."

"Callum?" The worry at once evaporates, and she breathes out a heavy exhale. The man beside her calms too, as if he knows who we are but is playing a dangerous game of pretend. His clock is ticking. "What are you doing here?"

"Come." Not that I wait. Before the last syllable passes through my lips, I'm in the truck and have her in my arms. *Home. She is home.* Our lips meet, her desperation near the same as mine while my hands wander and explore, from the back of her head down to her shoulders and then sides, where I pause. I touch her stomach and a heavy breath leaves me, my eyes cloud with tears. "Venus?"

"I'm three months, I think. We've been hiding it best we could, but my mother…she—"

"It's okay. I'm here now."

"She's my little cousin." At the sound of the other man's voice, I whip my head to the side and glare. He shrinks back, pretending to be defenseless. "I couldn't leave her alone in this."

"The fuck did you just say? Her cousin?"

"Yes." He runs a nervous hand across the back of his neck. "I'm on her mother's side."

"Is it true, Aliana?"

"No." Venus's voice is shaky. "He's my handler."

"And who the fuck orchestrated this?"

Casper raises his gun and points it at the git. He pales, shaking his head, hands up in the air.

"Callum, please. I just need to—"

"Who, Venus. Tell me, baby."

"I can't." My face turns to her, and the tears I see there kill me. "It makes it real."

"Your mum?" Keeping my movement slow, I pull her against me once again. I sway us a little while she lets out a sob, her tiny pregnant body shaking. "Is what Jorge said true? She killed him in front of you?"

"Yes." Aliana swallows hard, and I'm proud of her for trying to calm herself. The stress she's been under is something I will never forgive myself for. "After they took us, I woke up tied to a chair across from him. He was beaten, a little bloody, and by those he considered friends and family. Those he protected above me."

"Can you give me names?"

"I can tell you where they're all at."

"Good girl." I kiss the crown of her head. "They won't get away with this."

"It was Rigo, Gaspar, and my mother. Jorge and his wife were also there; they took us, but the latter is dead."

"Jorge's wife is dead?" Just to make sure I heard right.

"Yes." Aliana pulls back just far enough for me to meet her sad eyes. "She'd been sleeping with my father for over a year. Jorge pulled the trigger while my mother egged him on, calling him all kinds of names until he snapped and grabbed a knife, stabbing her to death a few feet from me."

"Oh, sweetheart." *Fuck*, she should never have seen something like that. Not her. Never her. "Jorge is dead, by the way."

"Good riddance. My cousin was a pig." *She doesn't know.* And for now, we'll keep it that way. The less stress, the better. "By the way, it was my mom that put this all together. Her and Rigo, who is also her lover, and I'm disgusted by the level of trash my family has become, and all for greed. They needed the money from that sale to disappear, while Gaspar wants me. They attempted to kill two birds with one stone."

"I'm sorry, love. I never wanted something like this for you."

"I know and I don't blame you. Y-you came for me," she cries lowly, her bottom lip trembling as she speaks. "I've been so scared. She kept threatening us and—"

"Baby, where are your brothers and Lindsey? There's a second team waiting to take off and grab them."

"Just Lindsey is with them. But why my brothers?" she poses the last as a question. *I'm missing something here.* "What about them? She told me they were in a new school…it was one of the agreements we made."

"Not here in London. Where are they?"

"They let me pick between Nicaragua or Sweden. I chose Sweden with the hope you'd find them first since that was one of the choices you gave my father."

CALLUM

I CAN FEEL Casper's eyes on the side of my head, but right now an explanation will have to wait. There are more pressing matters to deal with than my relationship status, and after all my men regrouped at the meet up, we detoured to a small building near Heathrow.

The place is isolated.

As if the owner closed shop recently and just left everything as is.

Exiting the car, I turn to look at Aliana. "I'm going to need you to—"

"If anyone is going to shoot her, it will be me." My little firecracker is back. It took us thirty minutes into the drive for her to go from weepy to fuming and every other emotion in between. And I'm proud of her, but right now, that baby inside her belly comes first. "Sweetheart, please. I'll drag her to the car if you want, but I need you safe."

"I'm the safest next to you."

"She's right." A female voice comes from our left, and Aliana's eyes fill with tears once more. "You will protect her like no one else will."

"Roe Roe, I'm—"

"Shut it." My eyes narrow at her tone, but I relax when I see the smile on her face. "So, he's dirty-joke dude?"

"Yeah. Just like one-night stand turned into a solo wedding?"

"Touché."

"Are we okay, then?"

"I don't know." Aurora turns an icy glare on me. "Do you love her, Callum? Plan to spoil her while also accepting that once every few months, we will be having a sleepover?"

It's hard, but I manage to keep my lips from twitching. "Aye."

"Then I see no reason why we can't get this show on the road. Let's get a move on."

My cousin chuckles at my perplexed expression. "Is she always this bossy?"

"Pretty much. From my understanding, they both are."

"Nice."

"Callum, can we get a move on?"

"Yes, dear." Aliana exits the large SUV, but before she takes a step forward, I'm kissing her again. Passionate and quick, enough to steal the breath from her chest. "Are you sure you want to come?"

"Please."

"Then give me your hand, love. You're a Jameson now, and we don't hide or cower."

"Aye," comes from the other two.

Giannis is a few feet away, smiling wide when we approach with a quiet Kray and Dwayne beside him. They have their weapons drawn, but I spot a smaller Glock at Martin's hip. At my questioning stare, he shrugs sheepishly and hands it to Aliana. "Just in case."

"Thank you," she breathes out before stepping away from me and then hugging all three men; Kray nods to whatever she whispers. All I'm able to catch is Lindsey's name, and I can't blame the man for the gratitude shining in his eyes.

She's his and has been missing just as long.

He already has orders to take a holiday as soon as we're done here.

"Ada Rubens is Aliana's kill. No one touches her, but she is not to escape. Is that understood?" Everyone taps their chest once in unison and then we're moving, walking toward our respective posts. Archie and the Collado brothers will maintain the back while Giannis and Dwayne cover the sides, and the rest walk inside as if strolling through an open garden.

They don't notice us at first. A grave mistake.

The man they hired to control my Venus is tossed at their feet with a clean slice across his neck. The gaping wound is large and gruesome, his body still warm, and the last of his blood trickles to the floor, creating the smallest of puddles. It's almost cute.

"Henri!" Ada screams, her eyes widening at the corpse. The others follow suit, and yet it's the older two of the trio that fail to look up. Gaspar is slowly trying to move away from them. *They truly fail at being criminals.* "What the hell is going on?"

"Hello, other," Aliana says from beside me, and Rigo's head snaps up a second before Ada Rubens's. "How have you been?"

"Mamita, I've been so worried." The tears begin, fake as the pearls around her neck. "How could you do this to your family? You killed my husband and now…now…" She pauses, a sob catching in her throat. I'm bored by her already. "How could you hurt me so? After everything I've done…fuck!" Ada's scream is loud, a painful wail, and it's because of the bullet to her right foot.

From experience, I know that stings.

"Tell the truth, or the next one will be to your face." Aliana's voice is devoid of all emotions. Her grip is firm, and I'm proud of her. "It's time for you to come clean. No more bullshit."

"I don't know…" My girl shoots past her head and Ada shakes, almost falls if not for Rigo keeping her upright. "Stop shooting!"

"The truth, carajo!" A tear slips down her cheek, but she's quick to wipe it away before retaking her stance. Her aim is now on her mum's chest. "Tell them how you blame me for not wanting to marry the man slowly moving away from you. Tell them how you forced me to watch you unload a gun on my dad's body, all the while saying I drove you to it. Tell them how you planned to make me abort this pregnancy before disappearing with the money to a private island while Gaspar made me his whore."

Never have I wanted to strangle someone so much in my life. To literally deprive them of oxygen while their body shuts down and eyes bulge out of their head.

I take a step forward, my intent clear, but Casper and Aurora grab my arm, the latter of which shakes her head and mouths *her kill*.

"Go on, Mother. Show your true colors."

"We were never meant to be parents, Aliana. That was our biggest downfall."

"Agreed."

My eyes shift to Kray when the oldest of the Collado brothers enters the building. I give them both the signal and they move quickly, one darting to the back where Lindsey is watching us from an office behind the three wankers. She's awake, but tied up, and I know Aliana will be happy once Kray gets her out of here.

"Callum, please!" Flavio's painful yell catches Rigo and Ada's attention. They watch as Collado lifts Gaspar off the floor and walks over to a large, dirty sliding glass door. "I'll disappear. I won't touch her!"

"Boss?" Collado asks, and I nod. Not a second later, Gaspar goes through the side exit and then doesn't move. He lies unconscious, small cuts littering his arms and face. Giannis is also there and while Rigo looks relieved, his son's face holds so much ire. "Do we take him to the car?"

"Not yet."

"As you wish, boss."

"Giannis?"

"Yes." He knows what I'm going to ask. I'm giving him the same courtesy as Aliana; Malcolm will just have to deal with it. Their kids get first right to claim.

"You or me."

"You." Rigo's son swallows hard; he looks at his father one last time and then turns his back.

"Son, you can't—"

"Silence." Everyone but my queen adheres to the command, her stony expression crumbling a bit. "I can handle them both. You don't have anything to prove."

"But I do. No more nightmares," she whispers, sad eyes glittering with tears she fights back. "She threatened our baby, Callum. A defenseless child."

"I know."

"Her daughter's child."

"I'll follow your lead, then."

"Thank you." Tilting her face up for a kiss, I give her one before aiming at Rigo's head. "Together, beautiful."

"Aye." A unanimous vote from every member of our family. Not the two pieces of shit crying and whimpering.

"You're our kids. You can't sentence us to death!"

"Stop this insanity. We can pay you!"

"Please, give us a chance to change."

"I don't forgive you, Ada." Her mother sobs louder—bangs on her chest as if in pain, while her daughter just sighs. "You're scum, worse than, and I hope you rot in hell for your crimes. Please know that I'll live my life to the fullest and become everything you never were: successful and loved. Fuck you."

She fires a second before I do, and we don't stop until the two bodies on the ground no longer move. They're not breathing, both with eyes wide open and blood pouring from their mouths, the multiple gunshot wounds visible on various parts of their body.

The first sob comes from Giannis. I know this is hard, but when Aliana walks over and they embrace, he crumbles. They both do, and we give them a moment. No matter how shitty both sets were, they are blood. It will always sting a little bit.

"So, Aliana?"

"I never hid it, Casper. You just didn't bloody pay attention."

My cousin scratches his jaw, lips thinning. "I'll blame my wife for the lack of awareness, and I extend a sincere apology."

"Oi, cut that shit out before she hears you."

"It would be just my luck, too."

"However, you can do me a favor to make up for the inconvenience…"

"Breathing or unconscious?" Casper asks; he knows me well. He's also no longer laughing but watching the small woman who's my world. My family. *Mine.* "I want him alive and delivered to the property in Dorset. His next job in this life is to be Zeus's snack."

"You and that large cat."

"I warned him, cousin. Told him he'd become my tiger's catnip." Aurora looks at us with a weird fascination, but I'll introduce her to my pets another day. When they're not hungry. "Come out to the property before heading home. It's a literal mini zoo."

Her eyes bug out. "You're serious?"

"Aye." I leave her with her thoughts on the subject and pick up Aliana, giving Dwayne room to step in as well. They'll be fine; it'll be rough for now, but what matters is that they're free. No more worrying. No more threats.

"It's over."

"You okay, sweet girl?" I ask, pushing her hair back from her face. She's lost a little weight since she's been gone, but the slight baby bump is unmistakable against my lower abdomen. *My baby.* "What can I do for you?"

"A burger and fries with a large cherry Coke?" For some reason, that cracks me up. Dear God, this woman is insanely beautiful. "I'm starving, Callum. It's been quite a busy few months."

"Then why the tears? I know this was—"

She places a delicate finger over my lips. "I'm not upset she's dead or traumatized by being the one to take her life. Not in the least. She's never been a mother to me. We never had that kind of connection. And before you ask, my father lands in the same category."

"And the crying?"

"Hormones, Mr. Jameson. I'm tired and hungry."

"Then let me get you out of here and fed." The emotions hit me hard then. The months without her, the constant worry, and I close my eyes while hugging her close. *I could've lost them both without ever knowing about the baby.* "I need you to know that I love you beyond all measure, Aliana. More than my own life."

"I love you, too. I've missed you." Her eyes tear up again, and she huffs at herself. It's cute. "This hormonal crap is going to be a pain."

I chuckle. "What can I do to make it better?"

"Never let me go," she whispers against my lips, kissing me once again, and I forget the world around us. Nothing matters but the treasures in my arms, clinging to me just as desperately as I hold her.

I'll never stop chasing her.

I'll never stop loving her.

Aliana Camila Rubens was born to be mine.

EPILOGUE 1
Aliana

SIX MONTHS LATER…

I STAND TO the side and watch with pride as Callum cuts his palm and let's a few drops of blood fall into a crystal chalice his uncle is holding. My eyes are riveted by him, watch every move he makes, and my heart fills with so much happiness as I take in the people inside the room bowing their heads.

My Callum.

My savior.

Their boss.

Closed fists bang on chests once and he follows suit, his gem-colored eyes flicking to me. But then again, he's always seeking me out. Even inside the same room, he needs me nearby.

Come, he mouths, and his father places a hand at the center of my back to help me up the walkway and then the small staircase which lead to him. The platform isn't large, but it's secure, and I have my own vows to make.

And while not as official and sacred as his, it's important for the wife of the boss to pledge her loyalty.

I'm his.

Today. Tomorrow. Always.

"Don't be nervous, little one. We're not like other families, and the women aren't shunned," his father whispers, tone affectionate and sweet. But then again, he's been like that since I came to live here.

One look at me, and I was claimed by the same parents that failed him. Weird, in a way, but the arse is having too much fun watching them fawn over me. He also gets a kick out of saying I'm the reason he's not the product of a broken home.

The two bickering old people have united with me as their goal.

Or better yet, to be the kind of grandparents that our child deserves.

"Easy for you to say, Abuelo." I'm out of breath already, but being nine months pregnant does that to a woman. "I'm the size of a whale, and everything makes me feel like a hundred-year-old chain-smoker."

My father-in-law bites back a laugh. "Would you prefer to be carried?"

"You wouldn't?" I turn to look at him, eyes narrowed. "I'll tell on you so—"

"He wouldn't what?" Callum asks from the bottom of the stage, his eyes dancing with mirth. "Carry you in front of all these people? You know the answer to that, Venus."

"Don't you dare!"

"My apologies, your majesty." And then, I let out a low squeal that makes those closest to the stage chuckle. Not at me per se, but how often I get caught in this type of situation. The moment he sets me down, though, I smack his arm and walk over to Uncle Jameson. He's another softie. "Get your nephew to leave me alone."

"You heard her."

"I did." Callum's tone holds no remorse. "Are you ready, love?"

"Yes."

He takes my hand in his, and together we face the men and women who work for the Jameson family. My family. Giannis and Dwayne are a part of that group now, as is Kray and Lindsey, who stand a few steps from the stage and to the left of Mariah and Casper.

Everyone is smiling. Happy for us.

"You will lay your life to protect her."

"Aye."

"You will respect her as you do me."

"Aye."

"I will never forsake my family. We are one blood."

"One blood." The last unanimous chant is loud, and it almost drowns out the music coming from the other room where politicians, heads of countries, and a few generals mingle and drink, unaware of what's happening within this room. We're celebrating more than just his blood oath, but the grand opening of Jameson Arms.

Don't let a country at war fool you. They all rub elbows in one way or another.

"My Venus," Callum's voice is reverent. So low no one else can hear, but I do.

"I love you, Mr. Jameson." However, the smile turns into a frown when I gasp a minute later.

"Aliana, baby?"

"Callum, I think…" I feel wet, not a lot, but like I had one of those accidents all pregnant women have. You sneeze or laugh at the wrong time and things happen down there. "Callum, I think my water is about to break."

"Are you sure?"

"Yes."

"Out," his voice booms, and everyone but our family leaves. They're crowding us now, worried, but Aurora meets my gaze, and she gets it. Gentle hands cup my face, thumbs rubbing across my cheek. "Are you in pain?"

"Not yet, but I feel off. Some pressure, but our doctor said that's normal." Callum's mom stands to our left, her hand massaging my lower back where I'm most uncomfortable, and I shoot her a small smile. "Thank you."

"I'm so excited, Aliana. My heart is racing!"

"Mum, let me get her to a seat. We need a—"

"Casper, honey. Don't just stand there. Please bring the car around the back."

"Gem, what're you—"

"I swear to God, if my best friend has our niece or nephew here because of you, I will smite you." At his wife's words, he nods dumbly but then jumps into action, rushing out of the room with all the men in this family on his heels. "Well, that lit a match under them. Pussies."

I'm surrounded by crazy people. I laugh at that, full-on giggles, but it quickly turns into a grimace as wetness rushes down my leg and feet. *So gross.* "Yeah, that was definitely my water breaking. I'm going to need a change of clothes."

"We have some in the car."

"Which one?" I ask, but Callum just shrugs and mouths *all of them.*

"You're that prepared?" Carefully, he picks me up, not caring about his clothes, and walks us down the stairs and across the room to a side exit. "When did you even have time to do all this?"

"While you sleep."

While I sleep. It's things like this that make me a believer in the possibility of a long and happy life with the person you love. Because only someone who cares will plan while you're asleep to make life easier. They'll sacrifice their rest and comforts so that when the moment comes, you never go without.

This man loves me for me.

With the good, bad, and ugly. Through sickness and health.

He holds me when I cry.

He understood my need to never discuss my family again, including Jorge being my brother and not the cousin I was led to believe all my life.

He respects, loves, and protects.

Callum is why I'm not afraid to become a mother. To take this step, because I know no matter what life throws our way, he'd never allow what happened to me to happen to our children.

He's caring and loving and so patient.

My brothers already lean on him. Look up to him.

And when its time to push a few hours later, it's his eyes I focus on. All I see and understand is his hand in mine, fingers intertwined, while my body handles the rest. The entire delivery lasts a few hours; there was one moment where my blood pressure was high and a concern, but then she cried, and I lost my heart to the Jameson charm all over again.

PAISLEY CAMILA JAMESON
SEX: FEMALE
WEIGHT: 6LBS 9OZ
HEIGHT: 19 INCHES

EPILOGUE 2
CALLUM

"ARE YOU SURE about this?" Malcolm asks, sitting back while watching the scene in front of him unfold. But then again, so is every other man I consider to be family. We're congregated atop a large deck with a table at the center just a few steps from me, but for this occasion, we stand. The veranda is all that separates us from falling into the den of my two favorite pets: one has lived with me since he was a cub, while the other I took in when the original owner couldn't keep up with its care.

My Hera and Zeus.

They're large and hungry.

Vicious and loyal.

To me. Only me.

And I treat them as if they are my babies, more so than the other animals that reside on my more than two-hundred-acre lot. There are various snakes, both poisonous and constrictors, while I also keep a few wolves. However, my Siberian tigers are who we watch today.

For over a year, I've babysat Flavio and Santis. Kept them in the same room, provided food and entertainment, while giving them a false sense of security that today won't be their downfall.

I never lied, but the more you make your prey wait, the easier it is to strike when the time comes. Complacency is a truly vile behavior, makes a person vulnerable—weak—but I did warn them.

A day. A week. Twelve months to the date.

None of that mattered in the long run, because they were always set to die.

The puppet master just hadn't chosen the *when*.

"Aye." Bringing the glass to my lips, I take a sip of my gift. The De Leon family has bought into the liquor industry, taking over a distillery in Cuba known for world-renowned rum. The amber glow alone is sexy while the taste is smoky with subtle tones of fresh pear and coconut, and while I'm not a rum drinker, this one I'm a fan of. "The information given to Aliana is accurate, and those are the codes that lead to their underground vault. One for each bank. Ezra verified it all, and he's never wrong."

"What you propose could change everything, my brother." Thiago smirks, and I know he's in. We've talked about this; Luna and Aliana have become close since our last trip to Miami, both women bonding over their growing up Latina. "The way we operate, live—how the world moves."

"The world." Malcolm shakes his head, but he's smiling. Santis and Flavio have been brought out to the enclosed space; they're sweating and complaining—waving their arms around and frowning. *They're still blind to their reality.* "We would be above the law."

"Yes. We would." My eyes look over to Casper, and he nods. He wants to make the move. "Aliana's father wasn't fully aware of either artifact's worth. The jade statue in Brazil, that one holds a heavy price tag, yes, but etched at the bottom is a set of numbers that belong to that government's missiles. Then, there's the vase in London. That beauty is the only way in and out of the underground vault, the same one where Spain and the United Kingdom have their secrets and crimes stashed away deep underneath their largest bank. We are talking about war, civilian, and every worldwide transgression committed, which isn't public knowledge between the two."

Javier chuckles, fixing his cufflinks. "It's a good start, but the US will hold some leverage. Our hit has to have ramifications for them as well."

"That's the beauty of it." A whistle rends the air then, and we all turn our heads. My animal's handler holds a large red flag high above his head, and I pick up the matching one, waving it twice. He knows to exit swiftly, and he does, backing away slowly so as to not startle my pets. "With treaties come favors. With alliances come expectations, and the US has skeletons in both closets."

Malcolm raises his glass, his eyes ahead while the others follow suit. "To immunity."

"Aye." Every family present agrees. This would change the world's dynamic, our stronghold in every bloody thing a government does or prosecutes.

Flavio and Santis look at the keeper, then at us and wave back.

Somehow, they've come to think we're friends.

We're not. They're nothing more than overgrown catnip.

And while they watch me, walking a little closer to the high, above-ground terrace we stand on, the keeper walks out and locks the exit. A whirring sound fills the air, a loud rattling of metal, and then white and orange paws come into our line of sight.

The Gaspar siblings startle and take a few steps back. They scream, nothing of what they say making sense, and it won't matter for long anyways.

Zeus and Hera stalk their prey slowly, lowering their bodies to the ground and inching forward. The Gaspar siblings freeze, but their eyes are on me, on the megaphone in my hand that Casper was so kind as to grab from the table.

It clicks on, an annoying whine that settles into a low static until I speak. "I warned you." Their heads shake, bodies moving closer to the enclosure's gate. "You had multiple opportunities to walk away, to stay clean, but you didn't listen. Here you will reap what you sow—just like your cunt of a father who aligned himself with people he shouldn't have—interfering with my family and the Boston organization."

Their family name will end here.

You don't make moves against this family.

You touch one—you bloody deal with all.

Flavio is angry, but scared. Santis is close to pissing himself, and yet, he's saying something I can't make out. He could be blessing or cursing me, I have no clue, nor do I give a bloody fuck.

However, the noises he's making Hera doesn't like, and hisses. Her nails dig into the ground, but both cats haven't lunged yet. These animals are hunters by nature; they wait and wait until the right opportunity arises. Or in this case, fucks up.

"I slit his throat." They both swallow hard at that, hands clenching. "Now, I'm going to make this fun. I'll have the keeper unlock the door and give you thirty seconds to make it out. You win, you walk out. You lose, my pets will pick their teeth with your bones."

I don't wait for their agreement and give the okay to unlock.

"Go."

Eyeing my tigers, they move a few steps and Hera remains low while Zeus rises midway, poised, yet he makes no move to attack. At the ten-second mark, though, both brothers turn around and run, pushing their bodies as far as they can, but it takes three full strides from each cat to reach them.

They pounce, forcing the men to the ground while locking their jaws at the back of their necks, shaking them from side to side. Horrified screams reach me, and I'm impressed by how far the sound travels when a true panic-induced cry for help is unleashed.

Zeus tosses Flavio aside like a rag doll, his body bouncing a bit on the ground, before pinning his chest with a front paw. Blood and spit dribble from the animal's muzzle and onto his prey, the latter of which is pushing with all his might but the beast remains unmovable.

For her part, Hera is already enjoying a chunk of flesh, taken from the still-alive idiot. It's from his leg, the thigh area to be precise.

Yet, this is nothing compared to what they deserve.

Yes, Flavio wanted to wed my Venus, but she would've become property of the family and would've been used as such. They spoke about it a week after their capture, unaware of Ezra recording this conversation. Back then, they had hope. Thought their organization—father—would come to save them, and they made plans.

The brothers wanted to share her. Lend her out. And eventually, when she'd become older and loose—their words—they'd whore her out to their seedier clientele with no limits to their depravity.

For that, I could never forgive them.

I'm being merciful by letting my pets feed on their rotten flesh.

Which they do. Piece by piece.

An alarm beeps from my mobile and I put my glass down, walking away without looking back, the others slightly behind me. I'm fixing my jacket and tie as I go. The stupid handkerchief on my breast pocket looks a little wonky, and I hope Aliana doesn't notice or she just might kill me at my own wedding.

Guests are beginning to shuffle in, each of the fifty chairs filling fast while Casper takes his place beside me. Our brothers find their seats in the first row on the bride's side, their wives all wearing cheesy grins while Luna smirks, camera poised to shoot.

They want my honest reaction to seeing my bride photographed.

I understand why a minute later when the traditional wedding march begins to play and my Venus pauses at the other end of the aisle. Everything stops for me. The air in my chest ceases to exist while the world fades away until she's all that's left.

My Aliana. My wife. Mine.

She smiles at me, and my heart beats inside my chest with the cadence of a war drum.

She takes her first step, and I'm able to breathe again.

She places her hand in mine a few seconds later, and I'm home.

Everything starts and ends with her.

Aliana Camila Jameson is the future I don't deserve but will fight every day to keep.

IVAN
DE LEON

The De Leons are a criminal dynasty.
No one makes a single move in South Florida without our knowledge,
and yet, it's not enough.

Not as a man. Not as a boss.
Not when I've vowed to lay an entire country at my little Mermaid's feet.

Every man has a path to walk, and Ivan De Leon's is set in stone. The price to pay for my decisions has been steep, but the gains are mine to claim, and I will. I've killed to be where I am—walked away from the most important person in my life—and now, one phone call changes everything.

Success comes with casualties. Hunger and desperation.

I've bled to be worthy of her.

I broke her heart, but I'll also put it back together again.

My little sirenita. My Amberlyn.

GLOSSARY FOR SPANISH & CUBAN SLANG:

Sirena/Sirenita: Mermaid

Viejo/Vieja = Old Man/Woman

Mierda = Shit

Chivato = Rat/Snitch

Coño = Fuck or Damn

Bebe = Baby

Cabron = Fucker

Mamajuana =
This Comes From The Dominican Republic And Is Made By Combining Rum, Red Wine, And Honey And Soaking The Mixture With A Special Tree Bark & Herbs. The Color Is A Deep Red, And Some Say It Tastes Similar To A Port.

Singao = Fucker or Asshole

Hijo de Puta = Son of a Bitch

Que Vola = What's Up

Acere or Asere = Friend

Tio/Tia = Uncle or Aunt

Salsa Rueda or Salsa Casino =
This style of salsa dancing originated in Cuba. Here, the couples form a large circle or rueda, and they execute turns, steps, and patterns in unison to the calls of the singer or leader.

Dear Reader,

When I started this series in 2019, I pictured the De Leon brothers as Cuban males with a Latino family dynamic—crazy cousins, funny parents, and endless get-togethers. Because no one parties like we do; what starts as a barbecue inevitably ends up feeling like a block party. LOL

Writing these books hit me with unexpected nostalgia. I was born and raised in Miami, and the people and places within these pages reflect my life and my stomping grounds: my friends and family. And sure, the whole crazy-mafia aspect is fiction and just for fun—an escape—but the longing to understand where your family comes from is real.

So, I dedicate this to the people who were never able to visit the places your grandparents talked about while reminiscing. To the countries our parents left behind to provide us with a better life.

And lastly, to my Abuelos—my Mima and Pipo—may you always rest in peace. We never got to take our trip to Cuba, to the city where you were born, but I plan to do it with Mom someday.

Elena XoXo

IVAN

THE CUBAN MALECON is beautiful at night.

Havana is nothing short of paradise.

And more so as its citizens come alive beneath the stars. The area from one end to the other is full—people young and old are dancing and singing, sharing with each other what they have even though it's illegal to do so by the government's standards.

They decide what you eat and when.

They decide what kind of business you are allowed to own.

You can be arrested for something as simple as speaking your mind.

There are no liberties here, because freedom means *they* lose power.

Those bastards sit comfortably inside the national palace and hold court surrounding a ridiculous round table, giving nightly discourses on a nonexistent threat that's dangerous to only one percent of the island's population. They fear everyone outside this country, and projecting that same emotion is how an abuser stays in control of a situation.

I'm the real threat within their midst.

And while I understand the notion that I hold no moral high ground, there are limits you don't cross. My family doesn't take kindly to abuse, not of innocent people, and their day of reckoning is coming.

In my grandfather's name.

In my grandmother's memory.

On the series of digits that grace our family's wrists in honor of a man who fought against oppression and demanded freedom.

Patria y Vida. Country and Life.

Their day is coming. The people here can taste it.

Smiles spread across those socializing near me, a few catching my eyes here and there while pretending it's just another hot summer night. The stone-built embankment runs for five miles and is an attraction that pulls in tourists and citizens alike; they come to relax and enjoy the cooling cocoon of never-ending sea mist while making deals.

The legal kind. The ones solved in alleyways and away from the military police who seems to be absent tonight.

This evening, though, those visiting the island have been warned to stay inside the National Hotel just a short walk from here. And while they watch from the windows and lobby, I stand right within the sight of the large fountain of said establishment in my black jeans and shirt with an old pair of combat boots on my feet. The tattoos on my arms and neck should be enough to pick me out of a crowd.

I'm not hiding.

The president knows I'm here and waiting.

A few feet from me, people begin to clap in key, keeping in tune with the salsa playing on someone's old-school stereo. It's loud and full of life, even catching the attention of a few vintage cars. The taxis are empty except for one driver, who passes and honks while a group of twenty-somethings begins to dance in a rueda formation.

They move in sync, turning to face their partners while staying in step. The count is the same as your standard salsa, but quickly changes when the couples begin to execute choreographed moves that are interconnected with each person—turns and dips and the occasional trick where the men lock arms in a circular pattern and the ladies sit atop their forearms.

The circle breaks when the song's chorus does, and those near us cheer.

Moreover, I find myself nodding along to the beat, humming low, when I see him. The man isn't wearing his normal military uniform, choosing instead to blend in—his guayabera and dress pants combined with a pair of dark aviator glasses are meant to make him seem harmless. It fails.

He's anything but.

A killer can sense another.

Those around me also take him in. They know who he is and what he's capable of.

General Ortega smiles at a woman not far from him, trying to seem nonchalant before moving closer. And to keep up his charade, I bring the bottle of Cristal beer to my lips and take a deep pull while looking at those still having a dance-off.

Ortega doesn't disappoint when he stops beside me, facing the same way. "You're playing a dangerous game, De Leon. One might say you're overstaying your welcome."

"Am I?" After another sip, I tip over the rest over his feet and soak what I'm sure are expensive moccasins. "I had no clue."

His face reddens, hands clenching at his sides. "What do you think all this will achieve? You're no one's hero, asshole. Instead, you're putting marks on innocent people."

"And you care about these people?" We both know he doesn't, and I snort, waving at an older man that I consider to be family sitting on the embankment's edge. He's my mermaid's uncle and one of the many eyes and ears here. "My, General, you're as corrupt as he is."

"And you're not?" I'm not blind to the way his right hand slowly reaches his hip—to the tight grip he now has on a small pistol. "The De Leon family has more blood on its hands than I do. A criminal should never point fingers, kid. That's something your family should've taught you by now."

"Is that so?" Turning my head, I meet his beady eyes and smile. Fucking idiot has fallen right into my hands. "Do tell me how to run my business. How should I bow to you?"

Two of my men give me a nod from over his shoulder, coming a little closer while those watching do the opposite. They make more noise, celebrating, while Junior brings out a syringe from his pocket and stands at the ready.

There's enough sedative in the small dose to knock him out and transport him without issue.

"Scum like you always ends up on his knees with a mouth full of steel, tears rolling down your cheeks. President Rodriguez won't be gentle either; he wants to see you choke and beg for mercy."

"What else?" His vitriol is unimaginative at best. Pathetic. "Will I be forced to kiss his feet?"

"No, but your puta will."

"You're wasting my time, Ortega. Say your piece," I say, and while on the outside I'm calm—my smirk in place—the ire within is barely contained. This is something every man in my position deals with at one point or another: the threat to a loved one.

My girl. My mermaid.

It's a test. Not my first either.

It also gives me a sick sense of pleasure to watch his composure slip a little at my nonchalance. He's expecting yelling and curses, for me to react with violence while I'm sure his men are nearby. Another mistake, and at this point, I'm going to tally them up and deliver my reprimand before I snap his neck.

"You're egotistical now, Ivan," he spits out through clenched teeth, voice low as to not attract attention. Ortega's not entirely stupid; he knows I have people here, but he just doesn't know who is who.

Is it the old man clapping?

The mom holding a rum bottle tightly in her grasp?

Or the young man kissing his girlfriend?

Any one of them is a possibility, but not the case this time.

"Will you ever finish explaining yourself?"

"I'm going to personally shove my gun against Amberlyn Ibarra's head, cabron. I know her schedule, where she sleeps, and who her family is here on the island. Working in that bail bonds office near the police station won't protect her from us." With two fingers, he taps his temple and smirks. "Our reach is just as deep as yours."

"So that means your wife and son in Curacao are fair game? What about the whore you keep here…Barbara, is it?" Tilting my face a bit, I give him an innocent shrug. "I'll bleed them both dry and then make you drink it, Ortega. Don't get cocky with me. That mouth of yours is already going to cost you dearly."

"Listen here, hijo de puta—"

"No one calls my mother a whore."

"Fuck you and your..." A snap of my finger and Junior stabs the needle into his neck before he can finish, injecting the concoction into the great general's system and then stepping back. "What the hell was that?" He brings a hand up to the pricked area, cupping it while frantically looking around. Eyes wide, he stumbles within a few seconds and mumbles something. It's unintelligible, but I'm sure a few curses were insinuated.

His hands dig at his side, but they're more than likely asleep and just keep dusting his sides.

I take his gun and phone, dropping the latter and stomping on it. The screen shatters, and he tries to say something but fails. Words come out, but they're garbled and my men shrug, not understanding the idiot either.

I'm sure it's some insult either way.

"What was that? Did you say something?" I grab Ortega's arm when he stumbles again, while my other guard, Israel, takes the opposite side to steady him. "Inebriated and while on duty. So irresponsible, General. Such a grave mistake, too."

There's anger in his eyes, so much hate, but both roll back and he slumps completely against Israel. The entire ordeal lasts but three minutes at the most. Those around us clap when he loses consciousness, still pretending, and I tilt my head toward the newly restored Ford Fairlane parked a few feet from us. The driver is my personal one while on the island and has his orders:

No stops until on the family compound.

And as they move toward it with the passed-out general, the crowd follows. Covering. They block the view and most of the street, the party growing while all traces of them being here is erased within a blink or two.

I'm left behind to stroll off at a leisure pace with a smile on my face.

President Rodriguez made a huge mistake today.

Never show your hand ahead of time.

Never leave your messenger without proper protection—men who can't be paid off.

Never threaten a De Leon or his girl.

IVAN

"**W**HAT THE FUCK!" General Ortega sputters, coughing up the old water from the hog pen Israel threw at him. He's alert at once, eyes screwed shut as I'm sure something nasty fell in there. "What's going on?"

I don't answer him. Instead, I sit back and get a little more comfortable.

We've been inside the family compound for a few hours now. The drive here didn't take long; our estate is located west of Havana on a private stretch of land not far from the Mariel port and with the gulf as our backyard. My abuelo made the first move to own property here, more for vacation purposes, but my father transformed the land into a fully functioning colonial monstrosity with a twenty-four-hour staff, a small airstrip—and a private jail at the back end away from the family communal areas.

No neighbors for miles.

No questions asked.

Only one way in and out of the premises.

We also have access on and off the port without bypassing security, something that worked perfectly fine—smoothly—until my guest's master became greedy. That doesn't sit well with me or Thiago; their fear, while attractive, can lead to stupid decisions made by the heads of this country.

I'll kill every one of them first.

Another rancid-smelling bucket of water is thrown on the near-naked man, the rivulets dripping over the side of his gurney and onto the floor. The noise isn't loud, but just enough to rouse the attention of the other residents of this land.

I've always been an animal lover, just like my viejo and his father. Working the land and tending to them is relaxing, a decompression from our day-to-day operations. It's also one of the reasons I've decided to move here permanently in a few weeks.

There's a freedom here you don't have in the city.

My brother can rule the 305 while I overthrow a government.

The Mariel port will continue to be our gateway to Miami. Our products enter and disperse from there, while I receive and account for everything here. It's how I pay back what I owe him while also following my own path.

Two bosses.

A few partners.

One familia.

To be worthy of her.

Moreover, we have plenty of livestock here, from cows to chickens, a few goats, horses, and lastly, hogs. Large ones. Hungry ones. The kind that always stay near the rear of the building and I moved their pen closer because of it, with a back door that lets them in and out.

The noises alone haunt those staying here as our personal guests; the shivers and soiling of themselves is quite disgusting. I'm used to the fact but do bite back a grin at the look that overtakes Israel's face.

Junior isn't fazed, though. Not when Miguel, his father, has worked for the family for years and is trusted. The kid's come into his own in the last few months working with me. Steadier—sure of himself—and has earned the right to move up in rank.

However, the newer of the two soldiers, Israel, a recommendation from Luna's uncle from his time with the Miami Police Department—his rookie partner before making the mistake of trusting another officer—is a different beast. That man took a small bribe from a celebrity needing to make the evidence against him—the drugs and guns confiscated in his possession—disappear.

Israel did a favor and caught the false charge.

He's been out now for a few months, and I offered him a position. His knowledge comes in handy.

"Hose him down." At my voice, Ortega turns his head in my direction and blinks. The wild hogs know my voice and a bit of screeching follows, causing the general to pale, body thrashing against the restraints. *Idiot.* "Calm down before I bring them in."

"Done."

"Cabron, let me go." Israel and Ortega speak in unison, but it's the general I'm focusing on.

"One second." Bringing two fingers to my lips, I whistle and the noise travels through the large space. It's sharp enough for my pets to quiet down, and I tilt my head to the side. My eyes never waver from him. "Now explain. Why would I do that?"

From my periphery, I see Israel walk toward the cell next to the hose spigot and step inside. He's in and out within seconds, dragging a piece of machinery behind him.

Smart man.

Ortega's tries to shift his face, to see what's happening, but Junior is quick to yank on the hospital bed's lever and force a half-sitting position. There's a grimace on his face right after, uncomfortable as the action stretches his arms back with how they're bound. It reminds me a bit of the way my hands were tied down before my gallbladder surgery a few years back.

Strap on each wrist. One across his waist.

He's unable to move much. In pain.

You have no idea what real pain is yet.

He swallows nervously, wrists trying to yank free. "You have no idea what you've done."

"I do."

"My president will never...*fuck*!" His scream reverberates through the large space; it's loud and full of pain. A small yet hard jet of ice-cold water smacks him in the face and he splutters, choking as the strength digs into his flesh.

Torturous. Painful. Such a thing of beauty to watch how something as simple as a pressure washer with enough PSI can be wielded as a weapon. Like butter, it will slice through every layer until reaching bone, and even that can be cut through with ease.

Israel is taking it easy on him.

I look over and give him a nod. "Increase it."

"Yes, boss." My guard fiddles with a button at the front of the machine and the fine-tip nozzle, shifting it a little to the right. In the background, I can make out the whine of my hogs; they dislike being kept out, but for now, remain calm.

They've been taught to be patient. They'll be fed soon enough.

"I'm going to kill every member of your family! Hijo de puta!" Ortega screams, trying to shift away, but Junior grips the back of his head. With strands of hair between his fingers, he holds the general still while I simply watch. From the right corner of his lip to his cheekbone, the skin gives way and the blubbering that follows is truly pleasing.

Makes me smile.

Blood pours from the wound and drips onto the plastic mattress, pooling a bit before his life's essence adds to the stained floor. It mixes with grime and filth and the more direct the hit digs into his cheek, I begin to see bone.

I raise a hand, and Israel pauses. "Rinse the rest of him."

"They'll be here any second now to rescue me. You're fucked, cabron."

"I'm shaking in my seat." My monotone grates on him. There's still plenty of fight in him, and yet it dies the moment Israel opens the water again. Pain fills his expression while rivulets of red run down his body, limbs shaking in their confined seat.

There's no true direction to my soldier's cleaning method. From the soles of the general's feet to his chest, there are quick and semi-deep slashes now littering his frame. He's been reduced to nothing in a matter of minutes—from a high-ranking member of the Cuban military to a whimpering pussy.

How fast the mighty fall.

Once deemed as clean as can be, Israel shuts the machine off and retakes his place a few steps back. Junior does the same, but not before bringing a rolling cart I have behind the bed to within my guest's line of sight.

Nothing covers the top, and the two items ready for me make him pale a little further.

"Talk." And while he swallows hard, his red teeth chattering a bit, I remove my shirt and lay it behind my chair. While he mutters under his breath what I know is a prayer for help to whatever deity he believes in, I shake out my arms and crack my neck.

I've been docile.

Keeping a tight leash on the monster within I've come to accept.

Because everyone has one. This evil that lurks beneath the surface, fighting to overthrow rationality, and I embrace mine.

It's been a part of me since my childhood. From the first time I witnessed my father slit a man's throat after catching him trying to sell us out, I knew we were different. That our norm isn't for everyone, but I learned quickly to thrive in it.

To protect what's mine. Just like every member of the De Leon family, we bleed for each other.

"Fuck you." That's his response, the open wound on his face gushing a bit with each word. Funny.

"Not my type, old man." Next, I remove the bracelet and Cartier watch on my wrist but leave the family ring. It's a thick gold band with our last name branded over the top, and right over the letter "D" there's a yellow topaz representing my mother's birthday. A bit eccentric from the rest of the family's; I consider my design to be a little more brutal when meeting a direct hit. My letters are 3D and with specific points meant to embed in the skin, tearing through flesh with each sharp edge. I flex my hand and then close my fist. "But you did mention someone I will kill for. Who's watching her?"

"I'd never betray my boss."

"You will." My steps are loud, the soles of my boots sloshing on the wet floor as I stop at the foot of his bed. He's following my every movement, fighting back the urge to cringe when I raise a hand and scratch my jaw. "Last chance."

"I'm not afraid." Yet his bottom lip quivers.

"Let it be known, you made me do this." Without another word, I walk to the tray and pick up a metal meat tenderizer. It's a little heavy in my hand, a very old kitchen tool my grandmother used and now I possess. She had a purpose for it, and I've eaten many meals where the meat melted in my mouth after a good pounding.

Now, though, it'll break down a different kind of flesh.

I make my way around him, from his head to his feet, pausing right beside his bare feet. These we did not strap, but he won't have much movement soon.

The first strike is right over his ankle, fast and hard, and Ortega disappoints me greatly.

His cries fill the space, and my animals outside once again get rowdy. Now, they thrash against the door, banging their bodies on the metal, and the sound nearly overthrows the general's pain-filled yells. I hit the same spot again, and then again, taking in how quickly the skin cracks and a fragment of bone slips through the opening.

He's also quick to pee himself once again, and I crinkle my nose. *Disgusting.*

My hard eyes meet his and still, his cracked lips remain quiet. I nod and trail the red-stained metal up his shin and pause at the knee. Waiting. Being hospitable enough to let him talk, but nothing comes out.

Nothing but whimpers of pain.

So be it.

The tap against his knee is a caress, very light, but I do enjoy the way he jumps in place right as I drop the mallet.

Holding a hand toward Junior, I wait for the next tool. This one, much like the previous, is meant to hurt, but the cross between hammer and sledgehammer is still comfortable in my grip. Easy to swing—same weight —yet the handle is smaller, fits better in my palm.

My fingers close around the sturdy base, and I arch a brow.

"He's the brother of a detective in the Miami P.D." Ortega licks his lips, shivering a little harder than a few minutes ago. "That's all I know."

"Liars never make it to the kingdom of heaven." The saying is funny coming from a man like me, but my mother drilled that into our heads while we were young. Be an asshole, a murderer, but your words should never be questioned.

A real man always keeps his promises.

Always admits to his wrongs.

Sins shouldn't be hidden under a veil of bullshit.

It's why the people here accept us so freely and without blinders. We give, provide, and protect, but discretion is the cost. Never bite the hands that feed unless you're willing to pay with your life.

De Leons value loyalty, not ass kissers.

They want to rise against and demand their freedom.

A mutual agreement that both sides respect.

"I swear it on my daughter's life. He lives in Hialeah."

"Hmmm." That's all I give him right before swinging the large steel hammer at his right, then left knee. One blow shatters both and he vomits, the sight of it slipping out of the facial wound quite disgusting. "Give him some water."

Ortega blanches, and the shivering increases. "Please stop."

This time, I don't hold my snort in. "Thought you said you weren't afraid of me?" Flicking my eyes to Israel, I shake my head when he goes for the power washer. "A bottle for the man, por favor."

Israel rushes over to a stack of room-temperature twenty-four packs and pulls one water out. He's back within seconds and untwisting the cap before placing it against Ortega's lips. And while the asshole rinses his mouth, spilling more than anything, I take my place near his opposite hand.

I'll give him points for having somewhat of a high pain tolerance. Laying the head of the hammer over his knuckles, I clear my throat and Israel retakes the bottle and dumps what's left on the floor. Ortega opens his mouth to say something, too, but I shake my head.

"I've given you every opportunity to come clean. To die with dignity and not as food for my pets, but you failed time and time again. So I'll do what you didn't and share with the class what I know."

"Ivan, I—"

One hard smack to the face shuts him up; Junior's hand is poised for a second hit. "He's Mr. De Leon to you." Nothing else is said, and I bite back a smirk. His father would be so proud of him right now, of how far he's risen in my ranks since starting at the bottom. "My apologies, boss."

"None needed." And when the guard retakes his place a few steps back, I refocus on a pathetic Ortega who looks nothing like the man threatening me earlier. How quickly that changed; he's a bloody, beat up, and scared man now. "From now on, all I want from you is a *si* or *no*. Do you understand?"

"Si."

"Good boy." Ortega doesn't like the praise, and his eyes narrow a bit; I remedy that by breaking the middle knuckle of his hand. Once again he screams, a sob catching in his chest, and I wait for the man to find his composure before continuing. "Now, tell me if I'm wrong." His nods are quick, as is the low *yes*. "Detective Jaime Uriel and his brother, Dalian, are related to President Placido Rodriguez through his current wife. They're her nephews from a dead older sister and have been in trouble a few times in the past. The only reason Jaime is on the force, and a detective, is through a heavy donation and favor called in by your boss to the now-deceased Miami mayor."

"Si." There's no hiding the surprise on his face.

Did he really think us to be so stupid? "Dalian is watching my mermaid."

"Si."

"They focused on her since she's not publicly claimed yet."

"Si."

That burns me with guilt; I put a marker on her head due to circumstances created out of duty. *This one's on me, and I'll right the wrong no matter what it takes. My sirenita will be safe.*

"Dalian and Jaime have asked for Amberlyn and control of Miami through us, as payment." Ortega hesitates and I break two fingers this time, my blows consecutive until the pressure of each direct hit makes the digits burst. "Did President Rodriguez offer those two singaos my girl on a silver platter to be at their service, if I was brought to my knees? If Rodriguez got control of the De Leon operations in Cuba?"

The pain is getting to him, and his eyes roll back. The blood loss from each injury is substantial.

"Bring the pigs in."

At those words Ortega perks up, eyes wide and full of tears. "I'll tell you everything. Just please...end this."

"Answer the question."

"Yes. He offered them the girl and a cut of your Miami profit while he controlled Cuba's."

"Why?" Below him, there's a lever that'll lower the bed and I kick it, bringing him closer to the floor. At just the right height, while Israel heads toward the only other exit. And when he does, the squeals become deafening. Animals are intelligent, can sense things we don't, and know what's coming. "Explain why a man like him would make such an ignorant move."

"Rodriguez is afraid." Ortega voice is low, and spit dribbles over his lips. He's slipping, but not as fast as he'd like. "People are talking, and the citizens are beginning to organize. He blames your family for this."

"So control the head of the beast, and the body follows."

"Si."

"Thank you, General Ortega. Your wife will be compensated for your brave contribution." No sooner has the last word left my lips than the sound of hooves fills the space. They rush to where I stand but don't touch me; instead, they focus on the bloody body atop the hospital bed with no way of getting out.

Not that he fights it. Instead, his limp body heaves in breaths while his eyes close.

The animals surround him, fighting for a bite, and I walk out when the bed topples over and every piece of him is covered by a hungry mouth. Nothing will be left behind, and once I cross the main entrance and step out into the warm night sky, those horror-filled screams of his disappear.

Tonight confirmed what we already knew.

It also cements my worry for Amberlyn and the life she'll have with me.

I can't allow her to be hurt.

"Placido Rodriguez has no idea how dangerous a man like me can truly be."

IVAN

"STAYING AWAY is an impossibility."

Using my copy of her house key, I walk in and only pause long enough inside the entryway to remove my clothing. Every single article is tossed aside like the nuisance it is, my boxer briefs holding the proof of my need for her in the few drops of pre-come that have slipped from the angry tip.

I'm hard for her. Always am.

I've been away for too long.

Cock in hand, I walk to her room at the end of the hall like the asshole I've become. Her door is open, a habit of hers from my late-night visits, and I kick it closed as gently as possible in my state. It's been four days since I've seen her. Too many, and I know this sensation—the feigning crawling under my skin—will only get worse when I move to Cuba.

Our expiration date is close, and she'll hate me soon enough.

I have no other choice, but first, I'll rid Miami of every cabron who's a threat to her safety, moves I've already put into motion.

After yesterday's incident with Ortega and then leaving instructions with the crew there, I flew right back onto American soil. Then made one small stop. Some people need motivation, and the proof of our talk is more than likely on my shirt or pants; a single punch broke his nose, and the idiot was a bleeder.

However, all other thoughts die when my eyes find her lithe body atop the bed, face down and with a strewn sheet across her ass and upper thighs. She's bare underneath that sheet; I know this just as I know she's already slick between her thighs.

"Motherfuck," I groan, voice low, yet she sighs in her sleep as if she's heard me. There's also the way she lifts one knee, further opening herself to me. Gifting me access to what I need to satiate our hunger—that primal fucking need for each other.

Amberlyn can't fall asleep without coming first, and I suffer when it's not around my cock.

She's a restless nymph with an appetite that rivals my own, and I live to see those light brown eyes roll back and her lips part in a seductive gasp— the feel of those thighs trembling around my hips and the sweet way she digs her fingernails into my back, leaving her mark behind.

Then, there are her toys for the days I'm not around. They range from the simple to light bondage—from intense to hours of teasing—and yet her favorite is the replica of my cock we made together two years ago. What started off as a joke, a teasing birthday gift, became a badge of pride for me.

Her desire for me makes me feel like a god.

Her need gives my life a purpose I didn't know had been missing.

Leaving you here is going to be so hard, sweetheart. My eyes adjust to the dark, the only source of light coming from the half-closed blinds. They give me just enough illumination to find her wand a few inches from her sleeping form, and I bite my lip. There's no doubt her pussy is wet and wanting. My favorite dessert. *Fuck, she's perfect.*

Taking the few short steps between us, I pause beside her nightstand and turn the bedside lamp on to the lowest setting. It's just bright enough for me to appreciate her beauty without waking her, and I walk back to the end of the bed and place a knee on it, and then the other. The mattress dips under my weight and then settles, slightly shifting as I crawl over her soft skin while removing the thin sheet. I'm careful and keep every touch lingering, maintaining most of my weight off while I enjoy the view beneath me.

She's soft, tan skin and long dark hair with bright scarlet highlights. Red has always been her signature style, from the fire-engine tones she used in her teens, to the now jet-black strands with delicate pieces in a lighter devilish shade that frame her delicate face.

The contrast suits her, even if I miss the way it looked in high school.

At least she keeps it long and wears it loose just the way I like it.

I reach out and grab the end of one loose curl and twirl it around a finger. "One day, I'll make everything up to you." It's my endless vow each time I come to her in the dead of night, the blood of an enemy still fresh on my skin. Not that she'll push me away. Instead, she loves me harder and then helps me wash away my sins. "My beautiful little sirenita."

I've kept my little mermaid a secret all these years.

The first time I kissed her was a week before Thiago turned himself in to the authorities, and I used her crush to our advantage. The first time I made her mine was on the anniversary of his imprisonment when she came to me, tried to make me feel better when my own guilt threatened to drown me, and I've never been able to put a stop to this affair.

Amberlyn has become my only. I won't touch another woman.

But I also know what this life does to people, and I owe her more than this. Than being selfish.

"You'll bear my last name one day. Take over the world with me." Lowering my body against hers, I keep her face down while positioning my cock at her entrance. Her skin is soft, and I shiver at the first contact; she's my heaven. There's also a hint of awareness in her, a small arch to her back and a pucker of those plump lips, but she's not fully awake and resettles. Nevertheless, when she's like this, all warm and vulnerable—this is when I lower my own guard. Love her the way I'll fight to make our future. "But not yet, sweetheart. Just give me a little time."

"Time?" Voice low and groggy.

Ignoring her question, I rub the engorged head of my dick against her opening, just letting her feel me. Letting her wetness coat, kiss my flesh. "You're so wet, bebe."

"Always for you." There's a hint of a whine when I slip the head inside and pull out. Once. Twice. Three times. "You're mean."

"And you love it."

Amberlyn smiles at that, eyes shifting toward the alarm clock, but stops when I nip her shoulder. *She doesn't deny it. Me.* "What time is it, papi?"

"Too early for you to be awake."

"But I need you." Those four words and her pout destroy any self-control I have left. Her body shivers beneath me when I grip her hips, pinning her against the mattress, but it's her face I focus on when I thrust inside. One smooth stroke and I'm nestled deep within her warmth while a peaceful smile graces her mouth. *Beautiful.* "I've missed you."

"*Fuck.*"

"I know." That curl of her lips stretches right before she bites down on the plump flesh and I watch the shift, memorize each sigh and whimper as if it were a slow reel—a private movie just for me. Time slows down as I take her body, never pausing the pump of my hips, fucking her hard and rough, yet all I can focus on is her pleasure.

On making sure she can feel me for days after. Craves me when I'm not here.

I'll never accept her loving someone else. *Wait for me.*

"You're my perfection, bebe," I hiss out after she clenches, her walls gripping me so fucking tight. Her wetness coats me, the sweet nectar grazing my balls and upper thighs and spreading more with each piston of my hips, the drops making a mess of her too. Amberlyn tries to move, to meet my thrusts, but my weight doesn't allow it. I'm in control of her pleasure. "So wet and tight just for me."

"Papi, I—"

"Tell me, Sirenita." I slam in deep and hold still, just giving her small flexes of my cock. "Tell your papi what you need."

But I know what she's missing. What she always craves.

"You. Always you."

Three words now sit on the tip of my tongue. Everything within me demands that I tell her, but I bite them back. The day I say them, I'll be hers. Can't have it any other way, and that can't happen until I settle my responsibility to our family.

Thiago gave up so much for us, and now it's my turn.

I need to eradicate any threat to her happiness.

One day, baby girl. I promise. "Good girl," I say instead and pull out slowly, dragging my thickness against her pulsing walls. The cool air of the room greets my slick cock. My balls feel heavy, but I'm focused on the way she trembles in anticipation.

And I let her while kneeling behind her. For a few minutes we stay like this.

No contact. No relief.

But it doesn't last long; I can't help myself and unconsciously start running my fingertips up the back of her legs, taking my time while following the path to her asscheeks. Her hips gyrate against the bed, a sweet offering, but still once I grip them tightly again.

With both hands I pull her up and onto all fours, her holes clenching—searching for my dick. *Motherfuck, she's a work of art. So mine.* My hand comes down over her right cheek and then left, a little harder than I intend, but she responds with a moan and a wiggle of her hips. I smirk at the sight. At the pink highlight of my palm on her flesh before slamming back in.

I don't pause or slow down or so much as breathe while fucking in deep and pulling out, riding her hard and fast like she craves. Because this is what we live for. What we both need.

It's a clawing need that tears us apart and then rebuilds the pieces into one being. One heart.

The slap of our skin is loud inside her room, obscene, but not enough.

I need more.

So does she.

A growl rips from my throat as I bring a hand to her neck and bring her up with me into an almost sitting position. My cock is nestled deep, her back to my chest, and the sharp breath she lets out at the change in angle brings a smile to my face.

Still not enough.

For a second my eyes shift to the wand not far from us, but jealousy licks at my blood. Toys can be fun when we play together, but not this time. Right now, there's an overwhelming urgency to imprint my touch into her every pore. Her soul. So I cup her with my other hand, fingers against her clit while pumping in and out.

Almost punishing as I take what will always be mine.

No rabbit or dildo or wand could ever replace what only I can make her feel.

Three deep strokes and she trembles.

Two rough circles over her trembling bundle of nerves and she tenses.

"Come, bebe. Give me what's mine," I hiss out, the sound primal and hungry. Her walls tighten at the demand and her back arches. It's near difficult to move, but I refuse to stop. Instead, I keep a rough pace while rubbing her clit. While watching the tantalizing way her bigger-than-a-handful tits, dusky-pink nipples hard, bounce for me.

"Papi, I'm so—"

I cut her off by tightening my hand on her neck, my lips now at her ear. Nip the shell. "Motherfucking come, love."

Amberlyn's mouth opens, but no words come out; she always comes so prettily.

She spasms, pussy so tight I bottom out and let her massage the come from me. And she does. These small gyrations and the feel of her juices coating—bathing my length—rob me of my senses. Everything within me throbs. So painfully sweet.

"Oh God," she moans, and brings one of her own hands down to cover mine cupping her. Amberlyn presses it harder, moving my fingers over her while pleasure rips me in two, and I empty every drop inside her warmth. We're a mess. Satiated and tired, but I refuse to pull out and slowly lower us down to the bed again and turn us so I'm curled around her much smaller frame.

No words are exchanged.

No declarations.

I know this always makes her sad, but I can't offer more until I make things right.

Soon. I mouth against the back of her head once I know she's asleep and pull her closer. Let my touch soothe her for now. Let it calm down my own urge to forget my commitments and drag us to Vegas to tie us together.

My phone beeps then from down her hall and I exhale roughly, closing my eyes for a few minutes. It pings again, Thiago's tone this time, and it's a reminder of what happened yesterday and the mess left behind by our livestock.

I should've reported to him the moment I stepped back on American soil.

I should've told him I'm okay and my crew is safe after visiting my forced-to-snitch friend, but I didn't. Couldn't. Not when the only thing that mattered was seeing—being with my sirenita and making sure she's safe and taken care of. Knowing someone has been watching isn't the issue, because as Dalian follows her, I have a tail on him. He'd never get close enough to touch, much less savor the sweet scent of sugar cookies that surrounds her.

It's that someone dared covet what's mine.

That's an insult to me as a man.

I'm a killer. Dangerous.

Bound by an oath and my own life plan, but more importantly, I protect what's mine.

I give myself another few seconds to soak up her sweet scent and warmth before slipping from the bed. Quietly, I fix the sheet and cover her before leaning over and kissing the corner of her mouth. Amberlyn doesn't stir but sighs, and it pains me to walk away once again.

One day I'll openly love and cherish this beautiful woman and lay the world at her feet.

I just need time.

"Be patient with me."

IVAN

SHE'S CLOSE.

I can feel her warmth from across the near-full room at my brother's rehearsal dinner two days later, and it's an indulgence I've imbibed in when I know it's wrong of me to do so. That I'm going to hurt her in the end, at least for a while.

Our timing is off. Our paths have a different timeline, no matter how much I want her.

Wish it were different.

Not when I'll be leaving the country without a return date after my brother comes home from his honeymoon. When after tomorrow I'll be in the shadows—out of sight— and life past those stolen moments is an impossibility until I remove all threats. But then again, that's always been the problem when it comes to Amberlyn. *My little sirenita.*

I can't say no. I let our relationship remain hidden for so long, and now, when I'm ready to settle down, I'll become that asshole once again.

She is my weakness. Always holds me captive with a mere look or the sinful curve of her plump lips.

I'm powerless against her. Can't fight the ever-present need for a taste.

Like every time I sneak into her bed, and all the ones before that. Because she's mine.

And because I'm also the man who adores her, yet leaves her just as fast when responsibility calls.

"If it's the last thing I do, I'll make us right. But first, I'm going to break your heart again."

The moment I crossed her threshold, front door closing behind me, I pulled my phone out and pressed number two. It rang twice before an audible click and then the rustle of wind met my ears. "You okay?"

"Yeah. I'm good." I look down at my shirt and there's a few specks of blood on it, not much since all it took for a friend of a friend to talk was a single punch to his nose and a warning: speak now or never do so again. *"Just had two stops to make before checking in. Everything good on your end?"*

"Jaime moved near the old courthouse in one of the new high-rises. Close enough to discourage and get around on foot if need be. Couple of precinct buddies also in that building."

"Coincidence?" Tucking the phone between my ear and shoulder, I make sure her lock is engaged and check the position of my camera there.

"Nothing in life ever is."

"Agreed." I walk down her corridor and toward the stairs, foregoing the elevator. Amberlyn lives on the eighth floor of a posh building with good security, but it's easily hacked. I've done so a few times, and I refuse to leave a single trace of my visit behind. Only we know. "One in Hialeah and the other in Downtown."

"Good source?"

"Ortega was very cooperative near the end, and the chivato confirmed."

My brother's snort is loud. "I bet. Heard you fed the masses."

"I did, but there's more to this. Their moves are either overconfident or—"

"You think there's a third location?" Thiago interrupts, voicing my thoughts. Then there's what sounds like a lighter sparking from his end. He pulls in deep and exhales just as quick before repeating the process a few

times, the action telling me it's a cigar. More than likely one I brought back from Havana on a prior trip. "It'd make sense."

"My money is on Homestead. Enough land and farming to hide."

"Hmmm." For a few beats he's silent, but I know my brother. He's thinking. Planning. "I'll send someone out tomorrow to have a look."

"There's also the matter of the fake money to take care of. That purchase was to test us."

"You think?"

"Yes." This one's personal. He knows Dalian...went to school with the brothers. "I think he's involved to some degree and also runs out of Hialeah."

"How soon?"

"Three nights."

"You think he'll bounce?" Another exhale, this time slowly.

"It'd be difficult to move his printing equipment. The machines are old and the local he's using is free. Owned by a friend who likes free weed and uses the fake currency to remain high."

"The connection to the brothers must be deep." Not a question.

"Henry's nothing more than a nuisance hiding behind false protection, brother. The man is a low-level criminal with the stupid penchant for paying for his purchases with his homemade cash." His mistakes are some-thing I'll make him pay for before his last breath. Just like I'll be seizing his operation and assets—real money and the counterfeit as payment to the De Leons.

"Okay. Get some rest." On his end, the sound of a woman comes through the line asking if everything's okay, and a pang of jealousy hits. It doesn't happen often, but I also can't stop it. I want what he and Luna have. How simple it is. The comfort in having someone on your side. "My wife says to behave and make the right choices in life."

A bark of laughter escapes me, yet that tightness in my chest intensifies. "I'm a model citizen. Honest and honorable."

"Sure, you are." Her voice comes through clear, and I know he's placed me on speaker phone. "Should I ask around and take a poll?"

"Be my guest, sis."

"Dork."

"Takes one to know one," Thiago grumbles something on their end that's too low to hear, something she giggles at, and I know it's time to get off the line. "All right, children. I'm done for the night."

"Three nights." Not a command. He wants confirmation.

"Yes."

"Brother, you look like a man about to commit a grave sin," Thiago says from beside me and I look over, then follow his gaze. I'm not surprised in the least to find his focus on his soon-to-be wife; she's his world. "Regret looks good on no one. Remember that."

"Never said it did." Luna's standing beside my own obsession, the women laughing at something another member of their group said, and I can't help but watch *her*. From her short stature to the sexy little black dress and stilettos from a designer she loves. The latter are in the same color, a gift from me on her last birthday—she rewarded me by wearing them and nothing else while escaping for a weekend trip to a private beach in the Gulf of Mexico.

I'm also aware of the way my hand rubs across my chest; I'm hurting us both. Moreover, I can't help but to be drawn in. There's something so pure about Amberlyn's carefree expression right now, the hint of pink on her cheeks tugging at my own lips. "But I have my own redemption to navigate when the time comes."

"Amberlyn's a sweet girl, Ivan." A waiter stops to Thiago's right, extending a tray with two drinks on it and a note. My brother picks up the small paper first and chuckles before pocketing it. "That woman will be the death of me."

No need to ask who he's speaking about. There's only one person in this world that can make him bend the knee. "How much is this going to cost?"

"Depends on how much we piss her off in the future." At my raised brow, he sends a wink in her direction. She's watching him too. "Luna wants us drunk. Says she needs new blackmail material for later."

"Jesus." The women in this family are insane. *But then again, I'm the same for Amberlyn.* A sobering thought because the truth is, I can't. Not yet. Taking her with me would be irresponsible, and while my men are loyal, until I have complete control over the island—more importantly, its government—I'd never put her in that position. "Then so be it." Taking both drinks, I knock them back while he raises a brow. "I'm sure she'll have plenty against me soon enough."

"Two more." He tells the waiter while grabbing the glasses in my hands and placing them back atop his tray. "And she's already pissed at you."

A rough exhale leaves me, and I scrub a tired hand down my face. "How many people know?"

"Those that matter." Thiago shrugs. "We also don't agree. Never have."

"I don't need you to." It comes out much harsher than I intended it to, my jaw clenching. The phone in my pocket also vibrates then, and it reminds me of each text I've ignored in the last forty-eight hours. All hers. All make the guilt worse.

> How's your day going? ~Mermaid

> I'm all sore and achy today. ;) ~Mermaid

> Is everything okay? ~Mermaid

> You know where to find me when you're ready.
> ~Mermaid

"True, but we care enough to warn you that there's an unnecessary huge wall you're about to slam into." Thiago's hand on my shoulder gives a squeeze, while his head tilts in my mermaid's direction. "What you do with the warning is your problem, but don't complain afterward. You crash and burn, and I don't know if she'll ever forgive you."

"Luna forgave you."

"She also knows I love her more than my own life." His eyes meet mine, his expression deadpan. "Can Amberlyn say the same?"

The answer is no, and that burns like acid in my chest.

I've kept her in the background for different reasons, possibilities that change depending on the scenario, but they're all the same. With Thiago in jail over a bullshit setup, I took over and as such, the threats toward me were large enough to crumble a weaker man.

She's seen the evidence of my car being shot at.

She's been there for Luna during Thiago's incarceration.

She agreed for the time being to silently stand by my side until normality returned to our family.

And maybe it's been selfish of me to keep us private and without the attention that comes from dating a De Leon, but not once have I given her a reason to question my loyalty to her. I'm also man enough to admit we can't continue like this.

I just need a little more time. "Cuba isn't Miami, Thiago. We both know what I'm walking into." While South Florida has always been great for business, the product we move through the island is vast and fast, two things others covet. Things are ever changing, the demand for the black-market weapons procured overseas and the perico Casper provides has quickly become a large percentage of our last quarter's earnings, and this has brought unwanted attention our way.

The US government is sniffing.

The Cuban regime wants to fuck us in the ass.

Many here want to make a name for themselves.

More so, I won't allow anyone else to pay for my sins. She won't become a casualty.

I'm here to bend both countries over and discipline them as one would a child.

The De Leon hand feeds and takes and will fuck you over without a second of remorse.

"It's a mess and won't be easy, Ivan, I'll give you that. But, keep in mind that the women in our lives are resilient and have bigger balls than we do at times."

"And stubborn," I mutter, but he hears. Fucker chuckles, too. "That woman is going to make me pay."

"Agreed." My brother shrugs. "They know who we are and accept it."

"I'm not doing this to be an asshole. They threatened her because of me, and keeping her close will only feed their ammunition—they'll know how important she is to me. All I want is her safety—just that."

"What if she walks, Ivan? That's always a possibility."

"Her feelings for me are what I'm holding on to." Have to. "Besides, between political greed and civil unrest—the kind of anarchy that will burn the country to the ground using the accelerant I provide—it's unsafe either way. I won't take the chance. Not until our family has complete control over the island."

"What about the threat here? Are you going to tell her?"

"No." My eyes narrow, the warning clear. He might be slightly older, but I've never been one to take his shit or be afraid. Respect is one thing, but betray me and I would kill my own blood. "That's not up for discussion. I want her free and happy and untouched by this. They'll also be dead before I go."

I'd never forgive myself if she spent a single moment of her life afraid or watching over her shoulder. That's my job.

"You forget just how much of a grudge she can hold." The waiter returns then with our drinks, and we each take a tumbler. He takes a sip and grins. "Remember when I crashed her car?"

This time I snort over the rim. "Is she still giving you the stink eye for that?"

"You know it's more than that." And I do know because every once in a while, my mermaid gives me the same hard look. What we asked of her all those years ago, to make Luna believe that Thiago cheated, still grates on her. More so, because I'm the one that talked her into it, knowing and using what was a crush back then. "Don't lose her. Don't repeat my mistake."

Without another word, my brother walks away and toward his fiancée, taking Luna's hand before pulling her out of the room. The reception fills with chuckles and his not-so-subtle flip off from over his shoulder is typical, but I'm more riveted by the quick look of longing that flits across Amberlyn's face.

It's there. So much sadness.

But then it's gone just as fast, and she says something to those around her that makes them laugh before excusing herself. I follow her every move; she's heading toward the bar when my father intercepts and then points toward the dance floor.

"Old fucker," I say, shaking my head as he twirls her three times fast before those around them join. There's an old-school merengue playing, and people begin to sing, moving their hips to the beat while my viejo begins a series of fancy turns. The faster he goes, the louder my mermaid's giggle get before passing her over to one of Luna's family members from the Dominican Republic.

My smile drops and body tenses. The hold I have on my glass is close to cracking it, even if they're doing nothing more than dancing. Even if the distance between their bodies is respectful.

Yet I hate it. Any male close to her.

I know him. He's an okay guy, a few years older than my twenty-six and with good hacking skills. He's related to the bride's mother somehow —I think a stepbrother—as Luna's grandfather continued having kids very late into his life.

They're a total of twenty-four kids with only sixteen alive.

They're also not the closest, something my sister-in-law wants to remedy by making him a part of the wedding party.

For the next two tracks, I don't move from my spot. Can't. Not when every single part of my DNA demands I pull her away from him and show the world she's mine.

And almost as if she senses my reproach, Amberlyn's smart enough to take a step back after the next song ends, and with a smile and turns to walk away. His eyes stay on her, though. I see the interest, but I'd never allow it.

Not in this lifetime. Not ever.

"Long time no see, primo." Mirabel slides in beside me, pulling my attention away from my girl. There's a sassy grin on my cousin's face, a tell of her amusement. "Did she finally kick you to the curb?"

"Your shoes are hideous." I have no clue if they are, but the woman is in the fashion industry and takes that shit seriously. And at the moment, if pissing her off gets her to shut up, so be it. The last thing I want or need is more meddling. "Dress is last season, too."

"Asshole." Not annoyed—there's too much mirth in her tone.

"Everyone has one." Bringing the glass to my lips, I knock back what's left and wave the empty tumbler toward a waiter who nods. "Speaking of...where's your husband?"

"No argument there, and at the bar talking shop with all the old men in attendance."

"What is he selling now?"

"A '56 Chevrolet Bel Air."

"Nice."

"But enough about cars and husbands..." she trails off and I look over, catching an arched brow and a smirk on her lips. "When are you going to make it right?"

"You're fishing for something that doesn't exist."

"Or am I calling it as I see it?"

"No clue what you're talking about." It's then I sense my sirenita close. The heat of her stare is coming from my back. There's this rush of something I can't quite explain whenever she's near, this electrical wave that settles on the tip of my cock and it flexes—fucking throbs against the zipper of my dress pants. My entire body, every muscle, tenses, and I exhale deeply. "Quit trying to annoy me."

"Sure I am." Mirabel's eyes scan the room, searching for something, and then she flicks them back to me. She knows. As Thiago said, they all do. "Where's red hiding now? I thought she'd be over after her spin on the floor. She asked me for information on this trip—"

"No clue. Don't care."

"Stop that. You love it."

"She's nothing more than an obligation." My voice is loud enough that it carries, and the low gasp from behind me makes my chest ache. *Please forgive me, little Sirenita. Trust me.*

Amberlyn

"*SHE'S NOTHING more than an obligation.*"

Heat flames my face, and it's from shame.

Embarrassment.

The way my heart breaks as I watch the man I've loved since my youth talk about me as if I were a nuisance and not the woman he slept with a few nights ago. But then again, I've always been an idiot—weak—when it comes to Ivan De Leon.

I've given him my first kiss.

My virginity.

My heart.

What has he given me in return?

I should leave. Move or curse at him for the pain currently building inside my chest—for how hard breathing is—but instead, my high-heeled feet are rooted to the marble floor beneath me a few feet from him. I'm unable to do anything but lean against the large pillar and watch as he laughs at my expense. The sound feels like the cut of a sharp blade, and not one of the usual butterflies he brings present.

Always from the fringes. It's what I've always done.

Since we met as teenagers and every time he's asked something of me, I've been there but kept at arm's length. Unless he wants to warm my bed, and then and only then, am I given affection.

A glimpse of what could be.

At first, that was okay. We agreed that the timing was off and with his brother in jail, it was best to wait. I stood by his side through numerous attempts on his life, rough nights, and dangerous meetings—I never questioned my place with him until recently.

Our relationship should've been celebrated once Thiago came out, yet I'm still waiting months later.

I've been a constant. I've been a fool.

"Don't be an ass, primo," Mirabel chastises, lips thinning as she cuts him a glare. "But then again, men are always this stupid. You'll be just like the rest, crying when Amberlyn walks away."

"She'd never." Not a single ounce of doubt, his voice hard. Almost angry at her audacity. "Her love keeps her here."

"But I'm learning to hate you just as much." The words leave me in a whisper, not that he can hear inside of the large ballroom where the rehearsal dinner with the entire De Leon family is taking place. Well, more party than dinner for Luna and Thiago's big day. The wedding is tomorrow at their home. The family is full of happiness and laughter is all around me, yet I feel as though someone died.

Suddenly, sweat dots across my forehead, and the room feels too small. Too many people.

My shame feels as though it's on full display and they all know.

Fuck, I need to get out.

"You look like you're in need of an escape."

There's no need to look over; I've known this woman just as long as anyone else here. "I do, but I'll be fine. This is your day and..." my head tilts and eyebrows furrow "...didn't I watch Thiago nearly drag you out a few minutes ago?"

"He just needed a little sugar."

"Sugar?" Voice low. It's hard to get the words out with the huge lump in my throat.

"What can I say? I'm so sweet." Luna snorts, her arm slipping through mine as she begins to pull me away from Ivan. Each step is painful, yet my lungs expand with a much-needed breath, and I don't look back no matter how much my heart demands that I do.

No one stops us as we make it outside and onto a large balcony overlooking the warm South Florida waters. And even though the daytime hit a high of ninety-five, the cool seventies gracing our skin now feels suffocating.

Maybe it's what happened. The harsh truth that's been smacking me in the face for years and I've been ignoring, hoping, and praying they were false. That he did feel for me and not that I'd played a game and lost; a mere puppet to be moved as he pleased.

"Talk to us." I've been so lost inside my head that I never heard Natasha follow us. I also have no idea how we ended up near the far left and sitting on a large stone bench a few feet from a set of stairs that leads to a small garden and then the beach. "What did Ivan do?"

"I'm not sure what you're talking—"

"Cut that out, chick. You two aren't as careful as you think you are."

"I'm pathetic." *How long have they known?* A self-deprecating laugh slips before I can school my expression, and my best friends each grab a hand. It hasn't always been this way for us; at first Luna thought Thiago cheated—another place where my feelings for Ivan made me stupid—but meeting them has been the biggest blessing. They're the sisters I never had. "And nothing that should surprise me. I should know better by now."

"Love makes us do and accept crazy things," Luna says, and when I turn my head in her direction, I find the striking brunette looking out into the late evening sky. The smile on her face is one I've seen before and holds a tinge of anger, but it's pushed back just as soon and replaced by understanding. "The men in this family are nothing more than stubborn idiots, I swear."

She's been where I am. Hurt by one of the brothers.

Yet, Thiago did what he did out of love. Out of the need, barbaric and stupid as it may have been, to protect her even if it meant pushing Luna away. His idiocy came from loyalty, while Ivan's is fake.

Obligation: I'm nothing more than an easy lay and someone he has no choice but to put up with.

"Or maybe I've been too blinded to see and accept my reality." The first tear rolls down my cheek, and they squeeze my hands in solidarity. For a few minutes we stay in silence, enjoying the clear evening sky, but it doesn't last long as I fight to swallow a sob. Hurt is churning and turning and is quickly becoming ire. At me. At him. At fate for putting him in my path. "I can't do this anymore," I say after a while and close my eyes, fighting to control my emotions. My voice is low. Breaking. "Can't keep putting myself in a vulnerable position when who I wish would catch me, always lets me fall. I'm worth more than that. Deserve more than late-night visits and empty words."

"You do," they say in unison, but then they give me the silence I need.

For the most part, I'm not the most emotional person. I'm more of a suffer-in-silence type of person, and yet, he's my exception. Ivan is a weakness I need to shake off, but in the past have failed to do so time and time again.

So while the clock sounds in the distance letting us know we're at the top of the next hour, I make up my mind.

I'm done.

Fuck him.

The sigh that leaves me is heavy. "Please don't hate me, Luna."

"I'd never, Lynnie. Just tell me what you need me to do." Turning my face toward hers, I open my eyes and meet her stare. Luna's giving me a smirk that says she'll get her fiancé to punch Ivan if I ask, and all I can offer back is trembling lips and more than likely ruined makeup. "You want me to have his—"

"I say we slash his tires." Nat cuts her off, and I shift my attention. She releases my hand before clapping once, then stands and paces—muttering under her breath while shaking her arms out like fighters do. "What if I add eyedrops to his coffee? Get his mom to serve him liver and onions for a month straight...she'd do it, too. That woman is brutal, and I love her."

I'm nodding, wiping my tears. They don't stop but have slowed. "Maritza is my shero."

"So payback it is? We choose violence?" Nat asks, and Luna laughs a bit. Crazy women.

No whining. No complaints. No hesitation.

It's why I love these two and would do anything for them. Their friendship is honest and giving. Never selfish.

"I don't want to walk down the aisle with him." Even as the words leave me, I can't help but cringe at them. My emotions are all over the place, and between the guilt and selfishness I feel for asking this of Luna, there's also so much relief. Distance is the only way I'll survive the next twenty-four hours. It's how I start getting over him. "I'll do it if there's no choice—"

"Done."

"That easy?"

"Yes." Luna didn't pause. Not one second of hesitation or analyzing. She gives a short, low whistle and Nat quits her pacing, pausing to meet her cousin's stare, head tilted to the side. "Ivan's your new partner, prima. You okay with that?"

"More than. I'll make sure to jam my heels into his toes the first chance I get."

Even with a little bit of smudged liner on my fingertips, I can't help but giggle. "I love you two so much. Needed this."

"You better." An older man I recognize as one of the family's most trusted guards pokes his head out, gets a headcount, but at the glares sent his way, leaves just as fast. Less than fifteen seconds. "That has my Thiago written all over it." The bride rolls her eyes, and we don't argue the truth. The man's the textbook definition of obsessed. I'm jealous of it in the best way: happy for her, but wishing I'd find someone as committed. "Now, Alvin will be your new partner. You know him."

My face scrunches up. "I actually don't. Who's that?"

"Do you trust me?"

"I do."

"Then don't worry, and let's get a few drinks in our system. The night is hella fucking young." Standing, Luna pulls me with her and loops her arm with mine while Nat takes up the opposite side. "Besides, I'm going to enjoy his reaction tomorrow. Ivan is going to be livid."

They walk me down the stairs and to a side door that says *Employees Only* that's unlocked and we step inside, following a short corridor that leads to a bathroom not far from the private party in her honor.

They're quick to help me fix my face and gather myself.

They're by my side when we eventually make it back inside, and I immediately catch his eyes. The honey color seems darker as he takes me in, and it feels like a dirty caress. Everything in me heats; no matter how much I fight the reaction, it's beyond me. Uncontrollable; a need that breaks me a little more as those words replay again.

And again.

Nothing more than an obligation.

"Goodbye, love," I mouth the words, and as if he understands, Ivan takes a step toward me. One step. That's all I get before once again, I'm given something I've come to expect.

Nada. Nothing. Emptiness.

He'll never be with me in the way I need. Love me with every fiber of his being as I do him.

Instead, the man I yearn for accepts another drink while his unoccupied hand goes inside his pant pocket. It's there for a minute at the most when my cellphone vibrates inside my wristlet, and I know it's him.

The same things he's done when around others; I'm number "1" on speed dial, and it's another means to control me. Keeps me thinking that I mean something—anything—more than what I am:

I'm his duty. Work.

I don't acknowledge it and give him my back, focusing instead on those around me and the drunken group dance taking place. They're laughing and off-rhythm while those who are still sober enough to not join egg them on. It's loud and full of happiness, and I don't want to be here.

"Here, take this and breathe," Nat says from my left, passing me a glass of red wine. "Knock it back, and I have the next one on its way."

"Thank you." Taking her advice, I sip it quickly but not fast enough to draw attention. The robust red is drier than I like, but the warmth that follows gives me something else to focus on, and I close my eyes for a second. It spreads, soothing my nerves a little while the empty glass is replaced. The first sip is a blind one. I just bring the glass to my lips and then snap my eyes to Nat when the sweeter spirit greets my tastebuds. Much lighter, the berry notes in this one is stronger, and I take another light sip. No rush.

The last thing I need is to end up drunk and in bed with him *again*.

That's also when I notice that Luna is now missing.

"Where did Lulu—?" A whooping chorus comes from the dancing group and when I shift my gaze over again, I find the bride and groom are busy showing the older people how to do the Macarena. Well, more her than him. Thiago just watches Luna with amusement while following her lead. "Never mind."

"I say we teach them how it's really done."

"Do you, now?" If she can tell my laugh is flat, Natasha doesn't mention it.

"I do, chica." Grabbing my arm, she begins to tug me along and I don't fight her. "Let's drink and dance and forget the bad shit for now. Don't let him steal your happiness, mami."

"You're right," I say and place my wine on a passing waiter's tray before joining the dancing to-be newlyweds. She turns her head in my direction, never missing a step with a raised brow, and I shrug. "You looked lonely."

"She's mine," Thiago grumbles, placing both hands on his hips but doesn't gyrate. More like hungrily watches Luna shake hers. "I don't share."

His bride blows him a kiss. "Cool it, Romeo."

Their playful banter reminds me of Ivan. Of that side of him that I see when it's just us, no work or family, and distractions are limited to our moans and teasing.

So I do what any friend would do in that instance and bury my jealousy deep—shake it off until this is all over. Taking up a spot on the dance floor, I finish this dance and three more after without searching for him. While ignoring the intensity of his gaze that slowly burns me alive. From one song to the next, I keep my pace and swallow down the hurt inside my chest that makes it hard to breathe.

I'm one of the maids of honor and will do my duty.
I will party. I will be supportive. I will live.
And even surrounded, I feel like an outsider now more than ever.
This is the final nail in my love for him.
I'm done.
He's lost me without ever appreciating how devotedly his I was.

Amberlyn

I FEEL RUN over the next morning, and it's not from a hangover.

No. This comes from heartache and self-reproach—from hours of over-analyzing everything we've been through while acknowledging the ever-present truths I've ignored. I'm at fault for not accepting them sooner, for thinking *he will come around* when Ivan's never given me any indication that I'd ever existed outside of the shadows.

I drank but kept it to a low buzz while Luna and Nat subtly watched over me. Their concern is sweet, but at the moment it's unhelpful as it unfurls along with my guilt, and the concoction isn't pleasant. No fuss from me and while they checked on me in between dances, I kept up the charade of being angry—not hurt—into the early morning hours. Instead of crying and venting, I put my feelings aside and did what a good best friend does when her girl is hours from getting married to the man of her dreams:

I smiled.

Laughed.

Hid my emotions.

Were they totally convinced? No.

Did Luna demand I let it out once we were back from the hotel? Yes.

However, I chose to hug her instead and then retreat into the guest room for a night of restless tossing and turning. Because when you're alone at night and without distractions, you can't escape reality and it's a vicious punch to the gut that knocks the air from your lungs.

I've gone from angry to hurt, and then consider taking a leave of absence from work.

Maybe being out of Miami for a few weeks would do me some good. The distance will help me with the ever-present clench in my chest.

Flicking my eyes to the bedside clock, I watch the numbers turn and the bright white lights announce that it's a little after eleven in the morning. Somehow, I managed to catch four hours of sleep and know it's going to be a long day. Luna and Thiago decided on a late-evening wedding, anticipating the all-out party the reception would turn out to be.

Hair and makeup will be here in another two hours, and I sit up against the headboard, try to get comfortable while breathing in deep and exhaling slowly. Right now, I need to get control of myself and my emotions.

The silence today is everything I want to avoid and I grab my phone, opening the Spotify app. Working in the bail bond industry has its up and downs like any job, but what drains me is finding those who skip and put unnecessary financial hardship on their families. It breaks a piece of my heart each time, and it's why I take those cases on personally.

The De Leon family is in business with my family as backers.

It's a mutually beneficial agreement that I've never questioned before. They get easy access to bail out anyone in the organization if needed, and we don't use outside insurance companies or local government programs, which makes it dangerous for those who choose to wrong our clients.

I'm loyal to those paying the bail, and our private backing guarantees the casualties are minor.

It doesn't stop many from trying, but the chase is never long.

Maybe that's the catch. Keep me complacent and easy to agree to just about anything as long as he's touching me. "Is that why?" No. It can't be. Won't accept it, because if I do, I'll hate people I've come to love as if they were family. "Please let there be any other reason. Don't let me be just another pawn."

Exhaling roughly, I choose my work playlist after the app loads and let a soothing classical composition run through me. There's something calming in the low cadence, how each chosen song in this list doesn't have large crescendos in their peak, but more of a soft melody meant to lull.

And it works. I can feel my muscles begin to loosen up and by the third song, I'm running through the day's plans while shutting off my emotions. The stylist will be coming here soon to the couple's home, and they'll set up in the main living room that's been emptied for that purpose. No fuss. No muss.

To be honest, it's kind of cute how Thiago's taken care of her every whim. Flowers, food, and location were all inconsequential when all he demanded is that she slept with him every night. No exception or night before separation as tradition dictates. No overnight planning sessions either; Luna has been by his side every day.

It's also one of the reasons she chose to have it at home.

The woman is as addicted and obsessed as he is.

"I'm never going to find a love like that if I stay here." My whisper travels through the room, echoing back the grief residing within my heart, yet there's also determination building within. It solidifies and almost feels as though it were a real entity—this being that pushes me to breathe in again and exhale my tension.

It's time I accept that Ivan isn't for me.

I need a man who wants to be by my side out in the open and with no stipulations.

Free. Honest. Raw.

My calm lasts as long as my solitude. Until the padding of feet comes closer, and I turn my head in the direction of the closed door. Then I put on my office smile.

The one that greets customers and makes them feel at ease in my presence. *I won't ruin her day.*

My best friends are anything but subtle on the other side, and their muffled exchange would be funny any other day.

"You open it." That's Nat.

"It's my day. You do it," Luna hisses.

"I can hear you," I call out.

Not a few seconds later, the door opens and Nat pokes her head in. "How's it hanging, chica?"

My lips twitch at that, and I can't help myself. "To the left and soft."

"Dork." Luna snorts, pushing her cousin out of the way before padding over to the bed and climbing in beside me. She's glowing. So happy. *I want that, too.* "By the way, Alvin's all set to be your new partner."

"Are you sure? What about the girl—"

"I have a back-up plan for everyone." Mrs. De Leon to-be winks and then lays her head on my shoulder. "Besides, it's a three-person switch and no hassle at all."

"Thank you." This leaves me on a long exhale.

"My pleasure, babes." I'm so blessed to have them in my life. How many women would do something like that, on the day of their wedding no less? But then there's my guilt for creating this problem to begin with.

Another reason to get away; I don't want to burden anyone. "I'm sorry."

"Stop that." She smacks my thigh hard and lifts her face toward mine, eyes narrowed. "I love you, and breakfast is ready. The others are starting to arrive. Just the women, by the way. Thiago kicked out anyone with a penis."

Remorse flares again. Did she ask him on my behalf?

"He doesn't need to do that."

"It was for me," Luna reassures, but I don't believe it. *Does he know? Do they all?* If they do, I know it wasn't because of Nat or Luna. This is all on me. My fault. I've spent years chasing after Ivan like a lost puppy. "The decorators are outside with the planner and with the ladies getting ready downstairs, it would've been too many people. My anxiety was high just thinking about it and Thiago reacted, almost shot Ivan—" At his name, I cringe but they don't call me out on it.

"Anyways..." Nat drags out the word, and I also don't miss the pointed look she gives her cousin. "Everyone's gone but the bridal party and Mami De Leon. They're downstairs and waiting, babes. We're going to eat, drink some mimosas, and get dolled up within an inch of our lives. You in?"

Not a question. More like testing how I feel.

"I am. I'm in need of a lot of coffee, not booze."

"How much are we talking about here?" Luna lifts her head and bumps her shoulder with mine. "Because I have the good stuff straight from Colombia; Alejandro sent it as part of his wedding present. Coffee and money. Can't ever go wrong with the two."

"Like an obscene amount, ladies."

"Obscene sounds good." Nat walks to the bathroom and comes back with a silk robe. My initials are over the right side and *Main Bitch 2* is embroidered on the back. I also notice it's just like hers, except she's number *1* by default as her cousin. "There's also pastries and tostadas and churros."

"You had me at pastries."

"I know." She tosses the robe at me, and I catch it before slipping from the bed. "Now let's go. We have a lot to do, and the bride needs to be ready early. We both know Thiago isn't staying away for long."

Closing the wrap and looping the belt, I walk toward the door and then look back from over my shoulder. "My money's on him barging in mid hair and demanding we get out."

"I don't think he'll make it that long."

"Hundred bucks?"

Nat winks, getting that I don't want to talk about me today. "Five hundred and you're on."

"Deal."

"You two suck." Luna's smiling, though. She scrambles off the bed and rushes to the door, smacking Natasha on the arm as she does. In a few strides, she's beside me and wraps her arm around my waist. Our eyes meet and I see concern in them, the last thing I want for her wedding day. "Tell me you're okay, and I'll make sure you win."

"I am."

"And you won't let him get to you?"

"He won't. Promise." *My heart can't take him being close again.* "So let's get you married."

"Yeah." Her smile widens. The kind of look she gets when she's about to be a smartass. "Let's go make an honest man out of Thiago De Leon."

———

"ARE YOU HIDING FROM ME, SIRENITA?" Ivan says from behind me fifteen minutes before the ceremony starts. I've been avoiding him, keeping myself upstairs while everyone else mingled or had a pre-wedding drink. I know he's been looking. The constant text updates from Natasha saying he'd grown irritated the longer I took.

And not just from her. His own mother told me as much.

> He's going to crack, mi niña. The De Leon men
> are all hard-headed, but they have one
> weakness. You're his. Trust. ~Momma Leon

That came in forty minutes ago, and it still eats at me. Because one thing is speculation, while another is having the proof that they all know.

My shame threatens to consume me once again, but I exhale slowly. *Just a few hours. Luna only needs me for a few hours.* "Not at all, Ivan." Not papi. No sentiment. The words spill from my mouth and they're dry— empty while I continue to stare straight ahead. "Just been busy."

"Hmmm." His deep hum dances across my skin, and it takes everything in me not to shiver. "Is that so? Are we lying to each other now?"

"Isn't that what you've always done?" I couldn't swallow back my bitter response, no matter how much I should've. The shrug that follows is meant to look unbothered, but I think I failed that too. "But that's not important. I've learned my place."

"Turn around." Tone heated. A hint of anger.

"I'm heading toward—"

"Turn around, Amberlyn. I need to see your face, beautiful." And, I do. My feet—body—move without my permission and on my next blink, it's his hazel eyes I meet. "Much better."

"I'm busy, Ivan." Slipping a hand into my dress pocket, I dig my nails into my palm. *Get a grip.* I don't want to be swayed by his good looks and height; at over six feet, Ivan makes me feel petite—like his doll. But then there's the tan skin, low fade, and hazel eyes while the tattoos marking his flesh tell a story I'm all too familiar with. "Can I go?"

"No." Expression calm, he stares at me with a heated intensity that makes my thighs clench. Can't help it. Can't stop it. Not when his masculine scent, this whiskey and woodsy panty-destroying weakness, surrounds me. Not when his eyes darken while roaming over me from head to toe and his tongue slides across his bottom lip. "You look delicious, bebe."

"Now isn't the time."

"The fuck is that supposed to mean?"

"Just that. We're here for your brother's wedding, not to mess around." Ivan swallows hard while his chest expands on a deep breath, but before he can give me some *line* meant to seduce—because I'm weak and want nothing more than to get closer—I turn to leave.

One step. That's all he allows.

Warm fingers curl around my elbow, grip tight, but before Ivan can turn me around again, two people arrive. And because I'm an *obligation* and nothing more, he steps back like I knew he would.

This time, I swallow hard. The act stings. "Exactly."

"We'll talk about this tonight, Amberlyn."

"No. We won't." Looking at him from over my shoulder, I give the man I love a rueful grin. "Now, go find your partner. She's up first."

"You're walking with me." His brows furrow and lips thin. Also don't miss the way his hands clench at his sides. "That's not up for discussion."

"Incorrect." That's when the man I danced with last night approaches. Nat is beside him, and they share the same sly look. *So he's Alvin.* Turning to face them, I widen my smile. "My new partner just arrived."

"Hello again, Miss Ibarra." Alvin's tone is deep and smooth and immediately puts me at ease. He's not interested in me romantically. If anything, he'd be checking out the mother of the groom. The man likes them older, told me as much last night after I caught him checking out Maritza, Ivan's mom.

I also warned him to never do that again. The De Leon men are protective of their women.

He'll never be like that with me. Not like Thiago is with Luna. Like Orlando is with Maritza.

"Hola, Alvin. Natasha." Immediately I lean forward and kiss Natasha's cheek, and when I pull back, she's biting her lips to keep from laughing. *You are so bad,* she mouths while I give a subtle shrug. I'm not doing anything. I'm clear on where I stand for once.

He's not mine.

I am not his.

"So, you ready to strut it down the aisle?" Alvin moves to greet me as I did Natasha, something common for any Latino, when I'm pulled back and into a warm chest.

"She walks with me."

IVAN

I SHOULD BE happy she's trying to keep her distance.

At ease knowing it'll make the separation easier, but I'm not.

Instead, I'm burning from the inside and have been since last night. *Goodbye, love.* I read her lips, saw the truth behind those expressively warm eyes, and it was a punch to the gut.

My resolve is weak. My need is too strong to contain.

And more so after watching my little sirenita walking down the stairs in a sea-glass, floor-length chiffon dress that complements her naturally tan skin. It's sleek and sophisticated with just the right amount of sex appeal—the halter neckline with the keyhole opening—that draws my eyes to the perky swell of each tit. No bra. Just a thin layer of fabric draping carefully over each, highlighting the way her nipples tighten under my attention.

But then again, they always have.

Amberlyn embraces her femininity and is open sexually without fear of judgement. As she should be. My mermaid isn't promiscuous, but comfortable inside her skin with the right partner…me.

Hungry and sweet. Motherfucking mine.

My eyes travel lower again, and I bite my lip at the high split in her dress, the way the material shifts and caresses her right leg. Smooth skin. So soft. "So beautiful," I say low, unable to stop myself. Even angry— burning with jealousy—I can't help but follow the tease of each curve when she leans over and kisses Natasha on the cheek. There's a look exchanged, a smirk from Luna's cousin at my girl, but then *he* makes an unforgivable mistake.

Alvin tried to put his lips near her cheek.

Over my dead body.

Their conversation is inconsequential to me. Her attempt to walk with someone else, to push me toward an amused Nat, and even the audacity to think I'd go for it, is insulting.

If she wanted me to feel the lash of this strike, Amberlyn won.

Before they can greet each other, my arm is around her waist, her back against my front. No hesitation. That primal part of me—the man who recognizes her as mine—nearly bares his teeth like an animal would.

"She walks with me," I spit out, and they each take a step back.

No one says a word, and I also don't miss the way Amberlyn shivers, how unconsciously she moves in a little closer. Even mad at me she seeks my touch, and it's something I treasure.

One day I'll make it all up to her.

One day it'll be her walking down the aisle toward me.

But then she freezes and tries to step away: a silent rejection. It stings. Her body language says everything she won't verbalize, and I hate it.

Abhor the most minuscule separation between us.

I've hurt her. Again. *There's no other choice. Not until they're all dead.*

Until I can bring their heads to her on a silver platter and then worship at her feet without restraint.

Maybe I should let her walk with him. Every cell in my DNA burns bitter at that thought.

Even now, her cold shoulder is more than I can take.

I've also accepted that living in Cuba while she's here will destroy me little by little. Many will bleed because of it.

"Let go, Ivan." Voice low, Amberlyn elbows me in the stomach, but I don't flinch. She stomps her foot over mine, the six-inch heel digging into the leather, and I smile. I like her a little violent.

Accept it like the gift it is. Means she cares.

"You walk with me, Sirenita. No one else."

"That's not up to you, De Leon," Natasha answers, yet I don't pull my eyes away from the woman in my arms. Can't stop focusing on how good her petite stature fits against my much harsher planes. "Luna decided last night that you'd be better off partnered with me. Alvin will—"

"Will be smart enough to not interfere. End of."

"Not your wedding," my girl hisses from between clenched teeth, the blunt end of her fingernails trying to find purchase on my arm, but the tuxedo prevents that. "Quit being difficult."

"Enough." Lowering my lips to her ear, I let out a rough exhale. We stay like that for a second or two, with me inhaling her sweet scent before speaking loud enough so only she hears. "Do you want me to show you what real stubbornness is, bebe? How crazy you make me?"

"No." A whisper, yet she still tries to move away. That won't do. While the other two watch, surprise on their faces, I turn and move us away.

There's a door that leads to a private weapons room on this level that only the to-be newlyweds and I know about. It's behind a bookcase and opens with the press of a button beneath the third shelf. There's an audible click and then a shift while Amberlyn gasps.

Grabbing the side, I pull it open just enough for us to fit. "Go on."

"What the hell is this?"

"Do you trust me?"

"With my safety? Yes…" those warm brown eyes meet mine and inside them, there's her love, but it's also tinged by the smallest hint of hate "…everything else, though? Not so much."

Fuck, that cuts, but nothing less than what I deserve. *One day she'll know the truth.*

"Please."

"Two minutes." I find it adorable when she tries to take charge.

Amberlyn walks inside and I close the door behind us, adding the extra lock to make sure she doesn't escape. Before I came to look for her, my brother went in search of his bride, smirk in place, and I'm more than sure they'll be busy for a little bit.

It's why I brought her here. Why I don't pause and take the few steps separating us before slamming my mouth down on hers like I've wanted to do since yesterday.

The kiss is possessive and urgent. It holds my apology and her denial.

And more importantly, this time she clings to me.

Her hands grip the lapels of my jacket while nipping my bottom lip before sliding her tongue against the flesh. And while she whimpers and fights me for control, I grip her hips and lift her off the ground, careful to not rip her dress.

Four steps and I'm across the room where a small table is nestled against the back wall. I place her atop it, not once removing my lips—breaking what I know will be the last kiss for a while.

This is a mistake.

I shouldn't.

"Papi," my sirenita moans into my mouth, and it's my breaking point. Between her rejection outside, her anger, and now that moan—*mother-fuck*. I'm feigning, my cock aches, but there's a bigger hunger I need to satiate.

No matter how much I want to bury myself deep inside her tight cunt, it's the taste—memory—of her pussy I'll survive on. What I'll fuck my hand to until we reunite.

Because she won't see me after today.

The hold I have on the skirt of her dress is tight, pushing it up and out of my way before Amberlyn's next intake of breath, but it's the way her legs part that I focus on. They spread of their own volition, her warm skin trembling beneath my fingertips as I drag them up her skin at a torturous pace.

Goose bumps appear and she shivers, her fingers never releasing my jacket. "What are you—"

"I need to make you come, sweetheart." It's a barely contained growl, my entire body thrumming with yearning.

"But the wedding." No real strength behind it. Also don't miss how her hips shift a little closer.

Gripping a thigh in each hand, I squeeze and bring my mouth to hers. Just press them, savor her every exhale. "Please."

"I should say no to you."

"Please." One word. My plea.

"*Fuck*," she moans, nodding once and I drop to my knees, lips against her right knee. The thin fabric is so breakable, delicate like my mermaid, and I carefully push it up to her hips with a gentleness that betrays the demonic thirst inside me.

I want her juices on my tongue. Drying on my skin.

Slowly, I nip her knee and then higher, sliding my tongue over the soft skin of her thigh. She's heat and temptation, and I inhale deep the sweet scent of her arousal, let it calm me.

It's a natural decadence that makes my mouth water and cock harden, throb behind the zipper of my pants. I can feel each bead of pre-come as it beads at the tip and then rolls down the underside while making a mess of the fabric.

I'm not wearing any underwear.

I want this torture. Deserve it.

"Spread your thighs, sweetheart. Let me taste you." She does so, careful with her shoe not to dirty my jacket. I could give less than a fuck if the heel tear the expensive garment. "Wider."

"I'm trying not to…oh God!" Amberlyn yelps when I pull her closer to the edge and throw both legs over my shoulder. *Beautiful.*

She's wearing white silk, the gusset clinging to soft lips, and right at the center is proof of her desire for me. The wetness pools there, soaking through and I don't hesitate, pressing my nose against the nearly translucent fabric.

Inhaling deep. Reveling in her need.

"Fuck, Amberlyn." A groan. A plea for mercy.

My mermaid's always bare and pink. The edge of labia peeking from the edge of her panties is fucking mouthwatering—so soft as they rub over my lips while I shake my head from right to left.

Her body trembles. Thighs squeeze me.

I can't live without her. Refuse to.

"Please." That one word sends a shiver down my spine.

"Move it to the side." Small fingers slide down her front while the other folds the front of the dress so it's out of the way and not scrunched up. Flowy material out of the way, she looks up and catches my raised brow, lips hovering over her cunt.

"What?" Breathy. Nipples hard. "You'll ruin it."

"Show me your cunt, Sirenita." Another hiss, this time as I watch two fingers slip beneath the edge. "Feed your papi."

"They'll be looking for us." Even as the words leave her lips, she does as I ask, exposing her slick flesh to me. "We shouldn't."

"Yes, I should." *Owe you this.* Not that I give her a chance to take in my words, my mouth lowers onto her wetness and I drag my tongue through her folds, groaning as her sweetness overtakes my senses.

I'm ravenous. Starved.

My patience is nonexistent, and I trace my tongue from slit to clit, nearly snarling as a sweetness uniquely hers caresses my senses. I'm lost to this ardor—a crippling thirst that dominates me.

Without Amberlyn knowing, I'm her puppet.

Tied to her.

The next pass of my tongue is rough, and so is the one that follows as I lose myself. All I understand is her softness and heat, the near painful throbbing of my cock. I eat her like the demon she's created: licking and nipping—lapping up every single drop.

There's no pausing to breathe or giving her a chance to catch her breath; I suck her bundle of nerves between my lips and flick the tip, watching how her chest rises and falls.

My mermaid is breathing hard.

Eyes on mine.

Teeth embedded into her bottom lip.

"Gorgeous," I growl against her heat, slickness coating my lips and chin as another rush warms my tongue.

"Papi, I'm—"

"Come for me." A command she fights, thighs trembling on either side of my head, and that's unacceptable. Bringing a hand to her pussy, I circle that tight little clenching hole.

"No."

"No?" I ask, sliding in one finger and then the other to the knuckle and stop. "Is that a challenge?"

"I'm angry at you." Out of all the things she could've said, that's the last I expected. Anything but that.

It makes me pause, but I don't remove my fingers. Instead, I pull back just enough to fully meet her eyes and let her see a little of what she's always been blind to.

I'm not perfect.

I'm an asshole.

But more importantly, this woman is my world.

"I know, and you have every right to be." That catches her off guard, head tilting a bit while the walls squeezing my fingers tighten a little more. Not that she says anything, but the doubts and hurt are plain as day to see. My girl might think she's unreadable, but I see what others don't. "I'm sorry, Amberlyn. It's never been my intention, but out of necessity, I'm the devil incarnate." Pulling my digits out, I circle her opening with the tips and then slam them in deep, immediately finding that one spot that I've tattooed with my name. "Just remember everything I said to you late at night. That you know a part of me no one else does."

Lips opening, she licks the bottom one and takes in a deep breath, ready to ask me questions, but I don't give her the chance.

"Ivan, what...oh *God*!" There's my sirenita. The gorgeous girl with the bright hair and love for the ocean that looks at me with nothing but love. Even if it's for a second, I saw it. With me, she's an open book.

But as the first wave of pleasure crests, she throws her head back and arches—legs widening a little more to accommodate me. So I can take what's mine and freely given, and I love her clit through each ripple while stroking my fingers deep. She's swollen and flushed, juices dripping down into my palm while her bundle of nerves throbs against my tongue.

Fuck, this is my heaven.

I can't live without her for long.

"So perfect," I groan deep before scraping my teeth over her sensitive flesh, reveling in the way that heated stare meets mine again. How those supple thighs tremble yet try to hold me in place. "Thank you, bebe."

Gentler now, I bring her down with slow licks and kisses after removing my fingers. With each, her breathing slows and body relaxes while that beautifully satiated grin gives me all the satisfaction I need. I've ignored my cock's throbs and the beads of pre-come that now stain my pants, how each flex against the zipper—the way she moans low in her throat—brings me closer to my own release.

Instead, I grit my teeth and bear this as punishment.

The next time I have her, she will be mine in every way a man can claim a woman.

Placing a final kiss on her clit and then wet hole, I pull back and stand. Then we're eye to eye, my still-wet lips a hair's breadth from hers, and I just watch.

Take into memory how sweet she looks a little disheveled. *Mine.*

We don't talk as I help her down and then fix her dress, both of us ignoring the slight wrinkles in her garment. We're lucky that the cut is made in a way that it hides them since the bodice is tight.

"I think we should head outside," Amberlyn says after a while and I nod, but when she makes to move past me, I halt her with a hand out. "Ivan, we really need to head out. We've been gone long enough."

Still, I don't budge and grin down at her. "Say you'll walk with me."

"Listen, I need—"

"Please." I bring the hand halting her exit up to her face and cup it. Relish in the way she nuzzles my palm unconsciously. *I know, baby. I know.* "Please walk with me, Mermaid."

Her entire body melts, and all anger evaporates for now. "Yes."

"Thank you."

Amberlyn

THE REST OF the wedding party is there when we arrive. They're laughing and smiling while he walks a step or two behind me, a warm hand on the small of my back. Not that they pay us any mind. Instead, they talk among themselves while the planner keeps watching the clock.

Most of these people are family members of the De Leons. A few are friends of the bride.

But they're all smart enough to avoid being nosy.

It also helps that Alvin and Natasha are keeping them busy with an impromptu toast while my heart feels as though it'll beat out of my chest. I'm sensitive and in shock. I'm a little lost, too.

He seemed almost desperate. More possessive than he's ever been.

What the hell is going on?

I thought he'd be happy with my decision to walk with Alvin. That he'd appreciate the distance—to not have to placate the lost puppy always following him around.

Was I wrong? Does he care?

Not that I'm given more time to dissect as a flushed Luna walks in with an apologetic look. "Sorry for the small delay, guys."

"We'll blame the groom," Nat calls out and I flick my gaze in her direction, catching her eyes for a moment. She's pulling Alvin behind her as she walks over to her cousin, but the quick glance my way warns me we'll be talking later. As does the bride, so many questions in the quick wrinkle of her nose and raised brow, but I'm not going to make today about me. They each share a quick kiss on the cheek and whisper something low so no one else hears, and then they nod. "All right, folks. Let's get me hitched and calm Thiago down. He's not a patient man…something that runs in the family."

The dig is clear, but other than Ivan clearing his throat, nothing happens.

"Yes, please. Let's line up and be ready to walk in five." Mercedes, the wedding planner, claps once and then lifts her tablet, pointing at pairs to come over. "Same placement as last night."

One by one, the matched partners move into place, and I follow, coming over to Luna first for a quick hug. "You ready to become the chain to his balls?"

"I was born to be." Her sassy response earns a chuckle from her brother-in-law who also gives her a small hug after I pull back. They don't exchange words, but the quick glare she sends his way makes the man nod once and then retake his place beside me, hand on my lower back.

The heat sears me. Feels so good.

But I fight the shivers back—how much I want to kiss him.

Because I heard him today. Those words while hovering over my core, they're something that I can't ignore, forget, or even begin to comprehend. They make no sense.

One minute I'm an obligation. Reduced to a nuisance.

And now…?

Truth is, I still don't know. There's also this hint of betrayal that looms at the edge of my mind: what game is he playing? *What do you want from me?*

Our stares meet then as if pulled by an inexplicable force, and time once again stops for me. I love this man, always have, but those doubts, that for years I've buried deep, can't be contained. My mind and heart are at war, fighting for domination now that the lull of my orgasm has faded, and I feel as though I'm being split in two.

"We're up next, Mermaid." My heart stutters at that, and the two low gasps from my girls mean they heard this too. That in my confused state, I didn't make this up. "You ready?"

"Yeah." Because what else can I say? Not at this moment. So instead, I take the bridal bouquet of white calla lilies he's holding out for me, no clue when or who gave this to him, and then shift forward.

Those behind me are staring. I can feel it.

I'm just as lost as they are.

"…your hand," Ivan whispers, bending a bit to my level and his warm breath caresses my cheek. This time, I can't control the shiver. "Amberlyn?"

"Huh?"

"Your hand, sweetheart. We're up."

A throat clears, and it's like I snap back into place on autopilot. My hand wraps around his elbow and in a few steps, we're over the threshold, the warm ocean breeze flowing all around us. He leads me toward the beautifully decorated arch, our movements in sync while his brother stands upfront by himself and anxious.

You and me both, buddy.

At that moment—heck, since he handed over the flower—it's like my mind has disconnected from my body and I move without conscious thought. Something's wrong here. I know it, but can't seem to shake it off.

Not that anyone can tell.

I'm smiling and greet the groom while my hand lingers with Ivan's for just a moment or two longer than they should. I also shrug when his brows furrow at Alvin walking with Natasha, not understanding why someone he met recently is walking with one of the maids of honor.

Yet the moment his beauty walks through the doors, he's done for.

You can see it on his face. This feeling of peace and completion comes from being close to the one you love.

Nevertheless, I can't help the way my eyes water at the sight. I'm crying in joy for them and sorrow for myself, a contradicting set of emotions that I hide behind a watery smile for the happy couple.

Ivan's also watching, but not them. It doesn't help my nerves, this anxiousness that creeps in when his words from last night and today mix. Confusion leads to weakness en route to heartbreak, and he's the one holding the guillotine.

Nothing more than an obligation.

It's never been my intention, but out of necessity, I'm the devil incarnate.

"I now pronounce you husband and wife." That snaps me back to the present, and I wipe at my damp cheek with the fingers not gripping my bouquet. "Mr. De Leon, you may now kiss you…never mind."

Laughter fills the large backyard, his mother's being the loudest. There are hoots and hollers, clapping as they continue to kiss without a care in the world.

A shoulder bumps into mine, and I turn my head. "You won the bet, by the way."

"Never a doubt."

"So cocky."

"No. Just smart." With everything but *him.*

"Tomorrow, late lunch?" In other words, we'll be dissecting what happened in the last twenty-four hours. Fine with me. At this point, I need someone to help me make sense of this.

"It's a date."

"Never a doubt," she parrots my same words, dipping her hand into the pocket of my dress and slipping something inside that feels like money. Nat also nudges me forward a second before someone grabs my hand, a touch I'd know anywhere, and winks. "You'll be paying, too."

MY HEAD ACHES a bit and my legs will be sore tomorrow, but it's worth it to see how happy my best friend is. The couple is dancing to a slow bolero being played by the band, an old romantic song that reminds some of us of where we come from, or a love lost.

This was a favorite of the De Leon abuelos, and it's touching to see their mother sing it to them. Her watery eyes shift from the couple to her husband, and lastly, to the man a few feet from me.

His presence is overwhelming. Hasn't given me the space I need to clear my head.

I chose this empty table near the back to relax after hours of nonstop running around because the actual ceremony was just a small part of today. You have pictures and toasts and avoiding questions while jumping in to help at the slightest infraction to help things move along smoothly.

If a vase fell because someone's tipsy aunt second removed bumped into a table? I got the person out of the way while the clean-up crew made it disappear.

If Luna needed a change of shoes? I ran upstairs in my death traps and grabbed her flip-flops.

But now that the night is almost done and people watch the final dance before they leave, I'm without a compass.

Lost. Exhausted.

He's also a lot closer than he was an hour ago, and I inhale deep, taking in that liquor and man scent that all women find attractive in men. *Not all men, though.* There's something about that combination on who you lay claim to that's near controlling in its pull.

It's woodsy and strong with just the right note of spice that makes my thighs clench underneath the table.

"Get ahold of yourself, dammit," I mutter under my breath and pick up my glass of wine, taking a sip. Then another, the crisp white flowing through me—warming me after my fourth glass. "You're not that girl. I'm not this weak."

The couple stops their swaying, turning to look over at the family matriarch while the rest of the guests begin to applaud. And I tag along, throwing back the last bit of chilled wine before pushing my chair back.

Yet before I can stand, a strong hand with a tattoo of a lion's head greets my line of sight. The fingers are extended in my direction before turning over, offering me his help to stand. My eyes quickly shift around the room and notice people glance away, his mother and father being two of them.

"You're bringing attention our way, Ivan." It comes out breathy and not the uninterested I'd been hoping to go for. Too much has happened, and my defenses are down—my anger at bay.

"You've always taken my breath away, Sirenita." That's his response. No hesitation and I narrow my eyes a bit, feigning annoyance to mask my anxiousness. This, his attitude and need to be close, is everything I've ever wanted, yet he's never given it to me before.

Why now?

Why after I heard him say that to Mirabel?

Is he trying to control me again? Straightening my back, I exhale deeply. "What's this? What are you hoping to accomplish by—"

"All I want is a dance, bebe. Just one."

"You're confusing me, Ivan. I want to hate you so much..." Trailing off, I try to step back and bump into my seat. For a second, I teeter on my heels, but then strong fingers curl around my wrist and with a gentle tug, I'm against his chest.

After the pictures, he'd removed his jacket and dress shirt, donning instead an off-white guayabera similar to his brother's tailored fit to be destructive for my ovaries. I'm sure this request came from his mother, a woman I'm currently cursing in my head as my hand lands on his pec and Ivan gives the muscle there a flex.

Bastard.

That cocky grin also tells me he knows what he's doing. "Come on, bebe. I won't bite tonight."

"That's a lie, and we both know it."

"Guilty when given the chance." The younger De Leon's imposing figure blocks any attempt of escape, not letting me move an inch while wrapping the other arm around my waist. "But I swear, all I want is to dance right now. I'll behave."

"What do you want? You're confusing me."

"To forget the world and my duty for one night."

"Okay." There's gratitude in his expression before he walks me to the edge of the dance floor where the lighting is dim. Not close enough to join the others, but our bodies are only a few inches apart and his soft exhales skim over my temple. *This is just a dance. No need to make a big deal out of it.* "This will either be a blessing or a curse."

"What was that?"

"Nothing." Thank God he didn't hear me; I've made myself a fool for this man enough times in the past. Moreover, I'm not looking for a repeat even if love makes you do stupid things, and there's no doubt in my heart that this is one of those times.

Ivan turns me twice and then pulls me closer. Not an inch of space separates us now.

My heart races and goose bumps rise across my skin. My core clenches violently.

I let him talk me into walking with him as my partner, stood by his side in every photo, and now I'm swaying to a slow song the band is playing. We're almost chest to chest, though my heels still don't make me tall enough, but being nestled like this feels right.

His strong arm is wrapped around me, and his scent lulls me into a cocoon of affection and safety I never want to leave. And yet, something is off.

It bothers me. This large elephant that's overtaken the room, yet neither of us calls out.

"Ivan, I can't do this anymore."

"I know."

IVAN

"**I**VAN, I CAN'T do this anymore."

"I know." Lowering my mouth to her forehead, I place three quick kisses there and then pull back. Every muscle in my body is tense, yet my arm around her is gentle, keeping her close these last few moments like the precious treasure she is. "Do you remember the time back in high school when I asked you to skip class and go kayaking with me?"

Her expression is perplexed, yet she nods. There's even a small curl on her lips. "You've always been weird and asked for more of me than you should."

"You were scared of the mangroves and thought a gator was hiding beneath us."

Sirenita smacks my shoulder hard but doesn't miss a step. "And you laughed at me and asked me to trust you."

"That day was the beginning of our adventures, wouldn't you say? We've skydived, raced bikes, and got our first tattoos together." My finger slides across her hip where there's a bundle of white mariposas, Cuba's national flower. Amberlyn shivers and bites down on her bottom lip. "Every time, I've been there. Never far, Sirenita."

Maybe I've been chauvinistic—it's been easier to keep her at bay—but this is the most I can offer. The hostile environment and bloodshed are unavoidable outside these walls; one goes with the other in a world dominated by greed, but keeping a clear head is what wins wars.

I'll remove the threat to her life.

I'll kill Rodriguez and his men for this.

And then I'll lay an entire country at my little mermaid's feet.

"What are you trying to say, Ivan?" If there's one thing my girl is, it's perceptive. Especially in her line of work: criminals are the best kind of liars.

"Things are moving in the background that need my attention."

Sliding my other hand down her arm, I skim her wrist before using it to turn her twice, stopping with her back to my chest. The last song ended and gave way to bachata, the melody a little bit faster, and we fall right into step. We gyrate, keeping to the basic three counts while I lower my face to her neck.

I inhale deep, and my groan isn't quiet. It's full of the hunger only she can create. "Yes."

"Okay." No more questions, and I leave it at that too. She's aware of who I am and what I do.

We stay in this bubble for a while, ignoring those around us who continuously shift their attention our way, while everything from merengue to salsa to house music plays well into the night.

I have no idea how much time passes, but the vibrating on my phone stops me.

Pulling it out with my unoccupied hand, I bring it up and let facial recognition open the screen. The message is from someone running surveillance on a building deep in the heart of Hialeah, a city neighboring Miami and whose population is heavily loyal to my family.

The eighties and nineties were great decades for business.

> Dalian Uriel is with your mark at a bar in Hialeah.
> They mentioned Mariposa Bail Bonds. ~ Cisco

They're dead men walking.

I'm not far from my exit on the Palmetto thirty minutes after the newly-weds departed, fingers twitching against the steering wheel while some club banger plays on a popular station. The dashboard's lit screen tells me I'm going well over eighty, yet the two cops I've passed have been smart enough to not stop me.

My mind, though, is on the look Amberlyn gave me right before I walked away after the first text came in. I knew exactly who Cisco was speaking about. They live in the same building, and my informant owes me a few favors.

And like the saying goes: *one hand washes the other.*

Mermaid picked up on the shift in mood at once and didn't ask questions. Instead, I was given a nod, a quick squeeze to the arm, and the space to leave while defeat mixed with exhaustion flashed across her expression.

There was also doubt. Worry.

She has every right to feel that way, and it burns me.

I've never regretted the life I was born into, not once, but tonight, a part of me wishes it'd be easier for us. But that's on me. My selfishness to keep us private and enjoy everything that came without the interference of our families has come back to bite me.

"Our day will come, Mermaid. I'll be back for you." Taking the exit with a sharp turn, I get off on Red Road in Hialeah and make the first left. I need this. The kind of release that comes from revenge, wearing the blood of an enemy on my hands.

Because this is more than anger.

I'm shaking as a deep-rooted rage—hatred—scorches my veins while driving down the deserted-at-this-time avenue. This area is a great mixture of new and old, from homes to businesses and everything in between while the east side of the city is known for its small factories and cafeterias.

My destination, though, is a small apartment complex near 49th Street and behind a shopping plaza.

That's where I find my informant, cigarette in his mouth while a pistol is tucked into the waistband of his pants. The tank top he's wearing barely conceals it.

"Acere," he calls out the second I step out after grabbing what I'll need, coming to my side of the vehicle. Cisco keeps his distance, eyeing my Glock and holster while extending a hand out toward me, which I take, giving it a hard squeeze. "Good to see you, bro."

"You been good?" I ask after releasing his hand, knowing he had a kidney stone issue in the past. Had to be operated on because of it. "Your family?"

"All good, thanks to you." A few years back, he saw himself in debt with a loan shark over a few default parlays and I paid them, with the agreement he do odd jobs for me here and there. Like this one: follow and report.

"Glad to hear it."

Cisco's phone pings then and he takes it out, showing me the message on the screen. It's from his older brother.

> The asshole just left. He's drunk and on his way
> to you. ~ Tito

Three dots appear right away indicating he's typing a second message, and it comes through before I can ask if Dalian is with him.

> Solo. Uriel is here and not alone. A woman came
> to see him. ~Tito

An image follows of a blonde woman no older than her late twenties with an arm sleeve of roses and thorns. She's sitting in his lap, whispering in his ear, while his hand is under the table. He's touching her, it's obvious, even if the empty beer bottles littering the wooden top block a bit of the view.

"He doesn't leave them until they're behind closed doors. I want a location."

"Understood." Cisco's already typing this before I'm done, pocketing the device before digging into the opposite pocket. There's nothing left of his cigarette but the butt now, and after smashing it onto the asphalt with the sole of his sneakers, he hands me something shiny.

"A key?"

"An apartment key, to be exact."

A grin tugs at my lips; I don't care how he got it. Instead, my body welcomes the rush of excitement that fills my limbs. It's heady. This lick of fire snaps at my heels and brings forth a different kind of pleasure.

Because every human has a beast inside—a vengeful demon that I accept—and mine demands payment in blood.

Never threaten what's mine. A lesson to be learned tonight.

"Gracias, Cisco. I owe you for this." His head shakes at that, but I pay my debts. This goes beyond what I asked of him, a man who made a mistake but isn't a criminal. This show of loyalty made him a friend. "Text me with an address when your brother gets it and pull back."

"If you need me—"

"I know. Appreciate it, too." With that, I walk away and toward the building with him coming up slightly behind me. There's a small click to the door after he swipes a card, the lock shifting, and then I'm inside after pushing a signal scrambler given to me by Casper's IT guy.

That British fucker is full of surprises, and this one has come in handy more than once.

With no record of my being here, I enter the elevator and wait for Cisco to push the floor's number. I'm going to eight while he exits on the seventh, leaving me with a piece of paper that reads: *number 808 and no neighbors.*

Cisco's response to my raised brow? *One just moved out and the other is still at the bar.*

I plan to leave a lovely present for Dalian and Jaime. They'll know I'm coming.

The door in question is at the end of the small hall where there's a circular ending and three separate entrances, and I slip inside the middle one without the worry of being seen. I find the entire unit in the dark, except for a small table lamp that illuminates a lonely grey armchair in the corner. It's made of corduroy from the looks of it; I find that it suits my purpose when it faces the entrance, and the bar cart is slightly to the right of it.

Funny thing is, for being a dipshit, this asshole has decent taste in liquor. There's an unopened bottle of expensive tequila, a few rums, and a whiskey that's got a good age on it.

Opening the latter, I take a sip straight from the bottle while removing my gun from the holster and placing it atop my lap. I also straighten the bracelet on my wrist, a gift from my brother, and undo the safety clip on it.

This could go two ways:

Quick and clean.

Or messy and agonizingly slow.

On my fourth sip, there's a rattle at the doorknob and I watch in silence as the man in question stumbles in, sloppy and drunk, singing to himself. He's unaware of his environment, the danger that lurks, and I almost snort when he manages to hit his toe on the entry table while tossing off his shoes.

Fucking moron.

"Buenas noches," I say, causing him to jump/fall against the door while I place the bottle atop the cart. Poor judgment on his behalf as I'd given him a slim window to run out the door and into the humid night, but to his surprise, the fucker managed to close it instead. "It's rude to not greet someone back. I expected more from someone with such fine taste."

The apartment is full of nice furniture, some paintings, and a gaudy coffee table that screams new money.

"H-how did you get in?" In response, I toss the key at his feet and raise a brow. He reaches for it while his body turns toward the door; the click of the gun safety being removed makes him pause, a pathetic whimper slipping past his lips.

"Get up and go to the rooftop terrace, Henry."

"Why the terrace?" Entire body trembling, his hands slip on the wall as he can't find purchase, yet I'd venture to say he's a lot more awake now than when he walked in. Eyes alert, he manages to right himself but doesn't move from what I assume he thinks is a safe distance.

He more than likely thought I wouldn't shoot inside of a building filled with innocent people on every floor.

Thing is—I would, and I will. Everything comes down to precision and choosing the right spot.

Say, forcing my gun into his mouth will end him, but not go through to the next floor. Not with the concrete noise barrier. That alone will help slow if not stop the bullet.

I'm not going to, but I could.

I believe in gun safety and firing responsibly.

"Because I said so."

"De Leon, this is unnecessary. I'm not the enemy."

"I like your fear." Standing to my full height, I take the steps between us and bend my head a little so we're eye to eye. "You have two choices. Are you listening?" His shaky nod is a good enough answer. "Follow directions, or take a trip with me downtown. Your call."

And because I'm a saint, I give him some space to consider his options. Not that he's the brightest crayon in the box, because the moment he thinks there's room to escape, the asshole goes for the door and yanks it open, rushing toward the apartment to the right of his door.

He bangs on it.

Screams out the names of who I assume is the neighbor on vacation.

Leaning against the doorway, I bring the muzzle of my gun to my chin and rub it there. "You'd think being a criminal would make one more aware of their surroundings. Check the whereabouts of those who live next door."

"Did you kill them?"

"The couple that moved out, or your friend?" My smirk irks him, yet I don't make a single move to grab the cornered animal.

"Whatever I did can be fixed."

"Seems you've sobered up well, since we're making deals now."

"Please."

"No." One word. Two letters.

So simple, yet incites so much fear, and his need to escape overrides common sense. My position places me within seconds from the open hallway and when the idiot makes a desperate last-second sprint, I clock him.

A single punch, bare knuckles, and the fucker goes down. The loss of consciousness is immediate. His body stiffens and drops, skull bouncing hard off the ground. He also lands a bit awkwardly on his shoulder and arm, the latter appearing off.

"This could've been handled with dignity, asshole." Grabbing a foot in each hand, I drag him back inside and close the door, locking it before maneuvering his limp body up and over my shoulder.

The top units in this building have access to a private rooftop terrace they share, mainly used for sitting out in the evenings on the large, shared patio set. That, or taking care of plants inside of a small greenhouse that's sealed, cooled, and irrigated in a very specific way.

But more importantly, it's private. Every noise is blocked by the small bit of traffic down below and the occasional plane above as we aren't too far from the airport.

No one to hear me empty my clip in his head.

IVAN

AN HOUR LATER the idiot rouses, groaning from his place on the floor a few feet from me. He's unaware, soaking wet from the hoses I pulled from his greenhouse after Israel confiscated every full-grown plant and the equipment.

The latter I'll toss somewhere or give it to a small farmer who's loyal to the family. This motherfucker purchased and used quality tools; it'd be a shame to waste them.

All in all, it wasn't much in the matter of bulk, but once ready for sale, the street value is easily twenty grand and I'll donate it to the cause. Because to remove a president in power, you need funds, weapons, and soldiers—in the end, this will be nothing more than a humble act of good-will from a dead man.

"How much did I have to drink last night?" His cough is rough as if he'd smoked heavily for many years. There's also a small gash over his right eyebrow from where I struck him, and it's bled quite a bit. *Not enough, in my opinion.* "I've never felt this fucked up."

Rivulets of red mix with the low setting of the water hose, flooding the top a bit before sliding over the side of the building. To anyone that comes up and discovers his body between tomorrow and the next few days, it'll look like a robbery for his illegal farming. Just another drug deal gone wrong, and the case will receive little to no attention.

The difference is that Jaime will know. The message will be clear to him and his family.

I'm coming.

"A lot, from my understanding." At the sound of my voice, his head snaps in my direction, and his eyes widen in horror. "Morning, sunshine."

"What the...*shit*!" He made a move to scramble back, but the dislocated shoulder doesn't help his cause. The weight he put on it when trying to gain traction causes him to slip and fall forward, hitting his face on the cold concrete floor. "Fuck!"

"You might want to be careful. That looked like it hurt."

Henry doesn't answer me, too busy looking around and notices two things: his marijuana is gone, and so is his phone, which I now have in my pocket. In all this, he keeps flicking his gaze in my direction, trying to guess my next move while I sit comfortably in a folding metal chair beside a patio table.

There's no escape. No help.

Just an executioner and the convicted.

"Please don't."

"I suggest you start talking. My patience is thin at the moment." Reaching into my front pocket, I pull out a pack of cigarettes and light one up. I'm not one to smoke often, but the relaxing atmosphere seems to call for one. The idiot flinches at the sudden move but settles; Henry tries to stand once again, but I hold a hand up. "You can explain from your knees, and I'd be quick to drop to them. Either you cooperate and make this easier on yourself, or I begin to unload my magazine. Trust me, you'll drop immediately with a blown kneecap."

"Killing me is not the answer, De Leon."

"No. It's not." His rough exhale almost makes me chuckle, but I keep my expression neutral. Emotionless. "It's just the beginning." Holding the cig between my lips, I inhale deeply and hold it a few seconds before exhaling through my nose. I also hold up my gun and point at his horror-filled face, and at once, he gets into position. Watching me. Body is shaking. Maybe going into a little bit of shock. "Now, you know why I'm here?"

"Yes."

"Tell me. I want to hear you say it."

Tears pour from his eyes, bottom lip trembling. *Pathetic.* "I paid for an order with fake bills. Lied and stole from your family."

"And? What else?"

"That's all I did. Te lo juro." *I swear it. I swear it.*

Leaning forward in my seat, I glare at him. "We both know that's a fucking lie. Your friendship with the Uriels is enough proof of that."

"Ivan, please. It doesn't need to be like this?" Henry says, teeth chattering while his body tries to shy away from the cold puddle he's sitting in. A quick tsk from me stops him. "Can you turn the water off?"

"No." Another deep inhale; this time I stretch my neck from side to side before releasing perfect 'O' rings of smoke. "Pick it up. I want it over your head while we discuss a few things." Shaky hands reach over the nozzle not too far from him. "And turn the setting to full power."

"Okay."

"Point it at your face, right eyebrow to be exact." Doing as I ask; Henry holds the sharp blast of water to his face and the gash I left earlier. A string of curses leaves his mouth, almost choking him as the water, tinged with red, rushes inside. There's coughing and sputtering as he tries to remove the jet, but I discipline him just as swiftly.

From my back pocket, I pull out the silencer attachment and shoot to his ear.

One shot, and it tears clean off. The torn cartilage now lies a few feet from him, and it's burned from the impact.

"Son of a bitch," he grits out, his hand loosening on the green hose to cup the injured area. Blood pours from the open wound at a rapid pace, and his hand becomes drenched—his arm and clothing bear the same fate. What was once a pale-yellow shirt is now red. Dark and bright. "How could you just shoot me? I'm cooperating."

"Pick it up and aim again, or you'll lose something more painful next time." One last puff, and I toss the remains at his head. The red ember bounces off his wet forehead and flops to the ground. "Remember, you hold the power here. How much you suffer is up to you."

"No more."

"Now."

"I'm begging you." Henry's face suddenly loses all color and then, like the pussy he is, the man bends over and empties his stomach. *Nasty.* Hacking and gagging, he unleashes hours' worth of drinking onto his front and below. "Please, no more."

"Pick. It. Up."

"Fuck," he screams out the second the sharp jet hits his cut and now the jagged cut where his ear once was. More water is poured, and the force of the stream opening the wound a little at a time while the floor is bathed in his life's essence, among other things. It's a foul smell. Henry looks pathetic. Nothing like the man who stole from my family conspired to help my enemy, and put my mermaid in danger. "Let's work something out."

The added pressure isn't helping the swelling either. The eye below the cut is half swollen shut.

My finger on the trigger twitches, and he flinches. "Like what?"

He licks his lips. Swallows hard. "I can pay—"

"First, what the fuck is your last name? I didn't care enough to memorize it." No sense in lying. That grates him, but he's smart enough to not react negatively. I'd kill him before finding out without giving a single fuck.

"Davila."

"Okay, *Henry Davila*." I smile and lower my Glock. "You have four minutes. This is your only chance to convince me that shooting you would be a mistake."

"I'll pay you double."

"Money isn't a problem for my family."

"You can have me work it off." Sweat trickles down his temple, mixing with the bit of blood there. "I'll tell you where they are."

"Now we're talking my language." Pressing the stopwatch setting on my smartwatch, I start running the time. "Convince me in the next three minutes, and we'll discuss other options."

"Okay."

"You can also lower the water. Take that as a gift for your cooperation."

"Thank you." Davila exhales roughly, dropping the hose. His shoulders hunch, and his hands clench and then open a few times. "They approached me with an offer to make a large amount of money while also allowing me to keep my counterfeit operations with police backing. I'd be essentially protected and rewarded, and all I had to do was hide Dalian here and do some small surveillance."

"Whose name are both apartments under?"

"This one is under my mother's." At my nod, he looks down as if he knows what he says next will piss me off. "Dalian's is under Amberlyn Ibarra."

That son of a bitch.

Every cell in my body vibrates in anger, yet I keep a tight rein on it. *Not yet.* "Who put it in her name? How did they get the information?"

Davila swallows, still not looking at me. "I did."

"Again, how?"

"A hacker I met online in a chat group. We exchanged goods."

"I see." Then I begin to pace. From one side to the other, while his bloodshot eyes follow. He jumps each time the hand holding the gun so much as twitches, but I ignore it for now. His audacity to involve others and obtain her information through a third party, one that could harm her as well, adds to my list of bodies.

"What can I do," he chokes out on my next pass, lips trembling. "Anything. Please, just ask."

For a second, I turn and give him my back. I'm a rational man, at times more than my brother, but right now the rage that consumes me is hard to fight back. So I breathe in deep and stare up at the night sky, taking in the many businesses on the street not far from us and those traveling through, a car here and there, but none the wiser to how close they are to a killer.

Life's funny that way.

As humans, we are complacent and unaware. Never truly seeing.

Instead, we ignore to protect our minds when that puts us in the most danger.

And then, occasionally, you run into an idiot like the one behind me.

He has the equivalent to the *I'm on vacation* syndrome. The it-will-never-happen-to-me mentality gets many in positions like this one: staring down the barrel of a gun and pleading to someone with no human compassion or morals not to hurt you.

"Anything?" I ask, looking over my shoulder at him. Completely filthy and pitiful.

"Yes."

"I want the name of everyone involved. I want addresses and details of each."

"Done."

"You have forty-eight hours, Davila. Get me this information and I'll discuss relocating you out of Florida permanently." Henry opens his mouth to respond, but I shake my head. "I'm not being understanding or have any desire to be. Don't mistake this for what it's not. Fail me, and I will not only find you but gut you and leave the body and entrails for all to see hanging off the Brickell Bridge. Understood?"

"Si."

"Then clean this up. The clock is ticking."

"Y-you're leaving?"

Too much hope in his voice and I laugh, the sound sardonic. "I am, but I dare you to run and hide."

Amberlyn

"MORNING, mi niña," Mom calls out the moment I step into the office early Tuesday morning. It's been two days since the wedding and since I last saw Ivan, and I'm worried. No text. No calls. Not so much as a late-night visit and it drills home the words I heard him say to Maribel.

Makes them real.

Not so much a mistake.

Not that he hasn't disappeared on me before, but there's a difference in knowing he's working and this time, having the fact he sees you as an obligation replay in your mind like an endless reel. It's why I took yesterday off; no matter how many times I went over what happened—heard—I'm left in a loop of confusion.

"Morning." It's a low grumble between sips of hot coffee, but she understands and then follows me toward the back where we keep a small lounge for those who work here. An employee is manning the front for now, and Mom wants to gossip. "I brought pastries and an omelet sandwich. Want half?"

"No, but I'll take a guava and cheese turnover." She makes a beeline for the coffee maker, her favorite mug in hand. "How was the wedding, by the way? Did you party that hard to call out yesterday?"

"Yes and no." Another sip from my latte, not looking at her yet. I'm keeping busy by grabbing a small platter and with the help of tongs, arranging the sweets for anyone working today to grab in between clients. Some days we are busy, and others it's a person here or there. "With all the last-minute wedding prep and helping Luna, I'm exhausted. Barely slept for a few days."

"Do you need an extra day? We're good if you do."

"Nah. Just need the caffeine to kick in…" unbagging my sandwich, I take a bite and chew, then swallow "…besides, I have two cases to catch up on. Court date is coming up, and I'd hate for them to skip. Both have a mom's signature on the debt."

"Gotcha." Mom studies me. I can feel the hard stare. The dissecting of my behavior. "Ask away, woman. What's got your curiosity?"

"You never answered my question, kid."

At that, I look over and raise a brow. "The inquisition hasn't begun yet. No clue what needs to be answered."

"Smartass." Grabbing a few pastries, napkins, and her coffee refill, Mom takes a seat at the small kitchenette set. Pats the seat beside her and waits for me to trudge along, and once I'm seated, she turns on the cheesy grin. *Yup. She wants to gossip.* "Okay, now tell me. How was the wedding…everything?"

"You were there, Mom," I chuckle before taking a second bite. When I don't say anything else, those eyes, so much like mine, narrow. Swallowing, I wipe my mouth with a napkin. "You're going to need to be more specific."

"Décor, food, and dances? Any surprises?"

"Same as the ceremony, catered from the restaurant and the couple's favorites, and they danced all night until leaving. Those two couldn't be pulled apart. So much so, the tossing of the bouquet happened right before she got in the car to leave for the honeymoon."

"Who caught it?"

"Is that important?"

"Yes."

She's an amazing woman, but nosy runs in all Latina mothers and it's best not to fight. The trick is always make them think they've won.

We were all standing in front of the house waiting for the newlyweds to drive off. Everyone there had a balloon in their hand with a wish for the couple, and as they descended, they were released one by one.

The idea had been mine. Something I saw in a wedding magazine and loved, and with how things are with me and Ivan—the lack of any commitment—I'd given Luna the suggestion. Something she loved and as they made their way through the group of family members and loved ones, she broke from the group and walked toward me and Nat.

Our balloon was a little different. The all-white plastic was hiding a naughty gift for the trip.

"I have a feeling this isn't meant for the public to see?" We shook our heads in unison, giggling a bit. "The extra streamers, glitter, and the three giant X's also give away that vibe."

"We thought so, too." Nat hands it to her, while Luna shakes her head. Even the man standing behind her snorts, the amusement and hunger for his woman clear to see. "More fun for us this way."

Luna shifts her gaze to me. "And you feel this way too?"

"Absolutely."

"I'm glad you do. Babe?" The bride holds a hand behind her, being blocked by her groom. There's a bit of rustling, whispered words from him that I can't hear, but beside me, Natasha groans.

"She wouldn't."

"Oh, cousin. I did." A few seconds later, I'm blushing and stunned into silence as I'm handed half of her bridal bouquet while Nat gets the other. Literally, she split it in half. No tossing, the woman just decided to hand it over to us. I'm going to kill her. "This is for my two favorite people—"

"What did you say?" Thiago growls, it's playful yet still full of jealousy. "Repeat that."

"Favorite after you, babe. Calm down."

And while they bicker a bit, Natasha taunting him with favoritism, my eyes search out his. Yet when I find him, I don't see the warmth in them from when we danced or the sweet smirk I'd been gifted after his mouth licked my release from them.

No. Nada once again.

Blank and uninterested and I shift away, smiling at some random person in the crowd. I'm sure I know her. Hell, I've been around for years, and yet, making out faces is past my abilities.

Instead, the flowers in my hands feel like thousands of pinpricks and I just keep repeating the words: trust me.

I'm brought back to the present by a throat clearing. "Well, kid. Who caught them?"

"No one caught them per se."

"Who?"

"Luna split it in half and gave the pieces to me and Nat."

"Oh, dear." That's it. That's all I get after answering, but the woman is smiling. Way too bright for this time of day. "That's one way to push her girls into finding someone to settle down with."

"And is that your way into peppering in that you want grandkids?"

Mom shrugs. "Maybe."

"Not happening for a long time, woman. I'd need a man first, and at the moment, I'm very much single." Those words feel wrong, yet the truth is the truth. The old saying *No puedes tapar el sol con un dedo* is appropriate. Covering the sun with one finger is impossible and burying your head in the sand makes it worse.

I was honest when I told him I can't keep doing this. Maybe we're just not meant to be, and I've been kidding myself for far too long.

"You need a man?"

"Yes. Unless you want me to adopt or go buy some—"

"Amberlyn!" Now she's red-faced, but there's sympathy behind that stare. Mom knows about me and Ivan, or better yet, I lied to her. Told her that *I* wanted to keep it a secret until taking over the business. That I wanted respect for my name and not fear because of who I dated. "Niña, behave. If your father—"

"What about her father?" Dad asks, walking into the room and straight for the baked goods. "Whose butt am I kicking?" At that, I burst out laughing and he looks over, giving me a wink. "What, kid? You know I could."

My father and mother couldn't be more different, yet they work. Where he's over six feet, Mom is barely five. While he's reddish hair and green eyes, my mom is dark hair and light brown eyes.

One is loud but believes in peace.

The other likes sports and enjoys a good fight. Kickboxing is his passion, as is being a bounty hunter.

She bails them, and he finds those who skip, while I'm certified to do both jobs.

"Last time, I gave you a black eye."

"I let you get that punch in." Coming over, he drops a kiss on my head and then pecks Mom's lips. So casual. They're in love, have always shown it and I look away, my eyes tearing up for a second. Blinking them back, I focus on my breaths but still catch the tail end of his response. "...your mother threatened to make me sleep on the couch if you so much as got a scratch in our last sparring match."

"Is that so?" My gaze shifts to hers, and I find understanding in them. There are also questions. A quick shake of the head and she nods, understanding that I don't want to talk about it. "That's mean, Mom. Poor Dad."

"Exactly, princess. Poor Dad."

"Oh, shut it, you two." Pushing back from her chair, she stands and walks over to the sink and rinses her mug. "I'm nothing if not sweet and gentile."

"Of course, love." Dad shakes his head at me and I bite my lip, fighting my amusement.

"I saw that, Joey."

"Yes, dear."

"Out, Joey."

"Yes, honey." With one last kiss on my head, Dad steals the other half of my sandwich and walks out, but not before calling out their plans. "Be ready for lunch by two."

Mom doesn't say anything for a few minutes; she's facing the wall while the water runs, and her fingers tap the countertop. But then she turns, and the sympathy is more than I can handle at the moment.

"I'm fine."

"Are you?" she counters, leaning back against the sink. "Is he?"

"To be honest…" I shrug "…no clue."

"What happened, kiddo?"

"Life. Reality." This is my cue to leave. Without understanding how we got here and what's true and not, I'm done speculating. What I need to do is talk to him. Confront this and let the chips fall where they may. Standing, I pick up my trash and then dump it before walking over to her. I kiss her cheek and meet her eyes; I'm not hiding. "But this mess is ours, and we will figure it out. We both need time, and I have clients to deal with. Just leave it alone for now. Si?"

Mom isn't convinced but smiles anyway. "Okay. I won't ask or interfere."

"Thank you."

"HEY, AMBERLYN." Anita, our front desk girl, taps on my door. "There's a woman out front who's asking to see you. Says it's urgent."

Looking up from my laptop, I scrunch my eyebrows. "One of my clients?"

"No. Never seen her before, but she looks…*twitchy*."

"Okay." Closing my computer, I sit back and crack my neck. It's been a long day so far with a few walk-ins and the two house calls I made, delivering court dates personally. Not something done by other companies, but at ours, we give people every opportunity to do the right thing. No excuse. We serve you a few days before and have you sign off a statement that says were made aware. "Offer her something to drink and send her in. Bring me a coffee, too, please."

"Right away." Anita pauses before slipping out. Hesitates.

"What's wrong?"

"It's not my place to—"

"You've worked here long enough to get a read on things. Speak your mind."

"Something's off about her, Amberlyn. I bet money on the fact she's under some influence—"

"Drugs?" I ask.

Anita nods, pursing her lips. "There are track marks and her eyes are bloodshot. Not the kind from crying, either. That, and her story makes no sense."

"How so?"

"Bar fight turned into arrest and the boyfriend is missing."

"Missing?"

"Yes."

"You pulled up the arrest records from last night?"

"Yes, ma'am. The name she's giving isn't in any Dade County facility."

"Send her in." Something's fishy, and I'm not in the mood for bullshit. "Pull whatever records you can on them both and bring them in with my coffee. Let's see what's this about."

Amberlyn

"THANK YOU FOR seeing me, Miss Ibarra," the woman says upon entering my office, taking a seat without me offering her one. She's pretty, about my age, but shifty—almost scratching her arms. There's also a lot of makeup on her face, her eyes are red, and the clothes she's wearing are better suited for a bar and not someone who's worried sick about a loved one.

She's a mess, yes, but not dirty after a quick perusal. Clothing isn't torn and her shoes are new; I'd say this is the first time she's worn them, too.

All in all, Anita is right; something's off.

"How can I help you…?" I trail off, needing her name.

"Sorry." A giggle and she holds out her left hand which I take, giving it a firm shake while checking out the ring. It's on the larger side and also obvious that she wanted me to look. Most people offer their right hands, rarely the left. "I'm Karen Lopez, but you can call me Ren—"

"I'll stick to Karen, thank you." There's a quick tightness around her mouth at that, but she quickly fixes her expression. "You wanted to speak with me?"

"Yes." Rubbing a hand down her arm, she tears up, and her bottom lip trembles as if on cue. In doing so, she failed to realize I noticed the needle marks on her arm, and they were fresh. "I can't find my fiancé."

"Okay." My cell phone beeps with an incoming text, but I ignore it. "Have you filed a report with the police?"

"They're the ones that took him from me!" Karen wails, covering her face with both hands while I reach into the right drawer of my desk and pull out a box of tissues, sliding it across my desk to her. Shoulders shaking and leg bouncing, she cries louder—nearly falling from the chair since she chose the one without armrests. "He's innocent!"

"Miss, there's not much I can do outside of posting bail," I say, keeping my voice gentle. Dealing with people under a lot of stress comes with the job, and while something is off, I'll give her the benefit of the doubt until proven wrong. "You do understand that, right?"

"But a friend of mine said you'd helped her." This is mumbled, yet I catch her peeking toward me.

"Please look at me."

"You got her a better lawyer and with your connections, the charges were dropped."

Connections? Lawyers? "Who is this friend you speak of?"

"Her boyfriend worked for the De Leon family." Not the name I need, but I'm understanding a little better. Either she wants special treatment or is trying to extort my company. Neither will end well for her if she doesn't tread lightly. "Last year he was picked up on carrying without a permit, a dumb charge, but she said you pulled some strings, and he was out before the following day."

"Name." The more she talks, the more I smell bullshit.

"I was asked not to say."

The last person I took care of was Ivan himself. He's who the MDP picked up, and before he was fully booked in, I had him out. It was a mistake by a rookie cop who didn't know the set of rules made specifically for the De Leon family.

There are certain concessions made for them. Miami doesn't want a bloodbath.

Moreover, it was his mother who called me in the middle of the night asking for help, not a girlfriend. I've accepted a lot over the years, but fidelity is the one thing I won't question.

Ivan knows where I stand.

What I'd never accept.

Dropping her hands into her lap, she wrings them together in a nervous action. More tears fall—faster—leaving behind black tracks of mascara in their wake. She's also a little more jittery. "Please. I don't know what else to do."

Coming around to Karen's side, I take the seat beside her, patting her back gently. "Please try and get a hold of yourself, Miss Lopez. There's not much I can do for you if I don't have the information necessary."

"Tissue, please."

"I've already laid the box out for you."

"Oh." That's it, but she does calm down. Creepily at once. "Didn't see them there."

"It's okay. I can see you're under a lot of stress."

"I am." She grabs a tissue from the box and dabs her eyes. Another to blow her nose. "They ruined our engagement celebration."

"Who did?" Trying not to cringe at the way she places the dirty tissues atop my desk. *Nasty.*

There's a knock at the door and Anita walks in with a manila folder, a bottle of water, and my coffee in a Styrofoam cup. "Here you go, miss." She places the water down first and smiles at Karen after she mutters a low *thank you.* "My pleasure. Please let me know if you need anything else." The rest is put beside my closed laptop before she walks out. Yet, before reaching the door, she tilts her head toward the folder, meeting my eyes.

Message understood.

A quick nod from me, and she exits. "Please continue, Karen. Who ruined your engagement?"

"I'm sorry, but can I have a coffee instead?"

"Sure."

Standing, I pause just outside my door and whistle. "I'm sorry, Anita. She'd like a coffee, please."

"Of course." Chiming comes from the front, and she rushes to greet whoever entered.

However, when I turn, I find a nervous woman. Pale. A little sweaty. Once again scratching her arm. "Are you okay?"

"Yeah." Clears her throat. "Why wouldn't I be?" *Because your fiancé is lost?*

"No reason." When I take a seat this time, it's back behind my desk. This is when I notice the papers peeking out from the folder, and the fact the coffee lid flap is open. The staff here knows I like the latter closed— keeps in the steam. *What the hell are you playing at?* "By the way, someone came in and Anita is helping them. It'll just be a few minutes for your coffee."

"Of course. No worries."

"So about your fiancé…"

"Oh, yes." Opening her water, she takes a deep enough pull to empty half the contents. "As I mentioned, we were out last night celebrating at a bar when we were attacked. We'd had a couple of drinks with some friends, nothing over the top…" she leans over as if sharing a secret, and I keep up the façade by grabbing a pen and opening the folder "…when some guy accused me of taking his keys. Mind you, I'd been sitting on Ramon's lap the entire time."

"Ramon is…"

"My fiancé."

"And his last name?"

"Isn't that in your paperwork already?" *Bingo. You looked.*

"That's not what I asked."

"Ramon Valle." Sulky, she sounds put off by my question.

"Where were you when this occurred?"

"I'm sorry, Miss Ibarra. I was told you were discreet and didn't ask for information, that this was an easy money exchange. Maybe I should've just called the officer that made the arrest." Karen begins to stand, and in an act of pure clumsiness, knocks over the water bottle. It soaks my paperwork and dribbles across and down onto my pants, but I remain calm. Too calm. "Oh shit! I'm—"

"Please sit down and collect yourself." Leaning over, I grab a few tissues and mop up the spill, then a couple more because it spread, before tossing all of it in the trash. A trash can that I hold up so she can also dump her used Kleenex.

"Thanks." Both are thrown in the bin, and I hold back the urge to Lysol the area. "Barging in and disrupting your day was never my plan. I'm just desperate to find him."

Taking a deep breath, I let it out slowly.

Also chuck the coffee in the bin, which makes her flinch.

There are two possible reasons why Karen made this visit, and I doubt it's pure love for Ramon Valle. Either she knows about my connections to the De Leons and wants to exploit that for gain I'm not aware of, or she wants to fuck mine or Ivan's family over.

The one common denominator in both is someone opened their mouth.

As a mistake? No clue.

As a favor to a worried friend? Maybe.

The problem will be in finding out the who, when, and why.

And I plan to do so.

"I know. I'm not upset, sweetie." Opening my laptop, I tap on the dictation app and give her a reassuring smile. "Now who is the officer you spoke of? I'll need his information to help you find Ramon and why he's not showing up in the system."

"Of course!" Karen quickly digs into her small purse, digging through before producing a small white card. This she lays on the desk and slides it across, careful to avoid the damp areas. "This is what he gave me. Asked me to call him if I had any questions."

Detective Jaime Uriel
Miami Police Department
Cell: 305-123-5847

"He was the arresting officer?"

"Yes."

"A detective?"

"Yes. That's him."

"I see."

"You think it's weird that an off-duty detective broke up a simple bar fight and then made the arrest."

"Yes and no. Being off duty doesn't mean they can't make an arrest or detain until another officer comes along. My problem is with him getting personal on this arrest. There's no large crime here, no reason for you to call him." While the dictation app continues to record what we're talking about, I pull Jaime Uriel's information through my phone. With a couple of clicks, his picture is on my screen. His bio is short, which doesn't give me much to go on.

I have his rank, years on the force, age, email, and phone number—different than the one on the card.

Next, I open the daily arrest report and check for any new inmates and scroll down the list. Anita already did this, but it never hurts to check twice, and still no Ramon Valle. Not in any of the jails.

"What county was this in again? Dade?"

"Yes."

"He's not reported to be in any of them."

"Christ, where can he be?" Tears form again, and they slide down her cheeks. "Please. I know you're busy and this isn't your usual case or work, but at the very least, can you call the detective? Maybe ask someone you know at any of the jails or precincts you might have a connection at?"

"Okay." At the very least, I will find out who opened their mouth.

Bails Bonds offices have to follow certain protocols and government regulations, and I can't have people sharing information—my business dealings—with anyone. Not even a family member. The wrong kind of attention could bring attention to my doors and worse, to the De Leons.

I'm not worried about myself, but him. Always him.

Karen exhales, her smile nearly ear to ear. "Really?"

"I'll see what I can find out for you, but I make no promises. Understood?" Opening the bottom drawer to my left, I pull out a basic NDA and pen, placing them in front of her. "Please read and sign. I'll need you to understand that anything shared through our interactions is to be kept private, and sharing business procedures outside of the parties involved will be cause for legal action on behalf of Mariposa Bail Bonds."

"No problem." Without reading a single line, she signs and stands. "I appreciate this. Anything you can do is appreciated, and money isn't an issue. My father will pay for it."

"I'll call you if I find anything. No guarantees."

"You'll find him. There's no doubt in my mind that you will."

ENTERING my home after a long day and endless phone calls—inquiries—I drop my shoes by the door and head straight for the kitchen. My footsteps are soft on the hardwood floors, yet inside the silence, it reminds me of a banging drum. This steady sound follows me. Torments.

It's easy inside the office to get lost within my work. To focus on helping someone, filing paperwork, and sometimes driving out to pick up a jumper.

Here, though, in my silence, it maddeningly comes rushing back.

My needs and desires. The lack of touch from the man I love.

His words and the limbo they've left me in while I haven't heard from Ivan in two days. Not a note, message, or smoke signal.

And this time, it stings worse than any other rejection.

"Maybe what he said to Maribel was the truth and once again, I fell for his act." In the kitchen, I open the freezer and pull out a bottle of vodka with a smile. Ice cold, it's just what I need and without hesitation, I remove the cap and take a sip straight from the bottle. There's not much left—at the most three double-shot drinks—and I take the bottle without a glass out onto the balcony.

The sun's slowly lowering as I sit on the lounge and take another small drink. From blue skies to darkness, it descends slowly while people begin to settle in for dinner.

Families talk. Couples share a kiss. Lovers curl around each other, offering pleasure while satisfying their hunger.

And here I am alone. Unsure of myself.

"He can't care for me and then turn around and hurt me this way." Something crinkles in my pants pocket as I shift and I slip a hand inside, pulling out a small white card. It's basic and like many I've seen in the past with the precinct information and officer's name.

"No reported incidents. Jaime Uriel is clean." Yet I'm unsettled. Something about Karen and the case—her fiancé who doesn't appear under anyone's detainment—worries me.

Those closest to me are not saints and have plenty of blood on their hands, but I'll be damned if anyone hurts them. Comes for *him*.

Because everything for me starts and ends with Ivan De Leon no matter how much I hate it at times.

The weakness. The pain. My never-ending cycle.

"He needs to know, though. What if something happens?" Grabbing my cell from beside the bottle, I press number one and wait. Five chimes and nothing. Straight to voicemail. Then I try a last time, but instead, my device goes off, and on the screen is a phone number I've only seen twice. I press the green button. "Hello."

"Miss Amberlyn Ibarra?" The man's voice is deep, a bit hoarse before they clear their throat. My skin prickles at the way he says my name, and I don't like it. Unpleasant. Ruins the slow buzz flowing through me while I also pick up the police radio in the background and the codes being shared. "May I speak to Amberlyn Ibarra."

"This is her, Detective."

"You've been expecting my call." Not a question. His tone is amused. "You can also call me Jaime. No need for formalities."

"I have a good memory, and your number crossed my desk today." *There's no reason for him to have my number or the informal interaction.* More cause for concern. "How can I help you?"

"Karen Lopez called me today and said you'd need my assistance. That something happened to her—"

"I'm not an investigator, Detective. We do bail bonds and bounty pick-ups when clients fail to show up. Nothing more." Either they're trying to catch me in some illegal activity or as an accessory. That, or they're after who I associate with. "This is something you or a superior should look into. Don't you agree?"

"My hands are tied, Amberlyn." Frustration is clear in his tone. I also don't feel comfortable with him using my first name. Doesn't feel right.

"How so?"

"Paperwork shows that I brought him in, when in fact, another officer did. I detained him, nothing more."

"Still doesn't explain why I'm being brought into this mess." Screw it, I pick up the bottle and bring it to my lips. My sip is larger than the last. "Again, I'm not an investigator."

"No, but as a bounty hunter, you have certain legal pull and allowances. I need to clear my name, Miss Ibarra, and Karen needs her other half. Can you help us?"

"Where's the arresting—"

"He's missing, too."

IVAN

"**W**HERE IS SHE?"

"At home, boss," Junior says, and a car door's alarm follows a few seconds after. He's stationed outside my mermaid's building and has been her tail now for a few days—since the morning after the wedding—and has my trust to protect her. Fail to do so, and he's aware of the consequences. Knows who will be pulling the trigger. "She seemed pensive on the drive home. Upset."

"That's later than usual." My watch reads a little before seven, and I frown. I've ignored her calls, stood outside her door at night, but haven't touched her since our dance. It's the only way to control my urges. This hunger that tears me apart, eats away at my flesh. Resolve. "Did something happen today at the office?"

"Yes."

"Speak." A knock on the open metal door announces their arrival, and Israel walks in with a reluctant Henry behind him. The latter has his bottom lip busted and his hands tied in front of him. He'd tried to run, as I expected, but the fear and stupidity led him to make a costly mistake.

He set fire to his *and* Dalian's apartment before running. Fucking idiot. Especially when I had eyes on him at all times.

Cisco gave me the tip while his brother followed him to a pay-by-the-hour motel near Okeechobee known for catering to those needing a quick fuck. Most of the rooms are set up with garages that lead to a private entrance, and Israel had a key made for the one Henry rented not two hours later.

The female clerk was more than willing to make one after a hefty tip.

"A woman came in today and was there for a while. She's not a client, but Amberlyn saw her anyway."

"And?" I point at the empty chair, but when Henry hesitates, he's forced by a single shove down. "Hold that thought." Placing the phone down atop a folding table, I press the speakerphone key before narrowing my eyes at the bruised man avoiding my gaze. "Okay. Tell me."

"Boss, you were right."

Scratching my jaw, I stand and begin to pace the twenty-foot container. We're inside the port and near the back end of the lot where no one will bother us. Or stop me when I leave. "Go on."

"It was the same woman your lookouts saw with Dalian and Henry a few nights ago." Where he's at, the evening breeze off the coast sweeps and makes noise. "Anita gave me a copy of what she came for and the police info pulled. Her name is Karen Lopez, and she's looking for her wrongfully arrested fiancé. You can guess who the detaining officer was."

A low hum escapes. No originality. "Jaime Uriel."

"Yes, boss."

"Where's Dalian?"

"I believe he's the missing-in-detainment fiancé."

"Of course. Thank you, Junior." Pressing the end button, I tilt my head and watch as beads of sweat roll down Henry's pallid face. There are stitches on his face from our last encounter and the wound to his ear looks infected, yet he's alive. Should be thankful. "You made a bad decision, Henry Davila. Running from me was foolish and irresponsible."

He swallows hard but doesn't answer. Wrong move.

"Answer when spoken to," Israel spits out, placing the muzzle of his gun against Henry's temple, and pulling the trigger. It's empty, just a click, but my guest understands the rules. He also pisses himself. *Nasty.* "Next one won't be empty, Davila. Understood?"

"Yes."

"Good boy." I struck a nerve with that remark. His right hand clenches. "Something you want to say?"

"No."

"Then lose the pinched face and start talking." Israel hands me a folded metal chair and I take it, open it, and sit across from him. There's a plastic table between us. "I'm waiting."

"My stepsister is in love with Dalian. Karen can see no wrong in him." I'm surprised; this is something I didn't know. Can come in handy in the near future. "The Uriel brothers use her. I know they do, and I was dragged in as a favor to her. To win *his* favor."

"Dalian or Jaime?"

"Dalian, but I have my suspicions she's slept with both."

"And you?"

"Guilty." Henry snorts, the sound is a bit sarcastic. "Not that she'd care if I die. We're not close. She was brought up spoiled, self-centered, and never wanting a sibling. As you can see, we also don't share last names and in her eyes, that makes me beneath her."

"Then why get involved?"

"Because Karen met them through me. I'm responsible for our downfall."

"You're right about that. You decided to help them, to put Amberlyn Ibarra in danger, and then you ran from me. All that was on you." Israel pulls out a manila folder from inside his suit jacket and places it atop the table; I open it. My eyes skim through the papers and I find names, addresses, and bank accounts with an accumulated wealth of well over five million dollars. "Why, Henry? Explain to me how going against me and mine was a good idea?"

"Honest answer?"

I wave a hand for him to continue. "Please."

"Greed. The offer was too good to pass up, especially with the guarantees they presented."

"Nothing in life is ever a sure thing, Davila. Not a fucking thing. "The blood on his lip has crusted a bit, and I also notice he's swallowing hard, thirsty, and I look at my guard. "Get him some water."

"Of course, boss." Israel exits the container while I sit back. One of the papers has my attention and I read through it. This one has information on safe houses here and in Cuba, and the backup plan to grab her grandparents there. Not going to happen.

"Keep going." Tone terse, it comes out harsher than I intend and Henry flinches back. "Relax. Right now we're just going to talk."

"Okay." His hands try to stretch, but the tight rope prevents that. Reaching into my back pocket, I grab my matte-black balisong knife and with a quick flick of the wrist, tear through the bindings. At the movement, he jumps and falls back, slamming his head against the hard metal. "Fuck. That hurt."

"I'm sure it did. Now sit." Another twist of my hand and it closes; I place it to my right. Henry scrambles up, nearly tumbling again before managing to right himself. "There are two names on this list I do not know. Who are they?"

"Cuban military smuggled in to protect the brothers." Angry rope marks surround each wrist and he rubs them, occasionally stretching out a hand. "They're from an alliance exchange; they were trained in an eastern European country to specifically work as protection to the president. However, Jaime bragged they'd be coming here, instead. And they did, on the day of your brother's wedding."

They're desperate. Don't know how to control me. Which can be a dangerous thing. Nervous—afraid—people make mistakes. Some are more costly than others.

"Why that day?"

"Jaime claimed the De Leons would be preoccupied. That's what Dalian wanted to celebrate—to them, their time had come."

"Yet, I had eyes on you and him. Could've killed you both that night."

"They don't know how close you are."

And that's because I never gave him the chance to so much as send them a text. I gave him forty-eight hours, but my men were always near. In plain sight of him, and he saw them at every turn.

"Correction—how close *you're* about to get me." Sitting back, I cross my arms over my chest just as Israel walks in. He hands Henry the water, who takes it and then sips, before retaking his place a few steps from the nervous man. I smirk at that. "How much value do you put on your life, Davila?"

"Not much at the moment. I'm a dead man."

"That depends solely on you."

"I-I don't—"

"Help me, and you'll live to see another year. Maybe twenty."

His smile is wide, so much relief in his features. "Okay."

"Smart choice." Yet I'm not sure he's understanding how much another betrayal will cost him. Grabbing my knife, I open it and flick it at his shoulder, the black metal blade embedding three inches deep. His scream of pain reverberates, bounces off the metal walls, and helps to calm some of the ire boiling within me. He's not absolved of all his crimes, a payment is yet to be made. "Learn your place, and do it quickly, Davila. We are not friends, partners, or associates. Fuck me over again, and I will deliver on my promise to hang your corpse over the Brickell Bridge. Go near Amberlyn or anyone I love, and I will chop off your dick and watch you slowly asphyxiate as you fight to breathe through the intrusion. Mind your choices, and know that I am always watching."

"Understood," he whimpers, holding his arm while not touching the blade.

"I'm glad we could come to an agreement." Turning my gaze to Israel, I give him a quick nod and he grabs Henry's arm, hauling the weak man up. My knife is still buried in his flesh and will stay that way until later tonight. For now, though, we'll take a ride. "Take him out to our boarding dock. I'll meet you there shortly."

A nod and they walk out.

I'm left alone with my thoughts. With the need to check up on her, and before realizing it, my cell phone is in my grip. Yet it vibrates before I can call, and it's Junior's name on the screen.

"Is she okay?"

"Yes, boss. Miss Ibarra hasn't left the building, but there's a problem."

"What?"

"An unmarked white SUV has been making the rounds in the area. I've seen it twice on her street, and the others watching the surrounding blocks have as well. They're looking for something." *Or taking note of any protection in the area.* "Do you want me to approach?"

"No, and keep out of sight. Let them think she's alone for now."

"And if they come near—"

"Put a bullet between their eyes and leave them to bleed out on the sidewalk as a warning. She's untouchable."

"Done."

"Is there anything else?"

"Thiago called and said he needs to talk to you."

"I'll get a hold of him now; thank you. Call me if anything changes." Hanging up, I pull up the camera to her bedroom on the app and find her asleep. No toys. No light sheen of sweat on her skin. *My sirenita.*

Knowing she heard the blasphemous words I'd said to Mirabel, that she was hurt by them, guts me, but knowing she more than likely believes them right now is a bitter pill to swallow.

But that's my penance. Her doubt. Anger.

But the one thing I can't allow to happen is for someone she loves to be hurt.

For the woman I love to ever be in danger or mourn her family.

I'd die for Amberlyn and those she holds dear.

They are mine to protect, too.

"I'll be back to you soon, my love."

Amberlyn

"THANK YOU FOR meeting me on such short notice, Miss Ibarra." Detective Uriel stands from his seat, holding a hand out toward me as I make my way to the table he's occupying the following afternoon. I take it, and a shiver runs through me. It's small and unpleasant and I pull it back just as quick, which he catches, face tightening a bit around the eyes, yet his smile remains in place. "Would you like anything to drink? I'm heading to the—"

"Here you go, Amberlyn." Lily places my café con leche down along with a large slice of red velvet cake before heading back to the counter. They know me here. It's a small bakery in a strip mall near the office that I frequent when needing a pick-me-up. They make the best sweets, and today is one of those days where indulging is how I'll get by.

I'm frustrated and miss him.

His smile. His touch. The way only he can make me come, and the tension left in his absence continues to grow.

I haven't touched myself either while thoughts of the last time we were together keep me awake. No toys or replicas of his cock. No release for this tension. And it's not just the sex; I need our connection. This all-consuming nirvana that his mere presence gives me. It's raw and sweet and us. *But was it ever real? Or was it all an act?*

"Amberlyn?"

The way he says my name snaps me out of my thoughts and I refocus, giving him a professional smile. "It's already taken care of." Taking my seat, I pick up the oversized white mug and take a few small sips since it's still very hot. "Now, what did you want to show me?"

"Does this mean you'll be taking the case?"

"I'm here, Detective."

"I need a yes or no answer, Miss Ibarra."

"This is me giving you the chance to explain yourself and gain my interest," I say instead while sitting back in my seat. For the first few seconds, there's quiet. He's studying me, and I flick my gaze around the semi-empty establishment before meeting his stare head-on. Detective Jaime Uriel is tall, and I'll admit many would consider him to be handsome with his tan skin, chocolate-colored eyes, and sharp jaw currently sporting a five o'clock shadow. Yet, he does nothing for me. Not so much as a twinge. *Will I ever be attracted to anyone but Ivan? Can I move on?* "That's the most you'll get from me at the moment."

"Noted." Tone terse. A hint of annoyance.

"Or we can end this here. This isn't my headache."

"Why are you being difficult?" he hisses, hands tightening into fists. There's also the restless leg, that moves him and rocks our table a bit.

Something about his presence isn't right. I'm a believer in following my instinct—heavily in tune with that tiny voice inside blaring out in warning, and I place my cell phone face-up on my lap. My father and mother are at the office today and will get here quickly if something were to go wrong. That, and I'm carrying my weapon in plain sight for him to see.

I caught him looking at my cross-body shoulder holster and the loaded SIG inside.

I'm not afraid to shoot. Have a damn good aim, too.

"What you decide to share is up to you, Detective. However—lie, and you'll make an enemy out of me." Again, the skin around his dark eyes becomes tight and this time, there's an added tick to his jaw. "Are we clear on this?"

"Are you threatening an officer of the law? Do you understand the implications—"

"I don't make a habit of saying things I don't mean."

A grin stretches across his lips at my response and his body relaxes, amusement coloring his features. "You're a spitfire, aren't you?"

In return, I level him with an impassive stare. "If I am or not, I don't see how that pertains to what I've been cited here for. Am I wrong?"

"You are correct." Bending to the right, he lifts a work bag and undoes the zipper before pulling out two yellow folders and placing them atop the table. No names on them, but one of the papers sticking out does have the city embossment in the corner. "We're here for business, and I apologize if I—"

"You're fine. I've had a few rough days, and I'm not at my peachiest."

"Are you okay?" While his tone is sincere, I'm still not sold on him. The man's job as a detective is to investigate, not pawn off work on a bail bond office and their bounty hunters. Bullshit seeps from every pore of this meeting, but I'll see it through. If he's a threat, I'll find out and deal with it myself if it comes to that. "Anything I can help you with?"

"No, but can you explain the need for my services?"

"Of course." Detective Uriel opens the first folder and shows me the picture of another police officer. Below his name is a handwritten note with the word *rookie*. The guy is of Latino descent and from the picture, he has a slim build with a recognizable tattoo of praying hands on his left forearm. His bio is short, having been officially on the force for a few months, and works in the Hialeah precinct. "This folder is on the rookie and the other is on the man I detained."

"Tell me what happened." I'm skimming down the few notes, nothing large. He's dependable, a likable guy by his peers. No wife. No kids. "I'll need full details, please."

"I was just having a couple of beers with a few friends, watching a Marlins game, when the fight broke out. It wasn't near me; I was on the opposite side but jumped in to help when it got too rowdy for the employees to contain."

"And you noticed this from across the establishment?" Opening the second folder, I skim down the perp's details. Young, male, and again of Hispanic heritage. Not much on him either, not even a speeding ticket. "Who was involved in the altercation?"

"After separating the two men with the help of my friends, I asked the owners what the issue was and if they wanted the police called."

"And they said yes." My gaze lifts to meet his. Uriel nods.

"They said yes."

"Hmmm."

"Good or bad?"

"More like I'll need a minute. Are you still going to get a drink?" Nothing to do with the conversation, but I need a moment to text Anita the names. There's a discrepancy between what the fiancée gave us and these reports. Same name, two different spellings. "I'm going to read through what you have here before asking more questions."

"Sure. I can go for a coffee." For a second, his eyes narrow but then relax. "Anything you recommend eating?"

"Sweet or savory?"

"A little hint of both." I don't miss the way he licks his bottom lip.

"Try the medianoche sandwich. It's legit the best I've ever had."

"I'll do that." He raps his fist on the table once and stands, pushing his chair back. "Be right back."

"Take your time."

Detective Uriel gives me another studying look before turning and walking toward the front. We're a bit out of sight of the counter and my back is turned to him, so I easily send off a quick text to Anita. Some things don't make sense; their insistence on my working with them is only a small red flag.

Angling my cell, I take three pictures of each document while pretending to read. Her reply is just as quick, her worry clear.

> Got it and already jumping into research. Do you
> need an out? ~Anita

Fingers tapping a quick *not yet* on the screen, I hit enter and place the device down before picking up the document with the perpetrator's name and info. As my eyes scroll across pictures from that night, I notice something interesting.

Uriel is smiling. As is the man being arrested.

In fact, they look more as if posing for a picture than someone documenting the altercation that led to this man's detainment. There's also the question of who took this photograph, and why was it included in this file?

Usually, you get a booking mugshot and detailed report. That's it.

"So what do you think? Can you help us?" Uriel says from behind me, close enough that I feel his hip graze my arm. That extra contact wasn't necessary, and he knows it, but I don't call him out on it. Not after he sits down. Nor when he takes a bite from the sandwich I suggested.

Instead, I smile, and it isn't a professional one. Whatever they want, I'm in and have all the time in the world to play.

I'm a woman scorned, vengeful, and who needs an escape from her problems.

"I can and will."

Grabbing a napkin, he swallows and wipes the corner of his lips. "Thank you."

"Don't thank me yet…" Uriel's head tilts a bit to the side, his mouth opening to say something I assume to be positive, but I shake my head "…you will, though. I'll find them both for you."

"Both?"

"The officer and perp are equally important, and both have stories to tell. Don't you think?"

"What if he's in on it?"

"Then all the more reason to find the guilty, and I won't rest until I do."

"Good." His tone of voice doesn't agree, though. There's a hint of something I can't quite put my finger on, but it raises goose bumps on my arms. "But I'm going to need a final favor if you will."

"Favor?" That word leaves a bitter taste in my mouth. Because the last time a man asked me for a *favor*, it hurt me and people I've come to care about like family.

What Ivan asked of me was a test—used my emotions against me.

I should have never agreed back then to pretend to help Thiago deceive Luna into thinking he cheated, even if it came from a place of love and worry for her safety. I'd rather know the truth than being fed bullshit, and I regret my stupidity over the need to please the youngest De Leon.

"It's nothing serious. All I ask is for complete discretion, please."

"Discretion?" My café con leche has gone cold, but I take a few deep sips anyway. "Explain."

"Amberlyn, if I get caught sharing private information…" he trails off, and I understand the implications. Yes, he can lose his job, but I bet a month's salary that he could give two fucks about that. This is larger than he's letting on; I'm more intrigued by his reasoning for targeting me.

Is my family being investigated and this is how they get inside?

Am I a key to information on the De Leon dealings?

What are you looking for, Detective?

"And that worries you?"

"Yes."

"Then so be it. I'll be prudent."

IVAN

S HE CAN'T SEE me, but I'm watching from across the street through the windows. They're sitting toward the back and beside a tintless glass. It's a little away from the main door, but in his idiocy, Jaime didn't pay much mind to the public view.

The again, why would he when his uncle sent two trusted hitmen to guard his prodigies?

This is where it becomes a simple lesson: comfort makes you cocky. Sloppy.

Or he's tempting me. Trying to draw me out.

The problem with that is—I know how to play this game.

"Where's the other singao that arrived with you?" The muzzle of my gun digs in deeper into the back of his neck, and his knees scrape against the dirty asphalt when he shifts away. He was easy enough to find, but what he has in size and skill, he lacks in common sense.

This isn't Cuba or whatever country trained him.

This isn't a simulator or controlled assignment.

My eyes and ears reach far deeper than this country or the island. One email sharing the photo, and plenty came forward with information. Seems they've been enjoying their time here, entertaining whores and gambling, the latter of which comes from casino footage of three establishments within city limits.

"Yo, no hablo ingles."

"Yes. You do." Junior, who's here just to remove the body before going back to his bodyguard duty, hits play on a small recorder from the bar they visited a few nights back. They were all there. Each of these assholes had a role to play, and the owners were more than willing to hand over the footage and erase the rest from their server for a small donation.

That video corroborates the audio Cisco and his brother provided.

"I wouldn't mind living here one bit," one man says while another chuckles in the background. You can hear music playing and the occasional cheer from those watching a game on a giant screen above the bar. "Acere, the pussy here alone would be worth the relocation."

"Amen." You can hear the clinking of bottles and what sounds like snorting after. "My brother, I never want to go back."

"Don't let my uncle hear you say that. He'd take offense." A feminine voice mingles with theirs for a minute or two, asking if they need another round, which is declined by Jaime.

"Coño, the ass on that one."

"Stay loyal to me, Pirro, and I'll make sure you have her and any other woman you want. Anywhere. Anytime."

"For her, I'd be loyal."

"And you, Silvio?"

"Keep me in la Yuma and I'll pledge my life to you."

"Now the question is…which one are you? Pirro or Silvio?" The man doesn't answer, and I'll wait a few more minutes. I'm too busy watching as Jaime walks away and my brilliant girl takes pictures of the folder in front of her and then sends off texts.

Whatever he's selling, Sirenita isn't buying.

Makes my chest puff out with pride; I know what she's capable of. How strong she is.

The entire time, Jaime doesn't look our way. Doesn't acknowledge the added security that he assumes watches his back and takes care of any issue that arises. *Dumb motherfucker.*

"Step forward." The moment I say this, the other person in attendance does as I ask, coming to a stop a few steps to my left. He's beside Junior and I look over, finding his focus on the ground. "Look at him, Henry. Meet his eyes."

The unnamed guard tries to stand, his fists clenched tight, but one strike to the back of his head ends that. He slumps, not unconscious but enough to know his place down on his knees. This soldier is a pet of the Rodriguez administration, and I'll teach him as such.

"Sir?" Henry asks, so unsure of himself.

"Name and rank."

"Don't you fucking dare, you piece of mierda."

"I thought you didn't speak the native language of this country." Not a question, but a sarcastic remark. The man is angry—nearly shaking—and my grin broadens. "What happened, asshole? Afraid?"

"Of you, hijo de puta? Never."

"You should be." One bullet with a silencer, right on the shoulder bone, and he cries out. Yet I'm quicker and stuff the end of the tie around his neck deep in his mouth, causing the jackass to choke. Gagging, he coughs around the material while I pat his cheek. "Breathe through your nose." Turning my attention to Davila, I urge him closer with a nod. "Do you know him?"

"Personally? No."

"In what capacity, then?"

"He's Pirro Cruz. One of the two men who came from Cuba under strict orders from the president to protect and help his nephews. He's the younger of the two and seems to get along the most with Jaime."

"Military or mercenary?"

"Both, and they speak fluent English. It's mandatory for anyone who works for Rodriguez."

"Thank you."

Pirro spits out the necktie then, dribble falling from the corner of his mouth. "You're a traitor to your people. You'll pay for this."

"He'll receive penance when I allow it. Not a second sooner."

"Boss, they're shaking hands," Junior says, and I look toward Amberlyn only to find her nodding at something Uriel is saying. The exchange is quick and when Jaime extends a hand, she takes it, but not before saying something that causes his grin to drop.

Sirenita, what are you getting yourself into? You're making it harder to keep you safe.

"Take his body and burn it. I want nothing, not even his teeth left behind."

"Yes, sir."

"Fuck you! You can't—"

My release is quick, and two shots to the back of the head end his time on earth. His body falls forward, blood splattering across the pavement and my shirt, but I only focus on the beautiful woman drinking coffee not far from me.

So beautiful. So mine.

I'm almost home, baby. Just a little more time.

My conversation with Thiago moved my trip up a bit and with a minor detour. My brother received an invitation to meet with President Rodriguez, and I've accepted.

"He's angry, brother. Very careless after finding his general's mangled body." Thiago's amusement comes through the secured line a few days ago. *He's outside and the wind is a bit heavy, but being they're so close to the water it's normal. His private estate isn't far from the family compound near the Mariel port. "You did quite a number on him."*

I snort at that. "Nothing they wouldn't do to one of our own if given the chance."

"Agreed."

"What's going on?" Taking out a cigarette, I light up and take a drag. "Why are you calling me instead of enjoying your honeymoon? By the way, when's your flight out to Tahiti?"

"A presidential invite arrived today via Amberlyn's family, and in two days." There's a pause, and I know what he's going to say. "I can post—"

"No." Grip tightening, I hear the plastic in my hand protest, nearly cracking. "Who delivered, and to what home?"

"Her grandfather arrived at the compound, and the maid called me,

Ivan. The old man had a busted lip and black eye." My brother exhales roughly. Even from miles away, his anger is palpable and mirrors my own. "Rodriguez wants to meet. Says we have a week to show our faces before he forces our hand."

"I'll be there when the time is right."

"You've always had my back. Let me—"

"Alone, Thiago. He's mine to deal with."

"I know."

I'll also be arriving with gifts.

The heads of his nephews, to start.

Fingering the beads at my wrist, I play with the latch and extend the solid steel wire within, thrumming it once. I've been saving this for someone special, and the who has been revealed.

And when Amberlyn stands from her seat, I step back into the shadows. When she exits after taking the folder with her, ignoring the tightness on Jaime's face, I watch her every step until she's inside her car and the tail-lights disappear around the corner.

Then from the dark alley, I meet his eyes from the inside the window.

The asshole waves at my silhouette, and I do the same. He's confusing me with his now-dead guard, and I smirk, still toying with the steel wire for another second before snapping it into place within the bracelet.

"Your hours are numbered, Uriel. Tick-Tock."

Jaime walks out the door and I turn, stepping inside an unlocked door a few feet away from me. It belongs to a laundry shop owned by a family acquaintance who's been nice enough to let me borrow the back room as storage from time to time. She's also old and crotchety, but Mom likes her, so I hold nothing but respect for the woman.

"Grab a clean shirt from my office before you leave, kid. I'll burn this one."

"Thanks." Pulling my soiled one off, I hand it over while taking a small, wet hand towel she's offering. Both items will be burned once done, but not before being soaked in commercial-quality bleach. "This one got a little messy."

"You, or the dead man I saw your guy dragging away?" Raised bushy brows assess me, lips pursing. "The deceased didn't look local, either."

"You're too perceptive for someone nearing eighty, Dora."

"No. I've just been around long enough to pick up on certain things." Turning, she walks over to a large metal drum that's rusty and has a caution sticker on the wall behind it. We're now inside the back room I use, away from customers, and with a filtration system that keeps the harsh odors away from those roaming the front. "You okay?"

"I will be." It's the truth. No use in lying.

"Good." Dumping my shirt in, she opens her palm for the towel, but I toss it in for her. I also open the lever that controls the bleaching agent, its strong odor infiltrating my senses at once. "God, that stinks. I'm getting too old for this."

"Blasphemy."

"Shut it and call your mother. She knows you're here."

At that, I raise a brow while closing the spigot. "How so?"

"Easy. I called her." She shrugs.

"Snitching isn't attractive, old woman."

"Neither is coming here without my favorite cookies." That pointed look is harmless to me. Her huff of annoyance tells me she knows it, too. Thiago, on the other hand, has fallen for it. "That's a horrible thing to do."

"You'll have three dozen first thing in the morning and dinner catered all week."

"Much better." Slowly, Dora walks over and taps my cheek with her small hand. Her expression is knowing. "Never make that mistake again, De Leon. I'm old and small, but mess with my sweets—our arrangement— and I'll complain to the woman you fear the most."

"And who's that?"

"Amberlyn Ibarra."

Amberlyn

I'M FLOATING, water lapping at my bikini-covered breasts while the sun warms my cheeks. The shore isn't far from where I am, and yet, I hear the group laughing—the loud music playing—as if I were sitting among them.

Instead, though, I'm in my own world.

Thinking. Daydreaming. Eyes closed while tipping my head back; I pretend I'm somewhere else.

Living in Miami is fun, and exciting at times, but to me, it's still not home. I miss Tampa, my family, and my friends there. I miss being accepted and not looked at like a favor they're doing. Like someone who tags along without being truly invited.

Not all do. Just a small few, but they matter more than most.

No one is outright rude, but you get that feeling. A look—a fake smile. If only they paid attention to where my eyes always wander. Who my smiles are really for.

Not that I don't understand; after two years, I'm still an outsider to them. Or maybe I try too hard.

Luna is as possessive as Thiago.

Natasha is protective of her family.

The rest follow the leaders.

While Ivan continues to ignore my crush. Yet his secret smiles when no one is looking give me hope. That maybe he sees me too.

"What're doing, Mermaid?" His voice comes from behind me, close enough that I feel his warmth on the back of my neck, and at once, goose bumps rise on my skin. Shivers rush through me. "Why are you out here by yourself?"

"Because I enjoy my solitude."

"I don't like it."

"But I do."

"What if I forbid it?"

That makes me turn, meeting his warm, soft eyes. Like he understands more than I want him to. "Why does it matter?"

"It does."

"That's not—"

"Come with me," he interrupts, hand raising to push a few wet strands of hair back and off my neck. Those fingers linger there and then trace from my neck to jaw before cupping my face. "You shouldn't be out here."

"Why don't you stay with me instead?" It's hard, but I fight the urge to nuzzle my face into his palm. "Maybe take a swim further out?"

"Swim?"

"Yes."

"Okay." His thumb traces over my cheeks before dropping and Ivan moves back, running a rough hand down his face. "Just promise me you'll stay close." I nod, but his eyes narrow. "Use your words, Mermaid."

"Why do you call me Mermaid?" I answer instead.

"Does it matter?" While the response could be taken as rude, his expression is playful, his grin delicious. "Would it make you happy to know?"

"It would." More than he could ever know. Since we met, that's been his name for me, much to the annoyance of almost every girl in our school.

Rarely does he use my first name. It's always *Mermaid this* or *Sirenita that*, and in Spanish, it sounds sinful coming from him.

This crush controls me. Ivan De Leon is my weakness.

"Miss Ibarra, I call you Sirenita because you remind me of a movie my little cousin used to watch on repeat." Once again, he steps closer. Our skin touches this time, and his hands grip my waist—fingers flexing against the mostly bare skin there. "It was about a pretty girl who loves the water and who has bright red hair and expressive eyes looking for acceptance. Always curious. Always sweet." Ivan lowers his face toward mine and inhales deep, this low, rumbling sound building in his chest. *What would it feel like to kiss his lips? For him to make that sound against my skin?* "I also call you Mermaid because when I look at you, I'm reminded of my favorite things. Is that enough of an explanation?"

"Yes." It's nearly a whimper, and his smirk deepens.

"Will you swim with me now?"

"Okay."

"Good girl." Heat sweeps across my cheeks and I turn my head away, hoping he doesn't catch my blush. Those words cause an ache in me, a need I try to control, but the pebbling of my nipples and clenching of my thighs are unstoppable; thank God he doesn't call me out on it. There's no doubt he noticed both. "Don't look away, Amberlyn."

And I return my gaze. As if I have any control over my actions.

I also swallow hard because the slight darkening of his eyes unnerves me.

"You ready?" Tone breathy. A slight whimper.

Ivan doesn't answer me. Instead, he turns and without a word walks us deeper into the warm waters. Moreover, I follow without hesitation. Let him lead me until my feet no longer touch the ocean floor and I lean over, hands gripping his shoulders to keep myself afloat.

We stay like that.

No swimming. No movement other than the gentle sway of waves.

Ivan and I watch the horizon while ignoring the world around us. In the distance, someone calls his name, yet he continues to look ahead with an arm low on my back.

Peace surrounds us. This quiet is comforting.

I never want this moment to end.

But then he clears his throat. "Sirenita, we need to talk."

"About?" Low. A little meek.

"A favor."

"A favor?"

"Yes." Regret flashes across his expression, but it's soon replaced by the smile that causes butterflies to take flight in my stomach. By a soft touch to my back, fingertips dancing up and down my spine while his mouth lowers to hover over mine. His exhale is my inhale. His scent infiltrates my senses and had I not been leaning on him, I'd have found myself submerged. "I need you to do something for me."

"Anything."

"Pretend to mess around with Thiago."

* * *

PRESENT...

I AWAKE WITH A GASP, my heart pounding while sweat beads across my forehead. My mouth is dry and my muscles are tight, thighs clenching, and the wetness there is unmistakable. As is my shame.

I'm needy and tired. Wanting and angry.

Yet my mind gives me no reprieve as the day our relationship crossed over the line from mild flirtation to indecent touches replays in my dreams like a punishing reel. Over and over while my body remembers that I haven't felt his touch in days.

No relief. No soothing words telling me it'll be okay.

Sitting up, I flick my eyes to the bedside alarm and groan when it reads a little over two in the morning. "Freaking detective and his stupid *I need a favor* crap."

Why did he have to use that precise word during our meeting three days ago? One I loathe, and yet, it was the beginning of *us*...

My affair with Ivan De Leon.

It reminds me of something I'm not proud of yet can't deny; he is my weakness. My ever-present inability to deny Ivan anything hasn't changed since then, and a part of me knows he'd do the same for me.

My battle: common sense argues with my heart.

His words to Maribel don't match the actions of the man I tried to reject before his brother's wedding. How he touched me—made me come for him with a desperation that rivaled the first time, and even now, I remember how easily I gave in.

Then. Now. Yet my clit throbs just the same. I feel the way my wetness soaks my underwear.

"When will he stop tormenting me?" I ask the silence of the room, but the reply is another memory. "This limbo is driving me insane."

Images flash behind my eyes. Our story. Him.

We were walking on the shore later that night and stop at one of the empty bodyguard towers, climbing up the steps to be away from public view. Giddy would be the only way to describe me, so freaking happy as he squeezes my hand and turn us so we're facing the night's sky.

"You're so beautiful, Sirenita. A perfect doll," Ivan croons, his voice low, yet the deep velvet tones slide across my flesh like a sinful sweep. At once, goose bumps rise on my skin, and my nipples pebble beneath the thin material of my bikini top. I shiver. Can't stop it. "You cold?"

"Little bit." A lie. Yet Ivan doesn't call me out on it. Instead, he moves so he's behind me with an arm wrapped around my midsection.

That's the first time I feel him.

All of him.

"Better?"

"Yes." This time it leaves me on a low whimper, and he chuckles, the low rumble causing his chest to rub against my bare skin. I'm in tune with his every minute shift. The rough exhale against the back of my neck a few seconds before he nuzzles me—leaves open mouthed kisses that make my knees weak.

Not that he lets me fall—I'm pulled tighter against his muscles while the hardness digging into my back throbs. Flexes in time with my pulsing clit.

"You feel so good, bebe. Always knew you would." Voice gravelly, he brings two fingers to my lips before dipping them inside, just the tip against

my tongue, before drawing them down my neck and chest. Lower, and Ivan caresses my skin—circling my belly button and the piercing there. He's toying with me. Causing me to squeeze my thighs together, and right when a moan slips from my lips, those same two fingers dip beneath the waist-band of my—

"Fuck me." My hand moves without prompting, reaching inside my bedside drawer for one of the toys I keep there. Fingers skimming, I feel the texture of one I know too well. The silicone girth and veins make me suck in a deep breath; my mouth waters and chest expands, yet it feels as though I can't get any air in.

I remember him.

The day he gave this to me.

How he used it to fill my pussy while buried deep inside my ass.

"No. No." A chant. A demand I force myself to follow and remove my hand, ignoring the need clawing at my flesh, tearing me apart. Instead, I reach a little deeper and grab my thrusting vibrator. It's not the real thing, nowhere close to Ivan's perfection, but it'll have to do.

With the click of a button, it buzzes in my hand, vibrating on a low setting. *More. Need more.*

It feels so good when I run it across my naked chest, nipples throbbing to the point my eyes roll back, and I bite down on my bottom lip. A hard shiver runs through me, and I'm wetter—hips lifting a bit and I lie down, situating myself so my back is slightly up.

My knees spread wide after I kick off my sheets so they pool at my feet.

My walls tighten and then release, anticipating the orgasm I desperately need. And when the tip of the toy touches just above my clit, I moan as warmth spreads through me. It's a gentle sweep, yet in my head, it's his lips that kiss me there.

His tongue dragging across my swollen bundle of nerves and tortures me with hard strokes. The vibrations pick up, a pulsing rhythm that makes me cry out when I circle my entrance. From hole to clit, I spread my juices as I remember just how he touched me that day.

Ivan wasn't tentative or slow, and petting me wasn't enough. No.

He slowly lowered to his knees as his hands pushed down the unbut-

toned cutoffs I'd put on after exiting the water. They didn't make it past my knees before his warm breath was teasing my flesh. I never got to fill my lungs with air before his tongue dipped over my clit and then my folds, those same strong hands yanking me against his mouth while the waves crashed behind me.

We were in our own little world and the darkness covered anyone from seeing how I was his at that moment.

"Fuck, bebe. So fucking sweet." That groan reverberated through me, vibrating against where I was most sensitive, and my body rewarded him with a rush of wetness. And the moment it coated his senses, I'm raised off the floor by two hands on my hips that forced me to ride his tongue.

"Oh, God," I moan as the silicone enters me, bottoming out while the air suction attaches to my throbbing clit. That's as far as I get while the air in my lungs gets trapped. In my mind it's his fingers inside me, two thick and unrelenting fingers thrusting, while his lips suck and nip at me. Sweat mists over my shaking form, a few drops rolling down my flesh and I arch, body strung tight.

I'm so close. It hurts.

But then I hear him as if he were here. Right next to me, that gravelly tone borders on a growl that's his tell before he fills me with his release.

"Come for me, bebe."

"Papi." It's a scream, my entire frame wrought tight a second before pleasure consumes me, and I let it. The torturous wave slams into me, and I don't know what's real or fake or even if this is all a dream, but it doesn't matter either way.

Not when a second later I let the vibrator fall and I'm languid. So spent I don't turn the toy off and simply kick it toward the end of the bed where it will eventually die off.

All I can do is melt into my mattress and close my eyes.

Yet the last thing I hear before succumbing brings a smile to my face.

"I'll be home soon."

IVAN

ROPES OF COME coat my hand and stomach, the proof of my inability to stop thinking of a woman I love more than rationality dictates. Maybe it's a sickness. An obsession.

I could give less than a fuck either way.

And the evidence of that is how I continue to stroke my cock as her breathing evens. How I wring out another spurt of my release while she sighs in contentment, body stretched out in her bed. Those sheets smell of her—a sweetness I crave more than anything in this world.

Again, my fist tightens and my eyes close. Another bead drops. It rolls down my fingers as I stroke up and then over then sensitive head when I hear her murmur *Ivan* in her sleep.

A shuddering breath escapes my lungs and my cock jerks, the near painful throb coming from the dissatisfaction of not being there. With her. Keeping my little mermaid cuddled close and warm.

"I'll be home soon." Gazing at her once again, I touch the keypad of my laptop and turn off the mic. She's mirrored on a large screen inside the penthouse suite of a hotel room in Atlanta after my short flight here, having connected the device to the TV from a remote private server.

The accommodations are large, ostentatious for the few short hours I'll be here, and not too far from the strip club where my enemy snorts his way through endless amounts of cocaine.

My job here is simple: grab and escort back home.

Nothing else. No more than a couple hours of sleep, yet the moment I open my camera inside her room—watching on the screen as she pleasures herself—that resolve always hanging by a thin thread whenever she's concerned snaps.

It's why I couldn't resist and let her hear me.

I needed to be the reason she came.

Yet my sirenita *destroyed* me. Hearing her say *papi* in that whiny tone, one that drives me crazy right before reaching her peak, is my kryptonite.

"Always mine." A ringtone blaring pulls my attention from the TV and I look over, finding Israel's phone number on the screen. He's stationed outside the club, monitoring who enters and who leaves. With my clean hand, I press the green button while ignoring a text from my father, then hit the speaker option. "Talk to me."

"He's here and not alone. There's a brunette with him and a man, one I've never seen before."

"Silvio?"

"No. This one is American and older."

"Okay." Grabbing the still-wet towel from my earlier shower, I wipe my hand and stomach before standing from the bed. I'll need a quick rinse before heading out, but for now, I wrap the bedsheet around my waist. I've made a mess, but it's her fault and I look over to where her figure still sleeps peacefully on the monitor. I can't help but bite back a chuckle when I find her hugging my pillow. She sleeps on the right, while I've always taken the left side of the bed. "Dalian doesn't leave. If he tries, shoot him. Blow out both kneecaps if you must, but don't kill him. He owes me a conversation."

"Consider it done."

"I'll see you in a few." Before I drop the phone, I read Dad's message.

> How was the flight? ~Viejo

Parents never stop worrying. Yet before I get the chance to respond, there's another text.

> Answer me, so I can calm your mother. If not,
> she'll be calling in sixty seconds. ~Viejo

I bark out a laugh, shaking my head. She would, too.

> Good, and I'll be driving back once I pick up. See
> you around two. ~Ivan

At once, three dots appear.

> At the docs or warehouse by 49th? ~Viejo

> Neither. We're taking a trip to the swamp. ~Ivan

THE PARKING LOT IS FULL, and the music can be heard from where I'm parked a few hours later. I'm next to a party bus; the lights inside are on, but the driver is long gone. He drove my prey here, and did a little coke, too.

Yet a few bills were enough to send him on his way. Alive.

"In and out. Keep it clean." I'm an asshole, but killing innocent people isn't how I get off.

"Yes, sir." Israel steps outside the all-white SUV with black tints and the two others traveling with us follow. They check their weapons and move to the back and wait for me.

It's late at night.

Those on our side of the world sleep, yet a few lurk.

Work. Party. Or fuck.

Dalian's mistake was doing all three without fear of being found. Every move he and his family took against mine wasn't well thought out. A trap with too many exit points, especially after the unhidden fiasco they created to reel in Amberlyn.

Bringing in the female as bait to gain Mermaid's trust, as though she—I—wouldn't see through it, almost makes me laugh. Almost, had it not pulled me away from my girl and forced decisions that keep us apart for now.

Pulling out my phone, I open the camera again. I just need to see if she's still sound asleep.

The sight that greets me tugs at my lips and my heart, and the owned fucker thumps harshly inside my chest. There she is, warm and sweet and waiting for me. Now she's snuggled up in a soft blanket that usually stays at the foot of the bed. It's big enough for her and in a dark purple tone she loves.

Closing my eyes for a second, I breathe in deep and then out, craning my head from side to side. All noises in the back minimize. They feel like a low thrum, yet I can pinpoint the direction of each: the guards at the back of my vehicle talking lowly, the two men laughing at something while walking past us, and then my breathing.

It's harsh, but not from nerves. No.

Rage flows through my veins and burns me from the inside. My hands clench, the phone in my hand making a low cracking noise, and I look down. The plastic groans again, and I drop it beside me on the seat.

I want my pound of flesh.

For her. For us.

The darkness in my soul, the baser instincts, demand blood. Retribution.

A sigh comes from my phone and I gaze down, seeing the microphone turned on. She can hear me, and I, her. Amberlyn turns then, just a slight shift, and gives another content sound. It's low, almost indiscernible, but to me, it's as if she's moaning beside my ear.

Beneath me. Sweaty and so fucking wet.

"Papi."

"Fuck, Mermaid." My voice carries and she stirs, almost wakes up, but then settles. Nestling deeper into the soft blanket, she grips my empty pillow beside her, and I turn the camera off. If I watch for even another minute, I'd head back.

I would murder every person inside that strip club just so I could end it all sooner.

Instead, I place the device inside my pocket and exit the vehicle. Those with me straighten and remain silent, eyes on the establishment while I tuck my gun in the waistband of my dress pants. They have their instructions and quickly fall into step behind me, Israel to my right.

The closer we get to the entrance, the music becomes louder, and a blaring guitar riff shakes the glass on the large doors. There's a bouncer there, and understanding dawns on his face when Israel hands him an envelope.

No questions. No pause.

We walk straight through and bypass the hostess waiting to walk us to a table. Or sell services.

VIP, dances, or an extra, if I go by the look sent my way.

Not interested.

The establishment is large with a few stages, but the main one is surrounded by men and three women. They're watching the show, some cupping themselves while throwing a few dollars on the stage, yet my eyes aren't on the two dancers kissing for the crowd.

It doesn't take long at all to find Dalian and company. I make my way over, ignoring everyone but them.

"What the fuck are you looking at?" a female's voice hisses and when I find their location, the one with Dalian isn't Karen. Yet she's hissing as if she's the wife, her twang unmistakable Miami, and more so when she adds a *fucking pata sucia* at the end. That's a 305 insult all day. While many outside the city culture won't understand, you're calling her dirty. One of those nasty women that will take off their shoes in a club or street and strut/dance without care where people have tossed garbage, drinks, and who knows what else.

For the women in Miami, that's a large insult. Cleanliness is drilled into your head since childhood and if you're willing to do that, how low will you go?

I find it hilarious.

Especially the lost expression on the waitress's face. "I'm sorry. What did you say? I don't—"

Before the brunette can answer, I slide into their booth while the others take a small table a few steps away. "Ignore her. They don't go out much."

"Oh. We get people like that in here occasionally." The blonde's smile widens, arching her back a bit after getting a good look at my face. "Is there anything I can do for you, handsome?"

"No. I'm here to pick them up."

"Limo driver?" She giggles, and the sound grates on my nerves—it's too nasally—but I keep my smile polite.

"Party bus." Dalian and the female shift uncomfortably to my left, while the other man remains quiet. "I'm parked outside."

"Those are fun. You got a business card on—"

"Excuse me, miss." A man taps her shoulder, and she looks over. "I'm here with a city employees retirement party, table of fifteen, and we need some service. We've been sitting for twenty minutes now, and no one has come by. Can you help me find our server or the manager?"

Talk about divine interruption.

He turns and glances at the table, looking apologetic. "Sorry for the interruption."

"No worries." I wave them off. "Go ahead, miss. We're fine."

"Are you sure?"

"I am." The two turn and leave while my guards stand. My eyes shift to Dalian first, and then the others. "Get up."

"Who the fuck are you?" The one I don't know sneers before raising a beer bottle to his lips, emptying what's left, and then burps. Disgusting. "You got balls, kid. But I'm not the one you should be fucking with."

That makes me laugh. Loud. "Know your place, *old man.* This isn't your problem, but I can make it so."

"Who the fuck—"

"Ivan De Leon."

Recognition dawns on his face; I notice the subtle shake of his hand still holding the bottle. "I thought you said he was in Miami. That they didn't know about our arrangement."

"Interesting."

"I want no issues, De Leon."

"Name."

"Kyle Montgomery."

Arms dealer, but his business is mainly with the US military. I've never met the man but know plenty, and it makes sense in a way. While I deal more with the narcotics department—you can call it perico, yayo, or simply cocaine—it's the same thing, but Thiago's brought black-market weapons into our arsenal. Untraceable and handmade, the pieces coming out of the Philippines are shipped to us using the scraps from the family yard in Hialeah and are better than anything you can find in the country. We provide the metal, but the supplier is a true artist and can recreate anything the large companies produce for a fraction of the cost.

Montgomery knows this. Has wanted to buy from us, but Thiago dealt with and denied him.

That's the only reason I've never seen his face before today: I trust my brother and his judgment in the matter while I've been watching our deliveries through our ports.

"You have some explaining to do, Montgomery."

"I meant no harm."

"Yes, you did." Sliding out, I stand and fix the watch on my wrist. "Let's go. We have a lot to discuss."

"Me too?" the woman asks.

"All of you." Dalian's been quiet, too quiet, and I find him looking toward the emergency exit. So does one of my soldiers, and I give him a nod. Within seconds, the muzzle of a gun is at the back of the bastard's neck and his two companions pale and nearly yell out. "Draw attention to yourself, and I'll kill you here. Don't tempt fate."

"You can't touch me, Ivan. My uncle—"

"Made a grave mistake in trusting an irresponsible cunt like you." Before the last word slips past my lips, there's a loud commotion near the main stage, howling, and Dalian is struck at the base of his skull. At once he slumps forward, his face meeting the tabletop and his empty glass cracks at the impact.

Blood begins to pool, and the woman whimpers.

Montgomery is grabbed from behind while Israel handles Dalian.

"Miss, I suggest you don't make this hard on yourself and follow me outside. I'm not going to hurt you."

"I'm just an escort. He paid me to spend the weekend with him through an agency," the brunette pleads, tears brimming in her over-made dark eyes.

"And as long as that's true, then you have nothing to worry about."

IVAN

"**Y**OUR NAME, please."

The woman sitting across from me on a picnic table is shaking, tears running down her face. Those ten pounds of makeup have begun to melt and the mascara tracks make her look like shit, so I hold out a napkin and bottle of water. She doesn't grab them right away; it's smart to be wary, but I don't hurt women.

Never have and never will.

In our family, if a woman is to be dealt with, my mother or another trusted female does. That's always been the rule, but this time I take the lead while my parents arrive. They've caught a bit of traffic.

We're away from the other two: a still knocked-out Dalian, and Montgomery, who's tried to buy his way out of this mess.

Placing the items atop the table, I push them forward. Now she grabs them. "Thank you."

"No worries." I give her a few minutes to right herself. Standing from the table, I walk over to Kyle and remove his blindfold. I'm not worried she'll try to run, not in the Everglades. We've brought her deep enough that one freaked-out wrong turn will land you face to face with a gator, or worse, a constrictor. Both will kill her. Both these dominating species have overtaken the wetlands and grow to be huge and aggressive. "Kyle, I'm going to ask that you please stop talking. When I'm ready to deal with you or hear out your plans to make amends, I'll let you know."

"Ivan, please. Let's—" My knuckles meet the bridge of his nose while the second punch lands on his mouth, busting his lip.

"Not another word. Understood?" He nods. "Good." When I turn back around, she's standing but her eyes are not on us. Rather, she's looking at a decent-sized banded water snake slithering toward a wet area not far from her. "It's harmless and nonpoisonous."

"Snake."

"Sit down. It's only passing through." When she doesn't, I pick up the animal gently and walk over to a bush farthest from her. There, I release it and return to take my seat at the table. "Now can you sit?" She does. Still terrified. "Your name?"

"Cindy."

"All right, Cindy, let's make this quick." At her quick indrawn breath, I hold both hands up while maintaining some distance. She's on the opposite side of the table and to the left, and I'm more than okay with that. "I'm not going to hurt you, but there are questions I need answered."

"Then I can go?"

"Yes."

"Okay." She adjusts the suit jacket Israel gave her, closing it tighter around her front. The water and napkin are in front of her, unused. "Ask me anything."

"How do you know Dalian Uriel?"

Her brows furrow and her fists close, yet I notice her hands shaking. "Who's that?"

"That would be the unconscious man on the grass."

"Pero like, that's not the name he gave me or the agency. His I.D. reads Wilmer Santos." *Bingo.* Only the natives use "pero like" instead of "but like" on everything. Just like *irregardless* and *supposably.* The lingo in South Florida is different, and most outside of the locals don't know these idiosyncrasies. Are the words said and spelled incorrectly? Yes, but we understand, and that's all that matters.

"Where do you work? And is Cindy your real name?"

"Craving Sugar, and yes."

"And your last name?"

"It's Johnson."

"Cindy Johnson from Craving Sugar?"

"Yes, sir." Grabbing the bottle of water, she twists the top and pours a little onto her fingers, then dabs her eyes while looking away. All that does is further smear her makeup, but she carries on like nothing and I don't say anything either. The silence stretches for a few minutes before she releases a sigh and meets my eyes again. "At first, it was a sugar baby/sugar daddy dating website, but recently, they've expanded into escort services for those needing an event or weekend companion. Those short-term contracts make me the most money, and that's how I ended up here."

My fingers thrum on the wooden tabletop. "Is the company based in Miami?"

"Yes, but they take clients nationwide. I work in the Atlanta area. Born and raised there."

"And you reside?"

"There as well." *Liar.*

While I've heard of the website, her story is too convenient. I also haven't forgotten how she insulted the waitress at the strip club, once again using terminology only Miami girls say. However, I don't call her out on this. Instead, I'll let the brunette walk and hang herself later.

"You're free to go. Thank you for your assistance." Standing, I point at one of the men who's standing guard over Dalian. He jogs over at once. "Get her on a plane back to Atlanta. First-class, and make sure she's compensated well for her trouble."

"What's going to happen to them?" Cindy moves toward me, calmer now. "Is this about a girl named Amberlyn?"

My head snaps in her direction, eyes narrowed. "How do you know that name?"

Cindy points a shaky finger at Uriel. "He spoke about her shortly after picking me up. Wanted me to wear a red wig, but I denied his request. And then—"

"Then what?" I snap and she jumps, yet a hand on my arm makes me pause.

"Let me talk to her, mi niño. I got it," Mom says from beside me. "You handle those two, while we go get a coffee and something to eat."

I nod, gritting my teeth. "Take one of my men with you."

"Miguel will go with us. He's in the car waiting."

"Okay." Without taking my eyes off the woman, I bend down and kiss my mother's temple. "She doesn't leave until I'm satisfied with what she knows. I don't trust her."

"Of course, son." Mom pretends to clean something from my collar, her lips barely moving. "You know I'm protective of our girls."

"Thank you." Rising to my full height, I give her and Cindy my back while Israel ushers them to the awaiting vehicle. Dad hasn't said a word all this time, but I catch his eye and he gives me a nod. We wait in silence for a good fifteen minutes while my guard comes back, knowing the women are gone and won't hear any of this.

The area we are in is mostly closed off to the public and leads to larger bodies of water where you're more likely to find dangerous animals. Not that the entire park doesn't have wildlife everywhere, but the deeper you go off trails and into the marsh, the terrain changes and so do the encounters.

No barriers separate you.

No illusion of safety.

"Wake him up." My father does the honors, landing a solid kick to his face with his favorite pair of church shoes, breaking the idiot's nose. For an old man who uses a cane, he's still strong and his violent tendencies are slightly below his son's. Not far, though.

"Motherfucker," Dalian groans from the floor, twisting on the ground while blood drips from his nose. A hand comes up to cup his face but then halts midway. His eyes open, the fact he's on a patch of dry grass and not in a comfortable bed inside of an Atlanta hotel hitting him. As is the harsh sunburn growing across his face and neck, then lower to his bare chest.

I can see the recognition on his face, the slight shake of his frame.

"Get up." At my voice, his face pinches tighter. There's fear in his expression, but more pronounced is the anger. "Now."

"Fuck you, cabron." That earns him a foot to the neck, pinning him down and cutting off some of his airflow. Dalian sputters and tries to push it away, but my father doesn't budge. "Get off!"

"No, hijo de puta," Dad sneers before adding a little more pressure. It's entertaining to see him this pissed. It's been a while. Orlando De Leon is strong, loving, and above all else, protective of his family. The only reason he's relaxed a bit is because of my mother. She wants to relax and enjoy what's left of their lives, and he lives to not disappoint her. "Fucking scum. I should chop your head off and ship it to your uncle."

"They'll be reunited soon enough."

Dad's gaze snaps to mine, and his lips curl into a grin. "I trust you have a plan?"

"Was there ever any doubt?"

"You've always been the more creative one of the two. Your brother's more—"

"Straightforward in his approach." I match his smile, and the men here chuckle. "We each have our strengths, Viejo."

"You are my kids, after all." Cocky bastard puffs out his chest a bit. "I expect no less."

"Funny." Shifting my gaze to Israel, I wave him toward Dalian. "Stand him up. We need to have a little chat."

A whimper comes from just a few feet to the left of Israel, drawing my attention. "Is there a problem, Montgomery?"

"Please let me go."

"Why should I?" While my attention is on the arms dealer, my men stand an unsteady Dalian up, but not before Orlando elbows him in the gut twice. The Cuban president's nephew coughs and groans, then sputters out a pained *fucking shit* before my father steps back. "This is your chance to save yourself."

"I meant no disrespect, De Leon. That's something I need you to understand, please."

"Go on." Pulling my shirt over my head, I toss it to a soldier near me. Next, I remove my gold watch, two rings, and then stretch my arms out.

The ink on my skin glistens under the hot sun, the story on my body an homage to who and where I come from.

The island. Our culture.

Yet the scripture on my neck comes from an old poem my mother loves written by a famous Cuban author. It speaks of the land, the treasures unseen by the eyes of most, but for those that know of its beauty strive to hold close.

Montgomery swallows hard, the blood on his face mixed with sweat and he licks it off his lip. "They approached me with an offer too interesting not to entertain."

"Isn't that always the story." Stretching, I extend both hands back and feel a pop at each shoulder. Feels good. "Get to the point."

"I was told your family had been overthrown…" He trails off when my eyes narrow on him. I take a step forward and he flinches back, falling to his ass from his knees. "I'm just telling you what they said."

"They who?" The bracelet I've kept on shines in the sunlight, the black azabache beads at the end near the clasp drawing his attention. These stones are used heavily in Spanish countries to ward off the evil eye. Babies especially wear them after birth, and Thiago gave me this special one as a joke since I'm the baby of the family. *Asshole.* Yet it does come with a special extra that I've saved for this piece-of-shit family. "Give me a name."

"Jaime Uriel."

At that, I snort and meet Dalian's eyes. "You're nothing more than a puppet they use."

"Fuck you, De Leon."

"No, thank you."

"You won't kill me. Motherfuckers like you don't have the…*Christ,*" Dalian cries out at the end, bending at the waist after my father stabs him once in his stomach. One. That's all it took for a few tears to fall.

"Pathetic." Turning back to Kyle, I wave him on. "Finish the story. Jaime called you, I assume?"

"Yes," he whispers.

"Louder. So everyone can hear you."

"Yes, he called with President Rodriguez on the line listening in."

"The fuck did you say?" Dalian's face pinches tight from his position, but he still hasn't straightened up. "That can't be true. My brother wouldn't lie to me."

Dad meets my eyes briefly, his knuckles white as he grips the teak cane tighter.

"I'm not lying. I have a recording of the conversation in my office back in D.C." Little Uriel's face becomes red, angry, but when the muzzle of a gun is placed at the back of his neck, he's smart enough to keep those lips shut and lower himself to his knees. Montgomery, on the other hand looks troubled. Very much so. "I never questioned the call or how they got my phone number—things in this business move fast—but Jaime did ask me to be discreet. To not tell anyone about the call, not even his brother, as he supposedly knew and wasn't interested in the details."

"And why do you think that is, Dalian? Are you discardable?" No answer from the man. "Continue, Kyle. Tell me everything discussed."

"Of course." Again, he licks his blood-stained lips. "Jaime assured me there had been a takeover of the De Leon operations and that you and Thiago stepped down. That the business had been sold for a reasonable sum to him after a bit of forcible persuasion, but you'd be staying on as intermediaries between them and the suppliers for the time being. From my understanding, your family agreed to keep a member safe and that your next shipment, which includes Mac-10s and other military-grade weapons, will be here next week and would be mine. I already have a client waiting for these."

"That's a lie! You're in a bidding war with a South American country; I promised you the rights to it if you doubled your original offer."

"What else?" I ask, not giving much thought to Dalian's outburst.

"I'd be given first right's refusal to all shipments following this first purchase."

"Hmmm." Walking over to Dalian, I crouch down and meet his blood-shot eyes. "Wonder why they made you their bait? What made them betray you?"

"They wouldn't."

"Are you sure about that?" He's right, but I'm not going to tell him that. Betrayal stings on his face, this pain-filled look that comes from family cutting deep, but I do keep my smirk. "Sounds to me as though you've been set up."

"Lies. All lies."

"Are they, though? Is Cindy as easy to manipulate?"

"They'd never." Yet at the mention of her name, he twitches. "She's loyal."

Exactly. She's dirty, and I'd bet my left nut that's not her real name.

IVAN

"Y OU'RE DUMBER THAN you look, Dalian." Eyes narrowing, he tries to rebut, but I grip his chin tight. The force grinds his teeth and hollows his cheek, while I hold a hand toward my father. "Knife, please, and text Miguel."

"Here you go, son."

"Thank you." I grip the blood-stained gold handle, weighing and testing my hold. "You'll get this back in a minute."

"Kill me, and you'll never find out our plans for your bitch." It's muffled by my grip, but I understand Dalian clearly and refocus on him.

"Keep talking."

"You can't protect her from us, Ivan. We know her schedule." Spit dribbled out the side of his mouth, and I smear it against the opposite cheek in mocking. "When she wakes up. When she eats. Every fucking thing Amberlyn Ibarra does in her day-to day."

"So you say, but I also know those you hold dear."

"They'd never betray me." His defiance is almost admirable. "I trust my family."

"Okay."

"Okay?" he asks, confused by my lack of taking his bait. I've played this game too many times to fall for his bullshit.

"If you trust or don't, it makes no difference to me."

"Let me walk, and I'll give you the chance to save her." A different tactic. *Next, he'll beg like the bitch he is.*

"No." With my unoccupied hand, I flick open the blade Dad passed over and dig the tip into his cheek, carving out a T, then an I, and finally, an O. The letters once put together, say *tio*, the Spanish word for uncle, and if his body is ever found, or just the cheek area, they'll look toward his family. And while President Rodriguez is the catalyst, those letters stand for Thiago, Ivan, and Orlando: the three male De Leons he tried to fuck over.

"We already have a grip on her," he hisses through clenching teeth, trying to shift away, but my hold doesn't allow that. Blood drops seep from the wounds and onto my fingers. They're not deep enough to have an open flow, but *drip, drip, drip* they do. Nevertheless, I pat them to make sure they sting a little more before releasing his chin. "One call from me or my brother, and she'll be taken and shipped to another country. She'll be used as a pet. Used like a—"

"Isn't that the job of Karen Lopez? Stepsister of Henry Davila?" At my response, anger flashed through his eyes, nostrils flaring. "From my understanding, she's looking for her fiancé at the moment. Crying and begging for help, while you rent a hole to fuck."

"You won't get a word out of her. She's conditioned to be loyal."

"I'm not the one you should worry about when it comes to her or Cindy, Dalian." My smile grows and I bite my bottom lip, sending the asshole a wink. "The De Leon women are ruthless when betrayed."

"Amberlyn isn't claimed." That idiocy isn't worthy of a response and I tilt my head to the side, casually standing from my position and walking to his back. There, I watch him squirm like the rodent he is. Dalian goes from cocky to scared. Human nature never fails to bring in the fight-or-flight impulse at the right time, and I watch as his eyes bounce from man to man, landing on a crying, sniveling Montgomery.

The man is now praying, the front of his pants soiled, and the stench of piss hits just as a warm breeze sweeps through us. *Why do they always pee?*

Bending at the waist, I lower my head just enough to place my mouth beside his right ear. "Just so you know, it was easy to find you and the woman you paid to suck your dick. The tip given to me paid its dividend."

"How did you find us?"

"Ahhh. There you go." With two fingers, I undo the latch on the wrapped-twice-around-my-wrist bracelet and it falls open, exposing a long, flexible wire hidden within. It's sharp and thin, just long enough to reach around a person's neck from side to side, and after gripping each end, I pull it tight against Dalian's neck. "Finally, an intelligent question."

"Stop!" His reaction is automatic as my knee digs into his back and I begin to saw from side to side. The flesh gives under the stress, cutting a straight line across his skin with ease and then deeper through the first layer. "You can't. No mas!" Both hands try to grip the wire, but all that does is cut his fingertips. The slickness of each doesn't help him find purchase, and I watch from above as his face becomes redder and redder, reaching an almost purple tint quickly.

A chuckle escapes me, my grip tightening. "Knew you'd be begging soon enough."

"What do you want, Ivan?" It comes out in between coughing—choking—but I don't ease off. "Ask, and it's yours."

"To know everything. Talk, and we'll come to an agreement at the end."

"You pissed off Tio Rodriguez and he asked us to remove the threat to his regime." A little deeper and a tiny bit of blood squirts from the wound, his coughing causing more of his life's essence to flow. Dalian tries to bring a hand up to the area again but a quick tsk from me and it falls back to his thighs. "H-he wants you and Thiago dead."

"Keep talking."

"We agreed, with one condition." His chest shudders, and I ease the pressure.

"Go on."

"Jaime wants your operations, and I, Amberlyn."

"Why?" When he's not quick to respond, I begin the side-to-side motion again, ripping through a little more flesh. "Last chance."

"Did you know I met her at a city function a few years back?" No. I didn't, but don't say this. Instead, I raise a brow as a silent request to move on with his story. Dalian exhales roughly, reality finally sinking in to that thick head. "It was a charity fundraiser hosted by the police department and my brother dragged me along. He wanted me to meet someone. Turns out that those someones were the owners of Mariposa Bail Bonds and their daughter, who's set to take over in a few years.

"Why did he want you to meet?"

"Because he knew her family is close to yours, and Jaime has always wanted to own Miami. In his eyes, they were an in. She could lead me to your family, or at the very least, introduce us."

"But that didn't work out, did it." Not a question.

Yet before he can answer, there's a rustling near the trees where I released the small snake earlier, and our heads turn in that direction. Nothing moves for a beat and it's silent, too quiet before a head slithers out.

It's large and so is the attached body, larger than any snake I've seen in the past. However, with all the invasive species that call these lands home, I'm not surprised that at some point we'd end up here.

Years ago, during one of the worst hurricanes the state has seen, there was total destruction in the city of Homestead. In 1992, Andrew, a category 5 storm, tore through South Florida leaving behind a loss of power, structures, fatalities, and lastly, the escape of many exotic animals that made their way to the swamps they now call home.

The breeding facility that bred pythons and other countless snakes created a problem.

One that now has made the need for a snake hunting season a reality in these parts.

Yet, this isn't what I thought it to be at first glance. No.

More than likely from another problem we have in this state, a lesson human beings haven't learned. We're not meant to own exotic animals such as these. They are easy to handle when small, but a specimen this large…at the very least fifteen feet in length, will kill you easily.

A green anaconda stares at us but makes no further move. It's coiled now and still, tongue flicking out to catch us in the air just outside the tree line. Everyone stills while watching the animal.

"Go on, Dalian. Tell me why it didn't work out with Amberlyn?"

"We need to go. That snake—"

"Is not the biggest threat here. Finish."

The animal shifts its head, and the pathetic cunt whimpers, "I'll help you stop him."

"I'm not hiring, but you have ten seconds to start, or I'll feed you to it myself." Still too afraid to talk, I force the metal to dig through a little more; the flesh now truly bleeds. The wound isn't enough to kill, but he's sitting on that razor's edge where another thin cut will bleed him out. "I can make this easy on you, or drag it out to the point you'll claw at your flesh and tear it apart just to end it. Tell me, Dalian. Now."

"She wouldn't even dance with me." He's choking, breathing labored as panic sets in.

"Is that all?" My men take a few steps back as the large animal slithers closer but not enough to strike. This is a waiting game.

"Please." Wheezing. Hands scraping at the ground, trying to find purchase and move back, but fail. "No mas. Por favor."

"All she did was turn down a dance? That made her your target?"

"She couldn't muster more than a hello, while I couldn't pull my eyes away."

"People always want what they can't have. It's a sin."

"We need…" he coughs and blood splutters, falling to the ground by his knees "…please. It will kill. I don't want to die."

"But you will, knowing Amberlyn Ibarra is mine. That you were never enough." Dropping the end of the wire from one hand, I pull it hard with the other and Dalian falls forward. His body is spasming, his breathing labored while I move out of the way, but not before leaving him with a final thought. "Henry Davila was your downfall. You told him where you'd be, and he told me after your last phone call."

Then, as I back away, another predator makes its way slowly into the small clearing. The gator is clearly more than eight feet, reminding you of a prehistoric beast. His hiss is clear, a warning to those in his domain and the snake takes notice, raising its head. How they interact reminds me of Georgie and Kline in the lake behind my parents' home; one testing the other.

For a few minutes, neither moves.

Both sizing the other up, but to my surprise, it's the snake that backs off. And while it coils into itself by the trees it emerged from, the gator moves toward Dalian at a speed I'm impressed by.

His head looks our way, another warning to back off his meal and we do.

One foot at a time, until the animal feels comfortable and clamps his jaws on the barely-alive scum. Teeth digging in, it overpowers the man in one death roll, breaking bones and tearing flesh while the younger Uriel gives one final scream.

You see the moment his body stops—eyes vacant—and that's when I turn to leave.

If it eats him or not, I don't care.

If Dalian is dragged into the marsh and torn apart by the various animals there, so be it.

I call this divine fate.

Meeting Israel's eyes, I nod toward a passed-out Montgomery. *No wonder his crying stopped.* "Get him up and in the car. We'll be heading out soon."

"Yes, sir." Israel rounds up the others and while they carry Kyle away, I look at my father.

"Will you be okay while I'm gone?"

"We'll be fine." Dad's pensive for a moment. I can see he has questions.

"Go ahead and ask." Leisurely, we walk back toward the tourist trails and parking area. "What's on your mind?"

"Are you sure this is how you want to handle the situation with Amberlyn?"

"Do I want to be away from her? No. No, I don't."

"But—"

"But I'm doing the best I can to make sure that woman never knows fear or the pain of losing someone she cares about. Staying away *is* how I prove my love. The only thing I'm guilty of is being selfish in my belief that she'll be there when I come back."

He nods, rubbing his chin. "Will you be back after D.C.?" I shake my head. "Then where are you going?"

"I'm going to personally deliver some bad news to President Rodriguez."

"Do you need me with you?"

"No, old man." I bump his shoulder with mine. "This is something I have to do on my own."

"You're carrying too much weight on those shoulders, kid. What happened five years ago was not your fault."

"We all have different points of view, and mine sees a picture that others don't."

"And the truth is, you're being stubborn. Let it go, and live."

"I am living." *I'm building our future.*

IVAN

I'M SITTING INSIDE Amberlyn's living room later that evening, watching as the sun begins to set while flicking my eyes to the front door every few minutes. The silence inside her home is comforting and brings forth a sense of peace I've been missing and couldn't help but return to.

Being here was never in my plans. Not until I could offer her what she deserves.

And maybe my father's right and I'm carrying five years' worth of recrimination, but failing my family isn't something I can get past. Did I save my father's life? Yes, but at the same time, I made a costly mistake that led to Thiago's arrest.

Stepping outside the Versailles Restaurant in Coral Gables after a last-minute fishing trip, I was full and tired. My job today was simple: guard the two old men talking shop and about my brother's ascension to head of the family. This man is a client, someone who buys large quantities of perico for private consumption while entertaining in the Bahamas.

Cocaine is his drug of choice, and we have the best quality. With imports from Colombia and the UK, the De Leons have managed to overthrow all other vendors while evading local police and DEA.

"So you'll have my order in two weeks?" We're at the client's trunk now, my eyes surveying the parking lot. "I know it's last minute, but there's a private swingers meetup I'm hosting and—"

"Done deal. You'll get it two days before." Dad extends a hand while with the other, he accepts a briefcase the older gentleman pulls from the inside.

The black case has a number lock, and I raise a brow. "I'll need the code to verify."

"Of course." He pulls out his phone and shows me the screen. 0916

Once the last digit is turned and set, the latch disengages, and I open the top. There's an envelope inside and after a rough count, I know the agreed fifty-percent deposit is there, if not a little more.

He'll get his briefcase back with the merchandise.

After my nod, Dad gives him a final handshake and steps back, a clear signal that we are done here. No further words are exchanged and the client leaves, getting inside his BMW while we turn and I press the fob to unlock our doors.

We each make it to our door; my father's hand is on the handle when the first shot rings out in the parking lot. Immediately, I move to his side and drop us to the ground, my body covering his.

The second round hits close, too close, and I pull my Glock from the back waistband of my jeans and fire in the shooter's direction. "Did the first one hit you?" I ask, keeping my voice low.

"No. At least, I don't feel anything."

That's not reassuring, but I focus on keeping him alive. Adrenaline courses through me. My hand wants to shake, but it's not fear. Not for myself, at least. Mom's face comes to mind, and I take a second to breathe in deep through my nose, then exhale.

I can't allow anything to happen to us. Mom won't mourn us.

Neither will Amberlyn.

She's been on my mind more and more as of late. I've always noticed how beautiful she is, how sweet, but have kept my distance. Haven't *allowed more than innocent flirting while everyone is oblivious to my attraction.*

Focus, asshole. Kill the asshole.

Lifting my head, I scan the area the first two shots came from and make out a pair of dark glasses, a mistake from the shooter as they reflect the moonlight, glinting as a target. I don't hesitate, moving a little to the side so I can get better aim.

We exchange fire at the same time.

His next fire zips right by my ear, while I empty my entire clip into the motherfucker. There's a specific sound that bullets make when hitting flesh, this low, almost thud before his body hits the ground. However, as he does, one more round dislodges and my father screams from beneath me.

Panic sets in and I drop my gun, not giving a fuck about anything but making sure he's okay.

"My leg, Ivan. Hijo de puta got my leg."

It was my bullet—my panic and forgetting to call for cleanup—that eats at me. That body with my bullet holes was dumped in Thiago's home and pinned on him because I forgot a simple rule.

He lost five years because of something drilled into our heads since we were old enough to hold a weapon.

An oversight like that is unacceptable.

Killing those threatening my woman and family is how I repay my sins.

The sun sets lower in the sky, filling the night with various shades of orange and pink with touches of purple mixing in. It grows darker by the minute, and I look over at the clock on the wall, noticing it's just after eight and she should be walking through the door at any moment. Later than usual, but the calendar on her fridge says there were errands to run.

My sirenita had mundane things to do and the fact makes me smile. It's what I want for her.

That the most she worries about is buying groceries, picking up meds from the pharmacy, and sometimes getting tires rotated on her car.

The latter is something I've taken care of for her in the past and failed to do so this time. It bothers me a bit, but I ignore it in lieu of the bigger picture: my sirenita is safe.

She's independent. So beautiful and strong.

I need her more than she needs me. A thought that's steeped in truth, and I can't deny a small part of me hates it. Abhor that her world continues without me, while mine revolves around hers.

I don't doubt her love for me, but my obsession—this need mauling at my chest—overshadows anything Amberlyn feels for me. It's what brought me here instead of stopping at my parents' home to handle the Cindy—or whatever the fuck her name is—situation. Why I barely showered in my penthouse overlooking the South Beach waters and didn't hesitate to unlock her door and sit in this oversized chair while waiting for Amberlyn to return.

That is what this kind of love does to a man. I can't stay away, no matter what vows I make for myself.

I'm crazy and irrational. Near desperate to feel her again, but won't.

Not until I can come back and place a diamond on her finger. Because I will. I'll lay the corpses of our enemies at her dainty feet before sliding my ring where it belongs.

For eternity. *Till death never do us part.*

Keys jiggle in the door and the knob turns then, her small fingers pushing it open while my heart picks up its beat. She doesn't see me; there's a couple of bags in her hands, nothing heavy, but when I stand, her eyes dart my way.

My mermaid screams, yet I'm proud of the way she quickly grabs her gun and aims at my chest while dropping what looks to be paper goods. "Don't make another move."

"It's me, bebe. Just me." At the sound of my voice, her shoulders drop, and the gun ends up pointing at the ground. Her chest, though, is rising and falling fast. Her lips part, words sitting on the tip of her tongue, but my sweet girl has gone mute. "Are you okay? Do you need to sit?"

I take two steps when the hand not holding the gun darts up. "Stop right there."

"Babe, you need to sit. I'll bring everything to the kitchen."

"Don't. Move."

"Okay." I'll give her a minute or two, but that's my limit. "Do you need some water?"

"Ivan?"

"Yes."

"Please grab my bags outside the door. I'm going to need a minute."

It's her professional tone, the one she uses while making phone calls or talking with clients. I don't call her out on it. Instead, I give Amberlyn a small smile and do what she needs me to. "Of course."

"Thanks." Without another word, she turns and heads toward her bedroom, closing the door once inside.

"That went well." Walking to her door, I grab the bags outside and head for her kitchen, depositing them on the counter. Then I go back for what she dropped and begin to put everything away.

One thing I learned soon after we began to date; my girl is organized.

Like the kind you see on social media with special containers for their eggs and orange juice. She rotates her stock, everything needs to be front-faced, and the newest in the back. It's a quirk I find adorable, and also know better than to mess with.

So I do as she does and make sure it's to her standards, with the shopping bags put away to recycle later.

My eyes shift to the clock and realize that thirty minutes have passed and she still hasn't come out yet. I worry. I also didn't miss the fact she took her gun with her. Not that I'm worried she'll harm herself—Amberlyn will shoot me, not herself—yet I can't help but want to check on her.

"Order dinner first." Pulling my cell out, I open my texts and send one to Junior downstairs.

> Pick up two pizzas from the place three blocks down. Tell them it's for De Leon and they know what we'll want. Get dinner for yourself, too. ~Ivan

His response is immediate. Not even thirty seconds later.

> On my way. Thank you, Boss. ~Junior

> Please leave it outside the door and knock once. I'll message you again before leaving. ~Ivan

Tossing my cell atop the counter, I make my way to her room. It isn't locked when I test the handle, turning it easily in my hand before I push it, and poke my head inside. She's nowhere to be found. The bed's empty, *but* then I hear it…

Water.

Her shower is on, and my naked and wet sirenita is inside.

I don't think twice about removing my clothes or making my way over. I'm hard and need to feel her against me.

Steam billows when I open the wooden door, yet it's the sight of her lithe form through the glass door that I focus on. The sight consumes yet lifts every single weight I carry while filling me with a different kind of demand.

That I take.

Own. Love. Cherish.

"Fuck, bebe." It leaves me on a pained groan and her head snaps in my direction, those piercing eyes meeting my own. There are so many emotions in them: anger and love being the dominating ones.

Those I can handle. Understand them.

But the tinge of disappointment that lingers behind the others is almost too much.

"Are you going to come in, or just watch?" The sassiness in her tone helps to ease this ache in my chest and I smirk, knowing my grin is one of the things she likes.

Amberlyn has always loved making me smile or laugh. Claims my eyes crinkle at the corners and it makes me adorkable. Her word, not mine.

Crossing to her shower, I open the glass divider and step inside, welcoming the hot water on my tired frame. It's been days since I've gotten a good night's sleep. It's been days of nonstop hunting and removing threats while finding every hiding hole and blocking them from our enemies.

I have one more Cuban sicario to find, but my gut tells me he's no threat.

Jaime Uriel will die by my hands.

I'm going to hand over the women to Luna, Amberlyn, and my mother.

All before decapitating the snake that President Placido Rodriguez is.

And all that while helping a country rediscover its footing and monetary position in the world.

"You look exhausted, Ivan." Her voice is low, almost tired, but I detect no anger. No resentment. "What's going on?"

"A lot." Reaching around her, I turn the water a little hotter and turn us, her back to my front. She fits perfectly there. Those sinuous curves mold against me and each shiver, every indrawn breath moves through me. *She's my heaven.* "Things I never want you to see."

"I'm not as delicate as you think I am."

"I know." Doesn't make things any better for me. If anything, I worry more. "But I've always wanted a different world for you."

"What about what I want?" While she keeps a calming tone, I can feel her strength. That fire draws me in, forcing my will to become one with hers. And while I'm a dominant man and I'll admit I'm hard to deal with at times, this woman owns me.

Turning her in my arms, I wrap both arms around her back and pull her in, chest to abdomen. Heads tipped toward each other. "What do you want, Sirenita? What do you dream about?"

"A life with you."

Four simple words. So honest. Pure.

Yet, they destroy me where I stand, and I can't stop myself from taking that sweet berry mouth in a passionate kiss. Our lips crash, and I'm reborn while branding her taste into my DNA.

Her tongue sweeps across my bottom lip and I shiver, yet my hold never wavers. If anything, it tightens while moving from her lower back to supple hips. They fit perfectly in my hand, so sexy—

The rain shower feature turns on and I pause, smiling down at her. "Did you switch it mid-kiss?"

"Guilty."

"Bad Mermaid," I growl against her lips, not upset in the least. This is something I've enjoyed about us—the ease and comfort to switch from playful to ravenous to nearly demonic with yearning. "Am I not enough to hold your attention? To blind you with need?"

"Ivan, you've always been my everything."

"Motherfuck, bebe." That's all I can say. No words would ever suffice, and I show her instead. Bending my knees, I drag my hands to her thighs and lift her and then tap the skin there. Amberlyn understands and wraps her legs around my waist while her back meets the still-cool-to-touch tile away from the still-running showerhead.

Her tan skin looks beautiful against the white. More so, when she arches, offering me her chest while gyrating in search of my dick. "I need you just as bad. Why can't you understand that?"

Dropping my forehead to hers, I try to remember all the reasons why we should wait. How I don't want to add another reason for her to hate me, but then Amberlyn sneaks a hand between our bodies and grips me, fist tight.

One stroke, and I growl. This animalistic sound builds in my chest, shakes every muscle in my body, and I pin her hips with mine, forcing her fingers to cease moving. She's trapped, yet I don't know if that's worse.

A sinful groan slips from her swollen lips. She's rubbing against her hand and my cock, searching for a release that belongs to me. "This is right. See that."

"Of that, there's never been a doubt, Mermaid."

"Then why stop." She's soft skin and warm eyes, so eager for me to impale her—wring an orgasm from her tight body.

"Because tomorrow I'm leaving again."

While her fingers flex around my girth, she cups my face with her other hand. "Will you be safe?"

"Yes." I throb against her palm, balls drawing tight. There's nothing I want more than to be buried deep inside her warm cunt.

"Will you come back?"

"Always."

"Then fuck me, papi. We'll figure out the rest later."

I don't respond. Can't. Not without blurting out four little words, and she deserves the world, not to be told in the heat of the moment and later abandoned.

The day I tell her is near. So close.

And while my lips mouth the words against the skin of her throat, loving the sweet flesh there with nips, I pray she sees my sacrifice. How much I adore her.

As if she understands, Amberlyn grips the hair at the back of my head and holds me tighter to her. "Ivan, I—"

"No words, mami. Just feel me." Lower, and my teeth drag against the top of her breast before attaching myself to a pretty pink tip. Her nipples throb against my tongue, swelling a bit, and I bite down hard enough to draw a short cry from her. "That's it. Let me take care of you."

Pulling her in deeper, I tease the sensitive tip with my tongue and then rake my teeth over it before applying the same attention to the neglected tit. Goose bumps rise on her skin. Her eyes become hooded. *Motherfucking perfection.*

My hands wander across her skin from ass to thigh and then back up before resuming the same path. My mouth leaves open-mouthed kisses across her breasts and then I suck hard, bruising the skin right above each nipple so she remembers me every time she looks in the mirror.

I do the same to the area between them and then back up to her neck where I bite down hard enough to break the skin a little. She screams, loosening her grip on me, and I position my cock between slick lips.

Hot. Wet. Heat.

She's velvety against me, feels so good, and I slide through her labia again, and again, her clit throbbing against my head on each pass.

Amberlyn is wet, and I'm drenched in her—us—the bead of pre-come and her juices mixing as I pull a deep moan from her. The sound so fucking decadent, I pause with the tip at her opening and breathe in deep.

Ambrosia, her name is Amberlyn.

"Need you inside me, papi. I'm so wet for you." Between the heat of the shower, her flushed skin, and those dirty words…

I slam in deep and hold still, knees nearly buckling when her walls stroke me. They pulse and pull me in deeper, her sharp cry and the way her hands grip my arms—nails digging into the skin—

"Motherfuck, beautiful." I'm breathing hard, trying to regain control, but I'm lost in the feel of her. She's slick, so fucking tight, and I take hold of her right hip with one hand while the other grabs her neck, fingers flexing as she swallows hard.

Those sinful eyes darken and her tongue sweeps across her bottom lip. Tempting. Pushing.

I pull out a few inches and stab in again, just short strokes and her eyes roll back, the walls of her sex tensing. They clamp around me, try to pull me in deeper, but I don't stop.

"More." Desperation sweeps across her features, thighs shaking while she tries and fails to gyrate in my hold. Instead, I press her harder against the wall, loving the small whine she emits. "Please, Ivan."

"Say you're mine. Only mine."

"There will never be anyone but you." No hesitation. Just her love open for me to see—feel.

Looking away is an impossibility and so is getting air into my lungs; I'm drowning in the open emotions clear on her face, and it's a heady yet humbling combination. Yet I never pause; I'll show her with my actions just how much she means to me.

And even as my chest burns, I thrust in deeper while grinding against her clit, forcing deep moans from the back of her throat. Those sweet orbs never move from mine but watch me as I take in how she falls apart a stroke at a time until I'm left with a quivering mess.

"Good girl." Another tight flex of her walls and I give her what she needs, stroking in deep this time while shifting my gaze between us. I'm watching her juices coat my cock, her upper thighs, while I stretch her in the most beautifully obscene way. It looks nearly painful, but when our stares connect again, the look of rapture on her gorgeous face tells a different story.

This is us without restraints, and I give in to my baser instincts; I fuck my mermaid brutally without reprieve. I don't stop or breathe; all I can focus on is the way she grips me and the slick juices that bathe my cock in claiming.

Because for as much as I own her, I'm hers.

We don't look away from each other, lips hovering as we inhale the other's exhale. I can almost taste her unique sweetness in the air around us while pistoning in and out of her pussy. A pussy that's squeezing just a little tighter.

"I'm close, Ivan."

"I know," I hiss through clenched teeth while she clamps down again. A small wave of pleasure crests over her—it's almost too tight to move—

but I buck my hips hard enough to move her up the wall before sliding down hard on my cock. "Come for me, Mermaid. Let go."

"Oh, God!"

"That's it. *Fuck*, bebe." The moment I ease my hold on her hips, she bucks against me, matching my every move. She's wild and lost in her pleasure, taking from me what she needs. "Give me what's mine."

My name falls from her mouth like a prayer while her muscles seize momentarily, her walls making it difficult to move while her orgasm takes her under. I give her a few seconds, ten at the most.

"Papi!" she screams, clinging to me as I pump in time with each pulse of her walls, chasing my own release. It's there, hovering close, and when the next rush of wetness almost forces my dick out of her, I lose control.

I'm almost feral, lip curling back as I force her to ride me, back sliding against the wall as I fill her with my come. Rope after rope, mixing with her own until the combined mess slides down my shaft and skims my balls.

And still, I ride her a little more until she's slumped against me, and this time, when my knees shake, I lower us to the shower floor. I let her curl up in my lap while I kiss her temple, my hands stroking her back and arms while the water soothes our muscles.

There's still so much to say, to talk about, but for now, I just want to stay like this and close my eyes.

Because when I open them again, it's time to tell her the truth.

Amberlyn

WE'RE SITTING ON the living room floor with our food spread out on the coffee table while I contemplate if eating a fourth slice of my favorite pizza is smart. It's sausage, pepperoni, black olives, and lastly…*pineapple*. Some might call it weird, but it's my thing and this man knows my weaknesses.

He's clever, I'll give him that.

Favorite food and cold beer? Check.

Warm guava cake and a slice of molten lava to split? Check.

Organized pantry? Double-check with a chef's kiss attached.

No shame in the fact I double-checked the moment we got dressed and he grabbed our food from a quiet Junior. At the time, I needed something— a few extra seconds to center me after the intimacy inside the shower.

Because even though he tries to hide it, Ivan let his guard down, and it was his openness that crumbled my walls. I couldn't deny the pull when he's being open and sweet—his actions showing me what he hasn't said with words.

"You know you want another slice. Go for it, Mermaid." He's smiling and more relaxed than the man I found sitting in my dark living room. Sure, sex is a great de-stressor, but it's more than that. I just wish I knew what the more was.

"Shut it."

"Make me."

"You more than anyone know I can hold my own." My quip elicits a foreign response, not the playful banter I expected. What I got was a man who put his sandwich down and grabbed me, placing me astride his lap as if I were a doll he can manipulate to his liking.

And as much as it's unwanted at the moment, my reaction makes me blush.

His strength—the way he can hold and bend me—has always been a turn-on.

"Behave, Sirenita."

"I've always been a saint, papi. The devil in this relationship is you." He tenses at the word *relationship* but before I can seize the opportunity and call him out, Ivan places a finger over my lips.

"Eat. We'll talk after."

"Promise?"

"Yes."

"Okay." Grabbing another piece, I bring the cheesy, salty goodness to my lips and take a big bite. Ivan, on the other hand, resumes eating his cold-cut sub while giving me indulgent looks here and there. Almost as if he enjoys spoiling me, but there's still something off.

Not negative, more like a secret I'm yet to be made aware of.

Once I'm down to the crust, I toss it on my plate and pat my stomach. "No mas."

"Overate?"

"Thanks to you!" With mock indignation, I slap his chest. "Go for it, Mermaid."

"Your imitation of me is ridiculous at best." His chest rumbles with a laugh while the fingers of his right hand skim up my bare thigh. There's also the flex of his cock beneath me, pushing against my bottom. One, twice...three times, and I can't help but blush. "Is that how I sound to you?"

The question is simple enough, yet I'm squirming. *He's doing this on purpose.* "No."

"This I got to hear."

"Not really." I try to move from his lap, but Ivan holds me in place while thrusting up. "I'm just going to put the leftovers away. Give me two minutes."

"I'll let you get up if you answer me."

Bastard. "To me, it's sexy," I say, voice low while trying to avoid his eyes, but the man is having none of it and with the tip of two fingers under my chin, he forces our stares to connect.

"Don't be embarrassed. To me, you're my kryptonite."

Why is this man so confusing? Why can't he just be straightforward?

I can't judge him based on actions when one minute he's ignoring me, and the next, worshipping me. When he caters to my pleasure and then lets small truths slip out that knock the proverbial floor from under me.

Buck up and ask him. It's the only way.

"Ivan, I—"

"I can't stay away from you, sweetheart," he says, tone gravelly. Just like when he's about to come, holding me a little tighter while breathing out a low *fuck* against my ear. "I'm tired and ready for more than what we've been these last few years."

"Why do I feel like there's a 'but' coming?"

"But there's something I need to take care of first."

"Does this have to do with where you're going after you leave me?" Ivan nods in response. "Does this have to do with the family? With all those trips to Cuba?"

"It does."

"Hmmm." For a few beats, we stay in silence, neither saying what we want. He's holding back, while my mind is running a thousand miles a minute. Yet, I can't help but come back to one thought. *She's nothing more than an obligation.*

She's nothing more than an obligation.

An obligation.

"Ask me."

His warm voice pulls me back to the present. "I'm sorry."

"I said, ask me. Anything, Sirenita...I promise to answer as much as I can."

"Why?" That's the only thing that comes out. A lump forms in my throat right after, those same emotions I've been pushing back—burying deep in the darkest recesses of my soul—slamming into me with the power of a wrecking ball. For a second, I'm back in that moment and listening to the man I love more than my own life talk about me as if I'm a nuisance. A pesky bug he tolerates. "How could you say that about me? Us?"

"Because I knew you were listening." It's his truth; I can respect that, but it stings worse knowing he said it to hurt me. I try to stand, though my legs are shaky. Once again, I'm kept in place by his arm around my midsection. "I'm an asshole, bebe. I know that and I accept all the fault here..." Ivan's warm breath is on my neck a second before he leaves a kiss over the bite mark from earlier "...but I need you to believe me when I tell you it's a lie. That all I was trying to do is push you away while I settled a few things."

"Settled things?" While I'm not okay with this, the hurt has lessened. It's becoming anger, a little resentment, but then it dies when I truly take in his expression.

Because I see him. Always have.

Ivan De Leon is loyal and protective, especially over those he loves. I've seen it firsthand, have been there when those walls came down and his family was threatened. His father. His mother. But it all came to a head when Thiago went to jail and at the age of twenty-one, he was stepping into the role of boss and righting wrongs that he was never at fault for to begin with.

I was there then. And damn everyone to hell, I'll be here now no matter the outcome.

Because that's what you do when in love. We give and give and give without asking for anything in return.

"Who's in danger, Ivan? Is there anything I can do to help?"

Lip curling up at the corner, he taps my nose. "I appreciate the offer, but we both know I'd never allow you to put yourself in danger. Least of all for me."

"You're worth it to me."

"I'm going to come back for you, but I have sins to atone for first."

Those words throw me back; I've heard them before.

"Ivan?" I'm shocked to find him outside the bail bonds office, leaning against my car after work. There's no one else in the parking lot; my parents left an hour ago while I finished filing some reports. "Is everything okay?"

"No." He exhales roughly, the billowing smoke from his cigarette swirling around him. He taps the end, breaking the ashes, and watches as they meet the ground before scattering in the wind. "The verdict came in today."

"I heard." And I did. It was all my parents could talk about. They were trying to see if bail could be posted while the lawyers appealed the decision.

Because of his family ties, no one was surprised, but Thiago has no prior conviction, or charges, and that goes in his favor. That, and the evidence presented was trash and anyone with two working neurons can see it. Then, there's the sentencing, which has been pushed back to a few weeks from now as they decide his fate.

Because of that, they can plea for a release while the appeal is presented.

No one thinks it'll work, but there's nothing to lose for trying.

"Had I not been stupid enough to leave evidence at the scene, none of this would be happening."

Leaning against my car beside him, I lean my head on his arm. "You mean the corpse of the man who tried to kill you and Orlando? You did the right thing and saved your lives, Ivan."

"It's not that simple."

"The blame is on the hitmen and whoever hired him. That's who should be paying."

Ivan's hazel eyes meet mine while a cruel smirk grazes his lips. "They will, Sirenita. Their lives will atone for my sins."

Suddenly, fingers snap in front of my face, and I find Ivan giving me a quizzical brow. "Lost you there. Are you okay?"

"Why are you punishing yourself for something that happened over five years ago?" I say instead as things click into place. The extra hours at work, the constant travel—his constant jumping in to take care of everything and everyone over the last few years, but it's worse since Thiago got out of prison. "You're still paying for something you're not responsible for, papi."

"I'm not—"

"You are." Shifting, I turn and straddle him before cupping his face. Immediately, he nuzzles my palm and I melt. That single action takes away any question or doubt; he does care. Yet, there's a piece of the puzzle I'm missing an answer for: me. "You did it when they locked up Thiago and you're doing it now. Stop hurting yourself."

"Bebe, I promise I'm okay. There's never a need for you to worry about me." There's a stubborn set to his jaw that I'm all too familiar with; he's shutting the conversation down. "Everything will be over soon, and I'll be back to fix this."

"Fix what?"

"Can you wait for me?" My nod in agreement isn't because I'm afraid to make him angry, but because I'm picking my battles instead. My love for him won't allow me to do anything but be what he needs, and I'll push, but not right now. "Thank you."

"I've always been your friend first, Ivan. That's not going to change."

"You're too good for someone—" He's cut off by the ringing of his phone on the countertop, and by the dark look that crosses his face, he's not happy. Ivan taps my thigh and I get up, walking toward the device, and pick it up. The screen reads *Israel* and I toss it over before picking up our mess. "What did you find?"

I try not to listen and give him space, but in between cursing and now pacing, there are a few things that stick out. This is also when he finishes getting dressed, and I miss seeing his tattoos immediately.

Hacker.

Leave tonight.

No D.C. and change of plans.

Dead.

And when he turns around to face me, I know this is where we part. Not as heavy as last time, and I'm somewhat at peace for the first time since my best friend's wedding.

"Promise me you'll call, Ivan. That's non-negotiable."

"Will it help you if I do?"

"Yes."

"Then you have my word." Ivan walks toward me with purpose and without another word, steals the air from my lungs with his kiss. It feels different from all the others before; I taste his passion, but behind it, there's something deeper. An emotion he's kept hidden but is now giving me a tease of.

His tongue runs across my bottom lip before biting down on the abused flesh. He nibbles, drawing a moan from me, and then steps back.

Ivan appraises me from head to toe, his want palpable, before turning for the door. Hand on the handle, he pauses. "You never answered my question, Mermaid."

"About?"

"My voice." The mirth in his voice tugs at my lips. "Tell me."

"Like sex and chocolate."

I hear his amused chuckle as he walks out, but what's important is his *wait for me, love* before the door closes.

FOR THE LAST forty-eight hours I've been on autopilot, reliving moments from his visit while going through the motions for those around me. I've also been going through my contacts in four precincts and haven't found a single hair of Karen Lopez's fiancé.

No one knows who her fiancé is.

There are no records of Ramon Valle being detained, much less arrested.

Not even a friend or family member on the news demanding answers, which leads me to believe I was right all along. This case is full of blaring warning signals and lies.

As if on cue, my office line rings. I look over, and it's Detective Uriel, and it's also not the first time he's tried to get a hold of me over the last few days. His last voicemail came hours after Ivan left my home, and his speech was a little slurred.

"You have to help me, Amberlyn. It's your duty and my—"

The recording stopped there, but the short message left me unsettled. More than when we met face to face; Uriel came off as scared.

"Are you going to pick that up, or do I forward your line to the front?" Mom asks, taking a seat across from me. Her eyes are on the paperwork I'm going through. "You've been off for days, kiddo. Talk to me."

"I don't know why I'm wasting my time with this case." A frustrated huff leaves me, and I crane my neck from side to side, the crick there growing more pronounced as of late. I'm beat. "If I could find this man, I'd feel better. Know that there's no danger—"

"Did you tell Ivan about this?"

"No."

"Why?" Mom gives me a pointed look. "You know he wouldn't hesitate to help you."

"We're on break." It's a weak excuse and total bull crap, and by the look she gives me, Mom knows this too. "Or maybe I just didn't get the chance. There was so much going on when I last saw him and I. . .*what*?"

"Like the hickey on your neck that you're failing to cover up with that scarf?"

"Mom!"

"What? You think I'm blind, or stupid?"

"It's not that." The phone rings again, but this time it's Karen's number and I hold a finger up. "Mariposa Bail Bonds. This is Amberlyn speaking."

"Can I please speak with Amberlyn? It's an emergency."

"Karen, it's me."

"I know." Voice low. So meek. I can also make out a male speaking nearby and the slamming of something, and my brows furrow. I also decided then to attend the call through the speaker option. "Is there any way we can meet today? Do you..." her breath hitches, the sound a little scared "...can we meet today?

My eyes meet Mom's, and she's shaking her head at me.

"My schedule is full today, but I am working on your case." Mom leaves for a second but comes rushing back with Dad on her heels. His mouth opens to ask what's going on, but his wife's hand slapped over his mouth prevents that. "I'm actually waiting on a phone call from a private investigator who's been helping me as a favor."

All lies, but she doesn't know that.

"Oh. Okay." Still off, she sounds nothing like the woman who came here begging for help. "Do you have any new information? Has anyone contacted you? His family?" A choking sound comes from the background at the word *family*, but it's covered by a sudden sob. "Karen, what's going on? Are you okay?"

"Yes." Sniffle. "It's just all so hard. I miss him."

"Understandable and expected, but please know I'm doing the best I can to help."

"Thank you." She mutters something that sounds like *no one can save us*, which my parents also pick up on. Dad grabs a notepad from my desk and writes something down while Mom grabs her cell and begins to record the conversation. "What you're doing means so much to me. No one else has given me any answers or even looked into this mess. I just want my love to come home."

"Let me call the investigator and see if anything has come up. If so, can you meet—"

"Please. I'll meet with you anywhere and anytime."

"Okay, Karen. I'll call you if I hear anything."

"Thank you, Amberlyn. For everything."

The call disconnects and our expressions mirror each other: worry.

"Something else is going on here, kid. Her reaction and wording make me think she's being forced into whatever this is." Dad scratches his jaw and turns the notepad around to me. "Call him."

"You think it's necessary?"

"If you don't, I will."

"Okay." At this point, I agree. Luna's uncle would be the best person to call. "Do we alert the De Leons, too?"

"Get ahold of Ivan or his parents. They need to know just in case."

"In case of what?" I ask. For the first time since meeting Karen and the detective, I feel a frisson of fear. "What do you suspect?"

Mom places a hand on Dad's arm while giving me a small smile. "Because I'd bet money this is an attempt by the feds to gain information or—"

"Or what, Mom?"

"Or an enemy trying to get close, mi niña. They might feel as though you are their in."

Amberlyn

"**G**OOD TO SEE you, Edgar," I say, bending at the waist to kiss Luna's uncle on the cheek. We're inside a restaurant owned by the De Leon boys, where the staff here knows me and a waitress is quick to place a Materva soda in front of me before giving Edgar his coffee. "Have you had lunch yet?"

He chuckles. "Already ahead of you. They're cooking my vaca frita as we speak."

"Damn, that sounds good." Neither of us has a menu.

"You thinking of ordering one?"

"No. I don't need to put in an order." There's only one thing I eat each time I'm here, and that's not changing today. "The imperial rice is all I ever get, and I'm not about to break tradition."

"Sounds good." Edgar smiles at a waitress while waving her over. She's not more than halfway to us when he points at me. "I'll take the vaca frita to go but blame this one for tempting with the arroz imperial. All. On. Her."

"Men." Jenny laughs. The older woman has been around for years.

Before I met the family. "Always blaming women, when they're the ones with constant cravings. Right, mi niña?"

"Amen." I hold a hand up and she high-fives it, giving Edgar a huff. All in good fun, but the man pouts until she smiles and then leaves to put in the added order.

"So."

"So," we say in unison, which I snort at. "This isn't a social call, and you know it. Might as well get to the point and enjoy our meal after? Sound good?"

"Go for it, kid. What do you need help with?" Edgar has been with the Miami Dade Police Department for years; he's respected and has the kind of in I need to get information on Detective Uriel. "By the way, is Ivan aware of this meeting? You know I'm loyal to the family."

"No. And I'm also not sure if what I'm going to tell you is cause for worry or not."

"Do you plan on telling the De Leons either way?"

"Yes. I haven't heard back from Ivan, but my next stop is Maritza or Orlando, depending on what you have to say."

"What's going on?" he asks, leaning forward in his seat while every few minutes sliding his gaze to the entrance. Edgar is in uniform, not sure if on duty or just got off, but the cop in him is ever vigilant. "Are you in trouble?"

"That's what I don't know." Opening my oversized purse, I pull out an envelope and hand it over. "The man in this file is missing, and his fiancée came asking for help. She believes that through my connection, I can find the detained prisoner that no one has ever heard about. Detective Uriel—"

"Has that asshole contacted you?"

"Yes. Multiple times over the same missing person." Tilting my head toward the file, I purse my lips. "The report and info are inside, all given to me by him and the fiancée, but something is off."

"You're not a private investigator."

"My thoughts exactly."

"I know him, and he's rotten. Jaime and his family hate the De Leons." *Fuck.* My gut instincts were right, and they're trying to use me against them. And right before I convey that, Edgar laughs at something, and I am lost. "Those motherfucking snakes."

"Excuse me?"

"Amberlyn, the person you've been looking for doesn't exist." That sinking feeling I had earlier returns, my eyes studying the grainy picture of the man he's pointing at. Then, he turns the page and pulls out one given to me by Karen of herself with whom she claims is Ramon, hugging her. "The person in this picture is Dalian Uriel, sweetheart."

"What the hell? Uriel?"

"Detective Jaime Uriel's younger brother." Edgar pulls out his phone and sends off a short text. Within seconds, there's a reply and he meets my eyes again. "I'm having someone pull records. Shouldn't take long. We'll go from there."

"We will?"

"You're not alone. Ivan would kill me—Luna's uncle or not—if anything happened to you." Then he gets an amused look. "Not to mention my niece. Luna can be intense."

Ignoring the mention of the younger De Leon, I raise a brow. "Does she know you're scared of her?"

"Her and Natasha." His bark of laughter catches a few eyes, but people look away just as quickly. "My daughter is trouble, too."

"I'll make sure to let them know."

"Good. Maybe they'll take it easy on an old man." Bullshit, but I won't tell him anything. I know that once he retires from the police department, he'll be working with the family full time. To what extent, I don't know, but he won't be a cleaner or work on the docks. "But back to your predicament." All traces of humor are gone as the phone vibrates in his hand.

Edgar goes through the information first, skimming it before handing the device over.

And right there on the screen is a picture of the siblings, maybe a few years back, at an event.

All of it comes back.

Why didn't I recognize him sooner? "Shit."

"What?" Jenny places our plates down, but I've lost my appetite. I feel stupid. How could I miss something so important? "Sweetheart, you've gone pale. You need me to call Ivan?"

"No." Grabbing my soda, I take a sip and hope the caffeine helps give me a boost. My hands are shaking. "Just remembered something."

"About the information I gave you?"

I nod. "I've met them before. Spoke to the younger one, in fact."

"Where?"

Noticing our untouched food, Jenny brings over some to-go boxes. "In case you need to leave."

"Thanks." Taking the offered container, I quickly shove my food inside before pulling out my credit card. "Just charge everything here. We need to go."

"Family doesn't pay."

"I'm not—"

"Just following orders, sweetie." Jenny doesn't stick around, and I'm left with Edgar, who looks at me strangely. As if he sees something I don't.

"Where did you meet him, Amberlyn?"

"You don't think that was a coincidence, do you?"

"Maybe. Maybe not, but either way, it's suspicious."

Taking in a deep breath, I let it out slowly. "It was at a city function my parents attended a few years ago. I was dragged along under the pretense of meeting officials and high-ranking officers whom I'd be doing business with. You know how it is. Everything is money and rubbing elbows and pretending to like each other for personal benefit."

"I do understand that."

"Well, as the future owner of Mariposa Bail Bonds, I needed to play the part. Get to know who my allies were."

"And?"

"And they were there. Both walked up to my parents and introduced themselves as detectives, claiming to be appreciative of a fugitive we found by mistake." I shake my head and take another sip of soda. "Dad picked up the wrong guy, but the man we turned in was also running from a double homicide charge. Our guy looked like him, down to the same bald head, but his criminal charges were all theft related."

"Did you socialize with them at all? Something other than being polite?"

"Edgar, I couldn't even muster more than a hello. Especially with the younger brother. He seemed too eager."

"Hmmm." Luna's uncle goes quiet for a minute, pensive, before standing and offering me his hand. He grabs our food bags and then walks me out, all the while his eyes keep shifting around. For a second, he pauses right beside my car with his eyes toward a section of vehicles farther down. Whatever he finds isn't a threat, but he nods at something or someone before looking at me again. "You were right to come to one of us, Amber-lyn. Whatever those two want, it has to do with you and the De Leons, and I won't let you be in danger. It's time to speak with the family."

"CALL HER. Let's gauge her reaction," Maritza says from her seat behind a large desk. We're inside her office in the De Leon home while her husband left to grab his wife a drink from the kitchen. They've been calm while we explained, understanding of my concern, but I don't miss the sympathetic looks she gives me here and there.

There has been no yelling or shouting orders.

No angry man with tattoos coming inside to grab and hide me away.

Where are you, Ivan? I need you.

It's been days and once again, no communication. His promise was nothing more than words spoken to the wind and disappearing just the same. And even when I called him before we arrived, my attempt was shut down after the third ring.

Disappointment sinks into me, but I shake it off. "She seemed nervous last time we spoke. Almost fearful."

"They must've known Dalian was missing then."

"That idiot has been dead nearly a week, and they're panicking." Not a hypothesis. That was a statement from Orlando as he walks back into the room, and it's clear they know more about the brothers than I ever did. "When was the body recovered, Edgar?"

"About three hours ago." Luna's uncle takes a bottle of water from

Ivan's father and passes it to me before grabbing another for himself. My stomach is in knots, though. I'm nervous. "I haven't been able to get ahold of my source inside. Right now, the media's reporting and the headline ties Jaime to Dalian, and they're asking the public if anyone knows how he was mauled by a gator."

"Where was the body found?" I ask.

"Deep in the Everglades by a now-traumatized park employee."

"I can imagine." Every person in this room has seen things they'd rather forget, but were unavoidable. Turning my attention back to Maritza, I give her Karen's number and wait as she punches the numbers in. No one talks as it rings, the speaker loud, and after the fourth ring, there's an audible click.

"Hello? Who's this?"

"It's me. Amberlyn."

"Hey. How's it going." No reaction. Very calm.

"Have you seen the news today?" I ask, hedging.

"No." Small laugh. "I'm just waking up. Felt very sick all night, think it's something I ate."

"Karen, they found the body of your fiancé at—" The phone sounds like it dropped, and I can hear the word *fuck* being repeated, but no crying. No, this is panic. Pure fear in the one word. "Karen? Miss Lopez, are you listening to me?"

"I'm dead," I hear her say this clearly and so do the others in the room, but before I can ask another question, I'm met with a disconnected call. Immediately, I try to call again but it goes straight to voicemail.

I try one more time and get the same.

"We need to find her."

"We do. Something tells me she's the key to understanding this mess," I agree with Edgar. "The sooner we take her into custody, the fewer chances of someone else nabbing her."

Standing from my seat, I pull out my phone and head toward the door. "Dad can help. He'll start mobilizing our resources to see where she could be hiding."

"I'll contact Ivan," a voice says, and my head snaps toward the female so fast my neck cracks. "He should be made aware of what's going on."

"Who the fuck are you?" The brunette is pretty and curvy, but the gleam in her eyes as they stare into mine hold malice.

"I'm a guest of the younger De Leon brother."

"Are you, now?" No one denies it, and I feel sick. "Since when?"

"A few days now." She's wearing a man's shirt but as my eyes water, I can't tell whose. Both Maritza's sons leave clothes here for emergencies. In fact, they have stashes everywhere, even in my home. "He saved me from Dalian." Her smile is wistful, as if remembering something that causes her heart to flutter, while mine feels as though it dropped to my feet. "I knew he would. Ivan promised to come back."

My heart clenches and the air escapes my lungs, yet I remain standing.

This betrayal stings, feels as though I'm being stabbed all over, and the look on Maritza's when I gaze back at her says it all. "Explain."

"Don't speak to my mother-in-law like that. Who the—" Before I can comprehend my actions, I have my hand around her throat and she's on the ground. I'm straddling her, my grip choking while she tried desperately to claw at my arms.

"Who is she?" The question is open to whoever wants to answer, but no one does. What I do feel is someone pulling me off, dragging me away and to the opposite side of the room. "Who is she?"

"Mi niña, you need to calm down. There's an explanation—"

I hold a hand up, and Orlando quiets. "I'm going to ask three questions, and I expect the truth."

"Of course," Ivan's mother agrees. Yet I also notice that she's now standing in the middle between me and the other woman. Edgar is helping the brunette up while Orlando is using his phone to message someone. "But we need to keep our hands to ourselves. Understood?"

Strike one. They are protecting her.

"Did Ivan bring her here?"

"Technically, yes. But it's not what you think."

"Why?"

Maritza's eyes plead with me to understand. To back down. "That's something we can't discuss with you. Just know that she's innocent and was under the Uriel brothers' thumbs."

"Are they involved?"

"That's something only my son can answer."

Strike two. His mother knows and doesn't care that I'm being torn apart where I stand.

"Why are you even discussing anything with her? Is she someone important to Ivancito?" the brunette cries, clutching at Edgar's sleeve while she put on quite the show. Had I been a spectator, I'd be laughing at how ridiculous she looks and the clear marks I left on her neck.

I wait and no one responds, which says everything. I'm no one to him.

I'm an obligation. Moreover, who knows what else he's done behind my back while everyone smiles to my face.

"Enough." The older De Leon cuts in, his eyes narrowed. Not at anyone in particular, but more at the situation. His hand holding the cell phone is clenching, knuckles white. "My son has been made aware of the issue and will call you. Please remember your role in this family, Miss Ibarra."

"You want me to leave?" Voice low. They've cut me deep with this.

"At the moment, yes. I'm sorry, mi niña."

"Not sorrier than I am. Never come near me again." With that, I turn and leave the room, ignoring the raised voices and what they're saying. Someone tries to follow me. They call my name, but I run out of the house as if the hounds of hell are on my heels.

I'm done.

She can have him.

They can all go fuck themselves.

I need to leave Miami. I can't be here.

IVAN

I'M STANDING ON a veranda overlooking the city of Havana a few hours before my meeting with President Rodriguez. The sun is high and the palm trees sway while the people below continue with their day-to-day activities as if there isn't a palpable change in the air. With the way they carry themselves, you'd never know that the standard government trucks parked outside are mine and what they're delivering to the bodega on the first floor of my building is much-needed food and medical supplies.

It's been a routine here for the last few years while we use the ports. The agreement was simple, but then Placido Rodriguez became greedy. Ambitious. Had he left well enough alone and let us give back in the memory of my grandparents, he'd be a powerful and obscenely rich man.

But human nature is one of envy and morbid hunger for what belongs to another, not once bothering to see that what you have is enough. Wanting more isn't the problem. It's all about how you go about achieving those goals.

The ten commandments are simple, and while I'm the poster child for most of those sins, I do understand that there's a place for everyone. That some basic needs should never be trampled on to become successful.

You don't starve your people.

You don't take away their safety.

And while I agree that ruling with an iron fist is necessary to stay in power, you also create bonds and loyalties to stay on top. Take care of yours, and they have your back. They'd take a bullet for the hand that feeds versus the one who abuses.

Taking in a deep drag of my cigarette, I watch another large, high-mobility truck drive down the street and turn out of sight. The two men inside the cabin are natives and dressed the part of military while delivering my weapons to a separate location. One where a select few have access.

Every political branch, including the army, is infiltrated by people in the De Leon pocket and they all have a role to play—to execute—for the country's takeover to work. Because the current administration's hold is on a timer, and the countdown is near done.

But not yet.

First, I have other things to address.

"Henry, come here." The man stands from his place inside. He'd been sitting on the couch for two hours now without moving much. There's been a twitch here and there, sweating, but for the most part, he's the perfect companion on this trip.

Silent. Dutiful. Nervous.

Moreover, he has every right to be.

"Yes, Mr. De Leon?" he asks, coming to stand beside me. I'm on the fourth floor of my building on a popular road that leads to a few touristy restaurants that serve food catered to their taste buds. It's old architecture and indoor water features inside of open courtyards where the waitstaff is taught to serve and entice while offering a milder taste of our cuisine.

"Dalian is dead." I've kept that tidbit to myself just to watch his reaction now, and he doesn't disappoint. There's a quick, indrawn breath and gripping on the metal railing in front of me. I also don't miss the abject look of horror that mars his features, but it's to be expected. They were close friends, the best of, and something as little as lying to me won't change that. "It was quite the spectacle."

"Oh."

"Is that all you have to say? Oh?" Turning so my back faces the veranda, I motion for Israel to collect my laptop. See, while this asshole was busy lying and feeding me bullshit, I began to look past what's in front of me.

There's always another picture. Another version of the same story.

Karen Lopez isn't his sister.

She isn't willingly sleeping with the Uriel brothers.

Yet Cindy Johnson, also known as Jasmin Davila, who's at my parents' home under surveillance with a long enough rope to hang herself, is related to the idiot. Actual sibling. The dots connected themselves. I just needed to look a little further into the theatrical performance they set up.

If anything, how quickly he was willing to sell his own best friend out to save his skin is testament to Henry Davila's lack of morals. His believing me to be stupid enough to fall for and not capitalize on his incompetence is his penance, not mine.

MacBook in hand, I unlock the screen and pull up a small feed—security camera from another business that shares parking lot space with the bar. Same bar where Cisco and his brother reported from, while these men partied. This is the beginning of their ends. Pressing play, I let him watch as the other Cuban sicario brought to protect them is attacked from behind by a now-dead Pirro while the woman, Karen, cries and thrashes.

She's calling out to the unconscious man. Begging them to stop, but no one listens, and all the while Dalian and Jaime laugh. The younger of the two Uriel boys has an arm around her waist while palming her tit with the other.

No regard for her distress. No shame in touching a woman who's clearly disgusted by you.

I have no respect for a man who abuses women, and Dalian deserved worse than what I gave him.

"I-Ivan, I—"

"Finish watching." I press another button and enlarge the angle. "Describe what I'm seeing."

"I'm sorry."

"You will be." A sardonic laugh escapes me. "Now, tell me what happened here."

"I'd gone by then."

"Go on. Amuse me with this story."

His eyes shift toward the exit. I see the intent to move away from me, but one blow to his leg from my boot sends him to the floor. "Not in the mood to talk now? All right." I snap my fingers at one of the guards, a man from the Cuban capital, and he forces Henry to his bruised knees. "I'll fill in the blanks for you."

"I'll tell you everything."

"You're disposable, Davila. A puppet." Placing the laptop on the ground, I pace the small space. All the while, his eyes are on me. Waiting for the strike. "I had men on you that night and they did as I asked—more than, but once I pulled them away, this happened. Not their fault, but mine, and I see that. Had I paid better attention, I would've noticed how Karen slightly cringed while on Dalian's lap. How when she came to see my mermaid with fresh heroin tracks on her arms, she was fidgety. Twitching and crawling in her skin while the woman has no prior record of drug usage. If anything, she's intelligent and resourceful—was only looking for a way to bring her husband here after his service. That's where your friends came into the picture…isn't it?"

"Yes."

"Who approached her?" I ask, even though I'm sure the answer is him. Because that's who this man is; a glorified gopher and nothing more. "Who made the offer to help her?"

"I did."

"And what did you offer? What was her role in this mess?"

"To act as Dalian's distraught fiancée while Jaime moved in on Amber-lyn." Henry swallows hard, tears falling from his eyes. "If she gave them this, they'd bring her husband to Miami and let them leave together with money and a secured home in Cape Coral."

"You used her."

"Yes."

"Sexually?"

Davila looks down, his fear palpable. "We forced her to get high and took turns."

Closing my eyes for a second, I exhale roughly. I have a mother, cousins, and a soon-to-be wife.

Had someone done something similar to those I love, I'd want them chopped up a piece at a time and fed as chum to the animals roaming in open water.

"What else do I need to know? Is there a hidden skill you've kept from me?"

"You know."

"I do." Birds fly over us before landing in the adjacent buildings. That's the old-world charm of this city; the structures are old and reminiscent of an era where this country was a tourist destination that rivaled the world's most exotic destinations and casinos. We're called the Pearl of the Antilles for a reason, and it's more than the long-standing Tropicana club. On this block, though, I own five buildings and they are occupied by those who work for me to distribute food and necessities from the capital to smaller cities and out to the more remote farmlands. "But I'd like to hear you admit it."

"I'm the hacker who stole Amberlyn's identity."

"Good boy." Reaching a hand toward him, Henry flinches but I simply pat his head. "Now pray."

"Let me work it off," he pleads instead. Wasting his breath. "I'm good at what I do and can be useful."

"I've told you before. Our organization isn't recruiting." Shifting a glance at the watch on my wrist, I give a short whistle and Israel comes forward with my gun. "Two minutes. Do we have word from Junior?"

"Yes. Karen is in his care."

"Good." After taking the Glock, I reach into my right back pocket and pull out a silencer attachment and affix it to the muzzle. "And Silvio Lopez? Have we found him?"

"Word is he's here on the island and held in a private high-security jail."

Henry clears his throat. "My uncle runs the president's personal prison here. I can get you in if—"

"Would you get my men inside and out safely?" I raise an amused brow. "Out of the goodness of your heart?"

"If it kept me alive? Yes." Low. Meek. Nothing at all like the man who lied to me and terrorized an innocent woman for personal greed. Where's that cocky son of a bitch now? "Just ask, and it's yours."

"Open your mouth." Expressions—from fear to almost relief—cross his features in rapid succession at the command. Yet he does it. He kneels on the cold ground while the sun beats down on the city, lips parted and eyes closed. The latter of which I didn't ask him to do. "Loyalty, Henry, is all that matters to the De Leons. What we pride ourselves on, from the lowest soldier to the head of the family. If we can't trust you, you are of no use and will be dealt with."

"I'll take my punishment." Opens his mouth further. *What the hell does he think I'm going to do?* Yet he's making this game of bull's-eye too easy.

Three steps separate us and I take two, stopping just shy of touching a wet puddle on the floor. *I hate when they pee themselves.* My aim is good, maybe even better than Thiago's. "You seem to be confused. Open your eyes." Muddy brown ones meet mine and widen. He tries to snap his mouth shut, but before he does, I've already fired, and the bullet breaks his teeth and tongue and exits out the back of his skull before he's successful.

The muted sound is barely discernible in the busy afternoon bustle where many pass the building below on their way to and from my store, and after he slumps forward, I turn and head straight for the door.

Those here fall into step behind me while dragging Henry's body. There's a cheap casket down in the bodega for him that I'll be taking with me to the meeting with Placido Rodriguez.

I couldn't bring Dalian back with me, but his best friend should suffice. I'll even give them enough time to bury the asshole before decapitating the president. Because that's the only way to get rid of a snake. A body is useless without the head, and his administration will crumble.

IVAN

WE MAKE IT to the Placido de la Revolucion a little after four in the afternoon and are met with a new general and his body of force on the steps. They're standing guard, weapons drawn while I walk past them but make clear eye contact.

His facial expression doesn't change, but there's a subtle tilt to his head no one else catches. Or maybe they do, and those here are mostly my men.

Either way, I make my way inside the grand door and into a large open room where those dressed in military honors line the room. They don't move. Don't blink.

It's quite impressive to witness.

The place is opulent yet a bit sterile, gleaming from corner to corner with history and the money hidden from its citizens. To think those in here feast while the nation starves.

And sure, things are a bit different with the youth finding ways to survive and grow—becoming entrepreneurs while pulling their families out of the molds they'd been forced into—but the country needs more.

As people, Cubans are resilient and proud.

Fighters, and as I stand inside this room, my chest swells with emotions I didn't expect.

I've always been proud of where we are from, but this moment is one I wish I could've shared with the generations that were lucky enough to see this. The future.

Patria y Vida.

"Mr. De Leon, President Rodriguez is waiting," a woman says, pulling my attention away from the flag slightly swaying ahead of me. "If you'll please follow me."

"Of course." Israel isn't with me; he's coming from another entry point with my gift in a special box. A demurely dressed woman in her thirties turns and I follow, walking past those in ceremonial uniforms while they stare straight ahead. She takes me and the four men with me toward the end of a long hall where a set of double doors awaits me. They're wide open and with the man of the hour sitting at the head of a long conference table.

President Placido Rodriguez is a greying, pompous motherfucker with a slight beer belly to finish his look. He stands when he sees me, fixing the cuff links at his wrists before holding a hand out in a very diplomatic fashion. He's smiling, as if he knows something I don't, while giving the escort a nod.

The door closes and so do the pretenses, my grip tighter than his. "I'd say it's a pleasure, but we both know that's a lie."

"Likewise, but I will insist we take a seat and talk like men." Placido eyes my men, more specifically their faces, and his grin morphs into a smirk. "Did your parents let you off the leash to play with the big boys? How generous of them."

"No more than your wife leaves you unsupervised so she can bend over for the gardener." My expression is neutral, unmoved by his earlier shot. "But her private extracurricular activities are none of my business. Heck, you might enjoy being a cuckold."

"You're skating on thin ice, kid. I could kill you, and no one would lift a finger against me." His old hand clenched. "This isn't Miami."

"I'm well aware of where I am, yet you're the one who seems to be confused." Opening my suit jacket, I pull out an envelope and place it atop the dark wood tabletop. "You're surrounded by your enemies, Rodriguez.

People who are waiting for the word—a reason to snap and slit your throat."

"And you're man enough to do so?" To his right is an ashtray and cigar inside the marked holder. The end is already cut, the sharp tool right beside it, and the president lights up. A few deep pulls and the end glows amber before it's overshadowed by his exhaled smoke. "We both know how this will end, Ivan. It's only a matter of time before Jaime and Dalian—"

"I didn't know the dead could walk, much less cause harm."

"What did you say?" The cockiness is gone and his voice shakes. Something the president tries to hide behind a cough, but it's too late. "Where's my nephew?"

"Morgue. In a gator's stomach." My shrug is nonchalant. "Both are true."

"You're lying."

"Are you willing to place a bet on that?"

"Hijo de—"

"Careful, old man. You're surrounded by your enemies; one wrong move and I will give the command." He's nervous. Sweating a bit. "Now, would you like the proof or are you willing to take my word for it?"

"Proof." Gritted teeth. The cigar is now back in the ashtray and wasting away. "How do I know it's not a lie?"

"Here." One of the men with me has my iPad, and it only takes a few clicks to open the browser and search. At once, headlines with links attached appear and I hand over the device. I don't care if he breaks it in a moment of rage. I'll buy another one. "Read one or several, but it won't change the outcome."

Rodriguez's face changes from pallid to nearly purple as the reality of what happened to his nephew sinks in. I'll do the same to Jaime and then him. He knows this. Yet he slams the tablet on the table so hard the screen cracks and shatters at the corner, but the image from the report on a local Miami station, a Spanish one at that, remains.

Dalian Uriel is dead.

Mauled. Unrecognizable.

"You will pay for this, cabron. From your mother to the puta you fuck, I will kill them all."

"Is this the route you want to go with me?" Standing from my seat, I tap the wood twice and the man to my left walks to a secret door no one but those at the highest level of intelligence know about. It's an exit made for the first family and the leeches who kiss their asses to escape through in case of a coup or assassination attempt.

Israel is on the other side of that door and the wooden box, half the size of a normal casket, is wheeled inside. It's plain white and has a few holes dotted in red where blood has begun to seep through.

"What's the meaning of this? How did you—"

"You have seventy-two hours to step down or bend the knee for the De Leon family, Mr. President. Seventy-two, and not a minute more." The lid is removed and inside, you can tell there's a male body about the age of Dalian. "And this is my gift to you. Henry Davila was Dalian's close friend and the snitch that told me where to find him when I pointed a gun at his head. You can burn him or pretend it's Dalian while having a fake service to mourn another life lost because of your idiocy and greed. Whatever you decide is on you, Placido, but remember one thing: I'm everywhere. I see everything."

"I won't let this go." Voice hoarse, he stands and leans over the table with both fists holding his weight. "What you've done—"

"Your call, and I could give a single fuck either way. Bend or die, it's up to you." Going around to his side, I place a hand on his arm and squeeze. "My deepest condolences. It didn't have to be this way, but the clock is ticking nonetheless. Make the right decision, Rodriguez. Don't be the reason your entire family dies at my hand. Take this as advice; I'm not the bad guy here."

I leave him to think and consider his options, then walk out of the room and the building without anyone asking questions or attempting to stop us. To be honest, everything was too smooth and when I get back to my chauffeur on the island, a sinking feeling hit.

He's worried. Wringing his hands together, but before I can ask, he tosses the cell phone I'd left inside the car at me. "Your father called me after you didn't respond. Says it's urgent and has to do with Miss Amberlyn Ibarra."

"WHAT DO YOU MEAN, you let her walk out the house?"

"Son, it's my fault. This is on me," Dad says, rubbing a hand down his face the same way I do when frustrated. "We thought she knew. That you told her, and she was just playing along to help Davila's sister hang herself. Even after she left, at first we thought it was her playing a part, until your mother called and found herself blocked."

"But Amberlyn doesn't know. I told you she isn't to be touched by my—"

"Papito, I'm sorry. I didn't mean to hurt her." The FaceTime call freezes momentarily, and Mom's blotchy face makes the situation worse. My ire cannot be contained; I'm shaking and what's worse, Amberlyn won't respond to any of my texts. I've been trying to get ahold of her since the plane took off, begging for her to reach out, but nada. *Is this what she feels when I've ignored her in the past?*

I'm an asshole for it. Deserve to feel the worry clawing at my skin because there are still risks I can't control.

A car accident.

Wrong place and time incident.

Fuck, even lighting strikes in Miami aren't that uncommon.

"This is beyond fucked up." Exhaling roughly, I type out another message to her and then one to Junior, the latter of which responding right away.

> I have Karen and should be in Cuba by tonight.
> Am I heading to Havana or the compound?
> ~Junior.

> Neither. Stay in Miami. I'm on my way
> back. ~Ivan

Three dots appear on the screen. Then the phone pings.

> Is everything okay? What do you need me to do,
> boss? ~Junior

> Try to find Amberlyn. No one knows where she
> is. ~ Ivan

His reply comes in just as fast.

> I'll start searching now. Karen will be kept at my
> apartment; she won't run. ~Junior

> Thank you. I'll call when I land. ~Ivan

The screen of my laptop unscrambles and my parents are there, still wearing upset expressions.

"My sirenita thinks I'm sleeping with and keeping a woman at your home? Do you realize how bad that makes me look?"

"I've never seen her so upset, Ivan. But again, we thought she was just playing along. We would've never let her go intentionally thinking that."

"Mom, to be honest…I don't know what to say right now. All I know is I need to find her."

"We fucked up, kid," Mom says and sniffs; she's been crying. Her face is blotchy while Dad looks miserable. "It all happened so fast, and I went along thinking nothing of it. I really thought she knew, yet her expression before running out is something I can't get out of my head. Baby, it's like she expected this and at the same time accepted it."

"Where was Miguel? Why didn't Edgar react?"

"Miguel was preparing for Cindy's transfer, and Edgar grabbed the bitch while your father sent that message to you. We were hoping you'd get in contact with Amberlyn to discuss what she came for, but instead, everything blew up in our faces." Dad passes Mom a Kleenex, yet she bats his hand away. She looks so sad. "I'm sorry, papito."

"Not your fault." Knocking back a drink, I pour another few fingers' worth of whiskey. "I'm the idiot that's let this go on long enough. She believes it because I've let her down."

"You'll find her. She has to listen." Dad tries to lighten the mood, to give hope, but the reality is much too somber.

Yet I refuse to lose her.

I can't and won't live without my girl. That gorgeous woman with the reddish-black hair and tattoos—with a sense of humor that rivals mine. She's sarcastic and beautiful and likes to read, but is ready for a night on the town just as fast. Amberlyn is the other half of my soul, taken from my rib as my perfect counterpart, and I will make things right between us again.

I love her. Simply and honest.

"I'm not letting her go either way."

"BEBE, PLEASE ANSWER. LET ME EXPLAIN." This is the third burner phone I've bought since landing. It's been twenty-four hours, and no one has seen her. Her parents don't know where she is, but know I'm involved and demand I make it right.

Not a promise hard to keep, but it'd be easier if the stubborn woman would just pick up the phone. Every time I call, she avoids or sends me to voicemail, and if I make her angry enough, I'm blocked.

Silly girl has no idea I'll burn through a million of these if it gets her to give in, even if it's just to curse me out. I'll take that any day over the silence. The cold shoulder.

I try again and get the same response.

Two rings and to a voicemail that's full at the moment. I'm more than positive ninety percent of those messages are mine.

The separation—this wall between us—is not something I can deal with. It's brewing, eating at me, and a part of me worries about the explosion that will follow our reunion.

Worry and anger mix while my love for her nearly suffocates me.

She'll be lucky if I let her out of my sight again.

Even my parents have noticed the change. I've always been possessive of her, needed her attention, but this surpasses anything I've experienced before. If what Mermaid wanted was to be claimed before, now she'll be handcuffed to me at all times. If what she needed was validation, now she'll bear my last name as proof of who owns her.

"Sir, I got Natasha on the phone." Junior rushes into my home office, phone extended toward me.

"Thank you." Sitting back in my chair, I place my legs up and cross the ankles atop the desk. The door closes and I breathe in deep before letting it out slowly, trying to calm myself so I don't snap at my sister-in-law's cousin. Nat is also my friend. Like a sister to Amberlyn. "Where is she?"

"Ivan, I think she just needs a couple days to cool off. Back off for a bit."

"Where. Is. She."

"I can't betray her trust. All you need to know is she's safe—"

"There's a plot to kidnap and sexually exploit her, Nat, by the nephew of Cuba's president. The man is a Miami detective, you know Uriel and should also be aware he's been missing since Dalian's body was found," I manage to grit out without completely losing it on her. This is my fault, not hers, but right now she's keeping me from what's mine. "Please, Natasha. Where is my mermaid?"

"Dominican Republic." Her voice is low, but I hear it clearly. As if she shouted the answer. "Amberlyn checked into an all-inclusive resort in Punta Cana."

"Thank you."

"Will she be safe?"

"She's mine, and I'd die for her."

TWO DAYS BEFORE...

MY PHONE RINGS again, the thirtieth time and counting, but I hit ignore and pick up my drink.

I'm stewing in my anger. Drowning in a heady concoction of regret and hurt that makes it nearly impossible to breathe, but I do. One inhale at a time while one of my best friends sits across from me at an airport bar inside of Miami International.

My flight leaves in three hours, but I've avoided being found thus far and I'm praying they heed my request to stay away. I don't want to see anything of them. Ever again.

A sardonic laugh slips from me, and I down what's left of my second sex on the beach. "Maybe that's what I need."

"What do you need?" Nat asks, picking at her order of chips and salsa. The girl is obsessed with them and never fails to order some whenever they're on the menu. "You've been muttering a lot, and I have no clue if I missed something."

"A good hard fuck with a stranger on the beach."

"Okay," she says, dragging the words out. "Not at all what I expected you to say."

"Couldn't hurt to give it a try now." I shrug, but even that is listless. It's as if all the air inside my words has been sucked out and I've been left to gape and choke until it's my time to die. "Casual sex could be beneficial."

All this time, for years, I trusted him. Blindly. Like a puppet.

Not once have I looked at another man, and not for lack of attention. Men have always flirted—threw out a cheesy line or two—but I never entertained the idea of being with anyone but Ivan.

How can I when he's been scaring away anyone who tries to get close since high school.

But there have been plenty of women who've tried and failed to date him. At least, I thought so until the chick inside the De Leons' home. His parents didn't rebuke her or try to defend me; I was the outcast.

Always have been. Always will be to them.

She's nothing but an obligation.

Well, screw them.

They can figure out the dead body's meaning, and the threat I want no part of. As of today, right this second, I don't care.

For years, I've silently fought my doubts over my importance in his life. My place.

I'll never be that ignorant girl again Can't afford to be.

"No mas. This is it for me."

"No more what, chica? Be more specific."

I haven't seen or heard from Ivan since he left my place. Since I once again proved my weakness and let him take me in the shower. *I begged for his touch. I instigated everything.* Moreover, for years I've accepted the scraps of attention without shame—to just feel him next to me was enough —and all of that is my fault.

How can a man take you seriously like that?

No reproach. No demands for an explanation.

Instead, I've always been there with my legs spread. Literally.

"I'm an idiot, Nat. A total fucking pendeja for continuing to put myself in this position." A flight announcement comes through the speakers, but it's not mine and I wave my now-empty glass at a waiter. The bar and grill we're inside of isn't far from my terminal, yet it seems empty suddenly, and I scan the surrounding areas just in case. *Nothing. He's not here.* And I let out a huge sigh of relief at that. Now more than ever I need to get away from my responsibility. From life. *Him.* "Why can't I just send him to hell and be done with everything? He doesn't deserve me."

The truth tastes bitter on my tongue because the pedestal I've always put Ivan on has crumbled and the rubble lies at my proverbial feet. It's left me shaking. Unable to breathe without feeling his absence.

"Maybe there's a good explanation?" By Nat's expression, even she doesn't believe it. Her response irks me, but before I can respond, my cell phone rings again.

At this point, I'm ready to break the device.

But it's not a De Leon this time. No. It's Jaime Uriel, and in the mental state I'm in, I have no patience for the man. It's why I answer while baring my teeth, welcoming the anger I hold for all males at the moment.

"What?"

"Amberlyn?"

"Again, Detective. What?" Our waiter places my drink down, and I take another healthy sip.

"Where are you?" His tone is aggravated, demanding, and today is not the day to test my inner gangster.

"How is that any of your business, Detective?" I demand, yet don't give him the chance to answer. I could care less about his reasons. "What I do or don't isn't any of your business, and since what *was* our agreement is now null after the man's death, I suggest you lose my number. Don't call me again."

"Where. Are. You?"

"On vacation…so fuck off." With that, I hang up and turn the damn thing off. My parents and Nat are the only ones who know I'll be out of town for two weeks and heading to the Dominican Republic. They're aware I'll be staying at an all-inclusive resort, but not which one. "That guy just rubs me wrong."

"He's pushy," she notes.

"Very much so, but he shouldn't be calling again." That call's put me out, and I push the drink aside before standing. Our bill isn't large, less than sixty, and I leave a hundred-dollar bill on the table before coming to Nat's side and pulling her up and into a hug. "I'm going to go sit at the gate. Love you, babes."

She squeezes me just as hard, rocking us a little from side to side. "You sure you don't want me to tag along? I've got some vacation time saved up and—"

"I need some time on my own."

"Fine." Pulling back just enough to see my face, she pouts. "Go be all alone and mopey while I dodge that man of yours."

"He's not mine."

"He is, Lynnie. And I have no doubt he'll be coming for you."

Tears build, but I won't let them fall and blink rapidly. "For the first time, I don't want him to come. A person can't live like this...I can't live like this, mami. I want more than empty words and false promises; Ivan will never be what I need him to be."

"Are you sure that's what you want?"

"Yes."

"Then I'll hold him off your trail as long as I can. Go find yourself."

***

PRESENT...

A WARM BREEZE sweeps over me while I nurse a shot of Mama Juana out on the water. I'm in a hammock watching the trees sway and birds fly over-head while silence surrounds me. It's both depressing and therapeutic, yet exactly what I need at the moment.

There's no escaping reality when the noises cease and you can hear yourself think.

And for forty-eight hours, that's what I've done on this private slice of paradise that I've paid a fortune for. I'm but steps from the warm Caribbean waters at all times and far enough away from noisy tourists and the horny men offering me a private tour of the island.

Guest and staff alike.

Since landing, I've been hit on and asked to become someone's Mrs. several times.

"Yet the one I want doesn't see me." I won't deny it's a blow to my self-esteem. That I wasn't enough to fall in love with, but that's life and if this place has taught me anything within my solitude, it's that there's a reason for everything.

Accepting reality hurts—that he's not the man I thought he was—and causes my chest to feel as though it's caving in, but there's a lesson in that, too. I'll survive. I'll be stronger one day soon.

So I close my eyes while enjoying the last sip of my spiced rum and repeat my mantra:

I am enough.

In the distance, a merengue song starts playing, and it's from a live band. It's soothing and lulls me; I'm safe enough here to let my guard down, and I do, sinking slowly into a nice, relaxing nap. It's easy to forget the world and those around me while the sun filters through the thin shade, warming my skin. While the water below laps at the shore.

This is what I needed.

Here, I find peace.

***

THE ATMOSPHERE IS OFF TODAY. I don't feel as alone with my solitude, and while swimming not far from the shore, there are eyes on me. The sensation is unmistakable, and goose bumps rise on my skin.

Hairs at the back of my neck stand up, too.

My first instinct is to think Ivan had something to do with this, but that notion is squashed just as fast. He won't come for me. I'm nothing to him.

Yet I can't shake the feeling while eating lunch out on my private deck or while sunbathing near a group of women near the resort's main activity area. It's also why I find myself heading toward the concierge service desk to ask them to search the surrounding areas around my villa.

"How can I help you today, Miss Ibarra?" the woman behind the desk asks, her smile so infectious and bright. But that's everyone in the

Dominican Republic you meet; they're happy and full of so much life—a positive attitude. "Are you finally ready to book a tour out to—"

"No, but I do need help with something."

"Of course. What can we do to make your stay more enjoyable?"

"I feel like I'm being watched." The smile falls from her face at that, but there's also a bout of nervousness that makes no sense. "Could you please have someone check the surrounding areas of my villa? Just as a precaution?"

"Of course, ma'am. I'll send security out there now, and again later tonight."

"Thank you. I really appreciate it."

"It's our pleasure. We want you to feel safe and happy during your stay with us." She taps a few keys on her computer, filling something out before giving me another warm smile. "I've just sent an alert to the head of security for us. He should be answering soon and will take care of it."

"Perfect."

"Are you heading back to your accommodations, or joining us for dinner this evening?"

"To be honest, I was thinking of going back."

"I insist that you don't, miss. Not until we get the all-clear from security."

"Okay." My stomach rumbles then and I laugh; since arriving here, this one isn't forced. "Which restaurant do you recommend? And I want authentic. Not something touristy."

"Lolo's is out on the pier and above the water. They serve the real deal, home cooking that our country is known for. Trust me, it's delicious."

"Sold. Do I need a reservation?"

"No. I'll take care of it." Glancing at my clothes, I grimace a bit. I'm in a simple tie-dye dress in different shades of yellow. "Will this be okay, or do I need to change? I didn't plan on going anywhere tonight."

"It's a casual setting. You'll have no problem with it." The woman grabs a walkie-talkie and sends out a quick call for a golf cart transport. Their response is quick, and the young man assures her it'll be less than five minutes before he arrives. "You're all set. I put the table under your last name, and the hostess knows to expect you shortly. Is there anything else I can help you with?"

"Not that I can think of."

"Great." Another mega-watt smile. "I'm glad I could be of assistance. If you need anything else, please don't hesitate to ask."

"Thank you."

"It's my pleasure."

———

"Wow," is all I can say, dropping my fork down after the final bite of the cinco leches dessert that's knocked me on my proverbial butt. It's sweet and a bit creamy with just the right amount of cake. "I'm in love with this."

But then again, everything about this place is amazing. Designed to make you feel as though you're out on the water, the entire restaurant is an open concept with nature providing the biggest draw. We're on the water with the late evening sky surrounding us while you can hear the water splashing against the pillars holding the place above the warm waters below.

From the waitstaff to the food, it's been an experience.

"We're glad you enjoyed the food, miss."

"Delicioso. Everything was amazing," I tell the waitress after she delivers my coffee and takes away my now-empty plate. "I'll have another of that to go or I'll be thinking about it all night."

She throws her head back and laughs. "You're not the first to request it. I'll get right on that…they'll be something extra too. You have to try the coconut dessert."

"Thank you."

"My pleasure." Once she leaves, I begin adding a little sugar to my coffee and begin observing the others dining tonight. There are a few older couples, but the majority I've run into are all adults. People are laughing and drinking and for a second, I'm a little jealous.

Always alone.

"Evening, Amberlyn," a male voice says from my right, and I'm startled, but more so because it's familiar. And when I flick my gaze in his direction, I understand why.

What the fuck? "Detective Uriel, what—"

"Jaime, sweetheart. Say my name."

"Again, Detective," I say, adding emphasis on his title, "what are you doing here?"

"I'm here to pick up my girl." That calms me for all of two seconds, when he's grabbing my arm on the next. His grip is tight as he tries to pull me up, causing the couple a table over to look our way. "Did you miss me, bebe?"

Coming from him, that word is all wrong. Disgust me and I shiver, something he mistakes for pleasure.

"Let go, Uriel. I'm not finding this funny."

"Neither was the death of my brother, but your cunt of a fuck buddy made sure I felt that blow." He bends down so his mouth is next to my ear, his hot breath causing my stomach to revolt. "And you will pay for his sins, amor. I'll take your pussy as deposit and your asshole as liquidation of said charges. Over and over again, Miss Ibarra, and you have the De Leons to thank for the cruel future you've been sacrificed to."

Yet a few seconds after the last word leaves his lips, there's an audible click of a gun, and men surround the table. It all happens so fast. One second Jaime has a grip on my arm, and the next he's on the ground a few feet from me with a vicious predator straddling his body and landing blow after blow to a now-unconscious man.

Those inside the restaurant look on in fear, while the staff seems unperturbed.

"What the fuck?" It leaves me and as if on cue, those eyes that haunt me turn and our stares connect. His hands are a bloody mess, while there are specks of red across his cheeks. His lips are curled up into an angry snarl, and yet he's never been more beautiful to me.

I sway in my seat and he's off Uriel's body in an instant, sauntering toward me. His gait is powerful, too much, and in my panic, I rise from my seat. "Stay back."

"Mermaid, I need you to calm down." Ivan grabs an untouched glass of water and napkin from a nearby table, making quick work of wiping his hands. The ease in which he does so show his comfort and quit wit, ridding himself of Uriel's blood quickly. Not completely, but enough you can't tell without inspecting carefully. "You know I'd never hurt you."

"Liar."

"Bebe, please. Let's cool off and talk. There's—"

For some reason, my world breaks at that moment and fight-or-flight takes over. There's one of his men to my right with a gun at his side, tucked into the waistband of a pair of dress pants, and I grab it before anyone can react. It also goes off just as quick, adrenaline making it difficult past the lies and betrayal—my need to hurt Ivan is larger than my body can contain.

"No one touches her," he barks out, the sound a little pained. "Step down."

"No, De Leon. You step back." My feet are trying to reach the exit, one step at a time. "No mas. We're done."

"The fuck we are," he roars, his harsh—angry—tone causing me to almost drop the weapon. "There will never be an end to us, Sirenita. I'll kill the devil himself to keep you."

IVAN

I DON'T THINK twice, tossing her over my shoulder in three strides while ignoring the punches landing on my back. My mermaid is livid, and I love it. Prefer this to ignorance.

That cold shoulder shit taught me a valuable lesson; she can be cruel.

"Put me down, De Leon. I'm not going anywhere with you!"

"Out," I hiss from between clenching teeth while her body squirms over the shoulder she lightly grazed with a bullet. It's not a huge wound, just stings, and I'll take care of it—and her for it—later. No matter what, we don't shoot at each other. I'll admit my girl has good aim and had she been calm, there's no doubt I'd be removing a shell and not planning the ways to fuck her into submission.

One by one, everyone inside the restaurant vacates without hesitating. The moment the last person leaves, I give Israel a nod and he picks up the unconscious waste of sperm from the floor, nearly dislocating his shoulder with the way he jams it into the table's edge. "I want him in the plane's cargo area within twenty. Make sure he's treated like royalty while you wait for us."

My sirenita huffs, but the hard punch to my side will leave a bruise. *Brat.*

She'll pay for that later.

On her knees or back. Maybe on all fours with her pretty holes on display.

I'm not picky at the moment. Not after living with the fear of not knowing where she's been for a few days.

"Yes, boss." With that, he exits, meeting Junior at the door and they make quick work of getting the detective out of the restaurant and then off the pier.

Now, it's just the two of us:

Alone. Angry. Hurt.

Her skin is soft against my fingertips as I slowly drag the pads of each up and down the back of her leg, pushing the back of her dress higher with each pass. I also don't miss the low sigh she emits after each caress.

"Are you ready to talk?"

"Yes." Low. Meek. It's completely false. Yet I don't hesitate and lower her to the ground, making sure to ease her slowly, rubbing my hard cock across her clothed front.

Christ, the sight that greets me once she's standing is delicious, and I step back. "Hola, bebe."

Hard nipples. Goose bumps. Parted lips.

"You asshole!" Amberlyn's hand connects with my cheek, and the sting feels like a jolt of electricity in my veins. Thrumming and heated. It's harsh and fast, leaving behind this all-consuming yearning for her touch. *I'll never be without her again.* "This isn't a date. He followed me here, like you, apparently."

"I've missed you, too."

"What part of *leave me alone,* don't you understand? Leave."

"No." I take a step closer while she moves back, trying to evade me, but I'm done. She wanted me, she has me. We're not leaving this island until she understands how devoted I am.

"Are you insane? That's an MDP detective you picked up. If they pin this on you, it'll bring heat the family doesn't need. What were you thinking?" She could care less about Uriel; this is just another weak attempt to create conflict, so I don't touch her.

"That you being in danger is not something I'll ever tolerate."

"Seriously? That's the best you can come up with." She gives me a sardonic laugh, a brave act, but I catch each shiver. The way her shoulders hunch in. "Why don't you go feed that line to the whore sleeping at your parents' house."

"Your life being in danger is idiotic?" Now I'm angry, nearly snarling the words at her. "Anything but you being safe and happy is unacceptable to me. Don't you ever say that shit again."

"Bullshit." This time she jams a manicured finger into my chest, mimicking my defensive stance, eyes spitting fire. "You left me. You broke every late-night promise."

"To protect you."

"Stop with the lies." Tears spring to her eyes but Amberlyn looks away, blinking rapidly so they don't fall. "What have I ever done for you to continue hurting me like this?"

"Bebe, not everything is as it seems."

"Just, fuck you." I hate the defeat in her voice. "If you ever cared for me, at the very least as a friend, leave. Go on with your life, and I'll do the same with mine." Her high ponytail has come a little undone and a few wisps of hair curl around her cheek; I want nothing more than to sweep them back but grit my teeth instead. "All you do is force your presence on me. Make me think you want me—more—but turn around and leave every single time. I'm done, Ivan. There's nothing more I can give you."

"You don't mean that."

"I do."

"Then you leave me no choice. I'm sorry." Whatever she sees in my eyes makes hers widen; there's a tinge of fear in them, and I hate it. This. Where we are. And I hold the blame, know that, but it doesn't stop me from advancing on her. "Run."

"What?" Voice shaky. Breathing choppy.

"You want me to chase you to the ends of the earth, then run. Just know that I will always follow."

"You're insane, Ivan. Just go. Stop this."

"Never, amorcito. I exist with you."

"Don't do this to me." This time a tear does fall, but when I try to wipe it away, she moves away. "I'm begging you."

"You are my heart, Amberlyn. Always have been, and always will be."

"I refuse to do this with you again, Ivan. You shouldn't have come here."

"So you expected me to sit back while the woman I love is taken? To let them have and abuse you?"

"Wait." The gun slips from her hand and goes off, breaking a large stone figure, but Sirenita just stares at me. She's trembling, hard. "What did you just say?"

"He's the nephew of President Rodriguez through marriage, sweetie. They were going to kidnap—"

"Not that." Heavy tears fall now. Lips trembling. "Please, I need you to repeat the first part."

My anger evaporates. Instead, what's left is a man splayed open and wanting to lay at the altar of his goddess to worship.

"I love you, Amberlyn. Always have, Mermaid."

"No. No." She's muttering something that sounds like *he's playing with me* right before making the biggest mistake she could at the moment. My girl ran. Literally took off as if her life depended on it, and I take a second to control my own emotions.

Her fear stings me as though she wielded a whip and cracked it across my chest. Yet there's also another emotion licking at my senses: pleasure.

I warned her I'd chase.

I'll prove my worth a thousand times over if it means she's mine.

Removing my shirt, I throw it over my shoulder and walk out of the restaurant. There's no doubt in my mind she's heading for the rented villa, but what she isn't aware of is a hidden pathway that connects those properties to this restaurant.

While she ran straight down the pier and toward the pools, I make a left and pick up the pace. Mermaid is quick, I'll give her that, and the last thing I want is to give her any inkling that I'm close or she'll veer off.

Through tropical foliage, I manage to keep ahead but once the main paths connect, I stop and wait. My girl's accommodations are on a private white sandy stretch of beach with an open-air jacuzzi and a lit pathway to the water.

Yet I never give her the chance to place a single foot on the smooth cobblestone, tackling her to the ground and twisting, landing on my back to take the brunt of the fall. Sand sweeps around us and settles, but the hellcat above me bucks and fights to stand while my teeth bite her neck.

"Get the hell off me, Ivan." Those fingernails dig into my chest while her lower half gyrates once, unconsciously, while trying to push herself up. It stings, but I don't complain. Not when she's in my arms again, scratching at my newest addition there: her name in my cursive hand-writing surrounded by mariposa flowers in red ink. "This isn't funny. I'm no one's joke."

"No, but you are my world," I croon low, releasing her for the time being. "I love you, bebe."

"You don't." Like a scared rabbit, she fidgets and looks for an escape. "I know you don't."

"Now who's the liar." *Fuck, she's beautiful when angry.* Those warm eyes blaze at my words, spitting fire at me while her hands ball into tight fists. *That's right, sweet girl. Burn me.* "But then again, you've always been a little blind."

"What did you say to me?" Her tone is acerbic. Incredulous.

"I'm calling you out on your bullshit." Her hand flies toward my face, intent clear, but I counter her move and yank Amberlyn against me. She gasps at the move and shivers from our contact, but I don't let another word of denial fall from those plump lips.

Instead, I kiss her. Fucking take what's mine and breathe for what feels like the first time in days.

And for all her fighting, she's right there with me. Kissing me as if she'll never get the chance to do it again.

Our tongues fight for dominance while hands remove clothing, tossing everything in a manic rush to feel. She's nipping my chin while I'm roam-ing, squeezing her bare ass with both hands before picking her up—rubbing her slick core over my cock while walking us to a swing set beside two white hammocks.

The water here barely reaches my thighs but lines her up perfectly to take me. It's a wide seat, could be for two, but dwarfs her lithe forms. She looks like the perfect sinful doll, and I growl out a loud *fuck* when Mermaid leans forward—nearly folding herself in half—to take my dick in her mouth.

Son of a bitch, her mouth is velvet heat, so soft while applying the perfect amount of suction with each swallow around my girth. The bulbous tip touches the back of her throat on the next bob, and I grip the back of her head, forcing myself a little deeper until she gags.

"That's it, mami. *Fucking hell*…just like that." I can feel her smile at my eloquence, the cockiness that makes her pick up the pace and depth until her nose touches the base of my cock. My eyes close and balls draw up, the first electrical shocks of my impending release striking me, but I pull out. Her pout is adorable right after, too. "Next time I come, it's to fill your cunt. I want you dripping of me."

Lips glossy with my pre-come, she smiles. "That was all you are getting from me, De Leon."

"You challenging me?"

"Just telling the truth."

"Then let me rectify that." A gentle tug by the back of her neck and she's arching her chest while I squeeze between her thighs. Her hooded eyes watch me. They beg me to make the pain go away, and I place a gentle peck on her mouth—tasting myself—while lining up. She's soaked. Tiny hole clenching in need as I rub my tip through soft folds. "I'm going to love you every day for the rest of our lives. There will never be another day where you doubt me, and if there is, then I've failed you."

"I don't need empty…*uh!*" That kills the stupidity she's convinced herself of.

I'm buried to the hilt in one smooth stroke, biting back a curse as Mermaid's walls grip me tight. They flutter around me, a pleasurable massage, but I pull out and thrust forward again. There's no rush. I fuck her with sharp, measured snaps of my hips and slow, dragging withdrawals. Moreover, she lets me with furrowed brows and parted lips, those eyes watching me. They shift from my face to neck and lower, all the while meeting me thrust for thrust.

I feel the change in her the moment she sees it. Her body is flushed with her desire, nipples hard, but before I can take a tip between my teeth, my girl pushes my head back.

Slim fingers lightly trace the cursive there, and her bottom lip trembles. "Why?"

"Because I love you." My own voice is hoarse, body wound tight, but I don't pause my pace. If anything, I take her just a little harder. "Because my life is empty without you."

"You hurt me, Ivan." It's a moan, a reproach, yet her thighs spread wider inside the swing. The momentum alone bounces her on my cock, an exquisite rhythm, and I grab her hip with one hand to slam in deeper. "How do I believe you?"

"Because you're the only person in this world that truly knows me, mi amor. You know that I'd do anything to keep you safe, to remove any obstacle in our way, to then lay the world at your feet." I swallow hard and with my unoccupied hand, place hers right over where my heart beats. "You own this, bebe. That cadence has always been yours, and I'm sorry for not telling you before. I fucked up, and I own up to it."

"I don't—"

"Look at me. Look at me and tell me what you see." It doesn't take long for the fear and reproach to leave her expression, I'm baring my soul, and Amberlyn can read it. Tears begin to fall from her eyes while she tightens, those fingers dig into my chest as emotions overwhelm, bring her to the edge, and I love her through the discovery. "It was never about you being enough, Mermaid. I'm the one who lacked in this relationship, and I let my personal pursuit of that worth ruin us. For that, I'm so sorry. Don't leave me again."

A sob wracks her body, pussy spasming as her orgasm breaks us both, and I slam into the hilt. The way her walls suck me in deeper—massage— brings me to the edge and we fall over together. I fill her with my seed, overflowing her small passage and when it seeps from around my cock, I reach between us and spread the drops over the top of her thighs and mound.

Then, I slowly rock us to prolong the pleasure.

Shivers run through her naked form, and my heart settles when she seeks warmth in my hold. Amberlyn lets me wrap her in my arms, nestling against my chest and the tattoo of her name. There, she turns her head to place a kiss across the inked skin and I smile.

At peace.

We're not perfect. There's so much to still fix, but this is a start.

The chance I needed to right our story.

Amberlyn

THE NEXT TIME I open my eyes, I'm disoriented and a little afraid. It's clear to me that I'm on a plane, strapped into a very comfortable seat, but I'm alone. "What the—"

"I'm here, bebe." Ivan's voice calms me at once and I rub my eyes, trying to gain more of my equilibrium. We were up late into the night; mostly him talking, but I get it now.

The man I love is as idiotic as his brother, but it comes from a good place.

I told him this, too. Because had he been honest, we could've dealt with the brothers back home while they tried to fool me with the whole fake detainee disappearance. That earned him a smack to his shoulder, which led to him hissing, and my freaking out after I shot him.

In my defense, though, I was—am—under a lot of stress.

And for his good luck, my guilt made me cuddle him after we took a shower and I dressed the wound. It's not large, but I burned the skin there while also causing a four-stitch gash. The resort has a good medical staff with a lot of patience because this man is hardheaded as all get out.

The compromise was they close the wound, and I clean it. I'm responsible for dressing changes and kisses to his lips for the pain and suffering he endured.

"When did we leave the island?" A yawn escapes and I arch, popping my arms out hard enough to hear a crack. "Why didn't you wake me?'

"After everything I put you through, you needed the sleep." There's self-recrimination there along with his own guilt, and now that he's open to me, I can't look away. Not because I want to punish him—not at all. I too have my faults in this mess, but because of the beauty that is his soul.

For a killer, Ivan is sweet and caring when it comes to those he loves.

Not loyalty. Not respect.

But only those he truly loves, and it's now unhidden and open when it comes to me.

It's not pretty words or promises. No.

It's real and raw, and he's willing to sacrifice his happiness at any time to make sure I don't feel the pain of losing a loved one. It was putting his own desires aside so that he could eliminate every threat he felt was sent my way because of who he is.

Yet in his blind love, my papi forgot that I chose him. His life. His worries. Every part of who he is and what comes attached to his last name.

Ivan De Leon has one fault above all others, though, and it's that he carries the weight of what isn't his to shoulder. Not alone. Not without those who care for him just as strongly and would happily take the world on for him.

"I love you, too." Because it's my turn to give. To be vulnerable in this new us. Last night when he said the words, I froze. My mind and heart were at odds and confused, but today it's clear and undeniable, and he needs my truth just as much as his healed me.

We're not perfect, but we will be.

I won't hold this against him.

But I do demand swift justice to those who sought to break us. That's non-negotiable.

His seatbelt is unbuckled, and Ivan kneels at my feet seconds after my confession, his smile wide. "Are you sure you're ready to say it back? You don't—"

"I've loved you since we were kids, papi. That's never changed."

"I'm going to spend the rest of my life worshipping you, my little sirenita."

"Only if you let me spoil you, too. We're even in fuckups and celebrations." Cupping his face with both hands, I lean my forehead on his. My smile wide and eyes watery; I let him see me too. "A team, Ivan. Nothing and no one will break that again."

IVAN

WE LANDED IN Cuba six hours ago with a quiet Jaime in tow and another body bag. This one belongs to Jasmin Davila after a quick encounter with Amberlyn where no words were exchanged between the two before the body slumped forward.

My mermaid hugged Mom like she hasn't seen her in years, both giggling a bit. They're wearing matching expressions, a mixture of relief and joy that my father basks in while her parents watch off to the side.

And when a second later my girl gives him the same embrace, I understand. He sees her and Luna as his flesh and blood, the Daddy's girl he never had, and thought she'd be upset with him over this.

"I'm sorry," they said in unison before wearing matching grins of relief.

"No, kid." The amusement dies for him then and my viejo kisses her forehead before pulling away, arms holding her at length. "You have nothing to apologize for. I know how stubborn that one is and should've surmised you didn't know. You are my child as much as he is, and I protect those I love. Never think differently, Amberlyn. We all adore you."

"Thank you."

"I also have a gift for you." Grabbing her by the hand, Dad walks my *mermaid outside to where the Davila female kneels. "Her future is yours to decide."*

"Dad, I don't—"

"A team, papi. Always." She also doesn't hesitate to grab my Glock *and empty three shots into the woman's head without pause. Then she shrugs as if it's nothing. "Lesson learned, don't talk shit. Flies don't enter closed mouths."*

"That's my girl." Her father and mine say in unison. Their smiles *proud.*

"He's going to kill you, De Leon. Mark my words." Jaime's trying to get under my skin. To play mind games, but in reality, is frustrating himself. My lack of engagement angers him. "We'll take turns using her holes, too. Right over your body."

"I'm sorry," my sirenita whispers and walks to where Israel walks with him. She smiles at my guard, all sweet, and asks that he breaks Jaime's teeth. Moreover, when Israel bashes the butt of his gun into the asshole's mouth repeatedly, Uriel cries, and I laugh. Hard. "What's so funny?"

"Not funny, love. I'm in awe of your ruthless tendencies."

She shrugs. "He's annoying."

"Agreed." I cut my eyes to Jaime once and what he sees quiets his sobs, leaving him a whimpering idiot while we continue to walk.

The city is awake and waiting. Demanding blood as retribution for what they've endured.

I hear the call. Embrace the darkness.

Many are waiting on my signal to approach the presidential palace, but I'll try to end this amicably and without any more casualties. Enough blood has been spilled on these lands, and while there's a part of me eliminating this man for personal reasons, there's another who's yearning for a better way of life for the people here.

I'm no hero. Will never claim to be, but sometimes justice comes under the guise of a monster.

Empty streets greet me all around, yet I can make out the ruffles sticking out from windows or holes in walls. Rodriguez has no idea how fine a line his future walks between my cruelty and total anarchy.

We walk up the stairs and into the large open lobby where Amberlyn's uncle and grandfather greet us with a nod. My girl smiles at them, so much love in her expression while controlled chaos ensues around us.

The newly appointed general stands proud with his men, all dressed in their military garbs, while traitors to the country kneel at their feet. He's one of those holding a gun to a member of the ruling party's head, his smile joyful.

Not at all the one of a man about to commit murder.

One by one, each gun goes off as I pass, and those bodies hit the floor, creating a haunting staccato to my entrance.

Each of these now dead citizens either killed, abused their power, or stole from those in a weaker position. A lesson for the next ruling class. I'll be watching.

"He's in the formal dining room. Placido has no idea what's going on."

"Thank you, General. Prepare for the elections."

"Gracias, Ivan."

"De nada. I'm not a saint."

"We know that, but you're fair. That's all we needed." He turns to start taking care of the clean-up process and then preparing for the future, while we walk straight into the private quarters of the Rodriguez family.

His wife is in Europe and knows to never return.

His extended family fled under threats of death.

Yet the man himself doesn't find anything strange in the mass fleeing of those he cares about.

"Buen provecho," I call out into the large room, and it echoes back to me, catching the president off guard. The coffee in his hand tumbles, burning him in the process to right it, and he hisses at the contact.

"What is the meaning of this! How did you get in?"

"And here I was simply just wishing you enjoy your meal."

"Guards!" he yells out, and nothing. "Guards!"

"No one is coming to save you, Rodriguez. Your time is up."

"Tio, do something," Jaime pleads through a busted mouth, his lip torn and hanging off to the side. Bruises litter his body, and the tank top and shorts combo we put him in show off each one. "You own the military! Call them to shoot these assholes!"

Junior locks the door, just in case there's a brave soul out there who still believes his propaganda, while I turn and kiss my girl. Just a sweet little peck to hold me over until later tonight.

She groans into my mouth, not caring who's present, and that makes me feel like a king. "End this, papi. I want to go home and start my life with you."

"I love you." A final taste, and then I place her beside Israel. The men with me know that she's to be untouched and will protect her with their lives. "Junior, open the bag in front of Jaime."

"Of course, boss." The large black bag has been kept away from him for a reason. We didn't want him to get suspicious, further stressed by the death of his lover. Jasmin Davila slept with both brothers, carried the same greed, and helped ruin a few lives in pursuit of a lifestyle she couldn't maintain on her own.

With the first few inches of the zipper open, her dark hair spills out and it's matted with blood. Her head follows, and Jaime gasps while Placido becomes shifty. Every room in this palace has a hidden escape, and he'll leave his nephew here to die without an ounce of remorse if it means he can escape.

"Try it, and I'll end it all now." That stills his movements while Jaime gags, violently vomiting what little is in his stomach at the disfigured sight of the woman who sucked his cock. Do I feel sorry for him? Not one bit. "Are there any words you'd like to say to her?"

"I'm going to kill her for this, you know. All of you, but I'll start with Amberlyn." His vows fall on deaf ears. It's as if he refuses to accept a reality where they have no power.

"No. You're not." Taking my place behind him, I kick the back of his knees and when he lands on them, I undo the ends of my bracelet and press the wire against his neck. The sharp metal embeds into the skin there, sliding through with ease as I pull left-to-right in a sawing motion. All the while, though, my eyes are on the president.

This is the by-product of his greed. Believing himself untouchable.

Jaime tries to fight off my hold, pushing back, but I dig my foot into his spine and use the imbalance as a counterweight. Within a minute I've torn open his neck, severing his jugular, and only let go, removing the wire when he spurts blood from the wound.

He'll choke on his blood, unable to breathe without blockage.

But before he takes his final bloodied breath, I lower to my haunches and speak loud enough that everyone hears. "Your brother died in a similar fashion, Jaime. I used the same wire that up until a few minutes ago only carried his blood. Dalian took his final breaths inside a gator's mouth, but I'd sentenced him to death before that. He died thinking you'd betrayed him."

"I'll step down and disappear. You won." Placido's voice is shaky, some might say stressed, but I know better than to believe an asshole like him has a heart. It's not grief he's facing, but self-preservation.

"No."

"I'll pay you to let me live."

"No."

"Then what can I do? Tell me, and I'll—" President Placido Rodriguez didn't get to finish begging for his life as Amberlyn raised the gun I'd given her from my collection and fired the first shot. Her decisiveness in stressful situations leaves me in awe of her. She did the same thing with Karen; Mermaid laid no blame on the woman who the Uriel brothers abused and forced an addiction upon.

Moreover, she offered to help them get settled after my guards retrieved her husband and reunited the pair shortly after we landed. And tomorrow, when they're back on American soil, I vowed to buy them the house this family promised and failed to deliver.

Following Mermaid's lead, I sank a bullet into his skull and then through his neck, as did those traveling with us. Every clip was emptied on a man worth shit, and who'd more than deserved the ending he got.

He ruined many lives and targeted my family, but his biggest mistake was threatening the safety of the woman intertwining her fingers with mine as we exit. She comes above all others, my biggest sacred rule, and I'd bring him back from the dead and do it all over again if I could.

Cheers ring out in the streets as we exit the palace. Many dance, some cry, and others drink to the end of an era not worth mentioning in the history books. No, it's time to remember what once was and what will be again: a culture of beauty and happiness.

Thriving people. A united community.

The devil lives among them now; I'll be relocating here with Amberlyn by my side to start our own dynasty. Thiago has Miami. I'll control Cuba. And who knows where the future generations will go.

Yet this place will always be home.

They'll live in peace, and I'll have my ports, and no one steps out of line.

I want a future here. With her, my sirenita.

In the back of the chauffeur's car, Amberlyn rests her head on my shoulder, still holding my hand. "Are you ready to start the next chapter with me, Ivan?"

A simple answer. No hesitation.

"Yes." What's more, I kiss her temple and nuzzle the soft skin there. "But I don't want one chapter, bebe." In my pocket, I've been carrying a ring since she disappeared. When I knew I couldn't let this treasure slip through my fingers again. "Today, tomorrow, and always. I want to own all the tomorrows we have left to share."

"Papi, that's so—"

"Marry me, Amberlyn Ibarra. Claim my future as I've already laid claim to yours."

"Yes."

EPILOGUE
IVAN

"**Y**OU'RE FREE TO go," I say, tapping the metal door keeping Kyle Montgomery trapped inside a small room in the basement of the private estate Amberlyn and I built in Cuba. He was smuggled in with Henry months ago, kept on the family compound, and then moved here when the accommodations were finished. I didn't kill him. Instead, I served as judge and jury while serving him with a one-year sentence that I'm ending today for good behavior. "My men will escort you home."

"I'm free?" He stands from the cot and walks to the metal bars of the door. This room isn't like the standard jail where my livestock roams and eats on the compound, but more refined. It's on the lower level of the main house; comes with basic human commodities and three meals a day. After all, I do plan to do business with the man.

He has connections. New routes to move merchandise.

Thiago also sees this now, and I plan to exploit every single one of them for my family's gain.

The U.S. needs him—the weapons he procures—and I want their money. For the name of every member of the Imperium to have legal immunity.

"You are."

"Thank—"

"Under one condition."

Apprehension dawns on his face. "What do you need?"

"Two things." Unlocking the door, I block the entrance and let him see the men standing behind me. Every member and their right-hand men are spread about the open area leading to this room. They watch him. Dare him to deny us. "You buy your weapons from the De Leons, and do what you're told and when. No questions asked. This is your opportunity to make a friend out of us, Montgomery. A friend helps and facilitates political advancements while an enemy will kill you, your son, and every male with your bloodline running through their veins." He's shaking, his eyes darting across each face before coming back to mine. "Do you agree?"

"Yes."

"Then welcome to South Florida. You'll be living here from now on." One of the guards from Miami comes forward and grabs Montgomery by the arm, leading him out and onto an awaiting plane that'll take him home. He'll be shadowed. So will his family. A single step out of line, and I won't hesitate to put a bullet between his eyes.

Just steps from the door leading upstairs, he pauses and looks back, brows furrowed. "What's the second condition?"

"You owe me quite the large amount of paperwork, beginning with the deal you had with Rodriguez and those prior. I want a legally binding trace to every weapon you've ever sold and the information on the buyers."

"I can do that."

"Then go and enjoy your freedom, Kyle. Your family misses you."

He's led out while the others begin to talk. We have plans.

Ambitions.

The Imperium is too large to contain, and many have taken notice.

We have a hand in every major industry except one: printing. However, acquiring Henry's machines have become the catalyst to change that as Malcolm will do more than just move and withhold money at his banks. The others approve as well. It transforms our plans a bit, but it'll be worth it to one day soon become the world bank and treasury. The Imperium's growth is what matters, as will our worldwide control over countries where it hurts them the most: money.

"You ready to get hitched the right way, bro?" Thiago asks, slapping my back while wearing a shit-eating grin. Singao. "It's about time, too."

"Fuck you." I know he knows, but I'll be damned if I admit it.

"Is that how you speak to my sister-in-law? No wonder I saw her flirting with—"

"Leave my son out of this, Thiago." Malcolm steps in beside us, just as amused. "Maximus is irresistible. Not his fault Amberlyn fell in love with his impeccable charm."

"This is where I leave you assholes. I have a bride to visit."

"You're not supposed to see her until after the wedding!" a British voice calls out, and I flip off Casper.

"So immature." That came from Javier. He's just as bad as the rest of them.

"Did any of you?" That quiets them all. Not a single peep. "Thought so."

Leaving them to talk, I quietly make my way up the stairs and onto our floor. Luna and Nat are with her, talking, but I bypass them and greet my mermaid with a passionate kiss.

Our wedding won't be a formal affair. Neither of us wanted it that way, and after going back and forth with our parents, they backed off. We live on the water and enjoy nothing more than cooking out, having a few drinks, and then taking a night swim when the weather allows it.

"You look beautiful, bebe." And she does. Amberlyn's wearing a floor-length white sundress with small sunflowers in the palest yellow, her feet bare. Her red hair is down, no more black chunks, and curly at the ends in a way that looks effortless. No makeup. No fuss. "You are simply perfect."

"As are you." I'm wearing an all-white guayabera and linen pants. Something I've discovered the woman currently biting her lips while eyeing my tattoos enjoys. Says they stand out more. "So handsome, papi."

"You ready to pretend this is our first time?"

"Our parents would literally kill us if they knew."

The day after I killed Placido Rodriguez, we wed on a beach in Varadero by the resort's Catholic father. We were lucky they had the service. Sometimes couples elope, and he performed the traditional vows with Israel and Junior as our witnesses.

After convincing Amberlyn to marry me today, she had one request: out on the water.

My mermaid wanted to feel the warm ocean lapping at our feet while the starry sky blessed this union. And I could never deny her. Not when she looks at me as if I'm her world.

She's wrong on that, though. I'm going to show her every day that I live and breathe for her.

I'll never take what we have for granted again. We do this together. Tomorrow. Always.

"Do you, Ivan De Leon, take this woman to be your lawful wedded wife? Do you pledge this before God and man, to love and honor, through sunshine and dark times? Do you promise to love and hold, forsaking all others until death separates you? If so, answer "I do."

"I do. In this life and every single one that follows."

"Good." The Catholic priest looks over at Amberlyn, smiling while my mermaid sniffs. A few tears fell from her eyes, and I wipe them away gently. "And do you, Amberlyn Ibarra—"

"I do. All of it."

The priest chuckles. "I didn't ask."

"We both know it's the same question, sir." Her gaze turns to mine. So soft and full of love. "I do, Ivan. Always, will."

"Then I guess I have—"

Whatever he said after didn't matter. It all became background noise because a few seconds later, I was kissing my wife. The future mother of my children.

Best decision we ever made.

That was the blank page we needed after so much heartache, and I wouldn't change it for the world.

Yet, we knew we'd have to do something like this at one point to make those waiting downstairs happy. Her father deserved to walk her down the aisle, and the mothers needed something to fuss over.

That is, until we have a mini mermaid or killer of our own.

Reaching around her back, I fist the airy material and pull it up, exposing her to the mirror behind her. "Fuck, I'm a lucky man."

"Yes. You are." There's a teasing tone to her, a naughty gleam in her eyes, and I spread her wide. Saliva pools quickly in my mouth and I swallow hard, tightening my grip on her bottom as white lace teases me.

I'm hard at once. Throbbing at the sight of my baby in a pair of crotchless panties that exposes her pretty cunt and puckered hole on display, the latter of which is stretched full by a green jeweled plug that's my favorite. It's a little on the small side, but enough to prepare her for my girth.

Amberlyn likes to wear it for hours when wanting to play. Tempt me to lose control.

I also can't help it and touch the area, tapping the end where her hole clenches around the smooth metal.

She's wet, and it coats her inner thighs. Her pussy is bare and wanting.

"Hands on the mirror, bebe."

"Ivan, we need to—"

"Hands on the fucking mirror." Bending a bit more, she spreads her legs and complies. This gives me access to her pussy, so slick and pink. I can't fuck her how I want, but she'll be walking down the makeshift aisle slick with me.

I run the blunt head along her lips, coating the tip twice. "Fuck, you're soft and wet. So ready for me."

"Your fault," she whines when I don't slip inside. "The last few nights you've been talking shop late into the night."

"My apologies, sweetheart." I tap her toy next and rub our combined juices over the green emerald. Not fake, and I desecrate it just the same. "You'll have me at your disposal for a month. We're leaving for Greece tonight."

"Oh shit!" she cries. It's a little muffled behind my hand as I cover her mouth. Her parents should be up here soon to get her. "That's amazing, papi. Thank you."

"My pleasure," I grit out before slamming in, not able to take the torture of simply grazing her slit with the head anymore. "Knew you'd be excited."

"I am," she moans, gyrating against me as I pick up the pace. We won't last long. Not with the way she's gripping me—it's near painful, but I punch through it. My next few thrusts force her onto the tips of her toes, her wild eyes meeting mine in the mirror, but it's the pure look of bliss on her face when I slip two fingers to her front and pinch her clit that my girl lets go.

Amberlyn comes hard, milking me, and I follow shortly after. All it took is to feel her juices graze my balls while her walls quivered.

I fill her with my seed and then rub it against her slit and thighs in between a few lazy pumps.

The smile on her face afterward is sweet and satiated. Well worth the fact we are late to our own casual-style wedding, and many give us knowing looks.

Not that I care; I wear her ownership of me with pride.

"Better, bebe?"

"Much." Turning, she lets the dress fall as it may and then stands on the tips of her toes to kiss my chin. "You ready to make an honest woman of me for the second time, papi?"

"Every day."

"And all the tomorrows."

OUTTAKE
Amberlyn

"HOW DO I let you talk me into these things," Ivan grumbles, giving me a glare when he's the one who bought the thing. "You owe me for this."

"Better yet, how do you figure it's my fault?" At my perplexed look, he only huff standing in the middle of my kitchen while holding his hard cock inside of a casting canister with the name *Clone-A-Willy* labeled on the front. "You're the one who got all upset because I was looking at a real-skin ten-inch toy. If anything, control the jealousy and you wouldn't be in this predicament."

"Are you really giving me lip as I clone my dick for you?'

"If the cast fits." His lips twitch at that response, and I lose it, doubling over while tears gather at the corners of my eyes. This—the ridiculousness of the situation—is us.

Ivan doesn't want to put a label on us, yet he can't stand the idea of me

751

so much as looking at anyone, or any toy, sexually. Hence, he's naked in my kitchen and making me a silicone copy of his *willy.*

"You're enjoying this a little too much, bebe."

"Same as you watching my tits jiggle when I giggle."

"Touché." Scratching at his jaw, Ivan purses his lips. "And I'll also admit I'm a little overwhelming at times. It's part of the charm."

"If you say so." Walking to the fridge, I open it and bend a bit to reach the last can of Dr. Pepper in the back. "Do you want a Coke?"

"Yes."

"Diet or cherry?"

"Doesn't matter to me." The gruffness in his tone sweeps across my skin and goose bumps rise, my nipples tightening into stiff peaks that rub against the cotton of my shirt. I'm not wearing anything underneath. Never do when I'm at home. "Fuck, I think it's almost done. Should be ready to pour soon."

"Okay." What else can I say? His dick is occupied, and that tone never fails to turn me on.

Behave, Amberlyn. Don't come off as desperate.

"Yeah, it's getting tight. And warm, too."

"Wonderful." *Calm your breathing. You can get off later.*

"Perfect pocket pussy if I could lube it up and move."

"Hmm." That's my eloquent reply, which was no more than a squeak while shoving my head just a little bit deeper into the fridge, pretending to search for something before standing back up. That same fridge has its door slammed closed a second later when a strong chest presses against my back. "Did you need something?"

"Your pussy riding my tongue."

"I thought we were—"

"Or you could bounce a few times on my cock, Mermaid. For research purposes."

"Research?" I parrot, my body feeling flushed. Sweat is beading at my temple. "You want me to compare?"

"Yes." Ivan lifts the now-filled container with the silicone substance and places it in my hand. *When did he mix the solutions? How did I miss it?* "Hold tight, and don't spill. I'm going to test a theory."

"A theory?"

"For research purposes, I want to see what it takes for my mermaid to lose control. I want to hear her beg for my cock, cry for it, but I'm going to gradually test her. Tease her." Fisting the back of my shirt, he stretches the material tight against my chest. The friction feels so good. "Turnabout is fair play, don't you agree?"

"But I haven't—"

"So you walking around without a bra or shorts is normal? You spend your days in nothing but these barely-there shirts and cheekies?"

"I'm at home, and it's comfortable."

His audible groan makes me press my thighs together. "Keep talking. What else do you do when—"

He's cut off by a knock on my front door and the sound of my mother calling my name. Gone is the heat from a moment ago, the sensuality that comes freely when I'm with him. I toss the willy-goop and container in the freezer while rushing to my laundry room for a pair of sweats.

Not that Ivan is any better.

The boy is dressed, all contents of our experiment gone, and now drumming his fingers in my kitchenette while drinking my Dr. Pepper. The last one. All innocent-like, too.

"Mamita, are you home?" she calls through the door. "I got juicy gossip about your cousin, Yuli."

Christ. Please help me.

This is too much, and when I meet Ivan's eyes again, he's chuckling to himself.

"What now?"

"I'm pretty sure we're going to have to buy another kit and do this all over again."

Elena M. Reyes is the epitome of a Floridian and if she could live in her beloved flip-flops, she would.

As a small child, she was always intrigued by all forms of art: whether it was dancing to island rhythms, or painting with any medium she could get her hands on. Her passion for reading over the years has amassed her with hours of pleasure, but it wasn't until she stumbled upon fanfiction that her thirst to write overtook her world.

She's a short and sassy Latina with an adorable pup, a kiddo that keeps her on her toes, and a husband who claims she'll cause him to go bald prematurely. Lol

Email: Reyes139ff@gmail.com

Elena's Marked Girls.
Come join the naughty fun.
Link: https://www.facebook.com/groups/1710869452526025/

Newsletter Sign-Up:
https://www.elenamreyes.com

tiktok.com/@authorelenamreyes

facebook.com/AuthorElenaMReyes

instagram.com/authorelenamreyes

bookbub.com/profile/elena-m-reyes

pinterest.com/AuthorElenaMReyes

amazon.com/stores/Elena-M.-Reyes/author/B00E3E26X8

ALSO BY ELENA M. REYES

FATE'S BITE SERIES

LITTLE LIES

LITTLE MATE

HALF TRUTHS DUET

HALF TRUTHS: THEN

HALF TRUTHS: NOW

OMISSION:

PART 1

PART 2

COME TO ME (2026)

THE HUNT (2025)

TERO (TBD)

BEAUTIFUL SINNER SERIES

Each book is a standalone.

Now Live!

SIN (#1)

COVET (#2)

MINE (#3)

YOURS (#4)

RISQUE #5

OWN #6

Beautiful Sinner Spin-Off

CORRUPT

MY SINFUL VALENTINE

SAVAGE KISS

ONE RULE

MAKE YOU MINE

(Marked Series)
Marking Her #1
Marking Him #2
Scars #2.5
Marked #3

(I Saw You)
I Saw You
I Love You #1.5

Teasing Hands Duet
Teasing Hands #1
Taunting Lips #2

SAFE ROMANCE:
Taste Of You
Doctor's Orders
Back To You

STANDALONES:
Craving Sugar
Stolen Kisses